MIS   RI

MISSOURI

MISSOURI

Variety Is the Spice of
Four Romances in the
Show-Me State

HANNAH ALEXANDER / TRACEY V. BATEMAN
FREDA CHRISMAN / JOYCE LIVINGSTON

BARBOUR
PUBLISHING

A Living Soul © 2000 by Barbour Publishing, Inc.
Timing Is Everything © 2004 by Tracey V. Bateman
Faith Came Late © 1997 Barbour Publishing, Inc.
Ice Castle © 1999 by Barbour Publishing, Inc.

ISBN 1-59310-902-4

Cover art by Conrad Zobel/Corbis

Scripture quotations are taken from the King James Version of the Bible.

Published by Barbour Publishing, Inc., P.O. Box 719, Uhrichsville, Ohio 44683, www.barbourbooks.com

Our mission is to publish and distribute inspirational products offering exceptional value and biblical encouragement to the masses.

 Member of the
Evangelical Christian
Publishers Association

Printed in the United States of America.
5 4 3 2 1

A LIVING SOUL

SOUL

Hannah Alexander

We wish to thank Sharon Heidlage, who first gave us the idea for A Living Soul
years ago when she worked as a counselor in a place like Alternative.
Thank you to Lorene Cook, whose attention to detail and
encouragement has helped improve this story.
Thank you to Mary Young for helping us with ideas for the cover.
Also, thank you, Rebecca Germany and Cathy Hake,
for your valuable input. God bless you all!

Chapter 1

The baby would die if Mother had anything to do with it. Kirby knew that. Mother hadn't changed in two years, hadn't even known what her own daughter was going through. This time she would know, but it would be too late. Kirby placed her hand over her abdomen and tried to feel some emotion, but she couldn't. It was just as well. Emotions got her into trouble.

She bent over the blank piece of paper and sucked on the end of her ink pen. What did one write in a suicide note? "Dear Mother and Father," she mouthed the words slowly as she wrote, then frowned and almost crossed them out. Why not call them Mr. and Mrs. Acuff? That was how she thought of them now. She felt so separate from them, so different. So alone.

A noise reached her from the other room, and she tensed. A knock. The doorbell chimed through the house, and she held her breath. It was Jenny, of course. Good-girl Jenny, who went to church, read her Bible, talked to God every day whether she needed to or not. They were supposed to go to the movies tonight with some of their friends.

"Sorry, Jenny, not tonight," she whispered, then waited until the noise stopped before she continued with the note. "I'm taking Dad's old junker on a drive tonight," she wrote. "I'm sure you'll see it again. . . . You just may not see me."

She reread the note and grimaced. It sounded like she was running away. Of course, they would know soon enough what had happened. But it still needed more. "I can't live with my past. Can you?" There, that would make them stop and think.

The small handful of tiny white pills in the pocket of her blue jeans would take care of everything. What good was her life anyway? She was a pain to her parents. She was disposable. All the guys felt that way. Use and dump. The instructions must be written on her forehead in letters that flashed on and off when she met a guy she liked. She thought Kyle would be different, but as soon as she told him she thought she might be pregnant, he ran off like she'd sprouted an extra head.

She had already cost her parents more money for a counselor than she was worth. That was why they'd terminated treatment. They'd stopped church a long time ago, only a couple of months after they started taking her. If they thought the religious goodness of those people would rub off on her, they would soon be disappointed—even though that was where she met Jenny. And that was how Carson Tanner came into their lives.

Kirby laid the note on the kitchen table, bent down to tie her hiking boots, and grabbed a bottle of juice from the fridge—had to have something to wash down the pills. Had to have a flashlight, too. . . . There would be one in the car.

Misty dusk gradually cooled the hot, muggy August evening as the mauve beauty of a Missouri sky battled for attention against the lush foliage of Jefferson City. Hungry nighthawks dipped and plunged within the reflected lights from the street.

Serena Van Buren lay on her back on a blue gray berber carpet, absently staring at the sunset through the plate glass window of her family room. Her thoughts drifted with the haunting bird cries that echoed through the growing darkness.

Tossing her head to chase a stray tendril of short, silver blond hair from her cheek, she stretched her legs out in front of her and glanced up at her mother-in-law, who stood by the window, arms folded across her stomach, fingers tapping in silent contemplation.

"I still miss him, Blythe."

Their golden cocker spaniel pup, lying curled up in a corner of the sofa, caught the caressing softness in Serena's voice. He raised his head and looked at her. She was lost once more in her contemplation of the sky when the animal stretched, leaped from the sofa, and boldly walked over to nuzzle her face. She absently raised a hand to keep his pink tongue from her lips.

Blythe turned and glared at the pup. "Rascal, get back." He turned a sorrowful gaze up at her, drooped, and slunk back to the sofa.

Blythe smoothed her gardening T-shirt down over her jeans. "Of course you miss him. You always will. But you can't just bury yourself with a dead husband." She sank into the overstuffed easy chair and swung her legs up beside her. "And don't start telling me about loyalty, either. Jennings was my own son, and I miss him, too." She hesitated, cleared her throat. "You're thirty-seven, Serena. It's time to be getting on with your life."

Serena stretched and yawned to hide an irrepressible grin. Blythe had preached this sermon before. "Yes, and you sure set a good example, didn't you, Pal? How many men did you go out with after Papa died?"

Blythe glanced away. "That's nonsense. I was a good twenty years older than you are when I was widowed."

"And still as active and beautiful as you were at thirty," Serena retorted.

"If you think I was beautiful at thirty, you haven't looked at our picture albums."

"Don't give me that, and don't change the subject. Life doesn't end just because you've had your sixty-seventh birthday, you know. If you wanted male companionship, you could have it, so don't preach to me about growing stale."

Blythe spread her arms. "Look at me. Who'd want an old raisin like this? It's just not the same."

Serena flashed her a warning look.

"Okay, okay." Blythe waved a hand casually. "All I'm saying is that a woman like you shouldn't finish her life alone. You're too young. It's been three years."

"I'm not alone."

"I don't mean the girls. You know the kind of companion I'm talking about." Blythe narrowed her eyes.

Serena chuckled. "Would you stop—"

The front door opened suddenly, then slammed as angry-sounding footsteps echoed along the hallway. Serena's older daughter, Jennifer, came striding into the room, her pretty, oval face flushed, her golden brown eyes flashing fire.

"Jenny?" Serena straightened. "Honey, what are you doing home so early? I thought you were going to eat after the movie."

Jennifer strode forward and flopped down onto the sofa, her long, brown hair tumbling across her shoulders in a loose cascade. "How can guys be such. . .such insensitive jerks?"

"Another fight with Danny?" Serena asked.

"Yeah, but Mom, it isn't just him. I'm worried about Kirby."

"Kirby Acuff? What did she do?"

"It's what she didn't do that worries me. She was supposed to go with us to the movies tonight, but when we went by to pick her up, she wasn't there. At least she didn't answer the door. And she never showed up at the movies, so afterward I wanted to go back to her house and check on her, but the guys didn't want to waste the time." The grim set of her jawline expressed her displeasure with her other friends.

She reached into the pocket of her white shorts and pulled out a ring. She held it out in the palm of her hand to show Serena. "This is why I am so worried."

Serena stared at the ring, a beautiful, glowing opal set in gold filigree.

"Mom, this was Kirby's prized possession. Her favorite uncle gave this to her on her fifteenth birthday. She came by the clinic today when I was painting the hallway, and she just gave it to me. She seemed really down."

Serena studied Jenny's face with growing concern. "Did she say why?"

"Just that she wouldn't need it, and she knew I always admired it."

"And she was supposed to go to the movies with you and your friends?"

"Maybe she went somewhere with her parents." Jenny shook her head, worry growing more evident in her expression. "I don't know. Her boyfriend broke up with her a couple of days ago, and I know that hurt her bad. Mom, in psych class last year we learned that when someone was thinking about suicide, one of the things they did was give their stuff away. Like this ring. I don't want anything to happen to her!"

"And Kirby's seemed depressed lately? Has she talked about killing herself? Has she given other things away?" Serena pulled herself up from the floor and sat on the sofa next to her daughter. "Honey, I trust your judgment. Do you think Kirby is in the frame of mind to do something like this?"

"I don't know. . . . I think so. I hate to accuse her of. . .but, Mom, we can't take any chances, can we?"

Serena picked up the telephone on the end table beside the sofa. "What's her number?"

Jenny gave it to her, and she dialed and waited. Almost before the first ring ended, someone snatched it up. "Hello, Kirby? Is that you?" came a man's frantic voice.

"No, Mr. Acuff, I'm sorry," Serena said. "This is Jenny Van Buren's mother, Serena. I think we've met at some school functions a few times."

There was a disappointed pause. "Oh. Dr. Van Buren."

"Please call me Serena. I'm sorry to bother you like this, but Jenny and I are worried about Kirby. Obviously she isn't there, and she was supposed to go out with Jenny and some friends tonight. She gave—"

There was a sudden shuffling on the other end of the line, and Serena heard a woman's voice raised in anger—or in alarm—in the background.

"Hello?" Serena said.

"I'm. . .sorry, Serena. We can't find her. She left a note on the kitchen table telling us she took my old car, and she hinted that we may not see. . .see her again. I'm not sure. . . . I don't know what to think."

Serena's concern deepened to alarm. "Is there any luggage missing? Are her clothes gone? What about shoes? Any indication that she might have run away, or—"

"Her overnight case is in the hall closet, and Carol says Kirby's hiking boots are gone."

"Hiking boots?" Serena echoed.

"Yes, but she wears them all the time."

"Mom." Jenny laid a hand on her arm, her brown eyes widening. "Kirby loves the Katy Trail. She goes hiking there a lot, and she's always trying to get me to go with her."

Serena covered the mouthpiece of the phone and murmured to Jenny, "But it's nighttime."

There was a cry of surprise over the telephone, and Serena heard Kirby's mother shout in the background, ". . .missing! They're gone!"

"Oh no," Mr. Acuff moaned. "Look, Serena, I've got to hang up now. We've got to call the police. Carol's sleeping pills are missing." There was a click, a silence, then a dial tone.

"What, Mom?" Jenny asked, grasping Serena's shoulder. "What happened?"

Serena replaced the receiver and turned to her frightened daughter. "Honey, Kirby's mother is missing her sleeping pills."

For a moment, Jenny's fear reflected across her face, spiraling out of control. And then, as if by conscious effort, she pressed her lips together and took a deep breath. "Okay, Mom. We've got to help look."

"Yes, we do. Give me a list of some of her favorite places, because if she's planning to end her life, she may want to surround herself with those things she loves the most."

"I already told you, Mom. The Katy Trail. She loves that place. She's always trying to get me to go hiking with her."

"Which trailhead?" The Katy Trail was a railroad track converted into a hiking trail, and it stretched across the countryside north of Jefferson City.

"It's where the trail goes through Hartsburg. You have to drive up Highway 63 eleven miles, then turn left. There's a sign."

Serena stood, and Blythe did the same. "I'll get my shoes on, and then I'll take the van and drive there. Jenny, you stay here on the phone and call more people. See if you can convince your friends Kirby could be in real trouble. Blythe, take your car and start checking the parks. She may have decided not to go all the way out to the trail, but I can't imagine she'd want to be around any crowds."

"I'll call Carson Tanner, Mom. He'll go. He's always trying to get Kirby to come to church."

Carson. Yes. The thought of him helped calm Serena's swiftly increasing stress level. "That's a wonderful idea, honey. Call Carson. He can help us search." She grabbed her cell phone, jammed on her shoes, and raced out to the garage.

Chapter 2

The old Ford was parked in the gravel parking area, and it was empty. Signs beside a small bathroom pointed both directions along the smooth trail, now swallowed in the darkness of night. All Serena had was her small flashlight, which didn't have the illumination she would have liked. But the car was here. Kirby had to be nearby.

She flipped open her cell phone and punched her home number. Jenny answered immediately. "Honey, the car's here, right where you told me it would be."

"Oh, Mom, did you find Kirby?"

"Not yet, but you need to call the Acuffs and tell them, and they'll need to alert the police. Did you reach Carson Tanner?"

"Yes, he's on his way out there." Jenny's voice wobbled, and Serena heard the tears in her voice. "I hope she's safe. I hope she hasn't. . ."

"I know—me, too. Which direction does she usually go? East or west?"

"She always goes west. She says she's always wanted to head the direction of Kansas and never stop walking."

"Okay. I'll be in touch." Serena said good-bye and hung up. The dusty white trail crossed through the tiny village of Hartsburg, and elderly homes hovered in the darkness. No one seemed to be out, and Serena decided not to waste time trying to find someone to help her search. She crossed an old railroad bridge and entered a deep passage of forest. "Kirby!" she called. "Kirby, are you there?"

No answer. No telling how far she might have gotten by now.

Serena first met Kirby Acuff about two years ago when Jenny brought her home from church one Sunday afternoon. Since then, the girls had become good friends and remained so, even after Kirby and her parents stopped going to church. Jenny had lamented several times how sorry she was that Kirby had no Christian influence at home and didn't always make the best decisions. Tonight's decision could be the worst—and last—of her life.

"Kirby!" Serena called again, farther down the trail. Still no answer. Time to pick up the speed a little more.

Not only had Jenny introduced Serena to Kirby, she had also introduced her to Carson Tanner, the church youth leader, who worked as an ER physician at St. Mary's. As Serena was an ob-gyn affiliated with St. Mary's, they had a lot in common. They had become good friends, taking lunch breaks together whenever possible—although, with their work schedules, that wasn't always a dependable thing. Their rapport had grown, but when her daughters and Blythe began to invite him to family dinners, Serena realized what was happening. She ended the relationship. She couldn't take it further; she wouldn't do that to a man again.

Under Carson's direction, the church youth group had doubled in size over the past two years. At least that was the information Serena received from her family. She herself had not attended since Jennings died three years ago. That was her biggest source of conflict with her children and Blythe. It frustrated her, and it hurt them, but she didn't know how to fix it.

"Kirby!" she called again. Still no answer, but she thought she heard a skittering of footsteps and a rattle of rocks. "Kirby, is that you? Please talk to me. Your family's worried about you. Jenny's frantic."

A whisper of sound. . .a sniffle, a soft moan. Serena rushed forward, shining her light back and forth across the trail. "Honey? Kirb—" She saw a patch of white, a fall of blond hair, to the left of the trail in the shadows. Serena stepped toward the girl in the darkness and felt the brush of a branch from an overhanging tree ruffle her hair. "Kirby, it's me. Serena Van Buren." She aimed her flashlight off to the side a bit so the girl wouldn't be blinded by the beam. "You have a lot of people worried about you."

Kirby shook her head, pursing her lips defiantly. She did not reply, but tears filled her eyes and dripped down her face. All this Serena saw in the glow of her flashlight as she stepped closer.

"I know about the note you left your parents," Serena said softly. "I want you to tell me if you're planning to hurt yourself."

Kirby dashed at the tears with the back of her hand, smudging thick mascara. "Leave me alone."

Serena stepped in front of her. "No, I can't do that."

Kirby glanced over her shoulder along the blackness of the tree-shrouded trail, as if she might bolt in that direction.

Serena reached out and touched the girl on the shoulder. "Have you taken your mother's pills?"

Kirby didn't look at her.

"I'm not joking here." Serena's voice grew firmer, more insistent.

Kirby glanced into her eyes, then looked away quickly. "No."

"Walk with me, Kirby. Come on. Use your flashlight and keep an eye out for snakes," she commanded with the same quiet authority she sometimes used with her daughters.

Like Serena's daughters, Kirby resisted for a moment, then turned and fell into step beside Serena. They walked a few yards in silence, toward the village, with only the echo of their footsteps to disturb the peace.

"Talking won't help this time, Serena," she stated sullenly, her voice hoarse with tears. "I'm not playing games."

Serena's worry grew. This talkative seventeen-year-old was unusually quiet—for Kirby. "Have you already done something to hurt yourself? Have you—"

"No, I haven't done anything, okay?" Kirby snapped. "I didn't expect to be hunted down like some wild animal!"

"You haven't been 'hunted down.'" Serena retained her "mother" tone. "You have friends and family who love you and want to make sure you're safe."

"Oh, sure." Sarcasm drifted heavily through the darkness. "Mother and Father wish I'd never been born."

"Difficulties with your parents can always be worked out. Jenny's worried. Do you mind if I call her on my cell phone to let her know you're safe?"

Kirby shook her head. "Go ahead," she said softly. "I didn't want to worry her."

Serena did so quickly, and when Kirby refused to talk to Jenny, Serena said good-bye and disconnected. Then she turned back to Kirby. "Tell me, why did you give your ring to Jenny? And where are your mother's sleeping pills? I've spoken with your father. The police are looking for you."

Kirby jerked to a stop, and her eyes flew open wide. "What! They called the police! What are they going to do, arrest me for grand theft auto?"

"Don't change the subject," Serena said. "They're afraid you're going to commit suicide."

Kirby's firm pointed chin wobbled, and her eyes filled with fresh tears. She turned and strolled along the trail again. Serena followed and waited and wished she had the right to pray. This girl desperately needed prayer—and she needed to be talking to someone who had a good relationship with God right now. Serena did not.

"What else did my parents tell you?" Kirby asked at last. "For instance, did they tell you how we played God with an innocent life?" There was a deep bitterness in her voice and a tone of intimate revelation. She had decided to talk.

"For instance?"

"Babies," Kirby mumbled. She wiped her eyes, streaking more mascara across her face.

Serena's throat tightened. She swallowed hard. This girl's pain radiated through the warm summer night like a mist.

Kirby took a deep breath. "I never told you, did I?" She stared hard at Serena, shaking her head slowly. "I never told Jenny." She walked along in silence for a long moment, sniffing, wiping her face with the back of her hand. "I had an abortion two years ago, when I was fifteen."

Serena felt the shock of Kirby's words all the way through her body, and she instinctively felt her pain. It took a moment to recover her equilibrium and voice. "You could have told me, honey. How I wish you had. I could have helped you. There are counselors—"

"We tried a counselor. Obviously, it didn't work."

Serena searched the agonized young face. "What do you mean?"

Kirby closed her eyes. "I'm pregnant again," she whispered. "And you know what? The guy who's the father broke up with me. Just dumped me flat."

Serena felt a lump forming in her throat. "I know it hurts, that it's frightening. I understand."

Kirby shook her head. "You can't know how it feels. Nobody can know what this is like unless they've been through it already and know they're going to have to do it again. Especially when. . .I can't help wondering if Mother would have gotten rid of me the same way if. . ."

"But she didn't," Serena countered softly. "And you're not alone." She stopped and reached out to the young woman. "Kirby, look at me." She waited until the tear-washed eyes slowly came open. "A lot of young women have felt the same self-hatred you're feeling."

"You think so?" Kirby's voice was filled with sarcasm. "You haven't talked to many girls my age lately."

"Yes, I have. Don't forget I run Alternative. I'm sure Jenny's told you about our free clinic. I talk to a lot of young women there and in my practice. Many don't struggle with it, I know, but many others do. They realize. . .they know. Kirby, I'll be here for you." She paused. "Are you sure you're pregnant?"

"I took a home preg test," Kirby said. "The last time, I was in the last part of my second trimester when I had the abortion. I even felt. . .felt kicking before Mom guessed I was pregnant and took me to the doctor. When my parents find out, they'll make me—"

"No." Serena's hands tightened instinctively with sudden outrage at the Acuffs. What had they done to their daughter? "They can't force you to have an abortion. No one can do that."

"You don't know my mother. She's like a rhinoceros on a rampage."

Serena studied Kirby's expression through the dim light. "Is she. . .abusive?"

"She doesn't hit me, if that's what you mean. She yells a lot. She's just. . .you'd have to see her to know what I mean."

Serena stopped walking and touched Kirby's arm. "Come see us at Alternative. We provide emotional support and even housing for unwed mothers. If you need some place to stay—" Should she be saying this? Was she trying to alienate Kirby from her own parents? But what they were doing. . .was trying to take a baby's life. "And we can find good homes for the babies."

Kirby watched her for a moment. "I guess I never thought about going there myself."

"Why not? It's a clinic for young women just like you, who are lost and frightened but don't want to terminate a pregnancy."

Hope flickered in Kirby's expression. "You'd really help me? Even if my parents—"

From the distance, a deep, male voice reached them. "Hello. . .Serena? Kirby? Are you out there?"

Serena called back, and as she did so, she felt Kirby tense beside her. "It's okay, honey; it's Carson Tanner. Jenny called him about you."

Kirby caught her breath. "What did they do, call the whole city?" Still, there was a hint of relief in her shaking voice. Carson had a special way about him that appealed to teenagers—and not just teenagers, but people in general. Patients trusted him. Staff worked well with him.

"I know he's kept in touch with your family," Serena said. "He cares very much about you. Do you think you could confide in him about the pregnancy? He's not going to judge, and I know he'll want to help you as much as possible."

Kirby hesitated, and a residue of tears sparkled in the glow of their flashlights. "But what if the test is wrong? Maybe—"

"At Alternative, we can give you a pregnancy blood test, and you and your parents can get counseling and help."

"But I don't want to tell my parents about this. You don't know my mother. She'll make life miserable for everyone if I don't do what she wants me to do."

"Aren't your parents friends with Carson?"

Kirby nodded. "Kind of. After I had my first abortion, they got desperate. They took me to a psychologist. That was a downer for me, so they went really nuts and broke down and went to church—you know, where Jenny and Emily go. We attended for a couple of months. Carson visited our house several times, and I know my parents liked him. He's even been to see them a few times since we quit. He doesn't harass us or anything; he just listens. My parents don't have a whole lot of friends. Mother doesn't get along with a lot of people, but I think she likes Carson."

"Why did they stop going to church?" Serena knew everyone had their reasons. She had her own.

"Mother said she got tired of hearing the preacher talk about sin and salvation all the time. He really blew it the day he preached on abortion. Mom freaked. That was it for them. I kept going with Jenny for a while, though, until Mom decided they might corrupt me." Kirby snorted in contempt. "Right. Like I'm corruptible."

Serena placed her arm around the teenager's shoulders. "My dear, I realize you don't have a very high opinion of yourself right now, but I think you're someone very special."

There was a surprised pause. "You do?"

"Yes. Let's hurry and meet Carson."

There was barely a second of hesitation, then, "I guess. . .I could talk to Carson about it." After another minute she cleared her throat and said softly, "So you. . .you know. . .you think I'm okay?"

"Very okay." Serena gave her a squeeze. "I've known you ever since Jenny brought you home that first time, and I love your sense of humor, your kindness to Jenny's younger sister, Emily Ann, and your interest in their grandmother's garden."

"Yeah, sure. You make me sound like a saint."

"No, I'm telling the truth. You're obviously desperate to prevent another abortion, and you obviously didn't want the first one, but killing yourself and your baby is not the way to change things. Two wrongs don't make a right. Two deaths don't make a life."

Kirby was thoughtfully quiet a few more yards, then said, "I couldn't do it, Serena. I wouldn't really be able to hurt my parents that way. I just don't—"

"Hello!" Carson Tanner stepped out of the gloom along the trail.

Kirby jumped, startled, and aimed her flashlight at him. He wore cutoff blue jeans and a white T-shirt. His short, black hair was spiked up in the back, as if he might have been sleeping before the telephone call woke him up. He looked tired. Those night shifts in ER could take it out of a person.

"Kirby, praise God, Serena's found you!" he exclaimed as he rushed forward and caught Kirby in a quick, enveloping hug. When he looked at Serena over Kirby's head, she could see the relief and joy in his eyes.

He released her and stood back. "Young lady, have you—"

"No, and you can cool it with the inquisition," Kirby said, focusing closely on his face, as if watching for his emotional reaction. "Serena's already said it all. No, I haven't taken any pills; no, I'm not going to hurt myself. . .and I don't want another abortion." Her eyes narrowed.

Serena held her breath as she, too, watched for Carson's reaction.

There was only a slight pause and no change in his expression. He held her gaze. "Sounds like we have some talking to do, my friends."

❧

Carson knew he couldn't let the shock show in his expression or in his voice. He'd worked with plenty of troubled teenagers, and he knew the games they sometimes played to get past an adult's defenses. He kept his voice deep and calm.

He was glad Serena had been the one to find Kirby. People couldn't help being drawn to Serena's compassion, and he was one of those people. Her obvious inner convictions reflected in everything she did, in spite of the fact that she seemed to have an emotional block against anything that had to do with God. Since she'd been very active in church before her husband's death, he couldn't help wondering if she was still angry with God for taking Jennings at such a young age.

Kirby touched his arm as the three of them walked toward the trailhead. "Carson, Serena and I have been talking, and I want you to help me tell my parents if I'm pregnant again."

"Of course I will," he said, feeling his stomach clench in protest. Kirby's parents could be on the difficult side—or at least Carol could be. Hal pretty much fell in line with whatever his wife wanted. But whatever they were like, Carson wouldn't allow Kirby to face this alone. He knew Serena wouldn't either. "Are you sure that you're pregnant? Have you had a test?"

"Serena said I could go down tomorrow to Alternative and have one, but I don't want to talk to them about it tonight anyway. Please don't tell them yet."

"They'll most certainly want to know why you're so upset tonight. It's my understanding that they've called the police, and they may very well show up here in the next few minutes."

Kirby rubbed her eyes wearily. "I just can't face it all tonight."

Hal and Carol Acuff were arriving at the trailhead as Carson emerged with Kirby and Serena.

Carol, a slender, frazzled woman with tightly curled blond hair, rushed ahead of her husband in the glow of their car's headlights. "Kirby! Baby, what you put us through!" She reached out to hug her daughter, but Kirby shrugged from the embrace.

Serena saw the darkening of pain in Carol's eyes as she lowered her arms to her side. "Why, baby? Why did you do this?"

Hal stepped forward with tears in his eyes and wrapped his arm around Kirby's shoulders. "We're so glad you're safe. You don't know how scared we were." He turned to Carson, and lines of worry seemed etched more deeply around his eyes than the last time Carson had spoken with him. "Thanks so much for coming out here." He nodded toward Serena, then reached forward and shook her hand.

Kirby darted a suddenly nervous gaze around the parking area. "Are the police coming?"

"No, we called them and told them we'd found you." Carol held out her hand. "Where are they?"

Kirby's eyes widened, and she blinked at her mother. "What do you mean?"

There was a waiting silence while mother and daughter attempted to stare each other down. Kirby broke the stare first and looked away. "I threw them away, Mother. I flushed them, okay?"

Carol watched her a moment longer, then sighed with obvious exasperation as she turned to Carson and Serena. "I don't know how to thank you. I'm sorry you've been dragged into our dirty little family problems like this."

There was an edge to her voice that made Carson uncomfortable. "Everybody has problems, Carol," he assured her. "Sometimes we need friends to help us sort things out, give us a shoulder to lean on. I've got to tell you, I've been praying hard since Jenny's call tonight. And I'll continue to—"

"Can we go home now?" Kirby's whole demeanor had changed. Her voice sounded abrasive, and Carson thought he detected that same edge to her voice that he'd heard in Carol's.

"First, don't you think you should apologize to Carson and Serena for dragging them out here like this?" Carol asked.

"I didn't drag them, Mother; they came out by themselves."

Carol shot her daughter another sharp glance, and the mutual antagonism was palpable.

This time it was Carol who broke the staring contest. "Fine, let's go home. We'll talk about this later."

Chapter 3

Serena awoke Friday morning just as dawn broke through the big bay window of her master bedroom. She slid from between rose-colored satin sheets and pulled the covers back to let the bed air. Later, when she was fully awake, she would make the bed so Blythe wouldn't feel compelled to do it for her.

She crept barefoot across the amethyst berber carpet to a long, low chest of drawers, the color of ocean driftwood. After selecting a black, one-piece bathing suit from a drawer, she slid out of her silky nightgown and pulled on the suit. Emily would come running through the house in a few moments, waking everyone up, cheerful and laughing. But Serena wanted to talk with Jenny first. She had still been upset about Kirby last night.

"Jenny," she called softly, pausing to glance through the open door at her pretty seventeen-year-old. "Honey, are you awake?"

Jenny stirred. A few tresses of her long, dark brown hair tumbled across her face, and she sniffed as a curl tickled her nose. She opened almond-shaped, golden brown eyes and gazed up at Serena.

"Morning, Mom."

Serena smiled indulgently at her daughter. "Good morning." Jenny looked fine this morning, not worried or upset. Perhaps the talk could wait.

Jenny stretched her long, slender arms over her head and yawned loudly. "I suppose you're going to drag me out of bed and throw me in that icy pool."

As she spoke, Emily Ann, her thirteen-year-old sister, came dashing down the hallway to stand beside Serena. Emily's grin was filled with mischief. "Yes, and I'm going to help." She was already dressed in her own modest suit, and her short, muscular legs carried her quickly to her sister's bed. She grasped the covers and flung them back. "Come on, sleepyhead, up!" Tossing her long hair behind her shoulders, she bounded on top of Jenny and tickled her.

"Okay, I'm up!" Jenny cried. "Emily!" she protested over her sister's giggles. "If you don't stop it, I'll dunk you when we get to the pool!"

Emily's soft brown eyes danced with glee. "You'll have to catch me first!" She dashed out of the room and down the hall. Seconds later there was a loud splash from the pool in back.

Serena and Jenny followed. As the three laughed and played in the water, the day warmed quickly.

A door closed on the private apartment attached to the house, and they turned to watch Blythe pass by in her gardening clothes, carrying a pair of trimming shears in her hand. Emily climbed from the pool and showered her grandmother with drops of water as she squeezed her long strands of brown hair. "Granny, aren't you swimming with us this morning?"

"Not this morning, honey." Blythe set down the shears and tucked an old white T-shirt into the waistband of her jeans. "I want to get to work on that garden before the sun gets too hot." The skin around her eyes creased as she frowned and glanced around the yard. "Now, where did that pup get to? Rascal! Where are you?" She wandered off toward her huge garden, which overflowed with vegetables.

"Uh-oh." Emily Ann pointed toward the rosebushes at the side of the house.

Rascal poked his muddy nose out from beneath a bush as he rolled in the damp earth, his golden blond coat no longer gold but muddy brown. Serena and her daughters watched as Blythe let out a howl of dismay and darted after the pup.

Rascal sped by the pool, missing the edge by a mere few inches, with Blythe no more than half a step behind him.

"Emily Ann Van Buren," she yelled as she passed by them. "If you find any more abandoned puppies in the ditch, just leave them there! Their owners know what they're doing!"

Emily giggled unrepentantly, then sighed when they all heard a yelp coming from the middle of the garden. "Poor Rascal."

Jenny snorted. "Don't worry about 'poor Rascal.' You should see Granny with him when no one else is around. I caught her feeding him a steak once. She even cut it up into bite-sized pieces so he could eat it better, and when she saw me watching, she turned red and jabbered something about the steak not smelling just right."

"Maybe it didn't."

"Granny had brought that steak home from the butcher the day before. If it didn't smell right, she'd have taken it back and demanded a fresh cut." Jenny chuckled as the pup emerged from the garden, his big, dark eyes darting from Serena to Jenny to Emily in a campaign for sympathy.

"Speaking of steak," Emily suggested, "why don't I fix steak and eggs for breakfast while you two get ready for work?"

As Emily climbed out of the pool to run, dripping wet, into the house, Jenny turned over on her back and floated out into the middle of the pool.

Serena watched her daughter thoughtfully as she began her water exercises. Jenny was so pretty—prettier than Serena had been at her age. Serena hoped she was also more mature. "Honey, are you still planning to go to the clinic this afternoon after you get off work?"

Water splashed as Jenny straightened. "What? The clinic? Oh, Mom, do I have to? A bunch of the kids are going down to the lake this afternoon, and I want to go."

"Of course you don't have to; that's why it's called 'volunteer work.' I just thought. . .well. . .I'd hoped. . ."

Jenny squinted at her in the sunlight, then her expression cleared. "Is Kirby going to the clinic today?" she asked softly.

Serena didn't reply. As a physician, she protected the confidentiality of her patients. As a mother, she wanted to share this information with her worried daughter, and Kirby was not her patient.

"Oh. You're doing the silent thing because of privacy rules. I got it. Of course I'll be there. I can leave for the lake afterward. Let's go get breakfast before Blythe feeds it to Rascal."

❧

The traffic light turned yellow as Serena approached the intersection. She sped up to cross before it turned red. She glanced sideways at Jenny. "Who was going to go to the lake with you this afternoon?"

"I don't know for sure. Danny said some of his buddies are going with their girlfriends."

Serena felt that old familiar worry tugging at her common sense. "Danny?"

Jenny shot her mother a long-suffering look. "So what if he is going?"

Serena pulled up to the curb in front of the print shop where Jenny worked three days a week. "But there are other kids going, aren't there? You know how I feel about you spending too much time alone with Danny."

"Oh, Mom, of course there are other kids going. At least, I'm sure there must be; Danny said there were." She climbed out of the van and shook several tendrils of hair back from her face. "Besides, you and Danny's mom are old friends. Don't you trust us?" She closed the door without waiting for an answer.

Serena watched her walk into the shop. "Yes, Jenny, I trust you," she whispered. "But I'm not sure I trust Danny Scott, even if Paula is my oldest friend." Making a mental note to call Paula later, Serena pulled back out into the traffic and drove toward work.

❧

"Good morning, Dr. Van Buren," Serena's secretary-receptionist greeted.

"Hi, Gail. You're early this morning. Did you get your car fixed?"

"Finally!" Gail grinned up at her, then stood and followed Serena into the inner office. "The phone's already been ringing for you this morning. It promises to be a hectic day."

"Of course," Serena replied dryly. "It's Friday, and we all wanted off early tonight." She sat down at her desk and shuffled through some papers left from the night before. "Messages?"

Gail pulled a watering can from the cupboard by the sink and watered Serena's jungle of plant life around the office. "Dr. Tanner called first thing. He wants to discuss last night's incident." She looked up from her work. "What happened last night?"

The buzzer sounded at the front desk, and Serena waved Gail from the room. "I'll tell you about it when we get a break this morning."

"You mean, if we get a break." Gail rushed out to answer the phone, closing the door behind her with a quiet *swish*.

Serena stared absently through the profuse growth of plants around the window to the large patch of blue sky outside. Would Kirby go to the clinic today, or would she allow her mother to convince her to have another abortion? If only Serena could talk to Carol for Kirby, if she could make her understand the pain Kirby was going through.

The private line buzzed, and Serena pressed the button to talk into the tiny, oblong speaker. "Yes, this is Dr. Van Buren. May I help you?" She picked up her pen and made a notation on one of the charts in front of her.

"Yes, you may, but what concerns me is whether you will." It was Carson's deep voice.

Serena felt a spontaneous smile warm her face. "That all depends on what you need."

"Well, it's a long story. I guess I need a sounding board."

There was an edge of worry in his voice, and Serena grew serious. "Is it about Kirby? Have you heard from her this morning?"

"Would you meet me for lunch? I hate to talk about this over the telephone."

Serena glanced at her schedule. "Sorry, but I can't today. I'll just have time for a quick sandwich at noon—if that."

"Probably not even that. Serena, you work yourself too hard."

Serena knew her family would agree. "I've cut my hours here at the office so I can spend more time at Alternative, but it seems as if my patient load hasn't eased."

"Have dinner with me tonight. We can talk about Kirby then. You can't possibly have patients around the clock."

"Okay, okay, I give up! What time, and where should I meet you?"

"Seven o'clock at your house. Good-bye, Serena."

The line disconnected, and Serena shook her head in exasperation, unable to control a playful smile that teased her lips.

She liked Carson. She had even had more than a twinge or two of physical attraction for him—after all, he was an attractive and strong man. Better yet, a compassionate man. In ways, he reminded her of Jennings; in other ways, the two were nothing alike. She couldn't deny the surge of excitement she felt at the opportunity to spend time with a man whom she had begun to admire deeply in the past few months, but there was an emotional barrier she had promised herself never to cross again.

The phone buzzed again, scattering her thoughts. This time it was Paula

Scott, Danny's mother, Serena's oldest friend.

"Paula, I was just going to call you," Serena greeted her friend warmly.

"Oh yeah?" Paula's casual voice came through the speaker. "I bet I can guess why. Is Jenny going to the lake with that monster of mine tonight?"

"Of course. Do you think she'd pass up a chance like that?"

"No, but do you know if any of the other kids are going?"

"Jenny said they were." Serena's earlier sense of foreboding returned. "Why? Do you have reason to believe they aren't?"

"If my son finds a chance to get Jenny alone, he'll take it. He's just like his father was at his age," she muttered.

Feeling old and tired all of a sudden, Serena leaned back in her chair and sighed. "I don't know, Paula. What are we supposed to do with them? Unfortunately, they're just like we were."

"Yeah, and look at the trouble it landed us." Paula echoed Serena's sigh. "The thing is, I can't keep Danny from going. He's eighteen, going on twenty-five, and he has his own car. If I try to stop him, we'll just get into a fight that won't solve a thing, and he would say, 'What's the matter, Mom; don't you trust me?'"

In spite of herself, Serena chuckled. "Where have I heard that before?"

"I think we invented the phrase." Paula paused thoughtfully. "Let me call some of Danny's friends' mothers and see if the other kids really are going. If they aren't, I can alert you."

"Then I can have another talk with Jenny. Paula, do you think we're overreacting because of our own mistakes?"

"Maybe just a little, but look at it this way," Paula argued. "If your mother had talked with you about things the way you talk with Jenny, maybe you wouldn't have that past. If mine had, maybe I wouldn't either." Paula had married Danny's father just two months before Danny was born.

"I have to hang up now. My first patient just arrived."

As always when with her patients, Serena became totally involved with her work, and the day sped by. She loved her job, loved working with people. She earned a good income, and she channeled much of it into the Alternative clinic downtown. Jennings had left the family well provided for and had taken out a generous insurance policy several years before his death. The interest from that investment helped keep Alternative going.

Situated as it was on High Street, with a teeming population surrounding it, Alternative attracted many young—and even older—pregnant women. Initially, curiosity brought them in. Word had spread in the past few years. More people were learning the value of new life.

❧

Serena stepped into the comfortably air-conditioned interior of Alternative late that afternoon and saw her older daughter in the waiting room, sorting through a box of newly donated baby clothes.

"Hi, honey. Has anyone come in yet?"

Jenny shrugged. "No, but Kirby should soon. I called her and told her I'd be here. We had a long talk, and she told me her parents are still really upset about last night." She frowned at her mother. "Aren't you off early?"

"I had a patient cancel the final appointment of the day. Are you still planning to go to the lake?"

Jenny bowed her head and sighed. "No. They wanted to spend the night, and I didn't think you'd let me since there were guys going, too."

"Good thinking, sweetheart." Serena walked over and sat down to help with the sorting. "Was Danny angry when you told him you weren't going?"

Jenny nodded in silence, and sadness was evident on her face.

"I'm sorry." Serena reached over and laid a hand over Jenny's hands. "I know it's hard, and I'm glad you had the strength to say no. So many girls don't."

Jenny grimaced. "That's why you have this place, but that doesn't make it much easier to turn Danny down. I really like him, and. . .and. . ."

"Growing up isn't easy."

Jenny shook her head. "Making the right decisions isn't easy."

They finished folding the clothes in companionable silence, and Serena stacked them in the back storage room. They often received donated clothing, baby items, and even personal care products for the women who were in need. As word had spread over the years about Alternative, more and more people supported them.

About twenty minutes later, the chimes played as the front door of the clinic opened, and Serena and Jenny both turned to find Kirby hesitantly stepping inside. They both got up to greet her, and her relief was evident.

Jenny walked over and gave her friend a long, hard hug. "I was beginning to think you'd chickened out."

Kirby's blue-eyed gaze darted around the clinic. "I almost did."

"Well, you're here now," Serena said. "I'll call Sharon from the back. She's our nurse on duty today."

Kirby tensed. "Can Jenny come with me?"

"Sure she can."

"Mother doesn't know anything about this, but she wouldn't shut up about it last night or this morning. I'm just glad she had to go to work today. If I'm not home before she gets off work, I'm dead. I can't wait around for the results. Can I call you?"

"Why don't you think about coming back in on Monday?" Serena asked.

Kirby groaned. "That long? Do I have to come in?"

"I'd like for you to," Serena said. "Are you forgetting that we're in this thing together? I want to be here with you to help you through it. There will be plans to make, and if the test is positive, we'll want to make arrangements for a medical examination."

A LIVING SOUL

"But can't you do that?" Kirby asked. "You're an ob-gyn."

"But I'm your friend first. In order to avoid a conflict of interest, I'll arrange for another physician to do the exam."

Kirby's gaze flickered to Jenny nervously.

"It's okay, Kirby," Jenny said. "Come on. Let's go find Sharon."

Later, after Kirby had left and the clinic was locked, Jenny stepped up beside Serena and watched through the window as traffic passed by on the street outside. "Mom, what would you do if I were pregnant?"

Serena thought about that for a moment, as she had many times before. "All I can say for sure is what I wouldn't do. I wouldn't panic and scream and hurl accusations at you. I would want to be there for you. And you know how I feel about abortion. Of course, the real question is, what would you do?"

A bemused smile crossed Jenny's face. "I'd tell you. Some girls can't say that about their mothers. Most of my friends' mothers would have panicked if they'd even asked the question."

"Most of the girls' mothers don't work with pregnant teenagers every day."

Jenny cocked her head to the side and frowned. "Some of them are volunteers here, remember? Jannell's daughter's in my class in school. There's just something different about you. You understand. Do you think it's different for us because you adopted Emily and me?"

Serena blinked at her in surprise. "No, honey, I don't think so. What on earth made you think about that?"

Jenny shrugged and went to get her purse. "I don't know. I guess lately I've been trying to see the differences between adopted children and natural children. I know Danny's getting tired of hearing it." She shrugged again, as if the subject didn't occupy too many of her thoughts. "Are we going home now? I'm hungry."

They drove through the heavy, noisy Jefferson City traffic in silence. It wasn't until they neared the suburbs that Jenny turned to look at Serena. "Mom, you know, I was just thinking. . .if you kept the clinic open later, you could reach more people."

"I've considered that, but I'd have to pay someone a hefty salary to stay downtown at night. Let's face it: I may make good money, and your father may have left us a safety net; but there isn't enough to double salaries, and I'm trying to cut my hours at work."

"Ask for donations," Jenny suggested. A mischievous expression crossed her face. "Or marry Carson Tanner."

Serena rolled her eyes. "Jenny Van Buren, wherever did you get an idea like that?"

Jenny eyed Serena innocently. "Well, Mom, don't you two see each other a lot?"

"I haven't gone out with him in at least a couple of months." She neglected to mention she was seeing him tonight. That was about Kirby.

"I don't know why not. He's gorgeous—that is, for an older man."

Serena parked in the driveway and climbed out. "You sound like your granny."

Jenny's golden brown eyes shone as she stepped ahead of her mother and threw open the front door. "How many times have you known Granny to be wrong?" she asked with a teasing grin. "Hi, everybody! We're home! Is dinner ready? I'm starved!"

Chapter 4

Serena felt like a girl on her first date when she opened the front door to find Carson standing there. Evidently he hadn't worked today, because he looked well rested and relaxed—not like a man who'd been rushing from patient to patient in a busy emergency room all day. He was dressed casually in jeans and a royal blue pullover that seemed to reflect the deep blue black of his hair. The gauzy material of her dress floated around her legs as she turned to lead him inside.

It was a very obvious coincidence when, just at that moment, Blythe came through the back door, followed by Rascal. Blythe's bespectacled gaze zoomed in on Carson, and she gave him a delighted smile. "Hello, Carson Tanner! Haven't seen you around here for a while." She took a swipe at her perspiring face and cast a warning glance at Rascal, who had a habit of sniffing legs.

"It's good to see you again, Mrs. Van Buren," Carson replied, his dark eyes warm and sincere. "It has been awhile, but you know Serena. Right now she's calling the shots."

Blythe walked toward them, then stopped and leaned forward conspiratorially. "Don't worry, I haven't given up hope for you." She shot Serena a challenging stare.

Serena glared back. Time to get out of here before Blythe could embarrass her further. "I'll get my purse and be ready to go. It'll just take me a second, Carson." As she dashed down the carpeted hallway, she heard Emily's voice.

"Hi, Carson! Welcome back. Are you and Mom going out on a date?"

Serena stepped into her bedroom before she heard the reply, but she couldn't miss the sound of Emily's footsteps pattering down the hallway to her sister's room.

"Jenny, he's here! He's here!" she squealed, with childish unconcern about the fact that her voice was loud enough to reverberate all the way through the house. She slammed into Jenny's bedroom, and Serena heard their muted giggles.

With a sigh of exasperation, Serena closed her own bedroom door and leaned against it. In any other situation she could deal with Carson on a strictly professional level, but it was impossible to behave professionally when her well-meaning family persisted in pushing her into a romantic situation with a man who, she had told them time after time, was merely a friend and colleague. What made it difficult was the fact that he had known all of them before he knew Serena. He was their friend, too, and he often saw them at church, and was closely involved in their lives as the girls' youth leader.

So why had she allowed him to pick her up here? He had given her no chance to refuse, but couldn't she have called him back? She sighed. She was always telling her girls not to say "if only" but "next time." Next time she would know better.

She stepped over to the mirror and fluffed the silvery curls of her hair. The problem was, her family—and perhaps Carson—were far too astute. He unsettled her. Jennings had been gone too long, and there were many things about Carson that fascinated her. She needed better control.

&

Carson felt like one of Dr. Doolittle's Pushme-Pullyou animals. Half the time he could feel the attraction emanating from Serena; the other half she very politely told him to back off. He knew she was confused right now. She undoubtedly still felt married to Jennings in some ways, even though he'd been gone three years. The grief would never disappear completely, but the living had to keep living. How did he tell Serena all of this?

He'd been intrigued by her from the first time he met her. She was so warm and vibrant, so caring about others. The more he knew about her, the more he learned to care for her—and he already loved her family.

Blythe had told him a lot about Serena's past, things that Serena would never have divulged. Blythe was the one who told Carson about Serena's intensity over her work and about the nights she sat up in the family room, staring out into the darkness, unable to sleep for worrying about her patients. Through Blythe, Carson had learned that Serena often came home in tears after leaving the clinic, heartbroken because she had failed with one of her patients at Alternative.

"You two have fun now," Blythe said as she followed Serena and Carson out to the front porch. "It's Friday night—no need to be in early."

Serena replied dryly, "Thanks, I'll remember that."

Carson chuckled as he preceded Serena toward his midnight blue Saturn in her driveway.

"Is something funny, Dr. Tanner?"

The chuckle turned into a full-throated laugh as Carson fell into step beside her and laid a casual arm across her shoulders. "Serena, you have a great family. For a mature woman, you certainly let them get the better of you. You and I are not opponents. Why don't you relax?" He helped her into the car and held her gaze. "You have nothing to fear from me."

"Of course you can see I'm terrified," she said.

Carson didn't stop in Jefferson City but drove west on Highway 54. The beauty of the countryside increased with each mile, flaunting its rolling, tree-covered hills and squared patches of green and gold, jeweled with farm ponds and dotted with huge round bales of hay. The serenity of the changing scenes seemed to ease something within Serena. When Carson glanced across at her, she had leaned back in her seat, a soft smile curving her lips.

She caught him looking at her. "Where are we going tonight?"

"I know a place, hidden in the trees, a few minutes' drive from here. It has excellent food and a peaceful atmosphere. You look like you could use some relaxation."

"Always the flatterer, aren't you? This place isn't, by chance, on a shore of the Lake of the Ozarks, is it?"

"My secret is out."

"Then I hate to tell you this, but it's more than just a few minutes' drive."

"It won't seem that long. A quiet drive is what we both need after last night."

"I thought you needed to talk about Kirby."

"Later, if you don't mind. It's a situation that worries me, and I don't want to lose my appetite."

As he drove, Carson darted a quick glance at Serena's profile. She could pass for a woman of twenty-two more easily than a woman of thirty-seven with two teenaged daughters. Perhaps that was because she was always so active. She didn't give herself time to brood.

"How's the clinic?" he asked, knowing that was one of the closest things to her heart besides her family. But that wasn't the only reason he was interested in Alternative. The idea of a clinic that produced a loving alternative to abortion, offering adoption services for childless couples, had appealed to him from the beginning. In fact, he'd donated anonymously through the church several times in the past.

"Busy. We've had a lot of girls come in lately. One of them was fourteen years old. You should have seen the look of relief on her face when she discovered the test results were negative." She shook her head. "Unfortunately, she could be pregnant in a month or so. It's almost as if the girls think they're immune to pregnancy. It's so difficult to convince a young girl about the dangers out there." Serena shook her head again. "How do you convince a know-it-all teenager that even if she never gets pregnant, the emotional scars she gets from her promiscuity will be with her for the rest of her life?"

"Not to mention diseases that could kill her." He paused. "I'm worried about Kirby."

"I thought you weren't going to talk about her until after dinner."

"Sorry, I can't help it. I called their house tonight and caught them while they were having dinner. I didn't talk long, but I could hear the tension in their voices. Carol seems like a woman on the edge—but then she's been that way ever since I met them two years ago. I hate to think Kirby is picking up on her mother's habits, but sometimes she sounds just like her."

"I don't know Carol or Hal that well," Serena said. "Kirby's been to the house a few times, a few sleepovers with Jenny, and she's good company."

"Do you ever wonder about the influence she might have on Jenny?"

"Of course, but Jenny isn't easily swayed."

He drove in silence a few more moments, then said, "I want to be with Kirby when she tells her parents she's pregnant."

"I think you should be."

"I just hope I say and do the right thing."

"Don't worry. You have a way with people." She turned and grinned up at him. "Especially women."

Carson had to concentrate on the road, but he felt broadsided by her mischievous smile and penetrating gaze. "You're a woman, and I don't seem to be making any headway with you."

"What do you call this date? You talked me into it, didn't you? And I don't date."

"Okay, I'm sorry. I take it back. I have you under my spell." He grew serious. "Alternative is a godsend, and you're the perfect person to have it."

"Sometimes I feel as if I'm just treading water."

"You do more than you know. You're good with Kirby and great with Jenny and Emily Ann. Your work with Alternative is enjoyable, isn't it? You're not having any problems?"

Serena leaned her head back against the headrest and stared out of the window. "No problems with the clinic."

"Could you use another helper? A counselor? Or floor sweeper?"

She glanced at him with renewed interest. "I could always use help at the clinic."

"Is a man allowed?"

"Allowed? That would be wonderful! Jenny was just telling me tonight that I should keep the clinic open later, but I don't think we can afford more salaries."

Carson's mind shot ahead. He could do something to help her there, too, but he wouldn't say anything about it just now. "Tell me," he said instead, "have you thought about Kirby staying with you if she needs to?"

Serena blinked at him in surprise. "Yes, of course she can stay with me. Why? Do you think Carol will throw her out?"

"I don't know, but it's a possibility if Kirby decides to go through with the pregnancy. She will need a lot of love and understanding."

Serena hesitated for a moment before answering. "I can give her that," she said quietly.

He turned off the main highway onto a narrow country road. "I don't doubt that for a moment, Serena."

The late evening sun had disappeared behind a thick growth of lush forest. Carson pressed a button, and the tinted windows of the car silently slid down. Serena took a deep breath. "Mmm, smell that. No exhaust fumes, no smokestacks, just fresh, country air."

They came to a break in the trees, and Carson stopped the car for a moment.

A green valley stretched out in front of them. Vivid blues and soft pinks coursed in and around the clouds. Serena sat as if transfixed by the beauty.

"God's artwork," Carson murmured. "Not only do we see it, but we experience it with all our senses. It makes me want to hold a worship service right here."

Some of the enchantment disappeared from Serena's expression. "It is beautiful all right."

Carson took his foot from the brake and allowed the car to coast down the steep hill again.

Serena turned sideways in her seat and regarded Carson thoughtfully. "How long have you been working with the church youth?"

"I started teaching Sunday school when we lived in Columbia thirteen years ago, when I was twenty-eight. Does that tell you how old I am?"

"Forty-one."

The tree line ended abruptly, and he slowed the car as they looked across the wide expanse of the Lake of the Ozarks. Serena gasped appreciatively as she stared across the glittering water, where millions of pink diamonds reflected the rosy hues of the lingering sunset.

"I'd forgotten how beautiful it is," she murmured.

"Has it been that long since you were here?" Carson followed the road that curved around the shoreline.

"The last time was just before Jennings died. The girls and I haven't been back since."

"My wife and I used to come here, too," Carson said. They rode in silence for a moment. He gazed out at the water as poignant memories forced their way through his mind—the calls and laughter of the boaters; the boats themselves, the sounds of their motors echoing across the valley; the mossy, slightly fishy scents of the water; and the ever-present green of the trees that surrounded it.

Serena looked up as a pontoon passed by them in the water. "We used to have a boat a lot like that one." She smiled. "The motor was so powerful, two people could ski behind it. If we'd known how much danger Jennings was in when he exerted himself like that, we'd never have bought the boat in the first place."

Carson knew Jennings had died of a heart attack. "He was so young, Serena. No one could have predicted it."

"One moment he was out mowing the lawn, seemingly healthy and vigorous, and the next moment he was lying on the ground without the strength to call for help. It was a shock."

"Jenny and Emily have come a long way since then," Carson said. He wanted to ask Serena why she hadn't, but he decided to keep his mouth shut for once.

They pulled up to an A-frame building with redwood siding, and Carson parked. "Hungry?"

"Starved."

"Then let's go in."

The Secret Cove specialized in seafood and steaks, and Serena quickly discovered that it was everything Carson had promised it would be, in service as well as in the deliciously cooked food. She ordered fresh rainbow trout and was not disappointed.

They spent the first few minutes eating silently, savoring each bite of the expertly cooked dishes. Quiet music played in the background, and the tables in the dining area were set far enough apart to give the illusion of privacy. Tall red candles, crowned by dancing flames, supplied the lighting. More than once, Serena glanced across the glow of the candles to find Carson studying her, and she glanced quickly away again, unwilling to be drawn by the magnetism she felt emanating from him.

"Has Blythe lived with you long?" Carson asked, finally breaking the silence.

"Since Jennings died. The girls and I invited her to live with us right after the funeral. She refused." Serena smiled at the memory. "She said she'd lived alone too long. She didn't want to be a burden to anyone. It was Jenny's idea to build an apartment onto the house, and it worked." She spread her hands in the air. "Blythe's been with us ever since, and I haven't heard a hint of regret from anyone. Of course, she didn't take my husband's place, but having her there helped fill a void for all of us. Blythe is a wonderful friend."

Carson pushed back slightly from the table after he finished his bass. "Yes, she is. You were especially blessed. But then so was she, to have you," he added quietly. "The death of a loved one is final and debilitating. I know—I lost my wife five years ago in an automobile accident."

Serena put down her fork and folded her napkin. "I'm sorry. I heard you had lost your wife, but I never felt comfortable asking about it."

He inclined his head as dessert arrived. As they slowly savored the rich, creamy chocolate cheesecake, Carson entertained Serena with humorous cases he'd had in the ER—without divulging names, of course. He kept her laughing until they were halfway home.

By this time, the sky was aglow with stars and a thin sliver of new moon. Carson left the windows of the car open, and Serena loved the silky soft feel of the night air against her bare arms. The sounds of tiny night creatures from the forest reached her ears, and the warm scent of a full-blown summer drifted and flowed with the breeze.

"Serena," Carson said at last, his tone growing serious, "I've been wondering something for a long time, and if you think it's none of my business, tell me."

"What's that?"

"The reason I think it might be my business is because of Jenny and Emily. I've grown to care very much for them these last couple of years—I care for all the kids in my youth group, but there's something special about—"

"You want to know why I don't go to church," Serena said.

He glanced at her quickly. "I don't want to offend you."

"You aren't. I'm not sure I can answer your question, though, because I'm not sure of the answer myself."

"Is it too painful?"

Serena met his gaze honestly. "You could be right; there is some pain involved in going."

"Three years' worth?" he asked gently.

Serena sat without answering for a few moments. There were old wounds there, much older than three years. It had been a very long time since she had actually enjoyed attending church services. Such a very long time...

She looked straight ahead at the road. "More than that," she said softly. "Maybe when I figure it out myself, I'll try to explain it to you."

When he slowed the car and turned onto her street, she felt his gaze rest on her for a long moment, and she felt like she was in high school again, coming home from her first date. Would he try to kiss her? Would he ask her out again? Everything within her dreamed that he would, yet the protective shield in her mind hoped he wouldn't. When they pulled into the driveway, she sat where she was, as if she'd been bolted to the seat.

"You have a wonderfully warm, embracing nature, Serena Van Buren," he declared softly, the deep, vibrating sound of his voice striking a chord of excitement in her heart. He took her hand in a gentle grip, but she still refused to meet his gaze. "When do you plan to start living your life again?"

Serena closed her eyes briefly. "I'm living my life."

"Through others, maybe, but not for yourself. Every patient you see receives a healthy dose of your compassion and understanding, but you have needs, too." He raised his other hand and traced the outline of her face with his fingers.

She shivered and pulled away. "Don't you do the same thing? It's been five years for you, and you haven't remarried." Her voice sounded shaky and unsure to her own ears.

His hand fell away, and the white gleam of his teeth revealed his sense of humor. "At least I'm making an effort to join the ranks of the living again. You're not helping me," he complained.

The warm strength of his voice seemed to spread an overpowering current of electricity through her whole body, and for a few seconds, against her will, she felt the urge to yield to his magnetism. With a burst of willpower, she pulled away and stepped out of the car. Taking a deep breath, she closed her eyes for a moment to steady herself.

"Good night, Carson," she said firmly as he climbed from his seat and came across to walk her to the door. "Thank you for—"

"Thank you, Serena," he said softly as he grasped her hand once more and raised it to his mouth.

She felt the shock of the tingling warmth of his lips to the tips of her fingers, then he released her and walked with her to the front porch. After she let herself inside, closed the door behind her, and stepped into the dark foyer, she heard a muffled giggle.

"Hi, Mom!" came a cheerful voice from out of the darkness.

Serena smiled. "Emily Ann, is that you?" Something slimy and wet touched her ankle, and she recognized the rough warmth of Rascal's tongue. She stepped down into the sunken living room and felt her way across to the sofa. "Why are you sitting in here in the dark?" She reached over and switched on a lamp. When she turned back toward the sofa, she discovered that Jenny was curled on the sofa in her nightgown, too. Both girls grinned broadly.

"We didn't want Carson to think we were waiting up for you," Jenny said sleepily. "How come you're home so early?"

Serena sat down on the cushion beside Jenny and slid her high-heeled sandals from her feet, fighting Rascal at every move. "It isn't early. What do you consider late?"

"Come on, Mom. I usually get home later than this when I go out," Jenny complained. "It's only eleven o'clock. What's the matter—don't you like him?"

"Of course I like him, sweetheart. He's an excellent person and a great youth leader."

"Mom, that's not what Jenny means, and you know it!" Emily exclaimed.

Serena aimed a playful tap at her daughter's shoulder and stood up.

"No, wait, Mom," Jenny pleaded. "We've been talking about it tonight. . . ." She patted the sofa in an invitation for Serena to sit back down.

With a wry grin, Serena looked at each daughter in turn. "What have you been talking about?" She sank down between the two.

Both were silent for a moment, and Serena waited patiently, already aware of what they were trying to say. She was touched by it, but also a little disturbed. Once again, they were getting their hopes up about Carson. They obviously adored him and talked about him all the time.

Jenny finally spoke, her young face serious. "I guess maybe we're different from a lot of families, aren't we? I mean we're pretty close."

Serena nodded. "Yes, honey, we're very close. We share a lot of love between us. I've been blessed a thousand times over with you two."

"But it's you, Mom," Jenny insisted. "You're the blessing in this family. If you and Daddy hadn't told us from the time we were little, we would never have guessed we were adopted. You've shown us the kind of love a lot of kids don't get from their own flesh-and-blood parents. You're the best thing that could ever have happened to us."

Serena grinned at her older daughter. "You can say that after you missed going to the lake because of me today?"

Jenny looked away. "It wasn't because of you, Mom." She glanced quickly at Emily. "There were other things involved. Besides, we've never been back to the lake since Daddy died, and I thought maybe I would wait until we could go as a family again."

"What Jenny's trying to tell you, Mom," Emily stated impatiently, "is that we don't mind if you marry Carson and make us a family again."

"Emily!" Jenny cried. "You have no tact! You weren't supposed to put it like that!" She turned to Serena. "What we are trying to say is that we want you to be happy. Daddy's been gone awhile now, and I know kids don't take the place of a husband, no matter how much they love you. You don't have to worry about us getting upset if you ever do decide to get married again. We just wanted you to know that."

"Yeah, we just wanted you to know that," Emily echoed her sister's words, looking up at her mother uncertainly.

"I do know that," Serena assured them. "But you need to understand that we are a family just the way we are now. I don't have to have a man in my life to fulfill me. We take care of each other, right?"

Jenny frowned. "Yes, but there's something to be said for men, too, isn't there? I mean, don't we need a chance to learn how to live with males as well as females?"

"There's not much difference." She squeezed them both tightly, then sat back with an arm around each girl. "Speaking of families, I have something to ask you, and I want you to think hard about this, because it affects us as a family."

Both girls sat up eagerly.

"No, it's not about my getting married again. It's about a teenager who's in trouble and may need a place to stay for a while."

"You mean stay here?" Emily asked.

Jenny tucked her feet beneath her nightgown and huddled closer to Serena. "Is it Kirby? Have you talked to her? I told Emily about it. If that pregnancy test is positive, her parents will freak."

"I hope not. Maybe Carson can work things out with her parents. I'll talk to your granny tomorrow."

"You know it'll be okay with her," Emily said.

"I'm sure it will be, but this is her home, too, and she should have a chance to give her permission."

Jenny kissed her mother and went to bed, but Emily lingered in the living room. "Mom, did you say you and Carson are both working on Kirby's parents?"

"Well, I'm not sure 'working on' is the phrase I'd use, but yes, we're both very concerned with the welfare of this family."

"You and Carson do work well together, don't you?"

"I suppose we do. Why?"

"Oh, I was just wondering. Don't worry—with you both working with Kirby's parents, they're bound to come around. Good night, Mom."

"Good night, Emily."

Chapter 5

C arson dragged himself out of bed Saturday morning to answer the strident ring of the phone. He'd intended to get up early, but not quite this early. It was barely light outside. He answered sleepily.

"Carson, you've got to help me. Talk to them! I can't take this!" It was Kirby Acuff's voice, choked with sobs, and it brought Carson totally awake.

"Kirby, what's wrong? Where are you?"

"I'm at home, but I won't be here long if this keeps up. I'll do it again, and no one'll stop me this time."

Carson could hear yelling in the background. It sounded like Carol. "What's going on there? Tell me what's happening."

"It's Mother. She forced me to tell her that I might be pregnant again."

"How did she force you?"

"She wore me down. She's been up all night long crying, pacing the floor, yelling at me. She's—she's crazy! I need you to talk to her!"

"All night?"

"Yes!"

Carson sighed and glanced down at a number beside his telephone. If Kirby was in an abusive situation, he could call the police to go to the house and remove her; but unless there was physical abuse, few people would take him seriously. "Kirby, listen to me. Calm down. Are you—"

"Please talk to Mom. I can't handle her by myself."

He could hear Carol Acuff's voice getting louder, heard muffled sobs, then Carol's angry voice came over the line. "Carson Tanner, is that you?" she snapped. "Nobody bothered to tell me my own daughter's pregnant again! How could you deceive us like this?"

"I did nothing to deceive you. I planned to be there when Kirby told you. Do you understand what your reaction is doing to Kirby right now, Carol?"

"That's none of your business! I'm just talking some sense into her that she should have had in the first place!"

"I'm coming to your house now."

There was a long silence, and then the sound of agonized crying. "How could this happen again? We did everything we could to keep her from. . . Oh, how could she do this to us?"

"Calm down," Carson said gently. "You need to take some deep breaths and give yourself time to think." He spoke with her as he would speak to one of the teenagers in his church youth group. "Why don't you sit down for a few quiet moments? I'll get dressed and come over so we can talk about th—"

"No." Her voice was firm. "Not here. Not now. I don't want anyone to see us like this."

Carson waited, holding the line, unwilling to release that tenuous connection to this desperate family that needed God's touch so badly. He heard Kirby's sobs in the distance, and Carol's quiet sniffles, and wondered where Hal was.

Hal Acuff was a quiet man with a quick sense of humor who allowed his wife to control their household. Carson wasn't one of those men who thought a man should be king at home—he loved the idea the apostle Paul had in the Bible of mutual submission. Unfortunately, Carol never submitted, and part of the fault lay with Hal.

Eventually the sniffling subsided. Carson said softly, "Carol, are you sure you don't want me to come over? Sometimes it helps—"

"No." Her voice had regained some of its iron. "We know what we have to do."

"Why don't we just wait until we can meet—"

"We'll go to the same place we went before."

"Is that Kirby's decision, Carol?"

"It's mine."

Carson curbed his growing anger. "It's Kirby's baby. Legally, she has total control over that life. Why don't you and Hal take Kirby down to the Alternative clinic Monday evening after you get off work. I'll come with you, and we can talk about it there."

"There's nothing to talk about. I've already made my decision."

"But Kirby hasn't made hers. She's the one who counts here." Carson forced his voice to remain calm. "The other night was a warning from Kirby. She was telling us that if she had to have another abortion, she wanted to die along with her baby. That's what she could—"

"Look, Carson, butt out, okay? I know how you and your church feel about abortion, and that's fine for you; but you don't have a teenager in your home who's about to ruin her life. Wait until you're in my situation before you start making any judgments."

Carson sighed wearily. "Fine. At least come with your daughter to the clinic Monday evening, if for no other reason than to make sure we don't 'poison' your daughter's mind further." He kept the sarcasm from his voice with difficulty.

There was a lengthy pause, then, "I'll be there."

"I'll tell Serena Van Buren to have a counselor waiting for us."

◈

The Saturday afternoon heat blasted down in waves from a cloudless sky. The luscious, fully ripe garden shimmered with layers of heated air, and the tiny, sparkling drops raining down from Blythe's hose scattered the sunlight into drifting rainbows. Serena settled back in her lounger and spread her arms over her head to catch more of the cooling drops. She watched with amusement as Rascal, sitting beside her, eyed one particular mud hole with careful nonchalance.

Slowly, cautiously, he rose to his feet and edged toward the tempting hole, all the time keeping an eye on Blythe's location in the garden. He opened his mouth and panted with anticipation as he lifted a paw to place it triumphantly in the water. . .but something went wrong.

With a loud shout, Blythe jumped from behind the tomato plants, wielding her trusty hose. With deadly accuracy, she caught Rascal in the face with a powerful stream of water, and he let out an indignant yelp before tucking his tail between his legs and streaking around the side of the house.

"Mongrel!" Blythe shouted after him as she walked over to the faucet to turn off the hose.

She pulled a bandanna from her hip pocket and wiped it across her mud-streaked face, then pulled a pair of shiny metal pliers from another pocket and sat down beside Serena with the nozzle of the hose between her knees. "This thing's shooting sideways again," she muttered. Beneath her deft touch and with the help of the pliers, the offending nozzle came apart.

"Rascal doesn't seem to think so," Serena replied dryly. "Blythe, you work too hard. Why don't you slow down?"

"What, and let this garden go to waste?" Blythe exclaimed. "That would be a shame, with all those kids starving in other countries." She shook her head. "Besides, what would I do if I didn't do this? I'm not one of those little old ladies who sit idly around drinking tea and eating cookies, waiting to die."

"You're not a little old lady, and I wasn't implying that."

Blythe worked a few seconds in silence, then glanced sideways at Serena. "The day I lose my usefulness is the day I hope the Lord takes me home."

"You'll never lose your usefulness around here."

"You're right; I won't. How will you and the girls manage after I'm gone?"

"You're not going anywhere. We need you too much." She paused thoughtfully. "Blythe, how would you feel if we invited another teenager to come and stay with us for a while?"

Blythe blinked at her. "You're talking about Kirby? Jenny told me about her. I think that would be just fine."

"And knowing you, you'll try to pick her brain about all her family problems."

"I resent that! I'll just let her talk, and she'll know I care enough to listen. I'm no gossip."

Serena laid a conciliatory hand on Blythe's weathered arm. "I didn't say anything about gossiping. You care about people. That's one of the reasons I know we could help Kirby. Still, if she wants you to know about her problems, she'll have to tell you herself."

"Fine, then I'll pick your brain. How was the date last night?" Blythe shot

Serena a sly glance and grinned.

Serena sighed. "The food was delicious; the drive down to the lake was peaceful, even if it did bring back a few memories."

"The lake?" Blythe stopped tinkering with the hose and peered at Serena over the rim of her glasses. "He took you to the lake? You don't call a drive like that romantic?"

Serena avoided Blythe's all too astute gaze. "Not in the least."

Blythe snorted. "Maybe not to you—"

"Hey, Mom!" Emily came out of the house in her swimsuit and ran barefoot across the wet grass. "My old speech teacher called. Remember Mrs. Jackson? She says there's going to be a school board meeting next Friday night, and she wants to know if you can attend and speak about Alternative for a few minutes. There's going to be a discussion group dealing with the problem of teenage pregnancy."

Serena reached up and smoothed long tendrils of hair away from her daughter's cheeks. She did remember Mrs. Jackson. She had been a volunteer at the clinic for a while, but her schedule was so busy, she'd had to bow out after about six weeks. Serena liked Bev Jackson.

"I suppose I could, but Mrs. Jackson could do a better job; and she knows a lot about Alternative."

"Please, Mom? She asked specifically for you." Emily lightly touched her mother's arm. "I already almost told her you'd do it. Besides, it's just for one night, and you've done it before." She glanced across at Blythe, and Serena could have sworn she detected a hidden signal pass between the two.

After a suspicious scrutiny of Blythe, Serena looked back down into her daughter's hopeful brown eyes and relented. "Okay, I'll do it. What time does it start?"

Emily launched into details, and Serena watched her younger daughter's animated expressions with swelling love. This was her sunshine girl, brown-skinned and always laughing. Emily Ann was the one with the tender heart who had rescued Rascal from a muddy ditch. She'd then willingly turned him over to her grandmother—not because she was too lazy to care for him herself, but because she knew, instinctively, that the pup would brighten the older woman's life when the girls were off to school and Serena was at work.

Serena watched her daughter step across to the pool and dive in. Emily was also the mischievous one, and right now that child had something on her mind—some hidden project—and Serena could only wait helplessly to discover what it was.

She glanced sideways at her mother-in-law. "Is there really a meeting next Friday?"

Blythe's eyes widened. "Serena Van Buren! Are you accusing your own daughter of lying? I'd be ashamed."

Before long, both women joined Emily in the pool. For the next two hours, the summer heat had little effect on them. Before they were finished, the pool was completely sheltered by the shadows of the house, and the heat had begun to surrender to the evening—only slightly, but enough to make them feel pleasantly cool when a breeze touched their damp skin.

"May I fix dinner tonight, Mom?" Emily asked as she climbed from the pool. She shook her streaming hair back from her face and squeezed out the excess water. "I thought up a recipe for barbecue cups that should be fun."

"Be my guest," Serena invited gratefully. "I don't know where you get all that energy." She watched Emily pat herself sketchily with a beach towel, then run inside, still dripping.

With a sigh of fatigue, Blythe heaved herself onto the side of the pool. Serena followed.

"How many teenagers offer to help out in the kitchen?" Blythe asked, a glint of affection lighting up her blue eyes.

"Two in this household," Serena said proudly.

Both women heard a car pull up in front of the house, then an angry young voice. "You're lying! Leave me alone!"

The car door slammed, and Serena and Blythe looked at each other. "Sounds like Jenny's home," Blythe said.

Chapter 6

Before Serena could get up to go see what had happened, Jenny came walking around the side of the house. Her head was tilted forward, as if she were deep in thought, but when she looked up, there were tears on her face.

Blythe stood up and glanced at Jenny, then back at Serena. "I think I'll go inside and see if I can help Emily."

Serena shot her a grateful glance and rose to meet her daughter. "Want to tell me about it?" she asked, rubbing a tear from Jenny's smooth cheek.

With a nod, Jenny walked over and slumped into a lounger. She stared morosely into the deep green of the garden. Serena sat quietly beside her for a moment, then asked, "Did you have another argument with Danny?"

"He's a pig!" Jenny erupted angrily.

Silently agreeing with her, Serena reached across and stroked her daughter's hair. "I've heard you say that before. What's he done this time?"

"Usual thing," Jenny mumbled. "According to him, I'm not natural because I don't want to. . .well. . .you know."

Yes, Serena knew. "You disagreed with him."

Jenny nodded. "I guess I've seen too much at Alternative." She paused. "Mom, I can forgive him for what he tried, but not for the nasty things he said when I refused." Her eyes again filled with tears, and she ducked her head to hide a trembling chin.

"What did he say?"

Jenny battled silently with her tears for a moment, then sniffed and raised her head to stare back into the garden. "Can I ask you something?"

"You know you can ask me anything. What is it, honey?" Anger at Danny Scott slowly built up within Serena. Even if he was her oldest friend's son, he was a spoiled, self-centered brat who had a lot of growing up to do. Jenny was discovering that for herself.

"I was four years old when you and Daddy adopted Emily and me, right?"

Serena frowned. What did Jenny's adoption have to do with anything? "Yes, Jenny. But you know we both loved you and wanted you very much. Has Danny said something to make you doubt that?"

"No, that's not it," Jenny said quickly. "He could never do that."

Serena nodded, waiting for her to continue.

"D–did you ever meet our real mother?"

The fear stabbed more deeply through Serena before she could ward it off. After all these years, was Jenny going to try to find her real mother? "Yes, honey, I met your natural mother twice before your daddy and I adopted you. She wanted to be sure you and Emily would have a warm, loving home."

Jenny glanced up hopefully. "Then she did care about us?"

"Very much."

"And our father? What about him?"

Serena bit her lower lip and hesitated.

"Mom?"

Serena sighed. "We never met your natural father. What little information we could discover about him led us to believe that he was too immature to shoulder the responsibilities of fatherhood." Serena knew this would not satisfy Jenny.

A quick snort of derision escaped Jenny's lips. "What took him so long? Did it take two kids for him to decide he didn't want them?"

Serena glanced across at her daughter. Maybe now was the time to tell her, though the man's problems still didn't excuse him.

"I get the picture, Mom. Our father never wanted us in the first place. He had four whole years to learn to love me, but he must have never learned."

Serena shook her head. "Honey, your father had a lot of problems, terrible problems, and he ended up in jail for robbing a convenience store to support his drug habit."

Jenny digested this in silence, not showing the shock or horror Serena might have expected. Her mind was only on one thing—her parents' desertion.

"And our mother may have wanted us in the perfect situation, but when the times got rough, she didn't have any trouble dumping us on you."

Jenny's face crumpled, and the sight made Serena's throat swell with tears. "I don't want to hear that, Jenny," she said at last. "It was the strength of your mother's love that brought you to us. Your mother wanted you and your sister to be raised in a happy environment. She didn't have the money to support you. There was no one in her family who could help her, and she was desperate. All she wanted was for you and Emily to have a good life." Serena reached across and raised Jenny's chin, and watched her daughter's expression change as the bitterness and disillusionment faded and hope replaced it.

"Then she didn't just get tired of us and dump us with you?"

"Is that what Danny told you?"

Jenny's eyes filled back up with tears. "He said I'd better be careful about how I treat him, or he may do the same thing."

Serena hugged her daughter close. "Honey, forgive me for talking like a mother, but would it be any great loss if Danny didn't come back? You're a strong, self-confident young lady; do you think you could go solo for a while?"

Jenny swallowed and sniffed, then wiped a hand across her eyes and cocked her head to the side. "You mean dump Danny before he has a chance to dump me?"

"Not exactly."

A faint flicker of interest showed in Jenny's eyes, and her mouth toyed with a smile. She leaned back in her chair with her hands behind her head. "Sweet revenge."

"No, that's not what I meant," Serena protested. "Even though he may act like a pig at times, he's a human being with feelings just like everyone else." Besides, right now Serena liked pigs better than she did the smart-mouthed boy who had hurt her daughter.

"You mean all guys are only interested in sex?"

"No, honey, although it does sometimes take up a lot of their thoughts at this age. What I mean is that revenge is not for you to take. I'm not suggesting that you break up to hurt him."

"Okay, okay, Mom. Don't worry. I was just thinking about it for a minute. I couldn't really do it, you know." Jenny frowned and shook her head. "I don't know; maybe I could. Not for revenge, of course, but just to get away from the pressure for a while."

"It's up to you, Jenny. I know it would be hard, but I'll be here for you whatever you decide." She tweaked a ringlet of Jenny's dark hair, then stood up and strolled across the lawn toward the house, leaving Jenny alone to think things through.

The pungent, smoky fragrance of barbecue sauce greeted her as she stepped in the house, and she glanced through the kitchen door at Blythe and Emily.

"Do you think we could use the good china tonight?" Emily asked her grandmother.

"I think this meal deserves it," Blythe replied.

Serena slipped past and left the two talking. As she walked through the quiet house, she relished the comfort of the air-conditioning. The scents of Blythe's flower arrangements drifted across from the den as she walked past it, into the bedroom, and pulled off her nearly dry bathing suit, then slumped onto the side of her bed.

"Oh, Jenny, how I wish I could do more for you," she whispered, glancing across at her older daughter's picture on top of the chest of drawers. "But you've got to make your own decisions right now. . . . I just hope you make the right ones."

She took a shower.

From somewhere in another room she heard the telephone ringing, and a few seconds later someone pounded on her bathroom door. "Mom! Hey, Mom!" Emily opened the door and traipsed into the bathroom. "Telephone. Guess who?"

Serena finished rinsing shampoo from her hair and turned off the faucets. "Hand me a towel, will you?" She held her hand over the top of the shower cubicle until Emily placed a fluffy bath towel into it.

"I'll give you a hint," Emily persisted. "He's tall, ve–ery good looking, and has the deepest, most masculine voice I've ever heard from an ER doctor."

Serena stepped out. "Hand me my bathrobe, and I'll find out for myself who this hunk is."

"Oh, come on, Mom. You know it's Carson."

"Oh, is that all?" Serena teased. "I'll have to tell him what you said about him. That should make his weekend. Thanks," she said as she took the terry robe from her daughter and pulled it on. She glanced at her bedside table, but the phone was missing. "Where's the phone?"

"Oops. I left it in the family room." Emily gave her a nervous look. "You wouldn't really tell Carson what I said!"

"Why not?" Serena led the way out of her bedroom and down the hallway to the family room. "What's wrong with letting a person know how you feel about him?"

Finally deciding her mother was teasing after all, Emily shook a reproving finger at her. "It's not nice to carry tales, you know. Besides, Carson already knows how I feel about him. Does he know how you feel?" she asked hopefully.

Serena merely grinned at her daughter as she picked up the receiver. "Hello, Carson. What can I do for you?"

"If you insist on holding such intriguing conversations with your daughter, at least hold them a little closer to the phone so I can catch every word," he complained from the other end of the line.

"You're a glutton for punishment," Serena retorted. "Don't you know eavesdroppers never hear good about themselves?"

"Yes, but at least they know where they stand. Besides, I just wanted to hear the sound of your voice again."

"I'll send you a recording," she retorted, shooing a deeply interested Emily from the room. "Better yet, why don't you just call my office number? My voice is on the answering machine."

"Should I also ask your answering machine to come to church with me in the morning?"

"Wouldn't do much good." In spite of herself, Serena could feel spirals of pleasure run through her at the warmth of his invitation.

"It doesn't hurt to try." He paused, but Serena didn't reply. "Do you have medical call next Saturday?"

She tried to remember her schedule. "I don't think so. Sally asked for weekend call this week."

"Then would you come to the lake with me?"

"I just went to the lake with you."

"Again. For the day."

"Are you kidding? A whole day away from town? I'm not sure I could handle the stress," she said dryly. "I can't remember the last time I've had the nerve to do that. What if one of my patients went into labor? What if we had a crisis at Alternative?"

"You have very competent help, and we can take a cell phone on the boat. You can be back to town in an hour if there's an emergency. Serena, give yourself a little break."

She expelled a sigh of exasperation. "You don't give up easily, do you?"

"Not when I want something badly enough."

She couldn't help it: She felt guilty, as if she were still a married woman who had just been tempted to step out on her husband. It was ridiculous, of course, but how would she be able to enjoy a day on the lake with Carson?

"No. I'm sorry," she said, and quickly changed the subject. "Have you heard from Kirby?"

"Yes." The disappointment was evident in his voice. "She'll be at your clinic Monday evening for the test results, and I hope you're there, because her parents and I will be with her."

Serena sat down abruptly as she digested this bit of information. "Her parents? She's told them?"

"Yes. I got a call from Kirby this morning during a family crisis after she told them about it. Carol's pushing for abortion, and she can push pretty hard, from what I understand."

Serena closed her eyes and sighed wearily. "What's that woman trying to do?"

"Carol is doing what so many other people do, Serena; she's hiding from the truth about Kirby's emotions and her own. She's closed her mind to it, and I haven't been able to reach her yet. We'll have a fight on our hands Monday evening, so be prepared."

"I will be, but. . .I'm glad you're going to be there."

"Well, well," he said approvingly. "That's a start."

Serena grinned. "Good-bye, Carson."

"Good-bye."

She replaced the receiver in its cradle and stepped across the thick carpeting to a window overlooking the countryside. She stared into the sky awash with gold, her mind and heart farther away than the clouds, on a tiny life she had given up so many years ago. . . .

"You and Jennings picked a good spot to build," Blythe said from the threshold to the kitchen.

Startled, Serena jerked around to stare at her white-haired friend, then nodded. "Yes, we did, didn't we?" She glanced back out the window as Blythe crossed the room to join her. "Of course, this place was farther away from town when we first looked at it. Jeff City has spread out quite a bit since then."

"Don't worry—you're not downtown yet."

"True, but sometimes even this sprawling neighborhood makes me feel hemmed in. I guess I'll always be just a country girl at heart."

Blythe murmured agreement. One of the many things they had in common was a true love for the open country. "You never did like living in town, did you?"

"Never. I remember the day—all those years ago—when Mom and Dad decided to move to town. I cried and carried on and made life so miserable, I thought for sure they'd leave me on the farm when they moved." More memories crowded in. "I had to spend my senior year of high school with strangers instead of surrounded by all my lifelong friends." Was that why she'd been so quick to accept friendship where it was offered—in the backseat of Greg Carter's parents' Buick? "I decided then that I would never do that to my own children."

Blythe grunted. "You've almost succeeded. Jenny graduates next year, and you don't act like you plan to leave before Emily does."

"No, I don't. If I show signs of doing so, you'll stop me, won't you?"

"That depends on what's most important at the time."

"There's little that's more important to a teenager." Serena slid open the silent glass doors and led the way outside. "Let's go see if we can find some salad vegetables to go with dinner."

Blythe hesitantly followed her. "I wouldn't advise it. Emily just finished chasing me out of the kitchen. I think she was afraid I'd mess up her menu." She glanced at the short terry robe Serena was wearing and raised an eyebrow. "I take it you're not going out tonight?"

"Not me." Serena inhaled, enjoying the soft fragrance of the air. "Mmm, smell that. Are those your roses?"

Blythe grimaced. "That's our neighbor's fabric softener coming through their dryer vent."

"Oh. Sorry. I guess you and the girls are going to church in the morning as usual?"

"Of course. And, as usual, I suppose you're not?"

"Not this time." She hesitated. "Maybe soon."

"How soon? It would be so much easier for the girls if you went with us." Blythe studied Serena's closed expression. "You can't keep blaming God for Jennings's death, you know."

"I don't blame God at all." Serena shrugged. "You know how it is when you lose someone you love: You tend to stay away from the things that remind you of them the most. Maybe I just feel guilty, maybe I blame myself for his death in some way. I can't help feeling that if I'd tried harder, God wouldn't have taken him from us." She shook her head.

Blythe raised a tanned hand and touched the backs of her fingers to Serena's cheek. "Don't give me that, Serena Van Buren. Jennings's heart attack wasn't your fault, and he would not want you to blame yourself. He loved you very much. You could brighten another man's life if you only let yourself. It's what Jennings would want."

Serena chuckled, threw an arm across Blythe's shoulders, and urged her toward the house. "Not nearly as much as you brighten my life, lady."

In the far, dark corner of a converted warehouse east of the city, a brown-haired, square-jawed young man named Edward stood watching his clan of workers with great pride. Most of them were teenagers, idealistic as he was, with a single focus in their hearts—to stop abortion, no matter what it took. From his informants across the city, he learned about which girls in the school system were pregnant. He tried to reach them with telephone calls, letters, or in person before they could make the wrong decision.

He had more difficulty during the summer months than the rest of the year because there was no school to throw the kids together. But one of his workers had informed on a friend of hers, Kirby Acuff. He had put a tail on the girl and discovered some interesting information: She had visited Dr. Serena Van Buren's downtown free clinic, Alternative.

Since she was a friend of the founder's daughter, she might just have been visiting, but Edward didn't think so. Kirby Acuff liked the boys.

Edward had always had niggling doubts about this clinic called Alternative. After all, if Dr. Van Buren hated abortion as much as she pretended, she was sure low-key about it. He'd never seen her at any of the protests at the state capitol building. He intended to do more research on the whole situation. Otherwise, how could he know Dr. Van Buren wasn't an abortionist herself?

He heard the ring of his telephone over the racket of his ancient printing press, so he reached over and jerked up the receiver. "Yes! Speak up!"

"What's that awful noise?" came Mrs. Jackson's answer to his greeting.

Edward smiled at the sound of the voice of one of his favorite teachers from high school.

"The printing press I bought last week with the money our group took in from the garage sales and bake sales this summer. I'm printing flyers for the meeting next Friday night. Did you get Serena Van Buren to speak?"

"Yes, her daughter just called. Emily also mentioned a Dr. Carson Tanner. He's an ER physician and youth leader at Serena's family's church."

"Youth leader, huh? Good. Thanks, Bev. I'll get back to you about the meeting." After hanging up, Edward returned to the printing press and turned it off. There would be time for this later. Right now, he had more investigating to do.

Chapter 7

The silence of the empty clinic weighed heavily on Serena's nerves, especially with the noisy rush-hour traffic outside the door. She glanced at her watch for the tenth time in the past half hour, then walked to the front window. The Acuffs would be off work by now, but they wouldn't have had time to get here. Out on the street, horns honked, traffic lights changed, and engines roared. Some of the storekeepers were locking up for the day, and Serena waved at a few of her acquaintances as they passed by.

She lowered the blinds. No need for every passerby to have a front-row seat for the coming meeting.

She walked back to the counter and read Kirby's file once more. Test results: Positive. Just as Kirby had expected. Perhaps the coming confrontation would prompt the Acuffs to seek help for the real problem in their family—if Kirby remained strong.

A dark-haired woman about Serena's age emerged from the back of the clinic, jingling a set of keys. "All locked up, Serena. Are you sure you don't want me to stay for moral support?"

Serena shook her head. "Thanks anyway, Sharon, but Carson Tanner is coming, too. I don't want the Acuffs to feel as if we're ganging up on them."

Sharon waved. "Just call if you need anything tonight or tomorrow." She stepped out and practically collided with Kirby, who was coming in.

Serena looked at the girl in surprise. "Kirby, I didn't think you'd be here so early. I thought your parents were coming with you."

The pretty blond stepped inside. Her face was pale, and dark circles deepened her eyes. "H—hello, Serena." She glanced around the big office, then stared at the entrance to the conference room. "I was supposed to wait for them, but. . .I wanted to talk to you alone before they arrived. I was afraid they might try to beat me here, though. That bus seemed to stop at every corner."

"Did you want to talk about something specific, or do you need moral support?" Serena stepped toward the conference room and gestured for Kirby to join her.

"Moral support, I guess. I need it after this weekend. I know what I'm doing is right, but my mother won't listen." Her gaze strayed to the shelves along the wall. They held replicas of an unborn baby in varying stages of development. "You don't have to tell me the results of my test. I already know I'm pregnant. I feel the same way I did the last time—morning sickness and all. And I'm grounded again, just like I was last time. It seems kind of silly, doesn't it? I mean, I can't get any more pregnant." She sat down beside Serena on a comfortable sofa.

"Kirby, there are other things that can happen besides pregnancy. I know your mother wants to do the right thing for you. What we need to do is prove to her that there's a living soul inside you, and that may be difficult to do." Serena studied the tension in the lines of Kirby's face. Would she be strong enough to oppose her angry mother? "To accept that," she continued gently, "your mother will have to accept what she's already done."

Kirby's chin jutted out. "But I accepted it, and I was the one who had the abortion." A tone of resentment entered her voice. "Mother acts as if she's the only one who's suffering. She acts like this is her life that's ruined, not mine. I made a telephone call today while they were both at work, and I found out all I have to do is go through some legal stuff and declare myself an emancipated minor. Mother can call all the police she wants, but she can't stop me. The police won't do a thing."

Serena hesitated. If Kirby did that, it might cause a damaging rift more permanent than the one they had now. Serena didn't want to undermine Carol Acuff's motherhood, but Kirby needed support. "This may be painful, and I want you to know before the meeting starts that my home is open if you need a place to stay, or if you and your parents need a few days to cool off and make some adjustments."

Kirby's eyes widened in surprise. "You'd do that?"

Serena smiled. "It isn't as if you're a stranger to us, Kirby. You've always been welcome in our home. As a guest of Jenny's, of course, you'd be treated like another one of my girls, with all the responsibilities and rules that go with it."

Kirby was thoughtful for a moment, then she shook her head doubtfully. "Mother would go nuts if I moved in with you. I think she'd rather see me try to move into my own apartment and starve to death."

The front door squeaked open, and Kirby stiffened. She and Serena turned to see Carson walk in. He wore blue scrubs and running shoes, so he must have driven straight from work. He looked tired, but when he saw Serena and Kirby, his face lit with a warm smile. "There you are. I was afraid I'd be late. We had a rush of traffic accidents thirty minutes before my shift was over, and I couldn't leave. Kirby, where are your parents?"

"Not here yet." The tension was back in her voice. She turned back to Serena. "I'm scared."

"There's nothing to be afraid of, honey."

"How about a prayer?" Carson said softly. "I'm a little nervous myself. I'm sure Carol and Hal will be, too."

"Better do it now, before they get here," Kirby said.

They bowed their heads, and Carson offered a simple prayer, asking for God's guidance.

Serena felt the peace of his words flow over her, and her own tension eased. It had been so long since she'd had the courage to ask God for something, but this time, in this situation, she knew it would be His will for Kirby to have this baby.

When Hal and Carol walked through the front door a few minutes later, their faces revealed the tension that was palpable in the conference room. "We're not staying long," Carol warned. "Just give the results of the test."

"I'm pregnant, okay?" Kirby snapped, her voice once again with that thread of discontent running through it, so much like her mother's.

Hal Acuff expelled a heavy sigh and looked sadly at his daughter. "Why, Kirby? Didn't you learn your lesson the first time?"

Kirby bowed her head and clasped her hands tightly together.

"What Kirby needs now is understanding." Carson looked from Hal Acuff to his wife. "She needs you to help her through this pregnancy and help her with decisions about adoption."

"No way." Carol's blue eyes grew cool. She studied her daughter's bowed head. "Kirby, do you want all of your classmates to see you waddle to classes during your senior year of high school? Is that the memory you want? Do you want them whispering and laughing behind your back?"

"I don't care what they say about me," Kirby muttered. "I can't take this baby's life."

"There's not going to be a baby."

"There already is one!" Kirby snapped. "You won't listen! You never listen."

Serena stood up and walked across to one replica on a shelf. She carried it over and held it out for them to see. "Kirby's in her second month. See the tiny baby in this piece of plastic? This is what your grandchild looks like right now. Its sex has already been determined. Its brain waves can already be recorded, and its teeth have already begun to form in the gums." She held it up so Carol could see it better. "It's a beautiful, miniature baby. That's fact, not fiction. I'm not making this up."

Carol stared at the tiny statue for a full five seconds, as if mesmerized. Her brows drew together. She pushed the statue aside and stood. "Why are you people doing this to us?" She walked to the end of the room and swung back. "Why us? Why are you picking on—"

"We're not picking on you, Carol," Carson said calmly. "We want to help you. Please just listen for a moment. We're trying to show you why Kirby threatened to take her own life the other night. We're trying to keep anything like that from happening."

Carol started to speak, swallowed, took a shaky breath, then apparently caught the compassion in Carson's eyes. She sat down on the edge of a hard-backed chair.

He continued, "Kirby can't emotionally handle another abortion, Carol. If she's forced to take this baby's life, I can't predict what will happen to her. We can save them both." He took the piece of plastic from Serena and placed it on the shelf, then turned back to Carol.

Carol glanced at Serena. Doubt entered her eyes for just a moment, then was gone. She slowly shook her head. "No." She looked down at her own hands. "Kirby can't do it."

"But it's not your decision, Mother," Kirby said. Her voice trembled, but the resolve of her words showed in her expression and the strong line of her chin. "If you don't want to help me, then I will move out."

Carol's eyes narrowed. "You're still a minor."

"I'm a pregnant minor. I have every legal right to protect this baby, and I will." Her own eyes narrowed at her mother, and for a moment their gazes did battle in silence.

"You don't have any money," Carol said at last. "You have no place to live—and don't get some crazy idea that I'll help you out."

Kirby swallowed and looked down at her nervously twisting hands. "I'll stay with Serena."

There was a long, shocked silence, then Carol exhaled as if she'd been kicked. Growing pain and anger tightened her facial muscles as she swung on Serena. "What are you doing?" she demanded. "I can't believe you people! Now you're trying to steal my daughter!"

"I'm not—"

"Stop it!" Kirby cried. "Mother, I'm not yours to steal. I want you and Dad to leave! I'm not coming with you."

There was another shocked silence so filled with anguish, Serena couldn't bear to look into Carol's eyes.

Carson cleared his throat. "Won't you both sit back down—"

"Fine!" Carol snapped. "Stay here. Go live with your precious Serena!" Tears sprang to her eyes, and she dashed them away with the back of her hand.

A frown spread across Hal Acuff's face. "No, Kirby's our daughter. We can't just—"

"She doesn't need us." His wife's voice shook as she glared at Serena. "Are you happy?"

"I'm not happy at all, Carol," Serena said. "But Kirby has made the decision to carry this baby to term. That's what we'll help her do."

Carol turned to her daughter, her face pasty white. Her hands shook, and her voice carried a sense of betrayal. "It's as if I'm not even your mother anymore. Well, that's fine with me! You've made your choice." She took a deep breath, straightened, and turned away. "Don't bother to come by and get your things. I paid for them; I'm keeping them. Let your new mother pay your way." Without looking at Serena again, she stormed out of the clinic.

Hal watched her leave, his face as pale as Carol's. He turned to Kirby, hands spread helplessly. "She doesn't mean it, Kirby. She's just. . .can't you just do—"

"No!" She put her hands over her face. "Just go," she said softly. "Go on with Mother. Maybe for once you can talk some sense into her."

"But I can't just leave you alone like this."

"I'm not alone." Kirby glanced hesitantly at Serena, then back to her father.

Hal shrugged and stepped forward to kiss his daughter's forehead. "You sure you'll be okay?"

"She'll be fine, Hal," Serena assured him. "She can stay with my family as long as she needs to."

He spread his hands again. "Then maybe I'd better go see if I can undo some damage."

Tears filled Kirby's eyes and trickled down her face as she watched her father walk out of the clinic in her mother's wake. "Oh, Serena, what have I done?"

Serena stood up and pulled the girl's unresisting form close and held her. She looked over the bright blond head to Carson, whose expression was sympathetic and whose physical presence lent her strength.

She gently tugged on Kirby's chin until the girl looked up at her. "Your mother's a troubled woman, and she needs our understanding and patience right now. I can't imagine how I'd feel if one of my daughters decided they wanted to live with someone else. Give her time to adjust. Maybe she'll come around."

Carson stood up. "I don't know about you two, but I could do with a nice, hot meal. Will you join me? My treat."

Kirby shook her head. "If it's okay with you, I'd just like to lie down. I'm so tired. I could rest right here on one of the beds in back while you—"

"Nonsense," Serena said. "My family is already fixing food. You can both come with me. I'll call home and tell them to set two more places, then Kirby and I can go shopping for a few necessities before we meet back at my house in. . .say. . .an hour?"

Carson inclined his head in agreement as the three of them walked together toward the front of the clinic. Serena and Kirby stopped at a shopping center for the supplies for Kirby.

On the way to Serena's, Kirby relaxed and started talking. "Mother has her temper tantrums, but she's never been as bad as this before."

"Not even the last time you were pregnant?"

"Nope, because I did what she told me last time. But she never trusted me again. She grounded me for a whole school quarter and wouldn't even let me go to a movie or a ball game with my friends, just church. And then she even put a stop to that." Kirby looked out the side window at the passing scenery. "I'm so glad Carson didn't give up on us. He's so. . .I don't know. . .kind. He's genuine, you know? He really does care about us, and even Mom picked up on that."

She stared out the window in silence for a moment, then said, "I'm not as afraid now. Now that I know I don't have to have an abortion, there's something inside me that feels so. . .safe. Something about it feels right. I know I blew it big time, but if I ended another life to cover up what I did, I. . .couldn't live with it."

Serena reached out and touched Kirby's shoulder. "I'll be here for you. Whatever it takes."

$\approx$

Edward drove from his parking spot near Alternative with a smile on his face. He couldn't help feeling pleased with himself. Within a forty-eight-hour period, he had discovered a lot of interesting things about Kirby Acuff. He had used acquaintances to find out information for himself and now knew Kirby's address, her telephone number, what school she attended. A friend of his who was a computer expert could find out more about Kirby's past in a couple of days. School records were next. All Edward had to do was hang around and listen a little more.

It wasn't just luck and perseverance that had put him outside Alternative at the right time to see the Acuffs enter the building, then see the parents leave later without their daughter. He shouldn't have tried to question them, though. That mother could be vicious, and he'd had trouble judging between the truth and her distorted picture of Serena Van Buren. To hear Kirby's mother tell it, Alternative was not a pro-life clinic but a place where Serena played out her own little God fantasies. He wouldn't make a decision about that until he knew more. Still, talking to Mrs. Acuff gave him a feel for the story he intended to write.

He knew he was definitely onto something good when he saw Kirby leave in Serena's van, and he knew God had a hand in it. Still, Edward needed more. He wanted to know more about Serena; yet she might balk at an interview, especially if any of Mrs. Acuff's bitter accusations were true.

Edward knew his methods were often questioned, but wasn't that just another sacrifice he had to make for the cause? He was willing. He didn't care what the whole world thought of him, as long as he carried out the plan.

$\approx$

Serena was proud of her family that night. Blythe had cooked one of her special recipes with veal and rice, and Jenny, when she heard they were having company, made her homemade blueberry ice cream. Emily met Serena and Kirby at the front door and grabbed Kirby in a hug, chattering incessantly. She escorted the older girl down the hallway to the room that would be hers.

"Hi, Mom," Jenny called from the kitchen doorway. "Is she here yet?"

Serena chuckled and pointed down the hall. "Your sister's already stolen her away. Go on back and welcome her."

"You mean you let Emily take her over already? Not fair! Emily!" she called as she followed in the wake of the other two girls.

With a soft smile on her lips, Serena stood listening to the friendly, muted voices of the girls in Kirby's room. The doorbell made her jump. Carson was here already. She stepped to the door, then hesitated with her hand on the knob for a moment before she braced herself and swung it open on Carson's tall form.

"Come in," she invited. Her gaze traveled swiftly down a casual, open-necked, red knit shirt and blue jeans, then moved back up to meet his eyes. They were watching her with undisguised admiration.

He stepped into the cool interior of the house from the heat outside. "You did well tonight. How's your guest doing?"

"The girls have taken her over. I think she'll be fine for now. I feel awful about Carol. I know she must be devastated."

"But I'm sure you understand this is necessary."

"Yes, but it's still painful." Serena led him into the family room where Rascal lay sprawled across the sofa in an attitude of dejection.

"What's the matter, boy; did they run you out of the kitchen?" She reached down and scratched his ears.

"Need any help with the food?" Carson asked.

"Are you kidding? In this houseful of cooks? I'll just go check on things and call you when it's ready."

Dinner turned out to be as good as Serena had expected, and she was gratified to discover that Kirby had shed the last of her misgivings and relaxed as if she were already a part of the family. Whenever the girl's face grew sober, Emily poked her from one side or Jenny whispered to her from the other, and the melancholy disappeared.

After an hour of talk, laughter, delicious food, and reprimanding Rascal-the-beggar under the table, Carson laid down his napkin and stood up. "That was a wonderful meal. Thank you for inviting me. I'd stay and help with the cleanup, but there are a few loose ends I need to tidy before I call it a night." He bent toward Serena. "I think Kirby will be just fine with the four of you. Want to walk me to my car? I could use a consult."

The sky was still bright when they stepped out the front door, and Serena felt a cool mist touch her face as a gentle breeze carried a spray from the sprinkler system in their neighbor's lawn. The fragrance of pine perfumed the air, and Carson inhaled appreciatively.

"I envy you, Serena. I wish I had an evergreen forest in my front yard." He chuckled. "I wish I had a front yard."

"That's a difficult thing to come by in a high-rise apartment, isn't it?"

"Very," he agreed. "But then, what's a pine forest or a nice house in the country without someone to share it with? An apartment building at least gives the impression of company."

"I'm sure you're right. This place would get pretty lonely without the others. I never lived alone. Is it difficult?"

Carson opened his car door and turned to look at Serena. "Very. It isn't so bad until you find someone you want to spend your time with—then it's very lonely."

Serena looked away.

"Don't get too attached to Kirby," Carson said.

Serena glanced back at him. "I'm already attached. Are you going to try to talk to her parents again?"

He nodded. "Neither she nor the baby needs the added pressure of her estrangement from her parents. As you said, Carol Acuff has problems of her own, but I think tonight might precipitate a change. You handled the situation very well."

"Kirby did most of it."

"Without your support, she may not have had the courage to do it," Carson replied. He touched her cheek in a tender caress.

The warmth of that touch sent a quick tingle of pleasure through her.

"You impress me, Serena."

"That just proves how little you actually know about me."

He got into his car and started the quiet engine. "Then I think it's time I got to know you better," he replied softly, then raised his hand in a half salute and backed out of the driveway.

With a feeling of bemusement, Serena watched until he turned a corner and disappeared from sight behind a stand of pine trees. The thing she had never expected to happen again was happening. If she weren't careful, she could easily fall in love with Carson Tanner.

&

The minute Carson stepped into his apartment, he switched on his desk lamp and sat down. There were three things he had to do before he went to bed tonight. First, he made a note to transfer funds to his checking account and write a sizable check to Alternative next week. He had always believed in what Serena was doing there, but after tonight, he felt a strong conviction to help her in every way he could. She was saving lives. This time his donation wouldn't be anonymous.

He reached for the telephone. He had already memorized the Acuffs' number. He dialed it and waited. It rang eight times before he hung up. Where were they? He'd have thought Carol would grab the phone at first ring, if she was there. If she wasn't there, where would she be? Barging in at Serena's to drag her daughter home?

He had seen the pain in Carol's eyes several times tonight, and in Hal's. If he could do nothing else, he might be able to ease some of that pain until they grew strong enough to see the truth for themselves: No one would take their place in the heart of their daughter.

He dialed Serena's number. Was he calling too late? Apparently not, for someone answered on the second ring. "Hello?" It was Emily's voice, and Carson smiled to himself at the sweet sound.

"Are the dinner dishes all washed?"

"Hi, Carson! Yes, the kitchen's spotless. Do you want to talk to Mom?"

"That would be nice."

"Okay, but first I want to ask you a favor, but promise not to say anything to

Mom." She didn't wait for him to reply. "Would you be interested in talking in an open forum next Friday night at a school board meeting? It's about teenage pregnancy."

He glanced at his calendar. He was free. "I'd love to."

"Good, because I promised Mrs. Jackson I'd probably be able to get you. I'll get Mom now and give you the details later."

Serena sounded tired when she came on the phone, and Carson took pity on her. "I won't keep you long. I just wanted to see how Kirby was settling in." *And to hear your voice again.*

"She's doing very well."

"Good. You wouldn't have, by chance, changed your mind about going to church, would you? We could use some extra prayers right now."

"No, Carson, I haven't. But thank you. You'll have to pray extra for me."

"I have been praying for you, Serena."

"That wasn't what I—"

"Are you trying to tell me how to pray?" Carson asked gently.

Serena hesitated. "No. I just feel that Kirby needs prayer more than I do right now."

"Maybe not. Good night, Serena. I'll be seeing you soon."

Chapter 8

As the summer advanced into August, Serena's patients complained about the heat. Blythe predicted the drought would kill her garden. Serena felt the familiar weight of depression drag her down as the calendar advanced. It was always the same. This time of the year was the most difficult for her and had been for all of her adult life.

Kirby settled into the household comfortably, but Serena often saw the sadness in the girl's eyes. For the first two nights, after Jenny and Emily went to bed, Kirby sat up and stared silently out of the bay window in the family room. Serena and Blythe, sensing that she needed time alone to adjust, stayed nearby, but they didn't pester her with questions or idle chatter.

Wednesday night, Serena sat down beside the pretty teenager on the sofa. "Can't sleep?"

Kirby shook her head.

"Want to talk about it?"

Tears filled Kirby's eyes, and she sniffed. "I feel so guilty for hurting my mother."

"That's natural," Serena assured her. "But you know what you're doing is the right thing. We need to give your mother time to realize that." She couldn't help wondering if Carson had spoken with Carol.

They sat in silence for a few moments, listening to the ticking of the grandfather clock. Blythe was in the kitchen baking a batch of cookies, humming a familiar gospel tune, and the sounds she made were homey, familiar, comforting—at least to Serena. She hoped they were to Kirby.

"It was nice to go to the youth meeting with Jenny tonight," Kirby said at last. "A bunch of the kids got together for pizza afterwards, and it felt good just to sit and talk about stuff. I've really missed that." She paused and glanced at Serena. "On the way home, Jenny told me again how she feels about God."

Serena kicked off her sandals and tucked her feet underneath her. "Jenny has strong Christian convictions."

"Yeah, I know. She always has, but I guess this time I listened better. She. . . told me that God can forgive me for my abortion, if I will only ask Him."

Serena nodded. "Did you ask Him?"

"N–no."

"Don't you believe He'll forgive you?"

"I. . .don't know. Maybe I don't know God well enough yet, or maybe I don't think I deserve to be forgiven."

"Don't you think you should let God be the judge of that?" Jenny should be in here talking to Kirby. Serena felt suddenly incompetent.

Kirby got up and stretched. "Maybe I'll go to church with Jenny on Sunday. Although now Mother says anyone who goes to church and calls himself a Christian is just a hypocrite."

After telling Kirby good night, Serena stretched out on the sofa and stared outside. She didn't go to church, avoided talking to God, and avoided talking about Him; and yet, when someone asked, she called herself a Christian. Was she a hypocrite?

Thursday morning Carson dialed the Acuff number. He had done so every morning and night since Kirby went to stay with Serena. He expected the same results as before—an answering machine—but this time Hal picked up.

"I was beginning to think you'd gone out of town," Carson said after he identified himself.

"We did, Carson. We went to stay with Carol's sister in St. Louis for a couple of days. Carol's pretty upset about all this. Kirby's okay, isn't she?"

"I was hoping you would call her and see." Carson tried to keep the sharpness from his voice.

"I would have. It's just that. . .well. . .Carol already thinks we're ganging up on her. I thought if Kirby called her first. . ."

"Your daughter's feelings are important here, too."

"I know they are, and I promise I'll call her as soon as I get a break this morning at work." Hal lowered his voice. "Carol's back in the bedroom getting dressed. She's more upset than I've ever seen her. She's cried every day since Kirby left. She blames Serena Van Buren."

In Carson's opinion, which he kept to himself, Carol was always eager to blame somebody besides herself, but that wasn't the compassionate Carson talking.

"Carol loves Kirby," Hal continued. "She just likes to be in charge, and when Kirby doesn't do what Carol wants, it upsets her. Kirby has her mother's stubborn streak, and so she rebels. It's my fault as much as Carol's."

"Have you tried telling your wife how you feel?"

"I've tried. . .but—"

"It might be what she needs to hear, Hal."

"Do you know how long things have gone on like this? We've fallen into a routine."

"Is the routine working?" Carson asked.

"No."

"I'd like to try to help you. We could set up some meetings with Kirby when the three of you feel you can handle it emotionally."

There was a pause.

"Will you think about it?"

Hal hesitated. "Yeah, I'll think about it."

❧

Kirby was still asleep when the Van Burens finished breakfast Thursday morning, and at Serena's request, Emily and Blythe took pains to be quiet while they did the dishes. Jenny didn't have to be at work until ten this morning, but she got ready early so she could ride to town with her mother.

"Why did you decide to go with me instead of letting Granny take you later?" Serena asked Jenny as they climbed into the van. "You know you'll have to wait around for two hours until the shops open."

"I want to talk to you alone, Mom," Jenny replied. "You have been so busy lately. It seems like you're never around anymore."

Serena glanced at her daughter in dismay. "I'm sorry."

"Mom, has something been bothering you?" Jenny asked.

Serena stopped in the process of buckling her seat belt. "What?"

Jenny shrugged. "You've been so. . .so quiet. And you've been going to work real early. Why?"

Serena looked into her daughter's questioning eyes for a brief moment, then sighed. It wasn't something she could talk about with her family. "I guess I just get so busy, I forget to take time for the most important people in my life sometimes." Serena rolled down the window and inhaled the fresh morning air. "I'm sorry, honey. I'll try to do better."

"Don't work yourself to death, Mom. We need you. You can't take on the whole world."

Serena patted her daughter's knee and backed out into the street. "I'll remember that. Now tell me what's on your mind."

Jenny sat back in her seat. "I took your advice. I broke up with Danny a couple of days ago. I would've told you sooner, but with all the stuff going on with Kirby, I decided it could wait."

Serena felt an immediate lifting of her spirits. No more worrying whether or not Danny would break down Jenny's will. "How did it go?"

Jenny grimaced. "Not exactly like I'd expected. Mom, he almost cried! I felt so bad. But I didn't let him talk me out of it, as hard as he tried."

"Are you sorry you did it?" Serena asked as they merged with the heavier city traffic and stopped at the first signal.

Jenny hesitated. "I don't know yet. I know I miss him. And I keep wondering if he'll go out with other girls."

"How will you feel if he does?"

"How do you think? Awful! But maybe he won't. He. . .he said he loved me and that if I didn't think we should go all the way, he could wait, if only I wouldn't break up with him. I just hope. . .I hope. . .oh, I don't know. . .I feel so lonely now without him. I hope I find out that he's sincere, but if he isn't, then it wasn't God's will for us to be together." She paused and stared out the window for a moment. "And there's something else, Mom."

"What's that?"

"Danny isn't a Christian. I mean, he says he is, and he's gone to a lot of the youth activities at church; but he doesn't actually live it, you know? If he did, he wouldn't be pressuring me like he is."

"And how do you feel about that?"

"I feel like there's something missing. It's like there's a whole section of my life I can't share with him, and it's the most important section."

Serena glanced sharply at her daughter. *The most important section.* "Jenny, you and I don't. . .talk about God very often either, since your father died."

Jenny continued to stare out the window. "I know."

The words sank deeply into Serena's heart. She completed the drive downtown in thoughtful silence. Jennings had been on her mind since she'd awakened this morning, and her sense of loss had been keen. His love had helped her forget the harshness of her past and healed some of her brokenness. Not all of it, but enough to face life. He hadn't ever known the depth of her pain, and she'd hidden it well, but his gentleness and joy lightened the burden she carried. When he died, she lost the peace he had brought into her world. She had placed so much of her faith in her husband, in his encouragement, support, and love. When she lost it, she felt as if she'd lost everything.

When they drove past Alternative, Jenny said quickly, "Stop here, Mom, and I'll open up this morning. Sharon will be here before I have to go to work, won't she?" The girl glanced along the street in both directions and opened her van door. "At least that man isn't hanging around today."

Serena shot her daughter a sharp look. "What man? What are you talking about?"

Jenny shrugged. "Probably nothing. I saw some guy hanging around the sidewalk a couple of times, and it looked to me like he was watching the clinic. Maybe I was just paranoid."

"I'm not sure I like the sound of this. What did he look like?"

Jenny shrugged. "I knew I shouldn't have told you. He didn't look bad. He was clean and friendly looking. He talked to one of the volunteers—I think it was Karen—when she left to go home the other afternoon."

"You mean he stopped her on the sidewalk?" Serena had trouble controlling the anxiety in her voice.

"Yeah, but she talked to him for a few minutes—I know, because I watched to make sure he wasn't bothering her—and she never acted upset. She was still smiling when she said good-bye to him. He's probably just taking a poll or something."

"Did he have a clipboard?"

Jenny frowned. "I can't remember. I'll watch for him today and see."

"You'll do it this afternoon, then. I'm not leaving you here alone this morning."

"Oh, Mom!"

"Close your door." Serena put the van in gear and pulled away from the curb. "You can wait at my office or where you work. It makes no difference to me, but I'm not taking any chances. I want to find out what that man wanted."

Serena called Karen Parker as soon as the first patient left her office but learned only that the strange man was polite, soft-spoken, and interested in the activities of the clinic. He had apparently known what Alternative's function was and seemed enthusiastic about it. He didn't sound threatening. Still, Serena wished she knew more about him.

After the third patient left that morning, Gail came into the office with the mail, laid it on Serena's desk, and proceeded to the sink for the watering can.

Busy with an information sheet on a new patient, Serena shuffled through the pile quickly, her mind barely registering the names on the envelopes until she came across Carson's return address. She slit the top of the envelope and pulled out a folded sheet of paper. When she opened it, a check fell out on her desk—in the amount of ten thousand dollars.

She gasped. She closed her eyes and shook her head, then looked back at the check, sure she must have imagined it. . .but there it was, written out in Carson's unmistakable handwriting.

It was for the Alternative clinic.

She picked up the letter that had come with it. "Dr. Van Buren," it read, "until I can be more personally involved with your clinic, I hope this can be of use. I believe in you, Serena, and I believe in what you're doing. Carson."

Serena leaned back in her chair and stared, unseeing, out her office window. A soft smile spread across her face. She reached for the phone to call him, but before she could pick up the receiver, it buzzed. When she answered, there was a short silence at the other end of the line.

"Serena, this is Carol Acuff. I want to know how my daughter is."

Serena hesitated in surprise. Things were happening a little faster than she could handle. "I think she's at the house," she said at last. "Why don't you call her there and find out?"

"Not right now. She'd probably hang up on me."

"I don't—"

"Just tell me how she is," Carol demanded.

Serena relented. "Kirby is fine physically. She's eating well, and she's getting along very nicely with my daughters. If you want to know how she's feeling emotionally, call her."

"What do you want from my daughter?" Carol asked with sudden bitterness. "Why are you going so far out of your way for her?"

"You already know the answer to that," Serena said quietly.

"So what's in it for you?"

Serena bit the inside of her lower lip to keep from snapping back.

"You were the one who sicced that jerk on me the other night, weren't you?"

Serena frowned. Was the woman losing touch with reality? "Who are you talking about?"

"That guy on the street. I walked out of the clinic, and there he was—asking me what was going on in there. What was he, a reporter? What are you up to? Did you write out the sermon he preached at me? All that garbage about abortion murdering babies. There isn't any baby, and you can't kill something that hasn't started living!"

Serena could feel the heat of her anger flushing her face. "Were you with Kirby through the abortion she had two years ago, Carol? Did you see them do the procedure?"

"Of course not."

"Then don't tell me it wasn't already a baby. Maybe if you'd been there for her—"

Serena broke off, appalled at what she was doing, what she was saying. The sound of a quiet sob snapped her attention back to the telephone. "Carol, are you still there?"

"It wasn't a baby," the woman said softly.

"Just keep telling yourself that," Serena said. "But while you're doing that, why don't you ask yourself where you would be now if your parents had opted for an abortion. Where would Kirby be?"

There was a swift intake of breath and then a snap as the line disconnected, and Serena felt a cold wash of shock at the harshness of her own words.

Chapter 9

Thursday afternoon brought a light, refreshing shower, and its effect was not only cooler temperatures, but cooler tempers. The tension that settled into Serena's neck muscles throughout the day disappeared. She stepped over to the window to inhale the fresh scent of rain and gazed with pride at the tree-lined streets and hills of Jefferson City. From where she stood, she could see the huge, white dome of the capitol building where it overlooked the sparkling Missouri River. The city spread over rolling hills, presenting an image of peace. If Serena had her choice of all the cities and towns in the country in which to work and raise a family, she would still have chosen Jeff City.

"Good night, Gail," she called as she locked her office door and walked across the carpeted floor of the outer office. "Is your car fixed yet? Do you need a ride home?"

"Running fine, but I'll go down with you anyway. I had a call today that might interest you." Gail turned off her computer and grabbed her purse as she stood to leave.

"A call? What kind of a call?"

Gail took out a ring of keys to lock the door, and their noisy jingle echoed through the empty corridor. "It seemed like just a request for information, but it was a pretty detailed request. Some man—he sounded young—wanted to know how many girls you saw at Alternative. He wanted to know how many volunteers you had working for you and what their names and addresses were."

"You didn't tell him, did you?"

"Of course not."

Serena pressed the elevator button. "Jenny told me about a man who's been hanging around outside the clinic." The elevator slid open, and Gail preceded Serena inside.

"What did he look like?" Gail asked.

"Young, slender, brown hair. He had the nerve to talk to one of my volunteers and to Carol Acuff."

"Maybe he's harmless."

"Or maybe not. What else did he ask you?"

"He flat out asked me if you ever arranged for abortions through the clinic." Serena stifled a gasp. "What did you tell him?"

"At first I didn't say anything; he surprised me so. I thought surely he'd at least know that much about Alternative if he was really interested—though I can't imagine why, unless he has a girlfriend or sister or somebody close to him who's pregnant. But you know what, Serena? I don't know if he believed me. He sounded really sarcastic when he asked me if I was sure about the abortions."

"If he ever calls again, give him to me. I want to have a little talk with this young man."

They stepped out of the elevator and through the revolving glass doors into the newly cooled, rain-washed air and walked toward the parking lot.

"He asked something else, too," Gail said. "He asked if Kirby Acuff was a patient here."

"And?"

"I guess I got a little huffy with him. Instead of just telling him we didn't give out that information, I told him it was none of his business and, if he wanted to waste any more of our time, he would have to make an appointment and talk to you."

"Good. Maybe you scared him off." Serena doubted it, but she could hope. This guy was beginning to worry her.

꧁

The telephone was ringing when Serena walked into the house an hour later, and she frowned as she rushed into the family room to answer it. Where was everybody?

A glance out into the backyard gave her the answer. Blythe was in the garden, and Jenny and Kirby were barbecuing steaks on the grill by the patio. As Serena lifted the receiver to her ear, she caught a glimpse of Emily dashing out from the side of the house, with Rascal tripping her up at every step. "Hello."

"Hello, Serena."

It was Carson's deep voice, and Serena couldn't control the leap of pleasure she felt. "Carson! I tried calling you today."

"Oh? If you'd called your clinic, you would have found me. I had some time and thought I might be of some use there."

"And were you?"

"You'll have to ask Sharon. I'm afraid I asked more questions than anything else, but I did learn a lot. Why did you try to call me? Is something wrong with Kirby?"

"No, I wanted to thank you for the check; but now that I have you on the line, I don't know what to say. How can I thank you?"

"I didn't do it for thanks. I wanted to invest in a good thing."

"Thank you, Carson."

"You're welcome. What I called you about was a date, but now it's going to sound as if I'm trying to buy one with you—and I'm not. Would you come out for a drive with me tonight?"

"But then you might think I was only going with you because of the money."

He laughed. "I knew that would cause problems. Come with me anyway."

"I'll tell you what: The girls are barbecuing steaks outside right now. Would you like to come over?"

"I will if you'll come for a drive with me afterward."

Serena smiled. "Okay. If a noisy dinner here with my family and a quiet drive afterwards will make up for the ten thousand dollars, then far be it from me to question your sanity."

"Why don't you try to figure it out for yourself? I'll see you soon." Without waiting for an answer, he hung up.

At Blythe's suggestion, the girls set up the table in the backyard. It was seldom cool enough to have a picnic this time of year, and they intended to take full advantage of the weather. Even Rascal sensed the party atmosphere and made a nuisance of himself as he dashed and played around their feet.

After a quick shower, Serena pulled on a pair of black jeans and a crocheted turquoise blouse. She cast a doubtful glance in her closet at her five pairs of sandals, then decided she would be more comfortable barefoot—she was always more comfortable barefoot.

The sound of a closing car door alerted her to Carson's arrival just before the doorbell chimes echoed through the house, and Serena felt the quickening of her breath. She glanced at the mirror one more time, gave her hair a final shake, and headed down the hallway to greet him. Her heart pounded loudly in her chest, and she pressed a damp palm against the denim material of her jeans as she swung the door open on its hinges.

What she saw sent her eyes widening in appreciation and her lips answering his broad smile of greeting. Her glance traveled slowly and appreciatively up his casual look. He wore black denim shorts and a white "Christ First" T-shirt. Her eyes traveled on up, only to rest on a frankly amused face. "You did say barbecue. . . ?"

"Sure did, and you look great." She turned to lead him out toward the back patio. "Are you hungry? The girls really got involved in their cooking today." She kept her eyes away from his and concentrated on breathing evenly, all too aware of his disturbing presence directly behind her. Tonight, more than ever, she felt his quiet magnetism.

The smoky aroma of sizzling steaks made Serena's mouth water when she led the way out of the house, and she eyed a large platter of them hungrily. Jenny—or perhaps Kirby—had been generous with Blythe's special barbecue sauce, and Emily had tossed a magnificent green salad of crisp vegetables from the garden. Blythe had spread a large red-checkered cloth over the long picnic table and was setting it with their finest china and silver. Serena raised a questioning brow when she noted their best crystal glasses set incongruously against the background of red and white checks.

"For a barbecue?" she asked Blythe under cover of the teenagers' loud welcome to Carson. "What is this, a celebration?"

Blythe glanced up from where she folded linen napkins. "Nope. No celebration, just good company." She glanced approvingly at Carson.

"Okay, everybody," Emily said, "it's ready. Come on, I'm starved!"

Carson asked the blessing for the food, and Serena's heart was touched by the simple sincerity of his words. He asked God to help Kirby become reunited with her family, and tears pricked Serena's eyes. She fought them furiously, unwilling for the others to see how sensitive she was just now. A beautifully grilled steak, thick with browned sauce, plopped onto her plate, and she jerked up to find Carson smiling at her.

"Join the party, Serena."

She returned his smile, picked up a fork and steak knife, and cut her T-bone into bite-sized pieces. She spooned out a large helping of Emily's crunchy salad, complete with creamy buttermilk dressing and sunflower seeds. Emily was proud of this salad recipe. It was one she had invented herself, and she'd even won an award in a contest at the fair last year.

Jenny leaned across the table with a small bowl. "Mom, dunk your cherry tomatoes in this sweet and sour sauce. . .and here, did you taste this corn on the cob? We roasted it on the grill with the steaks."

The low hum of talk at the table quickly grew to confused chatter, and Serena sat in silence, her glance roving from one face to the next. Blythe discussed a new recipe for homemade ice cream with Jenny, occasionally calling a warning at Rascal, who yapped for a handout. Carson joined in the conversation, surprising Emily and Jenny with his knowledge of cooking.

Blythe leaned toward Serena, her expression suddenly sober. "Have you had any phone calls from a member of the Save-a-Life group?"

"Never heard of them. Who are they?"

Blythe took a sip of her fruit punch. "That's what I wanted to know when some guy called here this morning looking for you. Now don't get excited, but I got curious enough to attend one of their meetings today."

"Sounds harmless enough. What happened?"

Blythe lowered her voice. "Kind of weird, if you ask me. Scary, even. This guy named Edward—didn't give a last name—seemed to run the thing. He led all kinds of chants against abortion. Some of it even sounded violent. They hate abortion, that's for sure, but they don't show much compassion. They were all pretty young. . .in their late teens, early twenties. The guy talked about God a lot, but I never heard him actually pray."

Serena thought about the man Jenny had mentioned hanging around the clinic and talking to Karen, who had accosted Carol Acuff and called Gail. "Did he say why he was trying to call me?"

"He heard about Alternative and thought you might be interested in joining their group."

"Did you set him straight?"

"Tried to. I told him you went about things peacefully, but he gave me some speech about banding together to get things done. They're talking about another meeting Friday night. I think I'll go again."

Serena set down her glass and stared at Blythe.

"Now don't worry," Blythe assured her. "I'm not getting crazy on you, but I'm curious. I'd like to know what they're up to. Ever heard of a mob mentality?"

"Of course."

"That's what this is. I met some people there today who seemed like decent folks until Edward got them all excited about 'the killers paying for their sins.'"

"And you're going back?"

"I'd feel safer knowing what's going to happen. You don't build that kind of heat in people without having a fire. I just don't trust them."

"Maybe I should go with you."

"Afraid I can't handle myself? Don't worry, these old bones have some life in them yet. You just have to convince them you know what you're talking about, and I think I can bluff them."

Serena nodded with reluctance. Blythe would do what she wanted anyway, but she had common sense. She could handle it.

The food vanished with amazing speed, and Emily jumped up when she saw Serena finish a last bite of steak. "Don't anybody move," the girl said as she ran toward the house. "Dessert is on its way." She disappeared into the house and emerged seconds later carrying a basket made out of a watermelon rind and filled with every fresh fruit conceivable, from bananas to kiwi to oranges. Emily's golden brown eyes shone with pleasure as she placed the salad in front of Carson and earned his immediate praise.

Serena watched the obvious display of affection between Carson and her younger daughter. Jenny and Emily needed someone like him—she needed someone like him to share her life with, to share her love, to share some of her burdens.

She nibbled on her fruit salad and watched the way Carson talked with the rest of them. He wasn't flamboyant in any way, yet his deep, quiet voice drew their attention the same way the glowing patio lamp was drawing moths in the fading evening light.

She bit into a tart, juicy kiwi and glanced up to find Carson watching her. He laid a hand on her arm and bent near. "I seem to remember your promise of a moonlight drive after dinner."

The tingling firmness of his hand and voice seemed to penetrate into her bones, and she nodded wordlessly. She slipped out along the bench and picked up dishes and plates.

"We'll handle the dishes," Kirby insisted, her blue eyes dancing as she took the empty plates from Serena's hands.

With a helpless shrug, Serena turned to Carson. "You win," she conceded. "Just let me get my shoes."

Chapter 10

Where are we going?" Serena asked as Carson backed onto the empty street.

"Good question."

"You don't know?"

"I don't have a clue." He shot her a teasing glance. "I just wanted to get you alone for a few minutes."

"Okay, but you're not going to take me on a moonlight hike in the woods or anything, are you? I'm only wearing sandals, and—"

"No hike tonight. The copperheads will be out."

Serena buckled her seat belt and settled back. She had to be honest with herself—she liked being alone with Carson Tanner. Of course, she would never admit that to him. Probably.

He drove the car around the winding streets of the peaceful suburb and finally merged with the sparse traffic on the expressway, heading away from the city lights. Country. Yes, he knew her well.

The night sounds of cicadas reached Serena's ears in a whisper through the closed windows of the car, and she listened contentedly. It felt good just to relax beside Carson. She gazed up at him through lowered lashes and bit her lip. She couldn't stop her imagination. What would it be like to spend more time with him like this? To have this to look forward to every day when she came home from work? To share—

No. She couldn't allow herself to go there.

"Deep thoughts?" he asked.

"Not particularly. I was. . .thinking about lots of things." She turned toward him in the seat. "Have you noticed how well Kirby seems to have settled in? She gets along very well with both Emily and Jenny."

The corners of Carson's eyes creased in a smile. "Do I detect maternal pride?"

"Do you blame me?"

"No. You have reason to be proud of them. I'm sure their friendship has helped her through this estrangement from her parents." He glanced briefly at Serena. "Until tonight, since the girls look so much like Jennings, I didn't know they were adopted. Emily told me."

"It's no big secret; it never has been. Even if we'd tried, we couldn't have kept it a secret. Jenny was four years old when we adopted them. She vaguely remembers her mother."

"You should counsel more adoptive parents. You've done so well with Jenny and Emily."

"Thank you. I think the girls are rather proud of the fact that Jennings and I actually chose them to be our children. It makes them feel special."

Carson slowed the car and turned off the expressway. "I think being loved by you would make anyone feel special."

"Being loved makes everyone feel special," Serena replied. "And since they're so attached to Kirby, she's bound to feel better than she did before. Life is so empty when you're not loved."

From the corner of her eye, Serena could see Carson nod in agreement; but when she looked across at him, the lights from the dash showed a frown marring his straight, black brows.

The narrow country lane entered a forest, and the headlights of the car reflected back at them from heavy foliage alongside the road. "I'm wondering how Jenny and Emily will react when Kirby returns home," Carson said.

Serena glanced over in surprise. "Is she going home?"

Carson stopped the car, switched off the ignition, and leaned back in his seat. "I called and spoke with Hal this morning. He was anxious about Kirby."

"So is Carol," Serena said. "She called me this afternoon to ask about her daughter, and I blew it, big time."

"Tell me."

"Well, I'm afraid I wasn't very professional." She hesitated, glanced at him, then looked away. She recounted to him the conversation with Carol, feeling her face flush with shame. "I'm sorry. I've become too emotionally involved with this situation. It's a bad tendency I have. I do it with patients, too."

Carson gently touched her cheek, and she looked up. "You may have gotten through to her when no one else could. Maybe she needs to see a show of force. Did you tell her how Kirby was?"

"I told Carol her daughter was fine physically, but that she would have to call Kirby and ask her how she was otherwise."

"Good." Carson slid the windows down with a quiet swish, and the night sounds of the crickets and cicadas came tumbling into the car with them. "I have a feeling Kirby may go home before she has the baby. I'll see if they'll talk to us again, kind of keep the communication lines open. But, Serena, I'm an ER doc, not a psychologist or family counselor."

"And I'm a hot-tempered ob-gyn doc, but I don't think Carol Acuff would agree to professional counseling again. It didn't help before. We'll do our best to convince them to try the counselor at Alternative. I really want them to have qualified, experienced guidance. If they refuse, it looks like they're stuck with us—if they'll let us help."

"We'll have to leave that up to God."

Serena nodded. The rich forest scents drifted through her window, and she breathed deeply. It smelled of dirt and hay and cedar. "How much longer do you think we'll get to keep Kirby?"

"It depends on Carol. It may be another week, maybe two. That is, if Kirby wants to go back home. She's pretty much in the driver's seat right now, because all she has to do is hold the 'emancipated minor' threat over their heads."

Serena hoped, for the sake of Kirby's family, that she reconciled with Hal and Carol and went back home, but a selfish voice inside argued with logic. Serena was growing more and more attached to Kirby and to the life that grew inside the young woman. How precious. How miraculous. To be a part of that. . .

"May I ask a personal question?" Carson laid an arm across the back of the seat. "Why did you adopt Jenny and Emily?"

"Because Jennings and I loved children, and. . .and we could have none of our own." She didn't feel it necessary to explain why.

"You made a good choice. I'm impressed by your girls." He paused, cleared his throat. "Sometimes I wish we had adopted. My wife and I couldn't have children either."

"I'm sorry." Serena looked down at her twined fingers and felt a sudden emotional heaviness. "That's not an easy thing to accept. I should know. I've lived with that same knowledge since I was a teenager." She raised her eyes back up to meet his through the darkness. "Did you feel terribly deprived?"

"I did at first, but there's much more to life and love than fathering children. I believe my wife was hurt much more than I was, but when I suggested adoption, she immediately rejected the idea." He reached out to touch Serena but drew back. "Now, seeing you with your daughters, I wish I'd tried harder to convince her to adopt. It's like you said, you seem to have a special relationship with them because you chose them. Speaking of your daughters. . .why don't you bring them and Kirby and Blythe, and come to the lake with me Saturday?"

"You already asked, remember? I declined."

"But I didn't invite your whole family. This is different. Would you consider it? You said you didn't have call."

The idea was tempting, but Serena shook her head. "No, Blythe is supposed to spend the day with an old friend of hers, and I don't think it would be a very—"

"Why not?" he interrupted, expelling a sigh of impatience. "Serena, until you give me a good reason why I shouldn't, I'm going to keep asking you to spend time with me."

The chirruping of tiny forest dwellers grew louder in Serena's ears, and all her other senses came alive in her awareness of Carson. He sat across from her, silent, as if waiting for her to argue. The clean male scent of him was strong in her nostrils, and she felt every fiber of her body reaching out to him—but still she held back.

He shifted slightly, and her heart skipped a beat when she thought he intended to move toward her. But he didn't. He just stared questioningly at her through the darkness. Her lungs felt empty of air, and she drew a shaky breath, fully aware of the raspy sound coming from her throat.

It seemed so long since Jennings had died, so long, and she had been terribly lonely. If she could just touch Carson, just feel the strength of his arms around her one time. . .

Of its own volition, her right hand reached across the expanse separating them. She stopped herself and drew back, but too late. Carson caught the gesture, and he grasped her hand before she could draw completely away. "No, Serena," he entreated. "Don't pull away."

He urged her closer, and incapable of resisting him, she allowed him to draw her across the soft seat into the arms she had so longed to feel around her. He drew her against his chest, and his firm lips came down on hers—and immediately she panicked and pulled back. Even in the darkness, she knew he must be able to see the pain in her eyes, so she closed them and ducked her head. "I shouldn't even be here, Carson. I still feel. . ."

"Married. I know. But you're not. Don't be afraid of intimacy, Serena. I mean emotionally, not physically. Well. . .I mean physically, too, I suppose, but. . ."

If it had been lighter in the car, Serena was sure she would have caught Carson blushing. She smiled. "I guess it's been a long time since either of us has dated."

"Yes, I guess it has. Longer for me. I'm afraid I'm extremely rusty at this, and I know that doesn't sound romantic; but the feelings are here, Serena. I could easily fall in love—"

Serena reached up and pressed her fingers gently to his lips. "No, Carson. You don't know what you're saying. You don't know me."

"Nothing I could discover about you now would change my heart."

Serena withdrew from him. "It's getting late," she said. "I have a long day tomorrow."

Carson slid back behind the steering wheel and started the engine. He glanced sideways at her. "Serena, no matter how precious Jennings was to you, he's gone and I'm here. My wife was dear to me. I loved her and supported her and protected her, but she's with the Lord now." He turned the car back toward town. "I'm more lonely since I've met you than I ever was at any other time in my life. I was ready to live alone, but when you came along, you upset all my decisions."

Serena looked across at him and laid her head against the soft headrest. "Tell me about your wife. Tell me about your past. Sometimes I think I know a person well, when in reality I know very little, because our pasts are what shape us. Where were you born and reared? How long were you married?"

Carson turned onto the expressway. "Deft change of subject. Okay, you win. I was born and raised down in the Missouri boot heel, close to the St. Francis River. Like most country boys in that area, I spent a lot of time along the river—

exploring, fishing, and swimming. I went to school in a town called Kennett. I suppose that's why I like Jeff City so much, because even though this city is larger, it has the same easy, countrified atmosphere as Kennett."

Serena watched the lights of the city appear on the horizon. "Don't you ever have the urge to go back to the country? I think I would feel stifled living in an apartment."

"Yes, as a matter of fact, I do long for the country life again. That's why I bought some land down by the lake a few years ago, before Judy's death. She was a city girl and afraid to live in the country. I felt sure she would change her mind when she saw what it was like, how peaceful it was. But then she was killed in the automobile accident." He fell silent, and Serena could empathize. For a few moments they rode in silence, until he pulled into Serena's driveway and turned off the engine.

"But that was five years ago," Carson continued. "This is now, and we're here. I wouldn't be anywhere else on earth at this very moment in time." He reached out, took her hand, and drew it to his lips.

The gentle pressure of his mouth sent a cascade of sensations through her, and she closed her eyes tightly for a second before pulling her hand away. "I've got to go in."

Carson got out of the car and came around to her side. He opened her door and took her arm, holding her eyes with his. "I think it's already too late to turn back," he murmured as she got out of the car.

She allowed him to lead her up the steps to the front door, and he turned to face her, gently placing a hand on each of her shoulders. The streetlights that reflected against his face washed out his natural tan and left him looking pale. "You know, you don't have to come with me to the lake Saturday if you don't want to, but your family is invited. Shouldn't they have the opportunity to accept if they want?"

Serena sighed in exasperation. "You don't give up easily, do you?"

"Alternative is in good hands. I know, because I've met some of your volunteers. Have faith in them. Serena, I told you, I'm a lonely man. I need companionship, especially since I met you. I enjoy your family very much. I have a cabin cruiser with room for everyone. If not for yourself, at least let the girls have some fun."

"Okay, I give up." Serena couldn't believe what she was saying. How long had it been since she'd been out of touch with the clinic for a whole day? But Carson was right, she had good people, and she needed a break. "Sharon can take care of things for the day, and she knows others to call if she needs help. I'll ask my family."

Carson drew her to him once again and kissed her, and the touch of his lips seared hers with tingling warmth that stirred a longing within her that she had never wanted to feel again.

"Good night, Serena."

Edward sat at his old electric typewriter and read what he had just written. He couldn't believe his good fortune. But wasn't this the way things were supposed to work? It paid to have friends in unusual places. For instance, computer experts who could hack into the clinics in Columbia and find one Kirby Acuff, age fifteen, who'd had an abortion two years ago. The same Kirby Acuff who was now associated with Serena Van Buren at Alternative and whose parents had left the place extremely upset just the other night.

It wasn't hard to put things together, especially not for Edward, who'd had experience at it. What concerned him now was that he might have come on too strong to Serena's mother-in-law, Blythe Van Buren. He didn't want to frighten them away. He wanted them on his side. He would have to keep things cool tomorrow night at the board meeting. Besides, he didn't want his Save-a-Life group to be a laughingstock. He had a mission to fulfill.

Chapter 11

Friday evening, Serena was tired. It had been a long, busy week, and she had been called Wednesday night to deliver a baby. It was always the most joyful part of her job, but also the most wearying. She dropped her purse on the kitchen counter and kicked off her shoes to carry them to the bedroom.

All at once, the angry sound of a loud car engine pierced the air, followed quickly by the harsh squealing of tires. Serena's brows drew together in annoyance. The front door slammed loudly enough to vibrate the windows, and someone stomped down the hall and into one of the bedrooms, slamming that door behind her, too. It had to be Jenny.

"Danny," Serena told herself with exasperation. She walked down the hall to her older daughter's room and knocked. "Jenny, I already know half the story. Do you want to tell your curious mother the rest?"

A few seconds later, a teary-eyed Jenny with windblown brown hair pulled the door open, looked at Serena, and stomped back to plop down on her bed. "What half do you know?"

"Only what the noises tell me. You and Danny had a fight."

Jenny placed her pillow onto her lap and punched it. "He asked me to go steady again."

Serena perched on the other end of her daughter's bed. "And you refused."

"Good guess," Jenny said, in a perfect imitation of her mother's dry tone. She placed the pillow behind her back. "He's threatening to go out with other girls."

"And?"

"And I told him to go ahead."

Serena watched the conflicting emotions in her daughter's face. "You're not crazy about the idea, are you?"

"No, but I'm tired of arguing with him. Besides, there's this cute new guy at church, and he's polite, and respectful, and you said yourself that I'm too young to go steady, and—"

Serena raised a hand to interrupt her daughter's flow of words. "You don't have to convince me."

Jenny crossed her arms behind her head. "You've always told me that love is more than physical attraction. Danny laughed at me today when I tried to tell him that there should be more of a sharing of spirits. Oh, speaking of the spiritual, there's going to be a great movie tonight; may Kirby and I use the van to go?"

"Sounds fine to me," Serena replied. "I don't think I'll need it tonight. I plan to spend a nice, quiet evening here at home."

As soon as Jenny went to take a shower, Emily Ann came banging in through the front door and stopped to stare at Serena. "Mom! Aren't you dressed yet? We've got to be there in forty-five minutes."

"Be where?"

Emily placed her hands on her hips, looking at Serena reproachfully. "Mom, you promised to be in the discussion group at the school board meeting. Don't tell me you forgot."

Serena gasped in dismay. "I already promised Jenny she could have the van to go to the movies tonight. I guess I'll have to use your granny's car."

"No, Granny's got a meeting tonight, remember?"

Serena grimaced. The Save-a-Life meeting. "Then I guess we'll have to call a taxi."

"You could buy Jenny that car she's been wanting so things like this don't happen so often."

"She's working to save money to buy that car. I wouldn't want to rob her of the thrill of doing it herself."

Emily shrugged. "Okay, Mom, but you better hurry and call that taxi. We don't have much time left, and I have to set up the refreshment stand." She turned and dashed back down the hallway to her room, then stopped and turned back. "Oh, by the way, did I tell you Carson was going to speak at the meeting, too?"

"No."

"Well, he is." She disappeared into her room.

Serena sighed. So that was the secret. Carson was going to be there. Sweet little matchmaking Emily had hopes for Carson to become a part of the family, and she was willing to manipulate everyone to see her dreams come true.

Forty-five minutes later, they stepped out of the taxi. It was a surprisingly large crowd for a school board meeting, but it wasn't hard to find Carson among the people. His tall form and dark head stood out, overpowering the rest—at least to Serena.

"See you later, Mom. Nicki's already up there," Emily said, pointing to a counter surrounded by large bottles of soda, coffee, cookies, and chips.

Serena watched her daughter skip over to the stand and crawl beneath the counter, chattering excitedly to her girlfriend as she did so, although their voices were lost in the crowd. The sight of Carson weaving his way toward Serena made her forget about her daughter's matchmaking tactics for the time being.

"Are you on the agenda for tonight?" Carson asked when he drew close.

"Yes, but I didn't realize I would be talking to a big crowd. This is just a school board meeting, isn't it?"

Carson walked with her into the large multipurpose classroom reserved for the meeting. "The topic of teenage pregnancy tends to attract attention. So does debate, and we're liable to have that tonight, with Dr. Wells in attendance." He gestured toward the slender, blond man who stood talking to Bev Jackson beside the lectern.

Serena glanced at the man in alarm. Dr. Wells performed abortions. He also lobbied for better access to abortions in Missouri and was one of the state's most vocal proponents of partial-birth abortion. Serena despised everything he stood for, and the feeling was probably mutual. She knew that, as the reputation of Alternative spread across central Missouri, its staff, and especially its founder, would be under public scrutiny. Her behavior tonight could affect the outcome of a pregnancy later. She needed to be civil.

Carson turned and glanced at a group of people walking in together. "I didn't know Blythe was coming."

Serena swung around in surprise to find her mother-in-law talking to a serious-looking young man by her side. Blythe was supposed to be at her own meeting tonight. Had the members elected to attend this one instead? Maybe the young man Blythe mentioned was asked to talk. Could that be Edward with her?

Two young women with Blythe carried stacks of leaflets, and when they entered the classroom, they started passing them out to everyone present. They wore T-shirts with the words ABORTION = MURDER emblazoned across the front. One of the girls handed a leaflet to Carson, who shared it with Serena.

It was in the form of a letter, introducing the Save-a-Life group. It announced plans to form a picket line the following week outside a clinic in nearby Columbia, which, in the words of the writer, committed murder on Missouri citizens. The byline was Edward. Just Edward.

The words were stronger than Serena would have used, not because she disagreed with his stand, but because her mission was different. Yes, she hated abortion, but her hatred of the deed couldn't be allowed to overshadow compassion for the people she was here to help. Her counselors shared the healing message of Christ with desperate, hurting young women. Edward might be able to stir up emotion, but what good did all that anger do? It was as if he was trying to incite hatred for the people caught up in the sin, instead of for the sin itself.

"Excuse me, Serena," Blythe said, approaching her. "Edward here has been after me to introduce him to you. He's—"

The brown-haired, bespectacled young man stepped forward and extended his hand. "Dr. Van Buren." His voice was smooth and well modulated—almost too controlled. "I've been an admirer of yours ever since I discovered Alternative, and even more now that I've spoken to one of your volunteers and seen you in action."

Serena was in the process of taking his hand. She froze. "Oh? When was this?"

"Different times. I'm interested in your work. I think I could help you—"

"And did you also speak with my secretary?" Serena knew she was being rude, but if this was who she thought it was. . .

Without answering, Edward held his hand out to Carson, who stood beside Serena. "You must be Dr. Tanner."

"Edward, did you speak to Mrs. Acuff outside Alternative last Monday night?" Serena asked, stepping in front of him and forcing him to look at her.

His light skin flushed easily, but he didn't seem abashed. "Yes, I just happened to catch her when she came storming out of your clinic. She accused me of working for you. Is Kirby going to keep her baby this time?"

"This time? You're a friend of Kirby's?" Serena wasn't aware Kirby had told anyone else.

"Yes, well. . .she doesn't exactly know me. I only hope she makes the right—"

"Excuse me," Carson said, "but how do you presume to know anything about Kirby's situation if she doesn't know you?"

This time the flush was darker, and Edward glanced around at the crowd uncomfortably; but before he could reply, the school board chairman spoke into the microphone and called Carson and Serena to the front.

Serena stared hard at Edward, then reluctantly turned to follow Carson to the tables set up for the forum. Who had broken Kirby's confidence, and why was Edward involving himself in her life? He was in the possession of information that had nothing to do with him.

One of the speakers ahead of Serena was Dr. Wells. He described what he did as a logical, compassionate way to rescue teenagers who were too young to handle parental responsibilities. He came across as an intelligent, caring person. Serena found herself wondering if it was possible to be that logical and not realize the presence of a human soul in the womb. She had to remind herself that her mission here was not to argue or debate, but to share with as many people as possible about Alternative. She struggled to keep her mouth shut.

Edward did not. Before Dr. Wells made his concluding remarks, Edward came marching down the center aisle with several of the Save-a-Life members. Blythe was not among them.

"I object!" Edward shouted. "You call yourself a doctor? You take lives for a living! You're a killer, a murderer!" His face was red and beaded with perspiration. He raised a fist in the air as he spoke. "You have no right to talk about compassion and responsibility. You should be behind bars! You should be executed. How would you like that, Wells, to be aborted from the earth the way you murder babies?" His voice broke, and passion and pain filled his eyes.

Bev Jackson sprang from her chair and rushed around the table to his side. She reached for him, but he suddenly swung around to face Serena and Carson. "Tell them, Dr. Van Buren! You know what I mean, Dr. Tanner! Why don't you tell them? You're both doctors. Is there any medical evidence to prove that partial-birth abortion is ever necessary?" Tears filled his brown eyes and spilled down his cheeks.

"No, Edward, there isn't," Serena said softly.

"It isn't taking a life to save a life then, is it? Abortion is a convenience in this country!" He raised a fist in the air. "And let the killers pay for their convenience!"

Bev grasped his arm and whispered something to him. He lowered his fist and shook his head as tears dripped down his face. His shoulders heaved, and she embraced him and walked with him out of the room. The members of his group stood looking at the crowd in bewilderment for a few short minutes, then followed him silently.

After a moment to regroup, the discussion continued. When it came time for Serena to speak, she described Alternative and the comprehensive help they offered for pregnant women—from room and board with volunteer families in the surrounding counties, to help with education, adoption services, and medical care. Carson followed up with his insight into the lives of the teenagers he'd worked with over the years in his position as a church youth leader.

The discussion ended peacefully, and several of the parents, teachers, and board members lingered to talk to Serena and Carson afterward. Serena was handing out her second stack of Alternative pamphlets when Edward entered the classroom once more. He saw her and came toward her, and the after-meeting chatter diminished around them. His eyes were red-rimmed, and his face was splotched from tears; and once again Serena felt a swell of sympathy.

"How did it feel to sit calmly by while that murderer was allowed to indoctrinate everyone in this room?" His tone held accusation, and his red eyes burned resentment.

"Excuse me, Edward?" Serena kept her voice low. "This country is founded on principles of free speech. I was given an opportunity to speak, and it was my intention to present my thoughts in a reasonable, thoughtful manner so anyone who heard Wells would also hear me and realize the truth."

"If I'd been asked to speak tonight, I would have done all I could to keep him from indoctrinating these people."

"You tried, and it didn't work, did it? I don't think a shouting match prevents anyone from having an abortion—it just makes people mad."

"It gets attention," Edward said, "which keeps the issue in the minds of the people, where it should be."

Serena held his gaze for a moment. "Edward, you're obviously passionate about your convictions, and that's admirable. I'm passionate about mine, as well. I think we'll just have to agree that we go about things differently." She held out her hand.

His thoughts were obviously active behind those intelligent, slightly disturbing gray eyes. He took her hand at last. "I guess this means you won't be at our protest in Columbia next week."

She smiled. "I will be waiting at my clinic for all those converts you send my way."

Edward didn't return the smile. He pivoted abruptly and stalked over to Bev Jackson. Serena watched the young man in confusion for a moment, then realized someone else had stepped up beside her. She turned and found herself face-to-face with Dr. Wells.

"Dr. Van Buren," the man said, extending his hand. "You handled yourself well tonight. I was afraid the meeting was going to turn into a free-for-all for a few minutes there." He shook Carson's hand, as well. "Your description of Alternative intrigues me," he said, still speaking to Serena. "I wonder if I might visit sometime and see your facilities."

"Of course," Serena said, puzzled. "Is there a particular reason why you're interested?"

His mouth tightened in irritation. "Surely you're not as narrow-minded as your young friend over there. I thought I might inspect your clinic, then possibly refer patients to you. Not all women should have terminations, you know."

"None of them should." Serena gave him her card. "Visit us anytime. I'll tell my staff to expect you."

❦

Carson could tell Serena was disturbed as he drove her home, and he was glad Emily had opted to ride home with Blythe. He needed time alone to talk to Serena, though they rode more than half the way in silence, since she was seemingly deep in thought.

"Am I a fence straddler?" she asked, not turning from her perusal of the lights of the passing city.

"You're kidding, of course."

She glanced across at him. "Edward was right tonight. I didn't protest when Wells described abortion as a perfectly acceptable birth control option."

"Neither did I. There is a time and a place for protest, Serena, and Alternative is your protest. How much stronger can your voice be?"

"Some of the things Edward said made sense."

Carson pulled into the Van Buren driveway, noting Blythe's car was still absent. He switched off the engine. "Edward is a young man in pain. Surely that was as obvious to you tonight as it was to me. He's passionate and idealistic, and I sympathize with him; but there's something else going on with him. Right now, however, I'm more concerned with you." He turned to face Serena, and he saw her startled gaze skitter away from his. "Something else is bothering you, or that little debate with Edward wouldn't make you doubt yourself like this."

She shrugged, clasping her hands together in her lap. "Maybe I'm a hypocrite. I look at things a little differently because. . ." She looked at him briefly, then took a deep breath. "Carson, you remember I told you that I didn't feel we knew each other well enough yet?"

"And do you remember what I told you? There's nothing I can learn about you that will change my mind."

"Yes, but—"

Lights flashed against the garage door, and Carson glanced around to find Blythe and Emily pulling up beside them.

"So much for confession time," Serena said dryly.

He laid a hand on her arm and squeezed. "Just remember what I said. Nothing can change my heart."

On his way home, Carson couldn't stop thinking about Serena. He was still disturbed as he stepped into his dark apartment and saw the red light flashing on his answering machine. Still picturing Serena's soft, intent eyes and firm, determined chin, and her exquisite instinct to help the lost and hurting, he pressed the PLAY button.

Carol Acuff's shaking voice rose from the speaker. "Carson, I–I've got to talk to you." There was a sniff. "I've got to know. . .about my daughter." She identified herself, then the machine beeped and kicked off.

Carson looked at the lighted dials of his desk clock, then picked up the phone and punched the Acuffs' number. Hal answered on the third ring. "Hello, Hal, this is Carson Tanner. Is Carol there? She left a message for me to call."

"Oh, Carson, what a mess." Hal's soft-spoken voice cracked with obvious strain. "She's gone out walking, and I'm worried about her. It's getting worse. She's picked up the phone to call Kirby at least ten times tonight, but she can't bring herself to do it. Last night she was muttering in her sleep about grandbabies." He paused for breath, and there was a shudder in his sigh. "She wants to see her grandbaby. I said something to her about it this morning, and she sat down on the side of the bathtub and cried for fifteen minutes. I think the guilt's about to kill her. I know this whole thing is about to do me in."

"Guilt?"

"Tonight. . .tonight she asked me if I thought we'd really ended a baby's life—Kirby's baby. What do I tell her?"

In spite of the pain Carson heard in Hal's voice, he felt a rush of hope. "Hal, your family needs to come to terms with the past. Talk to her about it, and let her talk to you. Opening the lines of communication is your first step, and it sounds as if that is happening. I know it's painful, but a lot of times there is healing in the pain. Your next step is to call Kirby. She desperately needs to know you care about her."

"I tried to call from work, but nobody answered. I didn't leave a message."

"Next time, leave one. She needs it."

There was a short hesitation. "I know I should have already. I just. . .it's sometimes so hard to know what's best, you know."

"Yes, I know. Now is the time to seek the truth. I'll be here for you as you and your family come to terms with it."

Chapter 12

Saturday morning, Serena awakened with the feeling of hovering darkness. A soft breeze pushed through her opened bedroom window, billowing out the lacy curtains. She slid out of bed and stepped over to the chair by the window to watch the dawn.

Ever since she was a little girl, this had been one of her favorite things to do, watching a new day promise a new start. She found no joy in it now. She felt as if she were seeking something in its beauty, and that something continued to elude her.

The pale colors in the sky deepened slowly, until its rose and bronze beauty penetrated Serena's unhappy thoughts. Some hidden mockingbird sang out, joined by a meadowlark, and then another, until the whole tree-filled yard echoed with songs. The muted ringing of a telephone marred the music for a moment, but someone answered it.

Serena stretched and yawned, consciously pushing her depression to the back of her mind. Her family deserved to see her happy today.

A timid knock sounded at her door, and Emily stuck her head in, her brown eyes wide and—for Emily—contrite. "Mom, are you mad at me?"

"For what?"

"Matchmaking."

"So you do admit that was what you were doing last night."

"Yes. Granny didn't think it was a bad idea."

"Don't blame it on your granny. I'll forgive you on one condition—I need a rubdown. Do you want to do it now or after I shower?"

Emily's eyes danced. "I'll do it now. Lie down on the floor."

Serena obliged, lying facedown and burying her chin into the amethyst berber carpeting. Immediately, her daughter's gentle hands moved over her back in an easy, circular motion, and she could feel herself melting farther and farther down into the floor. Tense muscles from a night of restless sleep began to relax.

Rubdowns were an old family tradition. When the girls were younger, they had always fought over who would get to rub down Mommy's or Daddy's back. It had been just one more expression of their love for one another.

"Mmm, just a little more on the right shoulder. Yes, that's it. Now down a little. There." Serena's words slurred as her whole body relaxed. Gradually growing aware of the silence—something unusual with Emily—Serena frowned into the carpeting. "Emily?"

81

"Yes, Mom?"

"Is something bothering you?"

The massaging stopped, and Serena turned over and sat up to face her daughter. Emily leaned back against the bed and gazed thoughtfully out the window. Her almond-shaped eyes held sadness, and Serena reached across and touched the back of her hand to Emily's cheek.

"Do you realize this will be the first time we've gone to the lake together since Daddy died?" Emily asked.

So that was it. Leave it to this sentimental child to remember something like that. Of course, Jenny had also mentioned it the other day. "Yes, sweetheart. That worried me a little. It might bring back a lot of memories."

Emily shook her head and looked up at her mother. "But don't you see? It could be a new beginning for us all, with Carson there."

A new beginning? Was that possible, with so many things from the old ending left undone, unsaid, unexplained? There were too many things about Serena's past that Jennings had never known about. Why had she kept secrets from her own husband?

Serena brushed long strands of brown hair back from Emily's face. "You like Carson a lot, don't you?"

Emily's eyes narrowed as she considered the question seriously. "Yes, I do. After Daddy died, I was sure I wouldn't ever want to see you with another man. You belonged to Daddy, and another man would make me feel like we were losing you to someone else."

"And that isn't the way you would feel with Carson?"

"No. He makes us feel included in everything. I can tell he cares for us. He's different from other men, isn't he, Mom?"

"Yes, he's different. He's very special." She reached down and wrapped a strand of her daughter's hair around her finger and twirled it absently. "But even though he's special, that doesn't mean he's necessarily going to spend the rest of his life with us." She released Emily's hair and sat back.

Emily turned confused eyes up to her mother. "Why not?"

"Because sometimes a woman can't do exactly what she wants to do. There are other people we have to consider besides ourselves."

"Like who? If Carson loves us and we love him, why can't we all be together?"

"Honey, love is a wonderful thing, but it doesn't always automatically mean marriage. I care a great deal about Carson, but marriage...isn't meant for everyone. I think he'll find, once he gets to know me really well, that I'm not right for him."

"Of course you are!" Emily protested indignantly. "You'd be right for any man!"

Exactly an hour later, the deep chimes of the doorbell echoed through the house, and Serena heard her younger daughter race out of her room and dash down the hall. "That's Carson!" Emily cried. "I'll get it!"

Serena, dressed in a hot pink short set, wearing her swimsuit underneath, followed at a more leisurely pace. In spite of Carson's instructions not to take food, she had decided to pack an ice chest with soda pop and fruit. She called a greeting to Carson from the hallway and proceeded into the kitchen, but she wasn't the first one there.

Kirby, her bright blond, uncombed hair shining in the sunlight that came through the window, was leaning against the counter with a glass of milk in her hand, staring out at the sky.

She glanced around at Serena and smiled. "Ready for the lake?"

Serena nodded, looking pointedly at Kirby's housecoat. "And you're not. Why?"

Kirby shrugged, avoiding Serena's eyes. "Call me chicken."

"You're not going? Why not?"

"Oh, you know, the usual thing," Kirby replied, her voice quivering. "I–I have some morning sickness, and I might get sick on the boat."

Serena stepped closer and studied Kirby's expression. "What else? There's another reason."

Kirby's face flushed a delicate pink. She took a deep breath and turned to look back out the kitchen window. "Mother called this morning." Her eyes filled with tears, and she set her milk glass down with a shaking hand. "I guess I'm feeling homesick again." She looked at Serena. "I'm messing up so many lives. I've been so selfish."

"You didn't do this all by yourself, Kirby Acuff. You can't blame yourself for the problems of the whole world. You aren't the source of all your mother's confusion right now." Serena leaned against the counter beside Kirby. "What did she say on the phone?"

"Not much. She just asked me how I was, if I'd been getting sick, if I was eating right."

"Does that tell you anything?"

"It tells me she still doesn't want to hear about how I'm feeling inside, where it counts."

"Maybe she's just afraid to ask. I imagine she's feeling guilty herself."

Kirby uttered a short, bitter laugh. "That'll be the day. For two years she's blamed everything on me. Why should she stop now, when I'm not even there to defend myself?"

"Maybe your absence has forced her to find someone else to blame. She's having to take a look at her own actions."

Kirby bowed her head as tears trickled down her cheeks, and Serena stepped forward and wrapped her arms around the girl. "Your parents do love you, Kirby, no matter what you believe. If they didn't, they wouldn't have been so upset." She released Kirby and stepped back, then reached up to tip the girl's chin until their eyes met. "These next few weeks are going to take some understanding on your part. You have to realize that they're weak, fallible human beings, just like the rest of us. They do and say things that hurt you, without taking into consideration the pain they may be causing you, because of their own pain. I imagine they're asking themselves why—and where—they went wrong. They're blaming themselves for your mistakes, but that's because they love you so much." Serena held Kirby's blue eyes with her own. "If your parents asked you to go back and live with them, would you go?"

Kirby looked down. "Not unless I could have my baby."

There was a quiet cough at the doorway, and they looked over to see Blythe standing there, dressed for the visit with Janet, her friend, in a cool linen shift and sandals. Her expression, however, did not reflect her excitement about the upcoming plans. Her eyes were somber, her lined face serious.

Serena stepped toward her with concern. "Blythe? Is something wrong?"

The older woman nodded her head sadly. "Kirby, I found something in your room I don't think you meant for me to find."

Serena felt Kirby stiffen beside her. "Wh–what's that?"

Blythe held out her hand. In the palm rested a little stack of tiny, oblong white pills.

Kirby caught her breath.

"I was doing some laundry and shook these out of the pocket of your jeans," Blythe explained. "These spilled out. What are they?"

There was a long silence. "It's. . .Mother's sleeping pills," Kirby said softly.

Blythe froze for a moment, then slowly lowered her hand to her side. "But I thought—"

"I had them in my pocket the night Serena found me on the trail." Kirby turned and raised a hand toward Serena beseechingly. "I'm sorry I lied. I said I tossed them, but I didn't. But I wouldn't have taken them, honestly." She hesitated. "At least, I don't think I would have. It's just that things were so hard at home, and I knew I could be pregnant again; and I didn't think I could go through it all over. Please don't turn me in."

Serena held her hand out to her mother-in-law, and Blythe gave her the pills. "Do you have any more of them, Kirby?"

Kirby shook her head adamantly as she held Serena's gaze. "No."

Serena stared at the tiny pills and felt a wave of defeat. "And you've had them all this time."

"I wouldn't use them now, Serena." Kirby's voice held a note of urgency in it. "I wouldn't have to. Now I know someone cares."

Serena shook her head. How could she have missed something like this? Kirby could have decided, in a moment of despair, to take an overdose, and she'd admittedly lied to her parents for years. It wouldn't be safe to leave her alone.

"You're right," she told the girl at last. "A lot of people care. Now go and get your clothes on. You're going with us."

"But I just—"

"I'm sorry, but right now you don't have a choice." Serena used her firm voice. "If you don't go, I will stay here with you, but I'm not leaving you alone today."

Kirby closed her eyes and bent her head. "You don't believe me."

Serena placed her hand over Kirby's. "Let's just say I'm not willing to bet your life on your honesty right now."

"I'll stay here with her if she doesn't feel like going," Blythe volunteered. "I can see Janet another time, and I have some work in the garden—"

"No," Kirby said. "I'm sorry, Serena. I'll go with you. I guess I just thought. . . I don't know. . .Mother might call again. Or I might call her. And I didn't want to get in the way—"

"Enough of that, young lady," Blythe insisted. "Get to your room and get dressed. I want to see a smile on your face when you come back out of there. You're going to have a good time today. You got that?"

A flush of embarrassed pleasure stole across Kirby's face. She grinned and ducked her head as she turned to leave the kitchen.

Serena slumped against the counter. "I can't believe I missed—"

"She didn't take them," Blythe said. "You caught her in time. And I really don't think she'll do it now. Do you?"

"No, but we believed her before, too."

"And she didn't use the pills, did she? We'll just keep an eye on her and keep the communication lines open." Blythe glanced toward the door and lowered her voice. "Serena, I just got a call from Aunt Myrtle, up in Nebraska."

Serena struggled to keep up with the switch in conversation, while Blythe announced that she was going to visit Myrtle and would be gone a couple of weeks. Serena opened the lid to the ice chest and checked the contents. "I'm not sure we can stand to be without you that long."

"Yup, I'm pretty indispensable, I know," Blythe replied with a teasing glint in her eye. "And the garden will probably go to pot, and Rascal will howl all night long, like he did the first week he was here."

"What about your Save-a-Life group? You'll miss the picketing next week."

Blythe shook her head. "There could be trouble there. You saw how argumentative Edward is, and the others follow his lead."

"He's young, immature, and inexperienced."

"He's trying to get attention any way he can," Blythe said. "I can almost understand him, though. You see, he got his girlfriend pregnant three years ago. He wanted to marry her and have the baby, but she didn't want to get married. She had an abortion. Really tore him up."

"Is that when he started this group?"

"No, it was already formed, but he joined it and gradually took over. You have to hand it to him; he has a way with people. He quadrupled membership within a year. He really believes in what he's doing."

Serena frowned. "I don't know. Something about him scares me. I think you were right about the mob mentality thing. It can be dangerous."

"Looks to me like he'll have to learn the hard way, Serena, and don't go suggesting I stay to keep an eye on him. He didn't listen to you the other night, and he won't listen to me. I'll be leaving Monday."

"Hadn't you better make sure you can get a ticket before you decide?"

"Ticket? For what?"

Serena frowned and looked hard at Blythe. "For the airplane, or the bus, or whatever transportation you plan to take."

"Don't need a ticket for my own car, do I?"

Serena frowned at her. "You mean you plan to drive all the way there by yourself?"

"Nonsense. I'm only going to Lincoln. That's less than a day's drive from here. The day I can't make that drive on my own is the day I've lost my usefulness. I'll start packing when I get home tonight."

Reluctantly, Serena murmured agreement. She knew from experience that it would do no good to argue. Once Blythe set her mind on something, she wouldn't be talked out of it. Still, it would have been nice to have Blythe continue her personal investigation of the Save-a-Life group. Something about that still made Serena very uncomfortable.

Chapter 13

The drive to the lake with the girls on board was every bit as beautiful as it had been last week alone with Carson. The morning sunshine and fresh air gave an atmosphere of newness to the rolling hills and trees of the countryside. The day was still early, and there was very little traffic on the highway—only an occasional farmer driving into town.

The aura of quiet peacefulness was only evident outside the confines of the Saturn, however. The interior seemed to be stretched to bursting with talk, laughter, excitement. Before she climbed into the backseat, Emily Ann glanced up at Carson, flashed a dimpled smile, and asked him about the skiing arrangements. His gaze was tender as it rested on her, and Serena allowed herself a few moments of unobserved enjoyment. Carson was a handsome man, with powerfully molded face, strong brow, and shoulders of a body builder—though he seldom indulged in weight lifting. He was not afraid of thoughtful silence, but neither was he afraid of sharing his heart in intimate conversation. Serena couldn't imagine how he had remained unmarried for five years after his wife's death.

Serena sighed. To her chagrin, Carson caught the slight sound, and his eyes raised to meet hers. He winked and grinned, then flipped on the signal, slowed the car, and turned right onto a narrower road that soon curved through dense forest.

"Oh, look, Mom. We're going to Horseshoe Bend," Emily exclaimed. "Are we going to Paula's?"

"No way!" Jenny called from the backseat. "We're not, are we, Mom?"

Serena cast her daughter a reassuring glance over the seat. "No, we're not going to Paula's." Poor Jenny hadn't completely recovered from her breakup with Danny, Paula's son. "Carson's boat is down here." She turned to Carson to explain. "Our friends have a cabin down here. When we used to come down, Paula always insisted we launch our boat into the cove beside her cabin."

They passed the golf course, and Serena fell silent, her mind awash with memories. She and Jennings had golfed many rounds on that course. It was beautifully kept, as it had always been, and at this time of morning it was nearly deserted except for the occasional avid sportsman.

There must have been a heavy dew last night, because Serena could see sparkling drops of water nestling in the short-cropped green grass and a mist floated in the recesses of the trees in the valley.

The forest of oak, elm, and hickory closed in around them once more, with an occasional narrow dirt road or grass path winding back through the trees. Carson slowed the car to take the curves and roughening road at a safer pace, and Serena opened her window to allow the fragrance of morning to enter the car.

As the conversation continued around Carson, he couldn't prevent himself from looking at Serena. She'd been reserved with him this morning, though when he looked into her eyes he saw a special spark of attraction there. Of course she had reservations. She was a sensible woman, determined to look at all sides of a relationship before committing herself. In his heart and in his mind, he had already done that. Now he needed to find the patience to wait for her to arrive at the same decision.

That old, familiar, mossy smell of the lake drifted in through the open window along with the sounds of boat motors and splashing water. When Carson pulled to a stop near the dock, he caught a glimpse of Serena's face and saw a wealth of expressions there. There was a wistfulness in her eyes, but the corners turned up in a slight smile, as if remembering the happy times she had spent here with her family.

"Did you come here a lot?" he asked Serena.

"Oh yes. Sometimes we came to this very landing and put the pontoon in for skiing or exploring. The exploring was always my favorite part; this lake is so interesting."

"I know. I like to do that myself," Carson replied. "The creeks and sheltered coves abound in this area, and I've spent a lot of long hours quietly drifting in and out of them."

"Hey, remember the day our battery went dead on us, and we had to paddle back to shore?" Emily asked.

"Yeah, and we only had one paddle," Jenny added. "Dad and Mom finally just jumped in the water and towed us to shore with the rope."

"I remember!" Serena exclaimed. "My shoulders were sore for days after that."

"And how about the time Dad decided to go ashore for a picnic and got the boat stuck in the mud," Jenny remarked. "We all had to get out and push."

"That was awful!" Emily remembered. "I kept feeling things tickling my toes under the mud, and I still think it was snakes."

"I don't think snakes go under the mud, do they?" Jenny asked.

"Well, let's not just sit here reminiscing, let's get out there!" Serena exclaimed.

Carson couldn't repress a faint surge of envy. Jennings Van Buren had enjoyed a wonderful, loving family and had spent those years with one of the most wonderful women in the world. He still lived on in the memories of his family, but he wasn't here to enjoy it. Carson vowed silently that, if given the chance, he would shower this family with as much love and support as Jennings had done.

He glanced at Serena and saw the wistfulness in her eyes. And the sadness. There seemed to be more in her expression than the grief of losing a husband. There was almost. . .guilt. He'd seen it before, but lately it had been even more often in evidence. He wished she felt she could talk with him about it.

The long morning shadows disappeared unnoticed amid the noisy, often hilarious excitement on the boat in the middle of the lake. Time passed quickly and easily for Serena as she watched her daughters graduate from the tube to skis, and it wasn't until both girls had skied together along a lengthy swath of lake that the blazing sun caught their attention.

They stopped for lunch at the unique floating restaurant, rested for thirty minutes, and hit the lake again. Serena only found a few moments to worry about how things were going at the clinic, and she resisted the urge to use her cell phone for a quick call.

Carson allowed Jenny to take the wheel for a few moments while he disappeared below deck, and when he emerged a little while later, he had changed into a pair of swim trunks. "Is anyone ready for a swim?" He took the wheel back from Jenny. "There's a good place just up in this next cove. There are even some good rocks for diving, if you feel like it."

As he turned the boat into the cove, everyone except Serena followed his example and rushed below deck. Serena remained seated beside him, all her concentration directed to keeping her eyes away from the rippling muscles of his powerful shoulders and legs.

He glanced across at her questioningly. "You're quiet today, Serena. Is something wrong?"

"Nothing at all. In fact, this is all too good to be true—you're too good to be true—and we can't continue to take advantage of you. You've spent this whole day pulling skiers, feeding us, and showing us the best places to swim. I haven't seen you ski, and judging by the assortment of equipment you have on board, you must enjoy the sport more than most."

Carson slowed and stopped the boat, then turned to look at her more closely. Once more, she thought she detected a hesitance in his manner, a question in his eyes. Then without a word, almost as if he couldn't stop himself, he reached across, drew her to him, and kissed her tenderly.

He released her. "If it makes you feel better, I'll ski after we swim."

"That's better," Serena said, struggling to maintain her equilibrium after his gentle assault on her senses.

"I'll tell you what," he said as he dropped anchor, "since you're feeling so guilty, I'll let you drive the boat for me."

"You trust me?" Serena teased.

"Yes, I trust you," Carson assured her, suddenly serious. "You are trustworthy."

She shook her head. He was wrong. So wrong. "Carson Tanner, you're far too special for my peace of mind," she whispered.

"Good. Keep thinking those nice things about me," he teased.

She looked away. Every moment she spent with him made things more confusing. She had fallen in love with him. . .and he thought she was trustworthy.

&

Edward and eight other members of Save-a-Life finished folding the last batch of flyers and stacked them in boxes to divide among the other members of their group and broadcast them across the city tonight. He was especially proud of this issue, though he was aware there might be some difficult consequences. That was okay, though. What he was doing was worth suffering for.

Sixteen-year-old Pam; the group's youngest member, gave him her stack. "Are you sure this is legal, Edward? Did the girl give you permission to print this? She might not want everyone to know her past."

"I didn't name names, did I?"

"No, but names were all you didn't put in here."

"Look at it this way, Pam, the story needs to be told. Besides, before long everyone will know she's pregnant."

"Sure, then those who know about it will also know everything else."

"Believe me, she won't be the only pregnant senior in high school."

Pam shook her head. "But what about Dr. Van Buren and Alternative? You're really raising questions in everybody's minds, and what if she's bona fide? You could ruin her whole program and hurt the cause. You did name names there."

Edward smiled and tugged a strand of the girl's hair. "If anything goes wrong, you can tell everybody you told me so, okay?"

Pam shook her head, turned away, and left with two of the other girls.

Edward's smile died as the others filed out of the room ahead of him. Sure, Pam was only sixteen. A kid. Badly as he hated to admit it, she had a point. It was too late to back out now, after he already had the flyers printed and the group prepared to pass them out. But Pam had a lot of common sense. She had worked on the school newspaper her sophomore year, and she had a good reputation for reporting the truth. Of course, it was just a school paper—but wasn't that all Edward himself had ever worked on? Maybe he should watch Alternative a little more before he made his final decision. Maybe he still didn't know all there was to know about Serena Van Buren. Maybe he would dig a little deeper, find out what kind of connection she had with that abortionist, Dr. Wells.

Chapter 14

On Monday, Carson managed to convince Carol and Hal Acuff to meet them for a trial family conference that evening at Alternative. As Serena drove downtown with Kirby, she could feel the tension radiating from the pretty teenager.

"Mother'll lose her temper like she always does," Kirby predicted.

"Possibly not. Perhaps she'll curb it tonight."

"Whether she does or not, I'm going to say what I think, Serena." Kirby crossed her arms over her chest.

Serena patted Kirby's shoulder encouragingly. Things would work out with this family. Carol Acuff wanted her daughter back, and she was a determined lady. If she had to show more unselfish love toward her family, Serena didn't doubt that Carol would eventually break old habits and find a way to reach out.

The familiar landmark of the capitol building appeared too soon for Serena; she wasn't looking forward to this meeting. She wished she wasn't so emotionally involved.

They both remained in a thoughtful mood until they parked close to the clinic, then Kirby glanced across at Serena, her blue eyes wide and apprehensive. "You sure they want me back?"

"Positive. Tonight's meeting will just be to pinpoint some problem areas."

To Serena's relief, the air-conditioning in the clinic had been left on, and she felt its invigorating coolness as she led the way back to the little conference area they had used exactly a week earlier. As before, the others weren't there yet, and the two of them sat down side by side on the sofa.

Kirby held out trembling hands and expelled a deep sigh. "Can you tell I'm nervous?"

"Your parents will be nervous, too. Your mother has had a chance this past week to think about some things. She may be having trouble dealing with them, just as you are."

"I know you keep saying that, but it's hard to imagine my mother admitting she's wrong." Kirby leaned her head against the high back of the sofa. "When I was a little girl, I believed she could do no wrong. She was strong, she knew what she wanted, and Dad and I always went along with her because it made life easier. I never resented it until I started high school. That was when she started getting on my nerves. She told me what classes to take, what clubs to join, and she was never satisfied with less than As on my report cards. After a while, I realized I didn't know how to satisfy her anymore, so I quit trying. I think my father realized a long time ago there was no pleasing her, so he just kind of went into his quiet little shell."

"That can change," Serena said. "You and your mother will have to learn to talk to each other. She needs to understand that you aren't a child any longer."

Kirby nodded. "Jenny's been talking to me a lot this week about God and about how He made us the way we are, with our own thoughts and feelings." Her voice tapered off as she stared thoughtfully out the window, then she asked, "Do you think if I told God I was sorry about the abortion and everything, He could forgive me?"

"Of course."

"And take all that away?"

"All what?"

"All the sin?"

"Yes. It will never be like it was before, and here on this earth you will always face the results of the choices you made, but you will have an eternity with God. You won't pay for those sins after you die." As she spoke, the front door opened, and she could feel Kirby tense.

"Brace yourself," the girl said softly as Carson preceded Hal and Carol Acuff into the conference room.

Carson gave them a smile and walked toward them. Serena could tell he was nervous by the tense set of his shoulders. "Hi," he said. "Hot enough for you outside?"

"Hi, Carson." Kirby dipped her head and studied her hands, clasped tightly in her lap.

Carol Acuff didn't say anything, but Serena saw the woman's face soften as she looked at her daughter. Serena got up from the sofa and stepped forward. "Hal and Carol, I'm glad you're here. Do you want anything to drink? We have a soda machine, and we keep cookies in the kitchenette in back."

"No, thank you," Carol said coolly as she lowered herself onto the sofa beside her daughter, where Serena had been sitting. Her eyes darted over Kirby, then back to Serena. "Well, she looks none the worse for her week with you," she observed reluctantly. "Has she been behaving? None of that staying out till all hours of the night?"

"Not at all," Serena assured the woman. "I think my girls have kept her so occupied, she didn't have time to get bored."

Kirby looked up at last. "We swim a lot in their pool, and Jenny and I went to a movie Friday night; but we got back early." She leaned forward. "Saturday we all went to the lake with Carson."

Carol cast a less than friendly look at Serena. "No wonder Kirby wanted to stay with you. Swimming parties, trips to the lake—"

"No one bribed me to stay with them, Mother," Kirby said with a scowl. "But

I did feel wanted there, and they didn't try to force me to do anything I didn't want to do or set impossible standards for me that I couldn't meet."

"Impossible standards? You mean like not getting pregnant? Apparently that's too much to—"

"Stop it!" Kirby stood to her feet. "I thought we were going to try to communicate. How many times did I tell you I was sorry? You don't listen! You never listen! What good does it do to try when I can never please you?" She paced across the room, arms crossed protectively over her chest.

Carol's eyes flashed fire. "As if you—"

"That's enough. Stop right there." Carson's calm voice was suddenly filled with steel as his gaze flickered from Carol to Kirby. "We came here to talk, and that isn't what we're doing. Hal and Carol, I feel I need to stress the value of having a professional counselor meet with your family for the—"

"No." Carol raised a hand to her face and rubbed her forehead wearily. "It didn't work last time; it won't work now." She shook her head and sighed.

Hal cleared his throat nervously. "Maybe if we tried again. Maybe if we tried harder this time. Obviously what we're doing isn't working. We've got to change."

Carol blinked at him, lips parting in surprise.

"You never listened to Kirby," Hal continued. He cleared his throat again and sat forward, hands clasped together between his knees. "You never listened to me either. Kirby never had a chance to make her own decisions. How could she learn—"

"How dare you talk to me like that!" Carol snapped. "Who was supposed to make the decisions for the family if I didn't? My houseplants have more backbone than you do! When's the last time you gave me any help with Kirby? When's the last time you ever punished her?"

Hal's face reddened. "Why should I punish her? You were always too glad to do it."

Carol gasped. "And you would have let her run out and play in the street, for all you cared about discipline. When I married you, I thought I was marrying a real man. Imagine my shock when—"

"Maybe you didn't let me be a real man," Hal retorted, his face splotching with color. "Maybe you didn't give me a chance. I could've handled the money. Just because you didn't agree with the way I handled it, you took over. And Kirby was a good baby, but you wanted perfection." He had lost all his nervousness now and was leaning forward in his seat, pinning his wife with his gaze. "Just because I didn't punish her doesn't mean I didn't help you with her. Many's the time I got up in the middle of the night to feed her, and many's the diaper I've changed."

"Changing diapers isn't all there is to raising a kid," Carol snapped.

Kirby laughed suddenly, a short, bitter laugh. "Would you listen to yourselves? I'm not a baby in diapers anymore. In a few months, I'm going to have a baby of my own. Mother, I have feelings and opinions, and I actually do have a brain, believe it or not. Can't you see that? If you can't, I may never be able to go back home with you."

Carol's face grew pale. "How can you say that to me?"

"Oh, stop the dramatics, Mother," Kirby snapped. "You've played that guilt game too many times. Why don't you concentrate on perfecting yourself before you fix the rest of the world?"

Carson raised a hand for silence. "Time for a cooldown."

"But she's—"

"No, Carol," Carson said firmly. "Stop and think about what you're saying. It's useless to place blame now. What the three of you need to realize is that you've all made mistakes. All of us do. Instead of pointing fingers, it's time to concentrate on learning from those mistakes in order to improve your family relationship. Carol and Hal, you can't continue blaming your daughter for a decision she made and now regrets. She needs your support, and you can give that only if you can escape the blame game."

"I agree with Carson," Serena said. "And if we may, we would like to continue working with you and Kirby on a weekly basis, no matter where Kirby lives. Just knowing you want her back has helped her, but it doesn't clear up a lot of the deep problems you still have as a family. She still needs guidance."

Carol stood and paced across the room, shaking her head in obvious frustration. She stopped to study a picture on the wall of a mother staring with delight into the face of her newborn baby. For a long moment, the others waited in uncomfortable silence. When she turned back, there were tears in her eyes. "You don't think this family is beyond help?"

"No, you aren't," Carson said. "You can have profitable family conferences; you can learn to communicate instead of shouting. Serena has a very caring, reputable family counselor on staff. We could schedule sessions in the evenings," he suggested and raised an eyebrow at Serena, who nodded, "so neither of you will have to take off work."

"We've got to do something," Hal said. "Carol?"

Carol shot her husband a resentful look, then bent her head. "What choice do we have if we want to get Kirby back?"

Serena stifled a sigh of relief, then glanced at Kirby. "You have a vote, too. What do you want to do about this?"

Kirby looked at her mother's bowed head uncertainly. "I want to try it. Maybe it'll work, if we all try to get along."

"Carol," Serena said, "if you spend some time on the phone with Kirby this week—maybe for just a few minutes every day—I think you'll realize how much talking does help. Try to listen to her as if she were a friend, an equal. I'm not saying you can't be a mother or that she won't have restrictions, but try as much as possible to treat her like an adult."

Carol leveled a cold stare at Serena, then turned to her husband. "Well, Hal, is it okay with you if we go home now?" Her voice was heavy with sarcasm. "We can set up another meeting next week."

☙

"Ouch! Rascal, stop biting my foot!" Emily jerked her spoon sideways at the dinner table and scattered droplets of soup over Kirby's plate.

Jenny poked Kirby with her elbow and giggled at a joke Kirby had just told. Serena sat back in her chair and sighed. At least there was a semblance of normal family life here for the lonely teenager to draw from. The peace was welcome. Now if only she could avoid getting any calls from the hospital tonight, she might be able to relax and rest, but before she finished her meal, the telephone rang. She sighed, laid down her napkin, and went into the kitchen to answer it.

"What have you done?" The voice was soft, strangely hoarse, intense. It certainly wasn't the hospital or a nervous patient. This woman sounded as if she were in shock. It was Carol Acuff. For a moment, Serena wondered if the woman had lost touch with reality. "I'm sorry, I don't understand what you mean."

"Why did you. . .how could you tell them?"

"Carol, what's wrong? What are you talking about?"

"I should never have listened to you! You said everything would be confidential, and now it's being spread all over the city!"

Serena glanced toward the dining room, where the others continued their conversation, unaware of the problem. "Carol," Serena said gently. "Just tell me what's happened. What's upsetting you?"

"Did you think I wouldn't be upset to find our family's life story in print, scattered all over town in those stupid flyers by that meddler?"

A cold suspicion grew in Serena's mind. "Who?"

"That fool who accosted me outside your clinic last week."

"Did you actually see a flyer?"

"I'm holding it in my hand! How could this happen?"

"Was the man's name Edward?"

There was a long silence, then, "I don't. . .I'm not. . .sure."

"Listen to me, Carol. I would never do anything like that, but I might know who did. The man who talked to you the other night? The first time I met him was last Friday night at a school meeting, and I didn't share anything with him; but he tried to question me about you. He told me he had spoken with you. Please believe I would never do this. Neither would Carson."

There was a sound of broken crying. "I sure didn't tell him all this."

"Why don't you read it to me over the—"

"Not now. I can't deal with this right now. It isn't bad enough that my own daughter has left me to live with some rich. . .just leave me alone." She hung up.

Serena dialed the number back. It was busy. She hung up and dialed Carson's home number. He answered on the first ring. "Carson, it's Serena. Carol Acuff just called me, and she sounds frantic. Remember Edward from the meeting the other night?"

"How could I forget?" he asked dryly.

"He's apparently printing more flyers, and this one has Carol very upset."

"Any idea what it's about?"

"Kirby."

"What about her?"

"I don't know, but Carol feels as if he's printed their family story."

There was a low, tired groan over the line. "This is getting scary, Serena. I've been checking out some Web pages online. There's an interactive site that makes me think of Edward. It starts off with a clear, pro-life theme; but as I pulled up more pages, the message grew dark, angry, filled with hatred, the way Edward behaved the other night. I researched some of the pro-life groups in central Missouri today, and three people have warned me to beware of Edward. He has some real problems."

"He could do a lot of damage."

"I think I'll drive over and visit the Acuffs tonight," Carson said. "I want to take a look at that flyer. Want to go with me?"

"I'll let you handle this one. I think Carol's had all of me she can take for one day."

✢

"Are you sure these will work?" Edward asked the man in the back room of an old storage building out in the country. He darted a glance over his shoulder into the shadows. This place was scary. This man was scary.

"They'll work," snapped the shadowed bulk in front of him. "Give me the cash. And this better not be a trick!"

"Trick?" Edward tried to keep the squeak out of his voice. He cleared his throat and handed the man the new bills he'd gotten at the bank just this afternoon. He was doing the right thing. He knew he was. The people of Jefferson City would be shocked out of their selfish, complacent attitudes. They would know what Serena Van Buren did down at that clinic.

"Now, could you tell me, just one more time, how to set these?"

"I told you once, and that's enough!" the man growled. "And if anyone finds out about this, I'll come after you."

Edward swallowed. "But I didn't write any directions down. What if—"

The shadow shoved the box of explosives into Edward's chest. "You didn't pay for written directions." He swung around and walked off, and Edward didn't have the nerve to try again. He could get on the Internet. Someone there would know.

Chapter 15

C arson wasn't sure of his welcome when he knocked at the front door of the Acuff residence, but when Hal answered the knock, he looked relieved. "Thank goodness, Carson. Come in."

Carol strode into the living room from the kitchen, hands on hips, her lips set in a grim line. Her eyes were puffy and red-rimmed from crying. "I guess Serena called you."

"Yes, she's worried about you."

"Please have a seat," Hal said. "We need to talk about this."

Carson sat down on the edge of a plush blue sofa and leaned forward, her elbows on her knees. "Serena told me how upset you were. May I see the flyer?"

Carol hesitated, then picked up a trifolded paper and handed it to him. "I don't know where this guy got his information."

"He said he talked to you outside the clinic last week. Do you remember anything you told him?"

Carol shook her head and sat down. Her face was pale and drawn, and her blond hair tumbled across her forehead in messy disarray. "I sure didn't tell him my life story, or Kirby's. Just read it, and you'll see what I mean. Doesn't make Alternative look too great either. The guy's crazy."

Carson read quickly, noting that the Acuff name was never mentioned, though it was Kirby's story. In a graphic, fictionalized account, it told about her past abortion, then hinted with sly innuendo that she was pregnant again. He expressed in vivid detail how upset Carol had been the night he spoke to her.

"She knew to look past that gentle, storefront facade, to the wicked lies within, and she came out a changed woman. What will happen to her daughter now? They thought they had found help. . . ."

Carson read on, his frown deepening when he came to the barely disguised character of Serena and the question Edward left dangling for the reader to interpret.

"Clinic founder. . .friend or foe? Is this clinic really pro-life, or is that just what she wants us to believe? There are many people in our country who want a baby badly enough to pay tens of thousands of dollars on the black market, but who will pocket the money for this girl's baby? Is that what this fight is all about, or should we delve more deeply still? The sympathies of this particular ob-gyn are in question. It has been suggested that this clinic could even be another front for the killers. Of course, that remark comes from an irate and frantic mother.

Draw your own conclusions. . . ."

Carson stood up, dropped the leaflet on the coffee table, and took a deep breath to control his mounting anger.

Carol slowed her pacing steps. "I didn't think I was talking to some stupid, half-cocked reporter that night." Her voice was defensive now. "I was mad, and who could blame me? My own daughter had chosen to live with someone besides me. I didn't mean. . . I didn't think. . . ."

"I know." Carson picked up the flyer, then threw it back down again.

"But we didn't know," Hal said. He stepped forward and hesitantly put an arm across his wife's shoulders. "Once Carol thought about it, she realized that you and Serena didn't know either."

"I wonder how many flyers they printed," Carol asked.

"Just be glad he didn't use your name."

❧

It had been two hours since Serena called Carson, and when the telephone rang, she grabbed up the receiver. She was surprised to hear Carol Acuff's voice at the other end of the line. "Carol, are you okay?" Serena asked with a rush of relief.

"I—I guess," the woman said reluctantly, then in a rush, "I don't guess you could have told that fool anything. I wasn't thinking too straight when I called. I—I'm s—sorry. I want to meet with you and Kirby again, the way we planned."

Serena didn't betray her surprise. "Good. Thank you. I would like to read the flyer, if you don't mind. Could you save it for me?"

There was a pause. "Well. . .it says some things you won't like. He even quoted me when I was angry last week. It may not be the best—"

"I promise not to hold it against you," Serena assured her. "But if we're battling an enemy, I would like to know how to prepare myself."

"Carson took a copy of it. I guess he'll probably show it to you."

Serena set up an appointment for the following week and hung up, elated by Carol's apology, worried about what might have been printed about the clinic. What if Edward frightened potential patients away? He was hurting the very cause he professed to support.

❧

Edward was either not at home or refused to answer Carson's persistent knock. After ten minutes trying at both front and back entrances to the man's apartment, Carson gave up—but only for tonight. Edward needed help, and Carson wanted some answers.

❧

The remainder of the week passed slowly, and Blythe's absence affected Serena the most. She hadn't realized how much she had depended on Blythe's easy companionship and common sense, on their peaceful evening ritual of listening to the girls splash in the pool or talking on the phone. As Blythe had predicted, the garden suffered without her loving hand, and Serena had no time to care for it.

Blythe would also have helped with transporting teenagers across the city to youth rallies and shopping for school clothes and all those wonderful summer activities that seemed to converge on them at once. Serena found herself especially busy with a new onslaught of patients at her office. Several women visited Alternative, and Serena was relieved that the flyers Edward published were, for the most part, ignored.

On Thursday, Serena received a call in her office from Jenny.

"Mom, can Kirby and I spend the weekend at Paula's cabin? She said we could use it, and she's going to be out of town."

"I don't know. . . ." Serena glanced at the clock. Her next patient was due to walk in anytime. "I don't like the idea of you two young girls being down there alone. The cabin does not have a phone. What if something went wrong?"

"Mom, what could go wrong? We can take the cell phone. There's a neighborhood watch down there, and all the doors have triple locks, which you know Paula never uses because it's so safe," Jenny reminded her.

"What do you plan to do all weekend, sit around the house?"

"Of course not. Paula said we could use the boat if we were careful. We won't go skiing or anything, but I'd like to explore." Jenny paused for a moment, as if thinking up more things to do at a moment's notice. "We could always go shopping at one of those tourist traps that have overpriced junk for sale, or to the amusement park in Osage Beach. If you want, I can call you Saturday night to let you know everything's okay."

Serena glanced at her clock again. "So what made you decide all of a sudden that you had to spend this weekend down at Paula's cabin?"

"Actually, it's for Kirby. You know she said she might go home next week, and her parents may not let her go anywhere like that. She's never stayed on the lake before, and for both of us, it's our last big chance for a little freedom before school starts."

"Who's going to be there besides you and Kirby? Any other friends?"

"No, just me and Kirby."

"Does Danny know you'll be there?"

Jenny hesitated, and Serena held her breath. "I don't know, Mom, but I don't think Paula will tell him. She knows how I feel about him."

"And how is that?"

"Mom, I thought you could read my mind. Besides, I told you just the other day that I didn't care if he dated other girls. . .or at least, that's what I told him."

"But you also admitted it might bother you. Honey, what would you do if he showed up at the cabin and decided he was staying, too? After all, it is his family's cabin."

Jenny hesitated again, then said, "Kirby and I would leave. It's all we could do. Kirby's just now beginning to listen to me when I talk about God, and if I were to compromise myself, I'd be proving to her that I'm the kind of a hypocrite her mother keeps telling her about." She added more softly, "Even if I wanted to stay, I wouldn't."

Serena glanced up worriedly as her next patient entered her office. "Okay," she said reluctantly, lowering her voice. "I guess you can go, but we'll talk more about it when I get home tonight."

"Thanks, Mom. Oh, I forgot to ask if we could use the van. . . . Will you be needing it this weekend?"

"Only if I want to go anywhere," Serena replied dryly.

"Oh. And do you?"

"Well, there's a sidewalk sale downtown this Saturday morning. . . ."

"Please, Mom?"

Serena's eyes flickered across the desk to her patient, who was trying hard to look disinterested in her conversation. "Okay, I suppose I could take a taxi if I really need to go anywhere."

"Great. One more thing I forgot to tell you. Dr. Wells visited the clinic today."

"Oh, really? Did Sharon give him a tour?"

"Yes. He didn't say much about it, but he said if he gets any women in his office who might be interested, he'll send them our way. Do you think he will?"

"I hope so."

"Oh yeah, and you know that guy who was hanging around outside the clinic the other day? He was back."

"Did he come into the clinic?"

"No." There was a pause. "But he was outside when Dr. Wells came in."

Serena nearly groaned aloud. That was all they needed. He would think they were an abortion clinic for sure now.

Chapter 16

Friday evening Serena sat cross-legged on the floor in the family room, folding a huge pile of donated maternity clothes while Rascal eyed her activity with concentrated interest. The puppy crouched beside the sofa until Serena had three neat stacks of blouses and jeans, then he romped across the floor with his floppy ears flying. With a growl of attack, he grabbed a pair of jeans in his sharp teeth and started to shake them.

Serena made a quick rescue before he could do any damage. "Dog! I'll send you outside if you're not careful!"

He turned and looked up into her eyes with sudden, soulful mourning.

"No more."

He scampered forward without warning and licked her face before she could stop him.

She never could resist a sloppy kiss. She leaned back against the sofa and scratched behind his ears. "Poor thing. I guess you miss Blythe, don't you?"

He licked her again and laid his head against her arm.

"Yeah, so do I."

"So do I," echoed a small, forlorn voice from the kitchen doorway, and Serena looked up to find her younger daughter slouching into the room, long brown hair tumbling across her face, mouth drooping.

"I know, honey." Serena released the puppy. "Don't worry. Granny will be back home soon. Isn't she supposed to call tonight?"

Emily plopped down on the floor and picked up a dress to fold it. "Tomorrow night."

"Where are Jenny and Kirby?"

"Back in their rooms, packing." Emily pushed Rascal away from the dress she held. "Did you know they're going to take Rascal with them? They've already packed the dog food."

"Yep. Sorry, sweetie, it's just you and me this weekend."

Emily folded another dress, then reached out absently and rubbed Rascal's head. She glanced up at Serena. "Hmm." Deep in those golden brown eyes, a little twinkle stirred to life.

That always made Serena nervous. "What do you mean, 'Hmm?'"

A tiny smile played around Emily's lips. She ducked her head and folded another dress.

"Emily Ann, what are you up to?"

"Oh, nothing, Mom. I just thought of something." She leaned back against the sofa and looked up at Serena. "With Granny and Jenny both gone, I won't have anyone to take me to church. I guess if you won't take me, I won't get to go."

Serena knew immediately that she was caught, but for a moment she played along. "Sorry, honey, we don't have a car. It won't hurt you to miss one service, will it?"

Emily's eyes flew wide. "Mom!"

"Gotcha." Serena chuckled as she heard the other two girls coming down the hallway. "I can't let my younger child backslide on me, can I?"

"You mean you'll go?"

"I'll go to church with you so you won't have to go alone."

"All right! Hey, Jenny, guess what," she said as the girls came chattering and laughing into the room. "Mom's going to church with me Sunday!"

Jenny's face reflected her sister's joy, and Serena realized once more, with a pang, how difficult her nonattendance had been on her family.

"Under one condition," she warned, indicating the huge stacks of folded and unfolded clothing around her. "That I don't get buried underneath all of this before Sunday morning."

Jenny and Kirby looked at each other, then sat down and started folding. "We can take this by the clinic on our way out of town," Jenny said.

"Good." Serena reached over and tore a slip of paper from a pad. "And here's the address of Memorial Baptist Church. They've collected four boxes of baby blankets, clothing, diapers, and a crib. I need you to pick it up on your way back into town Sunday evening and deliver it to the clinic."

"Sure, Mom."

"I packed an ice chest with food. It's on the kitchen counter. Don't forget to put it in the van."

Jenny smiled at Serena. "Steaks for barbecue?"

"And fruit and vegetables and sandwich supplies. There are a couple of board games on the counter I thought you might want to take with you since Paula doesn't have a television."

Kirby looked from Serena to Jenny and shook her head. "I'll never have that kind of a relationship with my mother."

"What do you mean?" Serena asked.

"You treat each other with. . .such respect. You can talk to each other. You do things for each other. There's so much love, and it just kind of spills out, you know?"

"Well, Kirby, we're starting to kind of like you, too," Jenny teased. "Maybe you could just hang around here with us."

"And while you're at it," Serena said, "pick out which of these clothes you want."

"You mean you're giving me maternity clothing?"

"Sure," Serena said. "You're pregnant, aren't you? Eventually, you'll need to size up."

The expression of dismay on Kirby's face made Jenny and Emily giggle. Kirby picked up a light blue dress, then discarded it. "Not my size."

"How do you know what size you'll be in a few months?" Jenny teased.

Kirby held the size tag under Jenny's nose. "I refuse to gain four sizes! If I do, I won't need this dress, because I'll hide in the house with the sheet over my head until I have the baby."

Jenny laughed, then sobered. "That would be awful. Then you couldn't even go to church with me."

Kirby picked up another dress and considered it. "Maybe your church wouldn't want me if they knew I was an unwed mother."

"Of course they'll want you," Jenny said. "Don't you remember what I told you about forgiveness the other night? If you seek God's forgiveness with a truly contrite heart, He'll forgive you; and if He forgives you, then who else has a right to accuse you?"

Kirby nodded, as if she'd been thinking about it for a while. "Serena, you believe that, too?"

"Yes." She did believe it. She'd believed it all her life, but for some reason she felt like a hypocrite saying it, because she knew, deep down, that she had been unable to apply it to herself.

Kirby picked up a pink sweater, fingered the material absently, and hugged it against her. "Serena, do you think my parents will go to church with me when I go back home?"

Serena folded a pair of maternity jeans. That was a good question. "You can ask about it during your sessions. Let them know it's important to you. Going to church is a personal decision for everyone. Your mother may not feel comfortable with it at first."

Jenny shot Serena a searching look but said nothing.

In spite of Rascal's continued interest in their work, they soon had the clothes sorted, stacked, and boxed. Each girl carried a box to the van, then loaded her own luggage and the things Serena had packed for them. They loaded Rascal last.

The van had just pulled out of the driveway when the muted ringing of the telephone forced Serena to set her armload of diapers on the sofa. "Uh-oh, Mom," Emily said, running down the hallway toward her room, "I just remembered that Granny wanted me to keep an eye on the garden."

Serena picked up the receiver. "Hello."

"What a surprise," came Carson's deep, teasing voice. "I felt sure your secretary would answer for you at home, just like at the office, so you wouldn't have to talk to me."

"I didn't want to pay her overtime," she teased. "Besides, I wasn't avoiding you. I just had a very hectic week, as you must know, since you referred a couple of patients to me from the ER."

"In that case, I'll get down to business. I just talked with Carol Acuff on the phone. She tells me Kirby and Jenny are planning a trip to Horseshoe Bend this weekend."

"What did she say about it?"

"That she wished she could afford to take her own daughter to the lake."

Serena shook her head. "What she needs to afford is time to listen to Kirby."

"She's trying, Serena. She's still jealous of you, but she wants her daughter back. I know that will all work out given time. Actually, that isn't why I called. I thought you might like a ride to church Sunday, since you were kindhearted enough to allow your daughter to use your only mode of transportation for the weekend."

"And Emily clued you in to this fact," Serena said.

"My matchmaking angel. Need a lift?"

"Emily and I can take a taxi."

"I'm cheaper, and I sort of already told your daughter I would be seeing her at church."

Serena sank down onto the sofa and sighed. She was getting a little irritable about Carson and Emily ganging up on her time after time, in spite of their good intentions. "Maybe I'll rent a car for the weekend."

There was a short pause. "Uh-oh," he said quietly. "I've crossed over the line, haven't I?"

Yes, he had, but she couldn't help being impressed that he'd picked up on it. "I read this book recently, Carson. It's called *Boundaries*, and it's an excellent book. It explains the need to set parameters in our lives."

"I'm sorry, Serena. I'm pushing too hard. I don't mean to make you uncomfortable." His deep voice held sincere contrition. "I need to remind myself that, just because I want to spend time with you every chance I get, I have no right to force you into anything."

She felt a smile nudging at her lips in spite of herself. "Yes, well. . ."

"And just because I think you're very special and beautiful and—"

"Okay, I get the message." She grinned. "Thank you, Carson. I'm still taking a taxi to church Sunday."

"I understand."

"Please don't get me wrong, I do appreciate the offer, but it's going to be difficult. . . . What I mean is. . .it's been a long time since I've gone to church."

"I know. I struggled with that after Judy's death. Serena, I know this sounds almost like blasphemy, but have you never forgiven God for taking Jennings away from you?"

She blinked in surprise. "Forgiven God?"

"Please don't take me wrong. I don't mean to say God actually needs your forgiveness, but that you might need to forgive. Several weeks after Judy died, I realized that I was still angry with God, and until I overcame that anger, I couldn't move forward in my life. In order to heal that breach, I decided to forgive Him. It was a simple act of letting go of the anger and reestablishing my connection with Him. It must not have been as sacrilegious as it seemed at the time, because He blessed me with a much deeper relationship with Him than I had ever experienced before."

"I think that's wonderful, Carson," Serena said softly. "But I don't need to forgive God."

"Oh?"

"It's. . .complicated."

"Do you want to tell me about it?"

She bit her lip and stared out the window, where she saw Emily working in the garden. "I haven't had a good relationship with God for. . .many years. Sometimes I wonder if I ever did, even though I was raised in a home that professed Christianity. Jennings and I got married when I was nineteen, and he put me through school. He was the most wonderful man. . .and he was four years older than me, already established in his family business. He became my whole life. He was a dedicated Christian, and we were active in the church. I said all the right things, volunteered for committees, worked in the nursery, and sang in the choir."

"How did you find time to complete your education in the midst of all that busywork?"

"I postponed it for a couple of years. Jennings helped me a lot with the girls and housework. But when he died, everything suddenly came crashing down. I realized that, during all those years of marriage, I had allowed him to be my connection to God. I lived my faith through him. My focus was on my husband, not Jesus Christ. Sometimes I wonder if God took Jennings from me because of that, but then I realize that isn't possible. My spiritual walk isn't worth a man's life."

"Your soul was worth a Man's life, Serena," Carson said. "Your soul, not just Jenny's or Emily's or mine. You are as special to God as any of us, and you're even more special to Him than you are to me."

For a moment, Serena couldn't speak. How could she explain to him that she had blown her chance many years ago? "Maybe we can talk more about it someday," she said.

"When? Every day counts, Serena. Every time you push God away, you build a thicker wall around—"

"Has anyone ever said you'd be a good preacher?"

"I'm doing it again, right?"

"Yes. Why don't we change the subject? Have you had a chance to find out more about Edward?"

There was a slight pause, and she could almost hear Carson's frustration over the phone line. "I haven't found him. He's apparently doing his best to avoid me."

"Jenny told me he was outside the clinic Wednesday. He was there when Dr. Wells visited."

"Oh no."

"I wonder what he'll write next." Serena saw Emily wander out of the garden toward the house. "Carson, I need to go. Emily's looking pretty lonely, and I'm going to take her on a walk and cheer her up."

"Would the two of you be interested in a late dinner?"

"Thanks, but we've eaten."

"Okay." He sounded disappointed. "I'd risk stepping over your boundaries again and ask you and Emily to go to Columbia with me tomorrow to a boring, all-day conference, but—"

"Carson." She couldn't help smiling.

"Yes, well, I'll probably see you Sunday at church then."

She shook her head. "You don't give up easily, do you?"

"No."

"Good night, Carson."

"Good night."

Chapter 17

Morning, Mom!" The sound of Emily's voice early Sunday morning scattered the last of Serena's dream, and she pried her eyes open, then squinted at the bright light that attacked her through the open window shades.

"Morning."

"It's going to be a beautiful day, isn't it? I knew you wouldn't want those old blinds closed, so I opened them for you."

Serena yawned and turned to press her face into the scented softness of her satin pillowcase. "Lovely."

"Come on, I thought we might go for a swim before we get ready for church," Emily prompted. "What do you think?"

For perhaps the first time in a year, Serena shuddered at the thought of diving into that cool water and exercising her sleepy limbs. Last night, along with many other nights lately, she had tossed restlessly, tangling her blankets into a hopeless knot. She'd probably had less than four hours of quality sleep—but there was Emily, her golden brown eyes shining, and Serena didn't have the heart to turn her down.

"Okay. You go on ahead of me, and I'll meet you there in a few minutes."

Emily raised an expressive eyebrow reproachfully. "You'll go back to sleep."

Serena grunted, then shook her head and slid out from under the clinging covers. "Okay! I'm coming! I hope you're satisfied," she grumbled. As Emily stepped out into the hallway, Serena slipped her nightgown up over her head and replaced it with a Chinese blue, one-piece swimsuit.

Emily led the way through the house to the pool, and Serena studied her younger daughter with sudden interest. "Have you been losing some weight? That suit doesn't seem to be fitting you so tightly these days." She indicated with surprise the modest green swimsuit her daughter wore.

Emily beamed at Serena. "It's about time you noticed. Granny put me on a diet about three weeks ago."

"Come to think of it, you look like you're getting taller, too. Let's measure you after this swim," Serena suggested. "I think my little girl is growing up."

Though she said it teasingly, she felt the quick sting of tears in her eyes. Her little girl was growing up. Her little girl. . .

As was usually the case, just a few minutes in her daughter's company was all Serena needed to feel alive and refreshed once more. After five laps around the pool, she felt energized enough to face her reentry to church without so much trepidation. She just hoped the energy would last. This was not a good time to face old memories.

"Mom, I wish we could call Carson and have him come and pick us up." Emily swam up beside Serena and grasped the side of the pool.

"Emily Ann, we discussed this yesterday." Serena climbed the metal steps and sat on the concrete. "I know you like to play matchmaker, but you're going too far." She squeezed water from the dripping strands of her short, blond hair.

Emily climbed out and sat beside her. "But I feel if I don't push, nothing's ever going to happen between you and Carson, and you're so perfect for each other."

"Don't worry," she said dryly, "Carson's doing enough pushing for both of you."

Emily brightened. "He is?"

"Yes." And Serena couldn't stop thinking about his words Friday night. If she continued to push God away, would the wall around her become insurmountable? Wasn't her real impediment an inability to forgive herself? Didn't her daughters deserve a mom who was spiritually strong and could continue to guide them in the truth—especially now, with their father gone? She couldn't continue like this. It was selfish. Her family needed her. The questions had haunted her all day yesterday, and the guilt overwhelmed her. What was the real reason she had avoided God all these years?

"Mom." Emily laid a gentle hand on her arm to get her attention. "Are you okay?"

Serena looked down into her daughter's tender, trusting eyes. "I'll be fine."

※

When their taxi pulled into the church parking lot, Serena spotted Carson's car immediately, and she felt a familiar tingle of warmth.

He met her and Emily just inside the church doors and, to Serena's relief, led them to a seat near the back, where Serena would feel less conspicuous. In spite of the low profile, however, members spotted her immediately. Within minutes she was surrounded by old, dear friends, former members of her Sunday school class, and choir members. They welcomed her back to church, asked where she'd been, and told her how much they missed her and wished she would return home where she belonged.

She felt welcomed. She felt overwhelmed and deeply touched. She felt more than that. She felt the hand of God reaching out to her, drawing her, and reassuring her. For the first time, she dared to open her heart to what He was saying. Could He really want her? After all she had done, after all the running and avoiding, could He still truly want to be a part of her life?

During a lull in the visits, Carson leaned over and whispered in her ear. "It does get to you, doesn't it?"

She glanced at him briefly. "Yes."

"Were you surprised by the welcome?"

She glanced around her old church, at the stained glass windows, the beautiful floral decoration at the altar, and the comfortable padded pews. What mattered to her now, however, were the familiar faces of old friends who had cared enough to call her for months after Jennings died, urging her to return and loving her through the grief.

"Serena?" Carson said. "Surprised?"

"No. Now that I think about it, I'm not surprised. I'm relieved. Nothing has changed."

"This is part of your family. They want you back."

Serena looked up at him questioningly, but before she could reply, the pastor came by to welcome them. Soon after he left, the singing began. Serena discovered that Carson had a beautiful bass voice, but the fact only registered superficially. Her mind was busy with his remark. They wanted her back—but did she belong here? Did she belong to God? If she did, why didn't she feel close to Him? Why couldn't she talk to Him the way Blythe or the girls did? Or Carson? Carson's faith was so simple, yet foundational in everything he did.

Halfway through the third hymn, her voice faltered. Sudden awareness rushed in at her, like a discovery of hidden treasure. Memories came together in a single thread of truth that stunned her. She stopped singing and felt Carson glance at her with concern. She didn't look at him. Emily touched her arm, and she shook her head.

Throughout her life, she had not experienced the faith that Carson and her family shared because she didn't own it herself. She'd borrowed her parents' godly rituals when she was growing up in that grim, cheerless household, but rules were enough for them. When she married Jennings, she'd adopted his enthusiasm for serving the church, but while she allowed his values to become her own, she had never taken them into her heart. With his death, her connection to the things of God had disappeared. She had never had that personal, one-on-one experience with Jesus Christ. She glanced at Carson, then away.

It didn't come as a surprise to her when the sermon that morning was about forgiveness. She often heard other people complain that they felt a particular sermon was directed at them, but this was the first time it had happened to her. She had no complaints. She listened hungrily to the pastor's words about God's forgiveness, never once feeling conspicuous or out of place, never giving it another thought as her soul drank in the words she had longed to hear for so many years. She'd heard it all before, but she had never felt they applied to her own life, never felt that God could forgive her until now. She bowed her head and said a silent prayer, repenting, releasing the burden she had held within her for so long, and the tremendous load of guilt slipped away.

When she stood with everyone for the invitation song, she felt hope rise in her heart—hope, and an intense desire to meet with the Savior she had so long rejected. She put her songbook down and stepped toward the aisle, then hesitated and looked back at Carson. He watched her expectantly.

"Would you come with me to the altar?"

He nodded and replaced his hymnal, his eyes never leaving her face until she turned to walk ahead of him.

As they knelt at the front of the church, she felt God's love encompassing them both, and tears of happiness came to her eyes as words of praise sprang to her lips. "Thank You, God, for sending Your messenger to talk with me." She reached across and squeezed Carson's arm. "Thank You for giving me the peace I've rejected for so many years, and thank You for Your forgiveness. Although I don't deserve it, please give me Your gift of life. I want to be Yours."

The congregation continued to sing as Serena raised her head and looked at Carson through the lingering tears. "Thank you," she whispered.

❧

After the benediction, Emily rushed down to the front of the church and flung herself into Serena's arms, her face wet with tears. "Mom, you did it! You did it!" She kissed Serena on the cheek. "Jenny and I have been praying for you for so long!"

Fresh tears rose in Serena's throat as she thought of her daughters, Blythe, and Carson, all praying for her. Now their prayers, and hers, had been answered. Serena felt clean, spiritually refreshed, ready for that new beginning they had told Kirby about. All the old depression left her, and she felt nothing but praise for God. She had been blind to Him for so long and had just now received sight. It was a wonderful feeling.

A friend of Emily's asked her to spend the afternoon, and Carson requested that Serena allow him to take her home. It was time for that talk she had been dreading. Somehow she didn't dread it quite so much now.

With growing certainty, Serena realized that, not only must she tell Carson about her past, but she must tell her family. It had been a secret for too long. She thought of Emily and Jenny, of their sweet, all-encompassing love for her. Nothing could change that. And Blythe was never one to pass judgment. Serena would wait until Blythe came home to tell them, but today she would tell Carson.

How would he react?

When he pulled into Serena's driveway and parked, she reached across and touched his arm hesitantly. "Would you take a walk with me? We have some talking to do."

He held her gaze, unsmiling. "Sounds serious."

She opened her own door quickly and got out. She knew she couldn't expect to feel perfect peace at a time like this, not when Carson's reaction could affect her so much, but she had expected to be a little calmer, hadn't thought she would have so much trouble breathing. This mattered so much. She reached the end of the driveway and turned onto the sidewalk in front of the house, her strides lengthening.

"Hey, want to wait for me?" Carson called from behind her.

She slowed her steps and allowed him to catch up. "Sorry. There's something I should have told you sooner, something I've been ashamed for you to know. It's why I've been a little hesitant about. . .about our relationship."

"A little?"

She smiled. "Okay, very resistant."

"And I've told you more than once that nothing can change my heart."

"Yes, but you have no idea. . . ." She turned to him and stopped.

"Don't you think it's time?" he asked softly.

"Yes." She turned away and stepped along the sidewalk once more. "Next Friday would have been my daughter's birthday. She would have been twenty years old now. . .if she were alive. If I hadn't aborted her." The words scattered into the air, and she caught her breath, suddenly wishing she could recall them.

Serena couldn't look at Carson. "I was seventeen at the time. There were complications during the procedure, which is why I can't have children." She kept walking. "It's the one thing I couldn't bring myself to forgive and I couldn't allow God to forgive. The pain was too great, and I think I wanted to suffer. I felt I deserved it. I felt that the suffering would take away some of the intense guilt I felt I couldn't live with. Jennings never knew. I kept that from him for so many years, and the guilt compounded, because I knew it was my fault, my choice, that also kept him from having children of his own."

Carson caught her arm and pulled her around to face him. His dark eyes held compassion. "That's what you've kept secret all these years? How could you have worked with all those women and shown such openness and empathy with Kirby when you couldn't find it in your heart to forgive yourself? The abortion must have been horrible for you."

"It was. I know I'll still have to struggle to continue to forgive myself. I'll live with it always. I'll never forget the loss." She turned to walk back toward the house, and Carson fell into step beside her.

"Why have you waited to tell me this? Surely you didn't think I would hold it against you. Who am I to blame you when God casts no blame?"

She couldn't answer.

"I love you, Serena. Nothing has changed except that I love you more all the time. I love your family. I want to marry you."

Serena's chest swelled with overwhelming happiness and gratitude, but she had to cover everything. "I could never have your children. You've never had children of your own."

"I'm not looking for someone to have children for me. You have two wonderful girls already, and if we decided to adopt, we could. You're the one I want to share my life with."

She slowed and stopped at her porch steps, then turned to look up into his face. He was telling her the simple truth. He wanted her as she was. She smiled and laid her hand against the side of his face. "You really want to marry me?" She didn't deserve the joy of looking into his eyes and seeing the adoration he had for her.

"I want to marry you, Serena," he said softly. "I've told you before, I'm lonely, and it's all your fault. I was settled and satisfied until you came into my life, then I realized how wonderful life can be with someone who is caring and giving and fascinating. You are so much more than I ever dreamed possible. Please marry me."

She leaned into the warm, embracing strength of his arms. "Name the time and the place, Carson Tanner. I'll be there."

Chapter 18

The hot Sunday afternoon sun dropped below a tree-shrouded horizon, leaving heat in its wake. Dusk fell as two men in dark clothing strode with careful casualness down the alley behind the strip of older buildings where Alternative was nestled. Both men were empty-handed. The taller, heavier man wore a light nylon jacket, zipped up to the neck, undoubtedly uncomfortable in the lingering humidity. He frowned at his smaller companion. "You sure about this?"

"Doesn't it make sense? Why go all the way to Columbia when we can gouge out the cancer in our own city? This is a silent cancer. Nobody even suspects what goes on here. But I know."

"Have you been inside the clinic?"

"Yes, I have. I went inside one day when the volunteer was talking with a girl in the back."

"Well? Did you see anything interesting?"

"Not then, but don't forget I talked to that Acuff woman, and she was really suspicious about the place."

"Yeah, but you yourself said the woman was upset because her daughter went to live with Dr. Van Buren."

"Sure she was, but I was still curious. What would you have been thinking when you saw Van Buren talking to Wells at the school?" He turned to his companion and waited for a reply, as if the answer had better be good.

"They could have been arguing."

"Or setting up an appointment to check out her clinic for a future death site. Get a clue, Freeman! That's your problem: You don't see trouble until it's smashing you in the face!" His voice rose with increased fervor. "And that monster had the guts to openly come right to this clinic to see her. He's spitting in our faces, don't you see that? He won't be killing babies on this street."

"Not at this address anyway."

"He was here for a long time, too, and he didn't hang around in the front. They took him to one of those back rooms." Edward stopped at the back door of the clinic. "She's a hypocrite!" His anger was palpable and growing again. "I wonder how many girls have their abortions right here in this place."

Freeman nodded in agreement, catching Edward's excitement. "Yeah, I wonder."

Edward tried the door handle and found it locked, as he had known it would be. "There's no one here to get hurt." He reached into his pocket and pulled out a thin strip of metal.

Freeman stared at it in surprise.

"I didn't just loaf outside this place for two weeks," Edward said. "I learned a little about jimmying locks."

The tool didn't work as efficiently as it could have, so it took Edward five agonizingly long minutes to jiggle it open and swing back the door. "After you."

Freeman hesitated and peered inside. "Dark in there. Can I turn on a light?"

"Maybe you'd better use your flashlight. Never know who might drive past out front."

Freeman did what Edward suggested and eased through the door.

"Uh-oh, I almost forgot." Jenny pressed the brake of the van and turned onto High Street. "We were supposed to drop these things off at the clinic. It's a good thing we've got the van. I can't believe how generous those people are at Memorial."

Kirby looked at her watch. "We're kind of late, aren't we? Won't Serena be worried? Why don't we call?"

"Okay, but we can do it from the clinic. Mom doesn't like me talking on the cell phone when I'm driving. This will only take a few minutes, then we can get on home. A couple of people are supposed to drop by the clinic first thing in the morning, and these things should help. Mom will understand when I tell her why we're late."

Kirby's blue eyes widened. "You're going to tell her Danny came to the cabin?"

"Why shouldn't I? Nothing happened."

"And she'll believe that?"

"Sure she will. Why not?"

"My mom never would."

Jenny hesitated, stopping at a light. "Mom knows I don't lie to her," she said quietly. She didn't look at Kirby, but she could feel the other girl's sudden tension.

"I do," Kirby said quietly. "It's kind of a habit I got into a long time ago. Now it's just natural. Mother wouldn't believe me if I told the truth anyway."

"Why don't you try it and see what happens? You didn't do anything this weekend you would have to lie about."

"No, but if I told her we went on that boat ride with those two guys—"

"Friends from church."

"That wouldn't matter to her. She'd think the worst."

They pulled up to the curb right in front of Alternative. Jenny switched off the engine and pulled her keys from the ignition. She opened her door, glancing behind the van to make sure no traffic was coming.

"Want me to help carry?" Kirby asked.

"I can get these boxes. Maybe you shouldn't be lifting heavy stuff. Besides, if you stay here with Rascal, he won't bark." Jenny glanced across the street, turned to slide the cargo door open, then spun back around to stare at Alternative's glass front. All was dark. But just for a half second she thought—

Rascal's sudden bark startled her.

"Jenny? What's wrong?" Kirby asked.

Jenny watched the building a moment longer, then shrugged and reached around for the box of clothes. "Nothing. I just thought I saw a light in the clinic, but it was probably just a reflection from a passing car." She glanced up and down the street, which was empty of traffic for the moment. The sky, totally dark now, loomed closely overhead without moon or stars to break its heaviness. Kirby had mentioned a cloud bank behind them on their way up from the lake.

Jenny shivered, though she wasn't cold. Even in Jefferson City, Missouri, downtown didn't feel like a safe place to be at night. She would hurry and drop off the supplies and leave. She warned Rascal to stay put and hefted the box to her hip, glad of the lights spaced closely together along the sidewalks. In spite of her command, Rascal leaped from the van and raced to her side, brushing so closely to her leg, he nearly tripped her. Having accompanied Serena often when she came down to lock up, he was familiar with the clinic. Tonight, though, he hesitated before he reached the front door. His front legs stiffened. Golden hairs stood up at the nape of his neck, and he growled.

Jenny stopped, heartbeats quickening. Then she shook her head in exasperation. "Silly! Are you trying to scare the life out of me? Stop fooling around!"

She set her box on the sidewalk and held her key ring up to the light.

Rascal barked.

Jenny ignored him, found the key, and stuck it into the lock.

Rascal barked again.

"Stop it, I said! You're not even supposed to—"

Jenny glanced up and saw—this time she was certain—a flash of light at the opening that led into the conference room.

"Jenny!" Kirby called. "What's taking you so long? Your mom is going to be really worried. What's wrong? You should have called her as soon as we got here. Tell me how to use this phone, and—"

Jenny whirled around, grabbed the dog, and bolted for the van, leaving the clothes sitting on the sidewalk.

"What is it? Are you crazy?" Kirby exclaimed. "Somebody'll steal that before morning!"

Jenny shoved Rascal into the back, closed the cargo door, and jumped in the front seat, her face pale, her heart pounding her rib cage.

"Somebody's in there!" She pressed the button that locked all the doors, then glanced at Kirby's disbelieving expression. "I'm not kidding! I saw a light, like a flashlight. Rascal saw it, too. Didn't you hear him barking?"

Kirby's eyes grew larger. Her face drained of color. "Let's get out of here!"

Jenny started the engine, put the van in gear, then hesitated. "We can't."

"What? What do you mean we can't? If there's some goon in there, we can't just sit out here and wait for him to come and get us!"

"No, but we can't drive all the way home and leave him there to burglarize the place or vandalize it. We've got to call the police. And Mom." She drove the van a short way down the street, pulled the cell phone from the glove compartment of the van, and dialed.

❧

For at least the tenth time that night, Serena turned from the window that overlooked the street. Carson had gone home hours ago, Emily was spending the night with a friend, and Serena had been unable to settle to the work she brought home from the office.

Where were Jenny and Kirby? They should have been home long before dark. Suppose something had happened to them? Serena had no way to get to them quickly. But what could happen? Jenny wasn't likely to do anything stupid. She was a good driver. The van had all new tires on it, and it was in peak running condition. That was another thing Blythe took care—

The telephone rang beside her. She jumped and grabbed it. "Hello?"

"Mom, this is Jenny. I'm down at Alternative, and something's going on. I went to deliver these baby things, and I saw a light flickering inside."

The cold chill of dread raced up Serena's spine. "And you're still there? Jenny, get out of there now!"

"I called the police, and they're already on their way. The silent alarm went off. Everything's all right, Mom, really. It's under control."

"And I know you, Jenny Van Buren. You'll try to play hero. Come home."

There was a pause, then Jenny said, "Can't we just lock the doors and sit tight until the police get here?"

Serena's heart pounded. She needed to get down there, and Carson could get to her faster than Jenny could. "Okay, fine. I'll call and see if Carson will bring me down there, but you sit tight and wait for the police."

"Okay, Mom."

"And lock the van doors."

"They're locked."

"Good girl. I'll be there as soon as I can. I love you, honey." She disconnected and dialed Carson's number.

❧

Edward peered over Freeman's shoulder at the dynamite that stuck out of a freshly drilled hole in the wall. "Why is this taking so long?"

"You want to destroy the supports, don't you? We've got to do it just right."

"But inside the walls? Is it necessary?"

"Yes. Are you sure the fire won't spread to other buildings?"

"Shouldn't—they're bricked. Besides, the fire department will get here in a hurry after the explosion."

"Explosions." Freeman straightened. "There should be three, if I've done it right."

"How much time will we have to get out of here?"

"How much do you want?"

"Ten minutes should do it."

"Go on to the door, and I'll meet you there."

Edward didn't use his flashlight to find his way. No sense in taking chances this close to their objective. He crept along the night-blackened hall with his hands out like huge antennae. He reached the door and pulled it open to a blare of blinding light, the sharp, metallic clack of a safety being released, and the resonant voice of a policeman advising him that he was under arrest. In a state of shock, he heard his Miranda rights read as he laced his hands behind his head.

They repeated the procedure a moment later when Freeman stepped out.

Jenny caught her breath and grasped Kirby's arm, scrambling back into the shadows behind the police car. "It's him! It's that Edward guy who wrote those flyers!"

"What was he doing in the clinic?"

"I don't know, but I'm going to find out."

"The police won't let you in right now, will they?"

"Maybe not, but I can try. Let's go around to the front."

Reluctantly, Kirby followed Jenny through the darkness, glancing back frequently at the flashing lights of the police car. They were halfway around when they heard shouts from the alley. Seconds later two more policemen ran around from the front with their guns out.

"It's okay, we got him," one of the officers announced. "He thought he could outrun us. Better keep an eye on these two."

"Come on," Jenny whispered, leading the way to the front. "They've got them under control, and now's a good time to try to get inside."

"But Serena will be here anytime. Can't we wait?"

Jenny stuck the key in the lock and turned. "That's why I want to check. Don't you realize how upset Mom will be if they've vandalized the place? Besides, what are you worried about? The police are here. We're perfectly safe." She picked up the box she had left on the sidewalk earlier and carried it through the door with her.

Kirby hesitated, watching Jenny switch on the lights. A policeman stepped into the main room from the back. Of course Jenny was right. It was safe. She was always careful, and the worst that could happen would be—

"Hey!" someone called from behind them. "Who are you, what are you doing in there? Get out—"

The ground lurched beneath Kirby's feet. A flash of light burned her vision. One millisecond later an explosion detonated in her ears. She staggered backward from the shock as the front windows shattered out onto the street.

A high-pitched wail followed the explosion, unrelenting, until Kirby realized it was her own screams. The scream formed a word: "Jenny!"

✎

Serena and Carson heard the explosion two blocks from the clinic. They saw the windows shatter, saw the lights go out. Figures bobbed and swayed, running through the darkness. Carson gunned the car through a stoplight.

Serena saw Kirby's slender, blond-haired form stumbling over the curb.

"No! Kirby, no!" Serena cried.

Carson honked the horn, and they screeched to a stop behind the van. They both jumped from the car in time for another explosion. And another.

"Serena!" Kirby shouted, running to them, choking on the black smoke that billowed into the street. "Jenny's in there! She went into the clinic!"

The words sent a shock wave through Serena. "Jenny," she whispered. "No." She stared through the shattered glass of the front window and bolted suddenly toward the front door. "Jenny!"

Carson grabbed her and dragged her backward. "Serena."

She fought his grip. "She's in there! What if there's another—"

Carson wrapped his arms around her struggling form. "You can't risk it right now. Look, the police are coming." He drew her more tightly still. "Serena, stop. You have to hold on for a minute."

She turned to him, met the deep fear in his eyes that matched her own. She grasped the front of his shirt, as if her grip would keep her steady, keep her from losing control. "Carson, we've got to get to her!"

"I know. We will."

Already they heard sirens in the distance. A uniformed officer came running toward them from the end of the block, gesturing for them to move back.

Serena struggled once more in Carson's firm grip, and he released her. She ran toward the policeman. "My daughter was in there! Please, you've got to help us. She ran into the building just before the explosion, and—"

"Are you Serena Van Buren?" the officer demanded.

"Yes. My daughter—"

"Jenny? Is that your daughter?"

She caught her breath and looked more closely at him. "Jenny, yes! Is she—"

"We've called an ambulance, ma'am. She was in the rear hallway when the first explosion detonated at the front of the building. Two of my men had just apprehended her for—"

"But how badly is she hurt? Take me to her."

"She says she's fine, ma'am. We just want to take—"

"She says she's fine?" Sudden relief weakened Serena's legs. She stumbled, and Carson put his arm around her shoulders for support.

"She didn't even want us to call an ambulance. I imagine it will just be a treat and release, but we didn't want to take any chances. I think your daughter will be okay."

❧

Two hours later, Serena opened her front door to find Carol and Hal Acuff standing on the porch, their faces tense. "Dr. Van Buren, thanks for calling us," Hal said. "We saw the news report on TV, but we didn't realize Kirby was involved until you told us. Is she here? Can we see her?"

"Of course, come on in. We're all still sitting around in shock." Serena stepped back and waited for them to enter.

Carol paused in front of her and searched her eyes. "I'm sorry about the explosion." Her voice was soft, and she was more subdued than Serena had ever seen her. She reached out and touched Serena's arm. "Are you going to be okay?"

"Now that I know Jenny and Kirby are safe. That's all that really matters. It looks like we'll have to have our meetings here for a while, or at my office downtown."

"The clinic was destroyed?"

"Totally." Serena heard her own voice wobble. She swallowed. "We'll rebuild."

Carol squeezed her arm. "Good." She paused, glanced toward her husband, then looked back at Serena. "We've done a lot of talking these past few days, Serena. And I've done a lot of thinking. I've had to. I can't stand the thought of losing my daughter because of my own stubbornness."

Hal stepped up beside her and laid a hand on his wife's shoulder. "What we're trying to say is that we'll help Kirby through this pregnancy. We want to do whatever it takes to make this family work."

"Tonight cinched it for us," Carol said. "I just kept asking myself, 'What if Kirby had been in that building? What if we'd lost her?' I couldn't stand the thought." Her eyes filled with tears. "I'm still struggling with the idea of being a grandmother before I'm forty, but I've got some time to get ready for that."

"Mom? Dad?" came a timid, wavering voice from the hallway, and the three of them turned to find Kirby standing there, her blue eyes—so much like her mother's—wide and questioning.

"Kirby." Carol's face crumpled, and the accumulation of tears trickled down her cheeks. "Oh, baby, we're so glad you're safe." She reached for her daughter, and Kirby rushed into her arms. Hal put his arms around both of them, and Serena quietly left them alone. They had a long way to go, a lot of healing to do, but she intended to see they got all of the help they needed.

She stepped into the family room and saw Carson sprawled out on the carpet between Jenny and Emily, laughing at Rascal's attempt to reach a cookie from the end table. Carson caught sight of Serena, and the laughter in his eyes deepened to something more powerful, filled with joy. He winked and beckoned her to join them.

Serena had never felt more complete.

HANNAH ALEXANDER

Hannah Alexander is the pen name of the husband-and-wife writing team of Cheryl and Melvin Hodde. They live in Missouri where Melvin has a doctor's practice. Be sure to ask them about their recent mission trip to Russia, with which they could certainly fill one or more books with stories.

TIMING IS
EVERYTHING

Tracey V. Bateman

To all my friends and fellow writers from American Christian Romance Writers who are waiting for your "babies" to be born. He truly does make all things beautiful in His time.

Love and gratitude to Chris Lynxwiler and Susan Downs for whirlwind critiques. You two are the BEST!

Chapter 1

The very last thing Esther needed to add to her already frantic schedule was her present conversation with her sister. It wouldn't be so bad if Karen would just say what she meant and then say good-bye so Esther could get back to work. But that wasn't her way—especially when single men were involved.

Resting her forehead against her palm, Esther closed her eyes in a futile attempt to thwart a fast-approaching tension headache. How could she wrap up this call before Karen roped her into another disastrous blind date?

"You've got to meet this guy, Esther. He just started working at the office, and he's so sweet."

Where was that aspirin she'd picked up yesterday? Esther pulled out her top drawer and rummaged around for the plastic bottle while Karen continued to tout the angelic attributes of the latest Mr. Right.

"He's not like the other social workers around here. And oh, Esther, you should just see him with the kids that come into the office. It's just so obvious that he's ready to settle down and start a family. I thought of you right away. Honest, he's perfect for you."

They always are. Esther released a heavy sigh into the receiver and glanced at her watch.

One twenty-five.

"I hate to interrupt, but I'm meeting a new client in five minutes, and my desk looks like a tornado hit it. I need to straighten it up before he gets here."

Never one to take the slightest hint, let alone a direct attempt to say good-bye, Karen continued as though Esther hadn't spoken. "A new *male* client, huh? Is he married? What does he look like?"

"Yes. I don't know. And I don't know. My assistant set up the appointment. To tell you the truth, I've never even spoken with the man."

"Well, make sure you smile while he's there. I just this minute got a feeling about this one."

Karen's "feelings" were legendary—and usually wrong. "You always have a 'feeling about this one.' Besides, what happened to the kid-loving social worker of two minutes ago?"

"Consider him a backup plan in case the new client doesn't work out. Let's talk about your hair. Is it brushed? You'd hate to meet your future husband with messy hair."

Esther patted her hair, which she had painstakingly coiled into a French twist at six-thirty that morning. With a quick glance at the clock, she felt her stomach tense with a desperate need to make a good impression on her new client, male or otherwise.

She debated whether to simply hang up on her only sister and best friend or whether she actually had the patience to have this conversation again. As much as she needed to end the call, she couldn't hurt her well-meaning sister's feelings. But perhaps a little hard-hitting reminder—again—wouldn't hurt. "Listen, Karen, when are you going to get it through your head that I am *not*, I repeat, *not* interested in getting married? Ever. Period. I enjoy being alone in my comfy sweatpants and Disney World T-shirt."

"I know, I know. Your perfect date is the Discovery channel and a huge bowl of Rocky Road ice cream. Spare me your diatribe on the benefits of bachelorettehood and how you're married to your career."

Esther chuckled. "I'm not sure bachelorettehood is even a word. As a matter of fact, I'm almost positive it isn't."

"Sure it is." Karen's voice rang with humor. "In Karen's Collegiate Dictionary, bachelorettehood is defined as the state of being an old maid. And your picture is next to the definition in glaring black-and-white."

"I prefer being thought of as maturely independent. Or independently mature. Either way, I'm happy as I am. And I wouldn't change it for anything in the world."

"You just think you wouldn't change it."

Esther hated Karen's all-knowing tone—the one that spoke of experience that she, Esther, lacked. And why shouldn't it? Karen had found her own Mr. Right during the hot, humid days of her thirteenth summer. She'd never even glanced at another boy after that.

A twinge of jealousy pinched Esther's heart. What would her life have been like if she had found the man of her dreams early in life and had spent the last twenty-five years married and raising children?

There was no time to ponder the probing and troubling question as Karen's lilting voice bubbled through the receiver. "Believe me, Esther, one look at Prince Charming, and you'll turn into a giggling teenager again."

"I was never a giggling teenager to begin with," Esther said wryly. "You're confusing me with you again. Anyway, dear sister, I have to run. My appointment will be here any sec. See you at Dad's on Sunday."

Esther settled the receiver back into its cradle just as her assistant buzzed her.

"Mr. Pearson is here." Thankfully, the nineteen-year-old used her professional voice.

"Thank you, Missy. Send him in."

Esther scowled at the papers scattered across her desk. She should never have allowed Karen to get her into the "I'm-happily-married-to-my-job" conversation. How in the world would Mr. Pearson ever trust her to keep tidy books if she couldn't even keep her desk clean?

She had thirty seconds—tops—to create the illusion of order from this chaos. Standing, she reached across her desk. Before she could lift a file, her elbow knocked against the large Styrofoam cup half filled with the cold latte she hadn't had time to finish earlier. A stream made a quick run toward her files and papers.

With a cry, she made a mad dash to save the papers. In her despair, she barely heard the door open.

"Uh, excuse me. I'm Tom. Should I come back later?"

"No." Grabbing at a box of tissues on her desk, she attempted to sop up the mess. "Come on in and have a seat," she said without an upward glance. "I'll be with you in a minute."

"Have an accident?"

A groan escaped her lips as the latte found a target. She snatched up the folder and quickly set it out of harm's way. "No, I did this on purpose," she shot back, then gasped and slapped her hand to her forehead. "Oh, good grief. I'm sorry. I just. . .I'm trying to save my papers."

"I completely understand. Here, let me help." His tanned hand, filled with wadded tissue, moved over her desk, sopping up latte. Esther breathed a sigh of relief while the tissue stopped the river from reaching any more papers before she could get them all off the desk. She set the messy, unkempt pile on a nearby file cabinet and settled back into her chair.

"I can finish," she said and, for the first time, glanced up. She caught her breath. "Oh, wow." The greatest-looking Hollywood actors and magazine models were all plastic surgery jobs gone horribly wrong compared to this guy.

Amazingly brilliant blue eyes stared back at her. Never mind that they looked at her as though she might be just a little more than nuts. He was beautiful. Prince Charming meets Andy Garcia.

"Wow?" Prince Andy repeated.

"Huh? Oh yeah. Wow, that's a messy pile of tissue. Let me throw those away for you. I have a trash can here at my feet." *Great recovery, Esther!* She smiled.

"Here you go." He plopped a sticky, wet mess of soggy tissues into her hand. "Not the kind of gift I usually give a pretty woman."

Esther felt a giggle coming from deep within and was completely powerless to keep it down where it belonged. She was mortified when the offending sound left her lips. Oh, brother. Karen was right. She was acting like a teenager. Time to get control of herself. Much as she hated to admit it, she was forty years old—too old to go crazy over a guy.

"Thank you for your help." She cleared her throat. "Now that that's all taken care of, let's discuss your account."

❧

Tom blinked in surprise at the new personality emerging before him. This enchanting woman had gone from unsure and even a bit ditzy to completely in control in an instant. This personality was probably better for his business, but the other one had made him smile. She hadn't even noticed in all the fuss that one side of her hair was falling from its twisty-knotted style.

"Mr. Pearson?"

He shot a glance back to her eyes.

Her brow arched.

Tom's face warmed at her obvious bewilderment. He'd been staring at her hair, debating whether or not to reach forward and test the shiny strands. They couldn't possibly be as soft as they looked.

She gave him a snap-out-of-it scowl.

"I'm sorry. I just couldn't help noticing that your hair is coming loose."

Her amber eyes widened, and she quickly patted her head. "Oh, brother. What next?"

Tom winced as she yanked the pins from her hair and let the rest of her dark tresses flow freely around her shoulders.

A lump formed in his throat, and he could almost feel the silky smoothness of her waves of hair.

"What's wrong?" she asked.

"Nothing. It's just that I've never seen that color of hair before. It's rare."

She snorted. She actually snorted. And to Tom it was an adorable snort. In fact, he wished she'd do it again.

"It's a special blend. Kind of a mahogany slash burgundy. I love it but not enough to call it rare in my hairdresser's presence, or she'll start charging me more." She smirked, and a dimple flashed at one corner of her mouth.

Tom swallowed hard. "Miss Young—"

"Esther."

"What?"

"Call me Esther. That's my name. Unless you'd rather we stay on formal terms."

"No, no. I'm Tom."

"You mentioned that."

A smile tipped his lips. "Esther. I don't usually do this. But I'm hosting a picnic at the park for the employees of Pearson Lumber this Saturday."

Esther nodded and glanced down at a document on her desk. "I see the cost. It's no problem. You can afford it."

Again, she glanced up at him and smiled.

Tom's returning smile began as a lurch in his heart and sort of exploded onto his lips. "Actually, I'm not telling you about the picnic to find out if I can afford it."

She raised a silky, delicate brow. "What then?" A look of understanding moved across her features. "Oh, I get it. I'm a new employee, and you're inviting me to join the crew."

"Not exactly."

A beguiling pink flooded her cheeks. "I'm sorry, it just seemed like you were building up to an invitation."

Clearing his throat, Tom fought the urge to chuckle. "I'm not very good at this. I'm asking you to come to the picnic. But not as my accountant. As my date."

Wide amber-colored eyes widened farther, and her mouth made an O. "Well, I don't usually—"

"Don't usually go to picnics? Go on dates? Eat barbecue? Mix business with pleasure?"

"That's the one," she said with a wry grin.

"Then I suppose you'll have to consider yourself fired."

A gasp escaped her lips.

"Just kidding. How about making an exception in this case?"

Tom wasn't sure if she had been shocked into it or not, but pleasure flooded him when she expelled a pent-up breath and nodded. "All right. But don't scare me like that again."

"You have my word. Write down your address, and I'll pick you up at one on Saturday."

Her look became guarded, and a slight frown creased her brow.

"Or you can meet me at the picnic," he offered.

"Yes. I'd prefer that. Thank you."

For the next hour, Tom struggled to focus on business while Esther went over his financial statements, making suggestions and praising his financial savvy. Disappointment clutched at him when she stood.

"I guess that's all, Tom."

Was it his imagination, or did she seem sort of reluctant to end the meeting?

She smiled that glowing smile once more, and suddenly moonlight and matching wedding bands flashed through his mind. He shot to his feet, scared to death at his last thought. Or had it been a premonition? A vision from God? A wish? A dream? A crazy hallucination brought on by lack of lunch today? The possibilities were endless. All he knew for sure was that in ten years, since the death of his wife, he hadn't come close to finding a woman interesting enough for so much as a second date, let alone matrimonial intentions.

This woman had certainly piqued his interest. Now it remained to be seen whether she could hold it. He couldn't help but wonder if God might have a second chance at love for him after all.

Esther walked him to her office door, gave him a sure-handed shake, and promised to see him Saturday at one.

Tom stepped into the sunlight, slapped his Stetson on his head, and sauntered toward his Ford truck, whistling a happy tune.

Chapter 2

No, that won't do. Too dressy," Esther muttered to herself.

She tossed the silky, black dress onto the pile of unacceptable clothing accruing on her bed and delved deeper into her closet. There had to be *something* suitable to wear to the picnic. Something that said, "Hey, I might be forty and unmarried, and so far I've liked it that way—but that doesn't mean I couldn't be persuaded to change my mind."

She groaned and sat back on her heels. Time was ticking away. She glanced at her watch to confirm that fact. Only an hour left before she was supposed to meet Tom at the park. How was she supposed to find the all-encompassing outfit, shower, cover her wrinkles, and appear as though she didn't have to work at it in only an hour?

The phone rang—a welcome diversion. Instinctively, she knew Karen's radar was in full swing. For the past three days, she'd purposely left her beloved sis in the dark about this so-called date because she didn't want to hear the I-told-you-so monologue.

But desperation called for a little humility—the price of Karen's expert clothes advice.

She checked caller ID to confirm her suspicion, then yanked up the phone. "Kare? I need help."

"What's wrong?" Karen's worried voice shot back through the line.

"I have a date in fifty-five minutes, and I can't find anything to wear. Don't ask questions; I'll fill you in later. Just tell me what to wear to a picnic!"

"Definitely Levis, your light blue summer sweater, and a pair of slip-ons."

"Hair?"

"Loose. Your hair always flows just the right way. If I didn't love you so much, I'd be insanely jealous."

"Okay. I have to go. I haven't showered yet."

"Wait!"

"What?"

"Don't you want to know why I called in the first place?"

"Sorry. Is everything okay at home? The kids? Brian?"

"Oh, they're fine. I wanted to remind you about your class on Monday."

"Like I could forget my last class." She grinned. After Monday she'd be licensed to become a foster parent. Hopefully, taking care of other people's children would somehow fill the void left by her own childless state.

"All right, one more thing," Karen said. "What was the new client like?"

Esther smirked and rolled her eyes, knowing full well her sister had called with that purpose in mind. The class reminder was only a convenient excuse. "He was passable."

"Passable?" Karen said slowly, as though trying to wrap her mind around what passable could possibly mean. She gasped. "I was *right*. He's your date today, isn't he? I told you I had a feeling about this one."

"Yeah, you're a regular prophetess. I have to get ready."

"All right. Call me when you get home. I want details."

❧

Esther's stomach flip-flopped as she pulled into the car-lined, gravel parking lot. She scanned the humongous park. Four baseball diamonds held Little League games in full swing. Six concrete slabs under green aluminum canopies hosted groups of barbecuers.

Esther frowned, wondering how she'd ever find the right group. *I should have brought a sign to hold up. Rescue me, Prince Tom. I don't know where I'm going.*

She was about to put the car in reverse and gun it back home when a knock on her window startled her. She jerked her head around, and relief flooded her. Her tall, tanned cowboy stood next to the car, waving. She rolled down the window.

"Hi."

"You made it!" Tom's delighted smile lifted her spirits, effectively erasing the angst of two and a half minutes ago. "I was afraid you might not know which picnic spot to go to. Have you been sitting here long?"

Cute, thoughtful, and unmarried? No one was that perfect. He must live with his mother, own fourteen cats, pick his teeth with his fork. . .something less than desirable. She wasn't lucky enough to hit the jackpot. "I just got here, as a matter of fact."

He offered her his hand like a knight helping a lady from her steed. Sudden warmth wrapped around her as she stood. Inches from his face, she could barely breathe. This combustible chemistry had eluded her in the past.

Was it just imagination fueled by her ticking clock, or could it possibly be that fortune had, at last, smiled upon her? Maybe Cinderella had finally found her prince.

❧

Tom felt like a teenager as Esther slipped her hand into his. He hoped his palms weren't sweaty. How could a woman reaching middle age be as beautiful as any twenty-year-old model—even more beautiful? This woman made every nerve in his body buzz to life.

He kept hold of her hand as they walked toward the picnic spot. It seemed like the natural thing to do, and she didn't protest. He didn't press his luck by lacing their fingers. But the feel of her hand in his felt alarmingly right.

"Thank you for inviting me. I haven't been to a picnic in ages."

Her soft, low-toned voice sent a shiver through him. "My pleasure," he managed around a boulder-sized lump in his throat.

"Where you going, Dad?"

Sixteen-year-old Chris's voice snapped him back to reality. Heat flamed his cheeks as he realized he'd walked a good twenty feet past his group under the canopy.

"Oops," he said, tossing Esther a sheepish grin. "Sorry. This is us."

"It's all right. I'm a little disoriented, too." Her cheeks flooded with pink as if she realized, too late, her admission. He squeezed her hand and turned her loose.

No sense having to explain to the kids why he was holding hands with a woman he'd just met. They were giving him enough of a hard time over this date as it was. And he was the one always telling them to take things slow. How important it was not to skip steps in dating relationships. Now he wondered how many of those steps he'd skipped by holding hands and thinking long-term on the first date.

"Everyone, meet Esther Young, the new accountant."

Chris grinned and stepped forward. "Hi, I'm Tom's son. Are you going to be my new mommy?"

Esther gasped as everyone in earshot chortled.

"Chris, go stuff something in your mouth," Tom commanded. He'd have a talk with the ornery kid later. For now he had to do damage control. His gaze sought his older daughter, who sat backward on a picnic table bench. He silently pleaded with her to smooth over Chris's attempt to be funny. Taking the hint, she stood and smiled.

"Hi, Esther. I'm Ashley. Dad's old married daughter. I work in the office as his secretary, so we'll probably be working together some."

Rather than relaxing under Ashley's friendly demeanor, Esther seemed to tense even more. "Nice to meet you," she said tightly.

Tom noticed her gaze shift to Ashley's slightly rounded belly. Was her tension from the realization that he had children or because they were grown? He leaned in close. "Ashley's twenty-two and married to my best contractor, Trevor. They're about to make me a grandpa in a few months."

Esther blanched, her eyes growing wide. "You don't look old enough to be a grandfather."

Or maybe she'd thought him to be younger than he was. Oh well, no sense putting the truth off. He wasn't ashamed of his age or his status as a soon-to-be grandfather. "I'm forty-five. Ashley was born when I was twenty-three, a year after I married her mom."

"I just turned forty," she murmured. "I suppose, technically, I'm old enough to be a grandparent, too."

132

As though the revelation was too much for her, she pressed her slender fingers to her collar.

Sensing her desperate desire to bolt from the picnic and most likely from his presence, he used a diversionary tactic. "Can I get you something to drink?"

She darted her gaze to him and wet her lips nervously. "Yes, thank you."

He escorted her to an empty spot at the closest table. "Tea or soda?"

Still looking a little shell-shocked, she stared at him. "Huh?"

"To drink? Tea or soda?"

"Oh, sorry. Anything diet if you have it. If not, unsweetened tea."

A woman who watched her figure. He liked that.

At the drink table, he took a plastic cup of ice. "Hi, Dad. Is that the dish you've been mooning over for the last three days?"

"I haven't been mooning." Tom turned to his middle child, Minnie. The soon-to-be twenty-one-year-old had that all-wise, all-knowing smirk that usually spelled trouble. Defenses alerted, he gave her a stern look. "Her name is Esther. And you be nice to her."

"I'm always nice." She popped a deviled egg into her mouth and gave him a closed-lip grin, making her pudgy cheeks fill out even more.

"Minnie. . .I mean it. Come and let me introduce you, but don't embarrass the poor lady. Chris already asked her to be his mommy."

Laughter pushed through her lips, and she shook her head, making her blond ponytail wag like a happy dog. "Wish I'd seen that."

Afraid she might try to one-up her younger brother, Tom gave her a stern frown. "I mean it."

She rolled her eyes. "Like I'd embarrass anyone."

Like she wouldn't. Tom grabbed a Diet Coke from one of the ice chests and followed his daughter back to the table. To his relief, Esther and Ashley seemed to be getting along nicely, and Esther seemed to have recovered her poise. He could always count on Ashley to ease any situation. She was like her mother that way.

"Esther, I'd like you to meet my other daughter." He stepped aside and let Minnie move ahead of him. "This is Minnie."

Minnie gave a wry grin and held out her hand. "Yeah, I'm the other one. Chris is the football star; Ashley's the former prom queen and the responsible one. And I'm the fat one. But rather than use that to identify me, we just say other."

Helpless in the face of Minnie's offended tone, Tom thought he'd die of embarrassment. Minnie's outburst was worse than Chris's goofing around. But Esther apparently chose to ignore the attitude and took Minnie's hand. Her eyes filled with warmth. "I'm so glad to meet you." She smiled and leaned closer. "Be honest with me. Are there any more of you? Because I have to admit, I didn't know your dad had even one child, let alone three."

Apparently still smarting from Tom's lack of a proper introduction, Minnie's eyes narrowed. "Do you have a problem with dating fathers?" The kid was gunning for a fight.

"No," Esther shot back. "If I did, I wouldn't be contemplating asking your dad to see a movie with me after the picnic. Do you have a problem with fathers dating? Yours in particular?"

Silence reigned over the table while everyone waited to see if Minnie would continue to challenge someone who could obviously hold her own in a verbal sparring match. Minnie scrutinized the woman for a second—then gave a tight-lipped smile. "It's not really my decision. He's a grown man. Excuse me. Mitch is waving at me down by the volleyball net." She shot Tom a grin and gave him a thumbs-up.

Esther cleared her throat, obviously as bewildered by Minnie's sudden change in attitude as everyone else around the table. "If Minnie likes you, that settles it," Chris said. "Now you have to be our new mommy. Minnie doesn't like anyone but Ben and Jerry. You know—the ice cream?"

"Yes, I'm aware of them—especially the Rocky Road." She gave a rueful smile.

"Believe me," the boy returned, giving her a once-over, "you don't know them as well as she does."

"That's enough, Chris." His son constantly berated his sister about her weight. And truth be told, Tom wished she'd take a lesson from Ashley and try to lose a few pounds, but he was smart enough to know that no amount of pushing would do it. She'd lose the weight when she was ready. In the meantime, they had to be sensitive.

Fun and laughter filled the table as the picnickers ate hot dogs and hamburgers and listened to Chris's stories about his recent summer football camp. Esther interjected her own funny stories about her sister and their cheerleading antics. They sat around the table until the sun sank lower in the western sky. Esther's quiet grace and quick humor utterly charmed Tom, and it was obvious she met with hardy approval from his children and employees.

As much fun as the day turned out to be, by the time Ashley declared herself ready to go home and put her feet up, Tom was more than happy to say good-bye and take the opportunity to get Esther alone. "How about a walk around the park?"

"Shouldn't I help clean up?"

"That's the advantage to dating the boss." He grinned. "All you have to do is show up looking gorgeous and let people wait on you."

She still didn't look convinced. Her concern tenderized his heart. "We have these get-togethers four times a year, and we rotate who cleans up. You can get on the list for next time."

She rewarded him with a heart-stopping smile and got up from the picnic bench. "All right. Then I'd love to take a walk."

They set off on a trail cut through a patch of woods at the outskirts of the park. Tom debated whether he could get by with holding her hand but decided against trying. No sense pushing his luck. He'd taken a little advantage of her bad case of nerves earlier. But now there was no good excuse to skip a step.

"I'm sorry I failed to mention the kids when I asked you to come with me today."

In the trooperlike style he was beginning to admire about this woman, she shrugged. "It was a shock. But there wasn't really time to give each other a rundown of family members. They're great kids." She grinned. "Even Minnie."

He chuckled. "Minnie's a handful. She was only eleven when her mom died. I'm ashamed to say that Ashley has always been a daddy's girl, and Minnie was closer to my wife. When Jenn died, Minnie sort of shut down. I didn't know how to deal with her. I'm afraid I still don't."

Esther gave him a sympathetic smile. "She's outspoken but otherwise seems to be a great girl. I bet you're being too hard on yourself." A branch crackled beneath her feet. "Of course I've never been a parent, so I could be wrong."

"Can I ask a personal question?"

She stopped and plucked a handful of Queen Anne's lace from the edge of the trail. "How come a girl like me never got married?"

He chuckled and sidestepped a rut, taking her arm to maneuver her around it. "Something like that."

A breeze blew from the south, lifting her hair up and around her face. She hooked a manicured nail around the invading strands and pushed them away from her face, tucking them behind her ear. Tom was utterly enchanted.

"I guess I just never found the right guy. I had definite goals about my career, and none of the guys I dated really got that about me."

As though unconscious of the effect she had on him, she continued to answer the question while he tried hard to pay attention. But there was this one wisp of hair. . . .

Unable to take it anymore, he reached toward her face. She moved back, her eyes wide.

Heat crept to his ear. "Sorry, you have just a strand here." He took it between his thumb and forefinger, marveling at the silky softness.

"Thank you," she whispered, her wide amber-colored gaze captivating him. He rested his palm against her cheek and took a step closer. With a quick intake of breath, she moved back. "I think we may be getting a bit ahead of ourselves."

He nodded and dropped his hand. "You're right. I'm acting like a hormone-ravaged teenager. I hope I'm not offending you."

She sent him an indulgent grin. "It's flattering, actually. But maybe a bit fast. I've been out of commission for a long time."

"Me, too. I'm always telling my kids not to skip steps, and here I am not taking my own advice."

"Well, don't worry," she said wryly. "I'll keep you honest." She cast a glance at her watch, then looked in the direction they'd come from. "I suppose I should get going."

His stomach twisted. He wasn't ready to let her go just yet. "What about that movie?"

"Movie?" She started walking back toward the picnic area. Tom followed.

"You told Minnie you were about to invite me to one."

A low chuckle fell from her lips. "I'm ashamed to admit that I only said that to gain the upper hand."

Disappointment washed over Tom like a cold wave. "I understand. You certainly met your objective. Minnie rarely gets shut down—especially when I've offended her."

"Wait," she said. "I don't absolutely have to go home right now. I'd love to go see a movie with you. But I should warn you: On Saturday nights, I turn into a pumpkin at eleven."

"So early?" Like he should talk. He hadn't stayed up past the ten o'clock news since Chris started kindergarten.

She nodded. "I try to get to bed early on Saturdays so I'm alert for church."

"Where do you attend?"

"Community Bible on Leland Street." She smiled again, her eyes sparkling in the fading light. "It's a huge building. You can't miss it."

Delighted at the welcome coincidence, Tom nodded. "I know. That's where the kids and I attend. Which service do you go to?"

"Eight-thirty. I'm an early bird."

"The kids like to sleep in, so we go to the contemporary service at eleven. It's pretty great."

"I've been meaning to give that service a try. Not because I'm dissatisfied with the more traditional one—but I always listen to contemporary praise-and-worship music at home, and I really enjoy it." She gave a low chuckle. "Besides, I wouldn't mind sleeping in a little."

"You should definitely give it a try. It's more laid-back. The kids love it."

She nodded. "I'll do that sometime."

The parking lot loomed ahead of them, and Tom saw that her red minicar and his blue truck were practically the only vehicles left. "So, do you want to ride with me to the movie?"

Her split second of hesitation nearly stopped his heart. Then she smiled, and he was able to breathe again. "I'll meet you over there. That way you won't have to bring me all the way back here afterwards."

"All right." Not that he would have minded the extra time with her.

She turned and unlocked her car door. Tom inhaled her flowery scent, lifted on the wings of another breeze.

"Okay," he choked out as she slid under the wheel. "I'll see you over there."

Climbing into his truck, Tom felt lambasted by the events of the last few days. He'd dated over the years, but his interest in a woman had never lasted any longer than the walk to the door at the end of an evening. Now he felt consumed by a desire to spend more time with Esther.

After ten years alone and raising three children who were pretty much grown, he'd assumed he'd be alone forever once the kids left home. Who would have thought God might have a companion for him to grow old with? A grin tipped his lips. He had the feeling that life was about to get real interesting.

Chapter 3

Esther stopped at the sanctuary entrance and scanned the seven-hundred-seat room—a futile attempt at finding the proverbial needle in the haystack.

A loud cough over her shoulder caught her attention. She turned and nodded her apology to the tall twenty-something male, who apparently thought he was being discreet in his attempt to inform her that she was holding up traffic.

She moved forward but continued to look for Tom's tall frame and brown hair, peppered with gray flecks. Her heart did a loop-de-loop at the memory of yesterday's date. They'd spent two hours watching a romantic comedy, and she'd been captivated by his genuine laughter during the funny moments. After the movie, they'd gone to a local coffee shop and closed the place down at midnight. So much for turning into a pumpkin at eleven. A smile touched her lips.

"Esther?" a soft voice called from the row of chairs next to Esther. Tom's daughter Ashley moved toward her, looking radiant in a pale green maternity dress. Her dark blond hair was cropped short and pushed up in the back. Her eyes, blue like her dad's, sparkled with obvious joy.

"Ashley. Hello." She worked hard not to look past the young woman to see if Tom was anywhere near.

"I've never seen you here before," Ashley said with a lilt in her voice. "Do you want to sit with us?"

Esther nodded, grateful to be out of the aisle. "I usually go to the early service." She slipped into the blue cushioned seat next to Ashley.

"Ahh. That explains it." Her eyes sparked with mischief.

Esther couldn't help but return the grin. "Explains what?"

The girl laughed outright now. "Why Dad went to the early service."

"Are you serious?" Esther joined Ashley's laughter as pleasure sifted through her. This situation was like something out of a movie.

The girl nodded. "If you two are going to be seeing each other, you'd better get your wires straight."

"I suppose you're right." There was no time to continue the conversation as the assistant pastor took the podium and greeted the congregation.

During the high-energy music service followed by a wonderful message, Esther felt her spirit lift to a place she hadn't been in a long time. She couldn't help but wonder if the prospect of new love was renewing her youth.

Ashley gave her a quick hug as they stood. "We'd love for you to join the family for dinner. Dad always makes tons of food on Sundays. Minnie makes dessert, and I bring a side dish and vegetable. Today I'm making my famous au gratin potatoes and green beans cooked in sautéed onions and mushrooms."

"Sounds great. You'll have to give me that green bean recipe."

Smiling with more warmth than Esther had ever seen, Ashley nodded. "Come to dinner, and I'll write it out for you."

"Oh no, I couldn't just drop in on your dad unannounced." The thought horrified her, and even more so because she'd actually taken a split second to consider it.

"Are you kidding? Dad will be thrilled. I haven't seen him really interested in a woman since—well, since my mother, I guess." The girl's tone moved from amused to wistful at the mention of her mother.

Esther touched the young woman's arm as tenderness surged through her. "I take that as quite a compliment, Ashley. Thank you."

A smile curved Ashley's lips. "It is. My dad's a great man. He did a fantastic job raising us alone. We were always at the top of his list of priorities, which is probably why he never got involved with anyone." Her eyes sparkled. "Until now, that is. I have a good feeling about you."

Esther felt herself coloring. This family certainly didn't hold back. "You should get together with my sister, Karen," she said wryly. "She gets feelings, too."

"I'd love to. We can compare notes." Esther joined the girl's spontaneous and infectious laughter. "Sounds like you and my dad are destined."

"Well, we'll see."

"So how about dinner? I could call Dad if it would make you feel better."

Feeling suddenly stifled, Esther shook her head. "Actually, I have plans today. Some other time, maybe."

Regret slipped over Ashley's face. "Sorry to put you on the spot."

"Oh no. Not at all. I appreciate the invitation, and I look forward to getting to know your dad better." She smiled. "And the rest of you. But I have a standing date on Sundays."

A sudden wariness clouded Ashley's eyes. Her brow arched in question. "A date?"

Esther could not hold back a chuckle. "With a very handsome, older gentleman—my dad. And my sister, Karen, and her family."

Ashley's suspicious expression morphed into relief, and she returned Esther's smile. "All right then. May I tell Dad I saw you?"

"Of course. And tell him how polite you were to invite me to sit with you so I wouldn't feel so awkward." She squeezed Ashley's hand. "I appreciate it."

"It was my pleasure. I hope you'll join the contemporary service again."

"You can count on it."

⬡

Later, as she sat in a lounge chair on Karen's deck watching the children splashing about in the spray of the garden hose, Esther closed her eyes and sighed.

"All right now, that's it." Karen's outburst interrupted the tranquility.

Esther squealed as ice chips landed on her bare legs. "Hey!"

"If you don't tell me what's going on in that dreamy-eyed head of yours, I'm going to give the kids permission to hose you!"

"I don't know what you mean," Esther taunted.

"Kids! Aunt Esther's hot! She needs a good cooling off."

"All right!" Ten-year-old Avery turned toward the house.

A sudden spray shot across the deck. Esther sucked in sharply as the cold water made contact with her warm skin. Laughing, she put up her hands in a not-so-successful attempt to ward off the onslaught. "Okay, okay! I give up. Call off your assassins!"

"Okay, kids, I think she's learned her lesson," Karen called to her squealing offspring. "If I need you again, I'll call. Now off with you. Go back to your own games."

"You're a horrible sister," Esther accused with a mock pout, wringing out her once carefully coiffed hair.

Karen tossed her a towel, waggling her eyebrows. "Ve haf vays of making you talk," she said in a poor German accent.

"Oh, please. Okay. I did go to the picnic with Tom yesterday."

"Finally!" Karen plopped into the patio chair next to Esther. "Now, start at the very beginning, and don't leave anything out."

By the time Esther had recounted the picnic, Tom's kids, the hand-holding, the movie, and finally the crossed church services, Karen's eyes gleamed with an excitement that matched the racing of Esther's heart.

"Okay, Esther. So now what?"

"What do you mean?"

"Is he going to call you?"

"I don't know." She wiped away a remaining droplet of water from her tanned leg, trying to appear as though she didn't care one way or another, but her heart didn't want to face the fact that he might not. You just never could tell with men. They all *appeared* to be having a good time. But that didn't necessarily mean anything. But then, he *had* gone to the early service just to be with her. The thought eased some of her angst.

"Well, didn't you discuss if one or the other would call?"

"No."

Giving an exasperated huff, Karen scowled. "He didn't say, 'I'll call ya'?"

A thick cloud of gloom threatened to darken Esther's excitement. Maybe Tom didn't plan to call her after all. Karen had a point. Wouldn't he have mentioned it if he were going to ask her out again?

"Maybe he saw my desperation and decided the run-don't-walk method of retreat was in order."

"Don't be silly." Karen peered closer and frowned. "How desperate were you?"

Esther tossed the towel at her. "Whose side are you on? You are supposed to reassure me, not add to my fear of rejection."

"Well, you already know that I think you're a real catch. This guy would be nuts not to call you."

"Please, I've dated enough nuts in the past."

Laughter, low and throaty, flew from Karen's lips. "Okay, I have an idea. Let's take stock of all the events." She lifted her index finger, poised to keep count of her points of emphasis. "One. He held your hand. Two. He asked you to a movie."

"Actually, I asked him. He just sort of reminded me."

"Same thing. That shows he wanted to extend his time with you. Three. Even after the movie, he kept you out until midnight, then the man—who is no spring chicken from what you've told me—"

"Hey, he's not *that* old."

"He's not *that* young either, and he still woke up early so he could spend another hour and a half sitting next to you. Poor guy. While you slept in and went to a late service, he was fighting sleep and is probably snoozing right now in his recliner while the football game plays on without him."

The image brought a twitch to Esther's lips.

"Oh, wow. This is serious." Karen's awe-filled voice broke through with crashing reality.

"Serious? I've known the man a couple of days!"

"I knew the first time I saw Brian that he was the man for me."

"You were only kids."

"Maybe so, but the moment he helped me off the ground after our bikes collided, I saw what he would be. To me, he was everything he is today. Steady, reliable, a wonderful husband and father, and the sexiest man alive."

Esther grinned and glanced toward the barbecue pit at the other end of the yard. The "sexiest man alive" rubbed his hand over his balding head as he nodded at something Dad was saying. His T-shirt hung large and long to cover his middle-age spread, and his legs below his knee-length shorts could cause an accident on the highway if the sun shone on them just right.

Karen's chuckle indicated she knew exactly what Esther was thinking. "He's mine. White legs and all, and I wouldn't trade that man for anything in the world."

"You're blessed, Karen. And I'm so glad you don't take it for granted."

Reaching out, Karen took her hand and squeezed. "You know, God had other plans for you all these years. But He knows how badly you want a family. Maybe Tom's entered your life for such a time as this, just like the Esther in the Bible."

Esther turned her attention to the three children who had tired of the hose and were now batting a volleyball back and forth over the net. Would this sort of life ever be possible for her? Or was it too late?

"I think you should call her tonight, Dad. How's she going to know you're interested if you don't tell her?"

Tom looked at his daughter's face, slightly puffy from her pregnancy, and grinned. "If she doesn't know I'm interested after yesterday, then she's thicker headed than I am."

"You can't assume where matters of the heart are concerned. You have to let women know you're still interested."

"Still?"

"Yeah."

"Are we talking about you and Trevor or Esther and me?"

Her cheeks pinkened. "I mean, a girl can't read a man's mind. Trevor hasn't told me he loves me in days. I'm starting to think he finds me repulsive now that I'm so fat."

His heart clenched for her. She was far from fat or even chubby, and her husband adored her. Anyone within a hundred miles could see the love and adoration shooting from him whenever she walked into the room. But maybe he wasn't communicating it.

"All right, I'll call Esther, if you'll talk to Trevor."

Tears sprang to her eyes, and she didn't try to deny her feelings of rejection. She nodded and offered a tremulous smile. "Deal."

Tom opened his arms, and she walked into them. Resting his chin on her silky hair, Tom felt a lump rise to his throat and his own eyes misted. Where had the years gone? It seemed like just yesterday, they were welcoming Ashley into the world, changing diapers, fixing bottles. And now she was about to do all those things for her own baby.

The thought of being a grandparent had gradually grown on him, and now he looked forward to bouncing the tyke on his knee and sending him home at the end of the day. The best of both worlds without the constant responsibility. At least Ashley and Trevor would have the benefit of a partner to lessen the load of parenting—not that he resented a single minute of the time he'd spent raising his three children. But it hadn't been easy. And he'd failed in so many ways.

Ashley pulled away from his embrace with a sheepish grin. Tom reached across to the counter and presented her with a box of tissues. "Thanks," she sniffed, taking two from the box. "I'm being silly, I know. These hormones make me nuts."

Tom took her shoulders and pulled her in so he could press a kiss to her forehead. "I know about those. Your mother cried at the drop of a hat when she was expecting you kids. But let me reassure you from a man's perspective. There's nothing more beautiful to a man than the woman he loves growing with his child. Unless it's the woman he loves holding his child in her arms. But you need to go and tell the father-to-be that you need to hear that he loves you." His eyes twinkled. "You'll probably hear it more than you want to from here on out."

"Ha! Not possible. Thank you, Daddy." Tiptoeing, she kissed his cheek. "I'm going to talk to Trevor right now. Go call Esther."

Tom smiled after his daughter as she waddled into the living room and touched her husband's arm. Trevor looked from the Cowboys game to her face. He covered her hand with his, and his expression softened with love.

Tom sent a grateful prayer to heaven. How many men would have asked her to wait until after the game—or at least until after the current play? God had blessed his daughter with a man who would love her first after God. Tom couldn't have picked a better man to take over the protection of his daughter.

He glanced at the phone, and his pulse quickened at the thought of what awaited him should he pick up the receiver and dial Esther's number. He'd been a little worried when he didn't see her at the early service. Lukewarm faith wasn't an attractive quality in a prospective wife for him. He wanted someone with a strong relationship with God. Ashley's news that Esther had attended the second service had delighted him.

Glad for the excuse of his promise to Ashley, Tom crossed to the phone and lifted the cordless off the charger. He pulled out the business card she'd offered him with her handwritten home number.

At the third ring, she answered.

"Esther?"

"Yes?" The confusion in her tone didn't bode well for his ego.

"It's Tom."

"Hi, Tom. It's nice to hear from you."

Okay. So far so good. She could have said, "Tom who?"

"Ashley said I should. . ." He winced. Bad, bad way to start. "I mean, well, she didn't make me. . ." Oh boy. He gathered a deep breath. "Do you want to go out again?"

"Are you sure you do?" Her tone was guarded, and Tom couldn't really blame her.

"Look, I'm sorry. I started off all wrong. I don't blame you if you say no."

"Wait. Do you want me to turn you down?"

"Well, no. It wouldn't have made any sense to ask you out if I didn't want to go out with you."

She gave a charming half laugh. "All right. Then my answer's yes."

"Yes?"

"Yes. Look, are you sure?"

Dropping into a kitchen chair, Tom released a sigh. "I'm really bad at this. Forgive me. How about if I stop trying to be smooth and just tell you the truth?"

"That sounds like a good idea."

"I enjoyed myself yesterday more than I thought I ever would again with a woman. I'm thinking long-term thoughts, and it has me a little rattled. But not scared. So you need to know up front that I'm not playing games. I have a feeling this could develop into something permanent, and that's what I'd like to explore."

"I–I see. . . ."

Tom groaned inwardly. What kind of an idiot was he? *Sayonara, baby. There's no way she's going to agree to a date now.*

"Are you still there, Esther?"

"Yes. I'm just trying to digest the information. That's a lot to put on a girl so soon."

"You're right. But neither of us are children. We're mature. . .grown-ups."

He cringed. Why not just call her old? "I didn't mean—"

She laughed. "I knew what you meant. But your honesty is refreshing. And I agree with you. This could very well lead to something long term. And I'm willing to test it and see if maybe God has a plan in bringing us together."

His heart jumped. "How about dinner tomorrow night? I know a steak house just off the interstate about twenty miles from town that has the best T-bone I've ever had."

"Oh, Tom. I'm afraid my week is full. One of my other clients is being audited, and I'll be working night and day."

"When will you be available?"

"Friday evening?"

Irritated at the thought of the long week ahead, Tom fought the urge not to press for an earlier date.

"All right. Friday. Can I pick you up at your house this time? Or is it still too soon? If you're more comfortable meeting there. . ."

"No. Not at all. Pick me up at seven." She gave him her home address.

Tom's face split into a silly grin even though no one was around to see it. No one had to tell him it was silly; he could feel it. He felt like a sixteen-year-old making his first date.

"Do you have an e-mail address, Tom? It'll be hard to catch me by phone this week."

"Uh. . .yeah. Wood4U." He gave her the ISP server name ending with dot com but didn't mention he'd never actually used it.

She laughed. "Catchy. Okay. I'll e-mail you this week and confirm our plans."

"Sounds good. I look forward to hearing from you."

"Bye, Tom, and thanks for being so open about your expectations. I'm so tired of the dating game."

The phone clicked before he could respond; but his heart lifted, and he felt like clicking his heels together. He headed into the living room, where Chris sprawled on the sofa watching the game in solitude.

Tom ruffled the teen's hair. "Chris! Come show me how to get into the e-mail program!"

TIMING IS EVERYTHING

Monday 9:30 a.m.

Dear Tom,
    Just a quick note to thank you for inviting me to the picnic on Saturday. I, too, had the best time that I can remember having in a very long time. I'm looking forward to seeing you again on Friday.
                                                        Esther

Monday 10:45 a.m.

Dear Esther,
    I'm glad you had a good time. You certainly made my day, but then I guess I already told you that. Ashley says to tell you hello. She seems to like you a whole lot. That's important to me.
                                                          Tom

Tuesday noon

Dear Tom,
    Ashley is a special young woman. It's easy to see she has a good father. I like her, too, and, yes, it's important to me that your children accept me if things progress to a long-term relationship.
                                                       Esther

Wednesday 11:00 a.m.

Esther,
    I'm sorry I didn't return your e-mail yesterday. We had a hectic day at the office. Hectic in a good way. We got the contract for the new community building.
    I've been thinking about your comment from yesterday where you said you want the kids to accept you. I have an idea. Would you consider having dinner at my house Friday night instead of going out? It would give you a chance to get to know everyone better.
    Let me know.
                                                          Tom

Thursday 7:00 p.m.

Tom,
    Congrats on getting the community center contract! I'm impressed. I, too, have had a hectic week, and I'll be glad to see it end. Dinner at your

house sounds lovely. What time should I arrive?

Esther

Friday 10:00 a.m.

Esther,

I'm pleased you have agreed to dinner with the kids. I'd warn you about Minnie and Chris, but you've already met them, so I'm sure you know what you're getting yourself into. I've already threatened Chris if he asks you to be his new mommy again. That kid is making my hair gray. LOL (Ashley said that's how you say "laughing out loud" in e-mail code).

I'm looking forward to seeing you around seven. I'm knocking off work a bit early to fire up the grill. We'll have those steaks after all. Only I'll be making them for you instead of ordering them.

Tom

Tom pressed SEND on the e-mail program and sat back in his office chair, smiling. Finally, the endless week was over, and he'd get to see the woman whose face had sweetened his dreams and distracted his waking hours all week.

"Daddy!" Ashley's weak voice drifted from the doorway of his office. Tom glanced up. His daughter's face was drained of color. She held onto the doorframe. "Daddy," she said again. "My head hurts so bad."

Tom shot from his seat and reached her just in time to catch her before she fainted. He picked her up and carried her to the office couch. The blood rushed to his head at the sight of his girl, unconscious and unresponsive. In a state of panic, he grabbed the phone and punched in 9-1-1.

Chapter 4

Caught in traffic, Esther glanced at the clock above the radio. *Seven-fifteen.* Four cars ahead of her, the light stayed red while the cross traffic sped through the intersection. Esther took the opportunity to smooth on face powder, a touch of blush, and lipstick.

She scowled at her reflection. This quickie makeup job was not how she'd envisioned her appearance for this evening. But an insistent client had barged in just before closing and demanded to see his books. No amount of reasoning could talk him out of it. Now, she was frazzled, late, and forced to wear the same outfit she'd had on since six thirty this morning.

The light changed from red to green. Esther tossed the cosmetics onto the passenger seat and prepared to accelerate. She gave a frustrated sigh as the car in front of her sat unmoving. Clenching her fists, she fought for control. *Don't honk, Esther. Under any circumstances. There will be no honking.* The car behind her wasn't as resolved to good manners and blasted its horn. Esther cringed as the driver in front of her glared through the rearview mirror before gunning the motor. When she finally parked alongside the curb in front of Tom's two-story frame home, she felt unkempt, unprepared, and unattractive. Still, her heart leaped at the thought of seeing him again.

After another quick check in the mirror—and a responding grimace—she got out of the car and headed up the walk to the front door. She rang the doorbell on the "Waltonesque" home. Minnie answered.

"Yeah?"

"Uh, I'm. . ."

"Oh yeah. Dad's new girlfriend."

A flush of embarrassment burned her cheeks. She forced herself to remain in control. "I wouldn't exactly call myself his girlfriend after one date and a few e-mails."

Minnie gave her a knowing lift of brow. "So what brings you by? Eileen, was it?"

Esther gave a tight smile. "Esther." *As if you didn't know!* "Your dad invited me to dinner. Is he around?"

"That's weird."

"What is?" As far as she was concerned, it was anyone's prerogative to walk around with a boulder-sized chip on their shoulder if they chose to do so—as long as they didn't infect her atmosphere with the sour attitude.

"Dad isn't here. As a matter of fact, he left a message on the machine. Something about not making it home for dinner and we should grab something ourselves."

Esther blinked at the girl, not sure she'd heard her right. "Your dad isn't coming home for supper? Did he mention me at all?"

Minnie shrugged and shook her head. "Sorry."

"I see." *What a creep!* He'd either forgotten, or he'd totally blown her off. Neither excuse was acceptable as far as she was concerned. A combination of anger and bitter disappointment mingled inside her.

"Do you want to come in and wait?"

Hard-pressed to keep her tone civil, Esther backed away. "I don't think so. Thanks anyway. Nice to see you again, Minnie."

"Sure," the girl muttered.

Tears pricked Esther's eyes as she walked back to her car. How stupid was she anyway? He'd been so convincing. She'd been sure he was on the level.

Stop crying! she commanded as one tear and then another slid down her cheeks. Oh, why at all times did the emotions have to fly out of control? More and more lately, tears flowed at the slightest pressure.

She yanked a tissue from her purse and looked in the rearview mirror—a futile attempt to fix her face before she drove through the nearest fast-food window. So much for a sit-down dinner with the family!

Just as she finished blowing her nose and cranked the engine, Tom's truck passed hers on the side of the road and pulled into the driveway. Too humiliated to face him, she slipped the car into gear and started to pull away.

"Esther! Wait!"

"Not on your life, buddy." She accelerated, but the car went nowhere. A growl rumbled in her chest as the engine revved. She'd put the car in neutral! The delay was enough so that Tom reached her car and opened the door she'd forgotten to lock.

"Hey, where are you going?"

"Home. Apparently you forgot our arrangements for tonight."

Crouching next to her, he shook his head. "No, I didn't. I left a message on the machine. Minnie was supposed to call you and explain."

She sniffed and looked unbelieving at his convincingly innocent expression. Peering closer, she frowned. Lines of fatigue etched the corners of his eyes.

"Is everything all right? Minnie only told me you wouldn't be home for dinner. I assumed you'd forgotten."

"Come on inside. We can order pizza or something."

Relieved beyond words that he truly had a legitimate excuse, she pressed her hand against his cheek, rough from a day's worth of growth. "Oh, Tom. That isn't necessary. You've obviously had a tough day. We can have dinner another time."

His eyes filled with emotion, and he covered her hand with his and brought it to his lips. "Come on. Please."

Her heart nearly leaped from her chest as he stood and tugged gently, pulling her to her feet. "A—are you sure?" she asked. No power on earth could have forced her to resist his simple request.

The presence of such an appealing, strong, and capable man made her knees go weak. When he laced his fingers with hers, she thought she might die right there on the spot.

He smiled, showing attractive, well-kept teeth. "I'm glad you didn't get the message." Without releasing her, he walked her to the door. When she thought he might turn her loose, he tightened his grip and led her inside. The door opened into a spacious living room. Minnie sat Indian-style on the couch, a huge mug in one hand, a textbook spread open in front of her.

"Hi, Dad." Her brow rose as she spotted Esther. "Oh, you waited for him after all?"

"No, I. . ."

"I got home as she was leaving. Don't be rude. Now why didn't you give Esther the message?"

The girl frowned. "What message?"

"The one I left on the machine."

"All I heard was a message that you wouldn't be home for dinner."

Tom looked at his daughter, suspicion clouding his eyes. He crossed to the answering machine.

"You don't believe me?" she asked, her mouth dropping open. She jerked to her feet, snatched up her book, and brushed past him on the way to the stairs. "I'll be in my room when you want to apologize."

Apparently undaunted, Tom punched the PLAY button, skipping through the tape until he found his message. "Minnie, I won't be able to make it home for dinner. Fix something for yourself or order in. I'm in a hurry, but I'll explain later. . . . Uh. . ." And the machine phased out.

Suddenly nervous to be witness to Tom's error, Esther looked at the floor, wishing she could slither away unnoticed. He still hadn't acknowledged his mistake. Curiosity got the better of her, and she sneaked a glance at him.

"I guess the tape ran out of room." He gave her a sheepish grin. "So, no one said I was perfect. Do you mind waiting alone for a minute while I go up and apologize to Her Majesty, the Queen of the Wronged?"

Esther laughed, relief making her heart light again. Nothing showed a man's true character more than the way he reacted to his own mistakes. "Not a problem."

"Thank you. Make yourself at home. Humble pie doesn't take long to consume, so I should be back quickly."

Alone, she perused the spacious room. The living room phased into a lovely yet simple dining area, and a double-door opening separated the kitchen from this room. Wooden floors, covered with two oval braided rugs, stretched over the entire area. A dusty bookcase boasted tons of books.

On an equally dusty curio cabinet in the corner closest to the front door, Esther spied an eight-by-ten-inch photograph of a much younger Tom and three much, much younger kids. She caught her breath at the image of a woman who could only be Tom's late wife. The woman smiled for the camera, a beautiful, confident smile that said, "I'm happy, in love, and thrilled to be living this enchanted life."

Suddenly feeling like an intruder, Esther walked away from Tom's memories and settled onto the couch to wait. When the door flew open a couple of minutes later, she nearly jumped through the roof.

Chris stopped short at the sight of her, then his expression brightened with recognition. A smile, identical to his dad's, split his face. "Oh, hi. Esther, right?"

She stood, relieved he wasn't playing dumb like his sister had. "Right." She smiled and took his proffered hand. "Nice seeing you again."

"Same here. So where's Dad? He didn't leave you all alone, did he?"

"He went upstairs to talk to your sister."

Chris rolled his eyes. "What now?"

"I guess you'd better let him tell you that."

"He'd better let me tell him what?"

Esther turned toward the stairs, but she heard Tom's boots clomping before she saw his face. Minnie was right behind him, her eyes red rimmed as though she'd been crying.

"What happened this time?"

"Mind your own business," Minnie snapped.

"Whatever."

"Are you two forgetting we have company?"

"It's, um, okay. Really." Esther felt like an idiot. This was going to be one awkward dinner.

As if sensing her hesitance, Tom cupped her elbow. Warmth spread through her arm. She smiled.

"Who's up for pizza?" he asked.

"I ate at Shermon's after practice," Chris announced. "I think I'll hit the books. Angsley's giving his first test tomorrow."

"Good luck," Minnie said with a sniff. "Angsley's the worst."

Chris nodded. He turned to Esther. "It was nice to see you again. I'm sorry I can't stick around."

Esther's heart warmed to his generous spirit. She smiled. "I understand. Good luck on the test."

She was rewarded with a dazzling grin.

Tom turned to Minnie. "How about you? Pizza?"

"I'm low carbing."

"Oh yeah. Well, what if we order you some hot wings?"

"Oh, sure. Eat pizza in front of me while I eat chicken wings."

Esther listened to the exchange and watched as Minnie reduced Tom to feeling like an unfit parent, all the while embarrassing him in front of a guest. Besides, she'd had enough. If she weren't a Christian and therefore required to walk in love, she'd be sorely tempted to tell off that girl. As it was, she felt it would be better to leave so Tom could deal with those in his house.

She placed her palm against his bicep. "Tom. I really need to be going home."

"Wait. What about that dinner I promised you?"

"Another time, maybe."

"Maybe?"

"Call me." She could feel his gaze upon her, burning a hole in her back while she walked to the couch and grabbed her purse. She headed for the door.

"Esther, wait a sec. I'll walk you to your car."

He cleared his throat loudly.

"Uh, Esther. Please don't leave because of me." Minnie stepped forward. "I'm just a grouch because of sugar withdrawal and. . .well, it doesn't matter. Suffice to say, I behaved badly. The truth is, I'm headed over to the hospital to see Ashley anyway. So you two order whatever you want."

"Ashley? Is she all right?" Esther turned the question to Tom.

He nodded. "I was getting around to telling you. She collapsed at work today. When I took her to the hospital, her blood pressure was through the roof. I've been worried about how puffy she's been but just figured she was eating too much."

"Is she okay?"

"They're keeping her a few days to try to get her to lose the water retention and get her blood pressure down. If not, they might have to deliver the baby early."

"How early?"

"She's only six months along."

The worry lines creasing the edges of his eyes struck Esther's heart like a well-aimed arrow. "I'm sorry. I'll keep her in my prayers." And she meant it.

"Thank you. Are you sure you won't stay for dinner?"

"I'm sure. I think I better get home. I have a full day tomorrow."

"Saturday?"

"Yes. I'm painting my guest bedroom."

"I'd offer to help, but Ashley. . ."

"Oh no. Don't think anything of it. Please tell her she's in my prayers."

"I will. Thank you."

Tom reached around her and opened the front door. Esther's heart sped up as he brushed against her. His gaze demanded hers, and she couldn't look away.

"Are you sure you can't stay?" he said, his voice soft and filled with emotion.

Still battling with the disappointment associated with the crashing of the high hopes she'd ridden all week, she nodded.

Tom heaved a long sigh and nodded. "I understand."

"I'm sorry."

"Let me at least walk you to your car."

They walked in silence until they reached her car.

He snatched her hand and lifted it to his chest. "I wish you'd reconsider. My kids aren't all that bad once you get to know them."

"Oh, I didn't mean to imply—"

"You didn't." He gave her a sad smile. "But I can put two and two together."

"Tonight was pretty overwhelming."

"I understand." His jaw clenched. "I have a busy, full life with three kids. I can't apologize for that. But I understand if you don't want to see me."

"I'm not saying I don't want to see you. Just that I need a few days to make sure I can deal with everything a relationship with you would entail."

"I understand."

I understand. Every time she heard those words of resignation, she felt about two inches high. "Take a few days to deal with Ashley. And I'll pray about us."

He nodded and smiled. "Should I e-mail you?"

"Please do. Let me know how Ashley and the baby are doing."

He reached out and laced his fingers through her hair, cupping her head. Esther felt the world stop spinning, and she stood unmoving, though her heart thundered like the hooves of a thousand horses.

"You have the softest hair."

Esther closed her eyes, relishing his touch and the sound of his husky, longing-filled voice. She knew all she'd have to do was lean forward and his lips would cover hers. With a shiver, she opened her eyes and stepped back.

Tom moved in closer until his face was inches above hers. "I'd like to kiss you."

She stared, unable to move. Unable to speak.

"But I won't. I know now isn't the right time."

A curious mix of disappointment and relief shifted through her. She glanced away.

"I'll let you go," he said softly.

Esther drove away, her mind whirling, trying to keep up with the new emotions running amuck. How could she be feeling so strongly about this man after only a week?

And why was it the first man she'd had any significant feelings for came with a jumble of complications?

Chapter 5

Tom clutched a stuffed elephant against his chest, praying fervently as his soft leather heels squeaked along the waxed hospital floor. Ashley's blood pressure had gone up and down over the last three days, necessitating a continued stay in the hospital. Tom had barely slept, barely eaten. And he'd worn a trail across his bedroom floor as he paced and prayed at all hours.

A petite twenty-something day nurse with a carrot orange bob and a smattering of cute freckles across her nose and cheeks came from Ashley's room and smiled, her eyes alight with recognition. "Hello, Mr. Pearson."

Tom nodded to her. Memories of his wife's final days slid through his mind. No one should have to stay long enough in a hospital that the staff knew family members by name.

The doctor had explained that Ashley's condition was extremely serious. Preeclampsia could easily escalate to seizures, organ failure, even death. Tom couldn't bear the thought of losing Ashley. The first few hours after calling 9-1-1 had been tense. And the last three days had been a jumble of highs and lows as her blood pressure stabilized and spiked, respectively.

Relief spread through him as he entered the room and saw his daughter sitting up in bed, laughing at a comedy/variety daytime show on the television. When she saw him, her countenance brightened even more. She clicked off the TV.

"Oh, boy, are you ever a sight for sore eyes. I'm dying for company."

Tom gave his girl an indulgent smile and set the stuffed elephant on the bed next to her.

"Oh, how cute! Thanks, Daddy."

Tom brushed a kiss to her cheek and dropped into the mauve, vinyl chair next to the bed. "How are you feeling?" The chair legs scraped the floor as he moved in closer.

"So much better." She held up both hands, wiggling her fingers. "See, the water retention is pretty much gone. My ankles are back to something resembling a human ankle."

"What's the doctor think?"

She sighed and leaned back. "Another day probably. My blood pressure has been good. They just want to make sure it stays near normal. When I go home, I'll have to stay on bed rest, though." A groan escaped her lips. "I don't know how I'm ever going to stay in bed that long."

"It's only for three months."

"Three months with only one of us bringing home a check?"

Tom's lips twitched. "You have a very generous boss."

Vehemently, Ashley shook her head. "No way. I'm not taking money from you."

"And I'm not going to let my daughter worry about having to pay the bills when she's about to give me a grandbaby."

He saw the softening in her expression as her eyes filled with tears. "We'll pay you back every penny."

Not a chance, little girl. "We won't talk anymore about it for now. The important thing is that you stay healthy and get that baby here healthy."

"I know. You're right. Trevor is already laying down the law. 'No cleaning, no cooking'—although I don't know what he expects us to eat—'no laundry, no violent or scary movies or books.'" She laughed. "I have a keeper."

"And I thank God every day for sending you a man who will love you the way I loved your mother."

A reflective look crossed over her features, and when she looked at him, her eyes took on a serious glint. "Do you still miss Mama?"

Tom sent her a tender smile. "She'll always have a very special place in my heart."

"What about Esther? You haven't said much about her the last couple of days."

A jolt shot through his heart at the sound of Esther's name. By the rise of Ashley's silky blond eyebrows, Tom knew she'd noticed his reaction. He breathed a sigh. "She's taking a few days to sort through some of the issues associated with a relationship with me."

"Issues?" Her face clouded. "She'd be lucky to get you on your worst day."

Tom smiled at Ashley's defensive tone. And his heart went out to Esther for a split second. She'd never known the joy of holding her own newborn child. First day of school, first dance, first child's wedding. First grandchild. She'd never known the joys and worries of parenthood.

Sympathy clutched his chest, and he rose to Esther's defense. "She's never been married. Never had kids. My life is a lot more complicated than a single working woman's."

Ashley stretched out, wiggling her toes beneath the light covers. "I don't know, Dad. She doesn't seem that petty to me. I think she just got a little freaked."

"Oh? And how would you know?"

She sent him a sheepish smile. "All right, so I wasn't exactly clueless about the other night. Minnie spilled the whole thing."

Tom scowled, reliving the entire incident.

"Minnie feels bad, you know. She was having a tough day." Ashley's tone pleaded for Tom not to hold a grudge. As if he could hold a grudge against one of his children, even one who constantly challenged him like Minnie tended to do.

"Yeah, no kidding. Who wasn't having it rough that day?"

"Anyway, I think Esther's just scared. If I were you, I'd definitely give her a call."

"I've e-mailed her a couple of times."

"Did she write back?"

Remembering the short answers, Tom sighed. "Yeah, if you can call it that."

"Okay. Listen. You need to take matters in hand, or she's going to do something you'll both regret."

"What would you have me do?" He gave her a wry grin. "Toss her over my shoulder and carry her to Vegas for a wedding?"

"Not a bad idea," she shot back, her plump cheeks pushing out farther, giving her a Shirley Temple adorableness he hadn't seen since she'd lost her baby fat around seventh grade. "But I was thinking more along the lines of a token of your affection. Something that speaks of a desire to raise the stakes of the relationship."

"Oh, good idea, Ash. Especially when she's running away. I'd say the last thing she wants is to raise the stakes."

"Maybe she just wants you to give her a good reason to see that being with you is worth complicating her life for."

"You mean chase after her?" Taken aback, Tom considered the possibility. "I've been giving her time to think."

"Ooh, bad choice."

"Hey, it's called respect."

"Send her flowers, Dad." She gave him a sassy grin. "I'd respect a dozen roses."

He leaned forward and chucked her chin. "I'll think about it."

Tom stayed until Ashley dozed. Taking care, he stood and bent over his daughter—the woman he would forever see as his little girl. She moaned and shifted as he kissed her head.

He left the room, his mind spinning with ideas. The image of Esther invaded his senses: her wholesome beauty and easy smile, the sweetness of her perfume, the silkiness of her hair, the melodic sound of her laughter floating on the breeze. A longing ache pressed his chest like a cement block. Should he send the flowers or leave Esther alone as she'd asked?

As he walked past the hospital gift shop, baskets of pink and white carnations, plants, and single-flowered vases called to him. He resisted the overpriced shop, but when he slid under the steering wheel of his truck, he turned toward the closest florist.

❧

With a half growl, half sigh, Esther clicked out of her e-mail program. Not one word from him. She'd been an obsessive e-mail–checking idiot all day at the office. Now, curled up with her laptop, trying to finish up some work at home, she couldn't stay offline. The e-mail program called to her with the taunting fear that if she stayed offline for more than two minutes, she'd miss a message from Tom.

"Stop being ridiculous," she admonished aloud.

It was her own fault. You don't push a guy away, barely answer his e-mails, and expect him to stay interested.

A frown played at her brow as she recalled their last meeting. He'd been so worried about Ashley. What if she'd taken a turn for the worse? Could that be the reason for his silence since yesterday afternoon? Esther stared at the computer screen, debating whether she should e-mail, call, or leave it alone. She reached for her cell phone just as the doorbell chimed, nearly sending her through the roof.

While her heart returned to a rhythmic beat, she cast a disparaging glance at her sloppy sweats and oversized Goofy T-shirt—her at-home uniform and not exactly the outfit she wanted to wear to open the door for anyone other than the pizza guy. And since she was eating chocolate chip cookies and vanilla ice cream for dinner, she knew it wasn't him.

She reached for the doorknob, then stopped as Karen's voice screamed through her head. *Never, ever answer the door without looking out the peephole. That's what it's there for!*

Obeying the voice in her head, she peeked out and frowned, her brain trying to process what she was seeing. Then realization dawned, and she smiled widely. A bouquet of flowers hid the bearer of the gift, but she could imagine who was standing behind the blooms. Breathlessly, she opened the door.

"Hi!" The smile died on her lips as the wrong Pearson man held out pale pink roses.

Chris gave her a sheepish grin. "From Dad."

"I see." Disappointment that Tom wasn't the one standing on her doorstep mingled with a sense of glee that he'd sent the flowers in the first place.

"Please come inside," she murmured, taking the offering.

"Thanks anyway, but I can't. I have a ton of homework."

"I understand. Thanks for being the delivery boy."

"You're welcome." Chris headed down the front steps. Then he turned back. "You know, Dad's a great guy. Worth a little hassle in my opinion." Without awaiting an answer, he jogged to his old, yellow Toyota and chugged away.

Burying her face in the fragrant blooms, Esther felt a surge of affection rising in her. If she was going to become involved in a ready-made family, this one—Minnie notwithstanding—wasn't a bad choice. Surely Chris and Ashley would make up for their sister's hatefulness. On the other hand, there was a lot to be said for an easy, uncomplicated life—one where no college-age girls infected her space with their spite, where she wasn't forced to share the attention of the man in her life. She chewed her lip and frowned. Of course, there was no man in her life at the moment, nor had there been for quite some time. Was being so picky worth the payoff of loneliness?

She stepped inside and leaned back against the closed door. The phone rang, and she ran to snatch it up. Her heart leaped when Tom's low voice filtered through the line. "Hi."

Swallowing hard, Esther could hardly breathe. "Hello, Tom."

"Chris just called. He said he made my delivery."

"Yes, he did. They're lovely. Thank you." Her knuckles grew white as she clutched the phone tightly, at a loss for anything else to say.

Obviously plagued by the same loss, Tom cleared his throat but didn't speak.

Esther took the initiative and baled them both out of the awkward silence. "So, how's Ashley?"

"Better, thank God. She'll be going home tomorrow."

"I'm so glad, Tom. I've been praying for her."

"We appreciate it. The doctor has put her on a strict no-salt diet, and he wants to see her every week. She's not crazy about being on bed rest for three months, but she's willing to do it for the baby's sake."

"I'm sure any price is worth it to deliver a healthy baby." She closed her eyes, and for a second she could almost hear the deafening sound of her biological clock ticking. Her mind conjured the image of herself, big bellied and swollen ankled. Oh, how it would be worth every second, every pound.

"So, Esther. I was wondering if you'd be interested in having dinner with us tomorrow night? We're having a welcome-home dinner for Ashley, at her house of course, so she can stay on the couch with her feet up."

On the verge of saying yes, Esther stopped short of doing just that as a twinge of nerves hit her full in the gut. The memory of Minnie's animosity and the frazzled state of Tom's home sent her scrambling for an excuse. Tom might be a great guy, but he came with complications she wasn't sure she could deal with.

"I'm afraid. . ." She cleared her throat, the pause long enough for her to consider what she'd just said. She really *was* afraid. Ice-cold feet—that's all this was? She almost laughed. Never once had she allowed fear to hold her back from something she really wanted. So why was she running like a frightened rabbit at the thought of a lovely relationship with the man who could very well be the one she'd dreamed of her entire life? Still, she needed to sort things through. Talk it over with Karen.

"I'd better not this time, Tom."

"I understand." The disappointment in his tone filled Esther with regret. But she needed time to think things through. She had never been faced with falling for a guy who had kids. She'd stayed pretty much off the market, convincing herself she was happily single. Married to her job.

"I'm sorry, Tom."

"It's okay. I really do understand. I'll talk to you later."

"Bye."

Esther's lip trembled as she hung up the phone. Without taking time to think about it, she punched in Karen's number. When her sister answered, Esther barely gave her a chance to say hello before she launched into her tale of woe.

"Esther! This guy sounds like everything you've always dreamed of."

"I know, but things were so chaotic the other night. And Minnie was so hateful."

"Look, relationships have their ups and downs. Smooth sailing isn't even possible. I might not have the stepchildren issue to deal with, but we have plenty of struggles of our own. It sounds to me like Tom is worth a little hassle in order to find love."

Esther gave a short laugh. "That's what Chris said."

"Chris?"

"His son."

"So you see. . .even the guy's kids think you two have something worth pursuing."

"I suppose you're right."

"Of course I am. Now how about giving him a call?"

"I might."

"Esther!"

"I have to go. Thanks for lending your ear."

"My pleasure. Call him."

Esther sat back on the sofa and picked up her laptop. After a futile thirty minutes of pretending to crunch numbers, she gave up and reached for the phone.

Gathering a deep breath, she punched in Tom's number. She let it ring until the machine picked up, then she replaced the receiver without leaving a message.

The memory of his hurt tone struck her anew. Had she blown it? Suddenly nothing was more important than hearing his voice. She wasn't above begging if she had to in order to let him know she was ready to push past her fear and pursue a relationship with him.

After a quick search through her address book, she found his cell number and dialed. She released a relieved breath when he answered.

"Hi," she said, her heart pounding against her chest.

"I'm surprised to hear from you."

"Happy surprised?"

He chuckled. "To tell you the truth, yes. But I can't talk right now. I'm in my car and just got to where I'm going."

Swallowing her disappointment, Esther nodded, though there was no one in the room to see her. "No problem. I'll try to call you later."

"All right."

The doorbell chimed as she pressed the button to disconnect. "What is this?" Esther muttered. This was the most action her door had gotten in one day for as long as she could remember. Without bothering to check the peephole, she flung open the door.

Tom's smiling face greeted her. "Hi," he said around an arrangement of carnations. "Roses didn't work, so I thought you might prefer these."

Esther laughed. "You mean you were outside *my* house?"

He nodded. "Can I come in?" His demeanor took on a seriousness that caused her heart to lurch.

Opening the door wider, she stepped aside. "Of course."

Once inside, he held out the flowers. "These are for you." His gaze sought hers with such questioning, she stepped back to escape the intensity of his ocean blue eyes.

"Th–thank you. I'll find a vase to put these in." Grateful for the excuse to escape the tidal wave of emotion rushing over her, Esther snatched the carnations and fairly flew to the kitchen. Her hands shook as she filled a vase with water. She didn't dare handle anything sharp, so she left the stems uncut.

Fighting for composure, she captured a quick glance at herself in the mirror above the sink. Horror filled her at the sight. Her hair had fallen from the barrette she'd used to pull it back at six-thirty this morning. The Goofy shirt and sweats didn't look any better than they had earlier, and her makeup had long since worn off—all but the black smears under her eyes where she'd rubbed away the threat of tears earlier. She'd be lucky if Tom hadn't taken the opportunity to run off while she was in the kitchen.

After finger combing her hair and wiping away the black smudges with a paper towel, she gathered a deep breath and pushed back through the kitchen door. The sight of him made her knees go weak. A light blue denim shirt rolled up at the sleeves revealed deeply tanned, muscular forearms. For a forty-five-year-old man, he looked pretty good in a pair of Levis and cowboy boots. His slow smile nearly caused her to have a heart attack.

"Have trouble finding a vase?"

"No. Just trying to fix myself up a bit before I came back." She gave him a sheepish smile. "It's been a long day. Do you have time to sit?"

He nodded. "Thank you."

He sat on the sofa, leaving Esther with a dilemma. If he'd sat in the chair, she could have taken a seat on the couch without a problem. But now she had to decide whether to sit next to him on the couch and possibly give him the wrong idea or sit in the chair and appear aloof, standoffish, scared silly, or all of the above.

A chuckle rumbled his chest, and he patted the cushion next to him. "Let's talk about why you decided to call me after turning down dinner tomorrow night."

Heat rose to her cheeks as she sat next to him. Shoulder to shoulder with Tom, feeling the warmth radiating from him, she had trouble forming a sentence.

Tom patted her hand. "Let me tell you why I came over with flowers after you shot me down an hour ago."

"I didn't exactly shoot you down," she replied wryly.

"That's a matter of opinion." He turned and faced her, his knee brushing against hers. Reaching out, he took a strand of hair between his thumb and forefinger.

Esther shivered at the intimate gesture. He peered closer.

"I think we have something promising between us. No woman has held my interest since my wife died, and I think this is worth pursuing."

"I agree," Esther said quietly, keeping her gaze fixed on his.

Surprise lit his eyes. "You do?"

She nodded.

"I was all set to argue my case."

"Your case?" Amusement lit inside of Esther. "Am I a judge?"

"You're definitely the one deciding the future of this relationship."

She nudged him with her elbow and sent him a saucy grin. "Would dating me be a jail sentence?"

He took her hand, its warmth filling her with all sorts of heady sensations. "No. If you give our relationship a chance, you'll be setting me free."

What was a girl to say to that? The laughter died on her lips. Twice she tried and failed to respond.

Tom smiled. "So why were you calling me?"

Finding her voice, she turned her hand in his and laced their fingers. "I wanted to tell you that if you're still willing, I'd like to explore where this attraction between us might lead."

"Then I think we're on the same page."

An overwhelming sense of relief flooded her. "I think we are."

"I'd give anything to kiss you right now," Tom said, his voice low and husky with promise.

And she'd give anything to make that happen. Despite the sirens going off in her head, she closed her eyes and welcomed a kiss, imagining the feel of his warm lips on hers. How many years had it been since a man had held her in his arms?

Instead of the expected kiss, she felt Tom stand, pulling her to her feet with him. Her eyes popped open, and she felt the blush rising to her cheeks.

"We have to get out of here. I'm just a man, Esther, and I haven't dealt with feelings like these in many years."

"Of course, I'm sorry."

"Don't be. You're a desirable woman, and I'm developing feelings for you faster than I would have thought possible. I just don't want to do anything to offend you or compromise you in any way."

Well, that did it. In an instant, Esther left her long-term romance with her job and transferred her affections to Tom, all the while imagining white lace and promises.

"Let me change into something more presentable, and we can go get some coffee."

She gathered a shaky breath as she headed for the bedroom, feeling his eyes on her as she went. There was no turning back now. She'd opened her heart to this man in a matter of minutes.

A smile tipped the corners of her lips, and confidence rose with each step. After all these years alone, just when she thought the romance train had passed her by, the Master Conductor had sent her the man of her dreams. The rest she'd deal with as she had to. For now, she was going to enjoy holding hands and seeing that wonderful smile flashed in her direction.

Oh, God. You are so good.

Chapter 6

The grill sizzled as Tom slapped another burger onto the already overloaded rack.

"Whose idea was it to invite twenty college-age kids and their appetites to a barbecue?" he asked with a lighthearted growl.

Esther, who had pitched in like a real trooper to make Minnie's twenty-first birthday bash a rousing success, patted his arm as she walked by. She set a bowl of freshly made potato salad on the picnic table and grinned. "You're a great dad, do you know that? Minnie's birthday is a big hit because of your efforts."

The mild irritation sifted from his chest, and he returned her smile. "Sometimes I think Minnie got the raw end of the deal where I'm concerned. Ashley is my first child and Chris my only boy. I don't always know how to relate to Minnie."

Esther touched his arm, sending warmth through his bicep as her hand lingered. "You'll figure it out."

He covered the grill and set the spatula on the side table. "I'm afraid it might be too late. She resents almost everything I do or say."

"It's never too late to mend relationships." Esther's eyes beckoned him to believe in her words. Tom shook his head, marveling at her beauty—skin that invited caresses, hair that caught the sun in shimmers of golden light, eyes a man could drown in. Thoughts of her filled every waking moment and invaded his dreams.

A pretty blush crept to her cheeks. "Why are you staring?"

He reached out and snagged her about the waist, pulling her close. "If I weren't staring, you'd have the right to ask me why. But I don't need a reason to look at you. You're beautiful. I can't keep my eyes off of you."

A smile curved her full lips, captivating Tom. They'd been dating for two months; and so far, he'd only given her a few cursory kisses on the cheek when he dropped her off, but he'd resisted long enough. He was going to kiss her. Now. And they'd just have to learn to resist anything more than that. Her eyes widened as he dipped his head. She took in a breath of air, her lips parting slightly. She didn't protest as he took possession of her mouth. On the contrary, she melted against him as though she, too, had been waiting impatiently for this moment. When she wrapped her arms about his neck, he drew her closer and deepened his kiss.

A low wolf whistle followed by a deluge of catcalls brought him to his senses, and he pulled away.

"Whoa, Mr. P., that was some kiss."

"Hey, who's watching the burgers?"

"Do you two need to be reminded you're to set an example for those of us who are young and impressionable?" Chris asked, a grin spread across his red face.

Tom glanced at Esther. Her gaze was averted to the deck floor. "All right. Enough teasing."

"Way to go, Dad," Minnie hissed in full earshot of Esther. "Did you have to humiliate me on my birthday of all days?"

Chris stepped forward before Tom could reply. "You're just jealous because you're not the one getting kissed."

"Why don't you be quiet and mind your own business?" she shot back, her lip trembling. She brushed past and slammed through the sliding glass door.

Watching her go, Chris shrugged. "I was just kidding."

"Greg didn't show up?" Tom asked.

Chris shook his head. "No. And Mitch let it slip that Golden Boy is dating Danielle Kovak."

Tom saw the question in Esther's eyes.

"Minnie has had a crush on Greg for six years," he explained. "But he's never noticed her. At least not that way."

Sympathy slid across her face. "I understand how she feels. That's hard on a young woman."

Tom couldn't imagine Esther having that trouble in a million years, but he refrained from mentioning her looks again, lest she begin to worry that he was only attracted to her physically.

He turned his attention to the burgers. "Okay, these are done. Chris, gather the troops."

"I'll go see if I can find Minnie," Esther volunteered.

Surprise lifted Tom's brow. "You sure? She's not in a very good mood."

A smile played at her lips, and she winked. "I think I can hold my own."

Could she hold her own? Esther's stomach turned over as she found Minnie's bedroom door and knocked. The girl could quite possibly eat her alive.

"What?" Minnie's voice sounded muffled.

"It's Esther. The burgers are done."

"Fine. Tell my dad to save one for me. I'll eat after everyone is gone."

Realizing Minnie wasn't going to ask her in, Esther gathered a deep breath and turned the knob. "I'm coming in," she warned as she pushed open the door.

Minnie scrambled to sit up on her bed. Her cheeks were wet from tears, and her chin-length dark blond hair clung to her face. "What do you think you're doing?" she demanded.

"I warned you." Esther's heart raced, but she returned Minnie's glare and took another step forward.

"I don't appreciate people walking into my room uninvited."

"Then you should have invited me in." She approached the bed. "May I?"

"Since you're not going to go away, you might as well."

Esther sat. "So the tears are over a guy, I take it?"

A scowl marred Minnie's face. "Listen, I don't need advice from someone like you."

Stung, Esther nodded, determined not to show her hurt. "Someone like me, Minnie? You mean a dried-up old maid?" It was on the tip of her tongue to tell the girl if she didn't sweeten her attitude, she might very well find herself forty years old and alone one day, too.

Minnie's bravado faltered before Esther's steady gaze. "That's not what I meant," she mumbled. Releasing a heavy sigh, she stared at her hands. "I mean someone who looks like you."

"I don't know what you mean."

Her lips twisted into a wry grin. "Do you think my dad is interested in your mind?"

"I hope he is," she said quietly.

"Well, all right. He likes you as a person, too. But I'm sure the looks were what attracted him in the first place."

Suddenly every word Tom had ever spoken about her looks flashed through her mind. Was their relationship only skin deep? Rousing herself from the troubling thoughts, she gave Minnie a stern glance.

"All right. Listen. You have twenty friends out there who love you. I understand how badly it hurts when you like someone and he doesn't like you back, but don't just run away and pout. It makes you look bad."

Lines creased Minnie's brow, and her eyes grew stormy. "I am not pouting, *Esther*."

"Oh, really?"

"Yeah."

"I bet if I went outside and took a vote, odds would be in favor of you hiding up here, moping over Greg Somebody."

"Big deal." Minnie flung the pillow across the bed, then she sat up. "You think?"

"What else would they think? Someone announces that the guy you have a crush on is dating someone, and you run inside and don't come back?"

Understanding registered in her blue eyes. She gave a grudging nod. "Yeah, I see your point."

"So, do you want to go back and join your party?"

A heavy sigh escaped. "I guess." She stood and glanced in the mirror over her dresser. "Fat with red splotches all over my face. I just can't win."

Esther's heart went out to her. "Go wash your face and use a touch of powder to cover your red nose."

Nodding, she walked into her bathroom, leaving the door open as she washed her face. She surveyed her appearance in the bathroom mirror and grimaced. "Too bad there's nothing to cover the bulges. Believe me, black isn't that slimming when you're my size."

Esther chuckled. "Believe me, it's not that slimming at any size. You are what you are."

Minnie came out of the bathroom, holding a compact of face powder. "Well, what you are and what I am aren't exactly comparable."

Drawing a deep breath, Esther decided to take a chance on the new camaraderie Minnie seemed to be offering. "You know, I have to watch my weight, too."

Predictably, the girl sniffed. "I don't see how you can even compare us, Esther. I don't mean to be rude, but I'm twice your size."

"Yes, but if I don't watch what I eat for the most part and exercise regularly, I'll gain weight, too." She gathered a breath and decided to take the bull by the horns. "Would you be interested in coming to the gym with me?"

Was that a hopeful glint in Minnie's eyes? If it was, it was so fleeting that Esther would never be sure.

Minnie shook her head. "I don't like to sweat."

"Neither do I. But it's a necessary evil if I'm to stay healthy."

"I'll think about it. Let's head back to my party before the guys eat all the burgers." She gave a short laugh. "One good thing about Greg not showing up, at least I can eat without being self-conscious."

"You know, Minnie, you underestimate yourself. Have you ever considered dating Mitch? If I'm not mistaken, he's got a thing for you."

A laugh erupted from her. "Mitch? We've been best friends since kindergarten. He's like a brother to me."

"I see." But what Esther really saw was the love in Mitch's eyes every time he cast his glance at Minnie.

Minnie moved toward the door, then stopped. "I appreciate your coming up here. Dad never quite knows what to say."

"Well, what man understands the complexities that are woman?" Esther grinned, and Minnie laughed.

"True."

Laughter around the picnic table died when they arrived back on the deck.

"Good grief," Minnie muttered under her breath. "What's their problem?"

Esther leaned in close and whispered, "Just smile and remember this is *your* party. You get to set the tone."

Minnie nodded. In an instant, she transformed herself from a sulking touch-me-not to a vivacious, outgoing young woman, sashaying to the table, grinning broadly. "Hey, did you leave a burger for me?"

Esther chuckled, watching the girl set a lighthearted atmosphere. Tom's breath against her cheek diverted her attention, and she smiled, turning to face him.

"How'd you manage it?" he asked.

"I don't know." She gave him a straightforward gaze. "I just talked to her without apologizing."

Tom's face reddened. "You think I coddle her too much?"

"I think maybe you feel so guilty about paying more attention to the other two children that you'll say anything to stay on Minnie's good side." She walked around him and grabbed a paper plate, then started loading a hamburger bun. She smiled over her shoulder. "Even if it means apologizing for something you didn't do."

"Are you trying to tell me how to raise my kids?" His responding grin belied the defensive words.

She nudged him with her elbow as she held onto her plate. "Never. I'm analyzing your parenting methods."

"Oh? And how do I stack up, Doctor?"

"Not bad. Not perfect. But certainly not awful."

"Not perfect, eh?"

Sending him a coquettish grin, Esther leaned in closer to him. "Nearly perfect."

"You're perfect," he said in a low voice.

Remembering Minnie's words earlier, Esther frowned. "Is that the only reason you like me?"

He drew back. "What do you mean?"

She shrugged and squirted ketchup onto her burger. She reached for onion slices, but remembering the earlier kiss, opted not to take the chance he might try again later and be offended by onion breath. "You love to tell me I'm beautiful. But you don't mention much else about me that you find. . .interesting."

Embarrassment caused her to falter under Tom's tender smile. She averted her gaze. He took her chin and raised her face to look her in the eye. "You think I'm only lusting after your beauty?"

Esther's cheeks flamed beneath his amused face, but she squared her shoulders and held her own. "Maybe."

"While it's certainly true that I find you attractive, I also love your humor, not to mention your intelligence—have you forgotten you take care of my finances?"

Seeing his point, Esther grinned.

Cupping her cheek in his palm, he continued, "I love the fact that you know God and serve Him with an honest heart. I love that you see beyond Minnie's surly attitude to the sweet girl beneath. I love that you are concerned for Ashley and laugh at Chris's nonsense. And, yes, I love to look at you because the wonderful, warm, funny person you are is all wrapped up in a gorgeous package. And if you have a problem with that, then you need to ask God why He made you that way and why He made me a man, because any man would enjoy looking at you."

With a short laugh, Esther pulled back and walked toward the deck furniture, away from the peering eyes of Minnie's guests. "They're not exactly beating down my door. Have you forgotten I'm an old maid?"

Tom chuckled and followed her, taking a seat next to her in the white-framed cushioned chair. "Lucky for me." He looked a little out of place on the pastel, flowery cushions. Esther wondered if it were time to replace the chairs and lounge, which had obviously seen better days—and had most likely been purchased under the watchful eye of his deceased wife.

Esther felt an instantaneous surge of jealousy for the unknown woman who had captured Tom's heart so many years ago and most likely still claimed a large part of it.

"How about coming back to the party?"

Tom's voice snapped her back to attention. "I'm sorry."

"You seem awfully far away."

There was no way she was going to admit to her train of thought, so she bit into her burger instead. A huge bite—one that would keep her mouth occupied for a while.

"Are you convinced yet that my affection is more than skin deep?" he asked.

Still chewing, she nodded, then swallowed hard. Tom handed her a can of Coke. "Here, take a drink before you try to talk."

She washed down the bite and gave him a sheepish grin. "I guess that's what's called biting off more than you can chew."

He groaned, rolling his eyes. "And did I mention your corny jokes are an endearing quality, as well?"

Feeling a giggle coming on, she smothered it with another bite.

"Hey, we're going to play volleyball. Do you two want to join us, or are you too busy playing footsie?" Chris's teasing words invaded the conversation, but far from annoyance, Esther felt only thanks. This got her out of the hot seat with Tom.

Setting aside her half-eaten burger, she hopped to her feet. "I haven't played volleyball in ages."

"Okay," Chris announced to the group, "Esther's the hole. Send the ball to her for a guaranteed point."

"Hey!" Esther gave him a playful sock in the arm.

Chris grabbed her and lifted her into a bear hug. "You're a great sport," he said against her ear. "I'm glad Dad found you."

Tears pooled in her eyes. He set her on her feet and sent her a broad wink before sauntering away. Esther watched him go, a wistful sigh escaping her lips. She should have had a strapping son—someone to fix enormous meals for and worry over as he dated girls who were clearly not good enough for him.

Warmth enveloped her shoulders, and she smiled at the feel of Tom's hands. "You okay? He's a little exuberant."

"He's a great kid," she said. "I was just thinking how proud his mother would be." She heard the longing in her tone but didn't care. Motherhood had never been a goal, not a real goal. Now, however. . .

Tom remained silent behind her, and Esther smiled, laying her cheek against the back of his hand, which still rested on her shoulder. She felt the gentle brush of his lips against her hair, and she closed her eyes, enjoying the intimate moment. And taking it for what it was—his assurance that he cared about her, that he understood her desire, but he wasn't ready to offer her the chance to become a mother.

The sun hung low in the sky, withholding some of its earlier warmth as evening approached and warning the volleyball players that they only had a few minutes of light in which to play their game. Fingers of pink and orange promised a beautiful sunset, and Esther breathed deeply of contentment.

Finally, her life seemed complete. She'd had her tough times, her lonely times. Surely, it was all gravy from here on out.

Chapter 7

The ringing telephone woke Tom from a deep sleep. Disoriented, he sat up straight, his heart beating a rapid cadence in his chest. He reached for the phone, glancing at the bedside clock. Three-o-six, in glowing red, marked the only light in the darkened room.

Who calls at three in the morning?

"Hello?"

Trevor's shaking voice filtered through the line.

Tom swung his legs over the side of the bed. "What's wrong?"

"A—Ashley had a bad, bad headache all day."

"That sounds like her blood pressure is up again. Did you call the doctor?"

"Yes, and she's doing better. . .but we should have known her headache meant her blood pressure was too high. We just didn't think."

"Okay, listen, Trev. Are you at the hospital?"

"Yes. They just took her to be examined."

"I'll be there in twenty minutes."

He hung up the phone and flew into action—praying as he dressed, praying as he pulled on his shoes, praying as he grabbed his keys and headed down the steps.

"Dad?"

Minnie's sleepy voice caught him just as he opened the door. "Hi, honey."

"Where are you going?"

"Ashley's in the hospital. Her blood pressure spiked again. That's all I know."

"Hang on. I'm coming with you. Chris! Get up. Ashley's in the hospital."

"I'll go warm up the car; if you're not out there in ten minutes, I'm leaving."

"Got it."

She made it in eight, Chris sprinting behind her carrying his gym shoes. They raced to the hospital in nearly zero traffic. By the time they reached labor and delivery, they were all three breathless. Trevor's face melted in relief when he saw them.

"They're going to induce labor. Her blood pressure is coming down, but it's still too high. The doctor is afraid that if he waits any longer, she could start having seizures."

"Why aren't they doing a C-section?" Minnie demanded.

"That's what the doctor wanted to do in the first place, but Ashley has her heart set on delivering the baby naturally."

"Is that safe?" Tom asked.

"Dr. Baker said they'll keep a close watch, and if she starts to have trouble they'll have to do the C-section immediately."

"What did Ashley say to that?"

"You know Ashley." He gave a shaky grin. "She's trusting God that everything will work out the way she wants it to."

"Can we see her?"

"In a little while. They're getting the IV in and starting the drip to induce her labor."

Chris pulled out his cell phone and handed it to Tom. "Do you want to call Esther?"

Tom started to reach for the device, then pulled back. "No. This is a family matter. I don't want to bother her."

Minnie made a face. "Get real, Dad. You know she's going to be family soon. If you don't call her, you're going to make her feel like you don't trust her with our problems. But you can't use the cell phone in the hospital, spaz." She headed across the hall to a pay phone.

She punched in some numbers.

"You know her number by heart?"

"Yep." She held up her hand to silence him. "Esther?"

Tom and Chris looked on and listened to the one-sided conversation, deducing that Esther was immediately concerned, was coming to the hospital, and was glad Minnie had called.

She arrived within an hour, her face void of cosmetics, her hair pulled into a ponytail. She wore a pair of faded Levis, a St. Louis Rams sweatshirt, and a worn bomber jacket. And she was the best-looking thing Tom had ever seen. He felt his tension release as warm air coming through the vents carried the scent of her sweet perfume.

A tender smile lifted the corners of her lips when she saw him, and she came to him, taking him into her arms. Tom buried his face in the soft curve of her neck. Minnie had been right. This woman was definitely going to be family. Soon.

"How is she?" Her warm breath against his ear sent a shudder through him. He pulled back and held her at arm's length.

"The doctor says her blood pressure is low enough for now. If it stays down she can deliver naturally. Otherwise, they're going to have to do a C-section."

"Can we see her?"

"Yes. We can go in two at a time."

"Should I wait out here so your family can see her?"

Tenderness welled inside Tom's chest at the uncertainty in her voice, the wondering whether she was close enough to intrude upon a family situation. "Chris and Minnie are in the cafeteria getting breakfast. Come on. Ashley will want to see you."

TIMING IS EVERYTHING

They entered the room.

Ashley's face brightened at the sight of Esther. "I'm so glad you came."

Esther moved to Ashley's bedside and pushed a strand of hair from the girl's forehead. "How are things going, honey?"

"The contractions are getting stronger. I'm starting to feel them." She smiled. "I guess that's a good sign."

Tom frowned. Ashley hadn't told him she was in pain.

"So I've been told," Esther said wryly. "Can I get you anything to make you more comfortable?"

"Just knowing you all are here means so much to me."

The automatic blood pressure machine kicked in. Ashley made a face. "Ouch," she mouthed as the cuff tightened. When the numbers displayed her reading, worry lines etched the nurse's forehead. "That's pretty high. How's your head?"

Tears formed in Ashley's eyes. "It hurts."

"All right," the nurse said, her tone leaving no room for discussion. "Everyone out except the husband. I'm going to call the doctor."

Tom's heart picked up, and his stomach began to churn. "What's going on?" he asked the nurse as they stepped into the hallway.

"Her blood pressure is spiking up, probably because of the pain from the contractions. I have to notify her doctor."

"Is she going to be okay?" He knew it was a ridiculous question, but he needed the reassurance. The nurse just gave him a look that clearly stated she wasn't making predictions.

Esther took his hand. "Come on. Let's go sit down. They'll let us know when they know something."

Tom allowed her to lead him to the waiting area. They sat on the cold vinyl chairs. He leaned forward and rested his elbows on his knees, forehead in his palms.

"She'll be all right, Tom."

"How do you know that?" he shot back. The quick hurt in Esther's eyes drilled into him like a bullet exploding in his chest. "I'm sorry."

"I understand," she said softly. But he could tell she didn't. He felt her withdraw emotionally, though physically she didn't move.

❧

Esther fought against the tears threatening to push their way to the surface. She truly did understand why Tom would snap like he did. He was wound so tightly with worry that Esther was surprised he hadn't yelled at the nurse. She didn't know what to say, so she remained silent and offered quiet support.

Tom took her hand. "I'm really sorry for snapping at you, sweetheart."

Esther drew in her breath at the endearment. She laid her cheek against his shoulder. "It's okay. Really."

"No. I shouldn't have barked at you. I'm just so worried." His voice trailed off. Esther raised her head to look at him but remained silent, waiting for him to continue. After a few seconds, he did. "Being a parent is the greatest joy and the greatest pain in life. There's no way to describe the feeling of holding your baby for the first time. You spend their childhood trying to find a balance between protecting them and not holding too tightly. They get married, and you think, 'Okay, now someone else will take care of her. I can stop worrying.' But I never stop wanting to take care of her. It's not that I don't feel like Trevor's a good husband. He is."

"She's been blessed to have two wonderful men looking after her."

Tom's eyes clouded with tears. "I've tried my best to make sure she's okay. But I realize how little power I really have. My daughter could be just down the hall having a seizure, and there's nothing I can do."

"Yes, there is. You can pray and trust the Lord's love for her. Remember, if you, as an earthly father, long to keep your daughter safe, how much more do you think her heavenly Father longs to see her through this situation she's going through?"

He nodded and squeezed her hand. "You're right. But knowing in my mind and releasing my daughter to God in my heart are two different things."

"It's called standing in faith. You are a man of faith. Search your heart and let God give you rest."

Chris and Minnie came into the waiting room. "Hey, they won't let us in to see Ashley," Chris said. "What's going on?"

Tom filled his children in on Ashley's condition.

Amid the barrage of questions, Trevor came into the waiting room, appearing shaken, his face drained of color.

Tom stood and went to his son-in-law. "How's Ashley?"

"They're prepping her for surgery right now. They're delivering the baby C-section. The doctor said if we wait, she might start having seizures." As though his legs were suddenly without strength, he sank into the nearest chair. "Oh, God. Please be with my wife and baby. Keep them safe."

Esther bowed her head with the rest of the group, and they followed Trevor's lead, each speaking aloud the prayer of his or her heart. For the next hour, they took turns pacing until the nurse arrived. A collective *whoosh* of relief left them as her smile registered.

"Mother and baby are doing well." She glanced at Trevor. "Congratulations, you have a six-pound, four-ounce son. He's doing great. We're going to keep him under the lamp for awhile and watch him since he's four weeks early. But he seems to be fine."

"And my wife?"

"Everything is returning to normal. That's the thing about preeclampsia. Once the baby is delivered, things usually straighten right up."

"When can I see them?" Trevor asked.

"The baby is on his way to the nursery right now, and you can see him through the glass. You should be able to see your wife in a couple of hours."

Minnie grinned broadly. "Let's go see the baby!"

Esther had never heard her excited about anything before. She smiled and nodded. "I agree."

Tom hung back for a split second, then acquiesced. "I guess if we can't see Ashley for a couple of hours anyway, we might as well go get a look at my grandson."

Esther looped her arm with his, and they walked to the next hall.

"Look, there he is!"

"Is he okay?" Chris asked. "He looks a little sick."

Tom chuckled. "All babies look like that when they're first born. Don't worry, he'll fill out and perk up in no time."

Esther watched the look of adoration on his face as he looked at his grandson. An invisible hand of longing squeezed her heart. *Oh, Lord. I want one.*

Once she'd spoken the words in her heart, she realized how many years she'd been afraid to pray that prayer. Afraid to admit to such a desire when she had no prospects of marriage anytime soon. Afraid the answer might be *no*. But as she peered through the glass at Ashley and Trevor's baby, tears streamed down her cheeks and hope sprang inside her heart. Would she hold her own child one day?

Tom's arm slipped around her shoulders, and he pulled her close. "Isn't he something?" he whispered close to her ear.

"He sure is."

"Thank you for being here to share this moment with me, Esther. It means the world to me."

"To me, too." And perhaps, if God willed, they would be sharing the birth of their own child in a year or two. A smile played on her lips as she closed her eyes and allowed herself to dream.

Chapter 8

If she hadn't been holding on, Esther would have slid right off the treadmill. The sight of Minnie standing in the doorway thrilled her beyond words. Dressed in black leggings and an oversized T-shirt, the girl looked ill at ease and shifted from one foot to the other. But she had pushed aside her angst and shown up.

A buff twenty-something guy walked past, gave Minnie a once-over, and continued on as though she weren't worth his time. Indignation clutched at Esther, and if she hadn't thought it would mortify Minnie, she'd have run after the jerk and given him a good piece of her mind.

As it was, Minnie's expression crashed, and she looked as though she might turn and flee at any second. Esther quickly shut off the treadmill and grabbed her towel. Patting the sweat from her neck and brow, she hurried over to the girl.

"You came!"

Pink spots appeared on her cheeks, even as relief washed over her features. "Yeah," she mumbled. "I'm not sure it'll do any good, but thanks for inviting me."

"My pleasure. There's an available treadmill next to mine. Are you ready to walk, or do you need to go to the locker room first?"

"I don't do women's locker rooms," she said, a wry grin playing at her lips. "I'll forever be scarred by my junior high and high school memories of skinny girls in their underwear."

Esther chuckled. "Me, too."

"Yeah, sure." Minnie gave her a look that plainly said she didn't believe a word of it but appreciated Esther's attempt to make her feel more comfortable.

"Okay then. Hang your keys on the little key holder there, and let's go get that heart pumping."

Rolling her eyes at her own attempt to motivate the girl, Esther shook her head. All she needed was a Minnie Mouse voice and she'd sound like Kiki, the gym's aerobics instructor.

Mindful of Minnie's lack of conditioning, Esther kept her own treadmill at a comparable speed, but increased her incline so she could still work at the proper level.

"So, how are things going?" she asked, resorting to the universal ice-breaking phrase. Not very original but, thankfully, it worked.

"Okay, I guess. I'm trying to wrap up a research paper that counts for half my semester grade in English."

"What's it on?"

"Obesity and the reasons girls get fat."

The plainspoken answer took Esther by surprise. But she also understood that Minnie was trying desperately to come to grips with her own physical condition, to find answers that might help her do something about her weight problem.

"And how's that going?"

Minnie gave a short laugh. "I'll tell you later when I can catch my breath."

After twenty minutes, Minnie was drenched in sweat and definitely looking ready for a little rest.

"How about going to the juice bar for a protein shake?" Esther suggested.

"Sounds good."

They grabbed towels and sat in a couple of stools at the counter. After ordering, Esther turned to Minnie. "So how is the paper coming along?"

Minnie shrugged. "Let's just say, I'm not entirely comfortable confronting myself. But I felt the Lord chose this topic for me. I mean, Ashley weighed less than I do when she went in to deliver her baby. Chris has eight percent body fat. Dad's thin, and so was my mom. As far as I know, there's not one genetic reason I should be overweight. And yet. . ." She glanced down at her body, then shot her gaze to Esther.

"Have you come up with any answers?"

"Yep. It's all Dad's fault." She gave a saucy grin, but there was a hint of truth in her eyes.

Esther nearly choked on her sip of protein drink. Her eyes widened, and she assessed Minnie's expression. The girl meant it. Knowing she had to tread carefully or risk undoing all the progress they'd made, she swallowed and focused on keeping her tone even. "How did you come to this conclusion?"

"Okay. It can't have escaped your notice that Ashley is Daddy's little princess. And Chris, well, he's the son. All men want that son, right?"

"I guess so."

"So that leaves me not only the middle child, but the unnecessary one."

"Unnecessary? Oh, Minnie, that's a little dramatic, don't you think?"

"I don't mean I'm not loved. I know Dad loves me. But fathers need one princess to shower love on, and they need a boy to pass on the family name to— plus all that manly information like woodworking, fixing cars, and so forth."

"Okay, I can see your point somewhat. But I'm not sure where you're going with it. And I don't believe you're unnecessary by any stretch of the imagination."

"When I was growing up, Dad had a special thing he did with each of us so that we didn't feel our mother's loss so much. Ashley wanted ballet and gymnastics. So he took her to lessons, encouraged her, went to recitals, all that stuff. That was their special time together. He played ball with Chris and helped him make go-carts, taught him to shoot a gun. Guy stuff. You know what our special time together was?"

"What?"

"Once a week we went to see a movie together. If nothing appropriate was playing, we'd go to a kid-friendly pizza place that had games and an arcade."

"That sounds like fun, Minnie. I don't understand your problem with it."

"Okay. What's the first thing you are aware of when you go into a theater?"

Perceiving how important this was to Minnie, Esther concentrated, wanting to get the right answer. She imagined herself walking into the theater, the smell of popcorn. . .ahh. . .

"Popcorn?"

"Bingo. I began to associate my time with Dad as a time to eat. That once-a-week outing with him was the best time in my life. All my happy childhood memories revolve around our times alone together. The happy smells and tastes of popcorn, nachos, pizza, Milk-Duds."

"I see your point, but I don't understand how you can fault your dad for wanting to spend time with you."

"I'm not really faulting him. It's just that his time with Ashley and Chris revolved around things they were interested in. He assumed I wasn't interested in anything, so he chose the easy way out with me and stuck with entertainment. The truth of the matter is that I wanted to take piano lessons. But he never asked me."

"Did you ever ask *him* for piano lessons?"

She shook her head. "I wasn't the type to ask for anything. But why didn't he notice that I always sat at Mom's piano and tried to pick out songs by ear?"

"He's not a mind reader, honey. And I'm sure he treasured those times with you and never thought about you not being satisfied."

"I know he did. He's a great dad. It's just tough not to be angry with him when I realize that I eat for comfort because food was the focus of my happy childhood memories." She grinned. "I'm also a movie junkie, and I love computer games."

Esther couldn't resist the playful tone. She laughed, then grew serious. "You know, Minnie, I think you should talk this over with your dad. He's trying to understand your relationship, too."

Her brow rose. "He talks to you about me?"

"You're talking to me about him," Esther replied, appealing to her sense of reason in an effort to thwart the righteous indignation of betrayed privacy.

Thankfully the ploy worked, and understanding lit Minnie's face. "I see your point. So you really think I ought to talk to him?"

"I do. Keeping things hidden causes more problems than it's worth."

"You're probably right. Thanks, Esther."

Esther smiled and continued to smile throughout the day. Parenting obviously came easy to her. She was going to be a great mom.

❧

Esther finally had all she could take of Tom's staring at her from across the candlelit table. This was their first dinner together at her home, and so far everything was perfect. His attention flattered her, and she normally enjoyed it, but not while she was chewing. She leaned forward. "Stop staring."

He cleared his throat and shifted in his chair. "Sorry."

Sending him an indulgent smile, she sipped her iced tea.

"How was your day?" he asked.

"Great. I got tons done at work. I'm gearing up for tax season, though. Right after Christmas, things really start hopping." Esther chewed the succulent prime rib and swallowed it down, debating whether or not she should bring up yesterday's conversation with Minnie. The girl had shown up again this morning, but had been tight-lipped, discouraging any kind of personal discussion.

She decided to approach the topic through a back door rather than bring Minnie up directly. "Minnie tells me Ashley gets to take the baby home tomorrow."

Tom beamed as he always did when anyone mentioned his little namesake. "We're having a welcome home dinner. You coming?"

"Is that an invitation?"

"Of course. Not that you need one."

"I'd be delighted then."

"Good. Maybe you can help keep things from getting heavy."

"Heavy? How could there be anything but joy at Tommy's coming-home party?"

He sighed. "Minnie is in another one of her moods."

"I noticed she seemed a little upset at the gym today."

"She came to the gym?"

"Yes. She's really serious about confronting her weight issues."

"Tell me about it. She's decided I'm solely to blame."

So the girl had spoken to him. Esther cringed. Maybe she shouldn't have encouraged Minnie in that direction.

"What'd she say?"

He repeated the things Minnie had confided to Esther the day before, only his eyes flashed with indignation. Guilty fear swept through Esther. She'd been the cause of this contention. Minnie probably never would have brought it up to Tom if Esther hadn't encouraged her to do so.

"Can you believe kids these days? It's not enough that we sweat to provide for them, worry to death over their well-being, cry over their hurts." He shook his head. "Even the ones who admit they had a good parent find something to blame us for."

"I don't think she was blaming you exactly, Tom." Feeling responsible for the entire misunderstanding, Esther felt she had to try to help patch things up between father and daughter.

Tom let out a short laugh. "Believe me. I'm to blame for every size above a six."

"Don't you think she's just trying to come to grips with her weight issues? It's difficult being a young woman her age as it is. But the added weight wreaks havoc with her self-esteem."

"I understand, but why not take matters into her hands and do something about it? I don't like being blamed just because she likes Twinkies."

Esther's defenses rose. "She is doing something about it. But some people need more than a physical response. Some people need to understand why things are as they are. For Minnie to lose the weight without understanding why she's heavy to begin with, she's likely to regain anything she loses."

"Is this our first argument?"

Taken aback by the abrupt change of subject, Esther had to take a second to readjust.

Tom smiled, and Esther couldn't help but respond in kind.

"I guess I got a little carried away defending her," she admitted.

"And I guess I got a little carried away defending myself. Come on, I'll help you clean up."

Some of the joy had been sucked from the evening, and she wished she could go back to yesterday morning and mind her own business.

Tom sensed her withdrawal but couldn't decide if he'd stepped over a line or not. He knew she was a little put out with him, but, for crying out loud, a man had a right to defend himself if someone accused him of being the cause of all her problems. He toweled a plate and set it in the cabinet and moved behind Esther. He slipped his arms around her waist and buried his face into the curve of her neck. She leaned her head back against his shoulder and released a soft sigh.

Tom swallowed hard, taking in the sweet scent of her perfume. "Look, I don't want us to be at odds," he murmured against her skin. "This is between my daughter and me. It doesn't have to be an issue with us."

She turned in his arms and laid her palms against his chest. "I have to tell you something. And you may not like it."

The worry on her face clutched at his heart. Mentally, he braced himself for what came next. "What's that?"

Averting her gaze from his eyes to her hands, she gathered a deep breath. "Okay, Minnie confided in me yesterday about all this. She told me about her research paper and about figuring out why she overeats."

"Yes?" Tom frowned, not entirely sure he liked where this was going.

"I—I actually thought she made a lot of sense."

That wasn't exactly what he wanted to hear. And she clearly wasn't finished.

"And I encouraged her to talk it over with you. I just assumed you'd be interested in hearing her out."

"And now you think I'm not only responsible for her condition, but an uncaring father, as well?"

She caught his gaze and pulled back. "I didn't say anything about you being an uncaring father. Nothing could have been further from my mind."

"But you think I made her fat?"

"I don't believe it was your fault at all. You were being the best father you could have been to her. Even Minnie admits that you were great. But no one can predict how a child's experiences will affect them. Even the good experiences."

"So you're saying I handled Minnie all wrong?"

"That's not really my place to say. But I think sometimes we have to give ourselves the opportunity to see a situation through someone else's eyes, even if we know in our heart that we did the best we could."

He tightened his arms about her and pulled her closer. "You know what?"

A relieved smile curved her lips. "What?"

"I wish I'd had you around a long time ago." He pressed a quick kiss to her lips. "I might not've made so many mistakes."

"I wish you'd had me around a long time ago, too. But not to thwart inevitable mistakes." She raised her chin for a kiss. Delighted, Tom obliged. She smiled and continued, "It just seems like a waste of time for both of us to have been alone for all those years when we could have been sharing our lives."

Her eyes widened, and she stepped back. "I didn't mean. . .I mean, I wasn't hinting."

Pulling her back into his arms, Tom muffled her rambling with a lingering kiss. He knew what she meant. Every moment they were together was precious time, and he regretted that he hadn't fired his former accountant and walked into Esther's office years ago. The soft warmth of her mouth beneath his invited a deeper kiss, but cognizant of the fact that they were alone in the house, he pulled away.

She sighed and laid her head against his chest. He stroked her silky hair. The words he'd been keeping in his heart for weeks suddenly spilled from his lips almost without warning. "I love you."

A soft gasp escaped her. She pulled back and caught his gaze. Her eyes shone. "You do?"

Taking her face in his hands, he returned her gaze, relieved to have the words finally out in the open. "I've only loved once in my life until now."

"I've never loved anyone before you."

Tom's heart thrilled at her admission. He pulled her close to him. "Say the words," he gently demanded.

"I love you." Her eyes misted; her lips trembled with the whispered words. Unable to speak, he lowered his head and covered her mouth with his. When he pulled away, they were both shaken and Tom knew he couldn't stay. They had planned a movie after dinner, but that was out of the question if they were to remain pure before the Lord.

"I'm going to go."

She nodded. "Yes, I think that's for the best."

"Don't walk me to the door."

Leaning against the counter, she watched him step back. Tom used every ounce of self-discipline he possessed to turn and walk through the kitchen door, grab his jacket, and leave.

In his car, he pulled his cell phone from his jacket pocket and dialed Ashley's number.

"Hi, honey, are you up for a little company?"

"Sure. I'm a bundle of energy waiting to bring Tommy home tomorrow."

"Okay, I'm calling Minnie and Chris. We'll be there in a little while."

He said good-bye and dialed home. "Minnie, get Chris and meet me over at Ashley's."

"Wait. Is Ashley okay?"

"She's fine."

"I thought you had a dinner date with Esther."

"I did. It ended early. Meet me over there. It's time for a family meeting."

Chapter 9

O kay, I blew off an entire afternoon of work," Esther groused. "The least you can do is tell me where we're going. I don't see what couldn't wait until dinner tonight anyway."

"The reason it couldn't wait," Tom said, with all the patience of Job, "is because I missed you." His heart-stopping grin nudged away some of her exasperation at being kept in the dark about where they were going. He'd come into the office thirty minutes earlier, picked her up in front of her wide-eyed assistant, and carried her to his pickup. Though outwardly she'd protested the Hollywood action, secretly she was swept off her feet in more ways than one.

The fall foliage flew past on either side of the small highway leading out of town, but Esther barely noticed its loveliness. "Okay, I mean it. I want to know where we're going."

"You're not very patient, are you? I hadn't noticed that so much before today."

"That's because you've never *kidnapped* me before today."

He grinned again. "We'll be there in about ten minutes, so just relax."

Scowling, she sat back and crossed her arms, feeling a full pout coming on. "All right, but this is under protest. And it had better be worth it."

"I think you'll be pleasantly surprised," Tom said wryly. He hummed along with the Christian radio station while Esther sat silently taking in the last days of autumn. He maneuvered the truck onto a small gravel road.

Esther forgot her protest as she took in the sight of the sun seeping through the red and gold leaves shielding the road like a canopy. She drew in a sharp breath. "Oh, how gorgeous."

He pulled to the end of the road where a field stretched out before them, bordered by evergreens and oaks. Tom shifted into park and killed the motor. He got out, walked around to her side of the truck, and opened the door.

"How would you like to have a picnic with me?"

"I'd love it." Placing her hand into his, Esther slid from the seat. Tom moved to the back of the truck and grabbed a picnic basket and a blanket.

A cool breeze lifted Esther's hair and blew across the back of her neck. She shivered.

"Cold?"

It was on the tip of her tongue to say no, but as he put his arm around her and pulled her close, she changed it to, "Not very."

"Now, was it worth it?"

"Every frustrating second. You should know I'm not patient in general. And I'm typically not crazy about surprises."

A laugh rumbled his chest. "You like surprises. You just don't like waiting for the surprise."

Nudging him with her elbow, she gave a sheepish grin. "I guess you're right. What a beautiful view. Where did you hear about this place?"

"Here and there." He set the picnic basket on the spread blanket and motioned for her to sit down. She complied, unloading chunk cheese, apple slices, deli sandwiches, and a bottle of sparkling cider. "Wow, you went all out. I'm impressed."

He leaned forward and brushed her lips with a quick kiss. "Good. I like impressing you."

"I like being impressed." Her giddiness emboldened her, and she initiated a return kiss.

Smiling, he sat back. They ate in the serenity of the deserted field, the silence broken occasionally by the call of geese overhead as they gave up their summer homes and traveled south for the winter. Tom glowed with pride as he talked about his grandson. And to Esther's profound relief, he admitted to clearing the air with Minnie after he got home the night before.

Tom pulled her against him, and his arms surrounded her from behind. They watched the breeze move the branches of the outlying trees, sending red and gold leaves floating to the already laden ground. Cradled in Tom's arms, Esther sighed with contentment. The sun caressed her face, and she closed her eyes, relishing the moment.

"I could get used to days like this," Tom whispered against her ear.

"Mmm. Me, too," she replied lazily, stroking the soft hairs on his arm.

"Then let's do it."

"What? Spend our days out here?" She gave a short laugh. "I'd never get any work done."

He pulled back and turned her to face him. "I mean, let's spend the rest of our lives out here."

"What are you talking about?" Understanding was beginning to glimmer, but Esther didn't want to allow herself false hope.

Moving in front of her, Tom knelt and reached into his front jacket pocket. He pulled out a ring box. He took a deep breath. "I know we've only been dating a couple of months, but we've both felt the intensity of the relationship."

Unable to speak, Esther simply nodded. There was no doubt what her answer would be. This guy was the embodiment of every dream she'd ever had.

Apparently taking her silence for hesitation, Tom hurried on, stating his case. "I don't think there's any reason to wait until we've known each other longer. I know enough to love you, and I want to spend my life finding out the rest of the details. This is my land, and if you agree, I'd like to build our house here."

He gathered a breath and commanded her gaze, a hint of anxiety evident in his blue eyes.

Swallowing back tears, Esther threw her whole heart into a loving smile. "I hope you know what you're getting yourself into. I'm pretty set in my ways. I'll probably nag you all the time."

He threw back his head and laughed. "I'll take my chances."

Breathlessly, Esther watched as he opened the ring box. Her eyes widened as she glimpsed the solitaire diamond ring. "It's beautiful."

"It's simple." He pulled it from the box and took hold of her left hand.

The stone sparkled in the sunlight. Anything but simple. This was the most beautiful ring in the world. The cool silver circle slipped over her ring finger, and to Esther it was as though the world had settled into slow motion.

"It's perfect," she said, not taking her eyes off the token of Tom's intent to marry her, to make her dreams of home and family finally come true. "Oh, Tom. You really love me?" She shifted her gaze to his and captured such a look of love shining from him there was no room for an ounce of doubt. A thrill rose inside of her, and she threw her arms about his neck. He held her in a tight embrace and rose to his feet, lifting her with him.

He held her out at arm's length. "I'd like to announce it at dinner tonight. Is that okay?"

A sudden fear shot through her. "What if they don't want us to get married?"

A laugh escaped him. "Are you kidding me? They're crazy about you. You've even managed to bring Minnie around. Why would they object?"

She shrugged, secretly delighted with his take on her relationship with his children. "Liking me as a friend of their dad's is one thing. Accepting me as the stepmother is entirely different."

Pulling her closer, Tom shook his head. "Trust me, sweetheart. We held a family meeting last night about this. There's not a dissenter in the ranks. You're in."

"You held a family meeting about this?"

"Yes."

"And what if there *had* been a dissenter?"

Lines etched his brow. "Well, I'd have listened to the objections and asked you to marry me anyway. But at least we'd have known who to look out for."

That answer was good enough for her. "All right. Then I guess it's all settled. We'll announce it tonight."

He gathered her closer and dipped his head. His breath mingled with hers a split second before he kissed her. Esther sensed the difference in the intensity of this kiss from all the others. As his lips moved over hers, they claimed her with a promise of what lay ahead for them.

Contentment welled up inside of her. Even in her sweetest dreams of falling in love, she'd never imagined such a feeling. In Tom's embrace, she closed her eyes and enjoyed the moment. She imagined shopping for wedding gowns, furniture, baby doctors, and experiencing all the baby "firsts" she'd never really believed would happen.

"So, how'd it go?"

Freshly showered and moving about his room in stocking feet, Tom held the cordless phone and smiled at the sound of Ashley's voice. "You'll have to wait until dinner to find out. Did you pick up my grandson from the hospital?"

An exasperated sigh filtered over the line. "You're going to make me wait? And yes, I picked up our darling. He's sleeping in his daddy's arms."

Tom could hear the joy in her voice, and his heart lifted at the sound. Thank God for His mercy.

"You know, Dad, if Esther answered your proposal the way I suspect, I wouldn't be a bit surprised if next year, we're expecting a new little baby brother or sister."

A burst of laughter shot from Tom. "Oh, sure. Cute, little girl."

For a moment, silence was his only answer. "Dad, have you and Esther discussed children?"

"We've discussed you kids."

"I mean starting a family of your own."

"I already have a family."

"Esther doesn't."

Tom breathed in a long, cool breath, frowned, then dismissed Ashley's concern. Surely, if Esther wanted children of her own, she would have mentioned it by now. The woman hadn't planned to marry at all until he'd come along, let alone have children.

"Dad? Are you still there?"

"Yeah. Listen, the only children Esther and I have discussed are you kids. Don't you think I'd know if she wanted a baby?"

"I don't know. Probably. Sorry for bringing it up."

"All right, I'll be heading over there in a few minutes. Anything I can bring?"

"Just Esther."

"That goes without saying."

"Okay. Love you, Dad. I can't wait until the announcement."

"Me either."

Tom couldn't shake Ashley's comments as he finished getting ready. He glanced at the baby photographs on his dresser. First Ashley, then Minnie, and finally Chris. For Tom, their childhoods had been filled with the wonder of learning to parent, teaching them the alphabet, that first bike ride without the training wheels. But he had done all of those things alone.

What *if* Esther wanted to have a baby? Did he have the desire or energy to go through that again? The thought of marriage to Esther filled him with images of passion-filled nights, long walks and talks, companionable retirement years. Never once had he considered the possibility of starting another family. Slipping on his shoes, he tried to reason with himself. Tried to consider the ramifications of fathering a child at this time in his life. What if something were to happen to her like it had his children's mother? Life was so uncertain.

If he and Esther got married soon and had a child right away, he'd be in his late fifties before the kid hit puberty, sixties before graduation. And what if he had another daughter? He'd be hobbling down the aisle with her at her wedding.

His brain echoed a resounding *NO.* He was ready to enjoy his grandson and ready to grow old gracefully with the woman he loved. More children were out of the question. If by any remote possibility Esther had something else in mind, he'd just have to be the voice of reason.

Shaking his head at the absurdity, he grabbed his keys and headed for the door.

A baby?
Not a chance.

Chapter 10

O h, Kare, look. Isn't this the sweetest thing?"
Esther pulled Karen aside to look at another baby outfit in the downtown shop. Her sister groaned but followed along as she had numerous times. For the past hour, they'd perused every rack and shelf possible and were now on the second time around. Esther was thrilled with her first visit to the Oh Baby! store.

"I can't believe I've never shopped here before. This shop is fabulous." She gasped in delight at a tiny red jacket. "Take a look at this. Isn't it precious?"

Karen scowled. "Esther, you're going to go broke if you don't stop grabbing everything you see."

"But it's an itty bitty St. Louis Cardinals jacket. It's so sweet."

Karen looked at the price tag and released an exasperated breath. "Yes and it's sixty-five bucks."

The arrow of reason hit its mark, and Esther replaced the little jacket on the rack. "You're right. But you should just see little Tommy. He's so adorable."

"I'm sure he is," Karen groused. "But you weren't nearly this gaga over my kids—and you know there have never been any three children born as cute as mine."

"Of course not," Esther humored, forcing herself to look away from a pair of baby sneakers with a popular logo stitched on the sides. "But when your kids were babies, I was just trying to get my business off the ground and couldn't afford these kinds of presents."

"We always loved whatever you bought—regardless of where you picked it up or how much it cost. Besides, we're supposed to be shopping for wedding gowns, not baby stuff. First things first, remember? First comes love, then comes marriage, *then* comes Esther pushing a baby carriage."

"These aren't for me," Esther insisted. "They're for Ashley's baby. Can't I be a doting stepgrandmother-to-be?"

Laughter bubbled from Karen's lips. "I can't get used to that. You're actually going to be a grandmother." She sobered and lowered her tone. "Have you and Tom discussed children of your own?"

A frown puckered Esther's brow. "No. Tom is very happy with his life. His daughters are grown, and Chris graduates this year. He's settled, you know? I'm pretty sure he doesn't want to have any more children."

"Well, how do you know for sure if you haven't discussed it with him?"

She shrugged, wishing Karen would just drop it. Not that she hadn't thought about the same thing every waking moment since he'd proposed, but voicing her concerns made them real; and she didn't want anything to spoil her lovely maternal fantasies. "A woman just knows."

"Oh, please."

Esther glanced at the determination on her sister's face and decided she might as well open up.

"Okay, for instance, the other night we had dinner with his kids to welcome the new baby home. He made a point of saying how much he loved little Tommy and how he gets to do all the fun baby stuff and then send him home with his mom and dad."

"Ouch. Well, did you tell him you want to have a baby of your own?"

Tears stung Esther's eyes, but she blinked them away as they approached the counter. After making her purchases for Tommy, she stayed quiet until they left the baby store and hit the pavement, headed toward the bridal shop a few doors down.

"Now, there are no salesladies listening," Karen said. "Have you spoken with Tom about this?"

Esther shook her head, and this time the tears came faster than she could blink them away.

Karen slipped her arm around Esther's shoulders. "Really, Esther, you can't go another day without talking to him."

"It's more than that. I—I'm not sure I can even have any."

"Okay, stop. Let's get a cup of coffee and talk about this before we go look at wedding gowns." Karen took hold of her arm and led her into a café.

"All right," Karen said, as soon as they had their lattes and as much privacy as the crowded café allowed. "What makes you think you might not be able to have children?"

"It's been two months since. . ." Esther hesitated and glanced around the room. She leaned forward and lowered her voice. "You know. . ."

Karen's expression registered understanding, and she nodded. Then her brow puckered. "You couldn't be pregnant, could you?"

"How can you even ask that? Tom and I are committed to God and to staying pure until the wedding."

"Esther, there could be a million reasons. Don't automatically assume. . ."

"This isn't the first time I've missed. It's been happening a lot this year."

"Then you need to go see your doctor and find out what's going on."

"I know. I'm just afraid of what she's going to tell me."

Karen chewed her bottom lip, a telltale sign she wanted to say something she wasn't sure Esther was going to want to hear. Esther braced herself. "What, Kare?"

"Okay. I was just wondering if you've given any more thought to foster parenting. Before you met Tom, you were convinced God was leading you to go through the training and get your license. Seems a shame to let all that go to waste."

Esther sat back in the booth, her fingers tracing the rim of her coffee mug. "I'd still love to do it. But I have Tom to consider now. I'm not sure he even wants more children of his own. How could I ask him to be a foster parent?"

"I understand. It's just that we need foster parents badly, and I noticed that all your paperwork is up-to-date in the office. You're ready to go."

"I am?" A sense of excitement rose inside Esther. The old enthusiasm.

"Yes. If you've decided against foster parenting, you should call the office so we can take you off the list of potential homes."

Esther hesitated. "I don't feel right about that. But to be honest, I'm not sure if it's guilt or a desperate need to share my life with a child—and the knowledge this might be my only chance to do that." Tears stung her eyes once more. "What if I can't carry a baby of my own, Kare? It seems so unfair."

Karen reached across the table and took her hand. She bowed her head and prayed for Esther to have peace, for God to be in control of everything concerning the situation, for Esther to have the courage to open up to the man with whom she'd agreed to share her life.

They were both crying by the time Karen said, "Amen."

⨇

Tom sat in the parking lot of the women's clinic, waiting for Ashley to come out. Since no one else was available to watch Tommy during her checkup, Tom had agreed to come along.

But the parking lot was where he drew the line. If not for the baby getting his picture taken right after Ashley's appointment, Tom wouldn't have come within two miles of the women's clinic. Especially considering the worrisome thoughts rolling around in his mind lately. So far, all of his hints about being too old to have a new baby of his own had failed to bring about the reaction from Esther he'd hoped for—agreement.

In fact, she'd been noncommittal each time he'd broached the topic, which led him to believe that Ashley may have been right when she suggested Esther would want to have a baby of her own.

Scrubbing his hands over his face, he let out a groan. He didn't want to do anything to jeopardize his relationship with Esther, but having another child was out of the question.

He glanced through the windshield, willing Ashley to hurry up. He felt ill at ease sitting in this parking lot. No matter where he looked, he saw women walking to and from their cars. Not even one male doctor walked through the parking lot. It made him feel like a peeping. . .well. . .Tom.

And every time he saw a dark-haired woman, he did a double take, thinking it was Esther. Like the one walking out of the clinic right now. He frowned and peered closer as the woman headed toward the pharmacy—she was a dead ringer. *Wait a minute.* That *was* Esther.

He honked. She turned, scanned the lot, then froze when she saw him. Mindful of the baby, Tom knew he couldn't go to her, so he rolled down the window and waved her over.

"Hi," she said, a little breathless from her fast walk across the lot.

Tom's throat tightened as he searched Esther's face. Her eyes were red as though she'd been crying, and the absence of makeup cinched his suspicion.

"What's wrong?"

"What do you mean?"

"Besides the fact that you're filling a prescription, which we'll get to in a minute, I can tell you've been crying. Is everything all right?"

She waved his question aside. "Just emotional, woman stuff."

"Woman stuff, huh?" As much as he'd like to pursue the matter, to make her realize there was nothing she couldn't share with him, he knew a brush-off line when he heard it. But he understood her timidity about such a personal topic. Tenderness swelled his chest. She had never had a real relationship with a man before, and he couldn't expect her to open up about private female matters so soon.

Eyes glowing, Esther spared him the necessity of the next line of conversation. "Oh, look who you have with you." Her expression softened as she peered in at Tommy. "He's growing so fast."

"Blink your eyes, and he grows an inch," he answered with a wry grin. "His mother is here for her checkup, and she needed a babysitter."

"That explains it. I thought maybe you were following me."

"I'm not. But I am a little curious. Are you okay? Physically, I mean."

Tom could tell it took quite an effort for her to drag her gaze from the baby and focus on him. "I'm fine. Why do you ask?" Was it his imagination, or did she seem a little defensive?

"You were going into the pharmacy. I thought maybe you were getting medicine."

A blush stained her cheeks. "Oh. Just filling a prescription."

"For?"

"Something personal." She smiled in an effort, he surmised, to take the sting from the "none-of-your-business" response.

"As long as you're fine."

"I am. But I need to pick up my prescription and get back to work." She leaned forward and kissed him lightly.

"Do you want to have dinner with me tonight?"

Her brow rose. "I thought you were going bowling with the men from church."

"I could change my plans."

"Oh, don't do that," she said quickly, a little too quickly as far as he was concerned. But she said it with such a beautiful smile that he couldn't hold a grudge. "To tell you the truth, I sort of looked forward to ordering Chinese food and curling up with my new novel."

"Sounds a little lonely to me."

She let out a short laugh. "Not to me. I haven't read a book in ages."

Stung to be replaced by words on a page, he nevertheless forced a smile and nodded. "All right. I can take a hint," he said, only half teasing.

She started to step back, but he slipped his hand behind her head and drew her to him for another kiss. She responded to his embrace but pulled away sooner than he would have liked.

"I'll see you later," she whispered.

A sense of foreboding hit him full in the gut as he watched her go. He didn't like the fact that she was keeping something from him. The thought struck him that he didn't really know her very well. Only three months. Had they moved too fast? His love-struck heart warred with the reason that had failed him since he'd met Esther. Was he doing the right thing? Or was he making the biggest mistake of his life?

❦

"So what did the doctor say?" Karen's call interrupted Esther's pity party. She sat wearing her *I love Goofy* T-shirt and her comfy sweats. She'd already downed way too much sweet-and-sour chicken, wontons, and at least three egg rolls. So now, the pain in her stomach rivaled the pain in her heart.

One week after her first appointment, Esther had returned for test results. The doctor had given her wretched news as far as she was concerned. "Perimenopause," she said dully.

"What?"

Esther sniffed and swiped at the fresh onslaught of tears with the back of her hand. "Perimenopause. That's what my doctor thinks is going on."

"Aren't you a little young for that?" Karen said, indignation edging her tone. "Maybe you should get another opinion."

"No, a lot of women in their late thirties and early forties get it. It's sort of a prelude to the actual full-blown thing."

"Wait. Honey. Calm down a second. I don't completely understand."

Esther gulped back a sob. "It means I'm getting old. The train's passed me by. Over the hill. Always a grandmother, never a mother. Does that make it any clearer?"

"The doctor said you can't have a baby? That doesn't make sense. Women older than you are having babies all the time."

"Yeah, well, some people have all the luck."

"You have no options?" Karen pressed.

"Fertility drugs to increase my chances each month—luck of the draw. Typical stuff for infertile couples."

"Well, see? It's not impossible."

TIMING IS EVERYTHING

Esther sighed and touched her palm to her forehead. "The doctor said I shouldn't put it off too long if I plan to get pregnant."

"Then you'll just have to talk it over with Tom right away."

A groan escaped as she voiced the thoughts she'd been avoiding for the past few hours—ever since she'd run into Tom in the clinic parking lot. "How can I ask him to go through all that trouble?"

"Esther, Tom knows you two aren't college-age kids. If you're going to start a family, you don't have time to wait. That has to have been on his mind, too."

"I don't know."

"Well, sweetie, I don't have to tell you this, but it bears saying." Karen hesitated, then went on. "You need to talk to Tom. The sooner the better."

Chapter 11

The first thing Tom noticed when Esther walked through the door, her arms laden with gifts for Tommy, was her tight smile. The sense of foreboding that had nudged him a few days earlier now kicked into high gear and slammed into his gut like a line drive traveling a hundred miles per hour.

He relieved her of the oversized load. "All this for one little baby?"

"Be glad my sister was with me, or I might have bought out the whole store." Shrugging out of her black leather, full-length coat, Esther gave him a sheepish grin, one that put him a little more at ease. He leaned down and kissed her upturned lips.

"Are Ashley and Trevor here yet?"

"Yep, they're in the family room with Minnie and Mitch. Chris should be home anytime."

"Thank you for inviting me for dinner before the shower guests arrive." Her smile lit up the shadowy places of his heart, and he felt a sudden sense of rightness. He'd most likely been overreacting to her vagueness.

"Look who's here, everyone." His announcement was unnecessary as Minnie and Ashley had already left their seats to give Esther welcoming hugs.

Watching his daughters interact with his future wife boosted Tom's optimism even higher. He inwardly mocked himself for being such a worrywart.

Esther glanced about the room. "Where's the baby?"

"Napping," Ashley replied. "Although I doubt he will be for much longer if the guys don't stop yelling at the TV."

"So who's playing?" Esther asked.

"Bears and Rams."

"Yeah, the Bears are getting creamed. But then, that's nothing new." Minnie tossed a sideways glance at Mitch and grinned.

"Just wait. The Bears are a great come-from-behind team. They'll pull it off." It was common knowledge that Mitch rooted for all the Chicago teams— out of loyalty, Tom suspected, to his grandparents who had lived in Chicago their entire lives.

As usual, Minnie couldn't resist pushing his buttons. Why that kid put up with her, Tom couldn't fathom, but they'd been best friends since childhood and Mitch never held a grudge. After a couple more derogatory comments aimed at the Bears, Minnie squealed as Mitch had all he could take without retaliation. Tom grinned in satisfaction as the kid pulled Minnie into a headlock and began knuckling her head. "Say the Bears rule."

"Never!"

"Say it!" Mitch doubled his efforts.

"Okay, okay. The Bears. . ." Mitch relaxed his hold. Minnie twisted out of his grip and tossed a victorious grin from half a room away. ". . .stink!" Turning, she sprinted from the room.

Chaos ensued as Mitch took off after her.

Tom shook his head and laughed, meeting Esther's amused gaze. "What are they, fourteen years old?" he asked.

"Don't wake up the baby!" Ashley called.

As though nothing out of the ordinary had occurred, Trevor kept his attention glued to the game.

"Want to go into the kitchen for some coffee? It would give us a few minutes alone to catch up on the last couple of days," Tom asked, slipping his arm around her slender waist.

Esther nodded. "Sounds lovely."

In the kitchen, she sat at the table while he poured two cups full of freshly made coffee. When he set them down, Esther glanced at him with a knowing smile. "I think you're going to be walking another daughter down the aisle before too long."

Tom blinked at her, trying to absorb her meaning.

Apparently picking up on his bewilderment, Esther laughed.

"Isn't it obvious? Mitch is crazy about Minnie." She shook a pink packet of artificial sweetener into her cup and stirred. "I can't believe you haven't noticed before now."

He shook his head. "You're way off base. They're just friends. Ask either of them."

"Trust me." She lifted her chin stubbornly. "Mitch is head over heels in love."

Amused affection surged inside Tom's breast. He leaned over and kissed her cheek. "You're cute. But, believe me, I know those two. Minnie is madly in love with Greg, and Mitch is in love with video games and math."

"Okay, have it your way. But when they announce their engagement, I expect a formal apology."

"It'll never happen, but if it does, I'll send an apology over the radio and dedicate a song to you."

"I'll hold you to it."

A burst of cold air shot through the kitchen as Minnie pushed open the door and stomped inside, soaking wet and shivering. "Can you believe that jerk?"

"What happened?" Tom asked. He was about to close the door when Mitch came in after her.

"He hosed me," she said, glaring at the offender. "In the middle of winter. He doesn't care if I die of pneumonia!"

Rolling his eyes at her dramatics, Tom cast a disparaging glance at the puddle of water at her feet. "You're dripping all over the place. Better go upstairs and change."

She sent Mitch another glare and stalked away, but not without the last word. "Jerk!"

"Bears rule!" Mitch called after her, obviously unaffected by her anger.

"They stink!" she called back from the steps.

Mitch shrugged at Tom, swiped a muffin from the counter, and headed back to the family room.

Sending Esther a triumphant grin, Tom sat back and folded his arms over his chest. "Oh yeah. They're just a step away from matrimony."

"I'm more convinced than ever that those two are meant for each other." A knowing smile curved her lips. "You might want to write out that apology so you don't get all tongue-tied once you're on the air."

Tom joined her laugher. Watching her sip her coffee across from him, he envisioned years of doing this very thing morning after morning. They would grow old together, enjoying each other's company. He sighed with contentment.

Esther looked down at the baby in her arms and swallowed hard, trying to keep the tears at bay. She'd volunteered to hold him to give Ashley a chance to eat a warm meal. While Esther rocked the baby in the wooden rocker, she couldn't help but pretend Tommy was hers. Hers and Tom's.

The scent of brown-and-serve dinner rolls mingling with the spicy smells of homemade lasagna made her stomach grumble. But Esther wouldn't have traded this moment for anything—even if she were starving to death.

When Ashley peeked into the room a little while later, Esther wasn't even close to ready to let the baby go, but he was beginning to stir and root around. "You're just in time." She smiled at Ashley. "I think he's hungry."

Ashley nodded. "I thought he'd be about ready to eat. Thanks so much. It was nice to make it through a full meal uninterrupted."

"My pleasure." Esther stood and handed the baby over.

"Dad said you should go eat now before Mitch and Trevor devour all the lasagna."

Esther chuckled. "I'm going." She leaned over and kissed the baby's head.

Ashley sat in the rocker. "Esther, can I ask a nosy question?"

"Of course."

The girl opened her mouth; then hesitation flickered in her eyes, and she shook her head. "Never mind. It's none of my business."

"Are you sure? I don't usually mind nosy questions."

A smiled curved Ashley's lips. "No. I better stay out of it."

Curiosity simmered, but Esther decided to let it go. If the girl was that hesitant, maybe she was right and this wasn't a topic Esther wanted to discuss with her future stepdaughter.

"All right. I better go eat so I can help clean up before your guests start to arrive."

"I'm looking forward to seeing Karen again."

"Thanks. I know she's looking forward to seeing you, too." Karen had recently begun attending the contemporary service, and she and Ashley had hit it off right away. "I'll see you in a little while."

Esther made her way back to the kitchen, a little nostalgic over her empty arms. She could still feel the warmth of Tommy's little body. A heavy sigh escaped, but she pulled it together before joining the merriment coming from the group sitting around the table. She forced a smile and stepped into the room.

"Finally, Esther." Chris stood and pulled out the chair next to him. She smiled at him and took the seat. "I need someone on my side, Esther."

"I'll help if I can."

"I think it's only fair that you and Dad give me a baby brother or sister."

Esther felt a jolt go through her, and she had to fight not to spew the sip of iced tea she'd just taken. "W–what?"

"I've been the youngest kid around here all my life. But now that Dad's marrying a younger woman, I think we need an addition. What do you say?"

Esther felt everyone's eyes upon her. Heat rose to her cheeks, and she tried to cover her horror by coming up with an evasive, yet witty remark. "Actually, I'm not much younger than your dad," she murmured, keeping her gaze firmly fixed on her plate of lasagna. Not exactly witty, but evasive nonetheless.

"Leave her alone, Chris." Esther glanced up at the sound of Tom's voice. His tone was harsher than she'd ever heard.

"Sorry, Esther," the teen mumbled. "I was just kidding."

"Sometimes your teasing goes too far." Tom's tone remained stern.

Esther caught his gaze and looked away from the questioning and dread she saw in the blue depths. Her appetite fled, and she stood. "I'll clean up. The rest of you better go hang balloons. Everyone will start arriving in an hour."

"What about your supper?" Tom looked up at her.

"I'm not very hungry." She couldn't bear to look him in the eye. Couldn't bear the thought that he might be reading her thoughts and have completely different ideas about their future together.

Surely God wouldn't allow her to fall in love with a man who couldn't or wouldn't give her a baby.

Tom herded the kids out of the kitchen and gave express orders for them to get the balloons done—without filling them with water first. He joined Esther in cleaning up. They worked together removing dishes from the table, putting leftovers away, and wiping down counters. He swept the kitchen floor while she loaded the dishwasher.

Their conversation remained light, a deliberate ploy, he suspected, to avoid a return to the topic Chris had broached—a topic he knew was going to have to be discussed very soon. She'd appeared noncommittal, and he couldn't gauge whether or not she agreed with Chris about giving the boy a baby brother or sister. He might have been joking, but that sudden light in Esther's eyes had been anything but funny.

Surely God wouldn't have allowed him to fall in love with a woman who wanted a child that he simply had no desire to father at this time in his life.

Chapter 12

These kids really need you, Esther." Karen's voice broke, and even through the phone line, Esther could tell she was crying. "I don't want to send them just anywhere. Please? For me?"

"I just don't know, Kare. My life is so complicated right now." Resting her elbow on the desk, she pressed the heel of her hand to her forehead. She hated how selfish she sounded. But how could she take care of two kids when her own life was so uncertain?

"Just for tonight? You have that spare bedroom sitting there empty. I promise I'll try to place them somewhere else tomorrow."

Releasing a heavy sigh, Esther felt her resolve waning. "All right. Give me a couple of hours to go shopping before you bring them over."

"Okay. I can keep them occupied that long. Thanks."

She pushed the button to get a dial tone and called Tom. Ashley answered. "Pearson Lumber."

"Hi, Ashley. It's Esther. Is your dad there?"

"Hi, Esther. He's out on a call right now. Want me to give him a message?"

"Yeah. Tell him I'm going to have to cancel our plans for tonight. Something came up."

"He'll be disappointed. But I'll tell him."

Esther gathered her belongings and left instructions for her assistant to lock up at closing time. Then she went to the grocery store to buy some kid-friendly cereal and snacks.

The children, a boy, aged five, and a girl, barely out of diapers, had just become wards of the state after their mother was arrested and put in jail. According to Karen, the little boy had been taking care of them both for three days when a neighbor discovered them alone. Their mother had been found strung out in a crack house. No one knew who the father—or fathers—were, and as far as anyone knew, the children had no other family.

Esther raged inside at the unfairness of it all. Why did God allow unfit people to have kids when decent people who would love and take care of them couldn't have children? She rejected the idea that maybe she should stop worrying about whether she could have her own baby or not and just adopt one of the many wards of the state who had no one to call Mommy.

It wasn't that she didn't sympathize with those precious children; it was just that she wanted her own flesh and blood. She wanted to feel a baby growing

197

inside of her, wanted to know the joy of nursing her child at her breast. Adoption would feel like. . .settling, somehow.

She picked up the groceries, bubble bath, junior-sized toothbrushes; then, on a whim, she headed to the toy department and loaded a cart with cars, dolls, books, and art supplies. She knew it was only for one night. But the thought of what those children must have gone through compelled her to provide things she was sure they'd done without in their short lives. Toys were more than a luxury. For children, they were a necessity.

Arriving home a solid hour before they were due, Esther cut premixed cookie dough and placed it onto a baking sheet. Once the treats were in the oven, she hurried to unload the rest of the groceries. She put the toys in the bedroom where the children would sleep and ran to shower and change out of her work clothes. She'd just finished drying her hair when the doorbell rang. Her heart lurched as she headed to the door.

The sight of the children nearly took her breath away. Karen stood behind a dark-haired little boy. His wide brown eyes stared up at her with uncertainty and even a bit of fear. Her maternal instincts ran into overload, and she offered him a smile. Much to Esther's delight, he returned the smile without reservation, showing surprisingly lovely baby teeth. The little girl clung to Karen as Esther stepped aside to allow the little group to enter.

With gentle hands, Karen pulled the little girl free and handed her to Esther. Rather than scream and fight, the child transferred her stranglehold from one woman to the other.

"Children, this is Miss Esther, and, as I told you earlier, she's going to be taking care of you tonight." Karen turned to Esther. "That's Tonya. She's two and a half and still has accidents, so I brought some diapers for overnight. And this," she said, ruffling the boy's hair, "is Chuck. He's five and very, very smart. Which you'll find out for yourself soon enough."

"Very nice to meet you both," Esther said, her heart wrapping around the warm little body in her arms and extending to Chuck, who seemed to be relaxing with each passing second.

"I made some cookies. Do you like chocolate chip?"

Chuck nodded vigorously.

"Did you plan supper for them?" Karen asked. "They haven't eaten yet."

"Hmm. I didn't think to start supper."

Disappointment and resignation passed over Chuck's features. Esther's stomach sank. The child obviously believed he'd be going without since she'd forgotten about dinner. How many meals had these children missed?

"I'll order pizza."

She grinned as his eyes widened.

Karen chuckled. "You're going to be popular. Cookies and pizza."

Esther waggled her eyebrows. "I have toys and coloring books, too."

"That's a lot of stuff for overnight guests."

"They can take them with them tomorrow." She knew Karen had thought she'd take one look at these angelic children, then agree to keep them as long as need be, but Esther wasn't ready to commit to that.

Karen gave her a disappointed scowl. "All right," she said. "There are two outfits each in the bag along with underwear and socks and pj's. I got them out of the freebie bags we have at the office."

Esther nodded. "Do you have time for some coffee?"

"No. I need to get home and feed my family. Besides, this will give you and the children time to get to know each other. I'll call you in the morning."

After giving Esther a quick hug, Karen patted Tonya's back and, once again, ruffled Chuck's hair before leaving.

"All right then, how about I call and order a pizza, and we can get to know each other? How's that sound?"

"Good."

She tried to set Tonya down, but the child clung to her like a spider monkey. She pressed a kiss to the child's dark head and laughed. "Come on, Chuck. Do you know your numbers?"

He nodded. "Uh-huh."

Esther smiled. "Then you get to push the buttons on the telephone."

A sparkle of excitement lit his beautiful eyes, and Esther's heart soared.

After ordering pizza, she turned to Chuck. "Can you grab the bag Miss Karen brought your things in? I'll show you to your room."

"See how strong I am?" Chuck asked, muscling the bag with one hand.

"Wow, you're a big guy. I'm lucky to have you around here."

The boy beamed under her praise.

"Follow me, strong man."

Esther's arms felt like lead, and Tonya's stranglehold was beginning to feel stifling. She hoped like crazy the toys would entice the child to let go.

"Is this my room?" Chuck asked, wonder thick in his voice.

"Yes. You and your sister's. Do you like it?"

He nodded, setting the bag on the bed. "Can I get on it?"

"The bed?"

"Uh-huh."

"Of course you can."

He climbed up, then didn't seem to quite know what to do. He glanced around and squirmed.

"Tonya, honey, would you like to sit next to your brother on the bed? I have some presents for you."

She tried to pry the child away, but she clung tighter.

"Don't you want to see your new toys?"

Feeling the little arms relax, Esther sighed in relief and took the opportunity to set the toddler next to her brother. She went to the closet and pulled out the bags filled with toys. She took them to the bed.

"Who gets them?" Chuck asked.

"You do, of course. Do you see any other boys in this room who might like this remote-controlled jeep?"

Wide-eyed, Chuck shook his head.

She pulled a soft, blond-haired, blue-eyed doll from a bag and stretched it toward Tonya. The little girl looked at her in wonderment and took the toy with painstaking slowness as though she expected Esther to change her mind and rescind the offer.

Esther's throat clogged as Tonya clutched the doll to her chest, her beautiful face split into a wide smile.

"What do you say, Tonya?" Chuck demanded, scowling at his sister.

"Thank you," Tonya whispered.

Esther ran her hand over the little girl's silken curls. "You're welcome, sweetheart."

Chuck nodded like a placated parent. Esther didn't have the heart to inform the boy that he had failed to thank her for his toys. Thanks weren't important today. Making the kids feel welcome, wanted, and safe mattered most. Manners could be dealt with later.

She sat back on the bed and watched while the children played. As soon as the children were asleep, she was going to call Karen. There was no way these children were going anywhere. In fact, her mind was already beginning to whirl with plans. In the morning, she was going to call the office and have some work faxed over, so she could work from home while she worked out child-care details.

Her heart leaped with the possibilities. The only question was. . .what would Tom say?

❧

Tom made a slight detour on his way home. When Ashley told him Esther had to cancel their date for that night, he'd been more than disappointed. He'd become worried. A quick call to her office had yielded very little information from Missy, Esther's assistant. All she could tell him was that Esther had gotten a call from her sister and shortly thereafter had gone home for the day.

Tom wasn't sure what to make of the news. He'd tried to call earlier, but there had been no answer. The next time, the line had been busy, so he knew she was home. Rather than call again and take a chance that she'd brush him off, he decided to drive by her house. Just long enough to assure himself that she was all right. She'd been acting strange lately. . .and there was that pharmacy incident. What if something were seriously wrong? Would she tell him?

He pulled his truck behind her car and headed to the porch. It took a couple of minutes for her to answer when he rang the bell.

"Tom. I thought you were the pizza guy."

"You canceled our date so you could stay home and order a pizza?" Hurt and bewilderment pushed at his heart.

Releasing a heavy sigh, she moved aside and opened the door wider. "Of course not. Come in. What brings you by that couldn't have been answered over the phone?"

Defenses rising, Tom stepped inside and glanced around. Nothing seemed out of the ordinary, unless he considered the scent of freshly baked cookies hanging in the air. "You've been acting different lately. I just need to see for myself that you're all right."

"Well, as you can see. . ."

Tom peered close. She seemed a little nervous, but not necessarily in a bad way. She had a glow about her that he wasn't sure he'd noticed before.

"Okay. I'm not leaving until you talk to me. Tell me what's happening between us." He took her hand. "Are you having second thoughts about marrying me?"

Her eyes widened, and her mouth dropped open. "Oh no, Tom." She moved easily and naturally into his arms. Tom closed his eyes and buried his face in the tender curve of her neck. He breathed in deeply, taking comfort in her familiar scent as relief spread through him.

He wasn't sure what made him open his eyes, but a sense that something in the room had changed prompted him to do just that. The sight that met him caused an immediate jumble of confusing thoughts. He stepped back but didn't look at Esther. Rather, he looked beyond her to the little boy holding tightly to a toy jeep with one hand and the other draped around the shoulders of a little curly-headed toddler. A beautiful little girl holding tightly to a doll.

"I need to explain something." She gathered a deep breath. "These are foster children. I—I got licensed to foster parent before we met. Karen called me today and needed a place for Chuck and Tonya. Well, just look at them. I couldn't say no."

Foster children? Dragging his gaze from the children, he faced the woman he loved—the woman with whom he wanted to spend the rest of his life, the woman who had been keeping secrets. The sense of foreboding that had been a constant companion of the past couple of weeks now morphed into a stinging sense of betrayal.

The doorbell rang while he was trying to digest the information. Esther roused herself and smiled at the children. "Now that's the pizza for sure."

Tom watched her navigate around him, grab a check off the table next to the door, and take care of the pizza delivery boy.

"Do you want to stay for dinner, Tom? We can talk after I bathe the children and put them to bed."

"I don't think so." He couldn't. He needed time to process. "I'll call you later."

"I'd prefer to discuss this in person," she said, tight-lipped.

"How about dinner tomorrow night?"

Her gaze dropped to the pizza box in her arms. "I'll have the children."

"Then, like I said, I'll call you."

Her expression crashed, and she nodded. "All right," she whispered. "Call me."

Tom walked to his truck as if in a daze. He needed to think—to sort it all out. Foster children were temporary, right? Kids came, stayed for a little while, then returned to their parents. But something in the memory of Esther's expression when she gazed upon those children answered all the questions he'd been warring with. Even if she gave these two back, she was definitely going to want children.

Sick at heart, Tom drove to the site of their new home. The foundation was laid; walls were up. But he had the sad feeling he wouldn't be carrying Esther over the threshold.

Chapter 13

"Esther, it's been four weeks since you and Tom broke up. Don't you think it's time to get back on the merry-go-round?"

Rolling her eyes, Esther hugged the phone tighter against her ear with her shoulder and fastened a piece of tape to the umpteenth Christmas present she'd wrapped that night. "The only merry-go-round I ever intend to set foot on again is the kind my lovely children will enjoy."

"*Your* children, huh? Be careful, Esther. Remember, their mother will get out of prison in a couple of years. You have to keep that in mind."

Esther's stomach tightened with dread at the very thought of that future day when she'd be forced to hand over Chuck and Tonya. "I don't see how any rational judge can allow a woman like that to have her children back."

"That's what rehabilitation is all about. She'll get clean, take parenting and job-skill training, and most likely be given another chance to do right by those kids."

"If she doesn't end up back in a crack house the second she gets out of jail."

"Well, for Chuck and Tonya's sakes, let's hope that doesn't happen."

"What if they don't want to go back? They'll have been with me a long time by then. Tonya probably won't even remember her."

The line crackled, the only sound between the airways for a few long seconds. Worry clung to Karen's voice when she finally broke the silence. "Maybe I should find them another home. I think you're getting so attached that you can't be reasoned with."

"No, don't be silly," she said quickly. "There's no point making them suffer just because I'm falling in love with them."

"All right. But be rational. If you get to the point where you think it's getting too intense, let me know."

"I promise. Are you all set for tomorrow morning?"

"Of course. Presents are wrapped and under the tree. Turkey is thawing in the fridge, as it has been for the past couple of days. Pies are baked. All we need now are you, Chuck and Tonya, and Dad, of course."

"We'll be there after the kids open all their presents and get some time to play with their new toys. I'm making blueberry pancakes for breakfast. Chuck saw them on a commercial the other day and asked if I knew how to make them." Esther smiled, remembering how the boy obviously hadn't wanted to come right out and ask her for them. She'd decided right then that they would be a surprise Christmas breakfast.

"That sounds good. I might show up over there for breakfast."

"The more the merrier, sister dear." She yawned. "I better go. I still have presents to finish and a camcorder to check out and make sure it's charged up."

"Okay. Make sure you get a shot of their faces when they see all the presents. And bring the tape with you so we can see it."

"I will."

Esther set the phone back on the charger. Tomorrow would be wonderful, and she couldn't wait to see the joy on their little faces when they saw the gifts she'd bought.

The clock struck midnight by the time she finished her wrapping and cleaned up the evidence.

With a yawn, she reached for the light switch just as the phone rang, nearly sending her through the roof.

A glance at caller ID sent her heart racing. "Hello."

"Merry Christmas."

Esther's stomach flip-flopped at the low tones of Tom's voice.

"Merry Christmas, Tom."

"I'm sorry to call so late, but I knew you were up."

"Oh? How'd you know that?"

"I saw the light on."

Esther ran to the front window, and her heart sank when she didn't see Tom's truck.

"You drove by?"

"Yes."

"You could have stopped."

His wonderful chuckle sent a rush of longing through her. "I would have justified a kiss under the mistletoe, but that would have only made things more difficult for us."

And what do you think this call is doing to me? Esther's heart cried out. She missed him. With every inch of her being. Missed his easy laughter, the conversation at the end of the day. His smile, his arms, his lingering kisses.

"I thought of you yesterday," he said softly.

It was to have been their wedding day.

"I thought of you, too." Her voice broke under threat of tears. "I'm sorry things worked out the way they did."

"Me, too, sweetheart. I blame myself for assuming you were at the same place in life as me just because you're close to my age."

"You're not to blame. I suspected you wouldn't want children for some time before we actually had that last conversation."

Silence hung over the line, long and dreadfully loud. Finally, Tom spoke. "Well, I suppose I should go. Ashley and Trevor are coming over early, and Trevor's folks are joining us later for Christmas dinner. The kids miss you."

"I miss them, too. Please wish them all a merry Christmas from me."

"I will."

❧

Tom pressed the button to disconnect the call. He'd driven home during his conversation with Esther and now sat in front of his house, truck motor running. With a sigh, he killed the engine and headed inside. The soft glow of the television caught his attention, and he headed to the family room. Minnie sat on the couch, a diet soda in front of her, a veggie plate next to it. He had to hand it to the girl: She'd set her mind to losing weight and was doing a super job of sticking with it.

"Hi," he said softly, so as not to startle her.

She turned. "Hey, where'd you go? I thought we'd watch *It's a Wonderful Life* together, but you left."

He shrugged and sank into the overstuffed recliner. "Just driving around."

She nodded. "Holidays are the hardest on those unlucky in love."

"I guess."

"I see Esther at the gym all the time. You should see those kids. They're adorable."

His lips twisted into a wry grin. "I have seen them. And it's not about cute kids. It's about kids in general."

"Chris ruined you for any more, huh? Can't say that I blame you."

Tom laughed. "You kids are great. Any father would be proud to have a dozen just like you. It's just too late in life to start from scratch."

"Not for men. Look at all those old movie stars marrying young wives and becoming fathers ten and twenty years older than you are."

He'd thought of it. Over and over. Until, for a while, it was all he could think about. A surefire way to get Esther back would be to give in and agree to have a child. But that was a deceitful way to get what he wanted, and he was afraid he'd resent the baby. Resent every cry, every diaper change, every feeding that took Esther away from him. Perhaps he'd grown selfish over the years, but now wasn't the time to become tied down to that sort of responsibility. This was the time in life when men bought sports cars and took up golfing. Midlife didn't have to be a crisis. He looked forward to it—without little ones, and, unfortunately, without the woman he loved.

❧

Esther woke up at 4:00 a.m. and couldn't go back to sleep in anticipation of Chuck's and Tonya's responses. She went to the couch and readied the camera for when the time came. By four-thirty, her eyelids began to droop. The next thing she knew, she was being awakened by light streaming through the window. She jerked awake. Expecting to find empty boxes and scattered wrapping paper, she sat up, bewildered to find Chuck and Tonya sitting together in the chair, quietly looking at a book.

"Merry Christmas, kids! Look at all the presents waiting under the tree."

"Yeah," Chuck said glumly.

"Well, honey, don't you want to open them?"

"They're not for us."

Esther frowned. "Come here and sit with me."

The children complied.

"What makes you think those presents aren't for you?"

"Mom said Santa didn't bring presents to kids like us."

A horrified gasp escaped. Esther couldn't help it. "Kids like you? What do you mean?"

He shrugged. "Poor kids."

"Chuck, do you remember how we learned the letters to your name?"

"Yes."

"I want you to go over to that tree and look on the presents. See if you can find your name."

Tentatively, almost as though he were afraid, Chuck moved to the tree. Tonya climbed into Esther's lap and watched her brother with curiosity, but no expectation.

Esther held her breath as he located a gift she knew had his name written on it. He turned to her, a wide grin splitting his dear, sweet face. "C-H-U-C-K. That's me, right? It says Chuck?"

Tears burned her eyes, but she forced them away. "That's right, honey. I want you to tear into that paper."

"Does Tonya have one, too?"

Hugging the little girl to her, she laughed. "Are you kidding? One? There are lots of presents under that tree for you both!" She rose and carried Tonya to the tree. Kneeling, she set the little girl down and started doling out the gifts. Amid the children's squeals of delight, she shook her head in wonder. How could she have ever considered adoption as settling for second best? No other children on earth compared to the two right here in her living room.

❧

"You want to what?" Karen's incredulous tone was to be expected, and Esther took no offense.

"Adopt them," she replied, keeping her tone deliberately even.

Karen pulled a pan of dinner rolls from the oven and set them on a cooling rack. "These children are not up for adoption, Esther. They have a mother."

"A mother who told them Santa didn't bring presents to kids like them. Do you realize this is the first real Christmas they've ever had? It would be cruel to send them back."

In frustration, Karen tossed the oven mitts to the counter and spun to face Esther. "That's not our place to decide. It's not our decision. Don't you remember any of your training?"

"Oh, who cares about that? You can't train the heart who and who not to love."

206

Esther's throat clogged, and she felt tears burn her eyes. "And I love those children. They belong with me."

"Listen. I can ask around. It's possible she would sign over rights if she knew someone wanted them. I'll check into it for you."

"You will?"

Karen gave her a tender smile. "Yeah. Merry Christmas. But don't get your hopes up."

"You might as well tell me not to breathe."

"I know."

The doorbell rang.

Esther frowned. "Are you expecting company?"

"Now, Esther, don't get mad, okay?"

"What are you talking about?"

"I invited Victor for Christmas dinner. His family lives in New York, and he didn't have time to go home."

"Victor?"

"The guy from the office?" Karen shook her head. "The social worker who started about the time you met Tom?"

"Oh, Karen!" Horrified reality bit her hard as she heard the front door open and heard Dad and Karen's husband, Brian, welcome the new visitor. "I can't believe this."

"Go wipe the flour off your face and brush your hair."

But it was too late. Brian escorted the poor, unsuspecting sucker into the kitchen.

"Victor's here, honey. He brought a fruitcake."

"How thoughtful," Karen gushed. "I'd like you to meet my sister, Esther."

Esther unconsciously swiped at the flour on her face that Karen had mentioned, with no idea whether she actually removed it or not. Victor towered over her, and his brown eyes were kind. He smiled, extending his hand.

"Very nice to meet you, Esther. Your sister sings your praise."

"Well, she's said some nice things about you, too."

"Can I take your coat?" Karen's voice intruded upon the niceties.

Victor shrugged out of a sheepskin coat, revealing a neatly cut outfit of dress slacks and a shirt and tie.

"I'll go put this away. You two get acquainted."

"I'm afraid I'm a little overdressed," he said, glancing at his clothes with a sheepish grin.

"Oh?" Then she nodded as understanding dawned. "Dad and Brian are Neanderthals. We can barely get them to dress up for church on Sunday mornings. Karen should have warned you the guys would be wearing jeans."

"I almost wore a suit coat. So at least I'm spared that humiliation in front of 'the guys.'"

Esther laughed. "It's pretty obvious why Karen wanted to fix us up."

His eyes took on a guarded look, and Esther felt her cheeks warm.

"I mean, we both have a sense of humor."

He pasted a polite smile on his face, and Esther could feel him tense. With a heavy sigh, she realized she was making things worse. Better just to come out and say it.

"What I'm trying to tell you is that I'm in love with the man I was engaged to marry," she blurted. "I'm not ready to date anyone else."

He looked so relieved, Esther felt a bit insulted.

"The truth of the matter is that I'm engaged to be married."

"You are?"

"Yes. We haven't told anyone yet. Her parents won't like the fact that she's moving here from New York, and I wanted to get money saved and buy our home so there would be that much less they have to worry about."

"Congratulations," Esther said, feeling the tension drain from her.

"Congratulations about what?" Karen asked, as she breezed back into the kitchen.

"Victor was just telling me he's engaged to a girl back home."

Karen's disappointment was apparent. "Engaged? You didn't tell me that."

"I was afraid you might not invite me to dinner if I told you I was off the market."

Esther chortled. "Serves you right for trying to fix us up. I told you I wasn't ready to date again."

Karen grinned. "Well, at least I got a fruitcake out of it, even if I'm not getting a new brother-in-law."

During dinner, Esther tried to stay in the conversation, but her thoughts transported her to Tom and his family. Were they watching a football game? Most likely. And laughing and joking as they always did.

How did little Tommy look in his first Christmas outfit?

And Tom. What was he thinking at this moment?

Today would have been perfect if only they had stayed together and kept their plans. Right now she'd be celebrating her first Christmas as Mrs. Pearson.

She excused herself from the table, went to the rest room, and cried.

Chapter 14

Tom couldn't help but smile at his six-month-old grandson, who sat in his stroller, enjoying the new warmth of early spring. His chubby fingers were wrapped around a teething ring, and he chewed voraciously, pausing occasionally to blow bubbles between his rosebud lips.

Due to an attack of spring fever, Ashley had decided to dive into cleaning every nook and cranny of her apartment and had recruited Trevor, Chris, and Minnie's help to accomplish the task. That left Tom with babysitting duty. Not that he minded. He couldn't get enough of the little guy.

"Tom?"

The familiar voice sent his heart into overdrive. He glanced up to find Esther staring down at him, her look of bewilderment matching the way he felt at the coincidence. "Esther. This is a pleasant surprise."

"Yes, it is." She glanced at Tommy. "Where's Ashley?"

Tom's heart sank. Was she disappointed to see him? It had been months since they'd even exchanged an e-mail. He missed her so badly at times, it was all he could do not to pick up the phone and ask her to dinner. But that wouldn't be fair to either of them. So, during those moments of weakness, he prayed for strength and wisdom. He had to admit, breaking up with Esther had done wonders for his relationship with God. And he didn't regret that for a second. He did, however, regret the way things had turned out.

"She roped everyone but me into spring-cleaning."

Amusement twitched her beautiful, full lips. Tom swallowed hard and forced his gaze back to Tommy.

"Well," she said, plopping onto the bench next to him. "Looks like we've been duped."

"What do you mean?" He drank deeply of her flowery scent, like a man dying of thirst.

"Ashley called and asked if I'd like to bring the kids to the park since it's such a beautiful day."

He threw back his head and laughed, feeling happier than he had in months. "My daughter is quite the matchmaker, isn't she? I wondered how she talked Minnie and Chris into helping her clean. They must have banded together."

"And used three innocent children to accomplish their plot."

"You brought the kids?"

She gave him a teasing smile. "Would I come to the park without them?

They're playing over there." She motioned toward the sandbox.

Tom smiled as the little girl dumped a shovelful of sand over the little boy's head. The boy stood, shook off, and sat back down without so much as yelling at her.

"Wow. He's a patient little tyke, isn't he? When my kids were that age, they would have been screaming for me to do something."

"Chuck practically raised her until they came to live with me. The only time he gets impatient is when she forgets her manners or does something he's afraid she'll get into trouble for." She leaned in and gave him a conspiratorial grin. "Not that she ever even comes close to getting into trouble."

She spoke of those children with emotion—just like every other mother he'd ever encountered. Joy mixed with pride—a recipe that exuded from her. Her smile seemed wider and even more genuine than he remembered. It didn't matter that these children weren't her flesh and blood. It was obvious that her love was fierce and real.

He couldn't help but smile. "Motherhood seems to agree with you."

She nodded. "It's wonderful. Much more than I ever dreamed really."

Tom's gaze rested fondly on her. Indeed, she glowed like a woman about to give birth. Her eyes shone with love as she looked at the children playing in the sandbox. She'd put on a few pounds, he observed, but the extra padding did nothing to diminish her beauty. In fact, it gave her a softer look, which he found extremely appealing—too appealing.

"How long will these two be with you?"

She breathed a sigh and fixed her troubled gaze upon him. Her obvious anxiety shot straight to his heart.

"What's wrong?" he asked.

"To tell you the truth, I'm trying to adopt them. But I'm afraid it might not materialize."

Tom couldn't quite analyze the emotions flooding him. Somewhere in his heart, he supposed, he'd hoped she'd keep the kids until it was time for them to leave and then she'd be satisfied and ready to settle into the rest of her life with him. Now he saw the idiocy and selfishness of such presumption. And he saw how badly it would hurt her if she were to lose those children. "What's the problem?"

"Their mother is in prison for drugs. She keeps waffling back and forth about signing away her parental rights."

"Sounds like she's not ready to give them up. Could she get help and be fit to parent?" As soon as Tom spoke the words, he wished he could take them back. She'd confided in him as a friend needing support. She didn't need to hear the other side of the story when she was already hurting. Her scowl testified to that fact.

Before he could find his voice and apologize, she launched her side of the equation like a rocket. Straightforward and to the point.

"She left Chuck in charge of Tonya for days at a time. A five-year-old! In my opinion, a woman like that doesn't deserve children."

"And yet God gave them to her." Tom cringed. What was his problem? This was not the way to win friends and influence people.

She sniffed. "Maybe God gave them to her because He knew I'd never find a man and wouldn't have any of my own. Don't you think it's possible He allowed her to have children so that I can have them?"

Stung and feeling the brunt of her verbal attack and implication, Tom averted his gaze to his grandson, who had dropped off to sleep.

"Oh, Tom. I'm sorry. I don't mean to sound so bitter. I really do understand why you wouldn't want to start a whole new family." Tears formed in her eyes. "I just can't stand the thought of losing those children. They love me, and I love them."

At the sound of fear in her voice, Tom finally caved in and put his arm around her. She buried her face in his neck, accepting the comfort he offered. He whispered against her ear the words he felt God wanted him to speak. "God has a perfect plan for you, Esther. You need to know that, even if Chuck and Tonya go back to their mother."

"I can't imagine why God would allow that," she mumbled. He could feel her tears on his neck. "It makes no sense to me."

"God's ways often make little sense to us, sweetheart. His ways are higher, His thoughts higher. But if we put ourselves into His hands, He makes our lives a work of art that He, the Master Craftsman, creates."

He heard his words, but applying them to his own life hadn't been so easy. Coming to the park alone with Tommy had brought back all the memories of bringing up his kids alone. No one to sit with and share the funny things they did that day. No one to share in the load. When he'd married his wife, they'd never dreamed that he would be raising their children alone. But he had. It hadn't always felt like God working and molding his life. Mostly it had been a lot of hard work. Although, if he were honest, he'd have to admit there were a lot of happy times, too.

Esther shuddered in his arms, pulling Tom back to the present. Tom's throat tightened. He pulled her back and looked her in the eyes. Tears stained her cheeks. He reached into the diaper bag at the back of the stroller and grabbed a Kleenex.

Taking the tissue, she swiped at her eyes and nose, then gathered a shaky breath.

"Thanks."

"You're welcome." He turned to look at the children she'd taken into her heart. They played contentedly, happily, as children should, without the worries their short lives had brought them. Would God allow them to go back to the woman who had neglected them? If so, what would that do to the woman he loved? He turned and caught the full force of her gaze, questioning, loving. He bit back the words "I love you." But he could feel himself weaken.

She broke their gaze and turned back to the children. For the first time, Tom could imagine his life in their house. . .the one that had just been completed. Only now he could see the swing set in the backyard, bikes on the porch, and a basketball goal over the garage.

What was happening to him?

"Okay, you need a bath, little boy." Esther glanced fondly at Chuck, who had tried to brush the sand from his clothes, but with little success. Her arms ached from the weight of Tonya's sleeping body. "Head in there and strip out of those clothes while I lay Tonya down. I'll be in to run your water in a sec."

"Tonya's going to get the bed dirty," Chuck observed, his little face twisted into a scowl.

"I'll clean it up later. I promise."

Apparently satisfied, the boy headed to the bathroom to do as he'd been instructed.

Esther laid the toddler on the burgundy-striped comforter and sat at the edge of the bed to remove the little girl's shoes. One baby-plump cheek was red from where it had rested against Esther's shoulder, and her hair was damp from sweat. Esther wanted to curl up next to the child, to feel her warmth and smell her baby scent. To hold onto these precious times that she feared might not last forever.

The phone rang, and she jumped, her stomach knotting as it did every time she got a call. That familiar sense of dread that Karen was calling to tell her the children's mother had made a final decision not to sign never failed to cause a rush of adrenaline.

She hurried to the phone and sucked in a breath at Tom's name on the caller ID.

"Hello?"

"Hi. It's—um—Tom."

"I know," she said, aware her voice sounded as breathless as she felt. Seeing him at the park had been a dream come true—the familiar dream. Meeting by chance. Tom taking her into his arms and telling her he still loved her. Today hadn't been quite like that. She'd snapped at him, then blubbered all over him. And now he was calling her?

"I know this is going to seem odd, but I wonder if you'd mind letting me take you and the kids out for pizza?"

Managing to stifle a gasp, she clutched the phone tighter. "I don't understand. Are you asking us on a date? Or do you feel sorry for me?"

"I—" He hesitated, and she held her breath until he continued, "guess I'm asking you on a date."

"I don't know what to say. You know I haven't changed my mind?"

"I know. And I can't say I've completely changed mine, but I have to tell you, Esther, I can't stop thinking about you. Life without you has made me very unhappy."

"Oh, Tom. Same for me." Her legs felt like rubber, and she sank to the couch next to the phone charger. "Seeing you again today was wonderful. But. . ."

"I know. You haven't changed your position on wanting children. I have to say, I don't know how I feel anymore, but I would like to at least explore the possibility."

Speechless, Esther stared at the opposite wall.

"Esther?"

"Yes. I'm here."

"I know it's a little unfair of me to ask you this when I'm not sure if I'll bail out again."

Her heart sank. Could she go through another breakup? "What exactly are you proposing?"

"I'd like to spend time with you and the kids. Casually. I promise I'll keep my hands to myself."

She smiled into the empty room.

"So what do you think?"

"Pizza sounds good. Give me an hour at least to finish bathing the kids and get myself ready."

"Okay, I'll see you in an hour."

Esther's heart sang a happy tune as she went about her routine, readying herself and the children for the date.

It couldn't be a coincidence that Tom was coming back at this time. This was everything she'd prayed for—everything she'd told God she wanted. Maybe she was finally about to get everything she'd longed for. Tom and the children would make her life complete.

※

Chuck was nothing at all like Chris had been at nearly six years old. Tom watched the sensitive child with growing admiration. His table manners were impeccable. He didn't ask for a thing but never forgot to say "thank you" to the waitress who delivered the drinks and pizza or to Esther for handing him a slice. Where Chris continually had to be told to wipe his mouth, Chuck wiped his own and his sister's, as well.

They would never have to worry about this kid embarrassing them in public. He allowed his attention to focus on Esther. She caught his gaze, and he realized she'd been watching him watch the kids. Her expression was tender as her lips curved—tender and a bit confident. He returned her smile. Perhaps she had good reason to be confident.

"Would you care to take a drive after dinner?" he asked.

Her brow rose. "Where to?"

"Can I surprise you?"

Lips twitching, she studied him for a second, then nodded.

"Well, look who's here." Tom turned to find Minnie and Mitch walking up to the table.

"Minnie!" The two women embraced. Then Esther reached out and gave Mitch a quick hug, as well.

"You look amazing!" Esther said.

"Thanks. I have you to thank for encouraging me to go to the gym."

"You had to do the work. I can't believe the difference."

"I think she looked great before she lost all the weight."

At Mitch's remark, Esther and Minnie exchanged grins, and Tom had the feeling he was being left out of a private conversation.

"Are you going to join us?" Esther asked.

Minnie turned to Mitch. "You want to?"

"Sure." He grinned and stood back while Minnie took a seat beside him.

Esther's pleasure at seeing the two of them worked magic on Tom's mood, and he found himself glad that they'd stopped by.

"So, how are ya, Chuckie?" Minnie asked the little guy.

"Good." He blushed and looked away. But that didn't deter Minnie.

"So, what have you been doing this week?"

He shrugged. "Playing." His eyes brightened. "Me and Tonya played at the park today."

"Oh, really?" Minnie tossed Tom a saucy grin. "My dad played at the park today, too, didn't he?"

Chuck glanced nervously at Tom, but obviously catching the teasing spirit of the moment, he giggled and nodded. Minnie tousled his hair. "You fit in just fine, sport."

Before Tom could do damage control to that statement, she switched her focus to Esther. "I haven't seen you at the gym in a few weeks, Esther."

Esther grimaced. "I know. I need to get back, but I've been swamped with last-minute tax filers and the kids. Certain things have had to get put on the back burner."

So that explained the extra pounds. Tom filed away the information. Perhaps he could relieve her a couple of times a week so she could hit the gym if she wanted to.

"So what are you two doing out?" she asked, her gaze darting to Mitch, then back to Minnie.

Minnie shrugged. "Just hanging out."

"Ha. It's a date," Mitch countered. "She's embarrassed to admit I finally wore her down."

Tom stifled a disbelieving laugh just as he noticed his daughter's cheeks brighten. "A date?" he said, unable to keep the incredulity from his voice.

Esther let out a short, almost imperceptible laugh. "I have a feeling I'll be getting an apology over the radio."

Remembering his bold promise to apologize and dedicate a song to her when Minnie and Mitch announced their engagement, Tom added his amusement to hers.

"What's that supposed to mean?" Minnie asked, her voice suspicious.

"Oh, nothing."

"So have you gone out to see the house yet?" Mitch asked.

His face twisted with pain, leaving Tom to assume Minnie had kicked him under the table.

"What house?" Esther asked.

No sense in lying to her or keeping her in the dark. "Ours." Tom hoped the longing he felt rising in his heart didn't disclose itself in the tone of his voice.

"Our house is finished?" Her gaze fixed on his. He loved the way "our house" rolled from her lips, as though they were still an *us*.

He nodded, and the rest of the world fell away as he became captured in the depths of her amber-colored eyes.

"Is that where you were going to take me tonight after dinner?"

"Yes."

"I'm dying to see it."

"Then let's go."

Chapter 15

Esther said a hurried good-bye to Tom at the door. The journey they had taken out to the house they'd planned to share had been an emotional one. And now that they were back at Esther's house, they both realized it would be best if she went inside alone. No sense in giving place to the devil. Or making it more painful if they didn't end up back together.

The phone was ringing by the time Esther and the children made it inside. "Chuck, honey, go brush your teeth and put on your pajamas." She set Tonya down, and the little girl toddled after her brother as Esther snatched up the phone.

"I've been trying to call all evening," Karen snapped at the other end of the line. "Why didn't you have your cell on?"

"Hey, Kare," she said. "Sorry. I forgot to grab my phone on the way out earlier. The kids and I were with Tom. He took us to see our house." She grinned, expecting her sister to pounce on the comment.

Instead, a nervous cough came over the line. "Listen, I have something to tell you," Karen said, her troubled tone searing into Esther's consciousness. She sat, bracing herself for the news she was almost certain was forthcoming.

"What's wrong? Their mother won't give in?"

"It's worse than that."

"What?" Her sense of foreboding caused nausea to rise in her stomach. What could be worse than that? "Tell me."

"I don't know how to say this."

Esther heard her slow intake of breath.

"Say it." The tears spilled over before Karen even spoke.

"It seems as though Chuck and Tonya's mother has family out there after all."

"What do you mean?"

"She has parents."

"What kind of parents let their daughter sit in jail while her kids go to foster care?" Esther tried to process the information amid rising fear and anger. Not an easy task to accomplish and remain reasonable. But she didn't care. If Karen was going where it seemed she was going, Esther didn't want to be reasonable. She refused to be reasonable. She couldn't bear what was coming with a logical mind.

Karen's voice broke as she continued. "Apparently the children's mother ran away from home when she found out she was pregnant with Chuck. She and her parents never got along, and she was afraid to tell them. So she left with her boyfriend instead, who of course didn't stick around very long. She recently contacted

216

her parents, and they've reconciled. They want the children, and she's signed over custody to them."

Panic rose hot and fast inside Esther, tightening her throat and causing her words to come out in a hoarse near scream. "That's not possible! They can't have them."

"Esther, you need to pull yourself together and think about this. Chuck and Tonya have grandparents who love them, sight unseen, and want to provide a loving home. We can't deny them or the children the basic right to be with family."

"How loving can they be if their own daughter ran away from home rather than telling them she was pregnant? What if they hit her?" The thought of Chuck and Tonya going into an abusive home nearly sent her running to her bedroom for suitcases. She'd run away with them before allowing them to be harmed.

"Esther, I've met them. I don't believe they're a threat to the children."

"You met them without telling me first?" The sense of betrayal she felt overshadowed any pain she'd ever dealt with.

"I didn't want to worry you unnecessarily," Karen replied, with no hint of apology. "And after meeting them, I have no good reason for keeping those children from their grandparents."

Reason invaded her fortress of emotion. Her hand trembled as she brought it up to swipe at the tears coursing down her cheeks. "H–how long do I have with them?"

"Just tonight."

"So soon?" She searched for an answer, anything that might buy her some time. "Couldn't we have a few visits with them so the children can get to know their grandparents first?"

"That's not the way things are done in cases like this one."

"Karen, what about God? How can we let them go to people who may not be Christians?" She grasped at this. Surely God wouldn't send the children into a godless home. "Chuck loves his classes at church, and he's learning so much."

"Esther, please. Stop tormenting yourself." She hesitated. "I'll tell you this much. Their grandmother said, 'Praise the Lord,' when I told her how safe and well cared for the children have been over the past few months. So I imagine they are Christians. I know it's hard, but you're going to have to deal with this."

"B–but what if they're scared? They don't know these people."

"They didn't know you either when they came to live with you." Karen's voice remained even, and Esther recognized the tone her sister used when trying to calm the people she dealt with on a daily basis. The knowledge made her uneasy and embarrassed to think she had to be "dealt with."

She forced herself to calm down. "All right. When are you picking them up?"

"In the morning. On my way to the office."

"I'll have their things packed and ready to go."

"I know this is difficult for you, but the pain will pass. I promise."

"You have a husband and three beautiful children that no one can take away from you." Esther knew she was being unfair, but how much more must she lose before God decided it was time to let her win? "You have no idea how I feel."

She dropped the phone into the cradle without saying good-bye. But she didn't care. Karen was obviously not on her side in this.

Chuck's voice calling from the other room pulled her from the veil of bitterness. "Mom? I have my jammies on. Will you read me a story now?"

Mom. Chuck had been calling her that for the past week. Only one short week to bear that wonderful title. *Oh, God. It's not fair!*

❧

Tom's heart raced as he sped along Highway 51 toward the "house." Esther had been hysterical when she called. Even in her worst moments, he'd never seen her more than a little nervous or upset.

The memory of her voice on the phone a few minutes earlier caused him to press the accelerator.

"Tom, can you meet me at the house?" she'd asked.

"Esther? Honey, what's wrong?"

"Please. Can you meet me?"

He'd pulled on his clothes and had made it to his truck in less than five minutes.

She was standing beside her car when he pulled up behind her.

He left the motor running and the lights on as he hopped out of the truck and hurried to her. In the glow from the headlights, he saw her face, red and swollen from crying. Her hair was tousled and her eyes wild with anxiety.

"Baby, what's wrong? Did something happen to the kids?"

She shook her head and motioned toward the car. He peered in through the window. Both children were sleeping peacefully in the backseat.

"Tell me what happened."

Sobbing, she fell into his arms. For several minutes, he held her. Each time it appeared she was pulling herself together and would tell him what was wrong, the tears began anew.

Finally, he gripped her arms and pulled her away from him. He studied her ashen face. "What's the matter?"

"They're taking the kids away."

"Who?"

"Karen."

"Your sister is taking Chuck and Tonya? Why?"

She gulped and swiped at her face with her sleeve. The childlike action slammed into his heart.

"Their grandparents have been located."

"I'm sorry, honey. So sorry."

She clutched at his shirt. "Will you help me?"

"Help you what?"

"I–I want to run away. Take the kids and just go to Mexico or. . .or Canada. Some place where they can't find us."

Horror gripped Tom's heart. "Are you crazy?"

She pounded his chest with her fists. Tom took hold of her wrists and gently pulled her back.

"I can't lose those kids! They're mine, Tom. Th–they call me Mom. They love *me*."

The determination in her face sent a shudder of fear through him. Who was this woman?

"Esther. You can't run away with them. Do you want to go to prison?"

"I won't get caught."

"Honey, you *will* get caught. And when Chuck thinks of you years from now, he'll only remember the woman who ran away with him and his sister. Is that how you want to be remembered?"

She stopped struggling and looked up at him with such grief, it was all he could do not to pack her and the kids up and do as she wanted. Anything to ease her pain. He pulled her to him and stroked her hair. "Let Chuck and Tonya remember you as the woman who took them in and loved them until they went to live with their grandparents."

She wilted against him as though she had no more fight left in her. Tom lost track of time as she sobbed quietly in his arms.

"Come on. Let's go back to your house so the kids can go to bed."

She nodded and didn't protest when he settled her into the passenger side of her car. "I'm going to move my truck out of the way, and then I'm driving you home."

By the time they arrived at her house, Esther had stopped crying, and she stared sullenly out the window. Tom glanced in the backseat. The children never even awoke during the ordeal.

"I'll carry Chuck in. Can you get the baby, or should I come back for her?"

"I'll get her," she said dully.

"Is your door locked?"

"The key's on the key chain in the ignition."

Tom took the keys and slid out of the car. He opened the back door and carefully pulled Chuck out. After he opened the door, he waited for Esther to precede him and then followed her inside.

She led him into the children's bedroom, where she deposited the little girl, kissed her cheek, and waited for Tom to lay Chuck down so she could kiss him, too.

He heard a sharp intake of breath and knew the tears were coming again.

"Come on," he said softly. He took her gently by the arm. "Let's go into the living room."

Dropping onto the gray overstuffed couch, she covered her face with her hands. "What am I going to do without those kids?"

Sitting next to her, he slid his arm along the back of the couch and rubbed her shoulder as she leaned her head back against him. "You'll make it, sweetheart."

"Don't you see? Chuck and Tonya were my future. After you and I broke up, I realized I'd never have children. But God immediately brought those two into my life. It was like He was saying, 'I closed one door, but look, here's an open door. All you have to do is walk through it.'"

Tom swallowed hard. He continued to rub her shoulder. "He didn't close that door, Esther. I did."

Her silky hair brushed against his arm as she turned to face him. "Either way, it closed."

"This evening when we had the kids out for pizza, I could see myself raising them. I could see us together as a family."

Her eyes filled with tears again. "That would have been wonderful."

He wanted to say so much more, but he sensed now wouldn't be a good time. She was vulnerable, and so was he. "I'm going to call Minnie to come over and stay with you tonight. I don't want you to be alone."

He reached over her to take the phone. She clutched his shirt as he hovered over her, balancing so that he didn't fall on her. He glanced down into her amber-colored eyes—those expressive eyes that said so much. Replacing the phone, he gathered her in his arms, taking her lips with his, exploring the passion he'd denied them both for half a year. She matched him kiss for kiss, pressing closer, tempting his control until he finally pulled away and stood. He turned away, unable to look at her mussed hair, her kiss-swollen lips. "We need to stop."

"Why?"

She rose and wrapped her arms around him from behind. He sent a silent prayer to heaven.

"Why? Because neither of us wants to sin, that's why."

"You still love me, don't you?" Esther's breath was warm on his back through his T-shirt. "Aren't we on the way to getting back together?"

He turned, and her arms slid around his neck. "I'd like to think so. But you're not thinking straight."

"I missed you so much." She leaned closer, and Tom's senses buzzed. "I just want to be in your arms. Is there anything wrong with that? We're getting married anyway."

He sucked in a quick breath. He'd hoped she wasn't suggesting they be intimate. He'd hoped she only needed his arms around her. To be close. But there was no mistaking her meaning. Taking her wrists, he pulled her away from him. "Honey, if we were married, I could hold you all night and try to comfort you, but we're not. I can't take you trying to seduce me. I love you and want you too much, and no matter how badly you're hurting or how mad you are at God, you can't justify sin."

Tears slid down her cheeks. "Oh, Tom. I'm sorry for throwing myself at you that way. Of course I don't want to sin. I just—I can't bear this. It feels like my heart is being ripped from my body."

Mercy replaced desire. Kindness replaced passion. He gathered her to him. "It'll be all right." He pressed a kiss to her temple. "I'm going to call Minnie now."

Thankfully, Minnie was still awake and agreed to come right away. Esther sat on the couch, hugging a throw pillow. She barely spoke during the thirty minutes it took for Minnie to arrive.

Tom bent down and kissed her head. "I love you, honey. I'll be back in the morning."

Minnie walked him to the door.

"Thank you for coming, sweetheart," he said, brushing his lips against her cheek, which now clearly showed cheekbones.

"I don't mind, Dad. Just make sure you tell Mitch where I am if he calls."

"So Greg's history, huh?"

"Oh yeah."

"I'm happy for you. Mitch is a great guy."

"Yeah, you'd think I'd have figured that out sooner." She glanced back at Esther. "What about you two?"

"I'm praying things will work out."

"So you might want to have more kids?"

Not exactly the conversation he'd have chosen to have with his daughter, but he guessed she deserved an answer. "I would have raised Chuck and Tonya, so I guess I am softening." He grinned. "Maybe Chris will get his wish for a baby brother or sister after all."

Minnie bit her bottom lip as she did when she was nervous.

"What?"

"I don't think Esther's going to have an easy time getting over those two. Go easy suggesting more kids."

"When did you grow up?" he asked, unable to keep the admiration from his tone.

"About the time Esther came into our lives. I hope we can keep her this time."

"Me, too, sweetie. Me, too."

Chapter 16

Thick clouds of despair settled over Esther from the moment Karen's car had pulled away taking the children. Now, two weeks later, she couldn't pull herself together long enough to do simple tasks. The phone rang, and she ignored it. The doorbell chimed, and she pretended she wasn't home, though anyone could see her car in the driveway. But she didn't care. Her reason for living was gone.

She knew she was in a heavy depression, but she was powerless against it. She tried to read her Bible, but the words were empty. The life she used to draw from the well-worn pages was gone, and she read familiar passages with a sense of boredom.

She tried to watch TV, but nothing appealed to her. So she kept it on for the noise but found no pleasure in the mindless jokes that usually entertained her. Books held no appeal either, and she stayed away from church. How could she sit on those padded chairs and pretend everything was all right when she was facing the darkest time in her life? From her years of knowing God, she was cognizant of the fact that only He could pull her through this. But she lacked the willpower to allow Him to do so. Not yet.

The doorbell chimed. She ignored it. It chimed again. She ignored it again. The persistent visitor banged on the door. Finally, curiosity got the best of her, and she glanced out the window. With a groan, she recognized Karen's minivan. After a few more minutes of banging, Esther got the message that her sister was not going away. With a heavy sigh, she pulled herself from her bed and shuffled into the living room. "I'm not really up to company, Karen," she called through the door.

"Too bad. I'm not leaving until you open up."

"Fine," she groused. She unlocked the door. "It's open."

"Unlock the storm door so I can come in." The determination in Karen's voice told Esther it was useless to argue.

She flicked the lock. "Okay. Come in."

Karen took one look at her, and her eyes filled with tears. "Oh, Esther." Without an invitation, she put her arms around Esther. "I'm so sorry you're hurting."

Pulling away, Esther went to the couch and plopped down. "Yeah, well." She wanted to say hateful things. Wanted to tell her sister she could have prevented them from taking away Chuck and Tonya, but she knew that wasn't fair.

Even through the pain and depression, she wasn't so far gone that she couldn't control her hateful tongue.

"When was the last time you ate?" Karen asked.

Esther thought about it and shrugged. "Yesterday, I think."

"Look at you. You're skin and bones. Go take a shower and get dressed. I'm taking you out for lunch."

"No way. I don't want to be around people."

"Too bad. Go take a shower, or I'm going to carry you, even if I have to call for reinforcements from the other people who love you."

"You wouldn't get much help. It's a short list."

Karen studied her for a minute, then took a deep breath. "It's your own fault for telling Tom to get lost."

"Hey, I thought you were here to console me."

"You thought wrong." Karen placed her hands on her hips. "I'm here to help you snap out of this depression. But I think this is more than just depression over the kids. It's gone on too long, Esther."

"What do you mean? What else is there?"

"Maybe it's due to perimenopause. I think you should call your doctor again."

"Give me a break."

"Think about it. This isn't like you. You've always rolled with the punches. Even when it looked like you would lose the business a couple of years ago. Remember? When Mom died, you took control and got everyone else through it. This just isn't like you."

She hated the possibility that she couldn't control her emotions because of a freak of raging hormones. Anger shot through her at the thought. On the other hand, if that were the problem, it would mean she wasn't going crazy. That she could get a grip on life again. Could function. Work. Love. Tom. . .

"Do you really think that's what all this is about?" Somehow it felt like she wasn't properly grieving over the kids if the depression was due to hormonal levels.

"I think this, on top of losing Tom and the kids, was too much. But your doctor will be able to tell you more about that than I can. Will you see her?"

Knowing she couldn't go on much longer in this state, Esther nodded. "All right, I'll call her."

❧

Tom had to make a fist to keep from picking up the phone and calling Esther.

"Believe me, Tom, I'm not the woman for you," she'd said to him the last time they'd spoken—the day the children had left her home.

He'd thought she'd be ecstatic with the news that he'd be willing to have a child if it would make her happy. Instead, she'd asked him to leave—had told him obviously God had decided she wasn't fit to be a mother. As much as he'd tried to figure it all out over the past four weeks, the answers eluded him. Her partner was taking care of all Esther's accounts for the time being, so he couldn't even pretend he needed to talk business with her. E-mails bounced back as though her inbox was too full.

"What more does she want?" he growled at the silent phone.

"You okay, Dad?"

Heat crawled up his neck as Chris walked into the kitchen. The boy gave him a curious look and continued across the room to grab a bowl and the cereal. "So, no luck with Esther, huh?" he asked with all the sensitivity of a high-school kid.

"No."

"Sorry, Dad. I really liked her a lot."

Tom smiled at his son. "Thanks. So did I. Loved her, in fact. Still do."

"Can't you tell her that? Maybe she'll change her mind. I mean, she was going to marry you. She must have loved you."

Releasing a heavy breath, Tom realized this is what he'd sunk to—pouring out his heart to his teenage son. But knowing how pathetic that was didn't deter him from opening his mouth. "I know she loves me. But losing those two foster kids really broke her heart."

Chris spooned a mound of Chocolate Dots into his mouth. "Well, maybe you ought to change your mind about having a kid."

Tom grimaced and fought the urge to tell him not to talk with his mouth full. When did kids outgrow that tendency?

"Believe me, I'm willing to have a kid if it'll make her happy. Anything to convince her to marry me."

"Well, I hope you didn't tell her *that*." Minnie appeared from the hallway. His life was an open book. She strolled to the refrigerator, grabbed a string cheese stick, and plopped into a chair across from Tom. She glanced at Chris and scowled. "Do you know how many carbs are in that junk?"

He grabbed the box, took a look at the nutritional information, and glanced back at her. "Yep." He shoveled another spoonful into his mouth.

Minnie rolled her eyes. "So, Dad, you decided you'd have a baby with Esther? Have you told her?"

Averting his gaze to the table, he nodded. "I told her." But after Minnie's outburst, he realized he'd been less than gracious about it. "But I think I might have goofed."

A groan escaped Minnie's lips.

"I think she might have gotten the impression that I was willing to have a baby as a favor to her rather than it being something I want, too."

Her brow rose, and Chris stopped crunching. Both stared, disbelief written across their faces.

"You mean you actually *want* to have a baby?" Minnie asked. "You weren't just giving in so Esther will marry you?"

"At first I think it was about giving in. But after I saw her with Chuck and Tonya, I could honestly see the two of us raising kids together."

"Wow. That's quite a change of heart."

Minnie's scrutiny forced the truth from him, a truth he'd known in his heart but refused to acknowledge in words. "It's been tough raising you three kids alone. There were nights I fell into bed for two or three hours of sleep before I had to get up and start another day."

"You did a great job, Dad."

"Thanks. But I was a young man back then. Still full of energy." He gave them a wry grin. "I'm not so young anymore. The thought of having a baby and then losing Esther sent me into a tailspin."

"And what changed your mind?"

"Well, mostly God. I know I'm not alone. If, God forbid, I lost another wife and found myself alone again, I have three adult children to help me."

"Hey, don't expect me to change a diaper!" Chris said, coming up for air from his second bowl of cereal.

"Don't talk with your mouth full, spaz."

Tom grinned. *Oh yeah. A lot of help they'd be.* Bottom line was that he had to somehow convince Esther that his objections weren't out of selfishness, but out of fear—and that God had helped him deal with that fear.

Chapter 17

Esther knew she should return Tom's persistent calls, but the truth of the matter was that he'd made her mad and she wasn't quite ready to let go of her anger. The last thing she'd wanted to hear the day she'd lost the children was Tom's self-sacrificing statement, and even now that she was feeling better, she was still ticked off.

The temptation to pick up the phone and tell him exactly why he'd said the wrong thing was strong from time to time. But she didn't know how to make him understand that she didn't want his *willingness* to have a baby, but his *desire* to have one. How did she explain that if he didn't truly want a child, then she'd always feel as though she'd forced him into it? She would always be insecure in the relationship and afraid that he resented her for essentially giving him an ultimatum—agree to give me a child within X amount of time, or you can't have me.

She glanced over at the phone and quickly returned her attention to the account on her computer. Today was her first day back at work, and she had a ton to do. If she worked fifteen-hour days for the next month, she still wouldn't be caught up.

A knock at her door pulled her attention away from her stress-filled thoughts. Heaving a sigh, she called, "Come in." Just what she needed—another distraction.

Missy stood at the door, her face hidden behind a huge bouquet of mixed flowers. "You are one lucky woman," she said, stepping in and setting the vase on Esther's desk. "Call the man back."

A smile played at the corners of Esther's lips. "Thanks, Missy." Unable to squelch the thrill shooting through her veins, she opened the card.

> *Tune in to* FM *91.7 at 2 p.m. today.*
>
> Tom

Esther grinned. *Time to pay the piper. Minnie and Mitch must have announced their engagement.* She wouldn't miss this public apology for anything in the world.

A glance at the clock revealed she had thirty minutes to wait, so she forced herself to return to her task.

She sighed, rummaging through a sheaf of papers. The next time she asked a client for an income statement and balance sheet, she would specify that she was looking for more than a shoebox filled with a year's worth of bank statements and check stubs. There were a few receipts turned in for good measure. These people ate more pizza than anyone she'd ever known.

Making a mental note to recommend a software program that might work a little better than a cardboard box in keeping records, she dove into the clutter with gusto, separating receipts into two piles—tax deductible and "You wish."

When Missy buzzed her sometime later, she barely even looked up as she pressed the button. "Yeah?"

"Your sister is on the line. Want to take it?"

A day at work wouldn't be normal, somehow, if Karen didn't interrupt something important. "I'll take it. Thanks."

She picked up the receiver and pushed the button for the right line. "Hey, Kare. What's going on?"

"Just checking up on you. Making sure you're not overstressing yourself."

Esther chuckled. At least she was honest. "I'm doing all right. But the stress is pretty high. My desk is piled up. You wouldn't believe it. Seriously. This client—who shall remain nameless in the spirit of client confidentiality—is the worst organizer I've ever seen in my life. I'm telling you, Kare, I asked her to send me her record files from her software program so that I could just convert her files to mine, and she laughed. Can you believe that?"

"Why'd she do that?" The lack of sympathy was more than evident, judging by the sound of Karen's amused laughter.

"She told me she uses cardboardware."

"Cardboardware? I've never heard of that."

"It's a shoebox."

Esther's comment was met with silence.

"Get it?" Esther pressed. "Cardboard? A shoebox?"

"Oh!" Karen started giggling. "I get it. That's kind of clever. Cardboardware."

Esther's frustration ebbed at the sound of Karen's laughter, and she found herself joining her sister. As they laughed, Esther's gaze traveled her desk until it lit on the vase of flowers. She gasped.

"What?" Karen said.

"What time is it?"

"Looks like about four minutes after two. Why?"

A groan escaped her. "I missed it!"

"What? What's wrong?"

"I have to go, Kare. I can't believe I missed it." Esther disconnected the call without saying good-bye. She flew to the radio. "Cardboardware," she muttered disgustedly as she pushed the scanner. It settled on the Christian radio station. She turned up the volume.

The DJ's voice blared through the speakers. "That was Tom. When a man admits he was wrong over the airwaves, you know he's in love. This song goes out to Esther from Tom. God bless you two."

Esther's heart sang along with the Christian love song. She would have given anything to have heard the announcement of Minnie's engagement, but this song proved that Tom still loved her. Her heart softened, and she let go of the anger she'd felt toward him. How could she blame a man if he didn't feel he wanted to start a whole new family after his children were already grown?

Strolling back to her desk chair, she allowed her thoughts to roam over the past couple of weeks. She'd made her appointment with the doctor and had blood tests. The results confirmed Karen's suspicions—she was suffering from a slight hormonal imbalance. Her doctor suggested a natural cream, absorbed through her skin, and suggested getting back into her exercise routine.

At first, Esther had been skeptical about the cream, but she had to admit, her life had come back into control when she started treatment. And aside from protesting muscles, it was great to be back at the gym four times a week.

She was feeling like her old self again—ready to rejoin life.

Chuck and Tonya were never far from her thoughts, but the searing pain she'd felt just weeks before was beginning to lessen with each new day. She'd resumed her daily devotions, and the Word had begun to speak life to her sickly soul. Finally, the craziness and pain of loss had righted itself in her mind, and she was able to put things into perspective once again. . .to breathe in and out without feeling like every breath might be her last. Or wishing it would be.

The joy she felt at the flowers and the love song from Tom eased the aggravation of the poorly kept records of her client as she worked throughout the afternoon. She watched the phone from time to time, wondering if Tom would call. After all, like the DJ said, when a man went on the radio to admit he was wrong, he must be in love.

By five-thirty, she realized he wasn't going to call. Had he decided that love wasn't enough to overcome all the obstacles they'd faced since meeting less than a year ago?

Maybe she should just cut her losses and move on. She'd lost the children and probably Tom. But at least she had her relationship with God, and her sanity had returned. Maybe God was telling her that should be enough—to be content with the life He'd chosen for her.

❧

Tom grabbed a mug from the shelf and closed the cabinet a little harder than he'd intended.

"I take it she didn't call." Minnie's accurate assumption ground into him like salt into a wound. He'd been watching the phone all day—ever since his radio debut. The female employees of the radio station had assured him that she'd race to the phone to call him. Boy, were they ever wrong.

"So maybe she wasn't listening to the radio."

"I made sure she'd tune in."

"I'm sorry, Dad."

He breathed a heavy sigh and plopped down onto a kitchen chair. "Me, too. I guess it's time to face facts. It's finally over for good."

Sweat rolled down Esther's cheeks as she finished her last mile on the treadmill. Reaching for her water, she switched the machine off, grabbed her towel, and stepped from the platform.

She headed to the locker room, stopping short at the sight of Minnie, lacing up gym shoes.

"Hey, Esther."

Was it her imagination, or was the girl a little cool?

"Hi. This is a surprise."

A shrug lifted the girl's now slender shoulders. "Summer semester. My classes are all in the morning, so I have to work out in the afternoons for the next couple of months."

"So I guess congratulations are in order."

Minnie nodded. "Thanks. It's been a long time coming."

"I knew it would happen."

"Yeah. It was only a matter of time. I really applied myself the last few months. I know Dad's happy that I finally got it over with." She laughed.

Esther smiled. "Don't bet on it. Your dad's going to miss you. Mark my words."

"Oh, I'm staying home afterwards, so he won't really have a chance to miss me."

"You and Mitch are going to live with your dad?"

"Mitch? What's he got to do with it?"

Esther frowned. "Aren't you getting married?"

"Married? No way." Minnie's cheeks stained pink. "Well, someday probably. But not now."

"Well, what did you think I was congratulating you for?"

"I'm graduating at the end of the summer instead of waiting for next year. I took a heavy course load last semester and decided to take summer classes. It's killing me, but it will be worth it to get on with my life." She frowned. "What did *you* think you were congratulating me for?"

It was Esther's turn to blush. Heat warmed her neck and cheeks. "I thought you were engaged to Mitch."

"Why would you think that?"

"Well, at your birthday barbecue, I noticed Mitch was crazy about you, but your dad insisted you two were just friends and always would be. So we made a deal that when Mitch proposed, your dad would go on the radio and admit he was wrong."

Minnie's eyes sparkled with amusement, and Esther could see she was fighting to keep from laughing outright.

"I know. It was pretty silly. But your dad went on the radio last week."

"Did you listen to that broadcast, Esther?"

"I missed the beginning," she admitted. "I caught the beautiful song he dedicated to me." Giving Minnie a sad smile, she forced back the sudden tears burning her eyes. "I thought he was sending me a message that he still loves me, but after a week without a call from him, I've gotten the message."

"What message?"

Esther was getting a little tired of Minnie's amusement. The girl might have the boy she loved, but that was no reason to be insensitive.

Gathering a steadying breath, she determined not to break down in front of Tom's daughter. "The song was obviously a farewell."

"If I'm not mistaken, he dedicated 'Our Love Will Last Forever.' "

"Yeah, that's it."

"That doesn't exactly sound like a farewell dedication to me."

"That's what I thought at first, too. I've been waiting for him to call, but I realized today he must have been saying that we'll always love each other even if we can't live together."

Minnie laughed outright. "Oh, Esther. This is priceless. Thank God He changed my schedule this semester."

"I don't mean to be uptight, Minnie, but this is really hurting me. I wish you wouldn't take it so lightly. Don't you remember how badly you felt when Greg didn't return your love?"

The girl sobered immediately. "I'm really sorry, Esther. But listen. You have this all wrong. Do you have plans right now?"

"I was going to shower, then go home and work some more."

"Will you come with me for a few minutes after you shower?"

"Where to?"

Minnie grinned. "Trust me?"

⁂

"Tom, I really hope you're listening." Tom nearly wrecked at the sound of his name coming over the airwaves. He'd only been half listening to the DJ as he drove through rush-hour traffic. Even now, he wasn't positive he'd heard what he thought he had. He reached down and turned up the volume. Sure enough, the sweet voice on the radio belonged to Esther.

"Tom, I hope you're out there, buddy," the DJ said. "Because this beautiful lady has something to say to you."

"I—I just want to apologize for not calling you last week when you asked me to. I didn't know anything about it because I got distracted at work and missed the first few minutes."

Tom's heart beat a rapid rhythm in his chest. That explained a lot.

"So if you really meant what you said on the radio, meet me at the house. You know which one I mean."

"Okay," the DJ said. "I hope you two will connect this time. Keep us updated, and God bless you. Tom, this is going out to you from Esther."

TIMING IS EVERYTHING

The strains of "Our Love Will Last Forever" floated through the truck. Tom made an illegal U-turn amid the blaring of two dozen horns. He hated to be the cause of more rush-hour stress for the other motorists, but he'd waited too long for this moment, and he wasn't about to miss out on his future.

❧

Esther pulled into the driveway half a minute ahead of Tom. He jumped out of his truck and was opening her car door before she could even kill the motor. He knelt in front of her, taking her hand. "I've missed you," he said and kissed her hand.

"Oh, Tom. I can't believe how crazy things have been the past few months. Can you ever forgive me?"

"Would I be here if I couldn't?" He tugged gently on her hand to help her from the car. "I need to ask your forgiveness, too."

"You? You've been so good throughout my craziness."

"Let's go up to the house."

Arm in arm, they walked toward the two-story gray-brick dwelling.

"You've built such a beautiful home," Esther said, her eyes misting.

They sat on the porch swing. "Now," Tom said, taking her hand and lacing his fingers with hers. "The reason I need to apologize is this. That morning the children left, I said something really stupid."

"You mean about us having children?"

He nodded, and Esther's heart plummeted. But she wasn't willing to lose him, no matter what.

"I understand. And, Tom, I know you're the man God planned for me. He waited until just the right time in my life to bring us together. And, though I admit I want children, the most important person to me is you, and I'm sorry I put so much pressure on you."

He released her hand and slipped his arm around her shoulders, pulling her close until his face was poised an inch away. "Esther, I love you." Their breath mingled just before he covered her mouth with his.

As Esther slid her arms about his neck, she felt the gentle peace of knowing she was exactly where she was meant to be. In Tom's arms. She wasn't ready for him to pull away when he held her at arm's length a moment later.

"Now, I need to tell you something," he said. "When I apologized, I meant for acting like I was doing you a favor by agreeing to have a baby. The truth is, I was disappointed when Chuck and Tonya went to live with their grandparents. I was really starting to like the idea of marrying you and adopting them."

Tears formed in Esther's eyes, and pain clutched her heart at the reminder of what might have been. "That would have been so wonderful. But I'm learning to submit to God's will, and I'm satisfied that Chuck and Tonya were never supposed to be my children."

"That's quite a revelation." Pride shone in his eyes, and joy rippled through

Esther at his approval.

She nodded. "All my life, I've done things my way. I planned a path where I'd get my business going well, then I'd get married and have a child. There was no room for God to have His way because I didn't ask His advice. I kept waiting for God to change your mind so that you'd want to have a baby with me after our marriage. Instead, God showed me that His ways are perfect, and I'll be happiest when I learn to walk in His will."

"And if I want to have a child?"

She hadn't expected that option. "I'm through asking you for something you don't want as much as I do."

"I want us to raise a child together." He gazed so intently into her eyes that Esther couldn't deny his sincerity. "After Chuck and Tonya, I realized my hesitance wasn't due to not being ready to walk into my golden years with you, but fear that something might happen to you and I'd be forced to raise another child alone."

Esther drew a sharp breath. "I never even thought about that."

He nodded. "God's given me peace. And to be honest, I'm looking forward to going through the process with you."

Excitement rose and then crashed. "Oh, Tom. I have to tell you something."

Concern creased his brow. "What is it, sweetheart?"

She explained the doctor's concern about perimenopause.

Tears were flowing by the time she finished. Tom brushed a gentle kiss against her temple. "If I'm not mistaken, what you're telling me is that it's unlikely you'll get pregnant without a lot of help, but not impossible."

She nodded.

"Can you trust me to just take it one day at a time? We'll pray for God's will and let nature take its course."

She nodded.

He reached into his front pocket and pulled out the familiar black box. With a sheepish grin, he opened the box. "I've kept it in the glove box since you gave it back." He plucked the engagement ring from the velvet confines. "Will you marry me?"

Tears blurred her view of the token. "Just try to stop me."

He smiled and slipped the ring onto her finger and drew her close, sealing the engagement with a heart-stopping kiss.

Relief flooded her. Peace. Contentment.

They sat on the swing, hand in hand, and watched the sky switch from blue to shades of pink and orange and finally gray. As she watched the sunset in all of its stages, Esther marveled at the perfection of God's timing.

She laid her head on Tom's shoulder and sighed when he kissed her head.

Her heart rested, knowing that her life was ordered along with nature. That God's love for her had planned her course and had given her the man of her dreams. The rest of her life would play out—in His time.

Epilogue

B reathe, Esther! One-two-three."

"I *am* breathing! Otherwise I'd be dead." There came a time in a woman's life—childbirth for instance—when she didn't need anyone telling her to breathe. If Tom didn't get out of her face in about two and a half seconds, she was going to send him from the room. His nervous energy was driving her nuts.

She cast a pleading glance at Ashley. The girl smiled. "Dad, Esther is only in early stages of labor. Natural breathing will get her through for now. Let's go get some coffee."

Coffee? That's all she needed—Tom strung out on a stimulant. She shook her head vigorously at the girl.

"Uh, on second thought, maybe caffeine isn't a good idea. We'll get you some milk or something."

"I can't leave my wife," he insisted. "What if she needs something?"

"I have the nurse's call button right here, sweetheart," Esther said quickly. "It might be a good idea for you to get some calories in you now. Later I'll need you by my side."

He bent and kissed her. "Are you sure?"

"Positive."

"I've been a pain, haven't I?" He sent her a sheepish grin.

She patted his cheek. "Only mildly. But I love you for it."

"All right. I'm going for a while. Have me paged if you need me."

"I will. I promise."

Ashley sent her a wink and herded the prospective new father from the room, leaving Esther to breathe on her own.

The phone rang next to the bed. Maneuvering her IV, she snatched up the receiver. "Hello?"

Minnie's voice groused over the line. "He wouldn't go to sleep without saying good night to you."

"Put him on."

"Mommy?"

Esther's heart soared at the sound of her four-year-old son's voice.

"Yes, baby. I'm so glad you called."

"Is Hannah here yet?"

"Not yet, but soon. Probably by the time you wake up tomorrow, you'll have a little sister. Won't that be fun?"

"Yes."

"Okay, I want you to go to bed now. I love you."

"I love you, too. Night."

Shortly after she and Tom married, Karen had called, needing a foster home for the child. Afraid to risk her heart again, Esther's initial response was to decline. But after prayer, she and Tom both felt the Lord's leading to take Jason into their home. God worked out the circumstances, and within a year plans were in progress to adopt the child of her heart.

She felt a tightening in her abdomen, accompanied by the telltale pain of labor—bearable, but stronger than before. Closing her eyes until the contraction ended, she concentrated on breathing. It wouldn't be long now before this child joined their family. A miracle. She and Tom had decided God's perfect plan was for them to adopt Jason and be content with raising one child together. But God had other ideas.

Before Jason's adoption was even final, she'd discovered she was pregnant.

The pregnancy went off without a hitch, and now they were down to the final stage.

One thing she'd learned in the last two years was that her course truly wasn't hers to set—that God had a perfect plan, a purpose, and timing.

Eight hours later, as she lay nursing her beautiful baby daughter, she knew without a doubt that God's timing had produced a life for her that all her struggle and manipulation never could have.

She glanced to the vinyl chair next to the bed and smiled at Tom, whose chest rose and fell in light sleep. As if summoned by her perusal, he opened his eyes and gave her a lazy smile. "Are you okay?" he asked, his voice husky from sleep.

"Wonderful. Go back to sleep."

"Love you," he mumbled even as his eyelids drifted downward once again.

"Love you, too," she whispered.

She leaned back against her pillow and closed her eyes. Contentment eased through her exhaustion, and she smiled. God had made all of her dreams a reality. In His time.

TRACEY V. BATEMAN

Tracey lives in Missouri with her husband and their four children. She sings on her church's worship team and writes full time through the week. Grateful for God's many blessings, she believes she is living proof that "all things are possible to them that believe," and she happily encourages anyone who will listen to dream big and see where God will take them.

FAITH CAME LATE

LATE

Freda Chrisman

*Dedicated to the memory
of our precious grandson
Josiah Daniel Chrisman
1981–1989*

Chapter 1

Y ou. . .you menace!" she shouted. "Are you blind?"

Ignoring other Kansas City shoppers, Julie Richmond bent down to collect her parcels strewn on the street.

"No, miss," he said, "I have good vision. Now if—"

"I have news for you, *mister;* you need glasses!"

"Miss, if you'll calm down and let me drive my car to the curb, I'll help you," he pleaded.

"Go on! You've done enough for me."

Uttering a disgruntled objection, the man retrieved a sack lying just under his silver sports car.

"Please, miss, we're blocking traffic. Let me—"

"*You're* blocking traffic! I am trying to recoup after almost being knocked down by a crazy driver!"

"I beg your pardon, miss. You shouldn't have stepped off the curb without checking to your left. The light changed; I had the right-of-way," he reasoned.

Anger consumed Julie's fatigue. *Another self-righteous male!* She dropped the last package into her shopping bag, got to her feet, and her eyes traveled way up to look at the man in front of her. He was not only a menace, he was gargantuan! Unusually tan for the month of May, he had black hair and penetrating brown eyes.

"Well," she spat, "what are you waiting for? Get in your car and stop blocking traffic!"

"I can't leave until I'm sure you're all right."

"Of course I'm 'all right.' Can't you see?"

The man gave her a slow grin. "You look great to me."

Julie's face burned. Clustering around them, a small crowd listened to their heated conversation. Some even chuckled at his remark. He added a final affront.

"May I take you wherever you're going? You may be more shaken up than you realize."

Julie took charge. "No, thank you! I'm perfectly capable of deciding if I need help, and I don't. Move your car, and the sideshow will be over."

She lifted her chin, saw the light was in her favor, and crossed the street with what dignity he had left her.

MISSOURI

❧

Her shopping done, Julie reached home an hour later. She heard them as soon as she got out of her car. What now? The house was well-constructed, like most of those built back in the thirties, but no house could completely muffle Sid and Ethel Richmond's arguments. Mentally turning off her parents' enraged voices, she went inside.

Never, never would it happen to her, she vowed, as she slipped up the stairs. Marriage was a joke as far as Julie was concerned. Her parents hadn't celebrated a single day of nonaggression in her memory. And they weren't the only ones. Most couples she knew had lousy relationships. They traded dirty slurs, cut each other down in public, cheated on their marriage, or all of the above.

In her room, Julie threw her carryall on the bed. Then, tossing back her long hair, she hung up her jacket.

"Hi, Julie. Did you just get home?"

It was Colleen, the baby of the family. She was graduating from Kinner High this month.

"Yeah, honey, and I have something for you."

Julie pulled a parchment sack from the carryall and, out of it, a pink velvet box. Glass shattered against the wall in the next room, and Colleen's eyes filled with tears. Julie frowned. Colleen usually got home about four o'clock. No doubt she'd heard the whole malignant session from the beginning.

"Forget them, Colleen. Close your mind. That's what I do. Here," Julie said handing her the box. "This will make you feel better."

Colleen's gift was an opal pendant in a gold filigree setting. They'd seen it in the window of Vontell's Jewelry, and Julie promised it to Colleen if she made valedictorian.

"Oh, Julie," her sister gasped as she opened the box, "it's the prettiest thing I've ever owned. Thank you!" She started to hug Julie, but raucous sounds erupted again, and Colleen's face clouded. "I wish they wouldn't ruin every evening, especially this one."

"Speak for yourself, kiddo. My evening's fine. I don't let them get to me the way you do. Neither does Lisa."

"Oh, Lisa! She's never home long enough to let them bother her. If she's not out with her boss, she's dating Curt when he's in town." Colleen sighed. "Curt's through with his tests at Washington U. He'll be home anytime."

Julie noticed Colleen's softened voice. "That's another thing that shouldn't worry you. Curtis Graham is Lisa's emergency kit, a fill-in when no one else is available."

"I'm not so sure about that. Curt's been home a lot lately. You remember his sister, Rosemary? She works in TWA reservations and gets a discount for him."

"Lucky guy!"

Julie regretted her offhand remark. The reason Curt came home so often was to see Lisa. But Colleen was deep in her thoughts.

"Rosemary says this was a hard year for Curt. I don't think the Grahams approve of all his dates with Lisa. They think he should study more when he's home. It's not his fault, though. She's the one who insists on going out. He'll be a great doctor if she'll stop getting in his way."

"Has it occurred to you that letting Lisa interrupt his study schedule speaks badly for his commitment to medicine?" Julie asked. "If he didn't fly home so often, he'd have more time to study."

Colleen looked away. "I don't mean to hurt your feelings, Julie, but you don't give any man the benefit of the doubt."

"I'm not hurt, and you're right. I've never met a man I felt I could really trust. Added to that, they're reckless, discourteous, and uninteresting."

Colleen's face flushed. "Maybe if you weren't assistant principal of a girls school. . ."

"Don't be embarrassed, honey. I understand what you're saying." She broke into a sing-song lilt. "You think my selection of men is limited by my job and that I'm a prejudiced woman who wouldn't recognize an interesting man if I saw one."

"I don't think that, Julie," Colleen returned softly.

Now she'd hurt her feelings. Julie hadn't meant to sound so cynical. Taking the pink box from Colleen's hand, she shared her latest frustration.

"I did meet a man. Today. He almost killed me with his car, the big oaf. He met the exact criteria I mentioned before."

Oddly, Colleen's face brightened as Julie's bleak criticism went on.

"I was crossing the street, going back to my car. When I stepped off the curb, out of nowhere came this *mutant* in his silly-looking sports car." Colleen was still smiling, but Julie was done. "Now turn around, and I'll put your necklace on you. Since the free-for-all next door has run out, let's enjoy a moment of peace. Are you excited about graduation?"

A smile lingered on Colleen's face, and Julie wondered why she was intimidated by it.

❧

Withering glares and bitter jibes charged the air between Sid and Ethel at dinner. Unnoticed by either of them, Colleen's hands shook as she ate. Their parents, day by day, gnawed at Colleen's self-esteem in spite of Julie's efforts to thwart them. Julie wished Lisa were there now. She always missed the choice battles. But there was a reason she did: She planned her days to avoid them.

When Sid was home from his territory, Lisa ate out with Leonard Sherry, her boss. Then they went back to work late at the office. He was the senior partner of Sherry and Winwood, Attorneys at Law. By the time she got home that evening, dinner would be over, the Richmonds would have quarreled themselves out, and Lisa wouldn't be expected at work until noon tomorrow.

"I see Lisa's taking dinner with the old man again," Sid Richmond observed, chewing as he talked.

Ethel shot him a frigid glance. "It's obvious, isn't it? She's not here. And why shouldn't she go out to dinner with Mr. Sherry? She'll have a steak."

If you'd called me, we could be eating steak, too, Mother, thought Julie. No matter, dinner would have been just as bad. Her mother was not a good cook. She didn't even like to cook. Julie wondered how Ethel could prepare meals for nearly thirty years and still put together a dinner as tasteless as the one they were eating. Everything was overcooked, except the meat loaf. It was a culinary disaster.

Julie searched for a safe subject. "How did your sales meeting go today Dad?"

Ethel snorted, and Colleen ducked her head to fork a piece of limp broccoli.

"Oh, those idiots came up with an agenda straight out of a comic book. If they'd let me handle those meetings, I'd show those college boys the *right* way to sell feed supplements."

"Go ahead, genius, tell us some of your big ideas," Ethel challenged with a smirk.

"Mother, please," started Colleen.

Julie rescued her. "Let's not quarrel, folks. The family's together, except for Lisa, of course. But we should make it a pleasant time. You know what the dietians say: Food digests better in a calm atmosphere."

Ethel sighed and rolled her eyes. "Not another lecture from the professor, I hope."

"No, Mother, I'm trying to promote a quiet conversation," she explained, maneuvering her potatoes away from the grease oozing out of her meat loaf. "We've all been busy today, and it's time to relax."

Colleen looked at Julie and smiled, but neither Sid nor Ethel was ready to call a truce. The malicious contest continued until dishes of lumpy pudding unmercifully ended the meal.

❧

Julie heard Colleen's door close. She put on an emerald satin robe over her gown and swept down the hall, brushing her hair dry. As she suspected, Colleen was stretched out across her bed, crying.

"Honey, honey, don't let them upset you," Julie cooed, dropping her brush to pull Colleen into her arms.

Clinging to her, Colleen sobbed, "It wasn't another quarrel. Curt came by to see Lisa. He just got in town. Julie, he hardly looked at me." Another shudder of tears.

"Honey, there must be guys at Kinner as good-looking and interesting as Curtis Graham," Julie consoled, stroking her sister's back.

"Not to me. Don't talk like I'm a baby, Julie. You know Curt's the only one I'll ever love."

Julie leaned back and eyed her sister. "How did the two of us ever wind up in the same family? You can think of nothing better than having a man in love with you, and I can think of nothing worse. An evening out to dinner and a concert or the theater is nice, but give me mine with a stalwart soul who bids me good night and *leaves*!"

"But you're twenty-seven," Colleen lamented. "Don't you ever let a man you go out with kiss you good night?"

"Sometimes I can't avoid it. After that, I'm busy the next times he calls."

"But you'll never get married if you keep that up," Colleen whimpered, and she cuddled in Julie's arms again. "You'll be an old maid."

"Bingo! I think you've got the picture. This lady will die happy, with her books and her travels and the best clothes she can put in her closet. Not everyone has to have a man to be happy!"

By bedtime, Julie had pumped up Colleen's spirits to the stage of all-out laughter. She'd done it before—lots. She could usually promote a cheerful atmosphere for everyone except her parents. They were impossible.

In her youth, she had wondered why the couple ever married. Now, she ignored the savagery and tried to create a healthier climate for Lisa and, especially, for Colleen. It was what kept her living at home. Because of her mother's frequent swings into irrationality and her father's chronic absence from duty, Julie was the backbone of the family.

Good old dependable Julie. She'd overheard that description of herself last week. Twenty-seven wasn't old, was it? And she was in good shape; she worked out at the school gym every day. She looked at her picture; the yearbook committee had presented one to each faculty member. Actually, it wasn't too bad.

Her skin looked healthy. Her hazel eyes were clear, although she thought their dark lashes and brows made them look too large. Still, her heavy chestnut hair was an asset, her nose wasn't bad, and her lips were not thin like an old maid's were supposed to be.

What the picture didn't show was her height. She was five-foot-seven. Not petite or beautiful like Lisa, she looked to a wide-open future based on intelligence and determination.

Five years before, Julie had taken her master's at Missouri University in Columbia. Breaking away had not been easy. The Richmonds objected only because they wanted her home, bringing in another paycheck. They'd miss her rent money. To Julie, a master's degree was essential, so she stood her ground.

At M.U. she held down an office job and studied harder than she ever had in her life. She made friends, loved the school, and regretted having to come home. Yet, in her two years at Pennington—"A Private School for Young Ladies," the brochures said—she'd grown to love her job as vice-principal.

Julie sat on the bed she had turned back and stacked pillows behind her. She opened her briefcase and, with reading glasses in place, spread a stack of student evaluations on the bed.

MISSOURI

Amelia Stewart—she was the first problem. Her teachers had given up on her. In the office she'd heard Miss Clay, her current instructor, commiserating with the teacher Amelia would have in the fall. It was not a happy conversation, hence the evaluation by Julie.

She opened the folder. Amelia Stewart was eight, and she came from a single-parent home. In those cases the source of trouble was sometimes apparent. But Amelia was a minister's daughter. Julie frowned. Well, no one was exempt when a child had problems. He might even be part of it.

A soft tap drew her attention to the door, and Lisa stepped inside. Her sister's navy blue suit emphasized a shapely figure and the sparkling blue of her eyes.

"Still working your fingers to the bone for the little monsters, I see. Must be a martyr complex."

"No, not at all. It's a pleasure." Julie placed Amelia's folder on top of the others, stacked them aside, and took off her glasses. "How did your evening go?"

Lisa glanced quickly at her. Satisfied the remark was not sarcasm, she sat on the end of the bed and slipped out of her pumps.

"We're getting together the last of a brief. It's always a race to the finish. Leonard goes to court on Monday." She ran her fingers through coppery hair. "How was it here? Did they take a night off?"

"Afraid not. Colleen was upset as usual. I picked up her necklace at the jewelry store. It turned out to be a good evening to give it to her."

"Did she like it?"

"She loved it," answered Julie.

Lisa leaned back on an elbow. "I suppose I'd better find something to give her. I haven't had time to think about it."

Julie wondered if Lisa planned to give Colleen anything at all; she'd only had eighteen years to think about it. But she gave her the benefit of the doubt. *You see, Colleen, I can do it when it makes sense,* she thought.

"Colleen needs to know she's loved, Lisa. A nice gift from you would help."

"You're right. She doesn't get much attention from the folks. What do they think about the scholarship to Lindenwood?"

"I haven't been in on the results. I've only heard the arguments, at full volume. When they ask her about it, Colleens swears she won't know until commencement night."

"Is it true?"

"No, the deed is done; Mom and Dad simply have to accept it," Julie replied. "Colleen's trying to hold off the explosion while Mother tries to persuade *her* she's not capable of living apart from the family. It's a replay of my university days and just as twisted."

"I suppose she probably will leave. But I don't think she'll make it out in the big cruel world either." Lisa lay back and stretched her arms above her head. "You wait and see; she'll be back before Christmas. I can get her a job at the office right now. She'll start as a typist, and they'll let her come back when she drops out of school."

"Oh, Lisa, don't even mention that to her. She already has a summer job at the branch library. Remember? She won't make as much as she would at your office, but she got the job on her own; and it's enough to buy some nice clothes to take with her. By fall I hope she'll look forward to leaving. I've already got her luggage. I plan to give it to her at the last minute to build confidence."

Lisa jumped to her feet, her eyes blazing with anger.

"I knew you'd do something like that—give her an expensive gift she'd be embarrassed not to use! And you'll make sure she stays there, won't you? Lindenwood is only a short commute from Curt's school. Don't you think I know she's crazy about him? Well, she can't have him; he's mine!"

Julie stood up, too. "I thought you liked older men—Leonard Sherry, for instance."

"I may end up with Len, but until I make up my mind, Curt is my property."

"Lisa, you can't own or manipulate people to suit yourself. You'll break Colleen's heart, and, if Mr. Sherry does propose, you'll throw Curt away."

Lisa's face flushed. "I have a right to make up my own mind!" A frown creased her forehead. "Be honest, Julie. Do you think a popular, handsome guy like Curt Graham could ever fall for a *chunk* like Colleen?"

"Surely you don't look down on her because of a few pounds?"

Lisa picked up her shoes and smiled into the mirror on Julie's dresser.

"I'm realistic," she said.

"Then be realistic enough to have some feeling for her. You're the fashion expert. Forget the competition and give her some tips on her appearance before she goes to school."

"A compliment! I'm thrilled! The god of us all has condescended to let someone else help her manage the family."

"That's a hateful thing to say. I don't manage the family; I try to keep a little harmony going. Stop thinking of yourself, Lisa, and help me."

Giving Julie an icy stare, Lisa crossed the room, yanked open the door, and slammed it behind her.

Chapter 2

Ethel was in a temper because Sid wasn't in town for Colleen's commencement. Appeasing her was impossible, so Julie retreated to her room to dress. Choosing an amber lightweight suit, she piled her hair on top of her head and added green earrings the shade of her eyes. Then, bracing herself, she returned to check on her mother's progress.

At the mirror, Ethel clutched and yanked at her shapeless attire. "I should stay at home!" she declared. Then, with unique logic, she added, "If her own father doesn't care enough to attend Colleen's graduation, why should I? I'll be the only one going alone."

"You'll hardly be alone, Mother. Lisa and I are taking you."

"It's not your responsibility to take me. Sid's supposed to take me. He's never around when I need him. I have to do it *all*."

Lisa appeared in the doorway. "I'm ready to go. I wore this outfit to the office today, but it still looks fresh; and it's almost new," she said, smoothing the sapphire pleats of her skirt with an approving look.

Glad Lisa was on time, Julie picked up her purse to leave. She was ready for a change of scenery. Her mother's clothes were shabby, but there was nothing Julie could do. She had offered to buy her a new dress, but Ethel refused. She'd wait until something more important than a high school graduation came along, she said. Julie hoped Colleen wasn't embarrassed. It was such a special night for her.

"Well, I'm ready. Come on! Let's get through this stupid kiddie exercise," Ethel ordered.

Sharing a look of resignation, Julie and Lisa followed their mother's heavy-footed exit from the house.

❧

Traffic was snarled around the high school, but Julie found a parking space not far from the auditorium. Even though they were early—Julie had seen to that—seats close to the stage were taken.

"Lisa, these seats are terrible," Ethel complained as soon as they sat down. "Go find some better ones. I doubt if they're all gone."

"I'm sure they are, but I'll check."

Julie knew Lisa didn't mind the attention she would get strolling down the aisle, even though, clearly, there were no empty seats. She was back in seconds, unsuccessful in her search but followed by Curtis Graham. Lisa gave Julie a smug look.

"Look who I found! Some of his friends talked Curt into coming, but he looked so bored I asked him to come back and sit with us. Here, Curt." Lisa patted the chair next to hers. "There's an extra seat right here."

Julie heard: *Here, Prince! Sit!*

Curt spoke to Julie and her mother. Then his fascinated gaze locked on Lisa again.

On stage, faculty and guest speakers filed in as the band struck up the processional. Their eyes straight ahead, Colleen and her classmates marched down the center aisle. With two other students she mounted steps to the stage and now sat facing them. Lisa and Curt were whispering together, ignoring the program. Julie held her breath and hoped Colleen wouldn't look in their direction.

The crowd quieted, and Principal Dayton announced the invocation by Reverend Alex Stewart. Julie's eyes shifted from Colleen to the tall man approaching the podium.

Reverend Alex Stewart? It was the man who had nearly run her down! Could he possibly be? No! He couldn't be Amelia Stewart's father! Nevertheless, Amelia's father *was* a minister.

Julie thought about the conference she had asked the secretary to schedule with him. Amelia's evaluation made it necessary; she'd probably need summer tutoring. But her request was made before their downtown confrontation on the street.

Remorse enveloped her. Never should she have allowed herself to get caught in such a position. She'd lost her temper and made a fool of herself before the parent of one of her students. Now, here in the auditorium, waiting for Colleen's valedictory speech, the episode seemed foolish. Julie gripped her hands and bowed her head as the *Reverend* requested, but she was hardly ready for prayer.

To her relief the tall man sat back down, and she focused full attention on the speaker. Seconds later she gave Alex Stewart a quick glance. He had zeroed in on their row and on her in particular. The slow grin she remembered was there again, and Julie felt her face burn. Lisa noticed her discomfort and jabbed her in the ribs.

"What's wrong with you?"

"Nothing!" Julie shot back.

"We'll talk later."

Irritated again, Ethel hissed, "Be quiet!"

Lisa paid no attention. "Later, I said."

Julie nodded and looked at her program. Colleen's speech followed ten minutes later, and Julie was in control again. She'd worry about Alex Stewart another time.

Colleen was nervous, yet she presented her speech well; and Julie was proud of her. Her rapt attention to the speaker was bound to signal the obvious for the minister, but Julie didn't care. How could she hold back smiles and applause when she was so proud of Colleen?

So focused

Following the ceremony Julie had no problem making a fast getaway. Ethel wasn't interested in socializing. Curt hurried Lisa out, so Colleen had little chance to see them together. She was invited, with other seniors, to celebrate the awards and scholarships they were presented. Since he'd come to the school, Principal Dayton and his wife entertained these groups annually.

So focused was Julie on getting her mother through the crowd, she glanced sideways at Ethel a second too long and ran full tilt into Alex Stewart. Overcome with frustration and embarrassment, she sat down hard.

"Ughh! Ah. . .excuse me," she muttered, not looking at him.

Her purse opened as she fell, and he bent down to help her retrieve its contents. Ethel, scolding, hovered in the background as people asked Julie if she was hurt. She was conscious of only one speaker.

"We've got to stop meeting like this," Alex Stewart said under his breath.

The silly remark brought Julie to her senses. How dare he be so cavalier! Duty or no duty, she had a consuming desire to forget school procedure and cancel the scheduled conference on the spot.

Dropping the lipstick and comb he handed her into her purse, she ignored his outstretched hand to help her rise, though she chided herself for wearing such a narrow skirt.

Once on her feet she reached for Ethel's arm.

"Let's go, Mother," she said, without glancing at Alex.

Julie heard a soft chuckle as she turned away.

Alex Stewart's eyes followed Julie until she disappeared into the crowd. It was the first time he'd even noticed a girl since Christi's death. Was God trying to tell him something by letting him meet her again?

When she stepped in front of his car that day, he thought he had injured her, and his heart almost stopped. Later, learning she was all right, he was euphoric with the possibility of getting to know her. In her anger she hardly tolerated him.

But, the next day, he took Amelia to school and saw the same girl get out of her car and rush up the steps at Pennington.

"Amelia," he asked as she snapped her tiny plastic purse, "who is that lady?"

The child stopped her move toward a good-bye kiss. "That's Miss Richmond, Daddy. Isn't she beautiful? I wish she was my mommy. You could marry her, you know. I really love her, and I pray for her every night."

He was taken aback and didn't answer right away. "You have to be patient and wait for things to happen, Amelia. God might not think she's the right person for me to marry."

FAITH CAME LATE

She crossed her ankles, clasped her hands in her lap, and stared straight ahead.

"I guess you're too busy to get a mother for me, aren't you?" she asked with a frown.

"No, it isn't that I'm too busy. God hasn't sent anyone yet," he replied, wondering what she was thinking.

"Sometimes you have to make things happen. You just haven't learned how to do it."

Alex laughed, but Amelia's voice had a hardness that made him uncomfortable for a moment. Feeling ridiculous, he dismissed the thought.

Tonight at the auditorium they had *collided* again. He'd found out her first name was Julie from the secretary who called about an appointment. He would be busy that day and was thinking of canceling. But now that he'd had a better look, he was eager for their little conference. He'd enjoy hearing how terrific his daughter was from Miss Julie Richmond.

⊗

Colleen's usually dull, golden eyes shone as she burst into Julie's room after the party.

"Oh, Julie, we had the best time! Mr. and Mrs. Dayton live in a lovely home, and they're so happy. They say 'dear' and 'sweetheart' when they talk to each other, and they touch hands and smile all the time. It was like heaven. I didn't know a couple could be as happy as they are."

Julie's heart tightened at the poignant longing in Colleen's voice. Decorations and refreshments were secondary. It was the tranquil marriage that impressed her.

"I was proud of you tonight. I knew you were nervous, but you carried off your speech like a pro."

"How did Mother take the presentation of my scholarship?"

Sitting on the bed, Julie laughed softly. "She choked and swallowed hard for a few minutes, but she pulled through just enough to complain about Dad all the way home."

"And you had to listen." Colleen kissed her sister's forehead. "Poor Julie."

She didn't include Lisa. Julie hoped Colleen's leaving would be the key to a new life for her. Tonight, though she'd probably seen Lisa with Curt, it had taken a routine circumstance—the example of a happy home—to charge her sister with excitement and joy.

⊗

Colleen and her mother were both in bed when Lisa got home. In the kitchen, Julie was warming a mug of milk to help her sleep and forget a tension-filled day and night. When Lisa didn't speak, Julie glanced up at her. Lisa's lovely face was void of color.

"What's wrong?" said Julie as she put down her cup. "You look like you've seen a ghost."

"I wish I had. I could handle that."

Julie pulled out a high stool at the breakfast bar. "Come and sit down before you fall down."

The dark blue of her eyes riveting, Lisa turned to Julie, who perched on a stool beside her.

"A while ago," Lisa said with difficulty, "I saw Dad with another woman."

"Lisa—"

"It's true. Curt saw them, too. They were getting into his car, and, believe me, it's not a mistake. They were together, laughing and enjoying themselves." Tears dropped from her eyes.

Julie felt a suffocating closeness. "But if you saw them for only a moment, you can't be sure."

"We followed them. They went to an apartment house on the south side, and they went in."

"Oh, Lisa." Julie slipped off the stool and wrapped Lisa's trembling body in her arms.

Dad would pull something like this, thought Julie. *It's not enough that our lives are complicated already.* She was furious, too furious to cry.

Lisa reached for a paper napkin to wipe her tears. "I know he's not much," she said, "but he's my father, and I can't hate him. I'm confused. I don't know what to do or say."

Julie's eyes were dry.

"What are we going to do?" Lisa asked.

"Nothing. We're going to let this ride until we know more. Mother and Colleen couldn't take it. I need to think about it and decide what our options are."

Lisa pulled away. "So, once again, it's Julie to the rescue! I find out about it, and *you're* going to handle it." Lisa crushed the napkin into a ball.

"All right, *you* handle it! *You* take the responsibility. What are you going to do first?"

Julie could see Lisa shrinking into herself. It was a situation she knew only as a lawyer's secretary, not as a personal problem.

"I don't know." Tears shone in Lisa's eyes again. "I'm sorry I said that, Julie. The legal side of separation and divorce is where I dabble." She gripped Julie's arm. "What if he's on his way out? What if he deserts Mother?"

"I suppose we'll cross that bridge when we come to it." Julie pressed her fingertips to her temples. "For now, let's get to bed before someone overhears us."

"How can you think of sleep at a time like this?" Lisa grumbled.

"I doubt I'll sleep any more than you will. The point is, we both need to calm down and see if any ideas come to mind."

Julie sounded a lot more optimistic than she felt.

⌘

Neither Julie nor Lisa slept. Julie noticed Lisa's swollen eyes and hoped hers didn't look worse.

Ethel served her usual inedible breakfast of greasy eggs and bacon, and both girls made a show of eating. At Julie's school there would be coffee and rolls for the staff, and she could disappear to work on the summer schedule. Lisa would do even better. Len Sherry, her boss, would order food sent in if Lisa even hinted she was hungry.

"How do you feel this morning, Mother?" Julie inquired and got a *Must you ask?* look from Lisa.

Ethel proceeded to tell all. "Miserable. Absolutely miserable. What with your father out of town, and worrying about Lisa getting in, I didn't sleep a wink." She would have continued, but Lisa cut her off.

"Maybe you can rest today," she suggested, glancing at Julie. "Is Dad coming in early?"

Ethel's laugh was sardonic. "Who can tell? If he happens to call, I'll know then. Otherwise, I'll expect the dear boy when I see him."

Ignoring the sarcasm, Julie asked, "After you've rested, Mother, why don't you make something special to welcome him home? Maybe you could make shortcake for strawberries. That's Dad's favorite dessert, and the berries are so nice this year. Colleen said they had a strawberry torte at the Daytons' last night."

"So that's what they served at their la-di-da party? Well, I'm not impressed. And I don't feel well enough to baby your father," said Ethel.

Julie tried again. "If you should decide on the shortcake after you rest, call me, and I'll bring the berries and whipping cream. Lisa, you'll be home for dinner, won't you?" she said, a slight threat in her voice.

Lisa obviously got the point. "Yes, I'll be here," she answered without enthusiasm.

"One of you go to the stairs and yell at Colleen," ordered Ethel. "Graduating doesn't mean she can sleep till noon. If she can't get down when the rest of us eat, she can make her own. She can wash the dishes, too. She'll be Little Miss High-Hat after getting that scholarship. Can't have that!"

❦

Julie knocked on Colleen's door and heard her sleepy answer. She opened the door.

"Wow, do you look nice!" said Colleen, sitting up in bed.

Julie was satisfied. She had decided on a royal blue blouse and skirt for the conference with Alex Stewart. Colleen's approval gave her confidence, and she thought how the same color would perk up her sister's drab wardrobe. Her mother wouldn't approve; Ethel thought Colleen too heavy to wear bright colors.

"You won't believe it, but I have a conference today with the man who nearly ran me down," said Julie.

"I *don't* believe it. How come?"

"His daughter is a student at Pennington. She has some disciplinary problems, and she was assigned to me for evaluation and tutoring, if necessary."

"Do you think he'll remember you?"

"I'm sure of it. Last night I plowed right into him at your commencement and fell with the grace of a giraffe. When he sees me, he'll remember," Julie said with a dour look.

Colleen shook with laughter. "I knew it! I knew there would be consequences from that meeting. You were trying too hard to convince yourself he was bad news."

Julie's face flushed, and she yanked her sister's covers off. "Stop giggling and listen to me. Orders are that you get yourself downstairs at once."

Colleen's face sobered. "Is she in a bad mood?"

"When is she not? Get dressed and, for all our sakes, try to keep things peaceful when Dad gets home."

A frown foretold a question from Colleen, and Julie went out the door to avoid it. She wished she had time to explain; it wasn't fair to leave Colleen out. The truth was, she wanted to clear her mind. Duty called, and today she would joust with the dragon.

Chapter 3

Julie's appointment with Alex Stewart was for ten o'clock, and her nerves grew more unsettled as the hour approached. Why? She had dealt with the same situation a hundred times or more.

Picking up a stack of letters on her desk, her mind still meandering, she carried them to the file cabinet. Was she apprehensive because he was a minister? He certainly didn't act the way she thought a minister should, dashing around in his jaunty little sports car and flirting with unattached females.

Julie blinked her eyes and shook her head. Had she actually made a mental note of his car? And the flirting bit—how did that get in there? The only unattached female she knew he'd spoken to was her!

Deliberately, she switched thoughts to her father's escapade the night before. How would her mother react if she knew? Ethel was a spoiled child who never grew up. Even their home was a gift from her parents.

Sid Richmond's upbringing was in stark contrast to Ethel's. He was his family's sole support after his father's death until two years before he married. Knowing about the house, he must have accepted Ethel's instability and left the rest to fate. But fate had been unkind, and her father had chosen an out.

The telephone buzzed. Julie answered, then cleared her desk and placed Amelia's folder before her. The door opened, and Nita, the secretary, stood calf-eyed, gazing up at Alex Stewart.

"Thank you, Nita," said Julie. "Would you bring coffee for us, please? Unless you'd rather have a cold drink?" she asked her guest.

"Coffee's fine, thank you." He smiled at Nita, who left with a rapturous look back at him.

Julie had not risen. It was meant to show him who was in charge. She nodded toward one of the chairs in front of her desk, and Alex Stewart sat down in the chair next to it. Julie's eyes lowered.

"Thank you for being so prompt," she said crisply.

"It was no hardship. My time is valuable, too."

Score one for you, thought Julie. No witticism today. That was good; they could get down to business. She opened the folder.

"I'm trying to understand why Amelia is having difficulty with the rules at Pennington. I'm not sure she's happy here."

"Is that what this is all about?" He sat back. "Because if it is, I'm getting a different story. She likes the school, and she tells me she loves you."

His declaration surprised Julie. Having talked alone with Amelia only twice, she hardly knew her. Why would Amelia tell her father she loved an assistant principal?

"That's puzzling," she said. "It seems she's playing a double role. Her disposition at Pennington is an unruly one."

"In what way?" he asked with a frown.

Julie took her time. "She talks back to her teachers, which encourages other students to do the same. Also, disruptions in her classroom take place on a regular basis."

"Are you saying she provokes trouble?"

Julie felt an explosion building and tempered her reply to defuse it.

"I realize this is upsetting for you, Mr. Stewart, but—"

"Please, call me Alex," he said, clearly trying to handle his feelings.

Nita brought the coffee, and Julie was spared addressing this threat to the reserved manner she'd assumed. When the girl left, Julie poured their coffee. He took it black as she did.

Continuing, she stated, "These incidents may be occurring because something is bothering Amelia inside. I hope, together, we can discover what it is."

"Yes, of course," murmured Alex.

He was distraught, and Julie had no explanation. Surely this was not unexpected; it was a conference after all. But his next words proved her wrong.

"You'll have to forgive me, Miss Richmond. I'm trying to deal with what you've told me. I love my daughter very much. It's impossible to think of her as a troublemaker.

"My wife left me before Amelia really knew her. I've been both father and mother to her; however, we've always had a good housekeeper," he said as if defending the idea that a hired caregiver was enough.

"What is Amelia's attitude toward the housekeeper?"

"Good, and Mrs. Blake has no complaints either."

Julie felt she was getting nowhere. His attitude was more serious, but he was still aloof, covering up for Amelia's conduct. In any case, she had to forget the father and think of the child.

"Then it's obvious that since other areas of Amelia's life are in order, we need to focus on the problem at school. You say she loves school. On what do you base that?"

"She never tries to skip. In fact, she's enthusiastic."

"All right," Julie said, making a note. "You also said she loves me. How do you know that?"

Alex set his cup on a side table and leaned forward, his elbows on his knees. "She prays for you every night, and she wishes you were her mother."

Julie felt her face warm. She sipped her coffee to keep from looking at him. Being a player in this scenario was not in her plan. It was a few seconds before she found her voice.

"I can't explain her affections for me. Amelia and I haven't been together that much," she countered.

"Maybe not, but what you said or did impressed my daughter to an unusual degree. Since you know how she feels about you, perhaps you can come up with some ideas of your own to help."

Irritated by the suggestion, Julie remembered that their conference was supposed to be for his benefit. He had neatly reversed the roles, and she had to get back on track.

"I will certainly try; although, these things sometimes happen when changes occur in the home." Taking one of her cards from a porcelain box on her desk, she held it out to him. "If you think of anything that might cause Amelia's attitude problem, I'd appreciate your giving me a call."

Alex whipped out his business card. "And I'd appreciate it if you'd do the same."

Julie got up, trembling, and followed him to the door. When she could no longer hear his and Nita's voices, she went to a large window that overlooked the front of the building. Seconds later he strode down the front walk to a modest, late-model automobile. *No sports car today*, she thought. Was he trying to impress her with his down-to-earth persona?

No, that wasn't right. He didn't know she'd seen his car today. At that moment, he turned and waved up at her. Julie backed away from the window, her hands balled into fists.

Seething, she grabbed the coffee tray and carried it to the reception area. Nita took it, her eyes on Julie's face.

"What's wrong, Julie? Didn't it go well?"

"It did not go well! I may as well resolve Amelia Stewart's problem myself— her father certainly isn't any help."

Two teachers listened at the door to the copier room. One was Miss Clay, Amelia's teacher the past year.

"Did you say Amelia Stewart?" she asked. "What now?"

Julie paced up and down. "I just had a talk with *The Reverend* Alex Stewart, that is."

"You're lucky. I tried, but he was always covered up with appointments or meetings and couldn't come in. Maybe I should have brought my problems to you in the first place."

"No, thanks! I don't want them either. He's impossible!"

Julie's voice had risen, and Mrs. Larabee, their elderly principal, came out of her office.

"Ladies, please. Someone might hear," she cautioned. "May I ask who it is you're discussing?"

"Amelia Stewart's father, ma'am," supplied Julie.

"Oh, yes. A likeable man. A pastor, I believe."

"I'm afraid I don't find him a likeable man. His daughter has problems, and you felt I could work well with Amelia. Since meeting her father, I'm not sure I'm. . ."

"I'm sorry, my dear. I can't give you a choice. We must learn to adapt to difficult situations. Isn't that what we teach our young ladies?"

Julie nodded, and things fell in place. Mrs. Larabee spoke from years of experience, and, of course, she was right. Julie had to work with Alex if she intended to improve Amelia's deportment.

❧

A week later, Colleen, dressed in jeans and a sweatshirt, was curled up in an armchair, reading. The doorbell rang. She sauntered to the door finishing a paragraph, but when she saw the caller, she wished she'd hurried.

"Curt!"

"Hi, Colleen. Is Lisa home?" the husky blond man asked, looking toward the staircase with hope that was all too obvious.

"No, I'm sorry, she isn't. Would you like to come in and wait?" Regretting the invitation, she said, "Or maybe it would be better to sit in the swing out here." She motioned with her hand.

"I guess the battle lines are drawn since last week, huh?" Ashamed her parents' quarrels were common knowledge, Colleen looked away.

"I can wait awhile, I guess. I have to get back soon though." The swing creaked and swayed forward as he sat down.

"When the days are as nice as they have been this month, I guess it's hard to stay buried in your books all the time."

"Huh? Oh yeah. I have to make myself stay at it."

"You have classes this summer, too, don't you? That doesn't leave much time for girls."

"Right. But I want to see your sister before I leave."

Colleen had heard that Curt and Lisa were together on the night of her graduation, but that night was such a happy one she put them out of her mind. She'd wanted to believe graduation from high school would make Curt notice her. Nothing had changed. To him she was still gorgeous Lisa's plump, uninteresting sister. What did it matter that her IQ was higher than Curt's?

"I guess you're happy about the scholarship to Lindenwood, aren't you? You won't be far from Wash U," he said, obviously making conversation as he peered down the street.

Colleen used the question as an excuse to approach the swing. Grasping the chain, she stilled her quivering hands. She'd never think of sitting beside him unless he asked.

"Yes, it's a good college. I want to go as far as I can in school. Maybe even a doctorate. Look where Julie's master's landed her."

"She's got a cushy job all right. But so has Lisa," he added quickly.

"Lisa only went to business school."

"I believe in everyone doing his own thing. Four years at a regular college would have bored Lisa."

"I suppose so. She wouldn't have met Mr. Sherry either," she said with a hint that the older man was special to Lisa.

"No, and that would have been a real shame." He missed the innuendo. "Sherry has done a lot for Lisa."

Calling over her shoulder as she headed for the door, Colleen said she hoped he wouldn't have to wait too long. Inside, a sarcastic quarrel held sway in the kitchen, and she ran quietly up the stairs to her room.

Leaning against the closed door, she scrubbed at her eyes as she cried for long, anguished minutes. How could Curt be so blind? She loved him far more than Lisa did.

In less than three months she'd leave for Lindenwood, at St. Charles. As he'd said, she would be close to his school in St. Louis. A lot of good that would do; he couldn't even see her when they were face-to-face.

Nagging her memory was what Curt said about the battle lines being drawn *since last week*. What did he mean? Lisa knew, and if Lisa knew, so did Julie. Colleen wished for Julie. She needed a shoulder to cry on. And she needed to know what Curt was talking about.

❧

Amelia's problems might be related to her academic work, so Julie started with her reading skills. She had a library of books she'd like to introduce to the child, but they should focus on the right subject. Amelia would read what she was most interested in.

She called Alex's house to make an appointment for time with the little girl. Expecting the housekeeper to answer, she was surprised when Alex picked up the phone.

"This is Julie Richmond."

"I know," he said softly.

Julie felt the air getting thin. "I called to talk about Amelia's choice of literature, and to ask if I might spend some time with her next week."

"Spending time with her is a great idea, but I'm afraid I can't tell you what she likes to read. I don't see her reading anything except her lessons for Sunday school."

"Do you have to make her read those?"

"Not exactly. She knows they're required for her class. It's the scaled-down version of our Bible study."

"But she has no shelf of books in her room that she escapes to occasionally?"

"No. Should I go out and select some books for her?"

"I'd rather Amelia did that. I'd like to see her on Tuesday afternoon. Would it be convenient to drop her off at school around one o'clock?"

"Certainly. I appreciate this, Miss Richmond, and I apologize for being so unmovable at our first interview. It's hard for a parent to face any imperfection in his child."

"I understand. But the first consideration should be your daughter. Our personal feelings are not important."

His chuckle brought back the memory of her inelegant fall at the auditorium, and she caught herself, mouth open, ready to give him a stinging résumé of his character.

Once she was off the phone, Julie calmed down. Their conversation had told her a lot. Alex probably ignored all but the spiritual side of Amelia's needs. And what about her report cards? Didn't he look at them? He knew neither what she liked to read nor her ability or comprehension. On top of that, his offer to supply the child with reading material meant merely filling a bookshelf. Didn't he spend any time with her at all?

Julie put Amelia's folder in the file cabinet, wondering about her exposure to music and the other arts. Had she ever seen a play or a concert, or visited an art gallery or museum? She made up her mind. This summer, Amelia Stewart would be introduced to the world of the senses: sight, sound, touch, taste, and smell. Julie would make up for Alex's oversight.

❧

Amelia Stewart bounced up the walk below Julie's window, and her father watched her until she was in the building, out of his sight. This time he did not check her window, Julie noticed. His total attention was on his daughter.

In seconds, Amelia knocked on her office door. Julie answered with a smile and invited the tiny brunette in. Her resemblance to Alex was startling. Her nose had not yet taken on the straight line of her father's; but her lips were full like his, and the same smile danced in her brown eyes. Julie couldn't believe she had noticed that many features of the man.

Still smiling, Julie led Amelia to a tea table she had ready. When she learned of Julie's plan, Mrs. Larabee had loaned her the mahogany table and English bone china tea set usually found in a corner of the principal's office. She also sent along demitasse silver, an Irish-linen tablecloth, and spice tea Julie knew was a favorite at Pennington. Mrs. Larabee's consideration was a distinct privilege.

It was immediately apparent that Amelia needed work on table manners. Yet as she absorbed Julie's suggestions, she showed finesse even Mrs. Larabee would approve of. Later, Julie got to the purpose of the afternoon.

"Amelia, it's Pennington's goal that every girl be taught poise and grace that will stay with her all her life." She explained both words to Amelia and continued, "We spend time with girls during the summer helping them reach that goal. You and I will be doing that this year. I hope you will enjoy it as much as I plan to."

"Oh, I will, Miss Richmond. I know I will." Amelia's eyes passed over the dainty plates of party sandwiches and lemon cookies, and the graceful teapot with its thin cups and saucers. Folding her napkin and spreading her hands in an outward gesture, she said, "I've never done anything like this before, and it was so nice."

In her mind Julie heard Colleen voicing similar words. *Alex and I have the same problem,* she thought. *We have deprived young people in both our homes, and it's not any more his fault than it is mine.* It startled her that she'd seen his side.

Opening the glass doors of an oak bookcase, Julie brought out a colorful book about a girl who wanted to be the queen of her country. Along with royal functions she thought so grand, the girl learned that a queen had responsibilities that must be carried out whether she felt like it or not.

Amelia expressed her gratitude with wide eyes. "I'll take good care of this book. You wait and see."

"I know you will, honey."

Julie pulled Amelia to her and gave her a hug just as Alex opened the door gently to look inside. The tender look he gave her almost melted Julie's heart. Almost. She straightened her shoulders and lifted her chin.

"Look who's here, Amelia," said Miss Richmond.

Chapter 4

Her father would be in from his territory that night. Though learning her new job at the branch library, Colleen had not forgotten that Lisa and Julie were keeping something from her. When she got home from work, Lisa was in her room, and Julie came home shortly afterward.

Beckoning to Lisa, Colleen headed down the hall toward Julie's room. Lisa hung up the dress she was holding and joined her.

"Have you lost your voice?" she asked.

"No, I don't want Mother to hear," Colleen murmured.

Julie stepped out into the hall. "She's downstairs. What's all the whispering about?"

Colleen herded the other two into Julie's room. Painted a warm ivory highlighted with forest green, impudent touches of gold and hot pink spoke of a free spirit in residence.

Colleen sat on the floor, leaned back against the wall, and waited until she had the attention of the other two. With a deep breath, she plunged in.

"Curt said something he didn't mean to the other night, and I want to know what's going on with the folks."

Julie looked at Lisa, who shrugged and dropped down to sit on Julie's cedar chest. She told Colleen the whole story. Colleen felt like crying, but she didn't.

"I'd heard some talk. I didn't want to believe Dad could be unfaithful, so I told myself they were wrong," she said in a choked voice. "But deep in my heart, I knew."

"That was a big load for you to carry, honey. Why didn't you tell one of us?" asked Julie, moving to sit beside Colleen.

"I thought if I kept it to myself, he might stop, and I wouldn't have to tell."

"Wish for the moon, Colleen," Lisa muttered. "What incentive does he have to stop? I've thought about this, and I can almost forgive him for wanting someone to love him. Mother sure doesn't, or at least she's never shown it."

"I guess I don't show much love for either of them," Colleen confessed.

"That goes for all of us," said Julie. "But let's face it, they're a hard couple to love. They've taught me one thing, though. Either get married and keep working at it, or don't get married at all. As for me," she declared, "I choose the latter."

Now was not the time to argue. Colleen concentrated on the problem at hand.

"I guess my next question is, does Mother suspect anything, and are we going to tell her? I vote no."

"I don't have the nerve either," said Lisa.

A sound at the door caused all three to turn. Ethel, her face pale, stood staring straight ahead. Knowing she'd heard their conversation, Colleen rushed to her mother as she slid down along the doorframe in a faint. Julie helped lay her down, and Lisa dashed to the bathroom for a wet washcloth.

"Do you think she overheard us?" she asked, folding the cloth and pressing it to her mother's forehead.

"Every word," said Julie. "How could we be so cruel?"

Colleen heard regret in Julie's voice; she was the family conscience. She gave them more direction than their parents.

"I never dreamed she'd take it like this," Colleen murmured. "What should we do?"

No one answered. Lisa grabbed a bed pillow, and Colleen helped place it under her mother's head. Julie covered her with a fleece blanket from her cedar chest.

"Shouldn't we call an ambulance or a doctor?" Colleen asked.

Ethel moaned and muttered indistinct words. Colleen knelt and took her hand.

"Mother, it's Colleen. Are you all right?"

Ethel's eyes traveled from one to the other. Her face wore a dazed, then a bitter expression.

"So you all knew about it. Everyone but me." The bitter expression changed to one of self-pity. "Why am I being punished like this? Lisa, you say you understand Sid wanting someone to love him. What about me? I need love, too; instead, he made a fool of me with another woman."

Brittle silence enveloped the room. *No one knows what to say*, thought Colleen. Minutes passed with Ethel mumbling, sometimes incoherently. Julie asked if she wanted to sit up or lie on her bed, and Ethel ordered them to help her to her bedroom. She wanted to be alone, she said, and the girls left.

Casting a backward glance, Colleen wondered if their mother should be by herself.

"She wouldn't try to. . ." Colleen couldn't finish. "Would she?" she whispered.

"No," said Julie, "I think she's adjusting to the shock. I'll check on her in a little while, though."

Colleen tried to remember. Was anything in her parents' medicine chest lethal? Ethel was a hypochondriac; she might have several medications that could end her life. But would she have the nerve? As Julie said, probably not. Once her mother absorbed what she'd heard, she'd scream and shout, but then she'd think of something more appropriate, Colleen decided. She might even lock her wayward husband out of the house.

Lisa and Julie made for the front porch, and she followed. Lisa propped herself against the porch railing while the other two occupied the swing. Sounds of twilight surrounded them.

"We've forced ourselves into a corner," said Julie. "We have to come up with some sort of strategy."

"Dad's supposed to come in tonight. Shouldn't we hear his side of the story before he sees Mother?" asked Colleen.

"Do you honestly think he'd talk to us?"

"Wait, Lisa! She might have something," said Julie with enthusiasm. "There's going to be a blowup the minute he and Mother meet. Let's try pounding some sense into his head before he talks to her. Maybe he hasn't considered how this affects all of us. After all it's our home, too. Aren't we entitled to try to hold it together?"

Good, thought Colleen. Julie was for it. Talking to their father might not work, but it was worth a try.

❧

Sid did not show up that night at all. The next morning Ethel was so upset Lisa faked a headache, called Leonard Sherry, and took the day off. Assuring her one of them would waylay Sid before he clashed with Ethel, Julie dropped Colleen at the library on her way to Pennington.

At school, she checked her calendar to see which day of her busy week allowed time with Amelia. Regardless of the family situation, the child was her project for the next six weeks. Every day, except that afternoon, was full. She called the Stewart home, got permission from the housekeeper to take Amelia to a children's play, and picked her up a little after noon.

"Daddy said you'd call me, Miss Richmond," Amelia chattered as she pranced down the walk to the car. "But I was afraid it would be like when *he* says we'll go somewhere and we don't. You know what he did when I told him that? He got down on one knee beside me, real frowny, and said, 'Do I do that, my little girl?' and I almost cried."

Another score for Alex, thought Julie. Mrs. Blake was still at the front door, smiling and waving good-bye to Amelia. The housekeeper did love the child. No doubt she did her best, but she was not Amelia's mother or grandmother; and the disparity in their ages might inhibit real closeness.

❧

The afternoon went well. Amelia was delighted with the play and wanted to relive every scene.

"Wasn't it beautiful when all the trees bowed down to the boy and girl, and the fairy came out of the sky all sparkles?" she asked. "I think I know what I'd like to be when I grow up. An actress! Yes, that's what I want to be."

"Then you need to read all the books you can because books, called scripts, are what plays are made of," said Julie. "Also, it would be a good idea to try out for the school play next year. That would help you decide if you like performing."

Amelia's expression darkened, and Julie knew she had hit on something.

"I probably wouldn't get a part. Caroline Basset gets all the main parts," she said with a sour voice.

"But wouldn't you be satisfied with another part instead of the main one? Sometimes it's those characters people remember."

"No! If I can't have the main part, I don't want to be in the old play."

A big fat clue to her attitude, thought Julie. "Did you read the book I loaned you?" she asked, dismissing the play.

"Yes, Miss Richmond, and I liked it. May I borrow another one?" Amelia's face was sunny again.

Julie turned onto Vivion and parked at a Baskin-Robbins ice cream shop. Inside, she ordered two small dishes of sherbet. Above them hung a cluster of pink balloons, and the boy at the counter told Amelia she could have one when she left. The child thanked him and popped a spoonful of sherbet into her mouth as soon as she sat down.

"Oh, it's so good," Amelia commented, using her napkin and good manners. "You have the best ideas, Miss Richmond."

"I don't think sherbet will spoil your appetite for dinner. Mrs. Blake wouldn't like that, I'm afraid."

"She wouldn't care, and neither would Daddy. They never scold."

And so your classmates suffer because you're never told no at home, thought Julie. Could this angelic child, dressed in white lace stockings and a candy-striped dress be a tyrant? With no knowledge of how to be less than number one, she got her way at school by causing turmoil and manipulating her classmates. Likewise, if she couldn't be the star of the school play, she wouldn't try at all.

Back in the car, Amelia's pink balloon bounced above her head while she charmed Julie all the way home. The car Julie had seen Alex get into at the school was parked in the drive. As they pulled up, Alex came out of the house with an expression so serious Julie wondered if he was angry with her for taking Amelia to the play. Surely Mrs. Blake had cleared it with him when Julie called about picking her up.

He opened Amelia's door, gave her a kiss, and sent her away with her balloon. Amelia waved to Julie when she reached the stoop of the modest ranch-style home.

"Don't tell me I've kept her out too late?"

"No, Julie, and I want you to remember how grateful I am that you've taken time to be with my daughter."

As he got into the passenger seat beside her, Julie wondered why he had used her given name and why his mood was so grave.

"Wh–What is it?" she stammered.

Alex settled back and studied her face. "There was a fire near my church last night. A motel burned, and three people died. I was called, and as soon as I knew the church property was in no danger, I went over to see if I could help." Alex took her hand. "An hour ago, they made a positive identification of one of the men." With his other hand on her shoulder, he turned her to face him. "It was your father, Julie," he said gently.

His voice seemed to get farther and farther away. Was she going to faint? *No.* She couldn't; she had to pull herself together and find out more. She was trembling, but her voice was as firm as she could make it.

"Does my family know?"

"Not yet. They let me come here because I wanted to be the one to tell you. The police will be at your house any minute. If you'd like me to, I'll come around and drive you home to be with your family."

Julie wanted to be in control, but she was shaking so that any fool could see she was not. Then the worst thing in the world happened. Alex pulled her to him, and her defense against tears crumbled. As he held her, stoking her hair, comforting her with words he might use with Amelia, she cried for herself and Lisa and Colleen, and for their mother.

Chapter 5

Lisa had a real headache after spending all day with her mother. She wasn't harassed, but the fact that she wasn't caused the tension. Ethel consented to eat a light supper, and Lisa had taken it upstairs. She was coming down when, outside, she saw a man, at least six-foot-four, open the door of Julie's car and help her out. It was inconceivable. Julie was hanging onto a man! And a handsome one at that.

Then an even stranger thing occurred. A police car drew up to the curb. Julie, the man she was with, and two policemen spoke together for a moment, then all four walked toward the house.

As they neared the front door, Lisa's impish demeanor changed to one of fear. The man with Julie opened the screen door as Lisa made herself walk toward them.

"I'm Alex Stewart. I'm—"

"Excuse me, Alex," Julie said with an awkward movement of her hand. "This is my sister Lisa."

Alex remembered his manners. "Lisa, I'm glad to know you. These men are here on official business." But Alex's concern was for Julie. He walked her to the living room couch, still holding her hand. "Julie will be all right. She's had a shock, and I'm afraid it will be one for you."

When the policemen broke the news about her father, Lisa listened and started to cry, sending Julie to her side. Alex rose, too, but an older woman at the head of the stairs caught his attention. Her face reflected anger beyond reason.

"Who are you?" she snapped at Alex. "What's going on down there? Girls! What are these men doing here? And what have you done to Lisa, Julie? Why is she crying?"

Alex was baffled by the woman's attitude. Julie had cried all the way home, and her beautiful face was cheerless and swollen. The older woman, maybe even her mother, was castigating her before she even knew what had happened. The two officers stared at Alex as if he should be able to explain.

"My name is Reverend Alex Stewart. I'm a friend of Julie's," he said, addressing the woman on the stairs.

One of the officers spoke up, "These ladies have received some bad news, ma'am. Are you Mrs. Sidney Richmond?"

Ethel nodded. She tottered and seemed to lose strength. Alex leaped up the stairs to support her, but Ethel shrugged off his help. He followed her determined stride down the stairs.

"What happened?" she screeched at Julie. "Did he run off with that woman?"

Still trying to make sense of the mother's attitude and her scorching questions leveled at Julie, Alex intervened.

"Why don't you have a seat, Mrs. Richmond," he suggested. "These officers will give you the details you want."

"Such as?" she spat at the policemen.

Alex watched the woman's face as the facts were reiterated. Her mouth screwed up like that of an aged crone, and she crumpled into a chair, her face in her hands. Julie spoke gently to her, but Ethel waved her off and called Lisa's name. As Lisa put her arm around her, Julie stood back, embarrassed.

It's because we're here, thought Alex. He suspected this happened often but not in front of strangers. He wanted to hold Julie and comfort her, yet he doubted she'd allow it. Instead, he took her arm and guided her outside.

"Let's sit in the swing," he said stoutly, not giving her a chance to refuse.

Julie sank into the seat of the swing, her shoulders slumped. Alex's arm dropped to the back of the swing behind her, and she didn't object. The evening had cooled, and Alex wondered if she merely welcomed his warmth. They rocked back and forth, listening to the muffled voices of the officers, Ethel's wails of self-pity, and the plaintive pleas for calm by Lisa. Julie's head rested against Alex's arm, and he was surprised but happy it was there.

A small, plump teenager with a stack of books in her arms strode down the street and turned onto the walk. There was no mistaking the family resemblance. It was Julie's sister, who had given the valedictory speech at Kinner High.

"Julie?" The girl hurried up the steps and set her books on the porch railing. One fell off. "Julie, what's wrong? Why are you crying?"

Alex retrieved the book as the girl sat beside Julie. Her voice trembling, Julie introduced them. Colleen pulled her skirt aside so Alex could sit down again.

Once more, he watched a Richmond daughter cave in at the news. Yet Colleen seemed to be mature enough to take it, he noticed. Clinging to Julie, she made no move to go inside, though her mother's frequent outcries were heard. Some were against the dead man, and Alex remembered what he'd heard earlier.

It wasn't the only thing he questioned. Why would a man, even a salesman who traveled a lot, be in a motel so close to his home? Was there more truth to Ethel Richmond's accusations than the others wanted him to know? Not one had mentioned another woman.

❧

Ethel insisted on seeing Sid's body. She got as far as the police morgue before passing out. Alex had offered to go with Ethel and Julie, and Julie accepted, more thankful than she cared to admit. When Ethel was herself again, Alex took her back to the car to wait.

Julie signed the necessary documentation, then clung to Alex's arm, drawing from his strength, until she could escape the place. On the way home she distanced herself from him again to regain her confidence.

Ethel went up to her room at once. Julie thanked Alex and offered a half-hearted invitation to stay for coffee. He accepted. In the old-fashioned kitchen, somewhat redeemed by a partial face-lift of the cabinets, Julie filled the coffee-maker and joined Alex at the table to wait.

"I suppose you realize by now that my father was seeing another woman. In his defense, I have to tell you—my mother is not the easiest person in the world to live with."

"She was a little testy when I first met her," said Alex. "But why does she give such latitude to Lisa and none to you?"

Julie blushed when she realized he'd picked up on a fact she'd tried to rationalize since childhood. She gave him what was, to her, the only answer.

"Lisa is so beautiful it's difficult for anyone to deny her preeminence."

Alex snorted. "Wait a minute. Is it possible you think Lisa is more beautiful than you are?"

Julie swept him a derisive look. "Don't try to flatter me, Alex. I haven't lived in Lisa's shadow for twenty-one years without realizing that."

"Who did the judging? Your mother? Your father? Lisa? Somehow I don't think Colleen falls in the group. She probably thinks you're as pretty as I do."

The shield around Julie's heart dropped abruptly into place. She was too smart to fall prey to a few compliments. Look where she was now, and all because of a man. Everything she had worked for was in jeopardy; her father's scandal and manner of death could cause her immediate termination at socially conscious Pennington.

She had no idea what would happen to her mother. Ethel had teetered on the edge of, yes, *madness*, for years. With her unnatural exhibitions of temper, grudges followed by violent acts of revenge, and contempt for everyone except Lisa, she couldn't manage what had happened.

Julie realized she must be stronger than ever. She would hold them together, through the embarrassment, through the funeral, and through the beginning of life without Sid. They would survive.

Alex listened to the silence and knew he'd made a mistake.

If he wanted to remain close to her, he would have to go slow. Julie's independent self wouldn't be smothered, and she didn't trust men because of her parents' tragic marriage. He understood, but it saddened him. God had the answer to her doubts, but it would be a long time before she was ready to believe that.

❧

Two days after his death, Sid was buried. Ethel didn't care who officiated, and, knowing no other minister, Julie asked Alex to conduct the graveside service. The story was carried in the newspapers, but Ethel refused to have them in the house.

Julie didn't need reminding either.

The insurance company had no Sid Richmond on its books. Aghast, Julie asked Lisa to investigate; surely, it was a mistake. Lisa came home angrier than Julie had ever seen her.

"Do you want to know the meaning of *rat*? I'll tell you the meaning of rat! It's a father who cancels his life insurance without telling his family. Two years ago! Can you believe it? A hundred-thousand-dollar policy, and he cancels it! Who do you think he spent the payment money on?"

Julie couldn't speak. Nothing substantial would come from Sid's company. He had used up his savings plan. She might soon be jobless, Colleen would need help with college, and the house and cars had to be maintained. With his secret life her father had plundered their future security without a thought for his family.

After shopping for books to begin Amelia's own library, Julie dropped her off at the huge red-brick building that was Alex's church. From a side door, he waved her down, trotted out to her car, and opened her door.

"Can you come in for a few minutes? I need to talk to you."

Julie drove into the nearest parking slot, and Amelia gave her a hug and left for a children's choir rehearsal. Alex guided Julie through the church labyrinth to his office.

It was a pleasant room, full of light. With floor-to-ceiling bookshelves, green plants beside a row of file cabinets, a huge desk with a computer monitor to one side, the office looked organized and ready for business. Why had she hoped it would be messy?

Once they were in comfortable leather chairs opposite each other, Alex apologized. "I'm sorry I can't offer you coffee. My next appointment doesn't like the smell." He sat back and sighed. "I have something to tell you." Then looking into Julie's eyes, he said, "The woman who was with your father was badly burned and has been in the hospital since the fire. I went to see her, Julie. She wanted me to tell you she's sorry for everything that happened."

Seething with anger, Julie stood up. Like a toy soldier, she walked rigidly to a window looking out on the parking lot. Her voice would hardly obey her brain.

"You can tell me that after the torment my family has been through? After what we may all go through yet?" She whirled to face him. "How could you do that? Tell me, *please*!"

"She's a poor, lost soul, Julie," he said, moving toward her.

"Are we talking souls that go to heaven or hell, or are we talking slimy souls that rob a family of decency and. . .and feed on innocent victims?"

"We're talking souls Jesus Christ died for," Alex said calmly.

"Oh! Yes." Julie laughed. "I forgot. Here comes the commercial.

"No, I'm trying to explain my position. Please, Julie, try to understand

Regardless of what people do, Jesus loves them. My aim in life is to reach everyone I meet with that message. You may not believe it, or care, but that woman did ask His forgiveness, and she accepted Christ as her Savior."

"Thank you very much, I appreciate the sermon, good-bye."

Rushing to the door, Julie opened it to see the upraised hand of a tall, unpleasant-looking woman about to knock.

"Please, Julie, don't leave like this," Alex pleaded, not at an angle to see the visitor.

"Well, really, Dr. Stewart! I can see now why my appointment was dealt with so casually," the woman chided, glancing at her watch. "I was supposed to see you six minutes ago, and I've been waiting since."

Alex's face held such distress Julie felt avenged. *Let his reputation take a few hits,* she thought as she dashed out.

"Mrs. Biddle, please, be seated. I will be right with you."

He hurried after Julie, who couldn't, for the life of her, remember the door they'd entered. He caught up with her, grabbed her arm, and spun her around. She thumped against his chest.

"Now you listen to me, young lady," he demanded softly. "I'm a minister. You learned that shortly after we met. But ministers fall in love just like everyone else." He put his other arm around her and loosened his grip on the arm he held. "I think I'm falling in love with you, Julie," he finished.

Behind them, Mrs. Biddle gasped. "Well! This is too much! Forget my appointment, Dr. Stewart!" Her heels clicked down a hallway out of their hearing.

"Great PR, *Doctor*. Any more surprises up your sleeve? How about your wife? You said she left you, but I haven't heard anything about a divorce."

"My wife died, Julie. It's easier for me to say she left. As for the 'doctor' bit, it's an honorary degree. I don't use the title because I didn't work for it. Like you, I have a master's. Mrs. Biddle is one of the few who addresses me as doctor."

With so much coming at once, Julie lost track of the crux of their disagreement. She knew she must get away from Alex before something happened they would both be sorry for. She wasn't ready for his commitment. Not at all!

"I suppose I should thank you, but I wouldn't mean it. If you'll let me go, I'll try to find my way out of here before any more of your *parishioners* check up on you," Julie spat.

"You may think that's funny, but that particular lady has a penchant for telephoning. By tonight's meeting here, a lot of people will know that I was holding beautiful Julie Richmond in my arms today, *in the church*!

"That's unforgivable, eh?"

"To everyone but my Savior."

"No more sermons, Doc. I'm immune!" she said as she stepped away from him. "Tell Amelia I'll call when I can."

Julie went through the door he indicated finally, and the exit was straight ahead.

❧

In a private conversation, Mrs. Larabee told Julie she was given a leave of absence "to come to terms with your tragedy and to decide what is best for your career." It was a cold sentence, and Julie held little hope she would be invited back. As she left the school, she felt as lost as a child in a dark wood.

Her mother had no questions when Julie returned home an hour after she left. Ethel moved from room to room like a ghost with no interest in the day's happenings. She had listened docilely to Lisa's explanation of the insurance and the Social Security checks she was entitled to. But as long as there was food to eat and her bed was available, Ethel cared about nothing else. Julie and her sisters worried that her mind was slipping away.

Not having seen or spoken to Amelia since shopping for her books, Julie felt guilty. Their great summer together was shattered by circumstances out of her control. One night Amelia called, but before Julie could get to the phone, Ethel made a vague excuse and hung up on her. Alex came to the house about ten o'clock that night.

"If I promise not to lay a hand on you or mention God's name, will you go out with me for a cup of coffee?"

They were on the porch, and Julie was hugging herself to keep from trembling.

"Aren't you afraid one of your *flock* will see us and tell?"

"I never was. But, as things stand now, it may no longer matter, in this church anyway."

"What do you mean?" Julie asked, aware he was sharing something close to his heart.

"I'm answering letters from other churches that have invited me to preach for them in the past."

"Why?" Her heart beat faster.

"Mrs. Biddle escalated our disagreement in the hall to a torrid love scene, and some of my people believed her."

Her eyes teary, she turned away. "I'm sorry, Alex, honestly."

Alex moved behind her and said in her ear, "Stop it, Julie. Think. We did nothing wrong. God knows it, and that's all that matters. This is in His hands now. If He wants me to stay here, I'll stay; if He doesn't, I won't. He's in control of my life, not people."

Moving away, Julie turned to face him. "I suppose you'd say I could use some faith. I may no longer have a job either. I'm on what's being called a leave of absence, but I doubt they'll ask me back."

Alex pulled her into his arms. "Marry me, Julie."

Twisting, trying to get away, she protested, "Don't be ridiculous! Marriage is

270

the last thing I need! Do you think I want to end up like my mother?"

"No, and I don't want that either. Stand still, Julie," he commanded with such firmness she stopped struggling.

"Marriage is given by God; it's not meant to be lived the way your parents did. I'm not saying we should be married right away. We have things to work out. But, please, won't you think about it? I want you as my wife and Amelia's mother."

Julie clawed her way free. "Amelia? How dare you! Men will use anything to get their way. Even a child." Her hands were fists at her sides. "You're not using *me*, Alex. Marriage wouldn't mend your life any more than it would mine!"

Alex started to leave. Turning, he looked back. "I had no idea I would ask this tonight. Someday, but not tonight. I only want to take care of you. Remember that, and that I love you."

He left. Julie couldn't understand why she was crying.

Chapter 6

Lisa's fingers flew over the computer keys, yet her mind wandered even as she produced letters and legal forms without error. Len said she was the best secretary in the building. With him in mind, Lisa took stock of her alternatives.

Julie would take no vacation that summer, Lisa was sure. It was not a time for the women to be separated; they were still resonating from shock. Reluctant as Lisa was to admit it, Julie managed the house admirably. Repairs and chores Sid had attended to, she hired done at less expense and inconvenience than when he was in charge.

It was the same with the bills and checkbook that, for obvious reasons, Sid had allowed no one else to touch. He made the household accounts sound so complex, Lisa and Julie were astonished at how simple they turned out to be.

Everything had changed, and Lisa was contemplating a different future. Curt was not the romantic knight she had daydreamed about, and he was barely a year older than she. He would have no real money until he became an established doctor, and that could take years. His family was well off, which meant an inheritance, but much farther down the road.

And Curt was skittish about taking money from his parents for expenses he thought unnecessary. They went to inexpensive places to eat, instead of the fine restaurants Len could afford, and they sat in the balcony instead of the orchestra seats on a rare *dress-up* date.

No, it simply wasn't practical to pursue Curt any longer. Colleen could have him, Lisa decided. Her opportunities lay with Leonard Sherry. Although he was nearly twice her age, he was still impressive.

Len wasn't tall like Alex Stewart, but he wasn't overweight as some men were at forty-one. His graying hair, too, had a certain appeal. Lisa didn't think of him as a handsome man, but his prowess in a courtroom was awesome. As Leonard Sherry's wife she would enjoy influence and attention from every quarter.

She had been in his home more than once. It was staffed by a group of devoted servants and was a showplace, reeking of old money and tradition. There was one drawback: Len's disabled mother occupied a suite of rooms, upstairs in one wing of the house. He rarely mentioned her, so Lisa believed she usually kept to herself and would present no problem.

Once she saw the unbalanced scale of assets as a Sherry versus the liabilities as a Richmond, she opted for a plan to marry. It took hardly any effort on her part, and she marched into the Richmond house one night wearing an ostentatious emerald-cut diamond.

❧

Julie was ready for bed when she heard Ethel's whoop of joy. Running down the hall with Colleen, Julie didn't know what to expect. Her mother seemed to have forgotten how to laugh; she must be hysterical. They burst into the room and saw Ethel dancing foolishly around Lisa. Posing in an occasional chair, Lisa crossed her legs and propped her left hand on her knee to display the diamond.

"Wanna see what Len gave me when I promised to marry him?"

Colleen flew to Lisa. "Let me see! Let me see!" she squealed as she grabbed her hand. "Oh, Julie, come look. It's dazzling!"

"Yes, indeed, professor. See what can be done with brains *and* beauty?" bragged Ethel. "Don't you wish you had what it takes to succeed?" Then she muttered bitterly, "Lisa's everything I could have been if you hadn't. . ."

Colleen backed up to stand with Julie. "Mother, why do you always criticize Julie? Whether it's good or bad, you use everything to harass her."

"You watch your tongue, little fatty, or you'll find yourself with fewer privileges!"

"And what would those be, Mother? She has hardly any, now." Julie's eyes glinted with anger.

Her mother put on a pathetic face. "Don't let her hurt me, Lisa," she whined. "She wants to. Look at her!"

Lisa lashed out in fury, "That's ridiculous! Julie would never do such a thing. It's wrong of you to accuse her. She and I don't always see things the same way, but we love each other. Stop trying to come between my sisters and me!" Lisa walked toward the hall. "If I had any qualms about marrying Len, you've cleared my mind, Mother. I'll do anything to get out of this house."

Julie knew it was true. She didn't think Lisa was in love with Len; she was fed up with her life at home, and he was the quickest way out. But he was rich and could afford the lifestyle Lisa wanted.

She heard a soft sound beside her and realized Colleen was crying. Listening to Lisa had, for the moment, chased her mother's hateful remark from Julie's mind. Calling Colleen "little fatty" was characteristic of Ethel's cruelty. Julie put her arm around her sister and led her from the room.

"Honey, don't let Mother hurt you," Julie begged. "I don't know why she takes pleasure in tormenting you and me; but she is our mother, and we're responsible for her. I try to do what I can to—"

"Julie, I know," Colleen interrupted. "You're always sweet to make up for her."

"It doesn't take away the hurt, though, does it? In fact, I seem to add to the fracas. But you'll be leaving for school in a few weeks; you'll be free to live a normal life."

"I can't wait," Colleen replied passionately. They passed Lisa's closed door. "Poor Lisa. What a celebration for her engagement."

Julie smiled slyly. "Maybe we should take her out?" she suggested, raising her eyebrows.

"Lets!" Colleen opened Lisa's door, and they slipped inside.

"We're breakin' out of this joint, baby," Julie murmured, in an imitation of Bogie. Then she smiled. "See how quick you can get ready. We'll take you for a little celebration."

Lisa was already grinning. Julie and Colleen dressed in jeans and pullovers, and, leaving a note for Ethel if she cared to read it, they left the house and got in Julie's car.

⊗

At a quick-stop market, Alex backed out of a parking space. He glimpsed a car traveling along the street that looked exactly like Julie's, and curiosity induced him to follow. It was Julie, and her sisters were with her. The girls stopped at an all-night restaurant and jumped out of the car, laughing.

Alex wanted to join them, but he could still hear Julie's angry rejection of his proposal when they last met. He parked his car out of their view and watched for a few seconds. Julie looked wonderful. Still maintaining her independence, she'd made the best of tragedy and helped her sisters do the same.

He couldn't resist being with her. A couple came out the door as he went in, and for a few minutes he and the girls were the only customers. He caught Julie's eye almost immediately. Her look of expectation surprised him. Following her gaze, Lisa and Colleen waved him over, and Alex slid into the booth next to Colleen and opposite Julie.

"We meet under different circumstances, Alex," said Lisa. "This time we're celebrating. I planned to call you later."

"What's happening?" he asked.

Colleen smiled. "Wedding bells are starting to peal."

Alex expression changed, and he looked quickly at Julie.

"No, not me," she said. "I'm against such rituals. It's our beautiful Lisa. Show him the hardware, sis."

Lisa shook her left hand before Alex, and he covered his eyes, palms out. Remarking that it was a shame the man couldn't afford something nice, Alex then said he knew Leonard Sherry to speak to and approved of her choice. No one offered Ethel's opinion, and he didn't ask.

The conversation remained light, and Alex enjoyed himself more than he had since the rotten business came up about his holding Julie in his arms at the church. In the meantime, several of the older deacons had begged Alex not to do anything rash. His spiritual integrity would prove itself to the membership, they said, and Alex decided to wait.

"How is Amelia, Alex?" Julie couldn't keep from asking.

"Reading as if there's no tomorrow."

Alex's smile ended. What a time to get *melancholy*, he thought. *Will I never let go of the possibility?* He'd had Amelia's heart examined again early yesterday; he'd make an invalid of her if he didn't stop watching her so closely. Because Christi died of heart disease didn't mean their daughter would inherit it. Nevertheless, he would not let it slip up on her the way it had Christi.

"Let's call this meeting to order, parson," Lisa teased. "I want you to perform the ceremony. Consult your calendar, and give me some open dates."

Julie's eyes were locked on him, and Alex was uneasy. Had she noticed his change of mood, or was she against his doing the wedding? The latter question had to be answered sooner or later; it might as well be now.

"I'd consider it an honor to perform your marriage ceremony, Lisa." Julie dropped her eyes, so he was unable to see the effect of his answer. "I will check my calendar and let you know as soon as possible. In the meantime, you might advise me of the size of the wedding and where it will take place."

"If Lisa is sure she wants to do this, I'd like to have it for them in our home," Julie interjected, and Alex wondered if she was against Lisa's marrying or if she was against her marrying an older man.

Lisa gave Julie a quick glance. "I'll have to talk to Len about that, Julie. He may want the wedding in his home. After all, a lot of his friends will be invited, and our house might not hold them all."

Julie said nothing, but it was clear to Alex that Lisa did not want her wedding at the Richmond home. Hoping Lisa's reply hadn't hurt Julie, he tried a diplomatic suggestion.

"I'd like to offer the facilities of my church if you want to think about that. If the sanctuary is free on the date you select, you can have it. If not, we have a chapel, which was the original sanctuary before we outgrew it. It's very nice and seats about two hundred," he said.

"I'd like a home wedding, especially at his home, but if Len wants to use your church, I'll let you know soon. Now, who wants to join me for chocolate mousse?"

❧

Julie unlocked the car, and they got in. She noticed Alex waited until their car was on the street before he drove off in the opposite direction.

"I thought you were going to choke when I asked Alex to do the ceremony," said Lisa. "I thought you liked him. He's the only minister we know, and I didn't think you'd mind if he did the honors."

"I don't," answered Julie. "It's just that Alex and I didn't part on the best of terms the last time we met."

In the backseat, Colleen leaned forward to get in on the conversation.

"I didn't know that, Julie, what happened?"

Julie could feel her face turning red. "It was personal, honey."

"Ooh, personal, eh?" Lisa quizzed. "Not even about Amelia. Just personal. *Verrry* interesting."

"Cut it out. I'm not saying any more."

Lisa sniffed and sat back in the passenger seat. "Shame. I'll just have to ask Alex."

Julie stepped on the brake. "Lisa Richmond, if you dare—"

"Don't worry," interrupted Lisa. "Your secret's safe with me."

"What secret? That's not fair. Let me in on this," begged Colleen.

"There is nothing to be let in on. I stand foursquare against marriage—always have, always will," vowed Julie.

"Famous last words," giggled Lisa, looking at Colleen.

Julie didn't even want to see Colleen's face.

Len Sherry did want the wedding in his home for his mother's convenience. Lisa was relieved. She knew Julie would put on a beautiful wedding, but Lisa wanted something better. Ethel was crushed, or so she said, yet she was easily persuaded that the Sherry house was the proper showcase for her new gown. The dress came from a bargain basement, and none of the girls liked the color; but it was new, and they were grateful she finally allowed them to buy it.

The bride gave her sisters a choice of soft yellow or green for their attendants' dresses, and they chose swirling, layered gowns of golden yellow.

On the day of the wedding, Alex rode with Lisa to Len's house but not before he had helped Ethel, Colleen, and, finally, Julie into their limousine. Julie had to keep her head when Alex whispered something for her alone.

"You look absolutely beautiful. How do you expect me not to love you?"

Julie didn't answer. His eyes held hers as they drove away.

Sitting on a mound far back from the road, the magnificent Sherry estate was enclosed by a stone wall and surrounded with historic maples, pines, and oaks. It reminded Julie of an ancient castle, gazing down with disdain on trendy, fashionable Kansas City. The limousines took them through iron gates guarded by security police. At the end of a long drive, uniformed attendants, who were parking cars, helped them from their automobiles.

Settling their dresses, they gave attention to the wedding coordinator's directions. Alex gave Julie a last look and went inside with an attendant to join Len. Julie wondered what the men would talk about in those last few minutes before the wedding. What did they have in common?

Decorators for the wedding had blended baskets of yellow mums with selected fall flowers and greenery. Placed alternately with the flower baskets, tall, golden baroque candelabra filled with creamy candles lined the walls and surrounded the altar set up at the far end of the room. In an alcove midway to the altar, a string ensemble played wedding preludes as those invited signed a guest book, greeted friends, and were seated. *Lisa has chosen well,* thought Julie.

FAITH CAME LATE

At the appropriate moment, Ethel, conspicuous in her orchid gown, was escorted to a seat in front, across the aisle from Len's mother, who had selected a beige lace gown. Mrs. Sherry's smile got none from Ethel, Julie noted sadly; but it was time for her entrance, and she made herself concentrate on her own part in the ceremony. Following Colleen, she then turned to watch Lisa.

The bride's tiny waist was accented by a bouffant skirt of yards of ivory satin. Beading and seed pearls embroidered her bodice, and sleeves of the same detail ended in points over her hands. Lisa's red hair, coiffed intricately on top of her head, held a gleaming crown. A cathedral-length veil cascaded from it. Len's gift, a diamond necklace, sparkled delicately against Lisa's creamy skin. She had never looked more beautiful. As he waited with his partner and another friend, a Jackson County judge, Leonard Sherry's eyes expressed Julie's sentiments exactly.

Julie prayed, in case Someone was listening, that this would be a good marriage. Maybe Lisa had done it the right way; she had looked at the facts and decided who could fill the specifics she considered important. Now, if she really tried. . .

Julie took Lisa's bouquet of white roses from her hands, and Alex started the ceremony. His glance met hers as he spoke the words of eternal love; Julie felt he was pronouncing vows for the two of them. The ceremony was pulling her in more than she wanted to be. At the proper moment she laid Len's ring on Alex's Bible with trembling fingers. Lisa put the ring on Len's finger, and suddenly she was no longer Lisa Richmond. She was Mrs. Leonard Sherry.

When Julie gave back Lisa's bouquet, her eyes again met Alex's, and the moment was charged with emotion. Hardly able to breathe, she followed the bridal couple back up the aisle. Would they never reach the end? Something she had never felt before was happening. She had to get away.

At the end of the gallery, Lisa and Len were enveloped by the crowd. The couple was kissing and being kissed; then everybody was kissing everybody. Julie saw Alex in the crowd near her. Then she felt his lips brush hers before he turned away to speak to Ethel.

Julie tried hard to fall asleep that night, but the memory of Alex's kiss kept her from rest.

Chapter 7

A week after Lisa's wedding, Mrs. Larabee telephoned Julie and made an appointment to see her on Friday. She gave no reason for their conference, so Julie feared the worst.

When Colleen came from work, she told her sister about the phone call, but not Ethel. Her mother would declare it another of Julie's *failures*, even though it was Sid's failure as a husband that was at the root of the problem.

"It probably means she's letting me go," said Julie.

As usual, Colleen was encouraging. "And maybe Mrs. Larabee and the board realize how efficient you are at your job. I'll bet it's an apology and they beg you to stay."

"I don't feel your confidence, Colleen. But you can be sure Mrs. Larabee will go through the formal procedure. She's a lady who likes things well organized, with all the loose ends tied up. I'll probably get a parchment certificate of termination with a black border." Julie tipped her head to one side and eyed Colleen up and down. "Are you feeling okay, honey? I think you've lost weight."

"Does it show?" Colleen asked with a smile. "I'm sure trying. I don't eat lunch now—I walk."

"Hey, that's a good idea, for a while anyway." Julie was worried about missed meals, as well as her safety. "Do you walk alone or with someone?"

Colleen's face flushed, and her eyes shone. "Well, yesterday Curt stopped his car to pick me up; instead, he got out and walked with me."

"That sounds promising," Julie said, urging her on with full attention.

"Not very. All he talked about was Lisa. Her marrying so suddenly was hard for Curt. I guess he thought they were closer than Lisa did."

"So? What are you waiting for?" asked Julie. "Now's your chance."

"Why do you think I'm skipping lunch and walking? And while I lose weight, I intend to make some other improvements."

"How about a short cut with a perm? That should be a good start," suggested Julie.

Colleen hugged her. "Oh, I knew you'd help. You're the best sister in the world."

"Don't forget the one in Aruba."

"I can't wait till Lisa comes back. Do you think she'll still be with us once in a while?"

"I think so. We're pretty close, you know." Julie laughed. "After all, you just can't resign from The Three Zanies' Club!"

Julie dressed in a conservative mint green outfit and tied her hair back with a chiffon scarf of the same color. Her cocoa shoes matched the bag she picked up as she left the house for her Friday appointment. If she was being fired, she wanted to go in looking as if she had a better job right around the corner.

Nita rushed to greet her when she arrived at the school and ushered her directly into Mrs. Larabee's office. The room, filled with fine antiques, was a proper backdrop for Pennington's principal, who came from one of Kansas City's pioneer families. Smiling, Mrs. Larabee rose from her desk to extend her hands to Julie.

"My dear Miss Richmond, how happy I am to see you."

The gesture astonished Julie. "I'm happy to see you, too, Mrs. Larabee."

"Please, be seated, and we'll get right to our business." Mrs. Larabee took a manila envelope from the console behind her desk. "Without going into details, the board of trustees and I request that you continue in your position as vice-principal of Pennington." She handed the envelope to Julie. "This contains the paperwork for an upgrade in your salary, plus a small bonus in consideration of your patience."

Julie's breath flowed evenly again. Until that moment she hadn't realized the stress she was under.

"Thank you, Mrs. Larabee," she said, holding down her exuberance. "I've missed not being here this summer."

"Yes, Amelia Stewart called the school several times to ask about you. Apparently she was unable to get you at home."

Julie frowned. She remembered only one call from Amelia the evening Alex had foolishly asked her to marry him. Was her mother deliberately keeping Amelia's calls from her when Julie's job was in jeopardy? She was behind on her activities with Amelia and would have to double up now that she was back at work. Promising herself to question her mother later, she concentrated on plans the principal was outlining for the coming year.

The interview ended with an elegant tea served by Nita, and Julie felt at home again. When she left, Nita glanced at Mrs. Larabee's closed door and walked out with Julie.

"It's a good thing you're coming back!" she whispered. "I shouldn't tell you, but things have gone from bad to worse around here. Her Highness got the total picture of the work you do when she had to pick up on it herself. I wish you knew how many times she asked me to call you, then backed out. We can't get along without you, Julie."

Julie drove away from the school in a state of euphoria. She had her job back! No one knew how happy it made her. *Forget Alex Stewart*, she told herself.

Vice-principal at Pennington was the position for her, and substitute teaching, now and then, made a good job even better.

She felt she could spend money again, so she stopped at a college shop to buy Colleen something new for school. Finding a royal blue blouse with a style similar to her own, she added a gold chain and earrings she thought Colleen would like.

Her mother was waiting downstairs when she got home. "I heard you talking to Colleen about your job. Did you get fired?" Ethel asked, her face sour.

"No, Mother. I go back to work Monday."

"Good. Now maybe that Stewart kid will stop calling." Ethel thumped up the stairs until Julie called out.

"Mother, why didn't you tell me when Amelia called?"

"That pest? Chatters like a chipmunk. I got tired of listening and hung up half the time." She laughed.

Trying to contain her anger, Julie raised her voice. "In the future, please, take down the information I need to call back. I bought you a notepad and pen for that explicit purpose." Her voice softened as she willed herself to calm down. "Has anyone else called that you've forgotten to tell me about?"

"Only the preacher. But I knew you didn't want to talk to him, and I told him so." Ethel continued up the stairs. "If you want anything to eat, go fix it."

Julie was trembling. Her mother was getting worse. No one treated her own flesh and blood the way Ethel did. Lisa got out because she could stand it no longer. Colleen would leave soon, and then she would be alone with her mother.

After trying twice to phone Amelia, she left her number on the machine. She checked her watch and decided to drop by the library. Maybe Colleen would go out for a salad with her.

☙

"Miss Richmond! Miss Richmond!" a familiar voice called, and Julie turned to see Alex and Amelia hurrying up the wide stone steps of the library.

"Hello, darling," Julie answered, dropping down to hug Amelia, not caring that she'd used such an endearing term. "I've missed you."

She glanced at Alex, and he mouthed, *Me, too?* Taking Amelia's hand, she turned away. Alex reached around her to open the door, and they stepped inside.

High-beamed ceilings echoed soft voices, and, hung by twenty-foot chains, lamps with frosted globes and ornate metal fittings lit sections of bookshelves and tables of readers. Julie loved the smells of the old library: aged leather, printers' ink, furniture polish, even a little dust.

A high voice assailed them. "Is that you, Dr. Stewart?" Mrs. Biddle came toward them from a side room. "Well, you and Amelia are here a lot, aren't you?" she said. "I saw you here last week, but I was busy and didn't get a chance to speak to you." Mrs. Biddle ignored Julie.

"Yes, Mrs. Biddle. With the encouragement of Miss Richmond here—you remember Miss Julie Richmond, vice-principal of the Pennington School, where my daughter is a student? She has helped Amelia push up her reading skills dramatically. We're here to check out another stack of books."

"Would you like to hear me read, Mrs. Biddle?" questioned Amelia with enthusiasm. "You can come with me to the children's section and help me pick out a book you'd like to hear. Then we'll read it while Daddy finds his stuff."

As Alex smiled and agreed, Julie could hardly keep from laughing. It was like watching a cartoon on television. Mrs. Biddle was the last person she'd expected to meet. And in the company of Alex? It was hilarious! She saw him fighting to keep his face straight, but how he had carried it off! Not a single ugly word, yet Mrs. Biddle was backing away, trying to escape both father *and* child.

Colleen spied them, and she parked her book cart to join them. Her eyes were shining.

"Hi, everyone! Julie, who's this pretty girl?"

"This is Alex's daughter, Amelia. Amelia, this is my sister Colleen."

"Are you the one Daddy married?" Amelia giggled. "I said it wrong! How do I say it, Daddy?"

He smiled and patted her head. "You're only a little mixed up, honey. I performed the marriage ceremony for Lisa, Colleen and Julie's sister.

"Oh. Do you work here?" Amelia directed to Colleen.

"Yes. Is there something I can help you with?"

"Tell you what," said Alex. "I'll talk to Julie while you two girls look for books. Okay?"

Julie spoke up. "Colleen, I came by to see if we might have lunch together if it's not too late. I have good news."

"Low man on the totem pole goes to lunch last." Colleen grinned. "I'll help Amelia find her books, and then I'll sign out."

Colleen and Amelia scurried away, and Alex turned to Julie.

"Am I mistaken, or has Colleen taken on a new look?"

"She has. Since Lisa's married, she's determined to make Lisa's old standby fall in love with her," Julie answered.

"How do you feel about that?"

"You know how I feel. I'm not interested in marriage, but it seems to be what Colleen wants. The boy's name is Curtis Graham. He's studying medicine at Washington U. and, as you know, Colleen will be at Lindenwood, in St. Charles—close."

"I wish her well." Alex rubbed the back of his neck and took a deep breath. "It's a shame your sisters can't persuade you to give a guy a break." He hurried on. "You wouldn't like to tell *me* your good news, would you?"

"You'll know it sooner or later. Pennington asked me to come back."

"That's good, Julie. I'm glad they woke up before some other school snared you. As a matter of fact, my congregation had a church-wide business session and, in a manner of speaking, gave me a vote of confidence. So it seems I've kept my job, too."

Julie was afraid to say *I'm glad*, so, smiling, she went back to her own situation. "I think I have my reinstatement figured out. Pennington couldn't stand the pressure of dismissing the sister-in-law of Leonard Sherry, who has friends on the board and is given to sharing his money now and then."

"And Julie Richmond just happens to be one of the city's most devoted educators." Alex let go his characteristic chuckle. "Maybe Lisa did me a favor, too. If the pastor insists on holding a single girl in his arms, it's not a sin if she's Leonard Sherry's sister-in-law."

The four gathered at the library exit to leave, but Alex was reluctant to let Julie go.

"We haven't had lunch. How about letting me take you two with us?"

"Please, Miss Richmond, do come," Amelia pleaded.

"I don't think—"

"I'd love to come, and I know Julie would, too," Colleen declared. "She just wants to be coaxed."

Alex saw the straight look Julie gave Colleen, but she took Amelia's hand, and they crossed the parking lot to Alex's car. Anticipating her move to the backseat, he took her arm. He unlocked the front door, handed her into the passenger seat, then tripped the locks for Amelia and Colleen.

The small restaurant was not far from the library, and Alex wished the trip had been longer. Having Julie beside him was a heady sensation. It was the first time they had been together since the wedding.

When they got out of the car, Julie stopped for a moment. "What happened to the fancy sports car you use for running down pedestrians? I never see you driving it anymore."

"It wasn't my car. Mine went in the shop for its warranty checkup, and a friend loaned me his little toy. Do you want me to trade mine for it?" he asked with mock enthusiasm.

Julie's laugh rang out. Alex clutched at his chest, and he staggered as if in shock. With puzzled faces, Colleen and Amelia turned back, but Julie shook her head and waved them off.

"You had to be there," she said, giggling.

After ordering salads for themselves and a hamburger for Amelia, Alex had a tough time getting Julie and Colleen's attention off his child. For some reason, Amelia was dominating the conversation instead of letting him talk to Julie. Then Julie told Colleen about the blouse and jewelry she'd bought, and Alex saw his chance.

"When do you leave, Colleen? And do you need a ride to the airport?"

"I leave from International next Tuesday, but I guess I'll have plenty of volunteers to take me." Then she added, "Would you and Amelia like to join the family to see me off? Lisa and Len will be back by then, too. If you think you can make it, I leave at six o'clock—evening, not morning."

Amelia begged to go, so Alex was thankful she was along after all. He looked at Julie, who was not taking the invitation well, and addressed her point-blank.

"Is that all right with you, Julie? Amelia won't mind staying home if you'd rather we didn't come."

The deliberate way he couched the question irritated Julie.

"Of course not," she said in a haughty tone. "The more the merrier."

On Monday, the newlyweds came home, and the family was invited to the Sherrys' for dinner. Ethel made a pretext of not wanting to go, but Julie knew she was dying to see the main core of the house and also what Lisa and Len bought on their trip. The Sherrys were in the living room with his mother when they arrived. In the foyer, Ethel whimpered softly and turned as if to leave. Knowing she felt out of her league, Julie took her arm to support her. Ethel jerked away and walked ahead. A wink from Lisa signaled Julie to ignore it.

"Hello, Mother," Lisa said, bussing Ethel's cheek. "Julie and Colleen, I brought some terrific things for you from Aruba. Uh. . .you, too, Mother." Lisa slipped her hand into the pocket of a striking gold-brocade hostess gown. A maid took away the Richmonds' purses, and, from the hall doorway, the cook caught Lisa's eye. "I see Juanita is ready for us in the dining room, so if everyone is hungry, we'll let Len lead the way."

Len gripped Ethel's arm, propelling her along, and went ahead with the two mothers, Juanita pushing Mrs. Sherry's wheelchair. Falling in behind, Lisa whispered to her sisters, "It takes planning, but how's that for gagging her before she gets off a shot?"

The three walked into the dining room, holding hands, smiling.

At dinner, Julie and the others heard a description of the Sherrys' honeymoon and of the resort, La Cabana, their paradise on the northwest white-sand shore of Aruba.

That Lisa was happy was obvious; in fact, she was ecstatic. The looks she and Len exchanged, holding hands at the slightest opportunity, the whispered words meant just for the two of them—Julie hadn't imagined that Lisa was so in love. Her sister's courage to cut the apron strings was a risk well-taken.

The Sherry environment also suited Lisa. To Julie, she was meant to be the lady of the mansion. She did wonder if two women could live amiably in the same house, especially if one had Lisa's temperament and determination. But she saw the warmth between the elderly Mrs. Sherry and the new one, and

Julie's heart took hope. Since Lisa had not known the love of a gentle mother, there could be a lifetime of affection between the two.

❧

Colleen's departure day arrived whether Julie liked it or not, and, drowning in sentiment, she expedited last-minute details. How she would miss Colleen! She'd be home for weekends, holidays, and vacations; but she wouldn't be there to talk to every day, and her interests would be different. Again, it drummed in her brain: Lisa was gone; Colleen was leaving. Her mother was the only company Julie would have at home.

When she was feeling sorriest for herself, Alex came with Amelia, and Julie again called up the presence of Miss Richmond. The Sherrys arrived, and while Alex and Len chatted and drank iced tea in the kitchen, the girls closed Colleen's luggage and tried for the last time to coax Ethel to go with them to the airport. Bluntly stating she couldn't abide the company Julie kept, she turned away and went to her bedroom. Julie hustled a belligerent Lisa and a disappointed Colleen out of the room.

"Mother is Mother," Julie reminded. "She has her world; we have ours. Listen! Great things are happening for the two of you. Enjoy them!" she said with a kiss for each girl.

She noticed Amelia standing quietly and wondered what she was thinking. For a child whose female parental model was a kind, sensitive housekeeper, Ethel's stubborn display and their attitudes toward her must have been distressing.

Julie bent down to her. "Amelia, darling, I'll explain all this to you another time. Trust me?"

Amelia nodded and gave Julie a comforting pat on the cheek.

❧

Colleen's face brightened when she saw Curt waiting for the same flight she was taking. Lisa introduced her husband, and Julie thought Curt acted with extreme discretion. Alex kept the conversation lively, and Len responded with his own wry sense of humor. Once more Julie admired Alex for his effort, this time to send Colleen away happily.

Even more enlightening, Julie caught Curt eyeing Colleen in her new red suit, draped with a brightly flowered silk scarf from Lisa. Unless she was mistaken, Curt was taking a fresh look at an old friend. If she knew Alex's God better, she thought, she would ask Him to give Colleen a break and let her have Curt. Maybe she'd hint that to Alex. *What? No way!*

The plane took off, and with it went a bit of Julie's heart. Seeing her tears, Amelia pressed close. Julie wasn't asking for sympathy, but when Alex's arm went around her waist, she didn't move away. She needed nothing but her job. Right? Yet each time she vowed to be strong and independent, she invariably leaned on Alex.

Chapter 8

To be sure she wrote home often, Julie bought Colleen a roll of postage stamps and gave her a mild lecture. A letter came as soon as she settled in at St. Charles. Although Colleen described the school in detail, most of her letter was about Curt. He picked up his car at the airport, she said, and drove from St. Louis to Lindenwood. Julie smiled. Letting go of Lisa must have been easier than Curt thought.

By the week following her return to Pennington, Julie had caught up on her records. She finished a long list of tasks she found waiting and did the annual reports due to the board of trustees. The principal simply wasn't up to the extra work.

After battling several hours of names, numbers, and applications for fall enrollments, Julie was tired and restless. Maybe anticipation of time with Amelia was the cause, she thought, checking her watch. Today they would spend the afternoon at the Nelson-Atkins Museum of Art. When Alex brought Amelia, however, he came inside because his child had plans of her own.

"Daddy has a meeting at four, but do you think we could go bowling until then?" Amelia asked.

It wasn't exactly a cultural event, but it was still an opportunity. Julie could analyze Amelia's disposition and reaction to any number of circumstances.

"Bowling is something I've tried a time or two, but I'm not very good at it," she said, eyeing Alex, who stood back, letting Amelia use her wiles without interference.

"You'll do good! And, look, you're dressed for it, isn't she, Daddy?"

Julie glanced at Alex, who gave her an up-and-down look, and she was self-conscious. Still, her chocolate brown skirt was full, and the beige loose-fitting top would be comfortable to bowl in. She took off her dangling earrings, dropped them in her purse, and spread her arms.

"Let's go," she said and took her jacket from a rack near the door.

Alex smiled and touched her back as she let Amelia lead the way. Julie had qualms about what she was getting into, but today she needed company. The grudge Ethel held against her had full rein now that the two lived alone. Julie had to admit: Alex and Amelia were an oasis in an extremely arid land.

⁂

The clatter of pins falling on thirty-six lanes, loud voices, music, a busy food counter—excitement in the bowling alley included a lot of noise. Nevertheless,

Julie looked forward to their contest. Alex had carried bags containing his and Amelia's equipment from the car, so he arranged for an alley and fitted Julie with shoes.

"Hey, Pastor!" A smiling teenage boy ran up to Alex.

"Hi, Keith! Are some of the guys with you?" Alex asked.

"Yeah." He pointed down the row of lanes, and three boys answered Alex's wave. "We just got here. We'll come over later to see how you're doing," he said, obviously challenging Alex.

"Okay. Let's see what *you* can do," Alex countered and clapped Keith on the shoulder. He turned back to Julie. "I'll introduce you to all the boys at once."

It was a ticklish situation, Julie felt. "Are you sure you want them to know you're with me?"

Alex did a double take. "Are you joking? I'm proud to be with you." He lowered his voice. "It's *our* lives, Julie."

Amelia had gone on and was almost ready when Julie sat with her in front of their lane. Her face red, the little girl stood up. Julie had been so preoccupied with her own thoughts she hadn't noticed Amelia's anger. She'd had the same expression the day she told Julie she wouldn't try out for the school play if she couldn't have the main part. What had upset Amelia?

Julie started changing shoes. "Amelia, will you help me get started and promise not to laugh if I throw all gutter balls?"

Amelia's face changed like quicksilver, and she laughed at Julie.

"You won't do that! I can't teach you much, but Daddy will."

On her first attempt Julie actually hit a few pins, but she knew in minutes she hadn't the bowling skill of Amelia and Alex. Despite Amelia's slow-moving ball, she'd made a strike her first time up.

"Why, that's wonderful, darling!" Julie whispered in her ear as Alex bowled.

"I guess that'll show those old boys I can bowl as good as they can with Daddy," she said, her face gathering darkness.

She's jealous of Alex's friendships, Julie thought. But how could her attitude be reconciled with the work her father did? Julie saw her opinion validated when the boys came over later.

Alex had an excellent relationship with the teenagers. They surrounded them when she was introduced, but Julie missed Amelia. She saw her sitting apart from them, watching other bowlers, and she remembered. If Amelia couldn't be the star. . .

The boys went back to their game, and it was Julie's time up again. She left a wide split. Alex came up behind her. Taking her arm, he demonstrated.

"You need to follow through, Julie. When you deliver, your fingers should slide out of the holes without jerking the ball. Then, after you release it, let your arm sweep all the way up like this." He raised her arm slowly. "You're aiming for a spot between the one and three pins."

Alex's nearness was suffocating; Julie laughed to dispel the feeling. "I'm happy if I stay on the lane, and you're giving me tips for an expert."

"Try it next time. You'll be surprised."

Julie did as she was told and made a strike, too.

Delighted, Amelia hugged her. "See? I knew you could do it!"

Alex made a move toward her, too, then stepped back. Julie wondered if it was because the boys from his church were there or if he felt she would resent it. Would she?

❧

Alex took Julie back to Pennington to get her car, and he apologized for leaving her. He had just enough time to make his meeting. Julie remembered that Mrs. Blake had loaned her car to her sister, so Amelia would wait at the church until Alex finished. Julie stopped him as he went around the car to leave.

"Since taking Amelia home will make you later to your meeting, suppose I take her out to eat and drop her at the house when we're through? Would you like that, Amelia?"

Amelia popped out of the car beside Julie. "Yes! Yes! Could we, Daddy?"

The look Alex rested on Julie's face was so tender she felt uncomfortable.

"If Miss Richmond wants you with her, I can't think of anything nicer— unless I were free to come along." Julie turned her head but not quick enough.

"Miss Richmond! Your face is all pink. Are you okay?" Amelia questioned in a crystal clear voice.

"Yes, p–perfectly," sputtered Julie. "I have to clean up my desk, Amelia. Then we'll go."

A glance at Alex told her not to look back. But she felt his eyes on her all the way up the walk.

❧

Occupied with another of Julie's books, the child waited without complaining until Julie finished her work. When she asked what she'd like to eat, Amelia surprised Julie by deferring to her choice. *So, she doesn't always insist on having her own way,* thought Julie. *Especially if she's treated fairly.*

Since there was little regard for well-prepared food in her childhood, Julie believed children should have a balanced diet. She passed up the fast-food restaurants in favor of a cafeteria she thought Amelia would like. She helped the child select her food but postponed dessert until she was sure Amelia ate a nutritious dinner.

A waitress carried Amelia's tray, and, finding a table in a small gazebo with hanging plants around the sides, Julie soon had them settled to eat. The meal was well along when she brought up the reason she had wanted to get Amelia alone.

"May I ask a personal question, honey?"

"Yes." Amelia was all curiosity.

"You didn't like it when the boys from your church showed up this afternoon, did you?"

"No!"

"Why not?"

"They're always butting in! Those boys and all the others get to be first! Daddy plays football or baseball or basketball with them. They even play board games at the house when Daddy could play with me. He'd *rather* play with those old boys!"

Julie hadn't meant to upset the child. She kept her voice calm and began again.

"Amelia, let's think about that. Your daddy has a whole congregation of people to. . .ah. . .help. Boys, especially, need ways to occupy themselves, so they don't get into trouble. You've heard about street gangs, haven't you?"

"Yes, but these are church guys," argued Amelia.

"Have you thought that maybe they would be joining those gangs if your daddy didn't take time to be with them?"

Amelia forked the last of her green beans and silently ate them. She looked at Julie and frowned.

"But, he's *my* daddy. He should be with me part of the time. He always has meetings, meetings, meetings! Sometimes we don't do anything together for weeks and weeks," she explained in exasperation.

Julie caught her hand. "Darling, I see where you're coming from, and I want to help. I'd like to talk to your daddy about this. Would you mind?"

The girl's expression was anxious. "What would you say?"

"I'm not sure. I'll have to think about it for a while. You trust me to do the right thing, don't you?"

"Yes."

"All right. Now, there's something I want *you* to consider." Amelia stopped eating to listen as Julie continued, "I think it would show how grown-up you are if you told your daddy you understand. That he can't spend as much time with you as he'd like, I mean. Do you think you could do that?"

"Well. . .yes. If you say so," came Amelia's reluctant assent.

"Good girl." Julie leaned toward her. "Now, with a clean plate like that, somebody's going to get dessert."

While Amelia enjoyed a banana pudding, Julie reviewed what she'd learned. Alex had a lot of responsibility; that was a given. Yet Amelia was his prime responsibility, and she needed him. She had to make both Stewarts learn to give a little.

Julie dropped Amelia off at her house, had a cup of tea with Mrs. Blake, then, reluctantly, she headed home. There were no lights downstairs, and the house looked lonely. She let herself in and turned on the light. Calling to her mother that she was home, she took the mail from a table by the door and saw a letter from Colleen.

Tucking the stack under her arm, she checked all the door locks before going upstairs. Her mother's light was on, but Julie didn't feel like approaching her yet. She set her shoulder bag on a chair and flopped on the bed. The mail dropped to her side. Lying back, she found she was exhausted, and something else.

For the first time, Julie was lonely. She was still in the job she loved, and school was starting. It was a busy time. Normally she was keyed up and had to make herself wind down. Tonight was different. It was as if everyone in the world, except her, had something to do, and she was bereft of an uplifting thought. Maybe Colleen's letter would pick her up.

Ripping open the envelope, she basked in the warmth of her sister's message. Colleen was happy. She found school exciting and challenging. She'd made friends already, and she'd had compliments on the wardrobe Julie helped her put together. It was a vote of confidence; Ethel had informed Julie her choices for Colleen showed no taste whatever.

Colleen had been out with Curt, and they had a date to go to the Gateway Arch and the Arch Odyssey Theater on Saturday. Julie smiled at the thought of Colleen in St. Louis, on a date with Curt. Her sister bragged that she had lost another three pounds. But what happened, she asked, when her new clothes got too big? Julie made a mental note to reassure her in her next letter. How she would adore buying clothes for a slender Colleen.

Ethel clumped down the hall. "Can't you tell a person you're home? I thought it was a burglar."

"I called out. I guess you didn't hear me."

"You thought you did. There wasn't a sound until you switched on your light and started rustling paper."

"That was a letter from Colleen," Julie said. "She seems happy at school. She's had a date with Curtis Graham."

"Colleen won't get him. She's a slob." Ethel turned toward her room. "Oh, by the way, that preacher called before you got here. Said he wanted to thank you for something. I wrote his number down, but you already know it, so I threw it away."

"Thank you, Mother."

Ethel didn't leave, and Julie knew her mother was waiting for her to explain why Alex wanted to thank her. It could only lead to an argument, so Julie kept quiet. She looked through the rest of the mail, placed the bills in a holder on her desk, and tossed the remainder in the wastebasket.

Knowing Ethel watched every move, it didn't surprise Julie when her mother criticized her handling of the mail.

"You think you're the big boss around here now, don't you? You're the only one who can take care of things," Ethel carped. "You might even try to get rid of me so you can take complete control."

Julie looked at Ethel in shock. "Mother! How can you say such a thing? What have I done except try to pick up the pieces since Dad's death?"

"You're taking over everything. Now that Lisa and Colleen are both gone, that makes it easier. I'll bet you want this house, too, don't you? Well, let me tell you—you'll never get it. Never!" Ethel was breathing hard, working up intense fury that had Julie close to tears.

"Mother, please don't say things like that." Julie reached for her mother's arm.

Ethel slapped Julie hard and shoved her backwards over a footstool. Julie's head hit the edge of a magazine rack as she fell against the wall. She was dazed for a moment, but she could still hear her mother's accusing voice.

"You were always there, making trouble, causing me to be sick. All your life! Causing trouble!"

Reaching for a chair, Julie got up, shaking. "Please, Mother, calm down. I don't want to take your house away from you. Don't accuse me of—"

"This house was given to me by Mama and Papa. And do you know why? It was the only way they could get Sid Richmond to marry me. Because of you, I had to give up my sweetheart to marry your father. Sid was the one who got me in trouble, and how I've paid for that mistake! But I made you pay, too." Ethel's maniacal laugh burst out. "You and everyone else."

Tears marked Julie's face. A bump had risen on her head, and her leg was bruised, yet the revelation of Ethel's hate hurt worse.

Her mother rambled on, excusing her moment of passion with Sid when Julie was conceived. Once he found out, the man she loved and desperately wanted to marry left town. Her parents gave her the house, on the condition that she marry Sid, and the older couple moved to Florida. Ethel never heard from them again.

Now, Julie understood. Her wounded heart continued to beat, but she felt nothing. Her mother had never loved her. She had lived only for revenge, and it was driving her out of her mind.

The telephone jingled. Trembling, Julie wiped her eyes and moved to the instrument by her bed. When she lifted the receiver, she could barely answer.

"Julie?"

It was Alex.

"I can't talk right now," murmured Julie.

"Julie, I can't understand you. What's wrong?"

"I can't talk right—"

"Don't mind me," Ethel shrieked. "I know it's the preacher. Well, he's welcome to you! Get out! I don't want you!" She went out, slammed the door, then opened it a fraction and slammed it again.

"Julie," said Alex, "I heard. I'm coming over. Get your jacket and go out to the porch. She must be losing her mind. Don't stay in there with her. Do you hear?"

"Yes, I'll go," she sobbed.

In less than twenty minutes, she was in Alex's arms. *He must have broken speed limits getting here*, Julie thought, but she was so grateful she didn't care. Her world had turned upside down. In his car in front of the house, Julie told him everything.

"You're not staying here, Julie," he said. "I'll take you to my house. No, you won't stand for that—I'll take you to Lisa's. But you can't stay here."

"Alex, I can't leave tonight. I have to be at work tomorrow. My clothes are here. My car. Besides, I can't just leave her. She's my mother. In her state of mind, she might even feel guilty and do herself harm. We both know she's unstable."

She felt Alex's arm relax. "You're right, of course. She's one of the most pitiful creatures I've ever met. But, Julie, you're the one who may be in danger. If you won't leave, will you at least let me go in and talk with her?"

"I guess when I knew you were coming, that's what I wanted. But, by now, she knows we've talked together, and she won't listen to you. I'm afraid she needs psychiatric help, Alex," she said.

"Leave it to me. There's a reliable psychiatrist in my church. I'll talk to him."

"No, not you, Alex. This is my problem. Lisa's and mine. We'll figure out something."

Alex smiled and kissed Julie's nose. "My stubborn little Miss Richmond. It took a crisis to get you back in my arms, but you're still going to handle everything. Let's see how you handle this."

He turned her face up to his and kissed her soundly. Julie remembered the effect of the brush of his lips at the wedding, but that was nothing by comparison. He pulled away, and in the glow of the corner streetlight, she saw him smile.

"It never ceases to amaze me that you can look so beautiful when you cry." He kissed her again.

This time Julie pulled away. "I have to go, Alex. There's a lock on my bedroom door. If I have to, I'll use it." Looking back at him, she said softly, "Our relationship has been a rocky one, Alex, but I do appreciate your wanting to help me. I'll call you tomorrow."

"Wait, Julie." He bowed his head. "Dear God, keep Julie safe tonight. She means more to You and to me than she knows. Help her to learn how much."

He spoke the name of Jesus, and a wave of peace swept over Julie that remained with her the rest of the night.

Chapter 9

Something has to be done. You can't live with her anymore," declared Lisa. Julie had made straight for the Sherry mansion the minute she got away from school. Now that she was here and had unloaded on Lisa, she felt like a coward. In this lovely living room with its muted rose and green velvets and its graceful dark woods, talk of last night's wild accusations and hysterics seemed far away—another world.

"Only a person who knows Mother well would believe me, Lisa." Propping her elbow on the sofa arm, Julie leaned her cheek on her fist. "Right now, I'm sitting here wondering why I came to you. I should be at home trying to patch things up instead of making you part of this ghastly mess."

Lisa's blue eyes narrowed. "You're just relieved because you talked it out. The problem is still there, and Alex is right—you should stay with me. Len will give us the legal angle, but we must have Mother placed where she can't hurt other people *or* herself." Touching Julie's hand, Lisa frowned. "She's getting worse by the hour, Julie. Don't you realize that? She has a mental problem. Her violence has gone past breaking dishes and throwing things."

"What about Colleen, Lisa? It would break her heart if we had Mother com. . .if we did such a thing. Alex suggested he talk to Mother. We could try that before we consider—"

"Alex will be home with Len in a few minutes."

Julie jumped to her feet. "Why didn't you tell me he was coming? I don't want to see him. Alex has no place in this!"

"Well, look at you," Lisa grinned lazily. "A guy finally got under Julie's skin."

"Lisa!"

"I calls 'em like I sees 'em."

"You've certainly called this one wrong. Yes, I was with Alex last night. But he's the one who insisted on coming over."

"You didn't say no, did you?"

"How could I? I had no one to turn to, at that moment. Besides, I wasn't myself. I was in shock after what Mother said." Julie sat on the edge of a chair away from Lisa. "Why are Alex and Len together?"

"He called Len, wanting to know how to protect you from Mother."

"And you let me go through this whole thing when you already knew about it? Why?"

"You needed to talk, and I thought I might get more information from you than Alex did."

"I'm leaving," Julie exclaimed, gathering up her things. "I don't want to be here when he comes."

"Too late. My lord and master just drove up," said Lisa, peeking through the bay window, "and the preacher is hot on his trail."

Julie's lips trembled. Lisa hurried to her, questioning with her eyes.

"Don't call him that, Lisa. That's what Mother calls him. Only she makes it sound awful, like a curse."

"I'm sorry, hon. I won't do it again. I promise."

They hugged each other, and Lisa kissed Julie's cheek as the men came through the foyer. Neither spoke at first, and Julie felt they knew it was a sensitive moment. Then Lisa rushed to Len and gave him a hug. Alex's eyes locked on Julie, but she didn't move.

"Are you all right?" he asked.

Julie nodded.

"That's a matter of opinion, Alex," Lisa declared as she and Len came toward them.

"Lisa's upset about what you went through last night, Julie," explained Len. "She's afraid for you." He invited Alex to sit down, and Alex pulled Julie to a couch to sit beside him. "In my opinion," said Len, "she's right. Why don't you move out, Julie? Get an apartment of your own."

"I thought of that, too." Lisa grinned and said, "My independent sister wouldn't be happy living with us, but an apartment's the answer for now. And we'll help, won't we, Len?"

"Of course. In fact, I own an apartment complex close to Pennington. Some of the suites are furnished. You could move in tonight if you like. There's no need to go back to your mother's house at all," he said.

Alex let out a deep breath. "For my part, I can think of nothing I'd rather she'd do than—"

"Wait a minute!" Julie exploded, facing Alex. "Whose life is this anyway? I'll make my own decisions, if you don't mind."

"Simmer down, Julie," Lisa cautioned. "No one's going to make you do anything. But you should have moved out long ago. I know—you wanted to protect Colleen. If Len hadn't rescued me, I might have stayed and wound up just like Mother—mean and vengeful. Let's go by there tonight, Len. We'll let her know Julie won't be back, and you can assess how dangerous she is."

"I'm not a doctor, sweetheart," Len returned. "But, Julie, I can bluff her into thinking twice about the way she treats you. Your mother must understand that her extreme behavior will not be tolerated."

Julie slumped against the back of the couch and closed her eyes. A tear slipped down her cheek, and she felt Alex's hand on hers. She'd lost her temper with him, yet he was still offering support. She wanted to move her hand, but she couldn't. Why was it so comforting to have him there? Simple. It was because she had wrestled with the problem all day long—alone.

She opened her eyes. The other three were looking at her, not pitying, but with sympathy and concern. Finally, Lisa broke the long silence.

"Do it, Julie, for my sake and for Colleen's. If she were here, she'd vote yes. When we go to the house, I'll pack some clothes and personal things for you, and we'll bring them here. You'll spend the night. Then, tomorrow, Len will get his manager to open the apartment for you. Right, Len?"

"Yes, and staying here tonight would be best. Lisa and I will help you get settled over the weekend." He stood up and took Lisa's hand. "Ready to see what we can work out with your mother?"

Lisa sighed as she got up. "I know I said I'd never go back, but I'd rather go myself than give her a chance to hurt Julie again."

Julie had never been so embarrassed. Alex was certainly seeing all their dirty laundry.

Lisa took Len's arm. As they left the room, she called, "We'll be back as soon as possible. Alex, keep Julie company. You'll want to know the results, too."

Julie wanted to throttle Lisa. She was making sure Alex stayed, and Julie wanted him to leave. They were ganging up on her. Without letting her decide what she wanted, the three of them had planned everything. It was infuriating! Her conscience told her Alex had done nothing, but she was mad at him anyway.

❧

With authority, Lisa said, Len convinced Ethel that Julie was not coming back. She had lingered in Julie's bedroom while Lisa packed the suitcases but made no move to stop her. She didn't ask about Julie and showed no remorse for striking her.

Hearing the details, Julie did feel remorse. She thought of the bills her mother had never paid, the checkbook she had never balanced, the monthly check to be banked, and dozens of decisions her mother would face for the first time. Ethel was so childlike and naive. What would happen if Julie weren't there to take care of her? She spoke of her concern before Alex left.

"I thought of those things, Julie," said Len. "I told your mother I would have them taken care of. She seemed glad to hand matters over to me." He straightened his shoulders, took a deep breath, and reasoned with Julie as an older brother. "Julie, your mother is an immature woman. A leader suits her fine. Live your own life now. It's time. Her attitude toward you is indefensible. Lisa says you were the one who took care of her even before your father died. That's a noble act, but misplaced. Long ago, she was the one who let herself be carried away; she didn't have to accept the house or your father. Apparently her handsome Romeo type wouldn't marry her, and she hadn't the courage to face the future with a baby and no husband."

"Give her credit, Len. That would be hard for any woman," Julie replied.

"Yet, today, thousands of single women in the same position do that," Alex countered gently. "They resist the pressure to have abortions, they keep their babies, and they live alone and raise them. It takes courage, but it's being done."

"As you said, that's today," Julie argued. "It was a lonely stand to take in her time."

"Len said it, Julie—Mother's immature. She's dependent on everyone," added Lisa. "Your leaving may be the best thing you could do for her. She may even learn to be a real person instead of a paper doll."

"It could start a change," said Alex as he stood up. "I need to leave. I have basketball practice in the morning with the church team before the boys go to school."

Julie remembered. "Alex, I need to talk with you about Amelia soon. I think I have some answers for you."

"Do you want me to stay now? I can, if you like."

"We're going to our suite right away, Julie," Lisa said.

"No, I need time to collect my thoughts. I'm too on edge right now."

"I'll help you and the Sherrys with the apartment. You can tell me then," he said, with a wave to Lisa and Len.

Frowning, Julie started to protest, but Alex was gone.

"Congratulations!" Lisa remarked. "If you keep that up, you'll send him away for good."

"He tries to run my life! I don't need him! I don't."

"Who are you trying to convince, us or yourself?"

Len spoke in a soft voice, "He was genuinely concerned for you when he called me, Julie. Alex Stewart is respected and well liked. You could do worse."

Julie was taken aback by Len's appraisal. Alex had a good reputation; she knew that. He was known in civic circles in the city and was on a committee or two. But, to her, his lack of time with Amelia gave those activities little merit.

"Len, I'm sure he's a good man. It's just that I'm not in the market for a good man. I love my independence. I don't want my future limited by a man. Can't either of you understand?"

Lisa snuggled up to Len. "I don't see my future like that. Len's given me life. I didn't know what happiness was until we were married."

Len's arm around her shoulders drew her close, and he kissed her as Julie looked on. Admittedly, Lisa was a changed woman; Len's love had changed her. But Lisa wasn't against marriage as Julie was. She didn't realize how rotten most marriages were.

"Suppose we give this a rest until morning," suggested Len. "I'll call home when the apartment manager contacts me, and you can move in. I'm sure there are things about the place you will want done, and we'll take care of them this weekend."

"Thanks, Len. I appreciate the way you've helped me," said Julie.

Lisa delivered a sly look. "Too bad you didn't tell Alex the same thing."

When Julie was in bed, she couldn't get Lisa's last sting out of her mind. Should she have thanked Alex? He had offered to help her move. In her determination to manage her own life, she was forgetting basic rules of courtesy.

But Alex took too much for granted. He staked claims where she hadn't given him permission. Always in the back of her mind was his proposal of marriage. If she didn't keep her distance, he might bring it up again. Why was everyone so eager for her to marry? She was happy; she wished they'd leave her alone.

Last night's feeling of loneliness came back like a judgment. How empty she'd felt! But that was a momentary thing. Normally, her mind and time were so occupied she felt her single lifestyle superior to most women's. They had their husbands. She had her work.

In an unbidden shift of thought, she wondered how she would feel twenty or thirty years from now. Would she still be proud of her independence? She wondered why she was analyzing. Had Alex Stewart's appearance in her life shaken her plan for the future? Every facet of that plan was set in a solitary world of her own choices.

Now, for the first time she questioned if she was right or wrong. The main obstacle that separated Alex and her was his God. That He came before Julie was clear. Her family had never attended church, not even on Christmas or Easter. Alex's prayer for her was a new experience.

She tried to rationalize the peace that enveloped her when he asked God to take care of her. There was no explanation. It was just there: instant, complete, satisfying. But she couldn't be a minister's wife. She imagined herself in a meeting with a dozen Mrs. Biddles. *No!* That was not the life for her.

What made Alex go into the ministry? He had education, looks, a good personality. Why tie himself down to a job where his behavior was constantly examined, and he was not free to live as he chose? Whatever it was, it had nothing to do with her. She could never accept allegiance to some superior being she couldn't see. There. She'd come full circle. Alex wasn't the man for her. She simply wasn't interested. Julie smiled and spoke out loud.

"Hey, God, if you're really up there, keep Alex Stewart away so I can go on with my life."

Saturday found Julie set up in a light-filled apartment on the eighth floor of Len's complex. When she learned he was practically giving her the apartment, she protested to Lisa.

"Look, I don't expect Len to charge me less than he does other tenants. I can pay my way."

"Have some respect for my position, please. How would it look if my big sister didn't get preferential treatment? Besides, you're free to do your own decorating, and have I got some ideas for you!"

"I'm counting on it. The first thing I want is a selection of plants. This place is so full of light it begs for them." The doorbell buzzed. "Aha! My first caller," said Julie as she padded to the door in her bare feet.

Suddenly conscious of her grubby jeans and blouse, her hair piled on top of her head yet escaping from a clip, and not a speck of lipstick, she opened the door. It was Alex, bearing a bouquet of yellow chrysanthemums in a white ceramic vase. His slow grin widened, and the light in his eyes danced roguishly.

"Tell me, Miss Richmond," he inquired, "is there any circumstance at all under which you would not look totally delicious?"

Julie felt the warmth of her finest blush. She pulled herself together and took the flowers he held out to her.

"Th–thank you. Come in. . .please."

Wearing a green knit shirt, khaki shorts, white socks, and Nike athletic shoes, Alex entered the apartment. He strolled through, looking left and right, until his eyes fell on Lisa, who was washing the cabinet over the kitchen sink. In a state of dishabille similar to Julie's, Lisa giggled impudently.

"Welcome to the real world, Parson. Grab a sponge. You can do the bathroom cabinets. Len had an unexpected appointment, so consider yourself recruited."

"Lisa! He's a minister, for goodness sake!" Julie chided.

Alex turned, took the flowers, and placed them on the dinette table. He caught Julie's wrist, and his voice lowered.

"Remember the little talk we had about what ministers do and don't do? It applies to washing cabinets, too."

Julie's face warmed again. "Oh, all right," she said, pointing to a plastic pail of sudsy water. "You wash. I'll rinse."

His eyes never left hers, and when he released her wrist, she still couldn't look away. Lisa finally broke the silence.

"Far be it from me to interfere, but would you two please join the workforce?"

⬭

Clean windows and cabinets, houseplants, and Julie's new vacuum had transformed the apartment by the time Len called from his client's office. He was bringing carryout food and would be there shortly, he said.

Julie wanted Amelia to see her apartment and to eat with them, so Alex left to get her. He came back showered, shaved, and changed into gray casual slacks and a striped cotton shirt. Len was not there yet. Amelia darted from room to room, clapping her hands with delight. At the dinette window, her look changed to one of disappointment.

"You can't see the school from here. Since you're so high up, I thought you might be able to," she said.

"I think I see enough of that place, don't you?" said Julie.

Amelia nodded, still frowning. "But I thought if you were sick and had to stay home, you'd know I'd be watching from school and praying for you to get well."

Julie bent down to kiss her cheek. "Only you would think of that, darling."

&

The doorbell buzzed, and Alex answered. Len stumbled in with a heavy box of food. Noticing his shortness of breath, Alex took the box from him and carried it to the kitchen. Len seemed exhausted, and he sat down with Lisa in the living room. Alex helped Julie unload the food, and she smiled with appreciation. It was a feast of Chinese cuisine.

"Sweet ribs." Julie sighed. "I can't wait."

"Then don't," answered Alex, and he popped one into her mouth.

Julie gnawed off a bite and laid the rib on a paper napkin.

"My, you're messy," said Alex. "You have a spot of sauce right there." Alex aimed a kiss near her mouth.

"Alex! Amelia's in the next room."

"You think that would surprise her, eh?"

"Alex Stewart, have you been talking to her about me?"

"No," he said, taking a bite of Julie's discarded rib. "She starts the conversations without any help at all."

Alex knew Julie saw the sauce that deliberately missed his mouth, but she glared at him and headed for the dinette to set the table.

&

She wouldn't have to cook for days, Lisa told her, and Julie agreed wryly, wondering how many days she could abide the same diet. Her guests were sipping glasses of iced tea in the cheerful living room of her apartment.

Green plants set off white shuttered windows and a white wicker couch and chairs upholstered in a flower pattern. Alex and Len had attached standards and shelves to one wall, and the colors of Julie's books, plus bright Dali and Picasso prints, underscored the charm of the room.

Amelia, listening to their conversation, climbed onto Julie's lap and fell asleep. Noticing Alex's frown of concern, Julie dismissed it until he rose to feel the child's forehead.

"What is it, Alex? Is she ill?" she asked anxiously.

"No, there's no fever, but I don't like to see her this tired. She's usually more energetic than she was this evening."

"Should we take her to an emergency room, Alex?" asked Len. "They could head off whatever might be wrong."

"No, Len, I'm sure she's okay." He went back to his chair and sighed as he sat down. "I have a thing about Amelia, and it goes back to her mother's trouble."

Julie and Lisa traded glances. It was a rare thing for Alex to mention his marriage, and they were both at attention.

"My wife, Christi, died six years ago with a rare heart disease. Her first symptoms were weakness and fatigue. When Amelia gets tired, I try to keep a lid on her activity. She was up late last night, so I wouldn't let her come earlier. No doubt she would have been fine, but I thought it best to leave her at home."

"Does she have regular checkups?" asked Lisa.

"She gets impatient with the number I have done," he said.

"But, Alex, we went bowling," reminded Julie.

"Doctor's orders. He wants her to have exercise. I'm the one who holds back."

Julie looked at the perfect little face and felt such love that she wondered how Ethel could hate her own daughter so much. She understood Alex's caution; he was a normal father. She looked up at him. As if he had read her mind, Alex's gaze was empathetic.

She thought of her own duty. Her job was to solve the problem of Amelia's bad behavior. Instead, she was getting more involved with Amelia *and* her father. Would she start excusing Amelia's attitude as he had? Len interrupted her musing.

"If you're definite about not taking her to a hospital, I think I'll take my child-bride home," said Len. "She looks tired, too."

Lisa and Len left with Julie's thanks, and Alex saw them to the door. Amelia woke and hugged Julie.

"You let me go to sleep and miss everything."

Walking back to them, Alex smiled at the mini-admonition.

Julie smiled, too. "Not much happened, darling," she said. "Just talk. Do you feel all right?"

"Sure. I'm never sick. The doctor says I'm a 'prime specimen.' Do you know what that means? I don't."

Julie told her it meant best of the best. As she passed Amelia's supine body to Alex, his arms rested on hers, and he didn't let go. Julie was caught in his gaze.

"Why don't you come to church in the morning? Eleven o'clock. I'll. . .we'll be looking for you," he said.

It was an unexpected request, and with Amelia, too, listening for her answer, Julie was thrown off guard.

"I don't know. . .but thank you for everything, Alex."

Chapter 10

Curiosity had gotten the best of her, yet still wondering why she was there, Julie parked her car and got out. She felt as if everyone in the parking lot and in the vestibule of the church was staring at her. She had dressed conservatively in a brown ensemble, but she was afraid to wear jewelry. What *did* women wear to church? Why hadn't she paid more attention to their Sunday garb? If she were overdressed, she would be noticed and gossiped about again.

Wishing she hadn't come, she followed an usher down the aisle to a spot about the middle of the sanctuary, as he called it, and looked around. It was a pleasant auditorium. Walls and pews were white with dark wood trim, and pew cushions matched the blue carpeting.

Alex and another man appeared and were seated a few seconds before the choir filed in. The congregation was singing when Alex spotted Julie, and his wide smile embarrassed her. She wondered where Mrs. Biddle was sitting and if she'd whisper that Julie was the one that Dr. Stewart had embraced, right in the church.

There were many things Julie didn't know about, but she stood when everyone stood and sat when everyone sat. Prayers were spoken several times, and Julie wondered if the people prayed at home or just at church. She remembered when Alex prayed for her; he talked as he would to a close friend.

Energy sparked from Alex as he approached the podium. Normally he wore sports shirts, sweaters, and jackets with slacks and jeans, but in a dress suit and tie, Alex Stewart's presence was overwhelming. Why hadn't she noticed at the funeral or at Lisa's wedding? Julie inspected a visitor's card until she gained composure.

Alex didn't address any particular section of the audience. His eyes seemed to take in the whole crowd. He talked about Jesus again, and it seemed Jesus had close friends called disciples. They helped Him during His time on earth, and they grieved when He was crucified on a cross. But Jesus had not stayed dead. Alex said He laid down His life for sinners and then took it up again. Jesus was alive!

Julie remembered the exact verses Alex read from the Bible. They were in the book of John, chapter 10, verses 17 and 18. She knew because she wrote the numbers on the visitor's card. No way would she fill out one of those. The usher who took up the cards would think she was chasing Alex.

She didn't know her way around the Bible, but she'd bet Amelia did. She' ask to see her Bible sometime when Alex wasn't with them. Maybe she'd buy a Bible of her own. She might even memorize those two verses to surprise Alex. Or would she?

At the end, Alex asked if anyone wanted to commit his heart to Jesus, and Julie was dreadfully uncomfortable. She had an idea Alex was saying it to her especially, but she lowered her eyes; and at last it was over. Julie felt her relief must be visible to the eye.

After the service, Amelia showed up sooner than Julie expected. Mrs. Blake hurried behind, but she couldn't keep up; and in seconds Amelia was hugging Julie's waist. They drew little attention, which surprised Julie.

People were busy collecting families and talking to each other, most of them on the run, and Julie felt at ease again. There seemed to be no special dress code. Some were dressed better than others, but that was not important, apparently, for they intermixed at will.

"Miss Richmond, we have to wait over here," said Amelia, leading Julie to a chair in the vestibule. "Daddy told me not to let you get away, and I won't."

Amelia's brown eyes probed hers as if to ascertain she hadn't gone too far. Julie had nothing else to do, so she waited. She complimented Amelia, who was "gussied up," as Mrs. Blake described her. They were almost late because Amelia put together three outfits before choosing the green jumper and blouse she had on. Mrs. Blake said Amelia wanted to look just right because she was sure Miss Richmond was coming. Julie was glad she hadn't let her down.

The crowd thinned, and Alex, tall, smiling, his eyes on Julie, came toward them from the center entrance. Amelia had informed Julie it was where her father stood to shake hands with people as they filed out.

"God answered our prayers, didn't He, Amelia?" he asked as he swung his daughter up in his arms. "Julie, Mrs. Blake has a wonderful dinner prepared for us. Right, Mrs. B.?"

"But—" started Julie, astonished that they had *prayed* she would come.

"Now, now, we'll hear no buts, Miss Richmond," said Mrs. Blake. "Lunch is in the oven, and I've baked the best raisin and apple pie in the world. Come along now."

Mrs. Blake crooked her finger and walked briskly toward the double doors that led outside. Amelia was grinning with the same satisfaction as her father. They were too much for her, Julie decided. A lady should acknowledge when she was beaten.

❧

Until today Julie hadn't seen all of Alex's house, and she found it utter pleasure. The furniture was not fragile like hers. It was big and wearable, indicative of a man's taste. The colors were neutral but accented with bold, vivid shades. His pictures were like him—the subject matter understood from first look. Were these things Christi had picked out, or had he thrown away everything at her death and purposely employed his own masculine judgment?

Lunch was as advertised—wonderful. The pie, with a scoop of vanilla ice cream, was beyond description. Julie wondered how Ethel had missed the mark so far, when with a little effort she could have produced meals like this one for her family.

Julie shut her eyes when they prayed before the meal. She had seen people doing it at church. Would they have another prayer when they finished eating, she wondered? No, there was nothing more.

Alex held her chair for her when she sat down, and he came to hand her out of it. Julie's emotions were playing havoc with her mind. In an atmosphere suffused with contentment, she was truly at peace. In the only family situation she knew, peace was nonexistent. Was it possible to have a marriage in which each day could occur without screams and accusations and threats?

"Penny for your thoughts," Alex murmured as they sat together in the living room.

When Amelia placed herself between them in play clothes that Mrs. Blake had ordered, Julie cuddled the little girl close. Looking over her head at Alex, she answered his query.

"I was thinking how peaceful your home is," Julie confessed. "You're a lucky man." She kissed Amelia's shiny bangs. "And so are you, darling."

"Daddy, don't you love the way she says darling?" asked Amelia, looking up at Alex.

Alex looked deep into Julie's eyes. "I love it, darling." Then he tousled Amelia's hair. "How would you girls like to drive out to see the fall leaves? They're beautiful in the country."

Amelia jumped to her feet, her eyes shining. "You mean you don't have a single meeting this afternoon?"

"Not a one. We have almost five whole hours together."

"Please, let's go, Miss Richmond. You don't have any meetings this afternoon, do you?"

"No, honey."

Amelia grabbed her hand. "Then come on, before the telephone rings and Daddy has to go somewhere."

Poor little girl, Julie thought. Even when she has time with him, she's never sure it won't be snatched away.

⌘

Some distance from town, driving down a lane on property belonging to friends of Alex, they came upon a small lake with a backdrop of maples that were gold and red. Soon the branches would be bare, but now they were breathtaking.

"Have you ever seen anything so beautiful?" Julie asked.

"Yes, it's amazing what God can create to show us His majesty."

"Majesty. That's just the word." She spread her arms wide to encompass the scene before her. "Just look at the majesty of the hills."

As Julie and Alex walked, crunching the fallen leaves underfoot, breathing in the smoky scent of autumn, Amelia chased a toad that hopped ahead of her along the bank. Alex smiled, and Julie decided the time was right to discuss his daughter's problems. She cleared her throat. Was she actually nervous?

"Alex, let's talk about Amelia." He stopped walking instantly, and Julie brushed back a strand of her wind-tossed hair. "I found out the day we bowled that Amelia resents the amount of time you spend with the teenage boys of your church. I realize it's necessary, but is there any way you could direct a bit more of your time to her?"

"Do you think that's the problem?"

"Partly. Amelia is disruptive at school because she wants the attention of the other girls. I haven't had a bad report on her this year, but Miss Clay, her teacher last year, says it comes in spurts. Alex, I suspect when she doesn't get the attention she thinks you should give her, she gets it at school any way she can. Being naughty does get attention from the girls *and* the teacher."

"It sounds right. But how do I know when she feels neglected? Or is a father supposed to grasp it instinctively?"

"I don't think there's a hard-and-fast rule. But maybe you could cut back until you feel, within yourself, that she's had enough time with you."

"Any clues on how to measure that?" he asked with a puzzled frown.

"I should think. . ." Julie's eyes narrowed as she looked across the lake, its surface rippled by the wind. "I'd say, when she sends you off because she has more important things to do and tells you so."

This time, Alex brushed back the tangle of hair from Julie's forehead. "Teacher, you're wonderful," he said with a smile.

Refusing to be distracted, she went on. "One more thing, Alex. Could you give her a private time at night—added to her prayer time, for instance—when she shares what she's reading? It would thrill her if you could trade ideas and let her show you she's becoming her own person."

Throughout, she had his complete attention. "Julie, Julie," he said. "You've really thought this out, haven't you?" Tracing her cheek with his fingers, he spoke again. "We both handle people. We encourage them, help them, correct them when we have to, and we love them. No wonder you suit me like a glove."

Julie backed off. "Let's not get carried away, Alex. We were talking about Amelia. Our personal lives don't enter into this. You helped me when I needed help. I'm merely returning the favor. All that stuff you said in church this morning separates us, and you know it. We live in different worlds."

"Why, Julie? What do you have against God?"

"I've never needed religion. I got where I am without praying about every step I take, and nothing has changed."

"That's because you didn't know what you were missing. Jesus came to fulfill our lives, Julie."

"My life, the part I control, is fulfilled. I have everything I need."

Looking down the bank toward his child, Alex shouted, "Amelia! Come on back now. You're getting too far away." He turned back to Julie. "As long as you don't have Christ in your heart, Julie, you'll never have everything you need."

"I think I've had all of this I want." She started to walk away.

"All right, Julie, I'll stop. But if you ever want to talk about this again, please tell me."

Don't hold your breath, she thought. But in her heart, knowing Alex to be an educated man, she wondered again how he could choose to *serve* an unseen God, who, as far as she could see, had no control over the world at all.

A letter from Colleen announced that Curt was driving her home for Thanksgiving, and by phone, Julie invited her mother to have dinner at her apartment. Ethel screamed her answer. If Julie wanted to have a Thanksgiving dinner, she could manage by herself. The answer wasn't a surprise, so Julie wasn't crushed.

Oddly, Lisa's response was indefinite. She wasn't feeling well, she said, and she doubted they'd be coming. Julie had never known Lisa to miss a party. Still, marriage had changed things; her sister was not the same girl.

Aware of the circumstances leading to Julie's getting an apartment, Colleen and Curt came to her instead of to the Richmond house. Julie beamed as she opened the door for them.

"Colleen! I've never been so glad to see anyone!" she exploded, grabbing her sister. "Come in! Both of you! I have hot mandarin tea, Curt. Come have a cup before you go back out in the cold."

Curt set Colleen's suitcase inside the door and helped her out of her coat. Julie was astonished at the amount of weight her sister had lost. She was beautiful from her shoes to her highlighted hair. Curt almost never took his eyes from her.

As they talked at the table, Julie got more clues about the couple's relationship.

"You look marvelous, Colleen," said Julie. "Don't you think so, Curt?"

"Too marvelous. I had to take a number for the privilege of driving her home to KC."

Colleen gave his hand a smack. "Curt, stop exaggerating."

"I'm not, Julie. She's turned into a femme fatale. I have to make her go out with me."

"Not because I am so utterly charming to other men. It's because you need to study, *Doctor*." Colleen turned on a proud look. "Julie, he made the highest grade in the class on his last test."

Noticing the intimate look Curt gave Colleen, Julie felt things were coming her sister's way at last. Despite her happiness with Curt, however, Colleen was concerned about the family crisis.

"Okay, Julie, Curt knows our problems with Mother, so let's get on with it. Where are we having Thanksgiving?"

Julie glanced at Curt. "Will you be with us, Curt? I warn you—it's going to be cozy because I'm having it here."

"Don't apologize, Julie. I think your apartment is gorgeous," said Colleen. "Don't you, Curt?"

"It's great. Only I'm afraid you can't count on me; the folks are looking forward to my eating with the family. We all hoped Colleen would be with us, but as things stand, I guess you want her here. I'd like to come over later though."

Julie nodded. "You know you're welcome anytime you can make it. I appreciate your bringing Colleen home. I've missed her so much, and, with all our troubles, I need a big dose of my sister, right now. Understand?" she asked plaintively.

Nodding, Curt grinned, finished his tea, and picked up his coat. "Good tea, Julie. Thanks." Then, speaking softly to Colleen, "Want to walk me to the door?"

Julie stayed out of sight until he was gone. A shiny-eyed Colleen giggled and hugged Julie when she was back.

"Did you ever see anyone so terrific? And he loves me, Julie. We talk about marriage as if it were some other couple, but we both mean it to happen for us someday."

"What a relief. I was afraid you would quit school and try to support him."

"No, I wouldn't quit. I need these four years to adjust to normal living." Colleen massaged her forehead. "I even dread Mother's coming here to eat. I'm afraid she'll make me lose my confidence all over again."

"We won't let that happen, Colleen, and she may not come. But don't worry—she isn't going to mess us up this time."

The telephone rang, and Julie answered.

"Hi. It's me," said Alex. "First, Amelia wants to know what time we're to come for dinner on Thursday. Second, Mrs. Blake wants to know if there's any way she can help you."

"Did you invite her, Alex?" Julie saw Colleen's quick glance and smile. "I don't want her troubling herself if she's not eating with us."

"I tried, but she wants to join her sister's family. What about that raisin and apple pie you enjoyed so much?"

"Mmm. . .I can't say no to that." Julie looked at Colleen. "Curt drove my sister home from college. They got in a few minutes ago."

"Tell her hello for me, and I'll see her Thanksgiving Day."

❧

Working with Colleen, Julie thought the holiday dinner turned out well. She anticipated a disaster since she was not an experienced cook, but Colleen gave her confidence; and no tragedies occurred. Ethel refused to eat with them if *the preacher* was coming.

To Julie, it was no contest. She owed Alex too much to renege on his invitation. He and Amelia came early, and Julie was surprised how helpful they both were and what fun it was. Her sister, seizing the opportunity, reminded her it would be nice to have them around all the time.

What Lisa had told Julie was understated. When the Sherrys tried to come for dinner, Lisa not only looked sick, she was sick. She made for Julie's bed as soon as she got inside, and Julie tucked a blanket around her. Once back in the kitchen, she sent Amelia to check on Lisa now and then.

Len said he was no good at cooking, so he sat on a high stool in the corner of the dinette, drank coffee, and gazed out the window. Julie thought he looked like a man with a troubled mind. Had he and Lisa quarreled? Minutes later, she heard Lisa in the bathroom, and Len rushed to her.

When he came back, he helped Lisa into her coat. "I'm taking her home, Julie. I shouldn't have let her come, but she did want to be here. Regardless of how this looks, it's actually a happy time for us." Lisa managed to answer his smile. "We're going to have a baby," he said, the words like syrup on his lips.

Julie and Colleen were ready to swoop down on Lisa, but she warned them away.

"Be careful, I may upchuck on you at any minute," she murmured. "I want to get the elevator ride over and go home. Sorry I'm such a party pooper, Julie."

Assuring her she was not, Julie asked Alex to go down with them to make sure they had no problems. He was gone several minutes and came back with a disconcerted expression.

The turkey Julie had taken up permeated the apartment with its savory aroma, and she handed Alex a carving knife.

Julie examined his somber face. "Wasn't she all right?"

He nodded, then looked toward Colleen and Amelia working in the dinette. "It's not Lisa I'm anxious about, Julie. It's Len."

Chapter 11

Thanksgiving day ended with Curt, Colleen, Julie, Alex, and Amelia playing a board game Amelia had persuaded her father to bring. Julie was anxious for a private conversation with Alex; he had not told her why he was worried about Len. But the others were having a good time, and she hated to interrupt.

The doorbell rang. Lisa and Len were back.

Lisa was smiling. "Yes, it's us! Expectant mommies feel nauseous one minute and not the next, more or less, so we decided to come back for what's left of the party."

"I've married a wild woman," added Len. "She can't stand to miss a good time." He hung up their coats and followed her into the room.

The mood got even lighter, and Julie felt her first dinner party and the evening a complete success. She wished her mother had come. She *might* not have spoiled the day. Who was she kidding? She probably would have.

Pulling his eyes from Len, Alex glanced at Julie as she went to the dinette for the coffee carafe. From the shadows she looked back at her brother-in-law. Alex was right; Len's color was not good. Julie had the feeling Len would be better off at home in bed. She should break up the evening so he could leave. Then, before she could think of a way, Alex handled it for her.

"No more coffee for me, Julie," he said as she started to refill his cup. "I have to get this little girl of mine to bed."

"Oh, Daddy, why? We're having so much fun."

"Because it's past your bedtime, and you need rest. Curt, it's good to see you again, and you, too, beautiful," he directed to Colleen, who glowed at the compliment. "Lisa and Len, I'd say the marriage is going to take."

"You can depend on it, Parson," said Lisa, hugging Len's arm.

"Sweetheart, why don't I walk Alex and Amelia to the elevator?" said Len. "They have the pie carrier, and the food Julie's sending, and the game," said Len.

"Sure. Help them all the way to the car, why don't you?"

Julie kissed Amelia and made sure her coat was buttoned, and the two men, each carrying something, followed Amelia out the door. Curt stood up.

"I need to get back to the house, too." To Colleen, he said, "If I ask Julie for some things to carry, will you walk me to the elevator?"

"I shall be delighted to walk you to the elevator, Dr. Graham," she enunciated, "even if you go empty-handed."

After Curt bundled up for the icy chill outside, they left, holding hands and laughing. Lisa leaned back and sighed.

"Aren't they perfect together, Julie? Colleen has made herself over. She looks wonderful."

"Yes," Julie agreed. "Curt told me she's popular with everyone. They see each other as often as he can get away, but his time is so limited Colleen says she feels guilty when he's out with her."

Lisa smiled. "I get the distinct impression that she's his cheerleader, whether it's by telephone, or mail, or in person. Colleen will make an excellent doctor's wife."

"As *you* have made an excellent lawyer's wife."

"The way I was going, I would have been a nonperson if I'd stayed around Mother much longer. Now I just want to love and be loved. But it is nice that I know something of the law. You have no idea how much Len shares with me, Julie."

"Sharing is what marriage is supposed to be about, isn't it? You're lucky your training suits him so well."

Julie was thinking: *That's what Alex said—I suited him like a glove.* Their conversation resembled that of two married women chatting. Only she wasn't married. Then, as if Lisa had read her mind, she said it out loud.

"Julie, as long as you can't or won't get rid of Alex, why don't you marry him?"

"I'm the confirmed old maid, remember?"

"Tell me one good reason you should not try to grab this great-looking man."

With a derisive look, Julie held up her fist. "You want reasons?" She extended three fingers in turn, "Number one, I don't want to get married. Number two, he's a minister. Number three, I could never be a minister's wife."

"You could learn to be a minister's wife."

"Oh, Lisa, that's not something you learn. It has to be part of a commitment inside. Alex wants me to believe in Jesus, and I'd never opened a Bible until I heard him preach. I went out and bought one—don't ask me why. I did it for no reason at all, so stop smiling. I know you and Colleen both think he's the one. But I'm still the same girl, kissed or unkissed."

"So, he kissed you, eh?" Lisa questioned with a sly look.

"Yes, he kissed me. You know when. I told you. I was in shock: After all those years of taking care of her, Mother had just told me to get out."

"That night was a turning point for you, sister dear. Your life has been changing ever since. So don't be dumb and goof it up. Maybe Alex's God led *him* to *you*. That's pretty strong stuff, and I don't think I'd mess around with it if I were you."

❧

Julie was about to undress when the telephone rang. It was Alex.

"I wondered if it was too late to get together again tonight."

"Alex, it's eleven thirty."

"Yes, I know, but I thought you might like to hear about Len."

"Of course I would, Alex. Forgive me."

"I'm downstairs in the lobby. Can we go to the coffee shop where we talked about Lisa's wedding? It's open all night."

"I'll be right down."

Julie ordered decaffeinated coffee, and Alex ordered the same. When it came, he tasted it, made a face, and set the cup aside.

Finally, he started, "Len's sick, Julie. He told me I could tell you, but under no circumstances does he want Lisa to know. She's under a specialist's care, in case she hasn't told you. Her nausea has pushed her almost to the point of dehydration. She probably shouldn't have been there tonight." Seeing her stricken face, he took her hand. "There's nothing you can do; everything that can be done is being done."

"Then what about Len, Alex? How sick is he?"

"It's his heart. The doctors want him to have a bypass, but he's afraid the nervous strain would cause Lisa to lose the baby. He wants to wait until it's born."

"But that's too long. If he's telling you now, you can bet it should have been done ages ago."

"Almost a year. Back then, he turned the doctors down because, even if it cost his life, he wanted as much time with Lisa as he could have. You've no idea how much he loves her."

"Yes, I do. She feels exactly the same. She's told me."

"Now that they're married, he says he can't bear to think of her losing the baby. He's looking ahead. If he doesn't make it, he wants her to have the baby to love and to remember him by."

"Alex," she cried. "Oh, Alex, what are we going to do?"

He slid into the booth beside Julie and put his arm around her. "There's nothing we can do, except pray and do as Len asks."

"What is he asking?" Julie murmured through her choking sorrow and tears.

"Our support. That's why he made an excuse to go downstairs with me. His partner, Dwight Winwood, will take care of his will and property if the worst should happen, but he wants me to take care of Lisa. I told him I'd do whatever he wanted, and he acted more at peace.

"He told me at the wedding he had given his heart to the Lord when he was a boy, and it was still as fresh in his mind as the day it happened. He wants Lisa to start going to my church with him," Alex finished as Julie wiped her eyes.

"I'll come, too. If I go, she'll go." Her eyes met his. "I'll try to learn more about this God of yours, Alex. If He's really there, it looks like we may need Him."

Throughout the holiday season, Julie kept in close touch with Lisa and Len. When Lisa's episodes of nausea permitted, Julie and the Sherrys went to church together.

Len had a good voice, and Lisa and Julie, without planning it, sat on either side of him to listen. One Sunday when they were walking from the church to the car, Lisa chided him gently.

"I love hearing you sing, Len. Why did you never tell me you had this great talent?"

"It's not great, sweetheart. I merely enjoy singing. You know I love music of all kinds."

Since they were eating out together, the Sherrys had picked up Julie that morning. All three shivered at the bitterness of the day. Though the sun shone through a cloudy sky at times, cold wind bit at Julie's cheeks as she spoke.

"This month is full of music at the church, Len. You should have joined one of the vocal groups," she commented and regretted it immediately. Len needed a low-key life.

"I thought about it, but my schedule doesn't allow the rehearsals involved. Besides, Lisa needs me home at night."

"That's right! But I would like to hear at least one program the choir is doing, wouldn't you, Julie?" asked Lisa.

"Yes, and I want to see Amelia's program, too."

"You and the parson's daughter are close, aren't you?"

"If this is the start of a campaign, I'm not getting into the conversation," said Julie.

"That's a guilty conscience talking. You know you should be letting Alex take you out more."

"Call off your wife, Len," Julie said, getting into the back seat as he held her door.

Len put Lisa in and walked to the driver's side. He started the motor and smiled as he backed the car out.

"I'm afraid you won't get much help from me, Julie," he replied. "I think you should go out with Alex more, too."

"Surrounded by conspirators!" Julie shot back. "My own family is trying to sell me out to a man with whom I have nothing in common, spiritually. I'm constantly looking up things in my little Bible to find out what he's talking about."

Lisa giggled over her shoulder. "I notice you qualified what you don't have in common. Don't fight it so hard, Sis. The man's in love with you, and he has a sweet daughter who adores you. How is she getting along in school, by the way?"

"Almost no problems now. Alex says it's because I'm in the picture, and she feels secure. But he'll have to keep her secure himself if I change jobs or move away."

Lisa's eyes widened as she turned to face Julie. "You aren't thinking of doing that, are you?"

Julie hadn't meant to address this, but she'd set her own trap. "Colleen says there's an administrative position open at her school. It would mean more money, to say nothing of a more appealing résumé," she explained.

"But why, Julie? No, don't tell me. It's to get away from Alex, isn't it?"

"No, not exactly. I—"

"Yes, it is—exactly that!" Lisa laughed and laid her hand on Len's shoulder. "Sweetheart, this is a momentous occasion. Julie Richmond has finally met her match, and if she doesn't escape at once, she'll have to turn part of her power over to *a man*. It's inconceivable!" she finished, giggling.

Len didn't dare laugh with Lisa. He agreed with his wife, but she was handling it the wrong way. He waited. Julie had no comeback and was sitting still, probably simmering inside. He knew his sister-in-law, and it was true—she liked being in command. Lisa, bless her heart, had just stepped all over her big sister's pride. Hoping Julie would forget all but what he was about to say, Len made a request.

"Julie, I don't know your reasons for wanting to leave Kansas City, and I'm sure you've thought it over from every angle. But I'd like to add one other fact before you decide." He patted Lisa's hand on his shoulder. "You know this wife of mine is priceless to me, and it will be several months before the baby is born. Julie, I'm asking you to give up the idea of leaving until well after that. Lisa will need you, and I need you. Will you do this for me?"

Julie could see Len's eyes in the rearview mirror, and she was sorry she had put him through such an ordeal. Naturally she couldn't leave. She was annoyed that she had shared something she'd only lately begun to contemplate.

Lisa had hit on the truth; the problem was Alex. She had seen him every week, and now she was accepted at church as the pastor's close friend whom he might someday marry. Amelia was starting to believe it, too. Julie was getting in deeper and deeper.

Did she refuse to commit her heart to the Lord and to Alex because she rejected a submissive role in life? Alex made no excuses when his messages declared a man was the spiritual leader of the home. If he was the spiritual leader, wouldn't that mean giving up all decision making? Wouldn't he hold the purse strings and insist she quit her beloved profession to participate in things he needed a wife for?

No! It was too uneven. The first thing she knew, she would be walking three paces behind and waiting at the door with his slippers. Julie shook her head as tears stung her eyes. It was absurd to think about. She'd wait until the baby was born and, in a reasonable time, start sending out her résumé.

"Yes, Len," she said firmly. "I'll stay as long as you need me."

"I hope you still feel that way after we eat," he said, looking straight ahead. "I've asked Alex to join us for lunch."

❧

Len drove to a seafood restaurant that was one of Julie's favorites. Not long after they were seated, Alex came. He had turned up his overcoat collar against the cold air, and the wind had mussed his hair. But he was the same handsome, in-charge person with whom Julie feared she was falling in love.

"Sorry I couldn't get here sooner," he said breathlessly, the cold emanating from his body as he sat down. "Lots of things going on at church. I'll have to get right back, I'm afraid."

Julie shrugged and gave the Sherrys a *see what I mean* look and picked up her menu.

"Oh, that's too bad, Alex," said Lisa with a pathetic whine. "We were hoping you could drop Julie off. Len needs to make a short visit to a client of his I've never met."

Alex bit. With a wide smile, he turned to Julie. "I always have time for that; consider it done."

As they chose from the menu, Julie could not catch Lisa's eye. How could her sister do this, she wondered. It was getting harder and harder to remain aloof when she and Alex were alone, and Lisa knew it. She was manipulating people, again. Worse yet, she was teaching Len. He was the one who invited Alex to lunch.

❧

They parted at the restaurant, leaving the Sherrys to "visit" a mythical client, Julie was sure. Alex turned on the heater in his car, and it sent out a blast of cold air. Smiling, he glanced at her.

"I don't suppose you could scoot over and share your warmth with me until the heater comes on?"

"I could, but it's against my principles."

"Ugh! Those principles of my little assistant principal again!"

She smiled at the word *little* and remembered how small she'd felt when he towered above her the day they met. Her hands trembled as she tucked her Bible into the side pocket of her shoulder bag. Alex was watching.

"Julie, is that the Bible you study?" he asked with a frown.

"Are you checking up on how much I read the Bible?"

"No," he said, "I wondered if you had a better one at home, but you carry this small one when you go out."

"No, Doctor, this is all. I have been reading it; although, I didn't think a Bible had to be a certain size or variety," she finished briskly.

He laid his hand over hers. "Julie, I wasn't criticizing; I was simply interested."

Minutes later they left the freeway and would soon turn onto Julie's street.

"There's something I'm interested in too, Alex. In the time we have left, why don't you explain why God made the man the spiritual leader of the home?"

"What brought that up?" he asked, chuckling.

"You did, several times in your sermons. You really believe t

"Yes, I do." His tone changed. "It's the father's responsibility to make sure his family is taught God's Word. Great women played important roles in the Bible, but it's the man God entrusted with his family's spiritual growth."

"Does that mean he's supposed to think for the wife, too?"

"No, God's Word teaches both men *and* women how to have a satisfying life. From Proverbs 31:10 to the end of the chapter, God pictures a woman helping her husband and children to be their best for the Lord. In return, she has security, peace, and contentment. But she doesn't sit in a corner doing nothing. God gives her a fountain of energy to be creative.

"Those verses were written centuries ago, but they're as timely as ever. God wants a woman to *honor* her husband, but he is to love *her* as Christ loves the church. Our minds are too small to imagine the extent of that kind of love; it's infinite. On top of that, Jesus liberated women with His love. They were mere property until He gave them freedom and status."

They had reached Julie's apartment complex. Alex drove close to the entrance and came to open her door.

"I can't tell you how much I would like to continue this conversation, but I have a rehearsal with the auditorium choir for the Christmas music. Will you read the passage I told you about? And make notes of any questions you have, Julie; we'll talk about them later."

"Yes, I will," she promised, delivering a straightforward look. "Do you realize that, at last, we've been together without bringing up the subject of romance?"

"Wrong," he said, pulling her to him.

Alex's mouth found hers. He kissed her ardently, and Julie didn't care that they were standing in a parking lot, buffeted by the wind, or that her purse had dropped, unnoticed, to the pavement.

Chapter 12

What to buy Alex was Julie's most perplexing Christmas gift. The price, how intimate, and what he would read into a gift were questions her mind shifted about without answers.

She had already given Amelia her gift. Julie purchased orchestra seats for Amelia and Alex to see *The Nutcracker*, performed by the State Ballet of Missouri. On the night before the performance, Alex managed a third ticket for her next to them.

It was a magical night. Julie bought a dress of midnight blue taffeta with a full skirt and a bodice trimmed with black velvet. A rhinestone pin and long earrings of the same stones glittered as she moved.

Amelia's dress resembled hers slightly. Although her full skirt was of green plaid taffeta, shot with a thread of gold, the bodice was solid black velvet piped in gold. Mrs. Blake had pulled back the sides of Amelia's hair and clasped it with a golden ribbon.

"Amelia, darling, you look good enough to eat!" Julie gushed to keep her mind off Alex when they appeared at the apartment.

Although he stood back to admire the two of them, in a black suit, white shirt, and maroon tie with black geometric figures, Alex was the handsome one.

Julie had to tell him. "You look wonderful, Alex."

"Now, Daddy, tell her she looks wonderful, too. Only call her *darling*, the way she does me," directed Amelia.

Alex's eyes were spellbinding. "You look wonderful, too, Julie darling."

"Now let's go," Amelia ordered, and Julie and Alex, taking the hands she offered, did as they were told.

❧

The review of the ballet in the *Star* gave it high praise. Alex concurred; though he had trouble concentrating as he normally would have. The lovely lady sitting next to him was more breathtaking than any of the sprightly beauties onstage. Amelia insisted he sit next to Julie for a reason. That reason had captivated him since the day they met, but Amelia laid it on the table.

"If she sits between us, we can both enjoy how good she smells," she whispered. "Grownups should sit together anyway, and, besides, I can see the stage a lot better than I could in Miss Richmond's seat."

Amelia winked at Alex with the subtlety of a child who had only lately learned the trick. He was sure both the man in front of her *and* Julie got the picture. Julie's usual blush and lowered eyes gave him an excuse to lay his arm across the back of her seat with a whispered comment of his own.

"I often wonder how men without clever daughters manage their social lives. I know I could never do it."

His remark brought a smile to Julie's lips, and he was fascinated, then thoughtful. *Lord Jesus,* he prayed silently, *You must mean to give Julie to me. I couldn't feel this strongly about her if it weren't Your will. Give me patience to wait until she sees You clearly and gives her life to You.*

On their way home from the ballet, Amelia didn't stop talking, so Julie, intensely aware of Alex, was relieved to answer yes or no at the appropriate times. Having Alex's arm across the back of her seat during the ballet was fatal to an unruffled composure. They stopped at an IHOP restaurant for hot chocolate to top off Amelia's evening.

"Miss Richmond," Amelia said as Julie wiped chocolate from the child's upper lip, "tell the truth now. Wasn't tonight the very best time you ever had in your whole life?"

Julie saw Alex waiting for her answer. Looking at Amelia, she said, "Yes, darling, it really was the very best time I've ever had."

"In your whole life?"

She glanced at Alex, whose eyes shone with merriment.

"Yes."

"I knew it! I told you, didn't I, Daddy?" She smiled at Julie. "I knew that's what you would say, and Daddy said we shouldn't get our hopes too high. But *I* knew."

"You'll have to convince your dad to have more faith, won't you?"

"That's exactly what I said. Also, he has to learn to pray about things more. That's what I did. And see? It happened!"

Julie's face warmed again because she knew this wasn't the last word. Alex's slow grin was there.

"That's right, Amelia. I guess if I want something a lot, I'll have to pray hard until I get it."

"Not only that, but if you want *someone* a lot, you have to pray hard to get *her,*" she said with subtlety equal to her wink.

Seeing Alex's embarrassment, Julie could hardly keep from giggling. Thanks to Amelia, he was getting back some of his own.

"I think you've carried this about as far as it needs to go," said Alex. "If you've finished your hot chocolate, we'd better get you home to bed."

The next day, Julie drove to her mother's to take a Christmas gift. The house looked more forlorn than usual. It was cold, and it was December; but none of the neighbors' houses had the dismal look of the Richmonds'.

As she walked across the porch, she noticed one end of the swing had fallen to the floor. Maybe her mother would allow her to send someone to fix it. Strange, Colleen hadn't mentioned it. Did that mean she hadn't been by? No, her sister would need encouragement even to drive down the street.

Her mother didn't answer the bell. Shifting from one foot to the other, Julie felt like a fool. The door had a new lock, and her key was of no use. She couldn't gain entrance to her mother's home. Mrs. Paine, next door, came out to speak to her.

"Keep ringing, Julie. She's there. She's up to her silly tricks again. Are you girls aware of how her mind is slipping?"

Julie nodded in embarrassment and kept ringing. Mrs. Paine went inside, and finally, the door opened a crack.

"Can't you take a hint?" her mother grumbled.

"I'd like to come in and talk to you."

Ethel hesitated a moment, then swung back the door and walked toward the kitchen. Julie knew it wasn't going to be easy. Alex had asked to come with her, but she refused, knowing that if he were along, her mother would not talk to her at all.

"Well, spit it out. What's on your mind?" Ethel asked, her eyes darting around the walls and ceiling.

Her mother's hair was uncombed, and her dress, blotched with food stains and grease, had not been laundered recently. How could the woman live like this? *She doesn't know how bad she is,* thought Julie, and her heart felt torn.

"It's almost Christmas, Mother. Aren't you lonesome for any of your family?"

"I don't have a family. They all died. Mama, Papa, Grammy, Grampa, my aunt Josie—they're all dead, all gone. Sid, too.

Evidence of her mother's decline was plain. She was living in the past.

"Mother, don't you remember your children? Lisa and Colleen, and me—Julie?"

"Oh, I remember you, all right," Ethel shouted. "The day I had you ended things for me. You took my life away, the life I could have had."

"All right, forget me. What about Colleen and Lisa? Don't you want to see them? Don't you care about them?" pleaded Julie.

"Yeah, I know Colleen and Lisa. But I'm going to forget about them, too. They don't care about me. People either hate you, or they die. Except Mama and Papa," she murmured with a smile. "They don't hate me. They love me."

"I know that comforts you, Mother. But I came to bring you this present and find out if I can help you in any way."

The present was ignored, so Julie set it on a chair. From beneath it, a cockroach tried a scratchy escape but was not quick enough. Ethel stamped on the pest with a triumphant cry and danced with delight before Julie.

"He thought he'd get away, but they don't get by Ethel. I watch for 'em all day long, and I kill 'em!" She laughed again. "I handle things around here now!"

Julie wanted to cry. The cluttered house was an eyesore. It was obvious her mother made no attempt to keep order. What could she do? What would Ethel allow her to do? She'd have to talk to Lisa and Colleen. One thing was definite—their mother's state of mind must be evaluated.

"How do you live, Mother? Do you shop for food and whatever you need, or do you have it delivered?"

"Whenever I need something, I call old what's-his-name that Lisa married, and he brings it by. Lisa doesn't know it, but he's my errand boy," Ethel cackled. "Can't you see Mister Fancy-Pants running up and down the aisles getting groceries? I leave out two or three things sometimes, so he'll have to make an extra trip." She laughed uproariously.

Julie dropped into a chair. Her legs would not support her. Len had turned over the paperwork involving her mother's affairs to one of his clerks. But having to do extra tasks for Ethel when his own health was in jeopardy? It was unthinkable! She shook with frustration. Lisa and Colleen had to know this at once.

No, she couldn't tell Lisa. Bragging that Len was the best husband in the world, Lisa might let him continue doing Ethel's work. With school and living away from Kansas City, Colleen could do little to change things. Julie's mind scampered along the perimeter of an answer, and she gave in to it. She had to ask Alex for help.

"I'm leaving now, Mother." Ethel had started upstairs, humming, as if she had forgotten Julie was there. "I'll call you as usual, and I'll be back soon."

Ethel didn't acknowledge her, and Julie left, worried and sad. Walking to her car, she turned again to the old house where she had grown up and saw its wretched look of despair. She'd have to get the swing fixed, or Len might be asked to do it. Tears misted her eyes. She unlocked her car as Alex drove up, and she knew he had been watching from someplace near.

He strode quickly to her side. Knowing her mother was probably watching them, Julie told Alex to drive to a service station two blocks over. They met at the station, and, as before, when Alex put his arms around her, the floodgate of tears opened. They got in her car, and he turned to listen.

"It was awful, Alex. My mother's losing her mind. She goes from the past to the present and back again. We have to do something about her care. I'm so ashamed. She actually bragged about making Len her errand boy. Can you believe she has him shop for her? She even causes him to make extra trips. We have to do something!" Julie was almost hysterical.

"Shh," Alex comforted, "we'll do something. Stop crying now and listen to me." He wiped her tears with his handkerchief, then put it in her hand. "We'll talk to Len first. But I'm sure he'll advise us to have your mother checked."

"It's all right to say it, Alex," Julie murmured. "I know her mental state has to be evaluated. And I know it's for her own good. You can't imagine the squalor she's living in. Mother has to be watched, and Lisa and Colleen have to accept it."

"I think Lisa will, but it will be hard for Colleen."

Julie started to cry again. "The house needs cleaning and exterminating, Alex. The porch swing has fallen on one side, and if it isn't fixed, Mother will ask Len to do it. He might have an attack just lifting it." Julie looked at him in alarm. "But, Alex, I'm not hinting that you should do it. If you did, I'm afraid she might come at you and—"

"We'll get it fixed, and the rest, too. I'll call Len when I get home. Maybe we can meet him at their place later."

"Colleen's out shopping with Curt. I'll go back to the apartment and wait for her. Call me when you get in touch with Len, Alex."

Alex started to get out, then reached back to touch Julie's cheek.

"It's going to be all right, Julie. God's already taking care of this."

Alex called before Colleen came, carrying a shopping bag full of gifts. She looked so happy, Julie hated bringing up their mother's problems, but she had to move quickly to spare Len. She'd have to watch what she said; Colleen didn't know about Len's heart trouble either.

After Julie told Colleen they were going to Lisa's that night, she followed her sister into the bedroom, gave her shoes a kick, and climbed onto the queen-size bed to sit cross-legged. Colleen opened a closet door and hung up her sweater and coat.

"Honey," Julie started, "we're going to Lisa's because I went to see Mother this afternoon, and I—"

"Julie! You went by yourself?"

"Yes, but it was all right. She wasn't happy I was there, but she wasn't violent." Julie dropped her head and picked at a fingernail. "She's worse, Colleen. I'm not sure she recognizes reality anymore. And she hates me. You'll understand when I tell you why. But it's her future treatment I'm concerned about, and it's not revenge. You do believe that, don't you?"

"Of course I do, Julie. I lived with Mother for eighteen years, remember."

"Alex knew I was going there today. He followed and parked where he could see the house. I needed someone, Colleen, as it turned out." Still clutching Alex's handkerchief, she stroked the corner monogram with her thumbs. "He talked to Len, and, tonight we're getting together to decide exactly what to do about Mother."

Colleen closed the closet door. The look on her face hurt Julie, but, as Alex said, Colleen was a mature girl. She would realize the urgency of the situation.

Her sister's answer was a total surprise. "I could have spared you this, Julie, and I'm sorry I didn't. I've shared your letters with Curt, and he prepared me for what might happen."

"Curt! Oh, Colleen, I hadn't thought of that. Thank You, God!" Realizing what she'd said, Julie was stunned, but Colleen only smiled.

"I think that minister of yours is affecting you more than you want to admit."

Julie couldn't argue. What she'd said was spontaneous. Was reading her Bible the reason? She hoped Colleen wouldn't tell Alex. He'd start preaching salvation, as they called it, to her. She sure wasn't ready for that.

Colleen wanted Curt to come to Lisa's with them, and Julie thought it was a good idea. A lawyer, a minister, and a medical student should help them make a clear decision. Making the decision didn't take long. Len had gone ahead of them and talked to Ethel's neighbors. He had a lot to share.

Their mother had committed one indiscretion after the other and was a constant worry on the block. She'd paraded outside in her slip when the weather was freezing, and she took newspapers from neighborhood yards every day. She started fires to burn leaves or trash and left them unattended.

Once, the fire department was called, and she was warned. That night, she called the property owner next to her. Julie had started the fire, she said. It was just like that crazy girl. If she couldn't have the house, Ethel declared, she'd burn it down.

Julie burst into tears, and Alex, aware of the others, hesitated only a moment before pulling her into his arms. The room was silent until she composed herself. Len cleared his throat.

"You're not the only one to take a hit, Julie. It seems she tells everyone I steal her money." The girls protested noisily, but Len raised a restraining hand. "Fortunately, I think my reputation can absorb the alleged crime."

Lisa was furious. "Julie and Colleen, as far as I'm concerned, that ends it. When she tries to get at my husband, I'll do whatever it takes to stop her."

Julie glanced at Alex and wondered what Lisa would say if she knew how her mother had used Len. *She must never know,* thought Julie. *She couldn't live with it if anything should happen to her husband.*

Len spoke again, "I'll need the complete agreement of all three of you if we act on this legally—"

"And medically, Len," said Curt.

"Right. So I must hear a vote from each of you."

Julie thought of the votes the three had taken all their lives. It was a childhood thing, then as they grew up they continued it in fun. This time was dead serious. She doubted they'd ever cast votes again.

"You already have my yes vote, Len," said Lisa tearfully.

Colleen, sobbing, turned her face toward Curt's shoulder. As Alex had done with Julie, Curt stroked her hair and let her cry. Lifting eyes to Len's, she gave him a nod.

"I want to hear you say it, honey," prompted Len.

"Yes," Colleen said firmly.

There was no question in Julie's mind what must be done, but when the bitter word had to be uttered, she couldn't choke it out. She knew why; she wanted her mother to love her. Now, she would never win her affection. Looking at Alex, she saw he had bowed his head and was praying for her. Her mind cleared, and her courage returned.

"Yes, Len, do what's necessary to give her the right kind of care."

Len nodded and took his wife's hand. "Lisa and I intend to have her house re-done in order to sell it." He addressed Julie and Colleen, "Since you two have such bitter memories of the place, I'm assuming neither of you wants to live there."

The girls shook their heads.

"Then the sale of the house should keep your mother in a good health care center for some time; especially if the money from it is wisely invested. Property in that area has risen in value over the years, and it should bring a good price.

"Now, be assured that every option will have the approval of you three beforehand. I don't want you feeling your mother was right about my stealing from her. Mrs. Richmond has gone down so fast since your father's death, I doubt if she will remember the house a year from now."

Julie saw Curt unconsciously nod.

"Have you any other questions?" No one spoke. "I'm sure you will have some later, but you're in a bit of shock at the present. Still holding Lisa's hand, Len looked at the three girls. "You'll regret doing this at Christmas, but some things have to be taken care of before they turn into a tragedy."

"You're right, Len," said Alex, "and I'd like to add one more thing. The Bible says we're responsible to give our parents good care. I hope you won't allow guilt to mislead you. Even though it's difficult, putting your mother in a care center is the kindest thing you can do for her in her condition. Be assured that what Len and I arrange, with Curt's help, will be good care. Now, would any of you mind if I asked the Lord to be with us in this?"

Len gave Alex the go-ahead, and Julie was grateful. This time Alex asked God to lead Len in preparation of the legalities of Ethel's case and to give him strength and wisdom from day to day. For the three girls, he asked for understanding and courage.

Julie relaxed, feeling new strength to believe in the future. Alex finished the prayer by asking that the Sherrys' baby arrive healthy and strong. He said, "In our Savior's name. Amen," and the prayer was over. Each couple talked quietly together, and Julie had no doubt they had done the right thing.

Later Juanita, the cook, brought in a tray of steaming cups of wassail. Julie sipped the spicy drink, thinking how obstinate she had been about accepting Alex's help. Now she wondered what life would be like without it.

Chapter 13

Anticipating a dismal Christmas, Julie and her sisters signed the necessary documents Len required for Ethel's immediate care. Painters and carpenters were not starting on the Richmond house until after the holidays. By then, Ethel would be settled in her new accommodations. Alex felt the abject pall that lay over the three daughters' holiday, but there was a flickering light in the darkness.

So that each sister could spend Christmas Day as she liked, gift giving was scheduled for Christmas Eve at the Sherrys'. Curt's family had claimed Colleen for Christmas Day, and Julie was expected at Alex's home. He told her Mrs. Blake had pulled out all the stops to give Julie the best Christmas she'd ever had.

He wondered if Julie and her sisters had ever experienced a real *merry* Christmas. Having her with Amelia and him, and a smiling Mrs. B. in the background, sent a warm glow through Alex's heart as he thought of it.

He had spent a lot of time in prayer about his relationship with Julie. Love had taken him by surprise. When Christi died, he had no desire for another woman to share his life. He wanted no one to take her place, and with Amelia to raise, his church, and Mrs. B. to keep his home in order, he was happy.

He smiled as he remembered the exquisite, angry lady he had met by accident and who'd stolen his heart in seconds. At their second meeting at the school, a glib remark burst stupidly from his mouth when what he'd wanted was to tell her he was glad they'd met again and to ask her to go out with him.

Julie was stubborn and chose not to admit something out of the ordinary had happened. Hanging onto her beloved independence, she came to him only when there was nothing else she could do. Each time she made it clear, though he was not convinced, that the barrier of his religion could not be crossed.

He prayed for the day he would present to her the Savior he loved. In an instant, she would see why no other way of life compared. Once she took that step, he knew she would be as eager as he to share her newfound faith with her sisters.

⤛⤜

Julie attended a vesper service Alex held before their Christmas Eve celebration at Lisa's. Since many were out of town, the church was only partially filled, and Julie sat alone, at the back of the big sanctuary. Putting on a facade of tranquility was beyond her when her mother had just been admitted to a health care center.

Despite her mood, the soft music, the candlelight, Alex's message of hope, and the final prayer of praise gave her peace. There was always the chance that her mother would get better; she had to believe that. Meanwhile, there were decisions to be made concerning her future and Alex.

Mrs. Blake and Amelia, seated close to the front, located Julie in the rear of the auditorium.

"There you are!" Amelia grabbed Julie and hugged her. "We were looking and looking for you. I was afraid you hadn't come." Her face registered a mood change. "I guess I let Jesus down. I prayed, but I didn't have enough faith."

Mrs. Blake left them, and Julie, concerned about Amelia's last remark, tucked the child in beside her to wait for Alex.

"Amelia, darling, why do you think you let Jesus down? You prayed, didn't you?"

"Yes, Miss Richmond, but I—"

"Let's start a new rule, today. Except at school and with your school friends, why don't you call me Julie? It will be your private name for me. You see, if you were to call me that at school, Mrs. Larabee might think you were being disrespectful. You understand, don't you?"

Amelia nodded, then put her hand over her mouth and giggled. "Daddy and I call you Julie at home all the time. Act–ual–ly," she stated, using her current favorite word, "we call you Julie *darling*. You aren't mad, are you?"

Julie's face repeated its warming trick. Amelia's latest information delighted Julie. She liked the idea that their pet name for her was used in the boldly stated, comfortable home. But Amelia hadn't answered her question.

"About letting Jesus down, Amelia, won't He forgive you?"

"Yes, Daddy says when we give our hearts to Jesus, He has already forgiven us. 'Course, we can't go around doing bad things on purpose. But when we do something wrong and we confess that we made a mistake, we're forgiven."

"You said you let Jesus down because you didn't have enough faith. Do you think not having enough faith in Jesus is a bad thing?"

"Oh, that's the worst thing. You *must* have faith in Jesus."

Her heart tightened, and Julie tried desperately to think of something else, instead of the faith she didn't have.

The Sherry estate glistened with holiday lights and wreaths at the gates, and, as Alex drove farther up the hill, cedar trees covered with lights blazed red and green. Splashes of red satin, greenery, and sparkling silver stars decorated the front of the house, and glowing candles lit the downstairs windows.

Like the candles, Amelia's eyes glowed, too. "Oh, Julie, look," she whispered in awe. "It's so beautiful."

Julie kissed the small hand on her shoulder while Alex viewed them with an approving smile. Julie suspected he imagined them married, with Amelia in the backseat, as now, sharing the panorama with her new mother. The thought didn't offend her.

Red was the color of the outfit Lisa chose for the evening. The sequined pattern of her jumpsuit disguised a bare hint of fullness. Colleen's dress was new; Julie had gifted her with a coatdress of amethyst, trimmed with jeweled buttons of the same color. It was obvious—Curt was awestruck.

Julie's own dress was of black lace with a sparkling jade lining. At church she had worn a black cape, buttoned at the neck, to hide it. Alex helped her out of the wrap as he spoke to Len and, turning, handed the cape to a maid. When his eyes fell on Julie again, they held such admiration that the price of the extravagant dress no longer bothered her.

※

Around the Sherrys' silver tree were gifts for everyone. Though the day started with her usual morning sickness, Lisa felt better as time went on, she told Julie, and now her enthusiasm stimulated the evening's celebration. Julie was afraid Lisa would exhaust herself, but her first Christmas in her new home as Len's wife was a miracle. She should enjoy it as she liked.

The dilemma of Alex's gift had finally resolved itself. Alex had lost his favorite pen, and Julie replaced it with a handsome rosewood pen and pencil set. His initials, tiny, engraved in gold, dignified the pair. Thanking her, he kissed her cheek. Julie bought Amelia a gold charm bracelet, to which she added symbols of a book, a teacup, a maple leaf, and, last, a nutcracker figure.

"I thought the play was my present! Thank you, Julie darling."

Alex's eyes enveloped Julie with affection.

A heavy box decorated in Amelia's definitive style came to Julie, and, inside, she found a leather-bound Bible. Julie, sure Alex had made the choice, sent him a smile of gratitude, but he shook his head and pointed to Amelia.

"She had her mind made up, and we shopped until she was satisfied."

Amelia's eyes sparkled. "Do you like it, Julie? It has lots of notes and maps and things."

"Of course I do, honey. Who wouldn't like such a lovely gift? Thank you!" Julie said, enfolding Amelia in her arms.

Len asked to see the Bible, and Amelia carried it over to him and stayed to point out her favorite verses.

A silver box came from Alex's pocket. He gave it to Julie, and her hands trembled as she opened the gift. It was a cameo necklace. The total figure was a dancing lady with a veil encircling her in the air as she moved. Julie had never seen a cameo like it. It was a stationary subject, yet it was as if she could hear the music and see the movement. Her eyes glistened with tears as she looked up.

Alex leaned forward. "It was my mother's, Julie. She died the year after Christi. The cameo came from the area of the volcano—Vesuvius—in Italy. I had the original chain replaced. It was so worn I was afraid you'd lose it, and, knowing you, I doubt you'd ever forgive yourself." His face softened as he looked at the cameo. "It is nice, isn't it?"

She nodded.

The lump in Julie's throat made it hard to speak. "This piece must be precious to you, Alex. Amelia should have it. You don't want to let it out of the family." Julie was talking to keep from crying; it was eerie how well Alex knew her.

Alex tipped up her chin. "Someday maybe you'll give it to her yourself if you want her to have it."

Julie knew all too well what he meant. His finger traveled along her cheek as he gazed into her eyes. A spell she couldn't resist was being cast. Probably he'd resent that metaphor; he'd told her he dealt with young people drawn into the occult, with their demonic studies of witchcraft. But that had nothing to do with the charisma drawing her to Alex.

"Hey, you two in the corner," called Lisa, smiling impishly as the maids gathered up their discarded Christmas wrappings. "Come join the party! Juanita's made a batch of hot punch, and we're in deep conversation here."

Alex stood up, held out his hand to Julie, and they joined the others. Juanita and Sarah, another kitchen maid, set out a buffet of holiday food, brightly decorated with the season's colors. Soon, with plates piled high, the group gathered to eat off trays around the fireplace, which blazed with pine-scented logs.

Mrs. Sherry also joined the group to eat. Then she was wheeled away to her suite by her personal maid and nurse. Lisa told Julie she hadn't agonized about Ethel as she expected to. Seeing how charming Mrs. Sherry was to Lisa, Julie thought how grateful her sister must be for a home in which the mother was a treasure instead of a trial. Len's attitude to his mother was a loving one, but clearly, Lisa had first place.

After the first round of eating, Curt moved next to Alex. "I want to ask you a question, Alex."

"Fire away." Alex propped an ankle on his other knee, sipped his punch, and gave Curt his full attention.

"Well, it's this." Curt seemed almost bashful. "At school they say man evolved from an animal. My folks object to that theory. How do you prove to a hardhead like me that God separated man from beasts?"

"Okay, for starters, let me ask you a couple of questions. Number one, if God didn't create man different, why have animals never built skyscrapers or made scientific advances? Number two, why are there no animal records such as those man has handed down from generation to generation? Also, man improves on the tools he uses, and he speaks multiple languages. I could go on, but how are those answers for now?"

No one spoke, and Curt laughed. "Hmm, Alex, I guess I'll have to think about that. I'll call you this week, and maybe we can talk over some other things I've wondered about."

"Anytime, Curt. Call my secretary, and she'll set it up."

What Alex said makes sense, Julie thought. If she gave him a chance, could he explain away the barriers that separated them? He must have good reasons for choosing the life he had. If she understood why, would she give her heart to Jesus, too? No. It was too scary. She believed in things she could see and touch.

⁓

Alex watched Julie and wondered what was going on in her mind. Except for Amelia, she was the most cherished person in his life. But she did not believe in God. He knew he wanted to marry her, and, given the opportunity, he knew he could make her understand why he was a minister. He had to make her see that it was more important than his relationship with her or his daughter. But it would be hard for her to accept until she knew Christ personally.

Len had purchased the board game they had played at Julie's, and the evening mellowed as the contest began. Curt and Colleen used strategies no one else had heard of, and Julie accused them of making up their own rules. Alex and the Sherrys chimed in to agree with Julie, and Amelia tumbled on the floor, laughing.

"Six grownups who are s'posed to know better, and they're acting worse than my friends and me!"

Such an insightful opinion from an eight-year-old produced a few seconds of dead silence, then hilarity.

Suddenly, Len's face sobered, his face took on a gray pallor, and he sagged against Lisa. Curt snapped to attention.

"Quick! Everyone, get up! Let him lie down on the couch."

Alex grabbed the game, and Juanita took it away. Lisa hovered in Curt's way.

Curt spoke gently, "Lisa, you need to let me take his pulse and listen to his heart."

Lisa stood up and watched Curt anxiously.

"Call an ambulance, Alex." Then to Lisa, Curt said, "You can help Len if you remain calm. He needs absolute quiet while we find the trouble. Don't you agree?"

Her eyes full of fear, Lisa nodded. Alex was back in seconds.

"They're on their way, Curt—five minutes."

Curt had moved Len's body to a position that allowed him to breathe properly, and he removed his tie and belt. He kept a constant check on his pulse, and in less than five minutes they heard a siren on the boulevard.

⁓

At the hospital, Alex's arm supported Lisa as he and Julie walked her from the emergency room to the waiting room of the Cardiac Care unit. Colleen and Curt had taken Amelia home and would soon be with them.

Restful colors of sand, soft blue, and green decorated the waiting room. Striped and solid-color pillows of the same hues were stacked in a corner rack for those spending the night. Reading material was available, but until a report surfaced on Len's condition, no one was interested. Julie doubted Lisa would leave the hospital even after they'd heard from the doctor.

Colleen and Curt arrived, telling Alex that Mrs. Blake had Amelia on her way to bed when they left. Curt volunteered to call Juanita and brought back welcome information.

Because she had not slept well the night before, Mrs. Sherry had taken a sedative before retiring. The ambulance driver killed the siren at the entrance to the Sherry estate, so she had not awakened. When Lisa realized her mother-in-law was unaware of Len's trouble, Julie saw a wave of relief sweep over her sister's face.

Two hours dragged by, and Lisa felt herself crumbling. Her marriage reviewed itself in her mind. She thought she was doing Len a favor when they were married. Of course, she wanted plenty back for that favor, but with her wedding, the scheming stopped. She had fallen in love with Len more than she dreamed possible. Wise, considerate, patient Len was the ideal husband, the knight in shining armor she had waited for, and, soon she would have his child.

Tears stung her eyes as she remembered the joy on Len's face when she came from the doctor's with the news. What she thought was a stomach ailment turned out to be the happiest event in their lives. Since then, the unity between them was incredible. Len couldn't die! He was part of her! He *must* live to see their baby.

Sitting together, Alex and Julie waited for signals from Lisa that they could be of help.

"Alex, why do you think this happened to Len? Was it God's will?" Lisa questioned desperately.

"I can't claim to know the mind of God, Lisa, but I know God wants to give Len His best. Did you know Len became a Christian when he was a young man?"

"Yes, he told me that before we started going to church. I didn't even know what it meant until he explained it. He's so wonderful, Alex. God wouldn't let such a fine man die, would he?" Lisa exclaimed.

"I can't tell you how many times I've been asked that in these circumstances, Lisa. But remember this, please—death to a Christian is not a punishment. It's the promise of Jesus he has waited for all his life. What happens to Len now is up to the Lord. Why don't we pray for him to get well." Alex bowed his head.

Lisa closed her eyes and listened. Alex asked God for a safe recovery for Len and for a return to the happiness Lisa and Len had together. He thanked God for Len's Christian ethics and for the opportunity of knowing him.

Lisa was glad the two men were friends. Maybe, during the day, they saw each other and talked about their religion. Religion was something she couldn't share with Len because she had never known the experience he described.

He wanted her to have that experience, but the thought of it scared Lisa. She wasn't good like Len. Now, though, as Alex prayed, she did, too. Promising God to try to give her heart to Him, she begged Him to spare Len's life and to let him live for their baby.

Alex asked the Lord to give them strength; then he added, "In Jesus' name" and said "*Amen.*" They sat back, Lisa trying with all her heart to remain calm.

Fifteen minutes passed. Finally, a small, motherly nurse from CCU slipped in to talk to them.

Jumping up, Lisa pleaded, "Oh, tell us, please!"

The nurse took Lisa's cold hands. "He's all right, Mrs. Sherry. The doctor would have seen you himself, but he had to rush back to ER for another emergency. He's confident the episode was a warning, but he wants to keep your husband in the hospital overnight.

"Mr. Sherry must take better care of himself, and he *must* get more rest. The doctor will be in touch with you as soon as possible with more details; but your husband is stable, and you may see him. You may even be able to have Christmas at home."

Lisa felt Julie's and Colleen's arms around her as she cried in relief. When she was able, the nurse took her to see Len.

Julie watched Lisa leave. "This was a near thing, wasn't it, Alex?"

But Alex wasn't there. Across the room she saw him kneeling on one knee beside a chair, his head bowed. Stunned, Julie realized he was thanking God for Len's life. *We all heard him beg God to spare Len*, she thought, *yet Alex is the only one who said thank You.* She glanced at Colleen. Her faced showed the same guilt Julie was feeling. They reached out to each other and bowed their heads.

Chapter 14

Early the next morning, Julie and Alex went back to the hospital. Julie had tried to get Lisa to go home with her the night before, but Lisa wouldn't be moved. She asked that another bed be brought into Len's room, yet, as she told Julie, it was impossible to relax and sleep. If she did, she feared Len's God would take him away from her. The bright day generated new assurance, and, to Julie's relief, Lisa looked alive again.

When Len was released, Julie and Alex drove the euphoric Sherrys to their quiet home on the hill. Dwight Winwood was getting into his car when they came up the drive. He waited for Alex's car to reach the front walk.

"Lisa," he chided, opening her door, "can't you take better care of your boss than this?" He clicked his tongue at her as she got out of the car. "How do you expect a man to have a happy Christmas when he's worried about his friends?"

Julie watched Lisa's face light as she spoke. "He's going to be okay, Dwight. The doctor wants him to take it easy for a while because he's been overworking. I intend to give him the best care possible."

Lisa's problem has taken her mind off Mother, Julie thought, as she watched Dwight clap Len on the shoulder and hug him. *If this hadn't happened to faithful Len, we would all be drawing on his strength to get us through the next weeks.* But Len had detailed Ethel's case to his partner, and now it would be Dwight Winwood's directions they would follow.

Once he was satisfied with Lisa's report on her husband, Dwight told Julie and Alex he would talk to all three girls before Colleen went back to Lindenwood. Dwight's serene temperament matched Len's, so Julie was sure he would handle everything to their mother's greatest good.

❧

Over the next four days Len began to feel better, and Julie saw Lisa's confidence return. The long talks he had with Alex helped Len regain vitality, and Julie wondered how Alex did it.

"What do you think they talk about in those sessions in the library?" Julie asked Lisa as they waited for the men to join them in the solarium.

"Religion, I guess. Len tries to share the Bible with me, but I just don't get it, Julie. Why is saying 'I want Jesus to come into my heart so important?' "

Julie's heart beat faster. So Len was saying the same things to Lisa that Alex said to her. Was she as cherished by Alex as Lisa was by Len? Yet both men were willing to risk a rift in their relationships to convince Lisa and Julie that Jesus should be first in their lives. Why *was* it so important to them?

❧

Julie and Alex left Len resting in bed with Lisa curled up in a chair at his side. In the foyer, they met old Mrs. Sherry and her maid coming out of the elevator, dressed to go outside. "It's good to see you again, Mrs. Sherry," said Alex. "Len seems to enjoy being at home."

"Yes," she replied. "I'm glad he's taking some time off. He looked so tired, but Lisa's making him rest. She won't let him do a thing for himself. You're lucky to have such a sweet, caring sister," she told Julie. "She's a lovely daughter."

Julie was barely able to manage a thank-you. Lisa had kept the truth of Len's illness from Mrs. Sherry out of love. How their lives had changed in the past months! Here was Lisa, given a second chance, living in an ideal home, expecting Len's child. Colleen and Curt were already looking forward to marriage, and she and Alex. . . As Alex steered the car down the long drive, Julie studied his profile and thought about the future.

"Just because I'm not looking at you doesn't mean I don't feel your scrutiny. What has you puzzled, Julie darling?"

"I saw you smile when Amelia called me that." Alex grinned, and Julie went on, "Lisa and I were wondering why you and Len have private talks." Alex's face sobered. "I think she feels shut out, and I guess I do, too."

Parking the car beside a tree at the edge of the drive, Alex turned off the motor.

"Mostly it's answers to his questions about God's Word. He wants to learn as much as he can."

"He's afraid he's going to die, isn't he?"

"No, not afraid, Julie. That's already settled for him. He wants to know his Savior better." Alex laid his hand on Julie's shoulder. "Len's concern is mostly for Lisa. He has arranged for Lisa and the baby to be taken care of, monetarily, but more than anything he wants Lisa to commit her heart to Jesus."

"She's having trouble with that. Lisa just told me. She's scared. So am I."

"Could I venture a guess why you are?" asked Alex.

It took a few seconds for Julie to give Alex a nod.

"The Lord is working in your hearts. The two of you, and Colleen, have lived in a maelstrom of discord most of your lives. Yet each of you is coming from a different direction. Lisa's treatment was less harsh, and Len came along for her. Because she was ready for his kind of love, marriage has been a kind of therapy for her. Colleen is young and will have several years close to Curt to unlearn some of the anguish dealt her. In fact, it's already underway.

"You, my love, built a wall around your heart because you were allotted the hardest blows. You did it to protect yourself. Your parents' marriage was an example that was always before you, so their failure became the standard by which you judge marriage. But the bottom line is, not one of you were given the chance to know God. Naturally, the unknown is scary to you.

"Don't turn away, Julie," he said, reaching for her hand. "Your parents' treatment taught you to be tough in a tough world, but they didn't give you the unfailing security you are entitled to—that is, belief in Jesus as your Savior."

"You're right about that, Alex. I don't recall His name ever being mentioned in our house. The way you talk about your God with such reverence has always astonished me, but the night at the hospital, when I saw you kneel and thank Him, I finally understood how much your faith means to you. It's like the air you breathe. You would never give it up."

"I couldn't. To me, there is no other life. Nothing else makes sense. God's reason for creating man was to be real to him in a person-to-person relationship. I want Him to be real to you, as Len wants it for Lisa."

Julie had no reply, but forgetting the fervor with which Alex spoke was impossible.

❧

The telephone was ringing when Julie let herself into her apartment. She ran to catch it and barked a hello.

"Julie," came a sobbing voice, "I need you. Come back."

"Lisa? What is it?"

"The doc–doctor is here. . . . He's dead, Julie."

"Whaat?"

"Come back, Julie, I need you."

"I'll be there as soon as possible."

Julie put down the phone in shock. Her hand would hardly obey her. Lisa must be mistaken. How could Len be dead? They had just left him! She had to get Alex. Her hand shook so she could hardly punch in the numbers. On her fourth attempt, she managed the right digits. Mrs. Blake answered.

"It's Julie, Mrs. Blake. Alex is on his way home. When he gets there, tell him to go back to the Sherrys'. Tell him I think Len is dead. I'm going there now."

Julie hung up, grabbed her purse, keys, and umbrella, and locked the door behind her. It was beginning to rain and she could feel ice in it. She drove carefully. It was no time for an accident.

The slow drive gave her time to think. Deep down, she knew Len was gone. *That's how death is,* Julie thought, her heart thudding. *One minute, everything is right; the next, nothing is.*

Could Lisa manage? She had security; Len had seen to that. But could she stand the shock of Len's death so soon after their father's? And what about the baby? Alex had said the baby would be Lisa's anchor, but what if he was wrong? Lisa was opening her mind, trying to understand why Len was so close to God, and God had taken Len from her. Was that a loving God?

Thoughts tumbled in Julie's mind until she could no longer think of Len's death. Finally, the entrance to the Sherry estate came into view. Julie took a deep breath and braced herself for what lay ahead. The first time she prayed, she had yelled at God, joking as she asked him to keep Alex Stewart away. Now, the one person she wanted to see was Alex, and she prayed that God would send him soon.

⊛

A maid let Julie into the house and hurried her to Lisa's sitting room. Lisa came toward her with tear-stained eyes.

"Alex will be here soon, honey. He's on his way," Julie said as she gathered Lisa in her arms.

Lisa couldn't speak, so Julie sat with her, mothering her as she had when they were children. They telephoned no one. Lisa wanted Alex to break the terrible news to Mrs. Sherry, before they called the funeral home.

The world has stopped until Alex gets here, thought Julie. *I've never wanted to depend on anyone; yet Alex was the first one I called, and it's so right.*

⊛

When Alex arrived, so did order. First, arrangements were carried out, and Julie made appropriate telephone calls, including one to Colleen and one to Dwight Winwood. Colleen and Curt dropped everything, rushed to the Sherrys', and ended up handling dozens of incoming calls. As Lisa and her sisters had loved Len, Julie realized, so had many others.

She saw Alex active at what he did best: organizing, encouraging, and reassuring. He comforted old Mrs. Sherry with words of innate compassion that gave her peace of mind.

Julie and Colleen walked Lisa through the motions of living. Silent in grief, Lisa clung to Alex when he was with her. Julie wondered how Lisa would have managed without his strength or, indeed, how any of them would have managed. Following the funeral, Julie and Colleen stayed at Lisa's house until Colleen and Curt left for school on the weekend.

The staff had moved Lisa to a second-floor suite near Mrs. Sherry's rooms, where Julie and Lisa were trying to relax after Colleen's heartbreaking farewell. A service of hot tea sat on a table between their chairs. Julie stirred artificial sweetener into her cup as she comforted Lisa.

"Colleen hated to leave, honey, but I think it would have been just as hard for her to go a month from now," she said.

"I wish we could be together all the time. But that's a childish wish. I have to face the future by myself. And when the baby gets here, I'll be responsible for him, too." Tears filled Lisa's eyes. "Len told me I didn't have to be alone. He said Jesus would guide my life if I gave it to Him. I didn't understand then, and I don't understand now," she sobbed.

Lisa's spirits were down, but Julie could pull her out of that. It was Len's statement about Jesus she couldn't explain. She didn't understand either. Mentioning the subject to Alex, even for Lisa's sake, was asking for another lesson in religion.

"I think we should visit Mother," Lisa said abruptly and got to her feet. "Why don't we go out this afternoon?"

"Sure," said Julie in surprise. "I. . .ah. . .don't want you to be disappointed, Lisa. She hasn't improved since you last saw her. In fact, she may be worse. I was there two days ago. . .but, yes, let's go again."

She wasn't sure Lisa was ready to see her mother in the guarded care unit. But it might take her mind off herself.

On their first visit to the facility, the three sisters were pleased. Len, Alex, Curt, and Dwight Winwood had made impromptu visits to the place at separate times, and Julie knew when the men recommended the center they felt Ethel would get the best of care.

❧

Shivering in the cold of the wintry wind, the two girls walked past neatly trimmed cedars surrounding the spacious brick building.

"I'll always be grateful to Len for handling Mother's affairs so wisely," Julie said.

"Don't say any more, Julie, or I'll start crying again," Lisa murmured.

Julie returned a wave from one of the patients at a dining room window. When they reached the entrance, a maintenance man, washing the inside of the glass doors, touched his cap and backed up to let them in. Smiling as they spoke to him, they made their way to their mother's special wing. A charge nurse recognized Julie and left the station to arrange for their visit.

When she returned, Julie and Lisa followed her to a room where a heavyset orderly Julie knew as Bud stood by the door. Inside, Ethel sat ramrod straight on the side of her bed.

"Mother," Julie said as they drew near.

Behind them, the door clicked shut, and Bud's face appeared at the double-glass square in the door. Ethel smoothed the material of her warm fleece robe and lifted a sleepy-eyed gaze to the girls.

"Do you know us, Mother?" Lisa asked.

"You're Lisa," Ethel murmured.

"Julie's here, too."

"Yes. She's Julie." Ethel pointed to her.

"You're looking well, Mother. Is it pleasant for you here?"

"Oh yes. Mama and Papa's house is very pleasant. I've always enjoyed living here. They gave it to Sid and me when we got married." Ethel's voice had a childlike quality.

Seeing Lisa's forlorn expression, Julie changed the subject.

"Is there anything you need, Mother? Anything we can get for you?"

"No, I'm fine."

Lisa examined Ethel's face with a pensive expression. It was a situation Julie had already dealt with. Day by day, Ethel had sorted out and kept only those memories that were important to her. Julie could see Lisa assimilating that fact.

"It's a bitter day outside, Mother. I'm glad you have a cozy home," said Lisa, glancing around the pastel-painted room.

"That's because Papa put in storm windows. Mama says we'll be as snug as a bug in a rug all winter," she replied with a smile.

The rest of the conversation followed the same vein, and twenty minutes later, Julie suggested they leave. She was afraid the emotional stress had consumed Lisa's energy. She had all but collapsed in her chair. So much tragedy was hard on Julie and Colleen, but Lisa was having a baby. Julie wondered guiltily if Lisa's doctor would have allowed this trip had he known.

"We need to leave now, Mother. I'll be back to see you very soon," promised Julie.

Ethel didn't move from the bed and didn't say good-bye.

Having stayed until Lisa changed into comfortable clothes and was resting, Julie left. But Lisa was far from relaxed.

The events of the past weeks were always there, repeating themselves, torturing her, not letting her sleep. She saw Len's face before her no matter where she was or what she did. Sometimes his beautiful singing haunted her, recapturing the bittersweet memory of his presence.

Everyone thought she was getting over his death, but she wasn't. Each day made living more unbearable. Why try? What was there to live for? The baby? Without Len, the coming of the baby held no joy.

She could escape, and she could take the baby with her. Alex would shame her for thinking such a thing. But Alex didn't know the pain she felt. He had once, but he had forgotten; or he wouldn't be in love with Julie. Men shaped up and learned to live again. She couldn't.

Alex and Julie would probably marry someday. But even if they didn't, Julie was strong enough to live her life any way or anywhere she chose. Colleen and Curt might be engaged even now, or they would be by the time Colleen finished school. Her mother was well cared for in the health care center. She had gone into a netherworld of unreality and was perfectly happy.

No one needs me, she thought, *not even Mrs. Sherry. She has all the money she needs to be taken care of, and if I. . .*Then she would have Len's money, too. Not even an elderly woman, crippled by arthritis, needed her.

She remembered the prescriptions for Mrs. Sherry that had been delivered the day before. There was a large bottle of Vicodin. She'd watched Nurse Williams lock the bottles in the medicine chest for security. But Lisa knew where Williams kept the key, and the nurse had taken Mrs. Sherry outside in her wheelchair.

Chapter 15

I'm sorry we hardly got outside," said Mrs. Sherry, "but it was just too cold today. Maybe it will be warmer tomorrow, and we can go out then." She frowned as she let Williams help her out of her heavy wraps. "I want you to check on Lisa right away. I'm worried about her, Williams. She's having a hard time."

"I know, Mrs. Sherry. It's not easy to pick up and go on, but it can be done. We both know that," said the nurse.

Williams situated Mrs. Sherry's wheelchair in her favorite spot by a front window. From there, she could look out over the dormant grounds to the orderly swiftness of traffic along the boulevard. Her patient felt less isolated when she could see the movement of vehicles and people. Mrs. Sherry had led a productive life, even in the early stages of crippling arthritis. Now Williams worked simply to keep her mind busy.

"Would you like something to read, or would you like me to read to you after I see about Lisa?" asked the nurse.

"Why don't you read from the John Donne collection? I feel like meditating on the quality of life," she replied.

Nurse Williams hung up her coat and started to leave the room. Suddenly, she heard screams and running feet in the hall. It was Peggy, Lisa's maid.

"Madame! She's done something to herself! Ms. Lisa! I brought up her dry cleaning. She acts like she's dead drunk!"

Mrs. Sherry seized the brakes of her wheelchair, turned it, and pushed herself forward. Astonished, Williams grabbed the handles and pushed her the short distance to Lisa's suite. In the bedroom, the girl lay sprawled on the bed. Williams tried unsuccessfully to rouse her. Lisa was unconscious.

"Her pulse is weak, ma'am. Her heart's barely beating!"

"Call an ambulance!" ordered Mrs. Sherry. "She must have taken something!"

Peggy snatched the telephone. Without Williams's help, the elderly woman, breathing hard, pushed her wheelchair to the opposite side of the bed. Lisa moaned.

As she fled from the room, Williams yelled at Peggy, "Try to get her up! Keep her moving! I'll be right back!"

When she rushed back, the maid had pulled Lisa to a sitting position, Lisa protesting with a faint "Noo. . ."

Williams set towels, a basin, and a glass of mustard-colored liquid on Lisa's bedside table. She wished for some ipecac, but the remedy she'd mixed worked almost as well. As the nurse stepped back, she saw an empty bottle near the skirt of the bed. The empty Vicodin container! But she'd locked it up!

"Quick, Peggy! Help me!" she bellowed. "We have to make her empty her stomach!"

Nearby, Mrs. Sherry watched with an agonized expression. Lisa fought against swallowing the liquid, but Williams forced it into her mouth. It started the process.

"Do it again, Williams! Don't let her leave us."

There was trembling in old Mrs. Sherry's voice that gave Williams new determination. She pressed the glass against Lisa's lips. Lisa fought harder this time. Good! Her senseless state might be losing its stranglehold. But Williams wasn't sure.

A siren wailed up the drive. Peggy had alerted the staff, and in seconds, two men in blue uniforms burst into the room. Williams went weak with relief. Her patient's beloved daughter stood a chance now.

❧

"Good morning, beautiful," Alex whispered.

At her desk, Julie flushed as she smiled and said, "Good morning," in her Miss Richmond voice.

Nita folded her steno pad and left the room with a grin.

"Alex Stewart, you'll have the whole school talking if you don't stop calling at the exact same time every day."

"If we were married, I wouldn't have to call you so often. Scratch that. I'd probably call you twice as often."

Another call saved her from answering. "Alex, hold on while I catch this other line."

"Gladly."

An anxious outburst erupted on the second line.

"Julie, this is Mrs. Sherry. Lisa tried to kill herself. An ambulance has taken her to St. Luke's, but I knew you'd want to go." Mrs. Sherry's voice trembled. "I love her, Julie. *Please*, keep me informed about my girl. I'll pray for her and wait to hear from you."

Mrs. Sherry hung up, and Julie pushed the button for Alex's line. "Alex, Lisa is in the hospital. She tried to kill herself!"

"Let me pick you up. I'll leave right now."

❧

By the time Julie got loose from school without telling why she was leaving, Alex was there. In his car, Julie clasped her hands to keep them still.

"Alex, I let her down. Why didn't I see how depressed she was?" she cried.

"One of the stages of grief is deep depression. My doctor reminded me, and I intended to talk to her as soon as possible. Instead, I let other things get in the way," he said bleakly. "If you're going to distribute blame, include me."

"But I'm her sister. I was seeing her all the time."

"You aren't perfect, Julie. We tried our best to help her, but we didn't get the job done. Let's trust God. He can still turn this around."

"You probably think if she had been what you call saved, she wouldn't have tried it."

"In some cases, saved people do commit suicide. But, Julie, it's not the one who is actively praying, studying God's Word, and serving Him with his life; it's the one who has wandered away from God or needs medical attention."

Julie nodded, wondering if Alex still prayed for her mother. Hadn't he said he wanted to reach all people? Lisa would need to talk to him before too long. Was it time for her to do the same thing?

❧

Lisa never left Julie's mind. With the help of Dwight Winwood, special consideration was given Lisa because she was Leonard Sherry's widow. Dr. Crandle, Lisa's doctor, told Julie that Lisa cried through the official questioning and her psychiatric evaluation. Julie yearned to hold her, but she didn't know what to say. When she was allowed to see her sister, Julie asked Alex to be with her, so he could carry the conversation.

In the quiet hospital room, filled with flowers from Mrs. Sherry, Dwight Winwood, and Julie, Alex squeezed Lisa's hand.

"Len's name is still protecting you, Lisa. Dwight made sure there were no leaks to the media. You're safe."

"You've been good to me, too, Alex," Lisa whispered between sobs. "I must seem pretty ungrateful."

Alex sat by the bed next to Julie. "No, Lisa, I think you're a little confused and need help. Do you realize how God blessed you by letting you keep Len's child? I'm sure Len wanted to see this baby, but he didn't get the chance. So, I think he died secure in the belief that his child was in the capable hands of the one he loved the most."

Lisa gasped and sobbed, "Do you think Len knows I tried to kill myself and the baby?"

"I don't know, Lisa. But I do know this. To take a life, even your own, is a sin. God's Word says so. They tell us the baby is fine, although you almost took away his right to live. But God still loves you, Lisa. He sent His Son so that sinners like you and me could be forgiven and have new life."

Lisa's eyes were locked on him; she was straining to hear every word. Julie listened silently. She didn't want to listen, but she couldn't help herself. Alex had such command of what he was saying.

"Now, Lisa, pay close attention, please. When you took that Vicodin, what were you thinking?"

As Lisa cried, words tumbled out about the futility of life without Len. By the time she finished, Julie felt she had been with Lisa through every minute.

She felt the agony. Why was Alex putting her through this?

Alex sat back in his chair. "So, you feel your life is over and you're completely worthless. Is that right?"

Lisa nodded, her shoulders shaking as she cried.

"Since you have nothing to lose, Lisa, why not turn that worthless life over to Jesus? You couldn't feel any worse. Why not see what the Lord can do for you?"

Lisa looked at Julie, then at Alex. "How do I start?"

Alex took her hand again. "Bow your head, close your eyes, and pray. I'll tell you what to say."

Lisa lowered her head and repeated after Alex, "Dear Jesus, I know I've done wrong things all my life and not just when I tried to kill myself and my baby. I ask You to forgive me. You died on the cross because God sent You to pay for my sins. Come into my heart right now, Lord Jesus, and make a new person of me. I ask in Your name. Amen."

Julie listened, her throat tight. Something inexplicable had happened to Lisa. Her eyes shone with a glow from within herself. She and Alex talked about Len's death, and suddenly Lisa's voice was steady as she spoke of the future with her baby. In a moment's turnaround, Lisa seemed to be a new person.

Julie felt like an outsider.

Evening was hiding the last rays of sun behind buildings taller than the apartment complex. Julie stood alone at a window looking down on cars and pedestrians heading home. No doubt most of the people had husbands, wives, or children waiting in warm houses to welcome them. No ponderous cloud of loneliness hung over them.

Colleen, involved with school and Curt, was almost too busy to write often. Lisa. . .her lifestyle had changed, and she was pulling away from Julie. She spent a lot of time at Alex's church—Lisa's church too, now that she was a member. At home she had no one except the servants and Mrs. Sherry. But Julie had questioned her about Mrs. Sherry the last time they were together and got a surprising answer.

"Does she ever come into the main part of the house?" Julie asked. "Do you ever see her?"

"Of course. Oh, Julie, she's been marvelous to me. The first day I was home, she told me, crying, that I was her real daughter. She remembered the night Len came in after asking me to marry him. He was so happy, and it made her happy, too.

"She said she had waited years for Len to find the girl he wanted." Lisa's tears shone. "She was prepared to love any woman of Len's choice, but when he announced that I was the one, she was overjoyed. Overjoyed, Julie! How could I not love a lady like that?"

So Lisa was not lonely either. She had Mrs. Sherry, a gentle woman who would love Lisa and her child. And Lisa had memories of a love she would never forget as long as she lived.

And what did she have? Her same old job, her same old independence, her same old. . .dull life! Why was life dull all of a sudden, when it had always been so satisfying? She'd seen what happened to Lisa. Faith in God had given her sister new enthusiasm for life.

Faith was what Alex said he would never give up. Alex. After years of saying she didn't need a man, she had to admit it. She was in love with Alex Stewart. And she wanted to believe as Alex and Lisa did.

The phone was an arm's length away. She resisted the temptation to call him. She had to think. Alex said faith in Jesus was an individual thing; she had to make her own choice.

In the living room she picked up the Bible Amelia had given her for Christmas. Curling up in a wicker chair, she turned on a light and read random verses. Romans 3:10 said: "It is written, there is none righteous, no, not one."

Maybe she did sin, but why did Jesus' dying on a cross forgive the things she'd done wrong? Alex said that was where faith came in. In the front of the Bible, Amelia had written a reference to John 3:16, and she turned to that verse.

Her heart tightened. "For God so loved the world, that he gave his only begotten Son, that whosoever believeth in him should not perish, but have everlasting life."

Alex believed that with all his heart. He'd told her God's Holy Spirit became part of him when he gave his heart to Jesus. She didn't understand, but she'd worry about that part later. Giving her heart to Jesus was first. But how did you give up yourself? She was getting nowhere. She had to talk to Alex.

Alex was praying in his study at home. He had eaten dinner with Amelia and had answered, it seemed, a hundred questions about his relationship with Julie.

"Why doesn't Julie darling love Jesus like we do, Daddy?"

Alex hadn't answered at first. When he did, it was a considered response.

"Julie has lived a life far different from yours, Amelia. You've always gone to Sunday school and church because your mother and I wanted you to hear God's Word and learn from it. Julie's parents didn't take their girls to church."

"But she goes now. Do you think she will accept Christ?"

"I hope so, honey. I'm praying she will."

"I am, too. But remember what we said, Daddy. We have to have faith," she warned.

Alex smiled—a child's abiding faith. Julie had watched Lisa turn her life over to Christ, yet it hadn't affected her as he thought it would. With her inquiring mind, she must surely have questions by now, but she hadn't called.

He loved Julie. So did Amelia. It made waiting harder.

He couldn't force Julie to talk about her salvation; she'd warned him off es. He prayed for that special moment when Julie knew, within hers... e needed Christ.

Alex sighed. He had to hear her voice. The telephone rang as he reached it to call her. Startled, he fumbled with the receiver.

"Hello?"

"It's me, Alex. I'm lonely. Would you come over and talk with me?"

An alarm went off in his mind. Could it be?

⤬

Her eyes were wide, searching, when she opened the door. As always, she looked beautiful, and Alex longed to take her in his arms. But if her call meant what he hoped, he wanted her to make it clear without any persuasion from him. They went to the kitchen where she poured two cups of coffee.

"I've been reading my Bible and thinking over things you've said in your sermons," she said as she sat down.

Alex placed their cups on the table and sat opposite her.

"Go on, Julie."

"I don't know what I'm supposed to do. Just saying give your heart to Jesus sounds so elementary. There must be more to it than that."

"Julie, have you ever done anything that you'd rather die than have other people know about?"

"Yes," she finally admitted.

"God already knows, and He knows about all the sins ever committed. He can't stand sin, so He gave us a way to be forgiven. He sent His own Son, Jesus, to earth but in human form so people could identify with Him. Jesus was perfect. He never once sinned. Yet He took our sins on Himself and willingly died for the wrong we have done.

"When we ask Him into our hearts, His forgiveness is so complete it's as if we're newborn babies. We don't know how Christ's sacrifice wipes the slate clean for us. But if we, in faith, believe it, God lets us know with certainty that our new life has begun."

Tears came in a rush. "Oh, Alex," she sobbed with a stricken face, "I've been trying to work it out by myself, and I made it so complicated. I should have come to you long ago. I *want* Jesus in my heart."

Alex stood up, and Julie did, too. He took her hands and bowed his head. She waited for Alex to pray.

"Lord Jesus," he said in a tight voice, "Julie has something she wants to tell You."

Julie never dreamed Alex would expect her to pray. She had never prayed a real prayer in her life. But he was waiting, and she found courage to speak.

"I want to accept You and know You forgive me of the things I've done wrong. Please forgive me, God."

Julie felt the dark cloud lift. It was cold outside, yet she felt warm and happy.

She couldn't describe it even to Alex. God's Holy Spirit didn't need explanation. He was there.

"Shouldn't you thank Him, Julie?" Alex asked softly.

"Thank you, God." Tears came again. "Thank You for this wonderful gift. And God, thank You for Alex. I love him so." Alex's arm stole around her, and he kissed her as they wept together.

❧

Wondering why Mrs. Blake was smiling with tears on her cheeks, Amelia took the phone from her outstretched hand.

"Hello."

"Amelia?"

"Julie darling!"

With a catch in her voice, Julie answered, "I've just learned what Jesus did for me, Amelia, and I've given my heart to Him. Now, it seems. . ." She stopped, and Amelia heard her father's voice urging Julie on. "Now it seems I'm going to be your mother, honey."

"When? When?"

Her father took the phone. "As soon as possible, sweetheart. We'll hang up now, and I'll bring Julie to the house so you can give her a hug."

Amelia felt like jumping up and down.

"Oh, hurry, Daddy, hurry!"

FREDA CHRISMAN

Deep in the south of Texas, Freda Chrisman and her husband pursue an active retirement. Two married children and six terrific grandchildren assist in the day-to-day process.

Freda is an active conference teacher and speaker. She is past president of the main chapter of Inspirational Writers Alive!—now with five chapters in Texas. Winning top awards in six writers' contests has been a joy, but helping beginning writers achieve their publishing goals is God's special blessing to this author.

She is a member of HOSTS (Helping One Student To Succeed), a ministry of The Master's Touch Program of her church. Together, the Chrismans serve the Lord with the one hundred member "Mavericks" class, Sunday school members whose mission is the true meaning of *Show, don't just tell*.

Freda is a member of American Christian Fiction Writers; the Faith, Hope, and Love Chapter of Romance Writers of America; and Bay Area Chapter 30, also a chapter of Romance Writers of America. That God chose her to write for Him has fulfilled a childhood dream, and writing inspirational fiction has led to incredible friendships. Freda starts the day with thanks for His grace.

ICE
CASTLE

Joyce Livingston

Chapter 1

Which do you like best?"

Carlee Bennett whirled around to find a handsome man standing beside her in the store. He held two colorful containers in his hands and wore a friendly smile. "Spray? Or bottle?"

"Oh, no contest," she quipped with an equally friendly smile. "Spray. That's what I use. I hate those bottles!"

"Hey, thanks for the advice," he replied pleasantly as he placed one of the containers back onto its shelf. "I've never tried the spray stuff, but it sure looks like it might be easier to handle than the bottle of saline I've been using. Am I ever glad someone invented contacts; I'd probably be out of a job without them."

She normally didn't pursue a conversation with a stranger, but he seemed like a nice enough guy; and his comment intrigued her. She gave him a quizzical look. "They won't let you wear glasses on your job? What do you do for a living?"

"Skater," he replied casually, as his eyes scanned the fine print on the spray can.

"Skater? What kind of skater?"

"Ice skater. I'm in Kansas City with Ice Fantasy at the Kemper Arena. Our last performance is tonight."

She turned to face him directly. "Really?" she asked in surprise. "I have tickets for tonight's performance. What numbers will you be doing? I'll watch for you."

He took a quick glance at his watch and dropped the spray can into his cart. "Wow! Didn't know it was getting so late. I gotta git. Thanks for the help." With a quick nod and a gorgeous toothy grin that highlighted his deep dimples, he took off down the aisle toward the row of checkout stands lining the front of the big discount store.

She quickly lifted a hand and called out to him, "Wait! You didn't say which parts you'll be skating in the ice show!"

He stopped long enough to turn his head and call back over his shoulder as he moved with haste toward the cash register and the waiting clerk. "Prince Charming! I'll be the guy in the white tights—without glasses!"

＊

At Kemper Arena, Carlee tightened her arms about her daughter's slim shoulders and pulled her close. "Keep watching! Remember what the book said?"

345

Four-year-old Becca lifted her shining face and smiled at her mother. "The prince will come and wake her up?"

"That's right!"

"That's dumb!" Eight-year-old Bobby clamped his hands over his little sister's eyes and grinned at his mom, who instantly pulled his hands away from the little girl's face.

"Bobby, stop! I wanna see the prince!" Becca buried her face in her mother's neck. "Mama, make him stop!"

For several weeks now the young mother had been excited about bringing her children to the ice show, hoping it would somehow brighten their lives. Today marked an anniversary of sorts—five years to the day since Robert had died. Four years, and Bobby was still having trouble understanding why his dad had been taken from them. It was good to see the children behaving normally, fussing at one another on a day that, otherwise, could have been a sad one for all of them.

She tousled the agitator's hair and gave him a sly wink. "Bobby, leave your sister alone. Watch for the prince, okay?"

The kettledrums rumbled; the music swelled to a loud crescendo, then dropped again as a lone voice sang, "I'll find my love someday—someday when my prince shall come. . . ."

"There! There he is—he's coming!" Carlee turned her daughter's head with one hand and pointed to the far corner of the big arena with the other. "See him, Becca? There! Right where the fog is thickest!"

Becca squealed with delight. "I see him! I see him!"

Out of the fog in a flash of speed and grace, clad in gleaming white satin, skated Prince Charming in all his glory.

"That's him, Bobby! The man I told you about." Carlee excitedly turned to her son, who was sitting on the edge of his seat watching the male skater. "Keep practicing and you'll be able to do a spread eagle like that." She pinched his arm lightly. "Yours is pretty good already, for an eight-year-old."

As the music slowed to a romantic pace, so did the prince as he performed an audience favorite—a long, graceful spiral.

Suddenly the music stopped, and so did the performer. An aura of anticipation filled the air as the hall became silent and the heavy fog crawled swiftly across the ice, creeping into all four corners, eerily hovering around the feet of the prince as he caught sight of Snow White. He pushed off with one foot and glided slowly toward the sleeping beauty.

"Isn't he gonna kiss her and wake her up?"

Carlee smoothed her daughter's hair and tried to mask her amusement as she viewed eyes watery with concern. "Just wait, Becca! Keep watching."

Deliberately, lovingly, the skater lowered his face to the maiden's pink lips with a gentle, lingering kiss, as a single violin played softly.

Snow White's lashes fluttered. The dwarfs gasped and began chattering to one another. She blinked her eyes, then opened them wide as she sat up and stretched—first one arm and then the other—followed by an exaggerated yawn.

The prince took her dainty hand in his and lifted it to his lips as she lowered her feet to the ice and stood before him. The bright blue bodice of her snug-fitting dress accentuated her small waist as the flowing red skirt fluttered and billowed about her slender hips. The perfectly matched couple began to move to the music—slowly at first, then more rapidly as they danced across the ice, the spotlight following their every twist and turn, ending with the crème de la crème, the phenomenal death spiral and a final kiss.

With the clanging of cymbals and the banging of kettledrums, the music ended. The bright lights shut off. The arena was encased in darkness as the crowd burst into thunderous applause. Spotlights exploded forth, penetrating the blackness of the room, moving in erratic zigzag patterns across the ice in a brilliant assortment of colors. But Snow White and Prince Charming were nowhere to be seen.

Becca tugged at her mother's sleeve again.

Carlee smiled at her daughter. "Be patient, Becca." The beams of light moved collectively to the center of the ice and focused there as Snow White skated into the lighted area, lifted one side of her long red skirt, and curtsied. The audience went wild with applause.

Prince Charming skated into the circle of light and bowed low. Again the crowd went wild, cheering, whistling, and clapping as they gave the pair a standing ovation. Then, out of the darkness, six miniature men skated into the light and dropped to their knees around the beautiful couple, enjoying their portion of the well-deserved applause.

Bobby counted aloud, "One, two, three, four, five, six. Someone's missing!"

"It's Dopey!" Becca shouted. "Where's Dopey?"

From a far corner, the little man skated clumsily into the spotlight, clutching a huge bouquet of long-stemmed red roses in his stubby arms. When he lifted them to Snow White, she bent and kissed him on the nose, to everyone's delight.

Dozens of spotlights in every color of the rainbow began to weave intertwining ovals as the rest of the Ice Fantasy cast skated onto the ice to receive accolades. "Ladies and gentlemen," the voice of the announcer echoed from the loudspeakers as the houselights came on, "thank you for coming, and drive home safely. Good night."

❧

A single hand wound its way out from under the Double Wedding Ring quilt and punched the snooze button when the alarm clock jangled. It was still dark at 6:00. Saturday wasn't a school day, so the kids could sleep in, but Carlee had to get up as early as she did every other day of the week. She fumbled for the snooze button a second time but decided against prolonging the agony and threw back the covers.

She'd barely finished her toast and was working on a glass of juice when she heard the key turn in the lock of the outside door and a tall, slender woman with salt-and-pepper hair entered the kitchen. " 'Morning, Mother Bennett."

The smiling woman placed a cookie sheet on the table and tugged at the fingers of her glove. " 'Morning, yourself. How was the ice show?" She lifted the linen napkin covering the pan. The aroma of hot, freshly baked cinnamon rolls loaded with caramel and pecans filled the country kitchen. "Can I tempt you with these?"

"Oh, my favorite! Mother Bennett, you spoil us." Carlee grabbed a sticky roll and kissed her mother-in-law. "When did you bake these? It's barely 6:15."

"Last night—reheated them this morning. I knew how hard this week would be for you. I wanted to do something special, to help you get through it. You'd better get going."

Carlee gulped her juice, wrapped the remainder of her cinnamon roll in a napkin, and wiggled into her heavy jacket. "See you at noon."

Once at the ice rink that she owned jointly with her in-laws, Carlee flipped on the string of lights and slipped into the little snack bar where the electric oil-filled heater waited to be plugged in. She filled the coffeepot, flipped the ON switch, and pulled her coat close about her neck.

The buzzer on the outside door sounded. A quick look through the peephole revealed four mothers with four children, each child holding a pair of ice skates. Carlee lifted the latch and held the door open as they filed in, one by one.

"Sure hated to get out of bed this morning," one of the mothers admitted as she sniffed the air. "Coffee smells good."

Carlee grinned and gestured toward the perking pot. "It'll be ready in a minute."

"Did you see the ice show at the Kemper?" a yawning mother asked as she plopped onto a stool and leaned her head against the wall. "That Dan Castleberry is a real hunk."

"Skates good, too," another added. "You agree, Carlee?"

She nodded, then turned her attention to the sleepy children, who stood watching like zombies. "It's time for you guys to get those skates on. Your patch is waiting."

"Don't you ever get tired of getting up this early to let people in to skate?" a mother asked a little later as she poured herself a second cup of coffee. "Sometimes I wonder if it's worth it."

Carlee pulled a caramel-covered pecan from her roll and looked thoughtful. "No, not really. Working at this rink makes it possible for me to take good care of my children and be home with them when they need me. I can't complain."

After Robert's death, Carlee had insisted that she carry her share of the load.

Her father-in-law couldn't handle it by himself. Their agreed-upon arrangement had worked out perfectly, with Ethel Bennett serving as the willing, available babysitter. Carlee was less than three weeks pregnant when Robert died in the plane crash; he never knew about his daughter.

In the little office with its clear view of the rink, Carlee sat and punched the calculator. Father Bennett ran the afternoon and evening skating sessions, but she was the one who tallied and recorded the sessions and filled out the bank deposits, just as Robert had when he was alive.

She watched with amusement as an overweight girl in her midteens struggled with her three-turns as her mother gruffly barked advice from the first row. *Please, Lord, don't let me ever do that to my children,* she silently prayed.

Praying for her children came easy; she'd learned at an early age to talk to God about anything and everything, even things that would seem foolish to most people. Only one time could she remember praying for or about something and receiving no answer: That had been prayer for her beloved Robert. Without realizing it, she began to sing softly as she worked, "Someday my prince will come. . . ."

It was five minutes past noon when Carlee slipped quietly through the kitchen door. A pot of homemade vegetable beef soup simmered on the stove. Mother Bennett's sweet voice could be heard as she sat in the rocking chair reading *Snow White and the Seven Dwarfs* to an appreciative four-year-old. The young mother tiptoed into the room and seated herself carefully on the sofa beside Bobby. Mother Bennett looked up, but Becca was too engrossed in the story to notice Carlee.

"And they lived happily ever after. The end!" Mother Bennett announced with a flourish as she closed the book.

Becca kissed her grandmother's cheek before leaping off her lap and into her mother's. Carlee cradled her baby to her breast and said gratefully, "Thanks, Mother Bennett. You're very special."

Her mother-in-law crossed the room and squeezed Carlee's shoulder affectionately. "So are you. Enjoy the soup."

Carlee watched as Ethel pulled on her coat and headed for her own home, only a hundred feet from theirs. Since Robert's death, Ethel had been coming over at 6:15 every morning to care for the children so Carlee could open the rink for the "patchers," as they called them. By now, it was a ritual. Carlee would return home, eat, and then Ethel would take some of the soup to Father Bennett. He'd eat, kiss her good-bye, and head for the rink in time to open at 1:30. At 4:00, 4:30, and 5:00, he would give private lessons, then run home for a bite of supper and be back at the rink by 6:30 to give a group lesson. Then he would open for the evening session at 7:30. But it was Mother Bennett who kept them all going. She worked quietly in the background, caring for the children all morning so Carlee could work and be home with them the rest of the day.

Chapter 2

When Carlee rolled out of bed Sunday morning at seven, a luxury she enjoyed only once a week, Mother Bennett was sitting in the kitchen sipping freshly brewed coffee. "How long have you been here? Why didn't you wake me?" The younger Mrs. Bennett poured herself a mug of hot coffee and plopped into the oak pressed-back chair.

"Came over early. I didn't mind the wait—I knew you could use the extra sleep. Besides, it's Sunday."

The young woman wearily rose to her feet and pulled on her heavy jacket. "That means I'd better hustle if I'm gonna close out last night's receipts and get the kids ready for Sunday school."

"Want me to go with you, Mama?" Bobby stood there, dressed in jeans and a flannel shirt, his feet covered with the worn cowboy boots he loved so much.

Carlee reached out a hand and grinned at her son. "Sure! I'd love the company."

The rink seemed exceptionally cold when they entered. She set about counting the admissions and preparing the bank deposit. Bobby placed the nickels, dimes, and quarters in the tray, counting them aloud as he deposited each coin. The two were startled by the sound of the buzzer. She checked her watch: 7:45. Maybe one of the skaters forgot what day of the week it was; who else would be buzzing on Sunday?

"I'll get it!" Bobby volunteered as he jumped from the stool and raced toward the door, ready to fling it open.

"No, Bobby! Wait!" his mother cautioned, her hands full of dollar bills, half counted. "Don't open the door!"

Bobby climbed onto a chair and peered out the peephole.

"Mom!" he shouted as he leaped from the chair and ran toward his mother, a broad smile dominating his freckled face. "It's Prince Charming! He's at our door!" He grabbed his mother by the arm and dragged her from the stool. "Aren't you going to let him in?"

Carlee drew back. "Bobby, stop! Prince Charming wouldn't be at our door, especially this time of morning. It's Sunday. He's miles from here by now."

Bobby was relentless. "Yes, he is, Mommy. Honest! It's him. I know it is. Come and see!" He released his hold and ran back to the peephole as the buzzer sounded a second time.

Carlee placed the money tray and the loose bills in the drawer and locked it securely, then hurried to the door. Sure enough, there stood Prince Charming, waiting patiently.

"See, Mom? I told you so!" Bobby tugged at the dead bolt on the door as his mother stood gazing out the peephole. "Mom, he's cold! Let him in!"

Carlee took one last look, then opened the door.

"Hi." The handsome skater smiled at the dazzled young mother and her son. "I saw your car parked by the door and hoped someone would be here. Do you rent ice time here at the Ice Palace?"

Bobby yanked at her sleeve. "Mom—say something."

"Yes. No. I mean, yes, we do, but not on Sunday." She felt like a dork as she stood in the doorway, her hair barely combed, her frayed jacket zipped to the neck. She was sure he didn't recognize her, not the way she looked.

The man smiled at Bobby. "Hey, kid, you a skater?"

Bobby returned his smile. "Yep. But not as good as you."

"Oh, you've seen me skate, have you? At the show here in Kansas City this week?" He stuffed his hands deeply into his pockets and shivered.

Carlee blushed and stepped back. "The building is cold, but at least the wind isn't blowing in here."

He strode in and closed and locked the door behind him. She should have been frightened, but after all, she had met him before, if only for a minute. And he *was* Prince Charming; surely Prince Charming would do them no harm.

"Let me introduce myself—officially." He winked at Bobby as he extended a gloved hand. "I'm Dan Castleberry."

Bobby stood straight and tall and reached out his hand to shake the skater's. "Hi, I'm Bobby Bennett. This is my mom."

Dan Castleberry shook the small hand vigorously. "Pleased to meet you, Bobby. What a fine, well-mannered young man you are." Then, looking at the boy's mother, the man did a double take. "You're the woman I met at Wal-Mart!"

Frozen to the spot, she responded with a dull, "Uh-huh," and nodded her head and wished she didn't look so dowdy.

"Well then, Mrs. Bennett, you may know Kansas City was the last stop on our tour; we've been traveling for two years with this production. I have three weeks off before we begin rehearsals for the new show." He looked at the boy. "I'm here to visit my parents, Bobby. They live in Overland Park. I need to start practicing my new role as the Beast." He laughed, screwed up his face, and crossed his eyes. "I'd like to stay in Kansas City and spend time with my parents. But I have to find an available rink in this area, or I'll have to go on to Florida to begin practice."

Carlee listened intently, trying to keep her mind from wandering to thoughts of him skating so beautifully in that white satin costume.

"So, I'll take any time you have available. And of course, I'll pay whatever the going rate is. I'd like to have at least an hour a day—more if I can get it."

Carlee pursed her lips awkwardly, wishing that, at the least, she'd put on a little lipstick. Well, too late for that!

"Mom. . ." Bobby nudged her side with his elbow.

"I'll—uh—have to ask my father-in-law," she responded weakly, still in shock at seeing the prince. "But I'm sure he'll work something out for you." She pulled Bobby in front of her and wrapped her arms about him, almost as a shield.

"I need to get started as soon as I can. Tomorrow, if possible." He grabbed the boy by the hand. "Hey, Bobby. How about showing me the ice?"

Bobby pulled away from his mom and led the man toward the big double doors. "Sure," he said with youthful enthusiasm.

Carlee hurried to the phone and called Father Bennett. "What do *you* think about this, Carlee? It'll have to be early in the morning—that's the only time an hour or more is available. You'll have to stay there with him. Are you willing to be there by 5:15? That's pretty early."

She grinned and shifted her weight from one foot to the other. "What's the difference?—5:15, 6:15, early is early! And he's willing to pay whatever we ask," she added as she peered through the windows of the double doors and watched her son's rapid-fire mouth. How she wished she could hear his conversation with the man.

"It's fine with me," he agreed.

The double doors swung open, and the man and boy came strolling through, laughing and talking like old friends. Sadness welled up in Carlee's heart. How much her son had missed without a father to talk to and be with.

Dan raised his brows. "Well, what's the good word?"

She pushed her hair from her forehead and smiled, first at Bobby, then at the skater. "If you can come mornings by 5:15, you'll have a whole hour. Is that acceptable?"

He rubbed his hands together briskly. "Great. And thanks, I appreciate it. I think my folks will, too."

She moved toward the door and unlocked it. "Sorry, but we have to leave, or we'll be late for Sunday school."

"Oops, I'm the one who's sorry! Hope I didn't keep you too long." He tousled Bobby's hair with his big hand before stepping through the open door. "See ya at 5:15 tomorrow morning!"

Bobby ran to his mom and gave her a bear hug. "Wow! Prince Charming! Wait'll I tell the kids at Sunday school!"

❧

Dan Castleberry sat in his car the next morning with the motor running, listening to the radio and thinking of his future. He checked his watch: five o'clock. He'd arrived early, anxious to start practicing his new assignment as the Beast. He drummed his fingertips on the steering wheel in time to the music. What if Mrs. Bennett had forgotten about him? No, not likely. He had a feeling she was more responsible than that. He'd liked the woman immediately, but he had wondered why any man would allow his wife to be out this time of the morning, meeting with a stranger. She had to be married; he'd noticed the wedding band on her left hand. And he'd met her son.

A bread truck pulled into the parking lot and stopped next to his car. The driver waved, placed boxes of buns on the empty rack standing beside the door, and drove off. Headlights splashed across Dan's face as a minivan pulled into the parking lot and parked beside him. The lone occupant, a woman, opened the door and stepped out. He smiled, waved to her, and turned off the engine.

Carlee returned his smile, waved back, and moved to open the door to the building. He followed her in, shut the door, and turned the dead bolt. A sudden chill ran down her spine; she was locked in the building at 5:15 in the morning, alone with a man she barely knew. She moved quickly to turn on the long string of flourescent ceiling lights, and the area was instantly flooded with a harsh, glaring brilliance. She could feel his eyes watching her as he stood silently near the door.

"Okay if I go on in and get my skates on?" he asked.

Suddenly she felt ridiculous. This was a business arrangement. He was there to practice—nothing else. "Sure. Of course," she called back over her shoulder and headed toward the snack bar. "You drink coffee? I'll have some ready in a few minutes." But her words were wasted; he'd already disappeared into the rink to lace up his skates.

When the coffee finished dripping, she poured two steaming mugfuls and slipped quietly through the double doors. There he was, etching perfect figure eights onto the ice.

"Come and take time out for a cup of coffee. It'll help warm you up," she invited as she placed his mug onto the smooth railing that surrounded the ice.

He finished the figures, then glided silently toward her and sipped the coffee. "Umm, good. Thanks." He leaned against the railing and held the warm mug between cold hands. With his skates on, he was nearly a head taller than Carlee, and she had to look up to see his smile.

"I know you don't know much about me, Mrs. Bennett, but I want to assure you—I *am* trustworthy." He took a big swallow of coffee and grinned at her. "You're perfectly safe with me."

She lowered her gaze to the floor to avoid his eyes. Had he sensed her fear? It wasn't that she was afraid; it was just that she hadn't been this alone with a man since Robert died, and there was something so intimate about meeting a strange man in a deserted ice rink at 5:15 in the morning.

"I know. . .I. . .uh. . .don't mean to keep you. From skating, I mean." She felt herself stumbling over her words.

He took a last swig and gave a slight chuckle. "You're not. I needed the coffee. Thank you," he said warmly.

"I'll go back to the office and give you some privacy," she explained as she pulled her scarf about her neck and began to head toward the doors with the empty mugs.

"I'm used to skating before an audience, remember?" He did a quick twirl and added, "Honest, I'd like you to stay. Maybe you can help me with this routine."

"Uh. . .sure." She lowered herself into a front-row seat. "What can I do?"

He winked a friendly wink. "I'll let you know."

She tightened the loop on her scarf, buttoned the top button on her jacket, and pulled her gloves onto chilled, stiff fingers, then watched in awe as the professional skater went through an old routine to loosen up. He stopped at the far end of the rink and stood watching her, then skated with strong, quick strokes directly toward her. As he came within a few feet, he quickly turned the edges of his blades into the rink's surface and showered the empty chairs next to her with a blizzard of finely shaved, snowy ice. "*Now* you can help me," he said with a mischievous laugh.

She brushed a few stray ice fragments from her sleeve and returned his smile. "How?"

He pulled an audiotape from his jacket pocket and handed it to her. "Can you put this on for me?"

She crossed the rink, loaded the tape player, and punched PLAY. The theme song from *Beauty and the Beast* filled the rink, and he began to skate. She slipped back into her chair and watched in amazement. From time to time he'd stop, listen to the music, and start again, as though receiving instructions from some unseen source.

The hour was up all too soon, but he quit right on time.

"All right with you if I leave the tape here?"

"Sure," she mumbled as he sat down beside her and began to loosen the laces on his skates.

"How about the skates?"

"Uh, I'll lock them up in the office," she volunteered.

The buzzer sounded on the outside door. The first group of regulars were ready to begin their patch session. Dan allowed the skaters to enter before exiting through the door, then closed it behind him.

"Who was *that*?" one of the mothers asked as she riveted her eyes on the closed door.

"Prince Charming," Carlee said coyly with a wink, leaving the stranger's true identity to their imaginations.

Chapter 3

He was sitting on the fender of his car when she drove into the parking lot. There were things he wanted to know about Carlee Bennett—like, where was her husband? Were they divorced? He caught up with her, took the key from her hand, and turned it in the lock.

"Been waiting long?" she asked breathlessly.

"Nope. Just arrived." He pushed open the door and stood back to allow her to enter, then locked the door behind them with a sheepish grin. "How can you look this great so early in the morning?"

She was both surprised and pleased by his question. She tucked a lock of hair behind one ear and smiled shyly. "Considering all the beautiful women you skate with, I must seem like plain Jane. But thanks anyway."

He stepped in front of her, spread his arms, and blocked her way. "I don't give compliments unless I mean them."

Carlee flashed an embarrassed smile and gave his arm a friendly pat. "Turn on the lights. I'll get your skates."

She filled the coffeepot and stood waiting for the water to filter through. By the time the last drop had fallen into the glass pot, he was already on the ice, etching perfect eights with his skate blades. When he looked her way, she lifted his mug to let him know it was ready and waiting.

This time he skated over and sat down on the seat beside her, their elbows touching. "Tell me about yourself, Mrs. Bennett. Does your husband skate?" He sipped the hot coffee nonchalantly, as though merely making conversation.

"Please, call me Carlee," she corrected through chattering teeth as she turned to face him, her bright eyes barely peeping over the upturned collar.

He fingered his empty cup. "Only if you'll call me Dan."

"Dan," she repeated slowly. "Were you named after your father?"

"No. How about Bobby—was he named after *his* dad?"

Carlee smiled as she thought of Robert. "Yes, he was." She tried to hold back a tear, but it ran slowly down her cheek.

Dan pulled the paper napkin from around his mug and gently blotted the tear from her face.

"Sorry," she whispered through a watery smile. "It's been four years; you'd think I'd have gotten beyond doing this—"

"He left you when Bobby was three?"

"No! He died!" Carlee protested as she turned quickly toward him and lifted

355

moist eyes to meet his. "Robert would never leave us; he loved us. We had a perfect marriage."

Looking as though he felt a little foolish, Dan continued asking questions. "How did he die?"

"Plane crash," she answered with a slight sniffle.

He fingered the handle on his cup. "Oh. Sorry."

The two sat quietly, sipping their coffee.

"You probably think I'm silly to be so emotional after five years." She forced a smile. "I miss him so much."

"I think it's wonderful. If anything ever happened to me, I'd want my wife to feel just like you do," he confessed.

She wiped away another tear but continued to smile. "You're married, Dan? To one of those gorgeous women in the show?"

He laughed, a good belly laugh. "No way! You should see 'em without their makeup!"

"Have you ever considered marriage?" she asked, amazed at herself for prying into a stranger's personal life.

"Marriage? No! I'm not about to ruin my life."

His comment surprised her. "That's pretty cynical."

"Not really. I've seen too many marital disasters. The last thing I want to do is get saddled with a wife and kids. No alimony and child support for *this* guy."

His statement threw her off balance and offended her. He made marriage sound like a cataclysm, something to be avoided at all costs. That was certainly not the way she saw it.

"But not all marriages are like that!" she defended as she turned down the collar on her coat.

"Name one that isn't," he scoffed.

"Mine, for one. Mine and Robert's."

"Oh, really? Are you trying to tell me you'd never considered cheating on your husband? Not even once?"

A deep scowl crossed her face and lingered there, all traces of any previous smile gone. "No! Never! I would never do that!"

He scanned her face, then frowned and said softly, "Next, I suppose you're going to tell me you were a virgin on your wedding day."

The heat rose in her cheeks at his comment. So personal. So blunt. "Yes, that is exactly what I'm telling you, Mr. Castleberry. I was a virgin, and so was Robert."

"And you believed him? That he hadn't—that there hadn't been other women before you? None of my acquaintances can truthfully make that claim. Most guys wear their conquests like a badge of victory. You'd be surprised how many guys brag about it."

This conversation infuriated her. "Does that include you?" she asked with fire in her eyes. She wanted to slap him for even suggesting there may have been improprieties in her life. Or Robert's. She clenched her fists angrily and answered his question before he could answer hers. "You needn't answer. But yes, I did believe him. We both were raised to have high standards, something that you apparently don't understand. I feel sorry for you, Dan Castleberry. To never love someone enough to trust them, to commit your life to them, to experience true oneness with your mate. Well, that's missing out on one of God's biggest blessings in life."

She could feel her heart pounding; rarely did anyone stir up her emotions like this. "Don't underestimate marriage, Dan. Granted, being married to the wrong person could be miserable. But if you're married to the one God intended for you—"

"Like Robert?"

She forced a slight smile. "Yes. Like Robert. Then marriage can be beautiful, especially if it's blessed with children." There, she'd said enough. Subject closed!

They sat silently, as he continued to finger the handle on his coffee mug and she stared at the ceiling. They'd been having such good, light conversation. It had turned so quickly.

She crossed her arms over her chest, breathed deeply, and tried to get control of her anger. How could he possibly understand her position on marriage? On life? Why should he? Her anger turned to pity. Without God's leading, life was merely living, years passing by with no true purpose.

Dan broke the heavy silence. "Hey, look. I'm sorry. I guess I come from a different world than yours. I didn't mean to come off so strongly. Guess I'm pretty opinionated." He shifted nervously in the chair. "And as to your question," he explained with a look of sincerity that said *I'm telling the truth*, he went on, "No, that did *not* include me. I have no conquests to boast about, no badges of victory." He lowered his chin and mumbled softly, so softly she wasn't sure she'd heard him right. "Not since. . ." But he didn't finish.

She allowed a slight smile to surface. "I need to apologize now. I have strong opinions, too. It's just that these things are important to me and close to my heart since I'm a Christian."

His hand reached awkwardly toward hers, and she felt the warmth of his fingers grasping hers as he gave them an apologetic pat. "You have nothing to apologize for. I'm sorry for my behavior, and I hope you'll forgive me."

He did come from a different world. Why should she expect him to share her perspective on marriage and fidelity? She felt sorry for him. He appeared to have so much, yet had so little. Disagreeing with Dan wasn't going to accomplish anything, and she wanted to be a testimony to him.

"I know you don't like kids, Dan, but Bobby thinks you're wonderful. He asked me if he was going to get to see you again before you leave."

"Hey," he returned defensively, "I like kids! I just don't want any of my own.

Sure, I'd like to see him. Especially since he's a skater." He bent over and tightened the laces on his skate. "Tell me when he'll be here, and I'll make a point to come by. Maybe I can give him a few pointers."

Her eyes brightened at the thought. "Oh, he'd love that! I could bring him by Wednesday afternoon after school—say about four o'clock? One of the patchers won't be in this week. Bobby could skate on her area. Would that work for you?"

"Wednesday it is!" he confirmed as he jumped over the railing and onto the ice. "Now, if you'll put that tape on the machine, I've got practicing to do."

Bobby ran to tell the neighbor kids when he heard that Dan wanted to watch him skate.

"Doesn't he want to watch *me* skate, Mama?" Becca asked as she brushed the long, tangled hair on her Barbie doll.

Carlee lifted the little girl and gave her a big hug. "Of course he wants to watch you skate, honey."

"Mama, does he wear his Prince Charming suit when he skates at our rink?" the tiny girl asked as she struggled to extricate the brush from the doll's hair.

Carlee tried to restrain a laugh. "No, sweetie. Just jeans and a plaid shirt, kinda like Bobby wears."

When Mother Bennett arrived Wednesday morning, Carlee was fully dressed and sipping coffee in the kitchen.

"You're up early." Ethel handed her daughter-in-law a brown paper bag, its top folded over like a lunch sack.

"What's this?"

Mother Bennett patted her hand and said with a curious smile, "I thought it'd be nice if you and Mr. Castleberry had some homemade chocolate chip cookies for your coffee break."

Dan was leaning against the door when Carlee arrived at the rink. His spirits had lightened since he'd thought over their conversation about Robert. The last thing he was interested in was a young widow with a son, but, although he was sorry for her loss, he was relieved to find there was no ex-spouse or deadbeat dad in her life. Losing a husband that way must have been tough on her. She seemed to have weathered it well.

"You're early," she chastised cheerily as she handed him the key and glanced at her watch.

"You're pretty," he replied as he unlocked the door and pushed it open with his shoulder.

She quickly entered and headed toward the coffeepot with her sack of goodies. "Flatterer."

"What's this?" He leaned over the counter and picked up the brown bag. "Goodies for our break time?"

She slapped his hand and grabbed the sack. "You'll find out soon enough. Now go!"

He saluted and headed for her office to get his skates.

The coffee seemed to take longer than usual to perk. By the time she carried the mugs into the rink, he had finished his school figures and was skating in a long, easy-flowing circular pattern. When he noticed her, he skated over and showered the area with the customary cascade of snowy ice, and as usual, she laughed and brushed it from her sleeve.

"You don't have to serve me refreshments every morning, you know." He took the hot mug of coffee and sniffed its pleasant aroma. "Umm. Just what I needed."

"Oh?" she teased as she dangled and swung the brown bag before his eyes, just out of his reach. "Look what I've got!"

"Give me that," he ordered with a twinkle in his eye as he lunged at the elusive bag. His cheek brushed hers in the process, and he backed off quickly, embarrassed.

She pretended it hadn't happened, opened the bag, and showed him the six giant chocolate chip cookies. "Mother Bennett baked these for us. Go on—take one. Don't be shy."

He pulled a cookie from the bag, took a big bite, and rubbed his tummy with his palm. "Thank Mother Bennett for me; these are great! Homemade, huh?"

She reached into the bag, selected a cookie for herself, and munched on it pensively. "Dan, you said you wanted to stay in the Kansas City area so you could spend time with your parents. Are you close to them?"

He took another bite and looked off into space with a melancholy look. "Not very. Traveling so much makes it impossible to see them very often. I call at least twice a week, but it's not the same as being with them."

She offered the bag, and he took a second cookie.

"You're close to your in-laws?" he asked. "And they take good care of your son while you're working here?"

"And Becca."

Dan looked puzzled. "Becca? Who's Becca?"

"My four-year-old daughter, Rebecca. Bobby's little sister. The delight of my life!" Hadn't she mentioned Becca? Dan raised his eyebrows in surprise, then frowned thoughtfully. "If Becca is four and Robert died five years ago, that means she was probably just a little baby when he died. She probably doesn't even remember her dad."

Carlee dipped her head and blinked hard. "Worse than that, he didn't even know about her. She was born eight months after his death. Neither of us knew I was pregnant at the time. Those were the hardest eight months of my life." She stood awkwardly and stretched as mixed emotions surged through her chilled body. "My in-laws live next door. Grandma comes over every morning. I come in here, work till noon, then go home. Want the rest of the schedule?"

He nodded.

She brushed the crumbs from her jacket and continued, "My mother-in-law goes home and fixes lunch for Father Bennett. He comes to the rink and works the rest of the day." She took a deep breath and let it out slowly, with a grin. "Then I come back the next morning, and the cycle begins all over again. It's a good, workable schedule for all of us, and this way, we can keep the business in the family. They want me to be with the children as much as possible, and they're willing to do whatever is necessary to help make it happen." She shoved the bag toward him once more. "Sounds boring, doesn't it?"

He shook his head and held up a hand. "No more for me; I've got skating to do!" He stood, grabbed the bag from her hands, and folded its top. "But I'll eat the rest of them when I finish. Keep 'em for me, okay? And don't forget to thank Grandma!"

Some of the patchers arrived earlier than usual; there was only time to shout a brief good-bye and a quick reminder that Bobby would be watching for him around four o'clock. Dan nodded and assured her he'd be there as he shut the door behind him.

The four mothers turned to watch him go, still not used to seeing Prince Charming in the Ice Palace.

Chapter 4

Gray clouds moved across the Kansas City sky as Dan Castleberry stared at the clock in the dashboard of his rented car; it was 3:30, and he was early. He'd never skated with an eight-year-old before. Could the little boy really skate? If Dan had a son, that's the way it'd be—he'd have skates on the kid as soon as he took his first steps.

Dan laughed aloud, a real belly laugh. A son? His son? Like he'd told Carlee, he'd never even considered marriage, let alone children! When you travel from city to city and country to country, spending only a week at a time in any one place, marriage isn't in your vocabulary. No, as long as he was skating professionally, marriage was out of the question. He'd have plenty of time for that later, when and if the idea of marriage ever appealed to him. But would he ever meet a woman he could trust? One he'd want to marry? One who wouldn't marry him, then take him to the cleaners for alimony?

The conversation he'd had with Carlee about her marriage to Robert replayed in his mind. He'd like a woman to be pure, to have kept herself for him only, like Carlee had for Robert, but he was nearly twenty-nine. Was there any woman his age who had remained pure? Not likely! He slumped in the seat, leaned back against the headrest, and closed his eyes as he mentally began to skate through his new routine.

❧

"Mom, do you think he'll remember to come?" Bobby asked from the backseat as they whizzed through traffic.

Carlee winked at her son in the rearview mirror. "Of course he'll remember, Bobby. That's the last thing he said this morning, 'See you at four o'clock!' He'll be there."

And sure enough, there was Dan's rental car, parked next to the building by the front door. Apparently hearing the sound of their engine, he straightened up and waved.

"Dan, I'm so sorry we're late," she called to him as she unbuckled Becca's seat belt. "Heavy traffic."

He locked his car and strolled over to where they were parked, never taking his eyes off the beautiful little girl.

"So, this must be Becca." He saw she was the image of her mother with soft, reddish brown hair and incredibly blue eyes.

Becca smiled and wrapped her arm around her mother's leg as she shyly

361

twisted a lock of her hair.

"This is Mr. Castleberry, Becca, the nice man you watched in the ice show. Remember? Prince Charming." She tugged at Becca's arm and tried to break free of her daughter's grasp. "Sorry, Dan. Normally she's not this shy. I think she's intimidated at meeting Prince Charming. We all are," she confessed reluctantly as she stroked Becca's hair.

"Well, it's nice to meet you, Becca. I hope we can be friends. I've never been friends with a four-year-old before." His warm smile might have been intended for the little girl, but it melted a proud mother's heart.

Carlee watched as Dan took Bobby's hand in his, opened the door, and disappeared into the rink.

By the time Dan and Bobby reached the ice, Carlee and Becca were already seated, waiting. Bobby had warned his mother that he didn't want her hovering over him during his time with Dan, so she'd chosen two seats that were several rows up and off to one side, where she and Becca wouldn't be quite so conspicuous.

Bobby stepped onto the ice first as Dan stood by the railing, watching. The patch didn't give Bobby much room to work, but he gave it his all. Carlee didn't watch her son. She watched Dan's jaw drop in amazement as he moved onto the ice beside Bobby and the two began to talk.

"That's the Prince Charming we've heard so much about?"

The young mother turned toward the voice with a smile as an athletic-looking man in his early fifties dropped into the seat beside her and pulled Becca onto his lap. Becca squealed with delight and pulled his cap down over his eyes.

"Hi, Father Bennett," Carlee said, nodding her head. "Yep, that's him. I think he's impressed with Bobby's skating."

He pushed his hat from his eyes and tickled his little granddaughter as she giggled and pulled away from his hold. "The kid's a natural; I've taught him everything he knows."

The threesome observed quietly as the professional ice skater worked with Bobby on his school figures, then they hurried toward the end of the rink when the two skaters left the ice. By the time they reached them, Dan and Bobby were already in their street shoes, laughing and wiping ice off their blades with an old towel from Bobby's bag.

Bobby smiled confidently at his mother and grandfather. "Hey, Mom, Mr. Castleberry said he'd teach me some more stuff before he leaves."

Carlee touched her son lightly on his slim shoulder. "Bobby, don't you think it would be nice if you introduced your teacher to your grandfather?"

Bobby took Father Bennett's hand in his. "Oh yeah. Sorry. Grandpa, this is Mr. Castleberry. Mr. Castleberry, this is my grandpa."

Short and sweet, just like a boy, she thought.

Dan Castleberry extended his hand with a broad smile. "Pleased to meet you, sir. I've heard many nice things about you and Mrs. Bennett—from Carlee and Bobby."

The older man accepted his hand and gripped it firmly. "Nice to meet you. But please, call me Jim."

Dan smiled. "Only if you'll all call me Dan, and that includes you, Bobby." He tousled Bobby's hair. "And you, too, Becca. Will you call me Dan?"

Becca twisted in her grandfather's arms and nodded her head, then leaned forward until her forehead touched Dan's and rested there. "Dan," she said with a giggle.

He looked pleased, his smile bright and warm.

"You in a hurry, Dan?" Jim Bennett asked as he lowered Becca to the floor.

"No, sir. Why?" He shifted his skate bag to his shoulder and lifted his brows.

"Got a few things I'd like to show ya," Jim answered with a friendly wink as he took Dan's arm and led him away.

Carlee watched them go, then called out after them, "Thanks, Dan. See you in the morning."

Dan spun back to answer. "You bet. I'll be there."

&

Jim Bennett led Dan Castleberry to his private office down a long hall, just beyond the skate room. "Oh!" said Dan appreciatively when Jim flipped on the lights.

The room was filled with rows of shelves supporting trophies in all sizes, colors, and shapes, each inscribed with the name Jim Bennett. The walls were covered with photos, most in color, a few in black-and-white. Many of them featured a man skating, spinning, performing jumps, spread-eagles, or spirals. The remainder pictured the same man accepting awards and shaking hands with dignitaries. The featured man was the same in each photo—Jim Bennett!

Dan was impressed. He had no idea that the Jim Bennett who owned and operated the Ice Palace was the same Jim Bennett he'd heard about all his years in the skating world.

"Why didn't Carlee tell me?"

Jim Bennett rubbed his chin. "Guess because she doesn't know a lot about me. Seems like I'm bragging or something. I don't talk about my past much. I quit skating professionally the year Ethel and I got married."

"But why?" Dan inquired with a puzzled look. "You were at the peak of your profession! Why'd you leave it?"

Jim smiled a secretive little smile. "Love, son. Love."

"Mrs. Bennett?"

"Yep. Couldn't expect her to follow me all over the world. We wanted to settle down and raise a family. So I quit, bought this rink—been here over twenty-five years now."

Dan watched Jim as he talked. It was obvious he'd made the right decision—for him.

"What kind of goals have you set for yourself, Dan?"

Dan leaned forward and looked at the man who'd blazed the professional trail before his time. "You're living it, sir! I want to own my own rink, maybe a couple of rinks. I'd like to train young skaters, maybe even steer some of them toward the Olympics." He leaned back with a modest grin. "I even have a name for my rink."

"Oh?" Jim moved to stand beside his guest. "What?"

Dan straightened in the chair, excited to share his dreams with someone who understood. "Ice Castle!"

Jim grinned as he rubbed the five o'clock shadow forming on his ruddy chin. "Good name! Catchy and appropriate. Owning your own rink is an awesome responsibility, but there's nothing like it." He raked his fingers through his hair thoughtfully. "Umm. Ice Castle. I do like that name."

Dan folded his arms across his chest and sat gazing around the room. Jim Bennett, ice skater extraordinaire, the owner and pro of the Ice Palace. It was too much to comprehend.

"You married, Dan?" His unexpected question came like a thunderbolt out of the blue, startling the young man.

It was a simple question, yet the skater felt uncomfortable answering it, and paused. "No, sir."

Jim seated himself in the straight-backed chair behind the cluttered desk, leaned back, and locked his hands behind his head. "Hate to tell you this, son, but you've been missing the greatest thing God ever arranged for man. A good-looking guy like you should have his pick of women. Is it that you haven't found the right one yet?"

Dan pondered the question. "I'm not sure. I've always thought of marriage as an anchor around your neck—being tied to one person, stripped of your freedom. Now I don't know, especially after a conversation I had with Carlee."

"You mean about Robert?"

"Yes, sir. Robert and their marriage. She made it sound like a good marriage was the ultimate goal in life. Talked like God had planned for them to be together."

Jim let out a long sigh. "And you don't believe her?"

"I honestly think *she* believes it, but could that be? Do you think God really cares about such things?"

Jim templed his fingertips thoughtfully. "Yes, Dan, I do. He's told us in His Word that He's concerned about even the littlest things in our lives." He smiled at Dan across the cluttered desk. "I even think He sent you into our lives."

❧

Dan Castleberry stayed at the rink much longer than he'd intended, watching and listening as Jim Bennett gave private lessons. He'd stumbled into a world he hadn't realized existed. In Kansas City, the home of his parents, of all places! He'd expected these three weeks to be routine and dull and that he'd be anxious to get back to join the rest of the cast and rehearsals. Now the time was passing all too quickly.

Carlee and the children had supper at the Bennetts' home that evening. With Jim Bennett, Bobby, and Becca talking about Dan Castleberry, Carlee and Ethel barely got in a word.

"I want to meet this young man," Ethel told her daughter-in-law as the two women cleared the table and loaded the dishwasher. "Maybe he could come to dinner on Sunday. Why don't you invite him?"

Chapter 5

Carlee told Dan about the invitation to Sunday dinner when he took his break from skating. He crossed his legs and leaned back in the bleacher-type chair, sipping his coffee, and without hesitation answered, "Tell your mother-in-law I'd be happy to come."

She was both surprised and happy. It had been months since either Bennett family had invited guests to their home.

"Now I have a favor to ask." He pulled a videotape from his pocket. "This is a rough run-through of the numbers I'll be performing in the new show. I'll be happy to pay you for your time. I need you to watch the tape while I skate, making sure I'm doing everything in the proper sequence. Could you do that for me?"

"Of course I'll do it, Dan," she replied eagerly. "And I'd never allow you to pay me for it."

"Yes!" he shouted as a doubled-up fist shot into the air, much like she'd seen Father Bennett do when something was going his way. "I'll pick up one of those portable TV-VCR units this afternoon."

"Great. I'm happy to help." She had a sudden flash of an idea and spoke before she had a chance to think it through. "Dan, do you have plans for this evening?"

He looked puzzled. "No. Why?"

At once she felt brazen and ridiculous. "Never mind."

"Oh no, you don't! You're not getting off that easy. Why did you want to know about my plans for this evening?" He crossed his arms and waited.

"Well," she began slowly, wishing she'd kept her mouth shut, "I was thinking, if you don't have any plans, maybe you'd like to come over for hot dogs." She really felt foolish inviting Prince Charming for hot dogs.

"I'll be there," he agreed without hesitation. "What time? I'll need the address."

His quick answer caught her off guard. "Oh, six, seven. . .whatever works for you," she mumbled incoherently.

A sly smile crept across his face. "Good! Hot dogs are my favorite food!"

❦

When Bobby got home from school, he took one look at the immaculate house and asked, "Who's coming?"

She greeted him with a sideways smile. "You're right; someone is coming for supper tonight. Now put your books away."

Bobby's brow furrowed. "Does that mean we aren't gonna have hot dogs? Remember, Mom, Thursday is hot dog night."

Before she could answer, Becca grabbed her brother's hand and blurted out, "I got a secret, Bobby. Wanna hear it? Prince Charming is gonna eat hot dogs with us."

"Mom?" Bobby ran to his mother and threw both arms around her waist. "Really? Is Becca telling the truth?"

"Would you like that, Bobby?"

His eyes sparkled. "Yeah. He's really coming?"

"Yes, he is. Would you like to help me build a nice big fire in the fireplace? We'll roast our hot dogs there."

The look on Bobby's face caused a tightness around his mother's heart. Was she making a mistake by allowing Dan into their lives? He'd be in Kansas City such a short time. She couldn't stand the thought of Bobby becoming attached to this man, only to lose him like he had his father. But that was different; Dan was only a friend, a short-term friend.

☙

Dan Castleberry stepped onto Carlee's front porch right at six o'clock. She hadn't been specific about the time, and he hoped he wasn't pushing it by showing up so early. He'd been excited about the invitation all day, ever since he'd left Carlee at the rink nearly twelve hours earlier. He'd even stopped at the florist on the way to their house and picked out a colorful bunch of flowers. He couldn't remember the last time he'd bought flowers for a woman, other than his mother, and usually he wired those.

No more angry words had passed between Dan and Carlee since that early morning at the rink when they'd discussed her virginity. Although the subject had never come up again, it hung heavily between them like an unseen veil. He hoped she'd think of the flowers as a peace offering, but he'd never suggest it to her. Her words had etched themselves indelibly on his being. He'd never forget them.

☙

Carlee checked the house one final time, with inquisitive little Becca at her heels. Everything was in its place. The porch! She hadn't swept the front porch! "Bobby," she ordered as she straightened the coffee table's magazines for the third time, "bring me the broom."

He did as he was told. She smiled at her son, grabbed the broom, and rushed out the door, only to find her expected guest standing on the porch, one hand reaching for the doorbell, the other holding a bouquet of flowers. The startled look that crossed her face was quickly replaced with a broad smile. "Sorry, you surprised me."

He extended the flowers awkwardly. "For you," he said with a smile that reminded her of the way Bobby smiled when he wanted to gain favor. The flowers remained suspended in midair, the intended recipient not quite sure what to do about them.

"Wanna trade?" Dan reached his free hand toward the broom handle, which she was holding onto for support.

"I. . .uh. . .was going to sweep the porch before you came. You know. . . leaves. Leaves have blown. . .up here." She knew she sounded like a bumbling idiot. What was wrong with her?

"You didn't have to do that for me. I really don't mind stepping over a few leaves," he teased.

The blush returned. It seemed to appear often since Dan Castleberry had skated into her life.

"Here. You take the flowers. I'll take the broom and sweep the porch for my supper. Fair trade?"

She relinquished the broom handle and accepted the bouquet. "Thanks— for the flowers. And, sure, sweep if you want." She added, "But it's really not necessary. Honest!"

Carlee and the children stood in the doorway and watched as he deftly swished the broom to-and-fro across the concrete porch. The flowers smelled sweet as she held them to her face and rubbed the velvety softness of their petals across her lips. No one had brought her flowers since Robert had died.

"There." He leaned the broom against the brick wall. "All finished! That better pass inspection, Mrs. Bennett; I'm hungry for those hot dogs."

She hadn't noticed, until now, how deep his dimples were. And she liked them. They fit him and his personality.

He followed her and the children into the house, then looked around, taking in everything in the living room. "It's just like I thought it would be. Cozy, cheerful, and warm."

Bobby tugged at his hand. "Come on, Dan. Mama doesn't let us play in this room."

Dan pointed an accusing finger at Carlee. "That so, Mama? You won't let us play in this room? Why not?"

" 'Cause we're messy," Becca volunteered as she pulled a naked Barbie doll out from under the edge of the chintz sofa.

Dan laughed as he lowered himself onto one knee and checked out Becca's unclothed Barbie. "Okay, now that you children have thoroughly embarrassed your mother, how about showing me your rooms?"

He swept Becca up in his arms and placed her on his broad shoulders as the little girl squealed with glee and hollered, "Whee!"

Dan turned to the young boy who was watching his sister with rapt attention. "Lead the way, Bobby."

Bobby looked to his mother for approval, then ran toward his room, followed by Dan with Becca wiggling on his shoulders and Carlee following close behind in a haze of emotions.

After the tour of all the rooms in the house, including the basement, which Carlee hadn't cleaned, their guest plopped himself down in the middle of the family room. He pulled Bobby down with him, playfully pinning the boy to the floor.

"Help me, Becca," Bobby called to his little sister as he struggled to get free.

A giddy Becca rushed toward the dueling duo and threw herself into their midst. Dan pulled her into the fracas as Becca's and Bobby's laughter filled the room and Carlee looked on, her heart bursting with emotion as she viewed the scene. It was difficult to hold back the tears of joy she was experiencing. But she knew she had no choice. None of them would have understood, and at this point, neither did she.

"Dan, wanna see my baseballs? They're in my closet," Bobby asked when he was too tired to wrestle anymore and needed a way to quit and still save face.

Dan looked pleased. "Sure. Can Becca come, too? Is she allowed in your territory?" he asked as he once again hoisted the little girl to his shoulders.

Bobby grinned impishly. "Okay. Just this one time."

Dan lifted his face toward Becca's. "You won't bother any of Bobby's stuff, will you?"

Becca answered by running her hands through Dan's perfectly moussed hair.

"Becca! Stop!" her mother cautioned.

But Dan and the two children didn't hear; they were headed for Bobby's room and the baseballs.

※

Bobby's room was as neat as a magazine photo. It was obvious his mother's cleaning hand had been there. Dan thought of his own room when he was Bobby's age. His mother had decided a child's room had no place on the second floor with the other perfectly kept bedrooms. She'd hired carpenters to close in the attic area and create a bedroom for her only son when he became old enough to "make a mess," as she called it. And once he'd moved into it, his mother had avoided his room. The cleaning woman knew more about its contents than she did.

"Dan, do you want to see my Bobby Richardson ball?"

Bobby's words brought Dan back to reality. He sat on the boy's bed with Becca still firmly planted on his shoulders as Bobby proudly held the marred baseball in his hands. He took it and examined it carefully. "It's signed!"

"Uh-huh. My dad bought it from a guy 'cause he knew I'd wanna keep it. He told me all about Bobby Richardson."

The skater gave Bobby his full attention as the boy pulled baseball after baseball from a box in his closet. Most of the balls had no monetary value, but they'd been signed by Bobby's T-ball coaches and friends who played ball with Bobby. He was as proud as if they'd been signed by Mickey Mantle himself. Dan handled each one as if it were special.

A wonderful aroma drifted through the house. Bobby placed his hand in Dan's and led him into the family room in time to see Carlee place a tray of steaming hot nachos in the center of the coffee table. "Thought these might tide you over till the fire gets going well enough to roast our hot dogs. And," she added as she offered a box of matches to their guest, "you are appointed chief fire builder, and Bobby will help you."

Dan lifted Becca from his shoulders and lowered her onto the sofa, then retrieved the badly abused Barbie from the floor and placed it in the little girl's lap. She hugged the doll tightly to her breast. He turned to Carlee with an amused glimmer. "Do all little girls like Barbie dolls?"

Before she could answer, Becca did. "Mama gots more Barbie dolls than me." Turning to her mother, she added, "Mama, show Dan *your* Barbie dolls."

Her mother turned crimson.

"Carlee, is that right?" Dan taunted as he sauntered slowly toward the wide-eyed mother. "Do you really have more Barbie dolls than Becca?"

"Show him, Mama," her daughter insisted as she swung Barbie in wide circles by her long, matted hair.

"Yes, Mama! Show me!" Dan mimicked in a high-pitched falsetto voice as he tilted his head toward the young woman.

Carlee lowered her head shyly, annoyed with Becca for revealing her secret. "Okay, maybe after supper. Right now, you three need to get that fire going."

"Promise? After supper you'll show me your dollies?" Dan kidded as the children giggled.

"After supper, I promise," she said, symbolically crossing her heart. "Now, get that fire going."

While they worked at building the fire, she made several trips to the kitchen, bringing in trays loaded with hot dogs, buns, mustard, relish, catsup, chopped onion, grated cheese, and other goodies. The final tray held a big pot of home-made baked beans. The wonderful scent of bacon-embellished beans in an open pot quickly drew Dan's attention from the full-blown fire he'd prepared for the hot dog cooking. Two exuberant children jumped into his lap. Their mother moved to push them off, saying, "Hey, kids. Leave Dan alone. Come on now! Get off his lap!" She tugged and pulled on Becca, who clung to Dan's neck and wouldn't let go.

Dan gently but firmly took hold of Carlee's wrists and pulled them away from the little girl who clung to him. "Carlee! It's okay. Really. I like it!" He pulled Becca onto his lap and circled his strong arms about her. She instantly stopped struggling and leaned her head against his chest, one small hand twisting at a lock of his hair.

He pulled her closer to him. "You know, Carlee, I never understood why my friends envied me for *not* having any brothers or sisters. My life was pretty lonely. I'd have given anything to have a brother or sister to fight with. I missed so much, and I always wondered why my parents never had any more children. Sometimes I thought it was because I was so bad." His slight laugh had a melancholy sound. "Maybe I was too much trouble for them." He rubbed his cheek across the top of Becca's head and sniffed the leftover fragrance of the baby's shampoo. "They don't know what they missed."

Carlee smiled and pulled Bobby onto her lap. The four of them sat quietly gazing into the warm glow of the fire. Dan gently slid his free arm around Carlee's shoulder and found himself envying a dead man.

She stiffened at the touch of his arm, but only for a moment. No man had been that close in five years. How she missed the strength, the security, and the love of a man's protective arm. She relaxed and found herself magnetically drawn to his nearness.

The fire snapped, sparks sizzled, and the room filled with a cozy warmth, but its origin was not the blazing logs; it was generated by the foursome on the sofa. It penetrated their minds, hearts, and bodies as they enjoyed one another's company. Carlee found herself enjoying the closeness a little too much, and it frightened her. She wanted to press herself into Dan's arm, to rest her head on his shoulder, to feel his breath on her hair.

But there was no place in her life for a three-week fling. And she knew there was no place in Dan's life for a woman with a ready-made family, not that he'd be interested in her. What did she have to offer that he couldn't find in any city, any state? No, she was a nothing in his world. How could she even think there might ever be anything between them?

"Dan!"

"Umm—what?" He'd been caught daydreaming.

"I asked if you'd mind if Bobby prayed before our meal?"

He pulled his arm from behind her and straightened himself on the sofa. "No, go ahead." He lowered his head and closed his eyes. A small boy slipped his hand into Dan's as a tiny hand pushed its way into his other hand. He sneaked a peek and found the children and their mother's heads bowed low as Bobby began to pray.

"Dear Lord, we thank You for this food our mama made. We thank You for Dan being here to eat with us. In Jesus' name. Amen."

When Bobby finished praying, Carlee pulled three hot dog holders from a long box and handed one to Bobby, one to Dan, and kept one for herself.

"Where's mine?" Becca asked, her lower lip curling downward.

Dan jumped in. "Oh, Becca. I wanted to cook yours with mine. Please? Won't you let me?"

Becca's disappointment disappeared, and she lifted two arms and encircled them about Dan's neck. "I want my hot dog cooked with yours," she told him with a winning smile that would melt a snowman.

"Mama, I'll cook yours with mine," Bobby volunteered with authority as he poked two hot dogs onto the long spike.

"Good idea," Dan agreed as he slid his free arm around Bobby's shoulder and gave him a wink. "We men will cook the hot dogs; you ladies prepare the buns. Right, Bobby?"

"Right," Bobby replied in a voice much lower than his usual one. She was surprised to see the young boy mimicking their guest. Her baby boy was growing up.

The hot dogs vanished quickly as the foursome laughed their way through supper. Carlee was amazed at the amount of food her children consumed and concluded it must be due to the joyful atmosphere created by Dan's presence.

"Anyone for dessert?" she asked after the hot dog mess had been banished to the kitchen. "Fresh apple pie loaded with cinnamon and topped with scoops of French vanilla ice cream?"

Dan, Becca, and Bobby all shouted, "Yes!" at once.

When it was served, Dan took one bite and frowned.

"What's wrong? Isn't the pie okay?" He'd been so complimentary about her cooking so far; what could be wrong?

He took another bite and closed his eyes. "Umm."

"What?" She couldn't imagine what was wrong; the pie tasted fine to her.

His eyes opened slowly, as if he were in deep thought. "I was trying to remember if I'd ever eaten any pie that was better than this pie. And you know what? I haven't!"

A pink flush rose across her face as Carlee smiled.

"This is fantastic," he added as he took another bite. "Did you really bake this, Carlee? From scratch? You're sure it's not from Perkins?"

She was both speechless and flattered by his compliment.

"Mama made the pie. I saw her," Becca said with her mouth full of ice cream.

"Becca," her mother corrected as she applied a napkin to her daughter's delicate face. "How many times have I told you not to talk with your mouth full?"

The little girl swallowed hard and pointed a finger at Dan. "He talked with his mouth full, too. I saw him."

Now it was Dan's turn to blush. "Caught me!"

After supper, Carlee settled the children in front of the TV to watch a new Odyssey videotape that had come in the afternoon mail. Dan watched as she moved about the room tidying up and rearranging pillows. When he caught her attention, he motioned for her to join him on the couch by patting the cushion next to him. The four of them watched and laughed together as the cartoon characters, Dylan and his friends, performed their antics.

"Bedtime!" Carlee announced when the tape ended.

"Aw, Mama, do we have to?" She'd expected rebellion; they'd been having such a good time with Dan.

"Tell you what," Dan proposed as he pulled them both onto his lap. "If it's okay with your mom, after you get ready for bed, I'll tell you a story."

Two children hurried off to don their pajamas as their bewildered mother looked on.

"Hope that's okay with you," Dan apologized.

A grateful smile curled across her lips. "I wouldn't have it any other way."

Two pajama-clad children leaped into Dan's lap and struggled to see who could hug him the tightest, as Dan buried his face in first one neck and then the other, giggling and laughing along with them.

"Which book do you want?" Carlee asked as she scanned the shelves that contained the vast assortment of children's books reserved for bedtime reading. "We have quite a selection."

His gray eyes twinkled. "Don't need one, thank you."

His answer surprised her. He'd promised them a bedtime story. Was he going to renege and disappoint them after such a lovely evening?

"Okay, you guys. Settle down. Time for our story." His voice was gentle yet firm as he opened his arms to them.

Two wiry children stopped their wiggling and seated themselves, Bobby on one thigh, Becca on the other. His long arms encircled them, holding them securely. "You have to promise that as soon as the story is finished, you'll go to bed without a word. Okay?"

Two heads nodded in agreement.

"Now, what shall it be? *Little Red Riding Hood*?"

"Yes!" Becca clapped her little hands as she wiggled on Dan's lap. "I love *Little Red Riding Hood*. Will you tell us about the wolf, Dan?"

Dan looked at Bobby. "*Little Red Riding Hood* okay, fella?"

Bobby grinned. "Yeah. Becca likes it. It's okay."

Dan kissed each child atop the head and began his story. "There once was a beautiful little girl with dark, flowing hair. . ."

The children sat motionless as Dan told the story of the little girl, her grandmother, and the wolf. He included parts of the story Carlee had never heard before, and she found herself as enthralled as the children. When the story ended, Dan again kissed each child on the top of the head, then lifted them both in his arms and carried them to their rooms. Carlee followed silently, not wanting to break the spell.

Becca was the first to be placed in bed. As Dan gently laid her on the Barbie sheets and covered her with the bright pink comforter, she pulled his face down to hers and gave him a forceful kiss on his lips and hugged him tightly. He hugged her back and whispered, "Good night, Becca."

"We didn't pray," the little girl protested.

Dan looked uneasy.

"If you'll put Bobby to bed, I'll pray with Becca," Carlee volunteered quickly, coming to his rescue.

"You got it," he replied as he hurried off with Bobby in his arms, apparently grateful for the reprieve.

Becca drifted off to sleep, exhausted and happy, almost as soon as she said "Amen." Carlee moved to the family room and settled herself in the corner of the couch, her knees drawn up beneath her chin. When Dan joined her, he was smiling.

"What?" His smile intrigued her.

"What what?" he said as he sat down close beside her, crowding her into the corner a bit.

"You were smiling; I wondered why. That's all."

He locked his hands behind his head and rested them against the sofa's soft back. "Didn't realize I was smiling. Guess it was just a smile of contentment. I never had an evening like this when I was growing up. Your kids are lucky."

They sat gazing into the fire as the flames furled and twirled and popped and crackled, spitting sparks wildly against the screen.

"It's hedge," Carlee said matter-of-factly.

"Hedge?" he repeated.

"Hedge pops and crackles like that, then spits sparks everywhere, but I like it." She gazed into the fire, enjoying the erratic behavior of the burning hedge wood. Eventually she lifted her eyes to meet his quizzically. "I have a question. How did you know the story of *Little Red Riding Hood*? Tonight I heard parts of that story I've never heard before. I was impressed. So were the children."

He winced. "It was okay? They weren't disappointed?"

She touched the tip of his nose with her fingertip. "You told it so well I've decided I'll never tell it again. I could never do it the way you did."

He let out a sigh. "Okay, I'll let you in on my secret. I've never read *Little Red Riding Hood* and my mother never read storybooks to me when I was a kid."

"But—how? How did you tell it like that?"

He angled his head toward hers and confessed, "I skated the part of the wolf!"

Apparently he realized she was laughing at his method of storytelling, not at him, and joined in her laughter.

Dan skating as the wolf conjured up hysterical images. He slid his arm across the sofa back and squeezed her shoulder. "I've had a great evening, but we both have to get up early. I'd better be going."

She rose to her feet to walk him to the door. Although she found herself wanting to ask him to stay longer, she resisted the temptation and thanked him for the flowers, now nestled in a crystal vase in the center of the coffee table. As the door closed behind him, she leaned against it and sighed deeply. What a wonderful day this had been!

Chapter 6

Dan Castleberry climbed in behind the steering wheel and turned the key in the ignition. The engine roared in response. He shoved the gearshift into reverse but kept his foot on the brake. He wanted one last look at the house—no, at the *home*—rising before him. The laughter had been contagious, and he found himself smiling smugly, as if he had been privy to an episode of love that only a few people could identify with. After this evening, he was anxious to dine at Jim Bennett's home on Sunday and meet Ethel Bennett. Yes, the Bennett family was a unique group of people. To think that there could be that kind of love between a young widow and her in-laws astounded him. So did such love between a mother and her children.

He'd never met another woman like Carlee. There was something so sweet about her—so pure. Just being with her gave him a feeling he'd never known before. How lucky Robert Bennett had been, to have a warm, caring woman like Carlee, who loved him so completely. He hoped someday he could experience that kind of love in his own life.

Carlee hummed as she drove toward the Ice Palace Friday morning. She hated to admit it, even to herself, but she was anxious to see Dan again. They may not see eye to eye on marriage and commitment, but he had become a good friend to her and the children. Marriage was the furthermost thing on her mind, too. She'd never find another man like Robert, but she felt safe with Dan. They understood one another's position; there was no room for a permanent relationship in his life, and she certainly wasn't interested in one either. Even if their relationship were more than a mere friendship, it could never develop into anything more than a mild flirtation, and that would end when he left Kansas City.

Her heart skipped a beat despite her thoughts, for there he was, leaning against the building as her headlights scanned the parking lot after she turned off the street. By the time she reached him, he was balancing the big tray of buns on one hand above his head and waiting for her to open the door.

"Oh, so now you're the bread man, huh?" she cajoled as she turned the key and shoved open the door.

"Yes, ma'am," he responded. He headed for the snack bar as she switched on the string of harsh overhead lights.

"I had a great time last night," he whispered into her hair as he passed her on his way back out the door.

"Hey, where are you going?" she called after him.

"To get the VCR! You promised to help me. You haven't changed your mind, I hope."

He inserted the videotape as he lowered the VCR onto the counter and plugged in the machine. "I thought we could run through it once—in here, while we drink our coffee—before I start my practice. That way we can discuss the various moves. Okay with you?"

She nodded her head. "Sure, crank her up. The coffee'll be ready in a minute." She pulled two clean mugs from the shelf while he commandeered two folding chairs. When the coffee was finished, she poured two steaming mugfuls, handed one to Dan, and seated herself beside him as he punched PLAY. The familiar theme music sounded from the VCR, and she sat spellbound as she watched Dan skate the entire routine on tape. Even without the costuming and special lighting, it was beautiful. He was extremely talented.

When the routine ended, the music changed and his image appeared on the ice with Valerie Burns by his side. "This is one of the pair numbers we'll be doing in the show. Kinda hard to practice those without a partner," he complained as he fast-forwarded to another of his solo numbers. "You haven't seen this one. I haven't even started practicing it yet."

She didn't understand. If he hadn't started practicing, how had he made the tape?

As if reading her thoughts, he explained, "We made it one small section at a time. The choreographer would show me the move, I'd skate it through a few times, we'd tape it, then stop the tape. By the time we finished and had recorded all the moves, we had the entire routine on tape. That's why it's so jerky—all the stops and starts. But at least it gives me the moves in their proper sequence so I can practice and begin to memorize them in the right order. This is only a start, but it saves time."

She listened intently; it all made sense but sounded difficult. But if this worked, who was she to question it?

They watched until the recorded part ended and the screen filled with snow. While she tidied up the snack bar, he carried the VCR into the ice area and set it up so she could watch from the front row and coach him as he skated.

It worked much better than she'd anticipated. If he'd falter or stop skating, she'd cup her hands to her mouth and shout out the move. When he stopped for his second cup of coffee, he complimented her on her help. "You knew the names of all the moves and called them out like a pro!"

She laughed. "Hey, my father-in-law *is* a pro, remember? I absorbed most of what I know by osmosis."

❧

Dan hung around the rink after he finished his session and watched her work before heading home. These days, there was no place he'd rather be than at the rink with Carlee.

When his mother came in from her round of golf, he asked her a strange question. "Where can I buy a doll?"

She lifted manicured fingers to his forehead. "Do you have a temperature, Daniel? I do think you are delirious."

He assured her he was not, but merely wanted to purchase several dolls as gifts for people who had befriended him.

"I think I would try the toy store in the Plaza." She shook her head sadly as he left the house and headed for the Plaza, as though she wondered whatever possessed her son to behave in such weird ways.

Friday afternoons in the Plaza were busy. His rented car circled the block twice, then pulled into the parking lot across the street from the toy store. He wandered past shelves lined with tin soldiers and ready-to-assemble models of cars, planes, and boats.

"May I help you find something?" a young man asked politely.

Dan lifted his brows and mustered his courage. "I'm looking for the Barbie dolls," he murmured so softly the clerk had to ask him to repeat himself.

He melted with embarrassment when the clerk pointed to the area beyond the checkout counter and loudly announced, "Sir, the Barbie dolls are right over there." Probably no one cared, but he felt as though every eye in the place was focused on him, the weird man who was shopping for Barbie dolls. He slunk past the clerks busily ringing up sales and rounded the corner. Sure enough, there were the Barbies, dozens of them. No, *hundreds* of them, with cars, boats, beauty shops, grocery stores, RVs, clothes, purses, lunch boxes, and items too numerous for him to investigate. He scanned the shelves from top to bottom, trying to decide what to buy for Becca.

"How about a Christmas Barbie for your daughter?" a nice lady wearing a name tag asked. "We just received a new shipment; every little girl wants those."

He started to explain that he didn't have a daughter, but deciding it really was none of the woman's business, he just let her think what she wanted. Actually, he was enjoying this. He'd played parts before—why not that of a father? He cleared his throat casually. "A Christmas doll? I think my daughter would like that." Inside he was shaking as badly as if he were stealing the doll instead of merely faking a daddy disguise. This daddy stuff was harder than he'd expected.

He wanted to buy a Barbie for Carlee, too. But which one? It had to be special, very special. "And I'd like another doll, more special than the Christmas doll. A real fancy one adults would buy for themselves."

The clerk smiled and pointed to a circular, lighted case. "Any one of those dolls would do nicely," the smiling clerk said proudly. "Is your wife a collector?"

"Wife? No. . .er. . .yes, she is." He'd succeeded in his charade as a father—why not be a husband? "Yes, she has a rather extensive collection," he said with all the calmness he could gather, hoping his face didn't give away his deception.

"Oh, does she have the latest Bob Mackie?"

Dan rolled his eyes. "No, only Barbies. She doesn't collect male dolls."

"Sir," she said rather indignantly, "Bob Mackie designs gowns for the Bob Mackie designer line of Barbie dolls. They are very much in demand by the most discriminating buyers."

He lifted his chin and faked with authority, "I knew that. Just a little joke, you know."

With a bemused smile, she asked, "Then, sir, do you think your wife would like the *new* Bob Mackie Barbie doll? Or has she already added this exquisite doll to her collection?"

"I don't remember for sure," he said thoughtfully. "If I purchase it and she already has it, can she exchange it?"

The woman's mocking expression never changed. "Of course, sir. Just be sure to keep the receipt."

"Then I'll take both dolls. Gift wrapped, please."

"Wouldn't you like to see the doll first, sir? Most of our customers want to see such an expensive doll before deciding to purchase it. We want you to be happy."

Expensive? How expensive could a little doll in a fancy dress be? "Yes, of course—I'd like to see it."

She carefully lifted an exquisitely dressed doll from the top shelf of the glass case and held it out for him to see. It was lovely. Even Dan could appreciate its beauty.

"This is one of Mr. Mackie's most unusual designs. And although it is the most expensive one yet, it's well worth the price of three hundred dollars. It's—"

Dan nearly strangled on her words. "Uh—did you say three hundred dollars?" He stared at the doll.

She reared back with a surprised look on her face. "Yes, I did. Surely you were aware of the cost of a Bob Mackie design since your wife is a collector!"

He faked a laugh. "I'm kidding again. Of course I'm aware of the price of a Bill Marker doll. I'll take it."

"Bob Mackie, sir. Bob Mackie."

Now his dander was up, and with a stern face he answered, "I knew that. Bob Mackie. Isn't that what I said?"

"Whatever," the woman said flippantly. "If you'll follow me, we'll ring up your items, and you may wait in one of those chairs over there while your purchases are being wrapped."

Dan registered a look of disgust. "I didn't say I was through."

She stopped in her tracks. "You want another doll?"

"No. A baseball. You do have baseballs, don't you?"

"Collector or to play with?" she asked coolly.

"Collector," he snapped.

"This way, sir."

Picking out the baseball wasn't nearly as hard as the Barbie dolls. He selected one with the name of a familiar player autographed on it. It was only thirty-five dollars and came in a hard plastic, see-through case—the perfect ball.

"I'll take it, and I'd like a second ball, a nice one that a boy can play with and not have to worry about losing it or getting it dirty."

When the clerk announced the total, Dan decided that being a husband and father could be a pretty expensive role.

"Thank you, sir. Your family is going to be very happy with the gifts you've purchased."

Dan smiled at the clerk, then exited the store with his selections tucked safely under an arm, his smile the width of his face. Shopping at the toy store had been an education, but he had to admit he'd loved every minute of it, especially the part he'd played as husband and father.

He saluted as he passed the huge stone teddy bear out front. "See you again someday, fella. If I ever have a wife and kids of my own, I'll keep your store in mind. Meantime, keep my secret, okay?"

He thought he saw the bear wink!

Chapter 7

The driver slowly pulled the rental car into the parking lot and dowsed its lights. The man behind the wheel stretched and checked his watch: 5:00 a.m. He twisted the dial until he found a country western station, leaned back against the headrest, closed his eyes, and began tapping his fingertips on the steering wheel to the beat of the music. A smile crossed his freshly shaven face as he thought of his shopping spree the day before, and he chuckled. What would Carlee think if she knew about his game of deception at the store? Dan Castleberry with a wife and kids? Now, *that* was a thought. He wondered if he'd really fooled the clerks. Probably. They didn't care who he was buying gifts for as long as his VISA card was good. When should he give them the presents? Maybe as a going-away gift. *His* going away.

Headlights passed quickly across his windshield as the minivan whipped into the lot and stopped next to his car. Carlee Bennett stepped out, her coat wrapped tightly about her to ward off the chill of the early morning winds. He wished she didn't have to work this early morning session, then realized she was there because of him. Otherwise, she'd be coming in an hour later.

She rapped on his window with her gloved hand. "Hey in there! Trying to use up all your gas sitting in my lot?"

Quickly he flipped the key in the ignition and stepped out into the cold. "Naw, just waiting to see if you have any goodies for our coffee before I make up my mind to come in."

She grinned and held up a white plastic bag.

He wrapped his arm around her shoulder and fell in step as they moved toward the door to escape the cold wind. While Dan carried the VCR into the ice arena to set it up for viewing, Carlee made coffee and retrieved his skates from her office. By now, their early morning routine was well established.

She loved having him there in the mornings. For five years, she had entered that blackened barn of a building by herself, and although she'd never told anyone, she'd been terrified. But thankfully, for the next few weeks she'd have Dan Castleberry waiting for her when she arrived.

"Five dollars for your thoughts."

Her daydream bubble burst at the sound of his voice.

"Did you say five dollars? I thought the price was a penny."

"Inflation."

"Corn-ee!" she shouted after him as he moved away.

Once seated in front of the VCR, she listened as his skates clicked across the ice in time to the music. And she watched to make sure his every move was in sync with the videotape.

At the end of the first routine, the skater showered her with the customary ice shavings, then hit the OFF button on the VCR. He towered over her as she sat on the cold metal chair sipping her coffee. "Well, where is it?" he demanded playfully as he shaped his muscular body into the form of the Beast. "Give it to me—now!"

She pretended to be frightened as she lifted her arms to shield herself. "And what will you do if I don't?" she asked in a high-pitched voice.

His body hovered over her as he answered slowly in a low, mellow voice, "I will strangle all your Barbie dolls!"

"Oh no," she said meekly in her normal voice. "I promised, didn't I?"

"Yep," he answered as he dropped into the chair beside her. "You promised, right in front of your children, that you'd show me your Barbie dolls after supper."

She pulled the bag from its hiding place under her chair. "Could I buy a little redemption with a surprise cupcake?"

"Surprise cupcakes, eh?" he questioned as he thrust his hand into the bag. "What's the surprise part?" He twirled the little cake in his hand, pulled the paper off, and took a teensy bite. "Good, but no surprise."

A crooked smile graced her lips.

He took another bite, bigger this time. "Hmm, marshmallow."

She loved these morning snack times. The two had so much fun. And no matter what she served him, he loved it.

"More," he commanded once again in his Beast voice and stance after he'd devoured the first cake. "Me want more!"

She rolled her eyes and handed him the entire bag.

He flashed those dimples and plowed into a second cake. She loved his sense of humor, his easygoing manner.

"If you don't ease up on those cupcakes, you won't be able to skate," she warned as he popped a third one into his mouth and followed it with a swish of coffee.

"Okay, okay. I get the message. Back to work, right?"

"Right!"

At 6:15, the patchers and their mothers arrived, right on time. Dan hung around and helped Carlee sweep and clean the snack bar and get it ready for the day. Mrs. Sweeney, who operated the snack bar, was visiting her daughter. Her sister was coming in to replace her but couldn't make it until 9:30. Carlee had told her not to worry—she'd make sure the snack bar was ready for the day.

"You're pretty adept at sweeping," she commented, remembering the sweeping job he'd accepted on her front porch.

"Learned it in the navy, swabbing decks."

She stopped her work. "You were in the navy?"

"Not exactly," he quipped with that ornery grin that brought out his dimples. "Skated the part of a sailor in a show."

She tossed a damp sponge toward him, and he caught it in midair. "Then swab, swabbie," she commanded.

It was amazing how much faster the work went when the load was shared. In no time the snack bar was shipshape. The "sailor" had done a good job.

Carlee poured two fresh cupfuls of steaming coffee and carried them to one of the round tables that circled the snack bar. "Dan, I don't get it. Here you are the lead skater in one of the best-known ice shows in the country, maybe the world, yet you come into my home and eat hot dogs. You play with my children. Now you clean our snack bar. Why?"

Dan smoothed his paper napkin and placed his cup squarely in the center, then raised his eyes to meet hers. "Carlee, to be real honest, I don't know why. I only know that I've enjoyed myself this week, and being here in Kansas City, more than I'd ever dreamed possible."

"You mean because of your folks? And the practicing?"

He leaned back in the chair and balanced it precariously on its hind legs. "No, I've hardly seen my folks. Their lives are much too busy to include me. And the practicing? I could have done that in Florida, like the rest of the cast."

Dan reached across the table and cradled both her hands in his. "It's you, Carlee. It's your family. It's this place. It's magical. I can't explain it to you. I only know that this has been one of the happiest weeks of my life, yet I haven't done a thing that's outstanding. Maybe you can explain it to me." He squeezed her hand appreciatively.

She pulled back, unsure how to interpret what he'd said.

Two patchers sidled up to the counter and tapped the little brass bell for service. Carlee left Dan sitting alone and went to wait on the girls. When she turned, he was gone.

It was pleasant to see the sun shining brightly as she locked the door behind her at the end of the morning session and strolled briskly to her minivan. A flutter on her windshield caught her attention; a note was anchored beneath the wipers. She flipped the blade aside and read:

> *I'd like to take you and the kids to dinner and a movie tonight. See you at 5:00. Call me if you can't make it.*
>
> *Dan*

Of course she could make it! She folded the note and slipped it into her pocket. And she knew the children would be thrilled when she told them about Dan's invitation.

Dan Castleberry found a note, too, from his mother. It was taped to his bedroom door when he arrived home. He was to call Brad in Florida as soon as possible.

Brad, his closest friend, was also a featured skater in the show. Dan phoned immediately. Brad and his fiancée had decided to get married the next Tuesday, in Florida, and he wanted Dan to be his best man. Dan assured him he'd be there. He'd never let his old friend down.

He phoned the airline and made his reservation.

The house was quiet when Carlee stepped into her kitchen at noon. Bobby tiptoed in to meet her. "Mama, Becca doesn't feel good. Grandma said she's gotta fever. She's hot!"

Carlee rushed into the family room and found her daughter nestled in Mother Bennett's arms in the rocking chair. She took the flushed child from Ethel and held her close. "Baby, baby. What's the matter with Mama's baby?"

Their grandmother stood by silently as her daughter-in-law cradled the child and strode about the room, planting kisses on the four-year-old's hot little cheeks. "I took her temperature; it was not quite a hundred. Do you think she's cutting more teeth?" Ethel asked gently.

Carlee smiled and nodded her head as she lowered herself into the softly padded chair and began to rock; it was the same chair her beloved Robert had been rocked in when he was a child.

Ethel backed away quietly with a slight wave. "Call me if you need anything. I'm going home to fix lunch for Jim."

The young mother rocked her daughter for the next few hours as Bobby exchanged cool, damp washcloths to cool Becca's brow. He was such a helper, wringing out the cloths with his strong little hands, then placing them on his sister's petite forehead. Carlee wanted to hug her son, too, but he was too busy being her little man.

At four o'clock, Becca's fever broke, and her tiny body cooled off. Her eyes were still droopy, but Carlee knew the worst was over. More than likely, it had been the teeth.

"Now can we go to McDonald's for supper?" Bobby asked as he gathered up the wet cloths. "Becca's feeling better."

"Supper!" his mother shouted as she put her hand to her forehead. "Oh no! I completely forgot—Dan wanted to take us out for supper and a movie."

"Yeah! Let's go!" Bobby cheered joyfully.

Carlee clamped her hand over her son's wrist. "Sorry, Bobby, we can't go; it's too soon for Becca."

Bobby's laugh turned to a frown. "Oh, Mama. Please?"

"We can't go, honey. Maybe Dan'll take us another time. Be a good boy and bring Mama the phone."

When Dan answered on the second ring, she explained about Becca's fever and asked for a rain check.

"No rain check!" he declared firmly. "But let me bring supper and a movie to you and the kids. Okay?"

"Really, Dan? You don't have to do this, you know." She should have known he would respond in such a thoughtful way; it was so like the man she'd come to know and care for.

"Do the kids like the Colonel's chicken?"

"It's one of their favorites."

"Then, chicken it is. I'll be there around five. Can I pick up a prescription or anything?"

Carlee smiled. "No. Just the chicken. Thanks anyway."

Bobby leaped through the house, swinging his arms wildly. "Dan's coming, Becca! Dan's coming!"

Becca raised her flushed face from her mother's shoulder with interest. "Is he, Mama? Will Dan hold me?"

Carlee lifted the damp little ringlets that encircled Becca's pink face and pushed them from her forehead. "Yes, baby. I'm sure Dan will hold you. Just get well, okay?"

The baby lowered her head onto her mother's breast.

When the doorbell chimed, Bobby ran to open the door. There stood Dan with a winsome smile on his face. He held two large sacks with colorful caricatures of the Colonel on their sides. Becca lifted her head when Dan came into the room and gave him a weak little wave and whispered, "Hi, Dan."

"How's my girl?" he asked as he placed his big hand on her clammy forehead. "Dan doesn't like Becca to be sick."

"Fine," came a tiny voice. She looked up and blinked slowly. "Hold me, Dan."

"Sure, honey. Dan'll hold you." He bent and kissed a rosy little cheek. "But don't you think we should eat first? Dan brought you some nice fried chicken. Your big brother is going to help me put the food on the coffee table—if it's okay with your mom." He shot a questioning glance at Carlee, who nodded her permission. "Then as soon as supper is over, Dan'll hold you for as long as you want." He stroked the little girl's hair lovingly.

"Yeah," Bobby agreed as he began taking the boxes and plastic utensils out of the bags and placing them on the table. "Dan and me are gonna fix supper for you girls."

The two *men* put cartons of coleslaw, baked beans, and mashed potatoes on the table next to the boxes of chicken, along with paper plates, napkins, and the utensils.

"Dan! You bought so much!" Carlee exclaimed when she saw the feast placed before them. "There's no way the four of us can eat all of this! You'll have to come back and help us eat the leftovers."

He smiled shyly. "I thought you'd never ask!"

The four enjoyed the impromptu fried chicken dinner. Even Becca nibbled on a chicken leg, but it was the mashed potatoes she enjoyed most. They barely made a dent in all the food. Dan suggested they make up a box for Bobby to take over to the Bennetts; the remainder was stuffed into the refrigerator for another day.

"That was thoughtful of you, Dan, sending that box over to my in-laws. Thank you for thinking of it."

"No problem. Just making brownie points."

Before she could question his comment, he changed the subject. "I thought about getting a videotape of *Robin Hood* for Bobby, but I knew Becca wouldn't like that. Then I thought about getting a tape of *The Little Mermaid* for Becca, but I knew Bobby wouldn't like that. So. . ." Dan moved to the coat closet, reached into his overcoat, and pulled a videotape from each pocket. "I got 'em both!"

Bobby cheered loudly. Little Becca's eyes brightened. Dan handed the videotapes to Bobby, then lifted Becca carefully from her mother's arms and carried her to the comfy old sofa, gently lowering himself into its corner.

Bobby loaded Becca's tape first, and the four of them watched *The Little Mermaid* while the little girl lay motionless in Dan's lap. Occasionally, she'd lift her face toward his and slip a warm little hand around his neck. He'd kiss one baby cheek and then the other, then each eyelid. She'd smile and go back to watching her video. By the end of the movie, she was sound asleep and her temperature was normal.

"Let me put her to bed," Carlee offered as she moved to take her baby from Dan's strong arms.

He shook his head. "No, let me do it." He carried Becca to her room and placed her carefully between the Barbie sheets, then tucked the pink comforter up under her chin before leaning to kiss her face.

"You should have a family of your own, Dan. You're great with kids."

"Just *your* kids," he said wistfully as he slipped an arm around her waist and walked her into the family room where Bobby was watching *Robin Hood*. They sat on the sofa, side by side, until the tape ended. Dan tucked Bobby into bed for the night and knelt on one knee beside the boy while the child prayed. When he came back into the family room, he walked directly to Carlee, took her by the hand, lifted her to her feet, and ordered, "Now, show me your Barbie dolls!"

She tilted her head to one side in question. "You're sure you want to see them? They're not exactly a guy thing."

"Positive. Lead on," he told her with a mocking grin.

She led him through her bedroom to a large walk-in closet and switched on the light. He thought he was back at the toy store! Shelves lined the walls along one side, and on them were more than a hundred Barbie dolls, all in unopened boxes. He quickly scanned the shelves looking for the Bob Mackie doll and was relieved when he didn't find it there.

"They're not opened?" he questioned with surprise.

She winced. "Bite your tongue! Of course not! It depreciates their value if they're opened. I only purchase dolls in perfect boxes. You know, mint condition."

He let out a long, low whistle as he moved along the shelves. "Where did you get all these?"

"Some I get when I travel, which isn't often. Most of them Father Bennett has brought home to me when he's attended skating championships. Others have been birthday and Christmas presents. They're all special to me." She lovingly brushed her fingertips across the top of the box with an oval front that rested at the end of the top row, and pulled it from the shelf. "She's the one who started it all—the 1988 Holiday Barbie. Robert bought it for me for Christmas that year as a joke, but I loved it. The next year I bought the 1989 Holiday Barbie as soon as it was released, and I've been collecting Barbies ever since. See? All my Holidays are lined up together on the top shelf. When Christmas comes, I'll display them in the family room, right along with the other decorations. Don't you dare laugh, Dan Castleberry!"

Dan symbolically crossed his heart with the index finger of his right hand. "I won't I promise! Are the Christmas dolls the fanciest ones they make?" he asked, hiding his new found education on collector Barbie dolls.

"Oh, my, no!" Carlee pulled a lovely bride doll from a lower shelf. "See this one? It's a bride doll, and its dress is by a designer named Bob Mackie. His are some of the most expensive dolls in the Barbie line. I have only this one, but there are a number of others by now. I had to have at least one Bob Mackie, and I won't even begin to tell you how much I paid for her. You'd never believe it!"

"Wow," he uttered as he looked at the beautiful doll clad in white, feeling a bit smug about his recent doll purchases. Soon, the newest Bob Mackie would be joining the beautiful bride doll. He could hardly wait to see Carlee's face when he gave it to her, confident he'd made the right selection. Somehow, the cost had become instantly insignificant.

Carlee pulled several other dolls from the shelves and explained about them to Dan. He listened intently as they moved from doll to doll. He loved the excitement in Carlee's voice as she talked about her collection.

She shoved the last doll back onto the shelf and grabbed both his hands in hers. "Don't say I didn't keep my promise. And, yes! I do have more Barbies than Becca. Satisfied?"

Dan gave her hands a quick squeeze. "Satisfied! I guess it's time I let you get to bed. You've had a long, hard day. Tell you what, I'm going to skip my practice session tomorrow morning. It's Sunday, and you deserve a break. That way you won't have to leave Becca."

She tucked her hand into Dan's and walked him to the door. "Thanks, Dan, you're a good friend. It meant a lot to the children to have you come over tonight. They would have loved to see you—with or without supper." She tightened her grip on his arm before opening the front door. "Good night. See you at Mother and Father Bennett's for lunch."

He stood in the doorway and looked into her round blue eyes. "You're quite a lady, Carlee Bennett." He bent and kissed her on the top of her head and lightly nuzzled her hair with his chin; it smelled like gardenias. He had an overwhelming urge to kiss her. She was so close; it would be so easy to take her into his arms. His lips nuzzled her hair again as she stood motionless; he was sure he could hear her heart beating. With one finger beneath her chin, he lifted her face to his and gazed into those beautiful clear blue eyes. Why didn't she say something? Anything? Slowly, he lowered his lips to her forehead, as gently as if he were kissing Becca's warm cheeks.

She just stood there.

He wrapped his arms about her and drew her to him. He half expected her to push him away, slap him, maybe tell him to leave. But, instead, she seemed to melt into his arms and welcome his embrace.

"Dan. . ."

He touched a finger to her lips. "Shh. Don't say it."

She leaned into his strong chest. Her arms lifted to encircle his neck as they stood there looking into one another's eyes.

"I need a drink of water," little Becca called out in her loud baby voice as she stood in the doorway in her jammies, the unclothed doll in her hand.

Carlee pushed away from Dan with a look of embarrassment. "Sorry. Becca needs me."

Dan smiled. "So do I, Carlee."

With Becca's untimely entrance, he'd forgotten to tell Carlee about Brad's wedding.

Chapter 8

Dan woke at six o'clock. Besides having trouble getting Carlee off his mind, he was worried about Becca. The little girl had looked so pale when he'd carried her to bed last night. He wanted to call to see how she was feeling, but it was too early. He hoped the children all felt fine and Carlee was sleeping in a little later than usual.

It was 7:00 a.m. in Florida where his friend lived, so he decided to call him instead. A sleepy voice answered. Dan tried to explain who was calling, and that he had made reservations to fly into Florida on Monday and would be there in plenty of time for the wedding on Tuesday, but he wondered if the message ever soaked into his friend's sleepy brain.

After fixing himself a cup of instant coffee, he wandered through the living and dining rooms of his parents' house and closely examined the abstract paintings that graced the walls. Each had been purchased as an investment, yet his parents hated them. Their only merit was the signature in the corner that provided their monetary value. Suddenly he hated them, too.

The ugly collection of abstract paintings cried out, *Look at me. I'm valuable! I'm expensive!* But Carlee's collection of dolls said, *Come share Carlee's love for me. Let me take you into fantasyland. I'm here for you to enjoy, to hold, and to appreciate.* At any price they were worth the cost. He chuckled to himself and said aloud, "Even the three-hundred-dollar one with the Bob Mackie design!" How he wished his mother would enter Carlee's closet and become like a child again, learning anew how to enjoy the simple things of life.

He waited till 9:00, then dialed Carlee's number. "Bobby, how's Becca?" he asked with sincere concern.

"She's fine. Mama's dressing her for Sunday school."

Dan felt a surge of relief. "Can I speak to your mother, please?" He heard a clunk as Bobby placed the phone on the table and went in search of his mother.

"Good morning, Dan. Would you believe Becca is feeling like her old self and chattering a mile a minute this morning?"

"Well, I won't keep you—don't want to make you late for Sunday school. I just wanted to know how Becca is; I was worried about her. See you at two at the Bennetts'."

As if on impulse she asked, "Come with us, Dan! To church, I mean. It doesn't start till 10:45. You have plenty of time!"

He hesitated, then reluctantly answered, "Naw. I haven't been to church since I was a teenager. I don't know the routine. I might embarrass you."

She laughed. "Haven't I been coaching your skating? I can coach you through the church service so you don't make any mistakes. Please. The children would be thrilled if I could tell them you'll be there." She paused. "I'd like it, too."

He teetered on the brink of saying yes.

"I'll send the kids on to Sunday school with their grandparents and wait for you here so we can go together."

He was convinced. "Okay, pick you up at 10:20. But don't expect me to make a habit of this."

❧

Dan Castleberry adjusted the rearview mirror. He was slightly nervous at the thought of attending church but looking forward to spending more time with the Bennett family. In the car's trunk, he'd placed the three gift-wrapped packages.

Carlee waved through the picture window when he drove into her driveway, then rushed to the door to meet him.

He took her hands in his and stood back and admired her from head to toe. "Wow, do you look terrific! You don't look like the mother of two feisty kids!"

Her cheeks flushed. She seemed to blush quite often since she'd met Dan Castleberry. "And what's a mother of two supposed to look like?"

"Not like you! You look—like a model."

"Dan," she asked coyly with a wink, "didn't your mother tell you your nose would grow each time you told a lie?"

"Been there. Done that," he retorted with a smirk.

"What's that supposed to mean? I don't get it."

Hands on his hips, he grinned that crooked little smile of his. "I skated as Pinocchio. My nose did grow—with a little help from the makeup department."

"You're incorrigible," she chastised. "And we'd better get going; the kids are probably driving Ethel crazy."

❧

Two eager children stood in the church's vestibule, watching for Dan and their mother. When the couple stepped into the church, Becca burst from her grandfather's hold, leaped into Dan's arms, and hugged him tightly. "I love you, Dan," she said as she snuggled her face into his neck.

Bobby took Dan's free hand and dragged him over to meet his grandmother.

"You've made quite an impression on my grandchildren and husband, Mr. Castleberry. I've heard nice things about you."

Now it was his turn to blush. "And you, Mrs. Bennett. Carlee has told me how unselfish you are, what a friend you've been to her, and what a wonderful grandmother you are to the children. But please—call me Dan. The kids do."

"Then, Dan it is! We'll expect you at our house around two o'clock." She patted his shoulder, then disappeared.

Jim Bennett extended his right hand as he leaned toward Dan. "She has a great dinner cooking. Come hungry!"

Carlee led Dan and the children into a back pew. It was obvious she was trying to make his church experience as comfortable as possible. People all around leaned close to say hello and to welcome him to their church. He was surprised at how comfortable he felt with these strangers. And he was proud to be accompanied by such a beautiful young woman and her very special children.

Becca refused to get off Dan's lap when Carlee tried to take her from him, and he was no help; he hugged the little girl even tighter. When they stood to sing the first hymn, Bobby moved past his mother to Dan's other side and snuggled in close to the big man when they sat down. The beautiful sanctuary, the stained-glass windows, the cushioned pews, the thickly carpeted floors—all seemed to say "welcome" with their beauty and warmth.

When the service was over, they moved out into the lobby with the other churchgoers, who smiled at them with friendly faces and extended hands of welcome. The pastor told them how glad he was that they were there and complimented Carlee on the regular attendance of her family, as he shook Dan's hand warmly.

"Now, was that so bad?" Carlee asked when they climbed into Dan's car and headed for home.

"It was okay, I guess," Dan answered without enthusiasm.

Bobby looked crushed. "You didn't like it?"

Dan reached over the back of the seat and poked the boy in the arm. "Just kidding. Of course I liked it. But I'm not sure I could take a steady diet of it, like you and your mom."

Bobby slipped two skinny arms around Dan's neck. "Well, I liked having you there with us."

Dan patted the eight-year-old's hands. "I liked being there with you, too. I like being with your family anywhere."

Becca look slighted, like she wanted Dan's attention, too. "I love you, Dan," she called out in her loud voice from her place in the backseat.

Dan felt a lump rise in his throat. Not even his parents said those words to him. In fact, other than Bobby and Becca, he couldn't remember anyone saying they loved him since his grandmother died. It touched him deeply, but he attempted to conceal that fact; such tender emotions were so foreign to him.

When they reached Carlee's home, Dan helped his passengers to the door, then excused himself, explaining he needed to get something from the car. When he returned, he was carrying the three gift-wrapped packages. The children danced happily around him. "Are they for us?"

Carlee looked embarrassed. Dan only laughed and enjoyed their childish enthusiasm.

He ordered the group to be seated on the sofa in the family room, then placed a bright yellow package with a green polka-dotted ribbon in Becca's lap. "Open it, honey," he told the smiling child as he knelt before her.

"Dan!" Carlee acknowledged with a frown. "None of us has a birthday. Why did you do this?"

He looked at the happy faces of the children and answered, "Because I wanted to. That's why! Now, Mama, be quiet and let me have some fun."

Becca pulled the paper with one big jerk and squealed when she caught sight of the beautiful Christmas Holiday Barbie. She ripped the doll from the box and hugged it to her and ran into Dan's waiting arms. "Thank you, Dan." She squeezed his neck and kissed his cheek.

"You're welcome, Becca." His heart was nearly bursting with joy at seeing Becca's cute little face express so much happiness.

Carlee's eyes took on a misty look. "Oh, Dan. The Holiday doll."

He placed the package with the cowboys on blue wrapping paper in Bobby's lap. "This is for you, Bobby."

The boy was a little more patient than his sister; he carefully pulled the ribbon and tape from the package before opening the box. He stared at the two balls, then at Dan.

"One for keeping, one for playing," Dan answered without being asked as he watched the boy's reaction to his gift.

Bobby picked up the see-through box and read the autograph. "Thank you, Dan. This is the best ball I've ever seen. Boy, wait'll my coach sees this." He held the box as if it would break and uttered "Wow" over and over.

"The other one is for playing catch. Maybe you and I can do that sometime before I leave. Would you like that?"

The boy ran to Dan and hugged him around the waist. "Yes, I'd like it. Playing catch with you would be the best present ever. Thank you, Dan."

Dan placed the package wrapped in pink foil with a pink bow in the young mother's lap. "Mama, this is for you. Open it."

She lifted weepy eyes to his. "I can't, Dan. You've done so much for me—us—already."

He touched her cheek. "Carlee, would you refuse my gift? When I went to all the trouble of selecting it just for you?"

"But. . .Dan. . ."

"Carlee, please open it."

She appeared to be reluctant as she untied the bow and removed the wrapping paper. He was glad they'd put the doll's original box into a plain white one before wrapping it; it prolonged the fun of watching her open the package. As she lifted the lid, she burst into tears at the sight of the beautiful doll. "Oh, Dan! A Bob Mackie!"

"Yep, the new one. Have you seen it?" he asked with pride.

She held the doll at arm's length. "No—oh, it's so beautiful!" She lowered it and put it back into the box.

"What are you doing, Carlee? Don't you like it?" Dan grabbed her hands to stop her as she shoved it away.

"I can't accept a gift like this, Dan. I know this doll was very expensive."

Dan lifted the doll's box and placed it back in her lap. "Carlee, I bought it for you; I want you to have it. I could've bought a cheaper doll, but I wanted you to have this one. This doll is yours, and I won't take no for an answer."

The young woman sniffled and rubbed at her eyes with her sleeves. "But, Dan—"

"No buts, Carlee!" he said in a soft but firm voice as he pulled a fresh hankie from his pocket and handed it to her. "And if you want to take her out of her box, I won't tell a soul!"

She laughed through her tears, then blew her nose on the hankie. "Oh, Dan. Didn't I do a good job educating you? Little girls open their doll boxes! Big girls don't!"

He seated himself beside her on the sofa. "You did an excellent job educating me; you just did it too late. I'd already bought these dolls before you showed me your collection. I was sure relieved to learn neither you nor Becca had the new Christmas doll and that you had no plans of buying the new Bill Maxwell doll."

Carlee giggled through eyes that sparkled with tears. "Bob Mackie, Dan! Bob Mackie!" She kissed him quickly on the cheek. "Thank you, Dan. I love her! I'll keep her forever!"

Little Becca yanked at his sleeve. "Can you help me, Dan? I can't get Barbie's shoes off the cardboard."

He gave Carlee's hand a squeeze, then dropped on his knees before the little girl and began to work on the plastic ties holding the doll's shoes fast. When he'd finished that project, he pulled the certificate of authenticity from the autographed ball's box and read it to Bobby, who listened with rapt attention.

Carlee watched him intently. He was an attractive man in his muted brown tweed sport coat. Dan was a sharp dresser. He was used to gracious living. Everything about him reflected the affluent lifestyle with which he'd grown up. Yet here he sat in her home, playing with her children. And, best of all, he had attended church with them.

He smoothed his hair where tiny fingers had tangled it. "What are you thinking? You look miles away from us."

"You. The kids. Thinking how lucky we are to have a friend like you." She patted him on the knee and rose to her feet. "It's nearly two; they'll be looking for us."

The four made their way, hand in hand, across the lawn that joined the two Bennett houses. Father Bennett greeted them at the door. "Welcome! Welcome!"

he said as he encouraged Dan to remove his jacket and make himself at home.

Carlee excused herself, and she and Becca hurried into the kitchen to help Ethel with the last-minute preparations.

"Look, Grandpa," Bobby said proudly as he followed his grandfather and Dan into the den. He produced the baseball from the little backpack that he wore everywhere he went. It contained all the things he loved most—a broken pocket watch, a picture of his father, a handheld video game. "Dan gave it to me. It's not even my birthday."

Jim took the clear plastic box from the boy's hand and examined it closely. "Well, I'd say this is some present. Dan must like you a lot to give you something this nice!" He nodded knowingly toward Dan. "And expensive!" When Jim finished reading, he slipped the paper and ball into its box and handed it to Bobby, who rushed off to show his grandmother.

Jim locked his hands behind his head and leaned back in the chair. "That was mighty nice of you, Dan. Meant a lot to Bobby to have you give him a present like that—for no reason at all." The older man closed his eyes and breathed a sigh. "What that boy needs is a father."

Dan nodded at his new friend's words. "Does Carlee ever date?" he blurted out. "I mean, does she have a boyfriend?"

Jim's eyes widened, and he looked long and hard at Dan before answering. "No, she doesn't date or have a boyfriend, although we've done everything we can to encourage her. She needs a life of her own; she's a beautiful young woman." He added with a smile, "In case you hadn't noticed. But she isn't interested in men. Says there isn't a man alive who would love her and the children the way Robert did. She may be right. They were the perfect couple."

Dan flinched. "I'd think men would be beating a path to her door."

Jim rubbed his chin. "They have been. She isn't interested. Her standards are high, and the guy'd have to be pretty special to live up to them. It's a heavy burden to raise two children alone. We try to help as much as we can, but she's an independent little gal."

"I've noticed that," Dan interjected. "She's quite a woman. Never met another one like her."

"Lucky the man that catches her, Dan. She'll make someone a wonderful wife. That girl is as special as they come." He stopped speaking when Carlee entered the room.

"Mom Bennett sent me to fetch you two hungry men; everything is on the table. The kids are already seated."

They followed obediently as the delicious smells from the dining room beckoned. Dan pulled the chair out for Carlee. Jim tried to lift Becca, to put her in her booster seat as he'd done hundreds of times, but she pulled away from him. "I want Dan to help me, Grandpa!"

Dan rushed around the table and lifted the smiling baby into the seat, then pushed her chair close to the table. Becca grinned and blinked her long lashes in his direction.

Bobby gave Dan a toothy grin as the boy slipped his hand into his new friend's hand. Carlee smiled and leaned forward as her hand slid into Dan's other hand, and the family circle was complete as Jim bowed his head and began to pray.

"Lord, we thank You for providing this food for us, and for Ethel who prepared it. We thank You for Dan, Carlee, Bobby, and Becca being with us at our table to share in Your bounty. We ask Your continued blessing in the name of Your Son. And we praise You."

Collectively, they all said, "Amen."

As a family, they laughed, joked, and enjoyed Ethel's wonderful meal. Dan stole a glance around the table at the happy faces. He couldn't remember the last time he'd had a home-cooked meal like this. Never at his parents' house. The cook had prepared the meals when he was a child, and now their meals were all eaten out in a fine restaurant or at the country club. This was, without a doubt, the best meal he'd ever tasted, and he told his hostess so.

"I'm glad you enjoy my cooking," Ethel said bashfully, embarrassed by his lavish praise.

"He likes Mama's hot dogs, too," little Becca announced proudly as she licked the butter from her second roll.

Her grandmother placed her hand on the tiny girl's shoulder with pride. "Your mother is a wonderful cook, Becca. She knows how to prepare far more than hot dogs."

Carlee threw her head back with a laugh and winked at her mother-in-law. "I must be a good cook; I learned everything I know from you—and you're terrific!"

With that, Jim stood up with his hands extended in the air. "Enough of this mutual admiration society. I suggest we wait on our dessert until later." Then, pointing to Dan and Bobby, he added, "We menfolk will build a nice fire in the fireplace while the ladies do up the kitchen. That okay with everyone?"

They agreed unanimously and headed for their designated jobs, full and happy.

❧

When the women joined them in the family room twenty minutes later, they found Jim asleep in one recliner and Dan, with Bobby in his lap in the other, reading the Sunday sports section. The rest of the newspaper lay scattered on the floor at their feet. A tear forced its way down Carlee's cheek. How much her children had missed, having been robbed of their father's presence in their lives.

❧

Late in the afternoon, the foursome walked back across the lawn. Carlee put Becca down for a much-needed nap, while Dan popped the Odyssey tape into the VCR for Bobby.

There he was, waiting for her on the sofa, when she came back into the room with two cups of freshly made coffee.

"You're spoiling me, you know." He took the cup and motioned for her to sit beside him.

"Enjoy it while you can," she said with a balmy smile. "You have only two more weeks—the first one is gone!"

"Not quite two weeks," he corrected dismally.

She frowned. "What do you mean?"

He told her all about his friend Brad and the wedding.

Her frown turned to a look of sadness. "When will you be back?"

"Don't know. I haven't made return reservations yet."

Disappointment crossed her face. "Oh," she said softly.

Dan didn't know what to say; he hadn't expected a negative reaction. He'd thought she would be glad to get a little extra sleep the few mornings he'd be gone.

"Thursday's Thanksgiving. The children and I were hoping you'd spend the day with us. You know, a turkey and all the fixings. I was going to cook for you." She lowered her gaze to the floor, apparently wishing she hadn't mentioned her plans.

He took her hand in his and pressed it gently. "You don't have to do that for me. Won't Ethel and Jim be expecting you and the children for Thanksgiving?"

She drew back slightly. "No, they're going to St. Louis to be with Ethel's sister and her husband."

"If I'd known. . ."

She gnawed at her lower lip. "It's okay. Really."

Dan lifted her chin with one finger and looked into her sapphire-blue eyes. "What if I come back Wednesday?"

That sparkle he loved so much returned to her face. "I wouldn't want you to change your plans for us."

"What do you mean 'for us'? I'd rather be here with the three of you for Thanksgiving than anyplace I can think of." He bent and playfully kissed her on the forehead. "Honest."

"Your parents are welcome to come with you."

Dan threw his head back with a robust laugh. "And miss the holiday buffet? To be with their only son? Surely you jest!" Their attitudes and lack of interest hurt him more than he cared to admit, even to himself.

"Dan, really. Do what works best for you. The children and I are used to being alone. We'll survive." If she were trying to mask her disappointment, she was doing a very poor job of it. It showed on her face.

"I *will* be back on Wednesday, and I'm honored to accept your invitation for Thanksgiving dinner." He stepped back dramatically and added, "If you promise you won't burn the turkey."

Carlee grabbed two pillows from the sofa and pelted him. He tried to duck, but she'd taken him by complete surprise. He quickly encircled her waist with his strong arms and held her tight. He could kiss her again so easily—she was so close, so desirable. Her lovely face was so near. . . .

Bobby looked up from his place on the floor, frowned, and said in a loud, authoritative voice, "No roughhousing in the family room!"

Chapter 9

One suitcase and one garment bag rested on the backseat of Dan Castleberry's rented car as he absentmindedly made his way toward the Ice Palace. He knew he was early, but he hadn't slept well. Was it the excitement of going back to be with his friends and the other cast members? Perhaps it was his leaving Carlee? A frown dug into his forehead. Maybe it was the three huge helpings of mashed potatoes and gravy or the four monstrous slices of roast beef. Or the two pieces of lemon meringue pie. He'd certainly eaten his share of Ethel's cooking, and then some.

So Brad was getting married. Maybe Brad was ready for it, but Dan wondered how a marriage could survive all the traveling. And the temptations. Brad skated pair numbers with many beautiful women. And his wife would continue to skate with the men in the cast. Dan wasn't sure he'd want *his* wife skating in skimpy costumes with any of those guys. He knew them too well—knew how they talked about women.

His *wife?* A smile came to his lips. He'd be an old man by the time he married, at the rate he was going. *If* he ever married. He was surprised to find Carlee's empty minivan already parked when he turned into the lot. He'd barely turned off the headlights when the rink's door flew open and she came running out, screaming and shaking uncontrollably, terror etched on her face. She flew into his arms and clung tightly, her speech erratic and garbled.

"There's a man in there! I—I saw him!" she screamed breathlessly.

Dan shoved her into the car and pulled the cellular phone from the glove compartment. He dialed 9-1-1 and quickly gave them the details. "Did you recognize him? Is he still in there?"

Carlee held tightly onto his arm as she shook her head. "No! I never saw him before! He just stood there and looked at me when I turned on the lights! I ran!" Her voice trembled with fear, and her face was deathly pale.

"You stay here. I'm going inside," he commanded as he broke her grasp and shoved her into his car.

She grabbed at his jacket. "No, Dan! Don't! Wait for the police!"

He pressed the Lock button, slammed the door, and ordered, "Stay in the car and don't open the doors for anyone!" He moved quickly to the trunk and removed a flashlight and jack handle and headed for the rink as Carlee watched, her face a mask of fear.

The overhead lights were still glowing when he entered the big building, but no one was in sight. He knew that if Carlee said she saw someone, someone was there. Where could he be? Was he watching from some hidden area?

Maintaining a cool head, Dan headed for the office, where the previous day's receipts were kept until they could be counted and banked. The man might be anywhere in the building, he realized, but the office would be the most likely place for him to go if money were his goal.

The lights were off in the office, but the door was ajar. Dan knew Carlee always kept it locked. Silently he slipped his hand inside the door and switched on the lights. No one was in sight, but the lock for the heavy steel cabinet where she kept the cash box had been pried off. Dan lifted the jack handle over his head and moved as stealthily as a cat on the prowl to the closet where he had stored his skates. If someone were still in the office, the closet was the only place large enough for a man to conceal himself.

What should he do? If he waited for the police to check out the closet and the guy wasn't in there, he'd be wasting precious time and the guy might get away. Or worse, he might see Carlee waiting in the car and go after her. No, he couldn't take a chance on that; he had no choice but to check out that closet. He crept toward the door, his heart pounding. With one hand on the knob and the other gripping the jack handle, he yanked open the door and found a scared, skinny young man crouched on the floor, the cash box tucked securely under his arm.

Dan raised the jack handle over his head with both hands and fire in his eyes. "One move and I'll split your head open with this thing! If you think I'm kidding, try me. I'm aching for a reason to let you have it!" He was serious, and he meant business. He knew if the kid were armed, he might go for his gun and he'd have to hit him. And he wondered, could he actually split another person's head open? If he had to? He hoped the police would arrive, and he wouldn't have to find out. But, as the vision of Carlee running and screaming into his arms flashed through his mind, he knew if he had to, he could. He'd do anything to protect her. If the guy made one move, just one, he'd use the iron.

The wail of approaching sirens could be heard, and within seconds, two police cars wheeled into the parking lot and screeched to a halt. Three officers jumped out, pulled their guns from their holsters, and moved cautiously toward the open door. The fourth officer ran to Dan's car to question the frightened Carlee. Dan heard them enter and called out in a loud voice as he hovered over the man, "We're in here. In the office. It's okay. I've got him!"

When the officers entered the room, they found Dan, still poised with the jack handle over his head, ready to strike the man on the floor of the closet if provoked.

"Good work, young man," one of the officers told Dan after they'd cuffed the perpetrator.

"But pretty stupid!" another officer added with a frown. "You could've been hurt, maybe even shot, coming in here like that. That guy might have been armed."

The first officer came to Dan's defense. "Hey, go easy on him. If this guy'd frightened my wife like that, I'd have gone after him, too. So would you, and you know it!"

Dan smiled nervously, his adrenaline pumping furiously. *Wife? No, sir. Not me!* he thought.

⟡

Carlee waited nervously in the car. *What was going on in there?* She gasped with relief as she spotted the man, his hands on top of his head, being led from the building by the three officers, followed closely by Dan, who was unharmed. She ran to him and wrapped her arms about his neck.

"You should be proud of your husband," the officer said. "He had the guy cornered—all we had to do was cuff him. Sure great to see a man lay his life on the line to protect his wife like that—even though he should've waited for us."

She tried to explain that Dan was only a friend, but they were too busy shoving the burglar into the police car to hear her.

After they'd gone, Dan grinned and pulled her into his arms and held her still-shaking body. "Let them think what they will—I don't care. I'm just glad you're safe." Then, with a wink of his eye, he added, "Remember when I said if you were a good girl Santa might bring you a Barbie? Well, this Santa has decided what you really need is a German shepherd!"

Once they were in the rink with the door bolted, Carlee phoned Jim Bennett to let him know what had happened. "Dan saved my life, Father Bennett! No telling what that man might have done if Dan hadn't been there when I came running out of the building. I was sure the thief was right behind me! What if he'd caught me before I got to the car?" Her body began to tremble once again, but Dan was there to hold her in the safety and security of his arms. After she'd filled in her father-in-law on the details, he asked to speak to Dan.

"Dan? I don't know how we'll ever repay you. I thank God you were there. If anything had happened to our little Carlee—well, I'm not sure how Ethel and I could go on without her. Thanks, son!"

Dan blinked his eyes as another strange emotion flooded his soul. Jim had called him "son" again. His own father never called him that. He felt so close to Jim at that moment—it was as if they had a true kinship. "I don't know what it was, Jim. I couldn't sleep and felt compelled to go to the rink early this morning. Do you believe in people being psychic?"

Jim laughed. "I wouldn't call it psychic, Dan. I'd call it being led by God. I'm convinced He sent you to be there at just the right time, to keep Carlee from harm."

Dan hadn't considered it that way. The thought of God's leading frightened him, yet consoled him. More of those mixed emotions he'd been experiencing since meeting the Bennetts. "I told her I thought Santa should bring her a guard dog."

"Good idea! Been thinking that same thing myself. Maybe we ought to keep one around there on a full-time basis. Sure would make me feel better about Carlee going in there by herself. I'll see what I can do about it."

When Dan hung up the phone, Carlee was waiting with their mugs of hot coffee. She was smiling, but Dan knew she was forcing a grin, trying to mask the fear that still surged through her body like ice water. He took the mugs and placed them on the counter, then wrapped her in his arms protectively. Funny, he'd been so concerned about protecting her, he hadn't been nervous or afraid for himself. He'd only wanted to get the guy who had terrified her so.

"What if you hadn't come early—do you think he would have followed me out the door? If he'd caught me, what—"

Dan put his big hand lightly over her mouth to keep her from finishing her sentence. "But he didn't! I *was* here. Jim said God sent me," he said reassuringly, surprising himself by his use of the word *God*.

She pressed her face into his chest as his arms encircled her body. "Oh, Dan. I praise the Lord that you were here."

The practice session was a total loss—his skating was erratic, his school figures lopsided. They decided to shut off the VCR and forget skating for the day. Their minds were too busy with what-ifs, although neither of them voiced them to the other.

"What time do you leave?" she asked as she slipped her hand into the crook of his arm. The fingers of his free hand gave her hand a gentle squeeze.

"Plane leaves in less than two hours. I should go pretty soon, I guess, but I don't want to leave." He lifted her fingers to his lips and kissed them tenderly as he looked into her wide eyes. "Why don't I call Brad and tell him I won't be there? I can't leave you here to open in the morning without me being here with you."

She lowered her head onto his shoulder as a smile curled her lips. "How do you think I've gotten along these past five years without you?"

He hadn't doubted that she'd gotten along without him—she was one of the strongest women he'd ever known. But somehow, he now felt responsible for her.

"Besides," she added confidently, "Father Bennett is going to come with me and check out the building the next two days while you're gone. I'll be fine. Just go and enjoy the wedding, and we'll see you on Wednesday."

It relieved his mind to know Jim Bennett would be with her. After all, he'd assured Brad he'd be at the wedding. "Okay. But promise me that if Jim isn't with you, you won't open the door."

She promised, but both of them wondered what would happen when he left for good.

Brad, Michelle, and a dozen other members of the cast of Ice Fantasy were waiting when Dan got off the plane in Tampa. They cheered and hugged one another, laughing and talking. Brad loaded Dan's things into his Porsche and suggested they all go for a beer. Everyone agreed, and they piled into their cars and headed for the nearest bar. The music was blaring when they entered—something about a brokenhearted cowboy whose woman had left him for another. Dan couldn't help but think it was probably the guy's singing that drove her away.

His old friend Michelle snuggled up next to Dan. He tried to move away but found it impossible with so many people crowded around the small table.

"Hey, honey! Beers all around and give me the tab!" Brad called to the waitress in a loud voice. When the beers were placed in front of them, Dan stared at his rather than drink it. Brad picked it up and shoved it into his hand. "You're the best man—aren't you going to toast the groom?"

When his friend put it that way, what choice did he have? Dan smiled his sheepish grin and lifted his glass. "Here's to Brad and Beth. May they have many happy years together." He turned to Brad, who was beaming with the attention. "And may their marriage last at least fifty years!"

The group fell silent. Brad rose to his feet and looked puzzled. "Come on, fella. I'm getting married—not facing a jail sentence. Fifty years with the same broad? Not me. We'll be lucky if we make it five. That's plenty!"

Dan frowned. "Then why are you getting married?"

"To make it legal, man. I figure five years, and then I'm out and on to greener pastures. Too many fillies out there, and I'm a young man."

Dan placed his glass on the table. Get married with the idea of bailing out in five years? He and Brad had never seriously discussed marriage before. He'd had no idea his friend felt this way. "How does Beth feel about this, Brad?"

The group at the table looked from man to man, their heads bobbing as if they were watching a tennis match.

Brad shrugged his shoulders. "Fine with her! Look, Dan, we all know in this crazy business we're in there are lots of opportunities to cheat on your spouse. Just the groupies alone offer endless possibilities!" He aimed a knowing wink at his friends, who nodded their heads in agreement. "We've decided that if we find someone else we'd rather be with, it's over. We'll get a friendly divorce!" He raised his glass to the others, who were listening intently while they guzzled their beers. "In the meantime, we can file a joint tax return and save a few bucks. Everybody wins except the IRS."

The group cheered in unison, and Dan felt sick. This is what he'd left Kansas City for?

"Hey, don't be a party pooper. Drink up! Have some fun!" It was Michelle, leaning on him, stroking his hair with her fingers. "Dance with me, Dan."

"Yeah," Brad agreed as he nudged Dan with his shoulder, "go dance with Michelle. You need to lighten up and enjoy yourself, buddy!"

Dan moved onto the dance floor with Michelle, then excused himself and left her standing in the middle of the floor. He had to get out of there. He felt that he was being smothered, that he didn't belong. He left.

For nearly two hours he leaned against Brad's car in the parking lot, waiting for a ride to the hotel. What was wrong with him? He loved parties! These were the people he partied with when they were on the road. They'd been in bars and clubs all over the world—Paris, London, Milan, Berlin, Singapore. What was so different about Florida?

Brad was a mess when he came teetering out of the bar; he was in no condition to drive. Dan tried to get his keys away from him, but Brad wouldn't give them up. Michelle was just as bad—after a few beers she thought she was Cleopatra. When Dan refused to get into the car with the two drunks, Brad sped off, squealing his tires as he left the crowded parking lot.

Dan stood there empty-handed. His luggage was in the trunk of Brad's car, and he had no idea where Brad and Michelle were headed. He waited ten minutes, but they didn't return. Others from their group emerged and offered him a ride, but they were as soused as Brad and Michelle. He turned them down flat. They couldn't understand his reticence. He didn't understand it either but attributed it to his early morning episode with the burglar. Somehow it had made him see life for the fragile thing it was, and he didn't want to waste it with a bunch of inebriated people.

He called a cab, and once in the hotel, he phoned Carlee.

"How are things in Florida?"

He took a deep breath and lied. "Great! Spent some time with my friends. Talked about old times—had a blast."

"I'm glad for you," she said sincerely. "Are you all going out for dinner together?"

He glanced at his watch. "Yeah, in an hour or so. Going to a great place. What'd you and the kids have for supper?"

"You'd never guess. Roast beef sandwiches! Father Bennett sliced the rest of the roast into nice thin slices and brought some over to share with us."

Suddenly he had an insane desire for roast beef. "How are the kids? Did you tell them about this morning?"

"Most of it. They think you're a hero. So do I!"

"I'm no hero, Carlee." He was sure he could detect a twinge of fear as she spoke. "I miss you guys."

"Sure you do! With all those beautiful women surrounding you, you miss us? How gullible do you think I am, Dan?"

He knew she was teasing, but he wished he could convince her he was very serious. He did miss them.

"Where are you going to have the bachelor party?"

He straightened. The bachelor party! He'd forgotten all about it! He'd planned to invite the men in their circle of friends for an impromptu gathering at their favorite pub, then the beer guzzling took place and Brad had spun off with Michelle. He had no idea where to find him. What could he do? He didn't want Carlee to know what kind of people he hung around with. She'd trusted him with her children.

"Better go," he said while trying to mask his anxiety. "Bachelor party won't wait. Call you tomorrow." He sat down on the side of the bed. He needed a plan.

The phone rang. He picked it up, hoping it was Brad. But it wasn't. It was Beth, and she was crying. "Speak slowly, Beth. I can't understand you. Tell me what's wrong."

The bride-to-be sniffled, took a few deep breaths, and began to explain the reason for her call. "I'm thinking of calling off the wedding, Dan, ending it with Brad. . . ."

He struggled for words. "Why, Beth? I thought everything was fine between you two."

"That was *before* I got the phone call!" Now her voice sounded more angry than hurt.

"What phone call?"

"From the anonymous caller who told me I could find Brad at the Coconut Motel—with a woman."

Dan fidgeted with the phone cord. "You know better than to believe someone who won't give you a name. It was probably a prank, a prewedding joke."

"I want to think that, Dan. But to be honest, I don't trust Brad. This isn't the first time I've had doubts about him. I know he's no saint, but is any guy these days?"

"But—he told me you two had an agreement, something about walking away quietly if the other person ever decided he or she wanted out of the marriage."

"He told you that? That's bunk. He knows I don't feel that way. He's made that stupid statement in front of all our friends. I thought everyone knew he was kidding. *I* thought he was kidding!"

"So what are you going to do?" Dan wanted to tell her about Brad and Michelle. Maybe the caller was right; maybe Brad *was* at the motel. But somehow he couldn't be the one to betray his old friend.

"Marry him, I guess. And hope the marriage will straighten him out. With all our family coming, it's probably too late to call it off, as much as I'd like to."

Dan placed the phone in its cradle and stared straight ahead. He'd only been away from these people for a week and a half. Now he hardly knew them. They were like strangers.

He wanted to call Carlee again—tell her about Brad. And about Beth's call. He needed to hear her voice. But he couldn't. He tried Brad's apartment and got no answer.

A rap-rap sounded on his door at eight o'clock that evening. There stood Brad with bloodshot eyes, looking guilty, suitcase and garment bag in hand. "Hey, man. What can I say? I'm sorry."

Dan glared at his friend, and all he could think about was Beth's call. "Where have you been? With Michelle?"

Brad lowered his head and rubbed the toe of one shoe on the surface of the carpet. "Dropped her off at her place right after I left you."

Dan wanted to believe him but found it difficult in light of his discussion with Beth. "Honest, Brad?"

Brad looked Dan directly in the eye. "Honest."

"Guess you know you've messed up with your stupid antics. I'd wanted to have a bachelor party for you tonight—get together with the guys—but you blew it. I had no idea how to find you. Where were you?"

"Driving around," he answered unconvincingly.

"In your condition? What'd you want to do? Kill yourself and maybe someone else? You were drunk, Brad."

Brad pushed past him and dropped onto the love seat in Dan's room. "Look, man. Tomorrow's my wedding day, so lighten up! What's the matter with you anyway?"

"Did you spend the afternoon with Michelle, Brad?" He had to know.

Brad reddened and squared his jaw. "Dan, why would you ask me that? Of course not!"

Dan wanted to believe him, but how could he? "Brad, have you ever been to the Coconut Motel?"

Brad stiffened. "That roach motel? Why would you ask?" He behaved as if he were offended that Dan would even ask.

Dan hoped his friend's response had been the sign of true indignation and decided to let the subject drop. "Never mind. How about dinner? My treat!" He grabbed the soon-to-be groom by the arm and ushered him out of the room. "Now, what do you want for your last dinner as a free man?"

Chapter 10

I t was Tuesday morning. Carlee woke at 4:45 and thought of Dan. He'd probably be sleeping still, exhausted from his bout with the burglar, the flight to Florida, and the bachelor party. She found herself wishing he hadn't gone to Florida. Had he left only yesterday? It seemed like it had been a week. She'd known Dan for such a short time—how could she miss him this much? She'd understood from the beginning that he'd be in Kansas City for three weeks and then he'd disappear from her life—probably forever. She'd been so careful to keep an impenetrable shell around her life. Yet Dan had worked his way into it without even trying. And without intending to, she'd welcomed and encouraged him.

Dan Castleberry was wide awake at 4:45 and wondering if Jim Bennett had remembered to set his alarm clock. The last thing he wanted was to have Carlee entering that building alone. Carlee. Hard to believe that less than two weeks ago, he hadn't even known she existed. Yet here he was, worrying about her. If Jim didn't get her a dog, he was going to. No woman should be out alone that time of morning. And to think that she'd been doing it for five years. But it was obvious she'd do anything for those kids of hers. He'd wanted to tell Brad about Carlee. She'd been on his mind throughout dinner. But what could he tell him? That he'd made friends with a young widow and her two small children? That the times he'd been in her home were some of the happiest times he'd ever had? That he'd spent big bucks for a doll? For two of them? And an autographed baseball? That he could hardly wait to get back to Kansas City to see her again and hold her in his arms? No. Brad wouldn't understand, never in a million years. Brad had known how important his career was to him, how focused his life had been. No, this was not the time to discuss Carlee.

Tom Cord, Ice Fantasy's administrator, phoned an hour later and, after the usual greeting, invited Dan to come to company headquarters at around ten. When Dan entered the office, Tom welcomed him, shook his hand, and motioned him toward a chair. Then he eyed him intently. "We've got a problem, Dan. With twelve cast members. I know they're your friends, but they've been hitting the bottle pretty hard." He moved around his desk, dropped into the comfortable leather chair, and steepled his fingers. "I don't know if it was because you stayed behind in Kansas City and he missed your influence or what; but Brad joined in big-time, and he's been on one big drunk since he arrived here." Tom Cord frowned as he closed his eyes and pressed back in his chair. "Dan, I know you haven't been a part of this mess. I've never even seen you the least bit tipsy. I've been watching this situation for some time now, and believe me, I'm not happy about it."

Dan slumped in his chair. He'd been afraid something like this was happening, but he'd tried to ignore it.

Tom continued, "I've warned the whole lot of them that if they don't straighten up, I'm going to have to replace them."

"But—"

"I can't have this, Dan. Ice Fantasy is a family show. We have a reputation to maintain. And I need people who are dependable. Not a bunch of drunks!"

Dan felt sick. "What can I do?"

Tom walked around his desk and stood facing his friend, a troubled furrow on his brow. "I honestly don't know, Dan. Brad is jeopardizing his career. I hope his marriage to Beth will be the answer—she's got a fairly level head."

Dan ran his tongue over suddenly dry lips. "I feel responsible. I was so caught up in my own life, I never even noticed how out of control he's gotten."

"He's a big boy, Dan. He's brought this on himself." Tom breathed a deep sigh. "Business is business. I hate to be the bearer of bad tidings, but I thought you should know. You being his best friend. Maybe you can talk to him." He placed a heavy hand on Dan's shoulder. "If he'll listen to anyone, I think it'll be you. He respects you."

Dan stood and extended his hand. "I'll do what I can, Tom. Thanks for clueing me in."

He took a cab to the hotel and scaled the steps to his room. The wedding wasn't until seven. he had plenty of time to call Carlee. He needed to hear her voice. The line was busy when he placed the call. He ordered room-service coffee, stretched out on the bed, and thought about his future. His long-range plans were right on target. He wasn't about to mess up like Brad and the others—he'd worked too hard, too long, to throw it all away foolishly. He smiled as he thought about Carlee. He missed being with her and the children, but skating was his life. And although he'd enjoyed being with her. . .

Suddenly he realized he wasn't being honest with himself. Carlee was much more than a friend! He'd devoted a third of his life to his career, but was it enough? Could he be passing up the love of a lifetime by walking away from Carlee Bennett? Could God actually have sent him to the Ice Palace like Jim said? He dialed again and waited. She answered on the first ring.

"Oh, Dan. I'm so glad to hear your voice. I've been thinking about you. How did the bachelor party go?"

He paused, wondering how much he should tell her and decided to come clean and tell her everything, including the part about Brad, Michelle, and Beth's phone call.

"Oh, Dan, I'm sorry. You two were such good friends."

"Well, not much I can do about it. I'm going to talk to him if I get a chance. But I want to hear about you. Did Jim go with you to the rink this morning?"

"Yes. But, Dan, he's not going to be able to do that every morning. It's too much for him—his schedule is so full. I told him that once you were gone, I'd see about getting a dog."

Dan stifled a laugh. "Are you saying I can be replaced by a dog?"

She giggled. "Oh, Dan, of course not. Father Bennett said he could take the dog home with him at night, and I could bring him back to the rink with me. What do you think?"

He breathed a sigh—at least she'd have some protection. "Sounds like a good idea to me."

"What time are you coming home tomorrow? The children and I will pick you up at the airport."

"Thanks. You sure you're up to it? The airport will be crowded."

"Couldn't keep us away."

At 5:30, Dan donned his tuxedo and took a cab to the church, where he was to meet Brad. It was a beautiful evening. It occurred to him that he should have invited Carlee and the kids to come along with him. He could have stayed on a few days longer and taken them to Disney World. Whoa! Back up! What was he thinking? How had that idea entered his head? Take kids to Disney World? This was Dan Castleberry, world-renowned skater. Confirmed bachelor. His mind must be slipping.

The chapel where the wedding was to be held was small and crowded. As Dan stood next to the groom, he hoped Brad had told the truth about Michelle and the motel, but the look on Brad's face when Michelle entered the chapel said otherwise.

All eyes turned to the double doors at the back of the church as the strains of "Here Comes the Bride" filled the room and Beth entered, dressed in a flowing gown of white satin and lace. That is, all eyes except Brad's. His eyes zeroed in on Michelle first, then flitted toward his bride. Only Dan noticed his distraction— no one else, not even Beth. She was too happy, too caught up in wedding joys to notice. Dan wanted to shout out, to stop the wedding, but he didn't. Instead he stood by, helplessly silent. When he heard the words, "If any person has just cause why these two should not be united in holy matrimony, may he speak now or forever hold his peace," his heart pounded violently in his chest. He reminded himself that he didn't actually know the truth. Brad had denied he'd spent the afternoon with Michelle in the motel. Who was he to accuse his friend? He watched as the newly wedded couple strode down the aisle. Mr. and Mrs. Brad Morris, the seemingly perfect couple. The wedding was over. All Dan could do now was hope for the best. The duplicity he'd witnessed sickened him.

He phoned Carlee the minute he got back to his room. A young boy answered. "Bennett residence. Bobby speaking."

Dan smiled when he heard the child's voice. "And how are you, Mr. Bennett? Are you taking good care of your mother and sister while I'm away?"

"Hi, Dan! When are you coming home?"

The word "home" made Dan sad. Home was wherever he was at the time. It wasn't Kansas City, where his parents lived. Or Florida, where Ice Fantasy was headquartered. He didn't have a home, not a real one. His home was a suitcase packed with his personal belongings. Home was somewhere off in the future when he would retire from the ice show and settle down.

"Tomorrow, Bobby. I'll be landing in Kansas City at 7:00 p.m. And I'm really anxious to see you and Becca."

"Great! Mama said we could pick you up in the minivan. Becca wants to talk to you, okay?"

He smiled as visions of Becca sitting on his lap, listening to his distorted fairy tales filled his thoughts.

"When ya comin' home, Dan? I miss you."

"Tomorrow, Becca. Tomorrow. And I miss you, too. Now let me talk to your mother. Okay, honey?"

"I love you, Dan," the tiny voice answered.

Carlee's voice could be heard in the background as she instructed the children to get ready for bed. Then, "Hi, Dan. We've been waiting for your call. You wouldn't believe these kids; they wouldn't go to bed until we heard from you. How did the wedding go?"

He gave her a run-through of the day's happenings, including the eye-contact episode between Brad and Michelle.

"You shouldn't feel responsible, Dan. He made his decisions himself. You couldn't have changed his mind even if you'd known about Michelle. We'll have to pray that his improprieties are a thing of the past, that he and Beth will have a wonderful, long-lasting marriage."

How like her, he thought, *always willing to give the benefit of the doubt to any person.* "Think prayer will be enough? It'll take a miracle to keep those two together."

"That's what prayers for, Dan. Miracles do happen!"

Dan had never prayed before coming into contact with the Bennetts. But now he welcomed it, as long as he wasn't the one who had to do it. "Hey, what am I doing, burdening you with all of this? You don't even know these people," he said apologetically. "The main reason I called, other than to hear your voice, was to tell you I'd be arriving at KCI at seven tomorrow night—if the offer to pick me up still stands."

"You bet it does—if you're sure it won't embarrass you if two eager kids come along. They refuse to be left behind."

The hotel room suddenly seemed cold and impersonal. He could hardly wait to leave it. "Thanksgiving still on?"

"Last time I looked at the calendar, Thanksgiving was still scheduled for Thursday," she teased. The warmth of her laughter seemed to beckon him to Kansas City.

Chapter 11

At exactly seven o'clock, Dan rushed through the walkway into the airport and was greeted by three smiling faces. He shook hands with Bobby, grabbed Becca up in his arms, and hugged Carlee. He was back in Kansas City and glad to be there. The trip to Florida had been stressful and exhausting.

The house smelled of pumpkin pie when they entered. Dan rushed into the kitchen and found two pies resting on the counter on cooling racks. "Just one slice?" he begged as he touched a fingertip to the top of one of the spicy pies.

"No," Becca said firmly as she tugged on his hand. "Mama said we gotta wait 'till tomorrow!"

Carlee smiled. "Dan is here now, children, and it's past your bedtime. I want both of you in your pajamas. Pronto!"

Two unhappy children obediently followed their mother's command, kissed Dan, and headed for their bedrooms.

She grinned at Dan. "*Now* you can have some pie!"

It was the best pie he'd ever eaten. And he told her so.

She beamed with pride at his generous comments.

Tomorrow he would experience the first home-cooked Thanksgiving meal he'd eaten since his grandmother died. His memories of his grandmother might have faded slightly, but he remembered her well. Yes, tomorrow would be Thanksgiving, and there'd be more pumpkin pie.

☙

Long, ragged bands of red and pink laced across the horizon and pierced the gray blue early morning sky as the sun began to peek through the leafless trees. It was Thanksgiving morning, and Carlee was up and out of bed to greet its arrival. But this morning, unlike most, she would be heading to her kitchen, not the Ice Palace.

As she sat on the edge of the bed tying her tennies, she caught sight of the wedding picture that had remained on her nightstand these five years since Robert was so quickly taken from her. She lifted the gold-framed photograph and hugged it to her breast. Memories of other Thanksgivings flooded her mind and her heart. Robert had been the nearly perfect husband; they'd been so happy. Why had God allowed him to die? She'd asked that question a thousand times. So had the Bennetts, but no answer had come. Yet in its place had come a peace, an assurance that God was in control. Reddened eyes stared back at her as she gazed into the mirror. Today was a special day—a dinner guest was coming.

∽∂∾

Dan Castleberry woke at sunrise, raised up on one elbow, and peered out the east window of his room. There was something he loved about a sunrise, and this one was a doozie. Long red and pink bands were spread across the horizon as though a painter were testing the colors of his palette, splashing them boldly across the canvas. Tossing back the covers, he stepped to the window and watched with wonder as the new day spilled out before him in all its splendor—clean, fresh, and new. He would spend the day with Carlee, Bobby, and Becca, a real family Thanksgiving.

There was no aroma of turkey roasting in the oven, no pies lining the kitchen counter, no cranberry salad chilling in the refrigerator at his parents' house. They didn't have a clue what Thanksgiving was all about. But did he? Had any previous Thanksgivings been meaningful to him? Where had he spent them? In cities where he hadn't known a soul, in restaurants too numerous to remember, with people he cared little about.

Suddenly, without announcement or fanfare, the sun's rays broke over the trees and filled his world with light. The darkness of both his thoughts and the night were banished by the arrival of a new day, brilliant and warm. A day full of promise and hope. Dan felt an inner joy. Today would be special; Carlee and the children would have a real family Thanksgiving, and he would be part of it.

∽∂∾

By ten o'clock the scent of roasting turkey and sage dressing filled the Bennett house. The salads were chilled, the corn casserole was ready to pop into the oven, the homemade Parkerhouse rolls were rising—dinner was well under control. Bobby and Becca were watching an Odyssey videotape, and Carlee was putting the finishing touches on the cheesecake. The sound of the Gaither Vocal Band filled the kitchen, and her spirits soared as she harmonized along with them. Dan was due at eleven, and life was good. On a whim, she crossed the room and dialed his number. He answered almost immediately. "Aha! You're sitting on the phone. Who did you think would call, Ed McMahon or Dick Clark?"

"Naw, what would I do with ten million smackeroos? What's up?"

She felt a little foolish calling him. Her mother had always cautioned that girls shouldn't call boys for no good reason. Funny she should think of that now. But Dan was hardly a boy. And she was way beyond the girl stage. Friends should be able to call friends, shouldn't they? "I was thinking about you, wondering if you were busy? I thought maybe you'd like to come over a little early."

"Sure, if you need help." His voice sounded eager.

She laughed into the phone. "You? Help in the kitchen? That's hard to imagine! I'll probably just have you sit on the stool and lick spoons. But I would enjoy your company."

"Tell the kids I'm on my way. Should I pick up anything? Bread? Whipping cream? Peanuts?"

"Just bring yourself—you're all we need."

Dan arrived fifteen minutes later and found two eager children waiting on the porch for him. Bobby ran to Dan's car with Becca three steps behind. The man stooped, grabbed a child in each arm, and swung them about in big circles before depositing them on the front porch.

He'd been so busy with the kids that he hadn't noticed the lovely young woman standing just inside the storm door, watching the scene with a satisfied smile. When he finally caught sight of her, he was sure he felt his heart skip a beat. She wore a soft white blouse and an ankle-length calico jumper, topped with a freshly starched red apron. He thought she looked like a page plucked from an *Ideals* magazine. He couldn't take his eyes off her.

Becca and Bobby held his hands and dragged him into the house while their mother held the door open for them.

"Dan, I'm so glad you're here," she said as she helped him remove his jacket and hung it in the hall closet.

"I'm glad I'm here, too," he stammered awkwardly, wondering why all of a sudden he found it difficult to express himself. What he really wanted to do was pull her into his arms and smother her with kisses.

Bobby and Becca tugged at his hands and pulled him toward the family room.

"No!" their mother said firmly. "There will be plenty of time for that later. I invited Dan over early to help me. He has work to do. You two go watch your video and leave him alone. This morning he's all mine. Now, obey me."

The two children dropped their hold on his hands and did as told. He watched, grinning, as they walked away. "They're good kids. I love being with them—you know that."

"I know. But for now, like I said, you're all mine. They'll have to wait their turn." She took his hand in hers and, with a sideways glance that melted his heart, pulled him into the kitchen and tied an apron about his waist. "Here," she ordered as she extended her open palm, which held a paring knife and a potato peeler. "Choose your weapon."

He considered the choices and selected the peeler. She pointed to a five-pound sack of potatoes waiting on the kitchen table. "Peel!"

Dan peeled potatoes while Carlee mixed the homemade garlic dressing and tossed the green salad. He hoped she wouldn't catch him gazing at her as he peeled away at the sink. This was all so new to him, watching a woman working in her kitchen and enjoying it. He'd always thought women hated this sort of thing. Wasn't that why take-out food and restaurants were such an important part of the American culture? Wouldn't it have been easier to eat out, as his parents would? Yet here she was, working away and apparently loving it. Would he ever understand Carlee Bennett? He'd never been around another woman like her.

With the potatoes simmering in the big glass pot in the microwave, Carlee showed Dan where the silverware was kept and began to set the table with her best china. The two stood back to admire their handiwork when they finished.

"I've never set a table before," Dan admitted as he adjusted one of the spoons he'd placed a little haphazardly.

She patted him on the arm. "Well, you did an admirable job, Mr. Castleberry—for a first-timer. I'm proud of you."

Funny. He'd received the applause and accolades of audiences all over the world for his skating ability, but this one small compliment from Carlee was every bit as important to him. He liked having her approval for the things he did. He liked everything about her.

"I'm gonna put that big pat of butter in the middle like Ethel did," Dan declared as he mashed the potatoes while Carlee stirred the gravy. "Umm, that was good."

The children placed the butter, salt and pepper, and relish tray on the table while Dan carried in the turkey on the big oval platter. "Where do you want this bird?" he asked as he eyed the golden brown treasure.

"At your place—at the head of the table," she answered with an impish grin. "You're going to carve."

Dan's eyes widened. "Me? Carve? I don't know how."

"The bird doesn't know the difference, and we won't tell. Will we, kids?" She and the two children snickered at his chagrin. "Here's the electric carving knife," she invited as she extended it toward him. "Have at it!"

Once the table was laden with all the Thanksgiving delicacies, Carlee directed everyone to their chairs. Dan was at the head of the table with Carlee opposite him, and a child sat on either side. Dan knew what was coming and took a child's hand in each of his own, while Carlee did the same, completing the circle. He hoped she wouldn't ask him to pray. He'd been worrying about that ever since she'd invited him. Praying aloud was not in his bag of tricks!

She gave him an understanding glance. "I'll say grace today." When she finished praying and they'd all joined in for the "Amen," Carlee said with a smile, "Let's eat. Dan, pass the turkey!"

He picked up the platter loaded with juicy slices of turkey, carved in ways no turkey had ever been carved before, and grinned. "Kinda mangled him, didn't I?"

"I think it's purty, Dan." Becca pulled a long, slender wedge of white meat from the platter and stuffed it into her tiny mouth.

"Becca, please!" Her mother grabbed a napkin and dabbed at the little girl's mouth. "Where are your manners?"

"Dan did it in the kitchen—I saw him," Becca accused as she chomped on the juicy turkey breast. They all laughed as the turkey began its trip around the table.

Dan took big helpings from each dish and platter as it passed by: steaming mashed potatoes smothered with melted butter; rich brown gravy; creamy corn casserole; sweet potatoes laden with brown sugar and melted marshmallows; hot, melt-in-your-mouth Parkerhouse rolls; thick red cranberry sauce; all the wonderful salads; and, of course, thick slices of tender turkey. Carlee watched with a look of satisfaction as Dan consumed mountains of food. It'd been a long time since she'd cooked for a man, other than Father Bennett. Dan's enjoyment made it all worthwhile.

He took the final bite of a buttered roll, sipped the last of the coffee in his cup, leaned back in his chair, and smiled at his hostess. "Carlee, this is the best meal I've had in my entire life! How can I ever thank you?"

She returned his smile. "By helping me clear the table and load the dishwasher, that's how." Dan stood and began scraping and stacking the dishes, eager to do his part as an appreciative guest.

"Dan!" she pleaded as she rushed around the table and grabbed him by the arm, "I was kidding—stop! Go on into the family room with the children and read the paper—or take a nap. I'll clean up in here."

He caught her by the hand. "Mrs. Bennett, you've spent no-telling-how-many hours preparing this delicious meal for the children and me, and now you expect to clean up after us while I read the paper or take a nap? No way! I'm in this thing to the end. It's only fair. Let's get at it."

For seconds their eyes locked. It was nice to share the good and the bad with someone. He had no one, and she'd lost Robert. Certainly, on this day, they could help one another.

The two worked as a team, scraping, wiping, cleaning, putting away, and loading until the kitchen was immaculate. She untied Dan's apron, then turned her back to him so he could untie hers. He kissed her lightly on top of her head, nestling his face in her hair. This time, without hesitation, she responded to his touch, turning and wrapping her arms about his neck. He bent and kissed first one eyelid, then the other. His lips brushed both of her cheeks as she leaned into him. He wanted to hold her forever, to never let her go. What was happening to him?

They parted, and without a word, Dan took her hand and led her slowly into the family room where the children were playing quietly on the floor. He pulled her onto the couch beside him, enveloped her in his arms, and there they sat, full and satisfied. Thanksgiving had been a success. All but the dessert had been devoured, and it would come later.

"One more week," Dan said under his breath.

"What?"

He tightened his arm and pulled her closer to him. "One more week and I'll be gone."

She pursed her lips and frowned. "I know."

"I'll miss you—and the children."

"I hope so. We'll miss you."

He cupped her chin with his hand and lifted her face to his. "Carlee Bennett. You've been a confusing influence on my life—do you know that?"

Her eyes searched his. "What do you mean?"

"I thought I had life pretty well figured out. Then I came here and met you and your family. Now I don't understand life at all." His lips brushed her forehead lightly. "Somehow the life I'd worked so hard to achieve seems pretty empty now. I didn't realize how true that is until I went to Florida for the wedding."

She sat straight up and turned to face him directly. "But you're the star of Ice Fantasy! You're able to travel the world, see new places, meet new people. And probably draw a good salary to boot. How could our routine, little lives have you confused?" She spoke as though she were the one who was confused.

He pulled her back into the cradle of his arm and tightened his grip. "I can't explain it to myself, let alone someone else. I don't understand what's happened to me."

She lifted her face and met his eyes. "Is it because of your friend Brad? He's made you second-guess your life?"

He paused and traced her eyebrows with his fingertip. "May have something to do with it. I'm sure his marriage will be nothing like what you and Robert had. I want a love like that, Carlee. Like yours and Robert's."

A little voice broke into their conversation. "I want some pie!" Becca clamored as she climbed onto Dan's lap.

"Okay. Okay. Why don't I help your mother, and if we're good, maybe she'll let us bring it in here and we kids can eat it on the coffee table. What do you say to that, Mama?" he pleaded on behalf of an endearing little girl and her brother.

Carlee cocked her head and frowned as if considering the offer. "You kids drive a hard bargain." She extended her hand to Dan, who took it gratefully, and the two walked arm in arm into the kitchen where the dessert waited to be served. "Okay, but ya gotta watch the crumbs!"

Chapter 12

The family and Dan shared a wonderful, leisurely afternoon together. After a late supper of leftovers, followed by a bedtime story, Carlee put the children to bed while Dan read the newspaper. Then he devoured the last sliver of pumpkin pie. "Umm, that pie could've won a blue ribbon!" he mumbled as he rubbed his tummy and pushed back in the recliner.

"With or without the huge dollop of whipped cream you put on it?" Carlee teased as she watched him relax in the chair.

He linked his fingers behind his head and closed his eyes. "Secret recipe? One of Mother Bennett's?"

"Off the Libby's pumpkin can," she replied with a giggle.

He opened his eyes wide. "Are you serious?"

"Dead serious," she said with a twisted smile as she lifted his empty dish and fork from the end table. When she came back from the kitchen, she found him sleeping contentedly in the chair. She kissed him softly on the cheek and settled herself into the corner of the sofa with her book.

A half hour later Dan opened his eyes. He looked around and rubbed his eyes vigorously. "What time is it?"

"Eight thirty, sleepyhead. You've had quite a nap."

He rotated his shoulders. "Why didn't you wake me up?"

"You looked so cute, just like a little boy. I couldn't bring myself to disturb you."

"Tell me, did I drool?" he asked as he sat up straight and rubbed at the stubble on his chin.

"No. But you did snore a bit." She diverted her eyes and smothered her desire to laugh aloud.

He lowered the footrest on the chair, leaned forward, and looked embarrassed. "Did I really?"

She faked a frown. "Sounded like a grizzly bear."

He crossed the room to the sofa and lowered himself onto the cushion beside her, then slipped his arm around her shoulders. "You wouldn't kid me, would you?"

"Now, would I do that?" she asked with a coy smile.

He grinned, then stood and extended his hand and pulled her to her feet. "I've had a wonderful day with you and the kids. I can't thank you enough for inviting me. And to think you prepared all that delicious food yourself. Well,

I'm impressed, to say the least."

She looped her arms about his neck. "Dan, I wanted you to come spend the day with us. I love having you here. You've filled a void in my life—a big, empty hole left by Robert." Fearing she wasn't making herself clear, she looked into his dark eyes and continued, "Not in the same way, of course. I loved him deeply. I never expected to find that kind of love again. Oh, I've put on a good front. No one, not even the Bennetts, know how lonely I've been." She brushed a lock of hair from his forehead. "I wasn't looking for a husband, Dan. Does that make sense? Can you understand what I'm saying?"

He tilted her chin upward toward his. "Sure, I understand. I feel the same way. I was pretty lonely, too."

She leaned her head on his chest and rested it there, enjoying his scent and the strength of his masculinity.

His chin rested on her brow. "Then I met Carlee and her children. My life changed. You've opened your home and your hearts to me, and I've felt—well, important. At times, even needed. I like that feeling. It's going to be hard to leave you. I could get used to your way of life pretty easily."

Things were progressing far beyond their self-imposed limits. Dan would be leaving soon. They'd each vowed to themselves that they wouldn't get entangled like this. "You'd better be going. You've got practicing to do in the morning, remember?" she whispered. She didn't want him to leave, but it was getting late, and she could feel her resolve weakening. She'd have to let him go when his time was up in Kansas City. She might as well get used to it now. There was no future for them together. To think otherwise would be inviting heartbreak.

He dropped his arms and backed off slowly. "Umm. . .okay. You're right. See you in the morning. And don't forget: You are not—I repeat, not—to get out of your car if you get there before I do. Promise?"

She smiled. "I promise."

He watched as she pulled his jacket from the closet. She looked like a little girl in the calico pinafore, not the strong, independent woman he knew her to be, and he wanted to hold her. To protect her. The thought of her being trapped in the rink with the man he'd captured made his blood run cold. He couldn't let that happen again. But how could he prevent it? In a few days he'd be miles away.

She held his jacket as he slipped his arms into the sleeves, then walked him to the door, where Dan held her close and they said their good-byes.

He leaned against the storm door after it closed behind him. Getting involved with the young widow and her children would ruin the master plan he'd laid out for his life. And it would mean getting involved with God. He wasn't ready for that, or ready to give up his career. But. . .

When she pulled her minivan into the lot at 5:15 the next morning, Dan was sitting in his car waiting for her. He insisted that she stay in her locked van until he'd opened and checked out the building.

After their wake-up coffee, he moved onto the ice and skated the entire hour without stopping. "Good practice. Felt good to get my skates on again."

"Uh-huh." She pulled her collar up and shivered.

He wrapped his arms around her and held her close. "That better? I get so warm skating, I forget how cold it is in here for you. You're not taking cold, are you?"

"No. I'm fine, Dan. I could've gone into the lobby where it's a little warmer, but I like watching you. You're a wonderful skater. I'm sure I'm the envy of the Kansas City skating crowd, being an audience of one to watch the famous Dan Castleberry skate. Do you think I'd let a cold building stop me? I'm no pansy, you know."

The buzzer sounded, and she was off to open the door for the patchers and their mothers. Dan put his skates into the office and left, saying he'd phone later.

Carlee was able to finish her book work in record time and wandered into the rink area to watch the patchers. After the last ones had shut the door behind them, she checked her watch and discovered she had more than a half hour to kill before the employees would arrive and she'd have to open the door. On sudden impulse, she ran to her office and pulled her figure skates from the closet shelf. It'd been months since she'd skated—entirely too long. She needed the exercise.

She moved through the doors, slipped off the protective rockers, and glided smoothly onto the ice with long, even strokes. It felt good, relaxing. Before long, she was moving rapidly across the surface, turning first one way and then the other, whirling and twirling comfortably. As she rounded the end of the rink, she caught sight of a face peering through the lobby window. It was Dan! He'd been watching her skate. When she realized she'd spotted him, he stepped through the doors and walked onto the ice to join her. She knew she was in for it now—her secret was out.

"Carlee! Why didn't you tell me you were a skater?"

She giggled, embarrassed yet pleased at his reaction to her hidden talent. He took her hands in his and held them tightly. "Tomorrow morning, Carlee Bennett. *You* are going to skate with me. And I won't take no for an answer!"

"But—"

"But nothing! You did say you'd do whatever you could to help me, didn't you?"

She stood there, without excuse. "I. . .I guess I. . .said that."

"I needed to practice those pair numbers, but it's been close to impossible without a partner. Now I have one. You!"

"Dan! I couldn't!" she protested as she backed away. "Skate with Dan Castleberry, the star skater? Never!"

He pulled her close once again. "Oh yes, you will. I've been watching you for some time, Carlee. I know what you can do, and I'm counting on you to help me," he explained as he released her hands and moved off the ice. "Oh, and thanks for giving me a key to the building. I would have missed your performance if I hadn't had a key. Tomorrow, Carlee!"

Carlee didn't see Dan the rest of the day, but he called her that evening. "Whatcha been doing?" he asked.

Her spirits perked up at the sound of his voice, and she relaxed. For some reason, the kids had driven her up the wall all afternoon with their magpie chattering. "Just put the kids to bed and fixed myself a cup of cocoa."

"Umm. With marshmallows?"

"Uh-huh, marshmallows. The big ones. What have you been doing today?" she queried as she took a sip of the rich drink.

Dan shuffled the charts on his lap. "Been going over the diagrams of the pair numbers so you can help me with them in the morning. You're gonna skate with me, remember?"

That very thought had haunted her all day. "How could I forget? I've been trying to come up with some reason, short of breaking a leg, to turn you down. You've got to promise you won't laugh. Or ask too much of me," she cautioned as she spooned out a marshmallow and popped it into her mouth.

"Forget it! You're committed. I don't expect you to do any of the fancy stuff, I just need you to skate the basic fundamentals of the routine. I'll be gentle, I promise." He asked about Bobby and Becca, and Jim and Ethel, then brought the conversation around to the true purpose of his call. "Carlee, you told me Bobby would be out of school Monday afternoon because of a teachers' meeting. I heard of a pretty little lake not far from here, near Lawrence. I thought we could go on a picnic, just the four of us. What do you say?"

She pondered his question. "Sure, sounds fine to me. The kids'll be excited—they love picnics."

"Not half as excited as the guy who invited them," he confessed in a half whisper. "See you in the morning."

Her body was chilled to the bone as she sat in the rink clutching her figure skates. It wasn't the temperature that caused the chill—it was the thought of skating with the star skater.

Dan left the ice and walked toward her, his hands in his pockets. "Ready?" He knelt as he began to loosen the laces on one of her skate boots.

"Not really. I don't think I—"

"Hush and give me your foot," he said firmly.

"But. . .you don't have to. . . ," she protested as she slid her feet back under the chair's rung, away from his grasp.

He held out his hand, palm up. "Oh, but I want to, Mrs. Bennett. Remember, you're dealing with Prince Charming. Snow White allowed him to put the shoe on her foot."

"That was Cinderella, you goof!" she stated with a muffled giggle as she extended her foot.

"Oh, yeah?" Dan laughed aloud with an impish grin. "Wrong fairy tale! I've been a prince so many times, I sometimes get my heroines mixed up. Sorry!" He placed the blade of her skate on his knee and began to draw the laces up snugly about her foot and ankle.

Carlee sat silently and watched him work. She wondered why God had allowed this man into her life. She could so easily fall in love with him. His gentleness, his concern for her welfare, his attachment to her children—everything she could want in a man. Well, almost everything. Two major things separated them. *Oh, well,* she reminded herself. *Be grateful for small favors. Having Dan in our lives for three weeks was better than no Dan at all.*

"Lovely lady, may I have this dance?" He extended his hand with a winsome smile as he motioned toward the ice.

"Sure. I guess," she stammered with uncertainty as she took his hand and rose to feet that seemed brittle and clumsy beneath her.

They stepped in unison onto the ice. Dan bent his arm and tucked her fingers into the crook of his arm, and they moved off, side by side, with long, steady strokes. After several revolutions around the rink, she began to relax and enjoy it.

"I have a feeling you've waltzed on skates before, right?" Without waiting for an answer, he did a quick three-turn in front of her and looped his arm about her waist, and they moved into a dance position. "Get ready now. . . ," he directed. "One, two, three, and glide."

"The Blue Danube"—one of her favorites. She started to hum softly as she and Dan whirled in long, slow circles about the glossy surface. It felt wonderful, like she was floating. With his firm arms guiding her, all she had to do was follow his lead.

When the music ended, they stopped waltzing, but he continued to hold her fast, his arm about her waist, her hand in his. For a moment, she felt dizzy. Not from the twisting and turning, but from the emotions that whirled in her head and heart, and she cautioned herself, *Get with it, Carlee. With him, this is business. You're only a prop!*

Dan lowered his face and buried it in her hair. "Now, was that so bad?" he whispered as his lips brushed hers.

She leaned against him slowly, her forehead touching his freshly shaven chin. "No. Actually, it was pretty nice."

"Carlee. . .woman of a thousand surprises." He planted a lingering kiss on her temple before easing his hold on her. What was happening? Why was he drawn to this woman, this mother of two? He was Dan Castleberry, a man at the pinnacle of his profession, a world traveler. He could have any woman he wanted. Groupies flocked to him, literally throwing themselves at his feet. This whole Kansas City thing with the Bennetts didn't make any sense. They had become the center of his life since he'd arrived. He rarely even thought of his friends in Florida. He stepped away from her, as if to force a separation between the two of them, and rubbed his hands together briskly. "I'd say you're a natural skater. Are you sure you wouldn't like to give this all up and run away with me and join Ice Fantasy?" he joked as they headed toward the coffeepot, arm in arm.

"Yeah," she chided with a nudge of her elbow. "Think they'd want my kids, too? I could furnish my own dwarfs!"

"Carlee, thanks," he said sincerely as they walked through the double doors leading to the lobby. "Honest. You don't know how it's going to help to have you skate these numbers with me. I know you didn't really want to skate with me, and if you'd rather not continue, I'll understand."

A timid smile curled her lips as she looked into his face. "How could I refuse? Of course I'll do it. That is, unless you're only trying to make me feel good and really don't want me to skate with you." She tapped his chin with her fingertip. "I'm a big girl. I won't cry if you tell me my skating stinks!"

He swung around and grabbed her up in a big bear hug. "Carlee Bennett, I can't think of another woman on this planet I'd rather skate with than you."

She lifted her face and peeked over his arm. "Good. 'Cause right now, I'm your only choice."

He gave her another quick squeeze before turning her loose. "Settled. Case closed." His boyish smile suddenly turned into a frown. "I just remembered I promised my dad I'd play golf with him and a couple of his cronies today. At the speed they play, it'll take all day. I'd hoped to spend some time with the kids today. Since Bobby is out of school, I'd planned to help him with his skating."

She patted his cheek. "I'm disappointed, too. Becca and Bobby had expected to see you today."

A hint of a smile began to form on his face. "You could invite me over for supper. They'll be done playing golf by then—unless they play by flashlight!"

"I might be persuaded to round up a pot of chili," she volunteered as she smoothed out a fold in his shirt collar.

His eyes penetrated hers. Having someone concerned about something as insignificant as a wrinkle was a new experience for him. And he found he liked it. No, he reveled in it. "I'd be mighty grateful, little lady. I've had a hankerin' for chili ever since I came in off the trail. And so has my horse!"

"Surely not John Wayne!" His impression lacked authenticity, but she appeared to be amused by it anyway; and she laughed, something she did often since Dan had first come to her door that cold morning.

"Nope! Clint Eastwood!" he cajoled as he lifted one eyebrow and cocked his head. "Couldn't you tell?"

Dan arrived promptly at 6:00 p.m. Two scrubbed and combed children tussled all the way to the door to see who would get there first to open it for him.

"Dan! Dan!" little Becca screamed in her high-pitched baby voice as Dan scooped her up and hugged her to his chest.

Bobby wrapped his skinny arms about Dan's waist and held on tight. "Hi, Dan," the boy said as he ducked back and forth, trying to avoid his sister's swinging feet.

Dan reached down with his free arm and wrapped it around Bobby, pulling the youngster against him. "Hi, Bobby. I've missed you!"

The little boy seemed to melt into Dan's body as he pressed close to the man, his arms entwined with the skater's legs.

The familiar lump rose in Carlee's throat. Just one week and it'd all be over. "Hi, Dan," she said softly, not wanting to take anything away from her children's welcome.

He stood there looking at her as if he wanted to lock this moment in his memory. "Hi, Carlee. Thanks for letting me come," he said almost sadly.

She wondered if he was thinking the same thing she was, if he was counting down the days. Could this time they'd had together possibly mean as much to him as it did to her, or was it merely a diversion for him—something he could laugh about with the other skaters when he joined them in Florida?

After a half hour of roughhousing on the family room floor, they all gathered around the kitchen table.

"I'll pray," Becca offered as she clapped her hands.

"No, me!" Bobby volunteered as he smiled at Dan.

Dan grinned mischievously. "No! Let me!"

All eyes turned his direction.

"Hearing you three pray reminded me of a prayer my grandmother taught me when I was little. I'd nearly forgotten it. But I think I can say it." He looked directly at his hostess for permission. "May I?"

She nodded, bowed her head, and folded her hands.

Nervously he began. "God is great, and God is good. Let us thank Him for this food. By His hand. . ." He paused as if he'd forgotten the next words.

Becca peeked at Dan with one open eye and filled in, "We are fed!" then closed it again quickly.

"We are fed," he repeated with a muffled laugh. "Give us, Lord, our daily bread." He raised his head proudly, as if he expected them to clap.

Something in Carlee's heart, a still small voice, seemed to say, *Don't give up. There's hope.*

The young couple sat gazing quietly into the fire after the children had been tucked into their beds. It seemed they no longer felt the need to talk to enjoy one another's company. It was enough to sit side by side, his arm about her shoulders and just be together.

"I've had a great evening. I love chili and the kids, but I've got to git."

"Chili and the kids? Sounds like a rock group when you say it that way." She grinned and snuggled her head onto his shoulder, savoring the moment. "Do you have to go?"

He stroked her hair, then stood. "We both have to get up early."

Carlee jumped up beside him, threw both arms about his waist, and squeezed tightly. He lowered his arms and thrust them about her shoulders. There they stood, motionless, embracing one another, neither understanding exactly why. They just wanted to do it. It felt right.

Dan cradled her chin with one hand while the other continued to hold her close, then lifted her face toward his. As if instructed by some unseen director, their faces moved slowly toward each other until their lips met, drawn by an invisible magnetism. But only for a moment. They separated quickly, as if they'd been taking something not theirs to take. Something forbidden.

"Oh, Dan." Carlee covered her face with her hands as she spoke. "We shouldn't be doing this. I'm too old to have a three-week fling. And I have children to consider. . . ."

He moved toward her, but she backed away.

"Maybe it'd be better if Father Bennett and I switched times until you leave. I can't bear to see you every day—to be so close to you. It's tearing my heart out."

"Carlee, we have so little time to be together. It's hard for me, too. I don't have any magical answers—I just know I want to be with you every moment I can. Please don't throw away what little time we have left; it's too precious!"

He took one more step toward her, and she nearly leaped into his arms. For an awkward moment they stood there, holding one another, their bodies pressed together in a warm embrace.

"Carlee," he whispered softly into her hair, "if you tell me to go, I'll leave Kansas City tomorrow and you'll never see me again. I don't want to hurt you."

"I–I know. . . ," she murmured weakly, all resistance gone.

He smiled that endearing smile that tore at her heart and caused her knees to go weak. "Last chance. What'll it be?"

"Oh, Dan—stay!"

His lips grazed her forehead, then lightly touched each eyelid, then the tip of her nose.

Her heart pounded wildly as his mouth sought hers and found it. How many times had she dreamed of this moment? Longed for it? Willed it to happen?

"Oh, Dan," she breathed in surrender. Never had a kiss been so sweet. It was more than she'd ever dreamed it would be, even if it had to last a lifetime after he was gone.

He held Carlee's hand as they walked slowly to the door. She bent slightly, and he kissed her on the top of her head as if she were Becca, then again drew her to him and kissed her tenderly with a kiss that brought out long-forgotten feelings of desire she'd thought had been extinguished forever.

She touched his lips with her fingertips and smiled with her eyes. "You will be skating tomorrow morning, won't you?"

"I'd rather go to church with you, if you'll let me tag along." His hands slowly stroked her spine.

Standing on tiptoes, she slipped one arm about his neck, and with an adoring smile, she kissed his cheek. "Good night, Dan. See you here at 10:15. And don't be late."

One final squeeze and he backed toward the door and closed it quietly behind him.

Carlee stared at the door. Dan was going to church with her, and it was his own idea. Praise the Lord!

Chapter 13

D an Castleberry caught an early morning glimpse of himself in the rearview mirror and smoothed his hair with his hand. Who would have thought he'd be attending church while in Kansas City? Twice, no less! And that he'd invite himself? He shook his head as he made a left-hand turn onto her street, then smiled, remembering the kisses he and Carlee had shared the night before. Deep in thought, he nearly missed Carlee's driveway. There she was in the open doorway, looking even more beautiful than she had the day before.

"Hi," she called out as she pulled the door shut behind her and tested the lock. "What a beautiful Lord's Day!"

Dan leaped out of his car, jumped the hedge, and met her at the foot of the steps. "Yeah, great, isn't it? By the way, you look terrific in red—you should wear it more often."

Her face flushed as she adjusted the shoulder strap of her bag. "Thank you. Somehow I felt like red this morning." She flipped the tip of his red paisley tie with her fingertips. "Looks like you did, too."

They laughed and talked and held hands all the way to the church. He in his red silk tie, she in her red wool suit. Becca and Bobby attacked Dan as the couple entered the lobby, and as the children expected, he swooped them both up in his strong arms and carried them into the sanctuary.

Carlee slid into the pew first, then Dan. He lowered Bobby down next to him. She tried to pull Becca from Dan's arms, but the little girl clung to his neck fiercely. "You promised I could sit next to Dan," she said in that loud, shrill baby voice of hers. People around them peeked over their hymnals and stared in amusement.

At the end of the service, church members shook hands with Dan and greeted him by name, as if he were a part of them. Jim caught his arm and pulled him to one side while Carlee visited with a group of women. "Hear you're going to the lake tomorrow. Good idea, son! You guys enjoy the day!" He gave Dan a hearty handshake and disappeared to find Ethel.

The Bennetts had been invited to a friend's house for the day, so Dan, Carlee, Bobby, and Becca went out for Mexican food. Then, after delivering them to their doorstep, Dan went on to his parents' house for the last Sunday he'd spend with them for a long time.

❧

Monday's weather promised to be as glorious as Sunday morning's had been. It was still dark when Dan and Carlee arrived at the Ice Palace, but the air had lost its nip and was perfectly still. The two walked arm in arm to the door as Dan related his day with his parents. Once inside the rink, he caught hold of her waist and spun her around. "Why don't we do it differently today? You know—break the routine."

She had no idea what he meant and raised her eyebrows questioningly.

"I'll make the coffee; you get the skates!" He placed his big hands on her shoulders. She backed off and grinned. "Sure. I'm game if you are." Then, gesturing toward the snack bar and the waiting coffeepot, she added, "Have at it."

The coffee was awful, but she drank it anyway. He took one sip, gagged, turned, and spat it on the ice.

"That's terrible!" he shouted as he grabbed the cup from her hand. "Don't drink that stuff—you might get sick and miss our picnic." His hands waved in the air in frustration. "How hard can it be to make coffee? What did I do wrong?"

Carlee pressed her lips together, determined not to make fun of his efforts. "Maybe it was the water. Hmm. Looks like you did everything right except for one thing." She lifted the plastic basket from the coffeemaker.

He looked puzzled. "What?"

In her hand she held a ruffled, circular piece of white paper. "You forgot to put the filter in."

The practice session went well as the two waltzed gracefully around the ice. Dan was pleased with his progress.

Ethel greeted them at the door when they went by to pick up the children. "If you'd been a minute longer, I would have had to tie them up," she said as she pointed to her grandchildren doing somersaults in the hallway at Dan's feet. "They were up at six and have been bouncing off the walls ever since. You'd think they'd never been on a picnic."

Dan pounced on the two wiggle worms, clutching one in each arm and holding them tight. They squealed with delight.

"Ready to head to the lake when you are," Carlee called out cheerfully as she headed for the front door, leaving Dan with two rambunctious wigglers in his arms.

"Hey, wait! Don't leave me with these squirmers," he pleaded as he hurried through the hall, carrying his precious cargo.

Dan was so good with the children that Carlee found it difficult to believe he hadn't been around kids all his life. According to him, he'd never even held a child before, yet he did it so naturally. And the kids loved him.

She scooted into the seat next to Dan, fastened her seat belt, and eyed the man behind the steering wheel. She was already hopelessly in love with him. As she touched her lips, she remembered the kisses they'd shared the night before—the kisses she'd longed for since that first day he'd invaded her life. If only Dan's career didn't keep him on the road fifty weeks a year. If only he'd allow God to take charge of his life. If, if, if. Too many ifs. They had the here and now, but there was no future for them. She knew it, and she was sure Dan must feel it, too.

"What?" Dan asked when he caught her studying him.

She lifted one finger to her lips. "Shh! They're asleep. Enjoy the silence while you can." She stretched her arms and gave way to an exaggerated yawn.

"Early morning skating getting you down?"

She wiggled her shoulders as she rotated her head in small circles. "Not the early part. I hate to admit it, but my muscles are sore. You're making me use muscles I haven't used for a long time."

He moved his hand to her neck and began to massage it with his strong but gentle fingers. "Too rough?"

"Ohh. That feels so good. Be careful, or I'll start purring. Mmm." She dropped her chin to her chest and enjoyed the firm kneading of her sore neck and shoulders. "Don't wear your hands out. You may have to continue this later," she cautioned as she cradled her hand over his and pulled it into her lap. His fingers entwined hers and stayed there. For several moments neither spoke nor looked at the other.

It was Carlee who finally broke the silence. "Dan," she said slowly and deliberately, as though something were weighing heavily on her mind. "I know this is probably all fun and games to you. . ."

He gave her hand an affectionate squeeze.

"What I'm trying to say, Dan, is that the children and I have loved having you here in Kansas City, spending time in our home. I know you'll probably forget all about us once you get back to the show—"

"And?" He shot a questioning glance her way, then turned his attention back to the road.

"Ohh," she moaned, disgusted with her inability to express her feelings. "I don't know what I mean. I've been confused since the first day I met you." She tried to pull her hand away, but he wouldn't let her, tightening his grip.

"Look, Carlee, I'll be honest with you. I selected Kansas City for one reason—to spend time with my folks. Fortunately, the Ice Palace afforded me the opportunity to do that and practice my skating at the same time. I never expected to meet you. Or your family. You came as a total surprise—a nice one!" He tapped the button on the cruise control and leaned back. "I've felt quite intimidated by you."

"By me?" How could he be intimidated by her?

"Yes. By you. I've never met anyone as—well, the only way I can think to put it is—pure. Yes, that's it. The word *saint* comes to mind when I think of Carlee Bennett."

She gasped. "Me? Pure? A saint? Hardly, Dan!"

He grinned nervously. "Don't interrupt me, please."

"But—"

"Like I was saying, I felt intimidated. I've never dated a girl like you. Oh, I don't mean married with children. I mean someone with your morals and high standards. I have to confess, I wish I'd known years ago what I know now."

"But, Dan. Don't you understand? It isn't morals and high standards. It's God! I don't have a list of dos and don'ts. I didn't stay a virgin because I had set a high standard for myself, or wanted to be Miss Goody Two-shoes, whatever that means. I stayed a virgin because I knew God wanted me to, and I knew He'd help me resist temptation. Don't get the idea that Robert and I were never tempted, because we were. Constantly!"

Her voice dropped suddenly. What was she saying? She'd never told anyone about the temptations they'd faced when she and Robert were dating, not even her best friend. Yet, here she was, spilling her guts to a man she'd probably never hear from once he left Kansas City.

Dan let go of her hand, put his arm about her shoulders, and drew her close to his side.

She wanted to be near him, to feel his body next to hers. If only she could make him understand. "Dan, I don't know why I told you about Robert and me. I'm sorry. I should never have brought it up."

He pressed his lips to the top of her head, then concentrated on the road again. "Carlee, let me say something I've been wanting to get off my chest. I decided when I was a young teen that I was going to have a career as a professional skater. You know about my goals—I spent all my free time at the local rink, skating and honing my craft. I decided early on that girls could only get in my way.

"When I was in the ninth grade, one of the guys in my class got a girl pregnant. They ended up getting married four months later when they were fifteen. That scared me so bad I avoided girls like chicken pox. But the first year I was with the show, when I was nineteen, I dated the daughter of the show's owner. We got pretty serious—I guess mainly because I was in awe of her father. Well, one thing led to another, and you can guess what happened. She told me she was pregnant. That really shook me up! I could see my whole career going down the tubes. I hated myself for my weakness and what I'd done to her. Then she called me and said she'd lied—she wasn't pregnant after all. Well, let me tell you, I ended things real fast! We broke up, and I know you probably won't believe this, but she was the first and last girl I. . ."

She felt a great sense of relief wash through her; for some reason she'd always assumed he was a man of the world with many conquests, but there had been only one.

Dan sighed, gave her shoulders a quick rub, and continued, "I've never been intimate with a girl since. Honest! I hope you'll believe me; it's important that you do."

She lifted her face to his and looked into the eyes of the man she'd come to know so well in such a short time. "I do believe you, Dan," she said earnestly as tears welled up in her eyes and trickled down her cheeks. "And I'm glad you told me." She straightened and kissed his cheek tenderly.

They rode along in silence. She could forgive Dan for his improper behavior with his teenage girlfriend. And God would forgive him, too. But first Dan had to realize he was a sinner and needed God's forgiveness. But was he ready to do that?

Chapter 14

Becca woke up and began chattering about the cows and horses grazing in the fields. Dan and Carlee sat quietly in the front seat, holding hands just out of sight of the children.

"Okay, troops," Dan said, "the lake is around the next curve in the road. We're almost there."

Suddenly there it was—a huge, beautiful lake, sparkling in the afternoon sun like a million diamonds. He turned off the highway onto a gravel road, then pulled up next to a concrete picnic table and stopped. Without a word, he opened the trunk and removed a stack of raggedy old quilts and a picnic basket. Two giggling children dropped onto the nearest quilt when he spread it out on the ground. Dan snapped a second quilt high into the air and lowered it like an open parachute. Carlee leaned against the car and watched, spellbound. "You think of everything. Wherever did you get such wonderful old quilts?"

He lowered himself onto a quilt and motioned for her to join him. "Borrowed them from Mrs. Sweeney," he answered with a chuckle as he began pulling food from the picnic basket.

After a satisfying lunch, the young couple settled onto one of the quilts while the children explored the shoreline and tossed rocks into the water.

Dan pulled the remaining quilt around the two of them, and there they sat in the center of the fraying red and blue Ohio Star quilt, covered snugly, with Carlee enfolded in Dan's arms. Two boats lazily crossed the big lake, dragging sagging fishing lines behind them, as the young couple watched. Three white egrets stood in the water, close to the shore, like statues. The two watched as the pristine birds moved forward cautiously, first on one foot, then the other, effortlessly, gracefully, barely breaking the water's surface.

"Look," Dan whispered as he hugged her close. "There. . .by the tree. Two little brown rabbits." Dan and Carlee sat so still, the rabbits wandered unbelievably close before they spotted the two humans and bounced away.

Carlee nestled her head under his chin. "Oh, Dan. This is the stuff real life is made of. God created all of this for our pleasure." Overhead, hawks circled, lazily gliding heavenward on unseen winds, while two children chased one another along the ragged shoreline.

"Carlee, what we were talking about earlier—I'd like to talk about it some more."

She nodded her head.

"Knowing you has caused some real problems in my life. I've. . ." He stopped.

She could feel her heart thundering in her chest and was sure he could feel it, too.

"I've—fallen in love with you."

Her heart did a flip-flop this time. That was the last thing she expected to hear him say. She felt breathless, unable to speak. All she could do was lift her head to face him in awe.

He pulled several pieces of dried grass from her hair. "I have, Carlee—deeply in love. I love you. I love the kids. I've finally admitted it to myself, but I don't know what to do about it. I can't give up my skating career; it means too much to me. I've worked too hard to achieve what I've got."

A heron swooped and soared overhead, but neither noticed. Carlee wanted to respond, to say something, anything, but the words wouldn't come. All she could do was pray.

"And I can't ask you to follow me from city to city; that would be impossible with the children. I would never do that to them, or to you. Even if you home-schooled on the road, it would be too hard for them to pick up and move every few days, or weeks at most."

Her heart burst with love, yet ached with grief. What could she say?

"And I realize that isn't our only problem. Your God is important to you. Your life is based on your being a Christian. I'm not even sure what that is."

She flung her arms about his neck and buried her head in his chest. She knew if she tried to speak, to tell him of her feelings and misgivings, she'd cry. She loved him so much. More than she'd realized. And like him, she'd been fighting her feelings and trying to deny them. This was the most open he'd been about the lack of a relationship with God.

He lifted her face to his and searched misty eyes. "Carlee! Say something. I need to know what you're feeling."

"Oh, Dan! I love you, too. My heart is so full of love for you, I think it will burst. Hearing your words, knowing that you love me, too, makes me so happy!" She gulped and wiped at her eyes with the back of her hand. "I've been thinking about the same things you have. Only I thought it was all a selfish dream. I had no idea you could love me. I fantasized about your love but never dared hope my dreams could come true."

He pulled her trembling body close to his own and smothered her eager, receptive mouth with sweet, tender kisses. She wound her arms around his neck and responded eagerly, returning each glorious kiss, her love for him taking command of the moment. If only the precious afternoon could last forever. A deep sigh made its way to the surface and erupted as fantasy was displaced by reality. "Oh, Dan! What are we going to do? Is there any hope for us?"

He pulled away from her and scanned her face as he pushed strands of hair, damp from her tears, off her lovely face. His own troubled countenance said it all—he had no answers. Their lives seemed to run on parallel tracks, side by side, but never coming together. "I don't know, Carlee. I just don't know," he confessed. "I only know I love you and want to spend my life with you. But how?"

They sat, locked in one another's arms, savoring every moment of their time together—time that was rushing past them rapidly. Five more days and it would be over.

"Why are you crying, Mama?" Becca asked as she climbed onto the quilt. "Did you hurt yourself?"

Dan wiped Carlee's tears away with his fingertips. "Mama's okay, Becca," he said as he pulled the little girl onto his lap. "Don't worry, honey. Dan's gonna take care of your mother." He gave Carlee's shoulders a squeeze. "He just doesn't know how."

He folded the quilts and loaded them and the picnic basket into the trunk while Carlee helped the children into the car and fastened their seat belts. He clung to Carlee's hand as they drove back to Kansas City, as if he were afraid he'd lose her forever if he loosened his grip.

She smiled and leaned close to him. "I love you, Dan," she whispered softly in his ear as he drove.

"I love you, Carlee," he mouthed silently as he kept his eyes on the road.

The children chattered all the way home, but Carlee and Dan scarcely heard a word the children said as they continued to sit silently in the front seat, holding hands, conscious of the few fleeting days they had left.

※

Dan Castleberry stood quietly by Becca's bed, staring at the little girl's sleeping face—so sweet and peaceful, so innocent—and wondered what it would be like to hear her call him Daddy. He'd never thought of himself as daddy material. But now, standing by Becca, he longed to hear those words from her tiny pink lips. He turned to see Carlee leaning against the doorway. "You have a beautiful daughter, Mrs. Bennett," he whispered as he slipped his arm about her waist and led her from the room.

As they passed Bobby's room, Dan leaned inside for a final peek at the boy. It was time for him to leave, but he couldn't separate himself from this family and the pleasure he'd experienced just being with them. Despite the joy they'd shared, he felt a sense of despair, a finality, hanging like a black cloud over them.

※

Carlee found it next to impossible to sleep. Dan's words kept filtering through her mind. *I love you, Carlee. I love you, Carlee.* They echoed over and over again, words she'd longed for but never expected to hear. When she would drift off to sleep, she would dream the words, hearing Dan's voice somewhere in the distance. *I love you, Carlee.* But each time she ran toward him, he would retreat, then begin calling to her once again. She'd run, but fall to the ground breathless, never quite able to reach him.

❧

Dan Castleberry twisted and turned in his bed, pulling the covers about his shoulders one minute and casting them off the next. Sleep eluded him as thoughts of Carlee filled his weary mind. His life had been so simple, so structured before he'd come to Kansas City. Now confusion reigned. He'd been secure in what he wanted and expected out of life. A wife and ready-made family had never been part of that picture. Yet now, that was exactly what he wanted. The only trouble was, he wanted his skating career, too.

❧

The two arrived at the rink at the same time Tuesday morning. They stood in the parking lot in the cool early morning air and embraced. Dan lifted Carlee's face to his and kissed her cheeks, her eyelids, her neck, then her lips—the perfect way for lovers to start the day.

Their skating was even more in sync than it had been the day before, and Carlee was glad she was able to please Dan with her skating ability. She held up her head proudly as they twirled and dipped across the ice to the music, his arm encircling her waist. When the hour was up, Dan slipped the protective rockers onto their skates, took her hand, and led her silently across the lobby to a chair. Unspoken words passed between them as they gazed into one another's eyes. Dan stooped and lifted Carlee's foot onto his knee and began unlacing the boot of her skate.

"You don't have to do that," she said with a slight frown as she tried to withdraw it from his grasp.

He clung fast to the leather boot and lifted sad eyes to meet hers. "I want to, Carlee. I want to do everything I can for you—our time is so short." He lowered his eyes and continued to remove her skates, then slipped her tennies onto her stockinged feet.

She watched this man kneeling before her, her Prince Charming. He would always be that to her, even if she never saw him again once this week was over. She leaned toward him, placed her arms about his neck, and planted a kiss in his dark locks. "I know, Dan. I know."

Dan's parents had requested that he spend the rest of the day with them. He phoned her late that evening, and after they'd talked about the day's happenings, Dan repeated the words he'd spoken on the picnic trip. "I love you, Carlee."

She took a deep breath and leaned into the plumped pillows she'd propped against the headboard of her bed. "I love you, Dan. I never thought I'd say those words—after Robert. But I mean them with my whole heart. I love you."

With a long, slow sigh, he stretched out across his bed and gazed at the ceiling. "What are we going to do about it?"

❧

Dan drummed his fingers on the dashboard of his car Wednesday morning.

He'd hoped Carlee would arrive early, too. He had to see her—had to spend every waking moment with her. How had he let himself get into this predicament? He'd fallen in love so fast he hadn't seen it coming—it just happened. He was hopelessly, totally in love.

Carlee drove down Clark Street. She considered how the past two days had changed her life. Dan Castleberry had proclaimed his love for her, and for the first time she'd admitted, not only to Dan but to herself, that she was in love with him. Despite the dilemma their love caused, it was a joy to have their feelings out in the open. But could she compromise her convictions? Dan was one of the finest men she'd ever known, but he'd made it clear he wasn't interested in letting God rule his life. Even if they could find a way to be together, dare she marry a man who didn't love her Lord the way she did? Maybe in time he would accept God on God's terms, but could she count on it? Hadn't the scriptures warned against that? True, Dan's career seemed an insurmountable obstacle, but so was his lack of a relationship with God. How many women had married men expecting them to change and found that they didn't? Too many, for sure. What about the influence of such a man on her children? A man without the same convictions about rearing children in the church?

No, as much as she loved Dan, she could never compromise; her children were too important. God had seen fit to make her both mother and father to them. He had entrusted them to her. She would not fail God. But why worry about it? With Dan's career in their way anyway, she'd never have to face that problem. She'd relish each minute she could spend with him now, and when Dan left Kansas City, things would come to an end and all she'd have left would be the wonderful memories. Precious memories of the times they'd spent together. She should probably end things now, before any more emotional damage was done. But she couldn't! She loved him too much. She had to be with him as long as she could. "Oh, God. . . make me strong!"

As she watched him skate, she tried to envision the number he would skate in the new show. Perhaps he'd wear a long cape over his broad shoulders. It would spread out like wings as he moved like silent wind across the ice, thrilling appreciative audiences with his skillfully executed jumps and spins. Maybe there would be fog whirling about his feet, as there had been in *Snow White*.

She thought of Valerie Burns and was filled with envy. It would be Valerie who would be held in Dan's arms, who would feel his closeness. No doubt there would be places in the program that called for the Beast to kiss Belle, and Valerie would be smothered with his kisses instead of her. She shivered at the thought.

"Cold?" he asked as he stepped off the ice.

She blushed guiltily. "No, just thinking."

He eyed her suspiciously, then pulled her to her feet and wrapped his arms about her. "About what? What would make you shiver like that?"

She clung tightly, basking in the protective strength that emanated from him, savoring the moment, a moment she'd cherish long after he was gone. "It's not important."

The young couple spent the day together. Mother Bennett had offered to watch the children till bedtime. Dan helped with the book work, then the morning session. They worked well together, like a well-oiled machine. The time went quickly.

Lunchtime found them at a nearby McDonald's, sharing French fries and sipping chocolate shakes like two infatuated teenagers. Dan watched as Carlee methodically dipped the tip of each fry in catsup before popping it into her mouth. Carlee smiled as Dan doused his fries with salt. Just being together made their meal as special as the most elaborate banquet. He wiped a dot of catsup from her chin with his napkin as she grinned at her hero.

After lunch they headed for the Plaza to select a gift for Mrs. Castleberry's birthday. Dan wanted to get something really special for his mom. It had been five years since he'd been home to celebrate the occasion with her.

"What should I get?" he asked as he pulled into the parking lot. "I end up wiring flowers every year, mostly because I'm on the road and it's the easiest thing to do. I don't want to do that same old thing, since I'm here in Kansas City. Any suggestions?"

Carlee looked thoughtful. "Does she like beautiful linens? You know, like tablecloths and napkins?"

A puzzled look revealed how little Dan knew about his mother.

"How about perfumes? No," she said, shaking her head, "that's too personal a choice when you don't know what a woman likes. Let's see. . ." She touched her fingers to her chin and stared off into space. "Jewelry? Dresser set? Handbag?"

He shoved his hands into his pockets. "Don't know. It's hard to choose something she'd like. She's pretty picky."

Carlee was glad he wanted this gift to be special. She felt she could tell a lot about a man by the way he treated his mother. Whatever his gift would be, it had to be just right. But what? Her face brightened.

"Dan! Do you have a good photo of yourself? Maybe skating and wearing one of your costumes?"

He studied her face. "Why?"

"Just answer. Do you?"

"Sure. Publicity shots. All skaters have those."

"A recent one? From here in Kansas City?"

He had no idea what she was leading up to. "Yes, in my briefcase. I have several four-by-five shots."

"Then I think I've got it!" she said, her eyes twinkling with excitement. "We'll take one to a photo-processing place and get it blown up to poster size and have it framed for her. She'd love it. Any mother would. What do you think?"

"Do you really think she'd like it? A picture of me?"

"Yes, Dan. I do."

He grinned, delighted with the idea. "Let's do it!"

They drove to his parents' house on Ward Parkway, just minutes from the Plaza. As usual, they were out. Carlee stood on the expansive porch of the grand, ivy-covered brick mansion as Dan fumbled for his key. "Dan, I've admired these lovely homes on Ward Parkway as long as I've lived in Kansas City. I never expected to know anyone who actually lived in one."

"They don't! Live, I mean. They exist here. You live in a *home*. They exist in a house."

He led her into the magnificent foyer with its marbled floors and gilded mirrors. She stared at her reflection, smoothing her hair and straightening the lapels on her jacket.

Dan moved up behind her, slipped his arm around her waist, and peered over her shoulder. "Mirror, mirror, on the wall. Who is the fairest of them all?"

The beginning of a smile turned up the corners of her mouth. "I bite. Who? Valerie Burns?"

"You, my love. Don't move a hair—you look beautiful just the way you are." He rubbed his chin against her neck.

"I know what you're thinking, Carlee. But you're wrong. I hated this place, still do. It was like living in a museum. No place to raise a boy. Bobby doesn't know how lucky he is. I'd have much preferred his life to mine. His mother puts her children first. I got leftovers from my mother's life. She just couldn't fit me in on her calendar." Dan pulled the photo from the briefcase and reluctantly handed it to Carlee. "Are you sure this is a good idea? What if she thinks it's a joke?"

She grabbed the picture from his hand and gazed at the handsome image staring back at her. "It's perfect."

They located the photo-processing center and left the photo for enlarging and framing.

"One jumbo fresh cherry limeade," Dan barked into the microphone when they stopped at a drive-in restaurant on the way back to Carlee's house. "With two straws, please."

They held the big container between the two of them and sipped as fifties music boomed from speakers hanging under the metal canopy. When the last drop was gone, Dan removed the plastic lid, retrieved the long-stemmed maraschino cherry, and offered it to Carlee. She grinned, then bit it from the stem.

He scrunched down in the seat and rested his head on the seat back. "It's Wednesday, Carlee."

She scooted close to him, her head against his shoulder. "I know," she said softly, her voice filled with emotion.

The jukebox was playing a love song. "Please release me, let me go," the crooner sang. Dan hummed along as they listened to the words. "You're going to have to, you know," he murmured as his fingers tightened around hers. "I'm your captive."

She pressed against him. "It's the other way around. You're going to have to release me. You're the strong one. You'll have to walk away from me, Dan. I may not have the strength to let you go."

For minutes they sat silently, oblivious to the cars parked on either side of them. Time was rapidly ticking away.

❧

Dan had driven Carlee to the grocery store to pick up bread and lettuce for Bobby's school lunch box. He watched now as she moved from the pantry to the refrigerator, putting things away.

"Water?" she asked as she took glasses from the cupboard.

He nodded, then watched as she filled them with ice and wondered what it would be like to share a home with her, to wake up to her each morning and help her with the dishes, buy groceries, do married-folk stuff. She was so. . .*comfortable*. Yes, that was the word for it. No pretenses. He was that way, too—when he was around her. So much of his life was lived on stage, performing in a role before an audience. People didn't know the real man or care who he was; they just wanted to be entertained. But Carlee was different. He knew she respected his talent as a skater, but he didn't have to be onstage with her. He could be Dan Castleberry, the man. And when he was with her, he felt like a man. She brought out his best, and he liked that.

"Dan? Ho, Dan! Where are you?" Her hand passed in front of his eyes, bringing him back to reality.

He grabbed her wrist, pulled it to his face, and kissed her palm affectionately. "I was thinking about you. About us."

For supper, they phoned for pizza. Afterward, Dan cleared away the mess and took it to the kitchen. Carlee was kneeling before the blazing fireplace, deep in thought, when he returned. He knelt behind her and used his strong fingers to manipulate her shoulders, kneading the muscles gently with his thumbs. "Tight," he murmured into her ear. "Relax."

"Umm. Wonderful," she purred. "Don't ever stop."

His hands moved smoothly from her shoulders to her back. "I don't want to stop. I love touching you."

"Oh, Dan. Why did we ever let things go this far? We both knew we were doomed from the beginning."

The room filled with silence, except for the crackling of the fire and the pounding of two hearts. Dan cradled Carlee in his arms and held her there as they stared into the flames and envisioned their dreams going up in smoke. Their love was at a standstill. It had nowhere to go. In three days, it would be nothing but a memory.

Chapter 15

Dan picked up Carlee at 5:00 a.m. Thursday. After their skating session, he swept the snack bar floor, did a few repairs around the rink that Jim hadn't had time to do, and sharpened four pair of skates for customers as they waited. It was nearly noon before he and Carlee's paths crossed again.

"Father Bennett'll be surprised when he sees all the things you've done around here," she said proudly, as she locked the door behind them. "It's a pretty big job for one man, running a rink like this. Are you sure you can't stick around? I'll bet he'd hire you as his right-hand man."

"Don't tempt me," he warned as he opened the car door and motioned her in. "I'm so crazy about you, if he asked me right now, I'd probably take him up on it."

With a melancholy look, she slid to the center of the front seat. "Oh, Dan, don't talk like that; your career is important to you. As much as I love you and want to be with you, I'm sure you'd always resent giving it all up."

They waited at the Castleberry house for nearly two hours before his mother arrived home. They'd propped up the poster-sized photo of Dan on the grand piano, and Carlee was admiring it when they heard the front door open and Dan's mother step inside.

"Happy Birthday, Mother!" Dan sang out cheerfully.

She reared back. "Daniel. You know I hate birthdays."

He pushed Carlee forward. "Mother, this is Carlee Bennett. She and her in-laws own the rink where I've been practicing my new routines. We've become—friends."

Mrs. Castleberry was so engrossed in removing her gloves, she paid little attention to the introduction.

"It's nice to meet you, Mrs. Castleberry. Dan was so pleased he'd be here in Kansas City for your birthday."

The elder woman smoothed her French twist as she lowered herself into a white brocade chair. "Oh yes. When is it you are leaving, Daniel? I've forgotten."

Carlee nudged his elbow and whispered, "The photo, Dan."

Dan lifted the photo from the piano and held it before his mother, beaming at his gift. "For you, Mother. Happy Birthday. I hope you like it."

The older woman sat staring at the handsome likeness of her son. "Daniel, whatever will I do with that huge thing?"

He looked devastated. Her words cut deeply into Dan's heart. He had so hoped to make her birthday special. He stood before her, disappointment etched on his face. "I'm sorry, Mother. Next time I'll wire flowers. If you don't like them, I won't know it, because I won't be here."

"Now, Daniel, you needn't be smart with me. You don't want to embarrass yourself in front of your little friend."

He tossed the frame onto the floor, grasped Carlee by the hand, and pulled her toward the front door. "Good-bye, Mother. Happy Birthday," he said coolly as he slammed the door behind him and they left the Castleberry mansion. Once outside, Dan pulled Carlee into his arms and held her so tightly she had to struggle for breath.

"Oh, Dan. It was all my fault. I'm the one who encouraged you to give her that picture. I can't bear to see you hurt like this. I am so sorry!" She wrapped her arms around him and stroked his cheek with her fingers.

"No, Carlee. I'm the one who's sorry. Sorry you had to be a part of that fiasco. I know my mother well enough to have expected her to behave like that. She's been that way all my life. A selfish, vain woman."

Carlee stood on tiptoe and kissed him on the tip of his nose. "She did one thing right. She gave birth to you."

He grinned, took a deep breath, and exhaled slowly. "Enough of that. Let's go celebrate her birthday our way. Without her!"

The two wrapped their arms about one another and walked toward the car. Time was too short to let Mrs. Castleberry's words ruin it for them. Her loss was Carlee's gain.

"Hey," Dan said suddenly as they turned into the Bennett driveway. "It's Thursday. Hot dog night! Do I hear an invitation for me to stay for supper?"

She grinned. "I might be persuaded to invite you."

Bobby, Becca, and Dan wrestled on the floor while Carlee assembled the food items in the kitchen. The sound of laughter should have made her happy, but it didn't. She couldn't get the episode with Dan's mother off her mind. She'd never forget the hurt look on his face, the rejection in his eyes. What a miserable childhood he must have had. No wonder he joined the ice show at such an early age; his home life must have been nearly nonexistent.

When the hot dogs were roasted and ready to eat, Dan suggested they all sing "Happy Birthday" to his mother. Becca and Bobby loved singing the birthday song and were happy for any occasion to sing it. But they couldn't quite understand how you could sing a song to someone who wasn't there!

After the children were in bed, Dan slipped out the door while Carlee was busy cleaning up the dishes.

"Got something for you," he said with an ornery grin as she finished in the kitchen. He put his arm around her waist and tugged her into the family room.

"It's not my birthday," she said, then wished she hadn't mentioned the "birthday" word.

He reached behind the sofa and pulled out a poster-sized photo, the same photo he'd given his mother.

"Here. For you," he said shyly. "I hope you like it better than my mother did. I had them make a second one."

Carlee's hand went over her mouth, and she blinked back tears of joy. "Oh, Dan. I love it!" The smiling face of the man who had skated into her life gazed back at her. "You don't know what this means to me. How can I ever thank you?" She lovingly took the big picture from his hands and stood it on the fireplace mantel. "It's going to stay right here where the children and I can see it every day."

"You—uh—don't think it's too big? Would you rather have a smaller one—to go on your desk?"

"No, silly! And if your mother doesn't want hers, I'll be glad to take it off her hands and hang it on my bedroom wall—so I can keep my eye on you."

He hugged her to him and rubbed his cheek against her hair. Her home had become a haven for him since he'd arrived in Kansas City, a place filled with love and warmth and security. Instead of love for his mother, he felt pity. She and his father and all their fine friends worked hard at finding happiness in things. But Carlee and the Bennetts had found the true secret to happiness. And best of all, they were willing to share it with him.

The flickering flames in the fireplace seemed to draw the young lovers to it as it crackled and popped its invitation to come and bask in its warmth. Dan pulled plump sofa pillows onto the floor and leaned into them. Carlee dropped beside him and curved into his beckoning arms. Neither spoke. Words were no longer necessary. There was an unspoken language of love between them and they understood one another completely.

It was Carlee who broke the silence. "If you want, we can spend the last two days together. Mother Bennett offered to keep the children, and Father Bennett said he'd take care of the rink."

Dan twisted a lock of her hair between his fingers and studied it intently. "Have you talked to them? About us?"

"Not really. But they know, I'm sure. They've always encouraged me to date. They want what's best for me."

"Oh, Carlee, Carlee. What have I done to you? I had no right to come into your life like this—with empty hands. I have nothing to offer you. Nothing but heartache."

Her fingertips pressed to his lips. "Hush! We did it together. I fell in love with you that very first morning you came to the rink. Neither of us was looking for the other. It just happened. It's no one's fault."

He sought her lips with his and kissed them tenderly as his hands caressed her back. Her lips tasted like fine honey from the comb.

His mind was awash in confusion. He had no future to offer her. None at all, with his lifestyle and career. Yet he wanted her more than anything he'd ever wanted. Wanted to marry her and be a father to her children. How could the most important things in his life be at such opposite ends of the spectrum? Maybe once he was away from all of this, he could forget her, put this all behind him. But in his heart he knew that would never happen.

"What if I give up skating?" he asked suddenly.

She look startled. "Give up skating? Give up your career? You'd never be happy, Dan. We both know that."

He traced her lips with his finger. "Then come with me, Carlee. We'll make it work—somehow. I love you!"

She shut her eyes tightly. "But the children. Oh, Dan—it would never work."

He watched as a lone tear escaped and ran down her cheek. "Is that the only reason, Carlee? Or is it also that I'm not a churchgoer? Are you afraid I might be a bad influence on your children?"

She appeared to be stung by his words. After a pause, she answered, "Not your influence, my love, you're a wonderful, honorable man. But faith is an issue with me. You've been very courteous when we've had prayer in our home. You've even attended church with me. But you've never made any claim to be a Christian. We've always been honest with one another, and I'll be honest with you now—I could never marry a man who did not love my Lord, even if all our other problems suddenly vanished."

He lowered his head thoughtfully. "Wow, you don't pull any punches!" He knew he'd never said no to God, but he hadn't said yes either. Maybe he didn't fully understand what God and Carlee expected of him. "Carlee. . . ," he said, needing to change the subject, "I've been thinking. You know what I'd really like to do my last two days?" He sat back, erect, and turned her toward him. "You've told me you like to put up your Christmas decorations in early December. I'd like to help you. Maybe the four of us could go shop for a tree, string popcorn—whatever you usually do. Could we?"

Her eyes brightened. "What a great idea. Oh yes!"

※

She was waiting in the doorway with Ethel by her side when Dan drove in at five the next morning. She ran to the car, scooted close to Dan, and slipped her hand into his. "I've been thinking. . .about us. We can be miserable about you leaving, or we can enjoy each moment we have together. I say, let's enjoy our time! What do you think?"

He was surprised and pleased. He'd been thinking the same thing during the wee hours of the morning when sleep had eluded him. "Sounds good to me."

"Okay," she began, her eyes filled with anticipation, "as soon as your practice is over, will you take me to breakfast at one of those all-you-can-eat places? I have this yearning for sausage, biscuits, gravy, pancakes, fruit—"

"Whoa!" he shouted. "What happened to moderation? You're talking Fat City!"

She lifted her chin and drew in a deep breath. "Today I want to throw caution to the wind—and pig out!"

"Once we've gorged ourselves, then what?" He'd expected their remaining days to be difficult. Apparently he'd been wrong.

Carlee's eyes sparkled. "Then we go find a tree! We can do it the easy way and go to a tree lot, or—"

"Or what?"

"We can drive out to a tree farm and cut our own!"

A frown furrowed his forehead as he considered the choices. "I say, let's cut our own! Now that that part's settled, what's our next project?" He angled his head toward hers and raised his brows.

"Mounting the tree in the stand and stringing the lights. You do know how to string lights, don't you?" She grinned.

"Want the truth?"

"Only the truth," she said as she jabbed his arm.

"I haven't the faintest idea how to do either. My parents hired someone to come in and decorate the house, including the tree. Is it hard?"

A serene smile blossomed on her face. "No, just takes time and effort. You'll do fine. I'll show you how."

That morning, he skated a flawless solo for an appreciative audience of one. When the music ended, he skated over to the front row, where she was waiting for him.

"Oh, Dan," Carlee said with a look of admiration as she reached both hands toward his. "That was beautiful!"

He cupped his hands over hers, lifted them to his lips, and kissed them passionately. "Sweetheart, your praise means more to me than that of any audience."

He'd called her sweetheart for the first time, and he'd said it so easily. She loved hearing it.

"Now," he instructed as he pulled her to him and onto the ice. "It's your turn." They stood in the center of the ice, their arms entwined, as they waited for their pair number to begin.

"This is the last time we'll skate this number together, Carlee. At least for now." He pressed his chin against her forehead. She could feel the beating of his heart. "I love you, Carlee Bennett. Never forget it!"

The music started, and they began to move as one, taking long, smooth strides across the gleaming ice, twisting and turning to the strains of a waltz. Never had Carlee skated as she did with Dan. There was something about being cradled in his arms that brought out the best in her skating ability. It was as though her feet never touched the ice but floated along beside him, moving as he moved, whirling as he whirled. They were poetry in motion. Their final skating session was the best one of all.

"The Christmas tree!" Becca squealed as she ran across the room and leaped into Dan's arms.

Bobby tossed his books onto the coffee table and stared at the perfectly shaped Scotch pine standing in the corner of the family room.

"I cut it, and your mom helped me string the lights," Dan bragged, his face aglow with pride. "Now I'm going to plug in the lights. Everybody ready?"

"Ready!" Becca shouted as she clapped her little hands.

Carlee gathered her children on the sofa, and the three watched expectantly as Dan ceremoniously pushed the plug into the socket. A mass of brilliant colors burst forth.

"Ohh!" they said in unison.

"Dan, it's beautiful!" Carlee praised as she shot him an adoring glance.

Dan carried boxes of decorations from the attic, and the happy foursome spent the rest of the afternoon stringing popcorn and cranberries and placing ornaments on the tree.

They hung angels made from white paper plates and snowflakes cut from construction paper. They placed reindeer made from twigs on the entertainment center. Dan and Carlee cut branches from the evergreens in her backyard and draped them in an arch over the fireplace, then added a string of red lights and big red satin bows. The final touch was lining Carlee's lovely holiday dolls across the mantel. Becca shrieked with joy and clapped her hands each time a doll was put in its place. "See, Dan? I told you Mama's got more Barbies than me. Aren't they pretty?"

He had to admit it—they *were* pretty. And the mantel was the perfect place to display them. The room looked magnificent, better than any Dan could remember as a child. A warmth filled him as he watched the children add the very last items to the tree—more of their homemade ornaments.

Carlee poked him gently in the ribs. "Aren't you wondering what's going to go on the coffee table? There's one more box on the shelf in the garage. Would you mind getting it?" And she added, "Be careful, it's fragile."

Dan retrieved the big box and carefully placed it on the floor by the coffee table. "What's in here?"

"You'll see." Cautiously she lifted the lid and began removing tissue-wrapped treasures from the box.

"It's a 'tivity, Dan," Becca declared with authority. "But don't touch—it will break if you do. No hands on it. Just look!"

Dan watched as Carlee carefully pulled the wrappings from Mary and Joseph and the baby Jesus, along with the wise men, shepherds, an angel, sheep, donkeys, and a cow. Last, she lifted the crude wooden manger from the box and placed it in the center of the polished tabletop. Her care with each figure amazed him and spoke worlds to him about her love for her Lord. His birth was the center of her Christmas. The tree and all the decorations took second place.

"I like your 'tivity, Becca," he said with misty eyes.

"Mama said He was borned and died for us," Becca said, her little chin resting on the table as she examined the baby Jesus figure.

"You gotta ask Him to come into your heart. Did you know that, Dan?" Bobby asked with childlike frankness as he dropped onto the floor by his little sister.

Dan flashed a glance at Carlee. "I'm beginning to understand that, Bobby," he said in an almost whisper.

He tucked the children into bed after he'd told them one of his famous fairy tales, then joined Carlee in front of the fire. She'd turned off all the lights in the room except the Christmas lights. Dan reclined on the floor and gazed at the radiant tree. "I think that's the prettiest tree I've ever seen."

Carlee stretched out beside him. "When all the trees at your parents' house were decorated by professionals?"

He slipped an arm over her shoulders. "Those trees didn't compare with this one. And I sure wasn't allowed to hang paper-plate angels and construction-paper snowflakes on it!"

"The children and I loved having you here with us, helping us decorate the house. Thank you, Dan. You've made this day one I'll cherish forever." Her voice carried the same element of sadness as his.

It was well after midnight when Dan rose to go back to his parents' house. "I don't want to go, Carlee. This place is magical."

"I know," she whispered softly as she tucked her hand into his arm. "When you're here, it's magical for me, too." She could feel her heart thundering. She was so full of love for this man, she felt her heart would explode. She tried to remember how she'd felt about Robert. Had this same love filled her heart? It was so long ago, it was hard to remember. Maybe it was because she and Dan couldn't be together, like forbidden fruit, that made love so sweet now. Whatever it was, it was ripping her to shreds inside. The thought of his leaving twisted in her like the jab of a knife. How could love hurt so much?

They stood in the doorway as Dan prepared to leave, holding one another, kissing, hugging as though there were no tomorrow. But there would be a tomorrow. And it would be their final day together.

Chapter 16

Dan Castleberry had already told his parents good-bye and was packed and ready to go to the airport by the time he arrived at Carlee's house at 7:00 a.m. for breakfast. Thanks to Jim, Carlee's family would be able to spend all day with Dan. Carlee had risen early, and breakfast was well under way when he arrived.

"Oh, yumm," he moaned as he caught the aroma of bacon frying on the big electric griddle. The smell filled the house and made his taste buds jump to attention.

Bobby and Becca ran, giggling and happy, to Dan and wrapped themselves around his muscular legs. He gathered the two wiry children into his arms and carried them to the cozy kitchen where their mother was standing at the counter, using two forks to turn the sizzling strips on the griddle.

"Hi. Sleep well?" she asked, her heart thumping wildly.

He took one of the forks from her hand and flipped over two slices, then scooted them alongside the others. "Nope. Couldn't keep from thinking about you, honey," he whispered into her ear as he sidled up next to her and kissed her cheek.

"It was the same for me." She rested her head on his shoulder with a sigh of contentment.

Becca broke the spell. "Orange juice, please."

Dan moved to the refrigerator and poured a glass of juice for Becca, then filled the other glasses on the table. Bobby took a sip, put his elbows on the tablecloth, and propped up his head with his hands, his lower lip drooping sadly. "Do you have to go, Dan? Can't you stay here with us?"

Dan pulled a chair up next to the boy's and put his hand on the lad's shoulder. "Wish I could, Bobby, but I've got to get back to my job with the ice show. I'd take you and Becca and your mom with me, but how would you go to school? I move from city to city every week or so. We've tried, but your mom and I can't think of any way it would work out."

Carlee lowered her eyes and absentmindedly moved the bacon around on the grill. "Bobby, it's very important for Dan to skate in the show. That's how he makes his living. He's a big star. You wouldn't want him to give that up, would you?"

Without hesitation, Bobby replied, "If he could stay with us, I would!"

The two tried to explain to Bobby what career meant and why it was important to Dan; but all he knew was that Dan would be leaving, and he didn't like it one bit. Neither did Becca.

They shared the big breakfast Carlee had prepared, laughing and talking about everything except Dan's leaving. Carlee couldn't face another discussion on that subject. His leaving was inevitable, and that was that.

The children watched a Saturday-morning cartoon while Dan helped Carlee clean the kitchen. "Carlee, don't move! Stay right where you are. I want to take a mental picture of you here in your kitchen, the place I've spent some of the best hours of my life."

She gnawed at her lower lip and feigned a smile. "Oh, Dan. I'll think of you each time I come into this room, or the family room, and remember the great times we've had with you. You've been such an important part of our lives."

"Have been?" He crossed the highly polished kitchen floor, threw his arms around her, and held her close, rubbing her smooth cheek with his freshly shaven face. "Please don't say that. It sounds so—final!"

The children were still watching cartoons when the two moved into the family room. Dan sat in the corner of the couch and placed his feet onto the ottoman. Carlee plumped the pillows, sat down beside him, and snuggled in as close as she could. They silently enjoyed each other's nearness as they watched the lights blinking on the Christmas tree, casting reflections on the shiny ornaments and tinsel.

Ethel and Jim came over to say their good-byes. Jim took Dan aside, and they talked quietly in hushed tones. When they'd gone, Carlee questioned Dan. "What were you and Father Bennett so secretive about?"

Dan appeared thoughtful but would only say, "Man talk."

For lunch Carlee prepared one of Dan's favorites—a chicken enchilada casserole with chips and a green salad—then served homemade deep-dish cherry pie for dessert. He reclined in the big chair, with Bobby and Becca cuddled on his lap, while Carlee cleaned the kitchen. He'd offered to help, but she suggested he spend the time with the children before she sent them over to the Bennetts' for the rest of the day. His remaining time would be hers alone. When the children had gone, she stood before him and held out her arms. "Hold me, Dan. Please."

He rushed from the chair and caught her up in his arms and held her. Could he ever let her go? When the time came, would he be able to walk away and not look back?

"I needed to feel your arms around me, Dan. I—I love you so much, it hurts. I can't bear to see you go." Pent-up sobs gave way to huge tears. No more being brave!

Her deep sobs broke his heart. He blotted her tears with his fingertips and wanted to cry along with her. His heart was breaking, too. He'd never felt this kind of pain.

She breathed a prayer aloud. "Oh, God, I love him so. Somehow, someway, please work this out. Please, God!"

The two spent the afternoon locked in one another's arms, thinking of what might have been.

⌘

At five, Dan bid farewell to the house he'd come to love, and closed the front door behind him for the last time. He and Carlee were silent most of the way to the airport.

The airport was crowded, and for once, the flight was on schedule. They said their farewells surrounded by dozens of strangers.

"I love you, Dan," Carlee repeated as she placed her palms on his cheeks and kissed him for the final time.

"I love you, Carlee," Dan whispered into her ear before he pulled away and entered the walkway.

She stood, waving, as the door closed behind him, separating the two young lovers. He was gone.

⌘

Dan phoned her every night the first week. She'd wait by the phone, willing it to ring, longing to hear his voice.

The second week, he phoned only four times. They avoided any discussion about their future. As much as Carlee craved his voice, she knew it was best that they begin to separate from one another. Nothing could come of their three-week romance.

⌘

Three days before Christmas, at two o'clock in the morning, Carlee's phone rang, waking her from a fitful sleep. It was Ethel, and she was crying. Jim was experiencing chest pains, and she'd called for an ambulance. It was on its way.

Carlee crossed the lawn and arrived at the same time as the ambulance. "Oh, Mother Bennett, I'll be there just as soon as I can get Mrs. Grimes here to stay with the children." Carlee shivered in the cold night air as she watched the emergency vehicle rush away down the street.

When she arrived at the hospital, she found the nearly hysterical Ethel in the waiting room. Ethel had been told nothing since they'd arrived except that Jim's condition was very serious. Carlee comforted her mother-in-law as the two women knelt together in prayer and begged the Lord to spare Jim's life.

The doctor came in an hour later. Jim had stabilized some, but it would be awhile before they would know how much damage had been done to his heart. The two women were allowed to go into his room to see him. The sight of all the tubes and machines hooked up to his body frightened them. He looked so ashen gray and lifeless.

"Call Dan," Ethel said firmly as she placed her hand on her daughter-in-law's arm. "Jim would want him to know."

Carlee rushed to the pay phone and dialed the number Dan had given to her.

When his sleepy voice answered with a weak "Hello," she blurted out the news.

A now wide-awake voice asked, "How bad is he?"

"We don't know. The doctor said it will be some time before they know anything—they're trying to stabilize him."

"I'll catch the next flight and be there in a few hours. Which hospital? How is Ethel doing? Where are the kids?"

"Dan, you can't come. You're in rehearsals!"

"We'll be off over Christmas. I'm coming, Carlee. Stay with Ethel; I'll take a cab from the airport. I love you!"

Built-up stress seemed to flow from her weary body. Dan was coming. And he'd said, "I love you."

The next two days were a blur. The three stayed at the hospital most of the time, leaving only long enough to shower and catch a few hours of sleep. Dan was very considerate of Ethel. She told him time and time again how important he had become to her. Her rock to lean on, she called him.

On Christmas Eve, Ethel insisted Carlee and Dan go home and relieve Mrs. Grimes so the children could spend Christmas in their own home. It was nearly midnight before the two finished wrapping gifts, but finally the last present was placed under the tree, ready to be ripped open by two eager children on Christmas morning.

"We'd better hit the sack," Dan said as he bent to kiss Carlee as she sat cross-legged on the floor, surrounded by paper, tape, scissors, and ribbon. He ordered Carlee to bed while he locked up the house and turned out the lights. Soon the house was silent.

She drifted off to sleep quickly, feeling safe and secure. Dan was in the house.

"Look, he's opening his eyes!" Ethel Bennett jumped to her feet and rushed to her husband. "He's squeezing my hand!"

It had been five days since he'd entered the cardiac unit, and other than a few flickers of his eyelids and a slight movement of his hands and legs, he'd shown little response. Carlee joined her mother-in-law beside the bed, and the two women wept for joy and thanked God for a miracle. The doctor had been reluctant to give them any encouragement about Jim making it. It had been obvious, even to the doctors, that God would have to perform a miracle in order for him to survive. And He had!

"I've got to tell Dan," Carlee said softly, so excited it was hard to keep her voice down to a whisper. She wanted to shout praises to the Lord. She rushed into the little waiting room and ran into Dan's open arms. "He's conscious! Oh, Dan, God has answered our prayers—he's going to live!" She buried her head in his chest and clung to him, absorbing his strength.

"He had to make it," Dan said firmly with a jab of his fist into the palm of his other hand. "I need him!"

Carlee thought his words a little strange but never questioned them. She was too happy. And Jim and Dan had become extremely close during their time together.

By the next morning, Jim was able to talk faintly, even laugh, but he still was very weak. "I knew you were here, Dan—I could hear all three of you."

Dan quit smiling. It pained him deeply to think how close they'd come to losing Jim. Jim had become like a father to him, in ways Carlee knew nothing about. He'd spent many hours at the rink with Jim during the time she'd been at home with the children—hours she'd thought he'd spent with his parents.

❦

The week between Christmas Day and New Year's Day was a busy time for the rink, but the rink was the last thing on Carlee's mind, or on Ethel's. Jim and his recovery came first, but she was concerned about Dan and his rehearsals, too.

"Don't worry about it," he assured her when they finally got down to talking about when he might leave and go back to Florida. "I'm a fast learner."

"Dan, you don't have to stay. Jim is getting better every day. They're going to move him to intermediate care tomorrow. Ethel and I can handle things here—you'd better go." It pained her to voice those last words. She didn't want him to go—ever! She'd said good-bye to him once already, and their second farewell would be no easier.

Later that afternoon he sat in a chair in the corner of the hospital room, staring out the window. He and Jim had similar backgrounds. But Jim had the one thing in his life Dan didn't have—a personal relationship with God.

❦

Once dinner was over and the dishes done, Carlee turned back the quilt on the bed in Bobby's room and suggested that Dan get some well-deserved rest. He would be taking the midnight to 7:00 a.m. shift at the hospital, then flying back to Florida. He grabbed her wrist as she turned to leave the bedroom. "Don't go. Please!"

She allowed herself to be pulled onto the bed, next to Dan, and found her heart racing wildly at his touch.

"I have to be near you, Carlee. This is my last chance. Stay with me," he begged, his eyes pleading with her.

She drew back, knowing her weakness.

He quickly raised up and propped himself on one elbow. "No, I didn't mean that the way it sounded. I just want you here till I fall asleep, that's all."

Her cheeks flared with pink, and she felt foolish to have misunderstood the meaning of his words. Dan had never said or done anything improper. He'd never asked her to compromise, and of course he wouldn't do it now.

"I'll stay," she said softly as she lowered herself back onto the bed beside him and pushed the hair from his forehead. For nearly an hour they talked, but eventually sleep overtook him and he drifted off. She'd been blessed with this kind of love twice in her lifetime. But like Robert, he was being taken away from her. She sat there watching him, praying for him, once more asking the Lord to let them be together.

When she awoke, the bed in Bobby's room was empty, and a note was propped against the basket of silk flowers on the kitchen table. He'd gone to the hospital to relieve Ethel.

Carlee and the children were waiting when Dan arrived at 8:00 a.m. to pick Carlee up. He waved to the two tearstained faces with their forced smiles as he backed the car into the street and headed toward the airport. Carlee moved as close to Dan as she could get, took his hand, and wound her fingers tightly through his. He swallowed hard and kept his eyes on the road.

After parking in the short-term parking lot, he grabbed his bags from the trunk and walked alongside Carlee into the terminal. They selected two chairs in the corner and settled down for their final few minutes together. Dan pulled her close and rubbed his cheek against hers as he'd done so many times before. Suddenly he laughed aloud. "I wonder how many of my so-called friends would believe that I could be so in love with a woman and, in all this time, all I've ever done is hold her and kiss her?" He cupped her chin and lifted her face toward his. "To some, lovemaking means sex. They only think they know love. Carlee, with you I've discovered what true love is, and we have it, dearest. They don't have a clue!"

A feeling of pride flowed though her. Living by God's standards was worth it after all. Dan respected her.

"I don't know how, I don't know when, but someday, Carlee Bennett, we're going to figure this thing out. I want you to be my wife—in every way. I want to be Bobby and Becca's dad. I know you know how to get answers from God. Please, ask Him to work this out because I love you, Carlee Bennett. You're my life!"

Surely God would work out their problems. Dan was so open. He'd even asked her to pray—that had to be a sign from heaven. Her hope for the two of them was renewed, rekindled by Dan's declaration of love and request for prayer.

The flight to Florida was announced, and he walked out of her life for a second painful time.

Chapter 17

On the last day of January, Jim Bennett walked into his house with the aid of a cane. He was on the mend. It'd been a rough month for Carlee. Managing the rink without him was no easy task, but she had to keep up a facade for the sake of the children and for Jim. She couldn't let them know how tired she was and how much she was hurting.

February came and went. Dan called at least four times a week, and they'd talk for hours. He begged Carlee to come to California to see the new show, but with Jim's physical condition so fragile, she knew such a trip would be impossible.

The first week in March, Jim gathered his little troop of staunch backers and told them, "We need to pray." He took his wife's hand in his and reached for Carlee's. "Lord, I thank You for sparing my life. And I thank You for each member of my family. You know, Lord, what I am about to tell them. Help me to say it, and help them accept it."

All eyes turned toward the man they respected and adored. What was he going to tell them?

Jim took a deep breath and looked around the circle at each one before he spoke. He turned to his wife first. "Ethel. You've been the perfect wife. You've stood by me through thick and thin." He patted his slightly rounded tummy. "Mostly thick," he added with a hollow laugh.

Next, he turned to his daughter-in-law, his only son's wife, whom he loved as a daughter. "Carlee, you've been the daughter we never had. We've loved you as much as if you'd been born to us. Our son loved you with all his heart. And we know you loved him with that same kind of love. It hasn't been easy, but you never complained."

"But, Father Bennett, what are you—"

He held up a hand for silence, then grinned at the two little ones, his pride and joy.

"Bobby, you're the image of your dad. The Lord must have put you here to take his place in our hearts. I'm proud of you."

"What about me, Grandpa?" Becca asked, her eyes shining expectantly.

The man nodded his head, then lifted his face heavenward. "Ah, yes. Becca. My shining light! I'm as proud of you as I am of Bobby."

"Jim?" Ethel asked with a glow of love in her voice as she slipped her hand in his. "What are you trying to say?"

451

He rubbed his eyes with his hankie, then stuffed it into his pocket. "I have a confession to make. I haven't been completely honest with you about what the doctor said to me."

"Jim!" Ethel's hand moved to her mouth. "What? What are you saying?"

"Whoa, Mother. I'm not going to die. At least not now. Not from my heart attack. But the doctor has said I *may* die if I don't change my lifestyle." He swallowed hard. "I've made a major decision: I've decided to sell the rink!"

"But, Father Bennett, I can run the rink. I've been doing it since Christmas," Carlee argued, knowing how much the rink meant to her father-in-law. "Please don't sell it. We can manage somehow!"

"No, Carlee," he said firmly. "You can't. The children need you. I've watched you push yourself these past few months. It's too much for one woman, especially when she has a family who needs her."

"But," she pleaded, "we could hire a permanent manager."

Jim shook his head. "No, I've thought it over, weighed all the pros and cons, and selling the rink is the only thing that makes sense. I've already contacted some interested parties; they're checking into it right now."

The two women made no further argument. How could they? Jim was right. To keep the rink would only prolong their predicament. His good health was the most important thing to both of them. Nothing should stand in the way of that.

Carlee unburdened her heart to Dan when he called that night. He listened, but as with their own situation, he offered no solutions.

She lay awake till the wee hours of the morning, feeling overwhelmed. Was God forsaking her? Didn't He care? Didn't He understand?

On Carlee's birthday, the UPS man delivered a cumbersome box, addressed to Carlee Bennett. There, packed among hundreds of foam pellets, was the newest collector Barbie doll. There was no card inside, but she didn't need one to know who'd sent the beautiful doll. Dan!

"Hey, how'd the birthday party go?" he asked when she phoned him that evening to thank him for her present. His question puzzled her. Ethel had given her an impromptu surprise party the night before, but how could he have known?

Later that evening, Jim Bennett called another family meeting, this time to inform them about the buyer he had for the rink. "We've already done the paperwork—the closing will be Monday, and the new owner will take over on Tuesday."

"So soon?" Carlee stared at her father-in-law. He hadn't said a thing to her about having a firm buyer. And they'd already signed the paperwork? The sale would close in just four days. She'd have to hustle to get her office in order and be ready to vacate the premises.

When Dan phoned, she filled him in on all the details as she knew them. "It's all happened so fast, Dan."

"How do you feel about this, sweetheart?" His voice was filled with concern. "I know you love that rink."

She sat cross-legged in the middle of the bed and stared at Dan's picture on the nightstand. "I loved it more when you were here. I miss you so much."

He let out a slow sigh. "At least then I won't have to worry about you so much. I wish I knew how to pray like Jim. I'd pray for you when I wake up early and think about you."

Dan wished he knew how to pray? Like Jim? *Oh, Lord God. Did I understand him correctly? Is all of this what it's going to take to get Dan into Your family?* Pushing down the joy that sprang up within her, she instructed him gently, "God is ready to listen, even early in the morning, Dan. He doesn't want eloquent words. Just words from our hearts. He's always ready to listen."

"Umm. In that case, I may give it a try," he teased.

The day the sale of the rink closed, Jim asked Carlee and the children to join them for supper. Ethel fixed his favorites: fried chicken, mashed potatoes, and strawberry shortcake.

The table was set for the five of them. Jim looked at the beautifully appointed table, then went to the china cabinet and took out another plate, cup, and saucer and placed them on the table with the five already there. "Better get another glass, and a napkin, and more silverware, Ethel," he said to his wife with a mischievous grin. "We have company coming for dinner."

"Jim!" Ethel said accusingly as she scurried to set the sixth place at the table. "Why didn't you tell me?"

"Who's coming, Grandpa?" Becca asked.

Jim smiled with pride, as if he'd pulled off the caper of the century. "The rink's new owner, Becca."

"You invited him here?" Ethel asked in surprise. "To have dinner with us? Isn't that going a bit far? Giving up the rink has got to be hard for you."

The doorbell rang as the five Bennetts stood staring at one another. Apparently their guest had arrived. "I'll get it!" Jim stated with authority. It was more of a command than an offer. "Why don't you all take a seat in the living room? I'll make the introductions there."

The two women and two children sat side by side on the tapestry sofa and waited. They could hear muffled voices in the hall. Perhaps Father Bennett was warning the new owner that the family hadn't been informed about his coming until the last minute.

Jim moved into the archway between the two rooms and leaned on his cane. "Family," he said with one of the broadest smiles they'd ever seen on his handsome face, "I want you to meet the new owner of the Ice Palace." He stood back and motioned toward the front hall as majestically as if he were heralding a king.

All eyes focused expectantly on the doorway as the new owner stepped into view. Four people gasped in unison as Jim reached for his guest's hand and drew him into the room.

"Troops, I'd like to present the new owner of the rink—Dan Castleberry!"

There stood Dan with a smile as broad as Jim's. The four sat glued to the sofa with their mouths dangling open. Surely they were dreaming. Could this be possible? Could Dan really be the new owner?

Jim shoved Dan toward them with his free hand while he leaned on the cane with the other. "Well, are you going to welcome our guest? Or just sit there and stare?"

Carlee flew into Dan's waiting arms. "Is this true, Dan? Are you the new owner?" She pushed back to search his face. "It can't be true. But if not, what are you doing here?"

He pulled her close and held her fast as Jim moved to stand by Ethel and the children. "It's true, Carlee. I'm here to stay. If you'll have me." He flooded her face with kisses as her in-laws looked on, smiling with approval.

"But how? I don't under—"

Jim Bennett dropped onto the sofa and pulled his wife down beside him. "Dan, let me explain. I'm kinda proud of my part in all of this. Not every day do I get to play Cupid."

Dan nodded as he dropped into the recliner and pulled Carlee onto his lap, along with two wiggling children.

"Dan and I had many interesting talks when he was here those first three weeks. He came over to the rink a number of times, and we'd talk about a lot of things. Dan is a fine young man. He'd put his personal life on hold while he worked on his career." He nodded toward Ethel, who nodded back as she patted her husband's hand. "I certainly could identify with that. His career was everything to him—that is, until he met our Carlee!" He winked at his daughter-in-law.

"Dan confided in me that he loved Carlee so deeply that he was considering giving up his skating with Ice Fantasy. I could understand that—I'd made that same decision when I met Ethel years ago!" He gave his wife an adoring grin. "However, that wasn't the only problem Dan and Carlee had. Carlee was a Christian—she had values and standards Dan didn't understand. Not that he disagreed with them, mind you, he just didn't understand her relationship with God. He'd never experienced it himself."

He aimed his cane at Carlee. "Carlee, on the other hand, had decided to put God first in her life when she was a child. That relationship has been the most important one in her life. More important than what she had with our Robert. And more important than her relationship with Dan."

He pointed the tip of the cane in Dan's direction. "Now, Robert was a Christian, too. So, no problem for them on that count. But it was different with Dan. He made no claim about God. That hurt Carlee; she'd promised God she'd never be unequally yoked to an unbeliever."

Carlee pursed her lips. What he was saying was absolutely true, but she'd never voiced it quite that strongly to Dan. Now she wished she had.

"I knew these two were meant to be together the moment I met Dan. So did Ethel." Ethel nodded.

"So I said to myself, I've got to work on that boy—explain God to him. And I did! I asked the Lord to send Dan to me if it was God's will and if I was supposed to talk to him. And, sure enough, Dan showed up at the rink while Carlee was home with the kids."

Carlee lifted Dan's chin with her palm. "I didn't know you spent time with Father Bennett. Why didn't you tell me?"

" 'Cause he wasn't ready, that's why! The timing wasn't right," Jim interjected. "Well, to go on with my story, Dan left for Florida, and I asked the Lord, 'Where did I go wrong?' You two weren't any closer than you'd been a week after he got here. I asked for another chance to talk to Dan, and the Lord gave it to me. I had a heart attack! The Lord answers in strange ways, believe me. Tell her, Dan."

Dan straightened himself in his chair, smiled at Jim, and took up where Jim left off. "Jim and I spent many hours together at the hospital. We talked about my long-range career goal to own my own rink someday and to be its pro. When the doctor told Jim he had to give up the rink or die, he remembered what I'd said. So—he called me!"

"Dan reminded me that buying the rink and moving to Kansas City would only solve half their problem—there was this thing standing between them about knowing God," Jim added.

Dan beamed at Carlee. "So, Jim said to me, 'That's no problem. Just say yes to God!' I said, 'You mean it's that simple? That's all I have to do?' He read a few scriptures, and I suddenly got it! I knew I was a sinner and I needed a Savior. God's plan of salvation was so simple, even I could understand it, with Jim's help." He gave a slight laugh, then became serious. "I finally realized I had to ask God's forgiveness. I knelt in my room right there while I was on the phone, and I confessed my sin and asked God's forgiveness and asked Him to be Lord of my life." Big tears formed in his eyes, but he made no attempt to hide them. "Carlee, I've been born again. Now I know what John 5:24 means, and I've taken it as my life's verse." He touched her face as tears flowed down his cheeks.

Carlee spoke with difficulty through tears of joy as her eyes searched his. "Oh, Dan, God has answered my prayer. But why didn't you tell me? You knew I'd been praying for you."

He wiped her tears away with his hankie. "We decided to keep it a secret between the two of us, to make sure the sale would work out first. So that no one would be disappointed."

"That's how you knew about my birthday party!" Carlee stated. "You two talked on the phone that night, right?"

Dan nodded. "Uh-huh. I almost spilled the beans."

She nuzzled his hair with her chin as she and her two children snuggled close to the security and warmth of his body. "But, Dan! How could you afford to buy the rink? I know the Bennetts are depending on the profits to take care of their living expenses for the rest of their lives. That rink has been their livelihood. Did your parents help?"

He laughed aloud. "My parents? Help me buy a skating rink? Forget it! I wouldn't even ask. No. I did it without them. They don't even know about it yet." He stroked her hair lovingly. "Carlee, I've saved every penny I could during the ten years I've been with the ice show."

"Except for the money you've frittered away on expensive Barbie dolls?" she chided with a playful jab to his ribs.

"Yep, except for that. My aunt set up a trust fund for me when I was a baby. That and the interest it's drawn, along with what I've saved and what my grandmother left me, was almost enough. Fortunately I have a prospective father-in-law who was willing to take a chance on me and carry the remainder. Right, Jim?"

"You bet! I know a sure thing when I see it," Jim Bennett said proudly as he peered at the happy couple.

"I still don't understand, Dan. Ice Fantasy? What are you going to do about that? They're counting on you!"

"All taken care of, kiddo. When Jim contacted me, I immediately went to Tom and told him I was buying the rink. I told him how much I loved you and how I wanted to spend my life with you and the kids."

Jim broke in. "He said, 'Go for it!' Right, Dan?"

Dan nodded. "Right! He brought in the lead skater from our show that's been touring Europe. I worked with him day and night and taught him all my routines. That's why I haven't called you as often as I'd have liked. No time! He's already taken my place in the new show."

She lifted her eyebrows questioningly.

"Beginning tomorrow!" Dan answered her unspoken question before she could ask it. "I'm here to stay."

It was more than Carlee could comprehend.

"Got any other problems you want solved? I'm your man!" Jim was happy to take every ounce of credit he could get.

Carlee slipped from Dan's lap and hugged him. "Nope, you old softy. You've solved them all. You're wonderful, Father Bennett. The best father-in-law a girl could have."

"Well, I have one more problem. A major one!" Dan warned from his place in the recliner.

The hugging came to a halt as three adults faced Dan. What other problem could there be?

"Only you can solve it, Carlee," he said as he crossed the room and pulled the love of his life from Jim's arms and into his own. "I haven't asked you to marry me. Not officially." He held her hand and dramatically dropped to one knee. "Carlee. I've already asked your father-in-law for permission, but I haven't asked you. Will you marry me?"

The overcome young mother reached down and kissed the lips of the man she'd loved since that very first day they'd met. The man she'd prayed for so many times. "I wish I could find the right words to express my love for you, Dan. This is the happiest day of my life. Of course I'll marry you!" She smothered him with kisses as two confused children watched, not sure what was happening.

"Then this is for you, dearest," he said as he unbuttoned the breast pocket of his shirt. "I was hoping you'd say yes, so I brought this with me. My grandmother's ring." He took her left hand in his and slipped the lovely ring on her finger. It fit perfectly. "I love you, Carlee, and I promise, with our God as my witness, that I'll love you and care for you till death do us part."

Becca's tiny hands tugged on his pant leg. "Dan, I love you, too—where's my ring?" They all laughed as Becca smiled, not sure why her words were so amusing.

Dan gathered his prospective family around him and enfolded them in his arms. "Actually," he said as he looked at each member of the precious little family he was claiming as his own, "I'm asking all three of you to marry me. What do you say?"

"Fine with me!" Bobby proclaimed quickly as he shook Dan's hand, eager to turn over his title of "man of the house" to this man he'd grown to love.

"I'll marry with you, Dan," Becca said as she hugged his neck and tangled her fingers in his hair.

His eyes met Carlee's. "And you, my love? Will you promise to spend the rest of your life with me?"

"Yes! Oh yes! A thousand times, yes!" Carlee threw herself into Dan's arms. "I love you, Dan Castleberry. God has given us our miracle!"

Epilogue

The day before Christmas, a big truck pulled into the rink's parking lot and carefully positioned itself. Its long crane cautiously lifted the giant sign and eased it toward the waiting steel poles. Two workmen standing in a cherry picker perched high overhead grabbed the sign and guided it toward the waiting platform where it would rest until welded in place.

Dan Castleberry and his wife leaned against the building and watched the process. Two children squealed and ran figure-eights around their legs as Jim and Ethel Bennett watched from the comfort of two folding chairs their new son-in-law had placed next to the building, where they could watch in safety.

"You feeling okay?" Dan asked his bride of six months as he pulled her into the warmth of his arms, with love and concern shining on his face for all to see.

"We're both fine!" she answered as she spread her fingers wide across her tummy and patted it gently.

"God has been so good to us, sweetheart." Dan placed his fingers over hers and nestled his face into her neck. "Think it's a boy?" He lifted her hand to his lips and tenderly kissed her fingertips.

She gazed into eyes filled with pride. "I hope so. I want to call him Daniel. After you, my husband."

"Mama! Daddy! Look, the sign is up!" Bobby shouted as he pointed to the magnificent new sign resting on its sturdy posts in front of the newly remodeled ice rink.

"What's it say, Daddy?" Becca asked as she ran to Dan and leaped into his arms.

He held his little daughter in one arm and hugged his wife with the other, as his son stood beside him with a skinny arm wrapped around his waist.

"Ice Castle, Becca. Ice Castle!"

JOYCE LIVINGSTON

Joyce Livingston is a Midwest native who lives in Kansas. She has six adult children, all married, and oodles of "good-looking, smart, and talented" grandchildren.

Looking at her calendar, you'd never believe that she considers herself retired. In addition to writing, she lectures and teaches all across the country about quilting and sewing. She is also a part-time tour escort, which takes her on "wonderful trips and marvelous cruises to fantastic places." Someone has to do the "dirty work," but she is sure to delight busloads of vacationers and earn their trust.

Before retirement, Joyce was a television broadcaster for eighteen years doing two variety/talk shows daily. This is where she was introduced to quilting, sewing, and a variety of crafts. From this, she published numerous articles on the subjects.

Through all this, Joyce says, "The Lord gives each of us gifts, some more than others. I feel my gift is to be an encourager and an uplifter to women of all ages through my writing and speaking, and in the countless other ways He presents to me as opportunities throughout my life. I am truly blessed!"

A Letter to Our Readers

Dear Readers:

In order that we might better contribute to your reading enjoyment, we would appreciate your taking a few minutes to respond to the following questions. When completed, please return to the following: Fiction Editor, Barbour Publishing, Inc., P.O. Box 719, Uhrichsville, OH 44683.

1. Did you enjoy reading *Missouri*?
   - ❑ Very much—I would like to see more books like this.
   - ❑ Moderately—I would have enjoyed it more if _____

   _____

   _____

2. What influenced your decision to purchase this book?
   (Check those that apply.)
   - ❑ Cover   ❑ Back cover copy   ❑ Title   ❑ Price
   - ❑ Friends   ❑ Publicity   ❑ Other

3. Which story was your favorite?
   - ❑ *A Living Soul*   ❑ *Faith Came Late*
   - ❑ *Timing Is Everything*   ❑ *Ice Castle*

4. Please check your age range:
   - ❑ Under 18   ❑ 18–24   ❑ 25–34
   - ❑ 35–45   ❑ 46–55   ❑ Over 55

5. How many hours per week do you read? _____

Name _____

Occupation _____

Address _____

City_____ State_____ Zip_____

E-mail_____